# READER'S DIGEST
# CONDENSED BOOKS

# READER'S DIGEST CONDENSED BOOKS

Summer
1971
Selections

**THE READER'S DIGEST ASSOCIATION
PLEASANTVILLE, NEW YORK**

# CONTENTS

# THE
# WHITE
# DAWN

A CONDENSATION OF THE BOOK BY
## JAMES HOUSTON

What happens
when three marooned
New Bedford
whaling men are
thrust upon
the gentle culture
of the Eskimo

ILLUSTRATED BY
## John Gundelfinger

CHAPTER
DECORATIONS BY
BAFFIN ISLAND
ESKIMOS

One day, near the turn of the century, several survivors from an errant whaleboat staggered onto a bleak, icy shore in the very heart of the Eskimo world. Frozen, starved, very near to death, three of the men were rescued by Eskimo hunters. Avinga, crippled son of the chief and narrator of the tale, relates the curiosity of his people as the strangers enter the life of the community. Gradually, as the brief spring and summer pass, they are fully accepted, especially by the young girls. But during the long, cruel Arctic winter, mischief arises, customs clash and passions flare. The aftermath is violent, the conclusion intensely moving.

*The White Dawn* blends adventure and romance with authenticity and profound meaning.

*Abstract from the log of the sailing bark*
Escoheag, *390 days outbound from*
*New Bedford, Massachusetts:*

*Tuesday, May 12, 1896.* Light wind blowing from the SE until noon when we sighted four right whales and put out all boats. All of them whales went into heavy ice and was lost to us. So ends this day.

*Saturday, May 16.* Wind still SE. Heavy fog banks to the south. Saw six right whales. Put out all crews. Mr. Jamison in the starbord boat struck and kilt his whale. The Portugese struck his whale good—but I saw it tow Billy's boat way up a long lead in the ice. Late afternoon the fog came over us. We hallooed on the horn and set out boats, but that night we did not find them. So ends this day.

*Sunday, May 17.* The damned fog cleared off this morning. Set out all boats searching, fired the gun in hopes they would hear us. No sign of them. So ends this day.

*Monday, May 18.* Wind stronger from the SW. Heavy ice moving towards us. Set out boats but not much hope. Late afternoon the search boats returned, and we left while we still could before ice reached us. It is hard to think that these six men—my third mate Billy, young Nathan, Daggett, the Portugese, the Indian, and Shanks—are all lost to us. God rest their souls in their cold graves. We is heading out of this bad-luck place to get back east to Baffin Bay. So ends this day.

9

I

WHEN I awoke, the first sound I heard was the south wind whispering and moaning, forcing its foul warmth against the front of the snowhouse. My dreams had left me with a feeling of terror, of something new and strange about to happen.

I rolled over on my back and drew the caribou-skin robe up over my naked shoulders. It was cold and damp in the big igloo. The seal-oil lamp was almost out and a fog caused by our breathing hung near the ceiling. I watched as the cracks between the snow blocks turned softly white with the coming of dawn. On the east side of the igloo I could see the melted places where the spring sun had licked the curved walls thin. The roof of the snowhouse would collapse soon now. Listening, I could hear the soft calling of snowbirds newly returned to the land.

I did not need to go outside to know the look of our land when the pale white dawn came creeping out of the east. In my mind's eye I could see the stone hills jutting steeply behind our igloos. The cursed south wind and the spring sun had wiped them clear of snow and dried them rich red brown. All the entrances of the igloos faced the sea, like seven dark eyes searching for food. Beyond the high meat cache lay our sealskin kayaks and our women's boat, long and sleek, lashed upside down on stone racks. From there the snow swept down over the beach until it reached the barrier ice that had been thrown up by the tremendous force of the tides. These shattered fragments of salt ice stood like jagged blue teeth

between the land and an immense field of snow-covered sea ice.

In the open sea beyond the ice swam seals and walrus, whales and seabirds; yet, in spite of all our magic charms, we could not have them. The loose ice was too dangerous to walk upon or to force a kayak through, and it had now been pressing against our coast for one whole moon and half another. We spoke of our neighbors, people living two days' journey from us. We knew they must be starving, and before their dogs died they would be forced to come to us for meat.

We were proud of our camp. With its seven snowhouses, it was the biggest on the whole coast. Other families gasped at the size of our igloos with their long tunnels and big snow porches and our rich abundance of children, meat caches, kayaks, sleds and dogs. You would need to count all the fingers and toes of two men to number our hunters, their wives, the old people and the children.

But still the weather was our master. It could help to feed us or starve us to death, as it had done to other sea hunters.

Sarkak was the only man who did not believe this. He was old and rough and powerful, and he acted sometimes as though he could control even the weather. He still had two wives living with him though four earlier wives had died, along with countless of his children. Three grown sons remained—good hunters, strong and willing to do his bidding; and he also had me, crippled Avinga, a bastard, half son, half slave to his household.

But I will speak of Sarkak later, of his greatness and his fierce jealousy. Now I wish to tell you what happened on that spring day and of the amazing days that followed. Imagine, I, Avinga, who was always the weakest, am the only person left alive from that whole camp. Even the children have died or have gone away.

Deep inside myself lies a memory so vivid and terrible that when it returns I sweat in the freezing blizzard and shiver in the summer's sun. I have never dared to recount all this until now.

AT THE dawning of the day that changed our whole lives, I arose early. Sarkak, surveying the weather, directed two of his real sons—Tugak, the eldest, and Yaw, the youngest—and myself to

11

take both of his sleds, harnessing five dogs to each, and go and open the last stone cache of walrus meat, which was up near the entrance to the long fjord. It was his custom to leave his meat cached far from camp, so he would not in some wild party mood be tempted to give all of us too much to eat. I was sent to help remove the heavy stones, for in spite of my crippled legs, or perhaps because of them, my arms were stronger than most men's.

Knowing that this was a season of quick violent storms and killing winds, we wore our inner pants and parkas made of caribou fawn skin, with the hair turned in against our naked bodies, and over these we wore sealskin pants and parkas, with the hair facing out to protect us from the icy dampness.

On our journey to the cache we saw no sign of life save one faint string of fox tracks. We loaded all the meat onto our sleds and then decided to return by another route over a high pass, where we would have a wide view of the broken sea ice. We hoped to see some opening where the tide might have forced the broken ice away from the coast.

As the two teams moved slowly through the immense white silence, I watched the hazy sun sink low and turn red. Each wind-carved drift cast a long blue shadow across the snow. Suddenly the dogs whined with excitement. We scanned the hills hoping it was a white bear they had smelled, but there was nothing there.

Then we saw tracks cutting diagonally across our path. The dogs scrambled into them, sniffing wildly at the fresh scent. My brothers jumped off their sleds and, kicking the dogs aside, silently examined every detail.

"*Kalunait*," said Tugak, using the seldom spoken word that means "people with heavy eyebrows," strangers from some distant place. None of us had ever seen a foreigner and yet we knew that we stood in the tracks of one.

"Four of them." Yaw gasped in excitement.

"Feet like giants," said Tugak. "That one staggers like someone sick or crazy. See there, he fell. Look how long he is."

We did not need to urge our dogs on. As the scent took us over the pass, we saw a man's form lying halfway up the opposite slope.

Silent and intent, like wolves, our two teams raced to where he lay face-down on the snow. The dogs knew as we did that the spirit had flown out of this body.

I held my team back and watched my brothers savagely beat their dogs away as they rolled the dead man over. He was young, and immensely tall and thin. His face was long and narrow, and when they drew off his tight black hat we could scarcely believe what we saw. A great mop of red hair! Red hair! Tugak pulled off the man's mitts; mitts not at all like ours, for they had five separate fingers and were made of trade cloth, not animal skins. It took both Tugak and Yaw to haul off the frozen coat. Under it, attached to a belt with a shining buckle, they found a broad sharp knife, its hilt bound with cord. Tugak grabbed the sheath and pulled it off the belt. It was the most precious thing he had ever touched.

Next we pulled off the big hard boots and the pants, and looked this strange man over in every detail. Seeing that he was in no way different from ourselves, save in his great length and body hairiness, we turned his body over in the position we had found it.

Lashing the clothing onto Tugak's sled, we shouted and thrashed the dogs away and started back onto the strangers' trail. Now there were footprints of three men. Two walked well, with long even strides, but the third man had sat down twice. If he did this often he would freeze to death. The tracks went to the top of a small hill overlooking the sea. Then the men foolishly had gone down toward the frozen sea, walking, not in single file as we would but side by side, each breaking his own trail, each using too much of his strength. Seeing that the trail led along the barrier of broken ice, Tugak ran forward, shouting at the dogs; but they disobeyed and scrambled to where, just ahead of us, lay a stiff cloth bag with a wide shoulder strap. Around the bag were many yellowish brown squares and black specks, and there were marks in the snow where a man had stumbled and fallen. The bag must have dropped off his shoulder. The three men must not have been together here, we thought, or the stronger ones would have helped the dying man. We could see where he had struggled onto his knees and then staggered on after the others.

13

It grew dark, and heavy fog drifted in around us. The freezing dampness turned the dogs' coats white and made us shudder, but we followed the strangers' trail along the very edge of the sea ice until we knew it would be foolish to go farther. Tugak cupped his hands and shouted, "*Iyoo. Iyoo.*" But there was no answer, only the cracking and groaning of the rising ice as the huge night tide swelled beneath our feet. It was time to go back to camp.

The dogs backtracked without any help from us and broke into a run when they caught the smell of home. We didn't stop them until we reached the center of the village. Then Tugak pulled the strange clothing from beneath the lashings of the sled, and drew the sheathed knife from his boot top, and we all crowded into the entrance passage of Sarkak's igloo. We tried not to make noise until, trembling with delight at the shock we knew we would cause, we flung all the riches into the lighted room: hat, jacket, pants, boots, knife, belt and shoulder bag. For a brief second there was silence, and then a great shout came from Sarkak.

"*Tikitut kalunait tikutuk.* They have arrived. The people with the heavy eyebrows, the foreigners, have arrived."

"Some of them have come to us dead," said Tugak. "But still they brought their gifts. Look in this bag. And what are these?"

"Those black specks?" said Sarkak. "Put some of them into the hot water over the lamp. They will make the water turn brown and taste delicious. They call it *teemik.*" He took a huge bite out of one of the hard yellowish brown squares, chewed for a moment, then blew out a mouthful of crumbs. "It tastes awful, but those people love this food. They prefer it to meat. No wonder, for when they have meat they burn it over a fire until it is tough as walrus hide."

By this time the hunters of our village—Sowniapik, Atkak, Poota, Tungilik, Nowya, and Okalikjuak—and as many wives and children as could stand had crowded into the big snowhouse to hear our unbelievable news. Sarkak sat quietly, examining the knife and carefully listening to the tale his eldest son related. On the bed beside him sat his middle son, his favorite, Kangiak.

"The man who dropped the bag, is he walking?" asked Sarkak.

"Yes. He is following the others. But they have no harpoon to

feel where the ice is thin and broken, so he may be dead by now."

"And the other two?" asked Kangiak.

"Perhaps they will be frozen in the morning," said Tugak.

"Go and get them," shouted Sarkak. "You, Kangiak, go with Avinga. And Yaw with Tugak. Bring them to me. Now!"

In all our lives we had almost never heard Sarkak shout with anger, and it terrified us. The women and children ran out, hiding their faces. The rest of us followed, eager to be away from him.

Kangiak helped me shove the load of frozen meat off the sled onto the snow, and we moved out at once while other men dragged the heavy slabs to the meat cache in the center of the camp. Oh, how I hoped that the foreigners were still alive!

We ran the sleds recklessly through the rough barrier ice onto the flat sea ice. We traveled throughout the dark night until we reached the edge of the floe ice, and there we waited for dawn. When it came and turned the fog pale gray, we saw them.

We saw two men, walking beside the long twisting crack in the sea ice that stretched beyond our sight. They seemed too big, the way things sometimes do in fog. And they seemed to float in the mist.

They stopped the moment they heard the dogs, and faced us as we started toward them. Kangiak sat up straight, and I could tell that he was nervous, unsure how to meet these strangers. "Now," he whispered, and I rolled off the sled and dragged myself like an anchor to slow the rushing dogs, roaring and driving them sideways with the whip. Only the big dog, Pasti, still tugged forward, trying to reach the strangers. Kangiak ran lightly toward him and kicked him sharply in the ribs with his soft skin boots. The dog dropped in his tracks, unconscious.

Kangiak pushed back his fur hood and walked slowly toward the strangers, the dog whip wriggling after him like a living thing. "*Tikiposi*," he called. "You have arrived."

The taller one answered something I did not understand. Kangiak called to them to come to him, but they did not move. Dressed in black, they stood silently like big awkward children.

Kangiak again called to them. "Come to our igloos for food," and he pointed back along our trail.

They understood his gesture and stumbled forward to our sled. Kangiak warned the dogs away from them. I sat on the sled and stared at them, hoping they could not see how I trembled. The first one smiled at me. His wolflike blue eyes were pale, as though they belonged to some spirit of the dead, and the lower part of his face was covered with yellow hair clogged with ice from his breathing. Then I looked at the second man, dark as though he had been burned in a fire. He, too, smiled, showing big white teeth. His eyes were dark, the color of a real man's eyes, and pierced through his left ear he had a shining yellow ring. He carried a bag across his back.

So, I thought, these are the *kalunait* who live south beyond the Indian country, half cousins to us, half children of the dog. I had heard of them, and now I had them sitting on the sled beside me, speaking strange words. I watched our team, wondering if perhaps the dogs could understand them.

Kangiak and I turned the sled with difficulty, for the two heavy strangers sat like old women instead of jumping off to help us, as real men would have. Then Kangiak called to the team. Pasti was conscious again and, like the other dogs, ready to go. It was not long before we found the third man squatting against a piece of ice, his face in his hands. The pale-eyed *kaluna* went to him and shook him gently. He was still alive. Kangiak drew off the stranger's mitts and blew on the man's hands and, raising his parka, held them against his own warm naked belly; together he and the tall stranger dragged him back to the sled. We wrapped a caribou skin around him, and tied his legs down to keep them from falling sideways and being broken against the rough ice.

It was after midday. When we crossed the bay, we could see all the people in the village waiting, motionless. They stared in horror, as though these were visitors from the world beneath. Women covered their eyes, and children hid behind their parents, and the youngest set up a wailing, as though they sensed the new danger that had come to all of us.

16

Sarkak stood quietly, his hood drawn over his face, his hawklike eyes appraising the strangers. Suddenly he revealed himself, stepping forward and pushing back his fur-trimmed hood; and I believe the two men instantly sensed that he was the man who held their lives in his hands. He stared at them, and then he cast his mitts onto the snow and raised his hands above his head, pulling the sleeves back to show that he concealed no weapon. He called out greetings, and the pale-eyed man answered something.

Sarkak then walked up and stood before these strange people, and I was shocked to see how their heads and shoulders towered above him. Sarkak had always been to me a giant, bigger in every way than all other men. The strangers looked down and smiled; and Sarkak looked up smiling, showing them the whiteness of his teeth. Without turning, he called to his wives, "These two will stay with us. Get them food now. That sick man, let him sleep in Sowniapik's igloo. They will care for him." And so saying, he led the two strangers through the crowd, who drew back to give them room. Sarkak might be small beside the *kalunait* but he seemed supremely powerful. I knew he was to be their master.

II

CROUCHING, we followed Sarkak down into the winding passages of his big igloo, through the meat porch, past the side rooms and finally into the big main room. There the two strangers could stand up straight again. They blinked as their eyes became accustomed to the half darkness of the dome-shaped room whose smoke-

stained ceiling kept out most of the light. I could see they were
partly snow-blind.

Sarkak's two wives were already sitting in their places on the
wide snow sleeping bench. It was high as a man's waist and took
up more than half of the whole round room. The women laughed
nervously, calling out, *"Taktualuk, taktuvingaluk.* It's dark in
here, very dark in here."

Their words were those they should say, for politeness, insulting
their own ability to maintain an even flame in the long stone seal-
oil lamps. But slowly I was beginning to realize that these
strangers understood not one word we spoke.

I was standing near the man with the shiny ring in his ear and
took the courage to say, quietly so others would not hear, *"Keenow-
veet?* What's your name?"

He only smiled, so then I knew he could not understand.

The two strangers were almost falling down with tiredness, and
yet their eyes were bright with excitement. They took off their
tight black hats, and everyone gasped. The pale man's hair was
long and yellow white, like nothing we had ever seen. The taller
man's hair was dark like ours, but tightly curled and bushy.

I tried to see the wonderful knives that they wore in their belts,
but both knives had disappeared from their sheaths and must now
be hidden in their clothing. Perhaps they did not trust us.

In the center of our wide bed, in the softness of our deep-piled
sleeping skins, Sarkak made room for the two strangers. Sarkak's
older wife, Ikuma, and Nuna, his newer and younger wife, carefully drew off the men's stiff, heavy boots and then their stockings,
torn and made of some coarse and evil-smelling cloth, and these
they handed to Nuna's mother, the old widow, to dry over her lamp.
We were all pleased to see that their feet were blue gray, not the
deadly frozen white we had feared.

Nuna's lips curled with disdain at the nearness of the ghostlike
yellow-haired man, but she pulled up the apron of her fur parka
and held his icy feet against her hot belly. Ikuma gently fed both ·
strangers some warm blood soup, which they eagerly drank, but
they could eat only a little of our raw walrus meat. We, who had

18

driven the sleds, ate our fill of it gladly, for it was our first unfrozen meal in two days.

After we had eaten, the other villagers came in. Sowniapik, to whose snowhouse the sick man had been taken, came first with his brother, Tungilik, followed by their wives and children and Akigik, the midwife. Next came Okalikjuak, the good archer, with his wife and daughter. Poota and his daughter, Neevee, stood by the entrance passage.

Sarkak spoke to the two men in a loud clear voice, asking them where they had come from. But they only shook their heads and made strange sounds. Years before, we all knew, Sarkak had seen many *kalunait*. It was when he had visited Big Island, a whole summer's journey from our camp, and there had been men there who hunted whales. He had climbed aboard their ship, carrying the skin of a white bear and a parka full of walrus tusks. These he had gladly traded for a few rusty iron nails and a small blue glass bottle that made the sun look like the moon when you held it to your eye.

Sarkak had often told us how these sea travelers would gladly give a bright bead just for the loan of a woman whom they always returned next morning, unharmed. We had never seen these whale-hunting men, because our tides were huge and the ice moved fast and the big whales did not come to feed on our coast.

Because Sarkak had traded with them we had always assumed he could easily speak with them. Now, finding that he could not, his brow knit with anger and embarrassment. This was a bad sign. He fell silent and would not speak to us. One by one the villagers left our snowhouse.

Sarkak motioned to me and said, "Avinga, go and sleep in the igloo of Sowniapik with the sick man. Remember that he belongs to us, to this household. Watch everything he does."

So for a time I went to live in the snowhouse of Sowniapik. I felt wildly excited. These foreigners had come from some far-off place and led different lives; now we had them, and we could keep them and grow to understand them. That first night I saw the third stranger lying there shaking with fever under the caribou skins the

women had laid over him. His eyes, when they opened feebly, were red-rimmed and glazed with snow blindness. The women laid a damp bird skin over his eyes to ease the pain and placed beneath him an amulet, a small ivory knife that would help to cut the fever.

Sowniapik's wife looked into his face and said with honesty, "You are dying. You will grow too hot, and you will die." But he did not understand her words.

That night and the next day the stranger I had been sent to watch tossed restlessly and cried out many times, and the women cared for him like a child. In the middle of the fourth night I was awakened by his calling. Probably he wanted water. Sowniapik's daughter Evaloo heard him, too. She sat up and dipped a horn cup into the stone pot. I could see the smooth curve of the girl's naked haunches as they flowed into her strong young back. She reached over me, holding the cup to the stranger's lips, and I felt the heat pouring down from her naked body. Then I saw her stiffen, and I could see that the stranger had grasped her by the wrist. I blew my hot breath upward between her breasts. It made her jump with surprise, and she jerked her arm away and recoiled into her furry sleeping place.

She whispered, *"Shogishiguluk,"* calling us bad children.

But there was laughter hidden in her voice; she knew at that moment, as did I, that this sick man must be getting well, for he was thinking of women. We were both glad.

SOWNIAPIK's wife was the first to call the brown-haired stranger Billy. He taught her his name by pointing at himself and saying it over and over again. Soon we were all saying it, the women in a soft musical way that sounded like "Pilee."

We could see on the fifth day that he was almost well again. When both of Sowniapik's daughters were in the snowhouse, Pilee's eyes never left them for a moment. He tried to talk to them, and Sowniapik tried to talk to Pilee, but nothing came of it. In the end we all laughed to hide our frustration.

Every morning I told Sarkak about Pilee's condition. On the day

he judged the brown-haired one to be well again, he told me to have a new snowhouse—big enough for three—built against our family's igloo. That evening he sent his two strong sons Tugak and Yaw to Sowniapik's igloo to bring Pilee carefully across the hard-packed snowdrifts to our house.

Sarkak should have spoken to Sowniapik before taking the stranger, but he did not, and I believe that much of the trouble in our camp started at that moment. For in taking Pilee without asking Sowniapik, Sarkak showed everyone that he considered these three strangers to be his personal property. He did not think of them as visitors, free men, who might choose their own home and friends.

With the coming of the strangers our luck seemed to change. A swift storm came and after it the sky was clear. A north wind blew over the land, and helped by the tide, it forced away the great fields of broken ice. The open sea now spread before us. Seals appeared in great numbers, as if by magic, and our hunters harpooned as many as we could eat. Our dogs grew fat again, and to hold the abundance of fresh-killed meat the kayakmen built new stone caches along the coast. It was a time of plenty, a time of feasting.

And suddenly, as if by magic, Poota's wife, who had seemed about to die, got up and left her bed. Had the foreigners some secret charm? We wondered.

I could see that they watched us closely, trying to understand our ways, as we did theirs. For many days they scarcely spoke to each other, and they seemed afraid to venture far away. But, surrounded with such plenty and the safety of our igloo, they could not help but relax with us. First they came to know Kangiak as their friend, then Sarkak, Yaw and me, and all the others of us who slept in the big igloo. My oldest brother, Tugak, was sleeping in Okalikjuak's snowhouse, for he was in a trial marriage with Meetik, daughter of Okalikjuak. Kangiak also was old enough to have a wife, but the girl who had been promised to him since her birth had died two winters before from eating poisoned meat, and Sarkak had not yet chosen one to replace her.

22

Nuna's mother must have been the most difficult one in our igloo for the men to understand. The old widow always sat beside the lamp on her side of the bed, staring into space or singing to herself. She had withdrawn into her own hidden world.

Slowly during the spring the strangers came to know Sowniapik, because he had helped Pilee, and they easily recognized Atkak, because he was strong and fond of laughing. They also came to know Poota, Nowya and Tungilik, and gradually understood who were these hunters' wives and children. It is little wonder if this took some time. We were all related in our camp, and our young people acted like common property in times of plenty. They ran as free as foxes and ate and slept in any snowhouse they wished.

The older children had been shy of the *kalunait* at first, but one spring morning I saw them leading the three men up the hill behind the camp to the small windswept plateau, where they liked to play when there was not too much snow. Many of the dogs followed, howling as if they were trying to sing, excited by the smell of these new people. I was glad the older children were there, for I could see that the strangers knew nothing of the nature of our dogs at all, seemed not to be aware, as we always were, that if a man fell down among them, they would grab him, and in their savage excitement tear at him. Indeed, this had happened to me, as I shall tell in a moment.

Soon we heard screams of delight from the hill, and Kangiak and Yaw went up to see what caused so much excitement. And then we heard them laughing, too; and none of them returned until early evening.

"They have a new game, a way of kicking a ball," said Kangiak as he followed the three strangers into Sarkak's snowhouse. "When we fully understood it, we will show everyone how to play."

INSIDE the igloo I watched the tall foreigners eating seal ribs. They did not seem to like the meat, and yet they were always hungry. The faces of the two pale men had turned red brown from the sun, and they now looked more like real people, except for the ugly hair on their jaws and their bushy eyebrows.

23

How they must have envied the smooth beautiful faces and the short compact bodies of our people.

When we had finished eating, we all sat together on Sarkak's wide bed. They listened carefully to every word we said and I imagined they were trying to learn our language. One night the big brown man put his finger to his chest and said, "Portagee. Me Portagee." So we learned his name, an easy word to say, for it sounded to us like part of a song. Now we had names for all three of the *kalunait*, for we had already called the other young man Kakuktak, meaning the white-haired one.

That evening when we were crowded onto the big bed in a warm and companionable way, I saw Kakuktak looking steadily at Sarkak, and I tried to guess what the stranger must be thinking of him.

Sarkak lay half-naked on a thick pile of soft caribou skins spread over the wide bed. His face and hands were brown as old used leather, tanned from countless hunts out on the glaring sea ice. His nose was small, his cheekbones so wide that they drew his eyelids upward into narrow slits. His merest glance was piercing and his voice was rough as sharkskin. He wore new sealskin underpants, scraped free of hair and white as snow. These were cut wide at the knees for running, in memory of the days when he had been the fastest dog-team driver. His sealskin boots, black and beautiful in their fit, had been chewed by his wives until they were soft as goose down.

Sarkak was born to lead men. Though the other six main hunters in our village were strong enough and wise enough to have camps of their own with other men to help them, they had chosen to stay together under Sarkak, surrounded by more plenty than any other camp could hope to possess, more food and laughter and dancing, and many women and girls to choose from. Visitors came often and stood in awe of Sarkak's riches and power, such as they had never dreamed existed.

Sarkak's three strong sons, who hunted for him, were his true riches. Kangiak, his favorite, was full of force like his father. The eldest, Tugak, and young Yaw were brute strong and willing to be led. Sarkak passed on to them his vast hunting knowledge of

the sea beasts and the birds. It was their only inheritance, yet it was thought by all to be more than enough. Some said that Sarkak could close his eyes and feel the changing migrations of the seals and walrus as they fed along the underwater reefs; and he understood the complex patterns of floe ice driven by wind and tide, the rhythmic movements that could either help a man to bring home heavy loads of meat or sweep him to his death.

Sarkak was a sea hunter, a wanderer, with no permanent houses and no lands, for how can a man own the land or the air or the sea? However, certain fjords and places on the frozen sea were recognized to be Sarkak's hunting places. And though he had no possessions, he needed to hold power over the men and women and children and dogs of the camp. I knew he had some hidden longing to dominate everything that lived. Indeed, to him the three strangers, with their big bodies and their sharp sea knives, were now personally his. They gave him power of a strange new kind. For who would not stand in wonder before a man who could command these giants from another world?

Sarkak's elder wife, Ikuma, was wise and durable. She had outlasted four others. She sewed and cared for Sarkak and advised him quietly when no one else was listening. His newer wife, Nuna, was younger than me by two winters, smooth as a seal, red-cheeked and full of laughter. Sarkak had chosen her to joke with and to warm him in the bed at night. My mother was his second wife.

In the year of my birth there had been a great killing of walrus, and Sarkak had invited many hunters on their way inland to join him in a great feast. Out of snow blocks our people built a huge dance house, and for five days and five nights they danced and ate and sang, and the girls and women lay with many men. I was born during the first storm of autumn and was carefully kept, for it was thought that I must be Sarkak's child. But as I grew older, it was seen that I looked in no way like him. When other hunters who had been at that feast came into our camp, Sarkak would say, "This one is surely *your* son." Then they would all laugh, for by that time no one really cared whose son I was.

In the next two winters my mother began coughing and grew thin and lost favor with Sarkak. He took a girl of only thirteen winters to sleep with him. Ikuma didn't mind and treated her like a daughter, for Ikuma always held the important first wife's place against the right-hand wall of the tent or snowhouse, and no young beauty could ever remove her.

When I could first walk and so left my mother's hood, my mother was coughing and dying. By this time she and I had the poorest places on the far edge of Sarkak's wide bed. Early one morning while everyone slept, I jumped off the big bed and ran outside. When people heard the dogs snarling, they rushed out just in time to kick the dogs away from me and save my life. I had been bitten many times; my lower leg muscles were torn away from the bone. Sarkak, in his rage, killed half the dogs in his team, for he believed that any dog that had bitten a human must be destroyed. People said I would surely die, but my mother kept me in her hood and nursed me. At last my legs healed, but they were not straight and I would have to limp forever.

Just when I could crawl again, my mother died. Sarkak was kind to me then. He allowed Ikuma to care for me and he taught me to walk on my crippled legs, to refuse to be weak. In certain ways I became stronger than other young men. I worked hard with my hands, stripping lines and scraping skin. When I learned to paddle a kayak, I strengthened my arms and the muscles of my back. At the same time my legs forced me to spend much time with the women. I learned secret things about them that most men would not believe.

But by the time the strangers came to us, I was treated more like a slave in the family than like a son. And so, when Kakuktak and Portagee first crowded into our igloo and I was sent to watch over Pilee in Sowniapik's house, I felt certain that my place on the family bed would be taken from me forever. I thought I would have to find a place to lie on the floor like a dog, but this great fear of mine did not occur. Instead, when Sarkak had a side igloo built for the *kalunait,* he gave them a position that was lower than my own.

III

THE *kalunait* had been with us for less than one whole moon when the domes of all our snowhouses collapsed under the strong spring sun. Suddenly the houses were filled with blinding light. I could hear people laughing and shouting to their neighbors. It was always like this when the roofs crumbled. We laughed at ourselves for our laziness in not cutting the domes off the igloos when we knew they would fall. We also laughed with joy at the thought of a new season. The strangers must have thought we had gone crazy, but soon they were laughing, too.

For a little while we lived within the crumbling walls of the snowhouses, and the women stretched makeshift roofs of sealskins over them. The sun grew hot, and the big tides carried away most of the heavy floes of winter ice. The sea sparkled deep blue in the sunlight. It did not grow dark at all now, and the sun at midnight only hid behind the hills to rise again.

Sarkak stood outside one evening, looking at the sky. "Bring me the new boots," he called to the women.

The children who heard him ran to their families and whispered, "We're going. Sarkak and the foreigners are putting on their new boots. Sarkak will break this camp tonight."

The children were right. It was time to move to the summer camp. Everyone began hurrying in and out, lugging out to the sleds armloads of caribou skins, bags stuffed with spare clothing, stone pots, drying racks and scraping boards. Ikuma, the first wife, wrapped her big stone lamp in a bearskin, and with the help of Nuna, the young wife, carried it out of the igloo and watched it

safely lashed onto Sarkak's sled. Kangiak and Yaw had the dogs all harnessed, and soon the people from every other household had lashed all their possessions onto their sleds, too. Dogs too young to pull ran free around each team. Bags full of squirming young pups were tied on top of some sleds, and children too old to travel on their mothers' backs were also perched on top of the loads.

We were ready to go, but still Sarkak waited. "The houses," he said. And Kangiak went with Sowniapik, Poota and Okalikjuak and destroyed the front passages of all the igloos and kicked new false entrances into the crumbling walls. This we always did, as the shaman had told us we should, to confuse any evil spirits that might wish to follow us, for our people are plagued by many evil beings: dwarfs and giants, strange birds and weird two-headed animals. To make the hunting go well and to avoid sickness and disasters, we are careful to do the things our shaman tells us to do.

Kangiak drove the first sled, breaking the trail that all the others would follow. He walked or trotted, calling out directions to the lead bitch. Sarkak rode grandly behind Kangiak, perched high on a white bearskin which covered the load. He proudly saw his son's growing ability to command dogs and men. Near Sarkak walked his two wives, one on either side, their huge hoods elegantly puffed with wind.

Behind the women the three strangers, foolishly fearless of hidden holes in the ice, talked loudly as they walked. Yaw's sled followed, heavily loaded. Nuna's mother and I always rode on it, for she, like myself, could not run, and when one of the strangers grew tired, he also rode with us.

After our sled came the other six teams in a long curving line. All that remained of our village, as a sign that we had once lived there, were our boats, lashed upside down on their high stone racks. We rode through the long half-light of the spring night and into the soft brightness of early morning, for we knew that as the sun grew warm the trail would soon grow soft.

Finally we could see the end of the fjord, the big gravel bank where we would make our summer camp. Now we could hear the surest sound of spring: the wild roaring of the river. It was still

completely hidden by the snow, but we could hear it gnawing blindly at the winter ice. The young people and stray pups ran out ahead of the sleds, eager to begin our summer life.

The three strangers must have known that this was the place we sought, for our things lay scattered, just as we had left them the year before—fish spears, tent poles, old stone lamps and blubber pots. Everyone hurriedly dragged the driftwood tent poles into position, and helped to cover the poles with sealskins and then place heavy rocks around the edges to hold the skins down against the often violent summer winds. We put up eight tents in all, with entrances mostly facing south toward the fjord.

There had never been any pattern for the position of our new homes, but for the first time in my life I noticed a curious separation in our camp. Sarkak's big tent and the smaller one for the three strangers rose on one end of the high gravel bank. But Sowniapik, Tungilik and the other hunters took theirs farther toward the river. A child could throw a stone the length of this split within the camp, and yet it was there.

We all ate quantities of seal meat when our tents were ready, and then slept the long day through. When we arose that evening, we heard the first calling of the geese returning to their summer nesting grounds. Everyone started imitating their sound, "*Kung-o, kung-o,*" and the big birds answered like old friends. We held up our arms to them in greeting, and the strangers called to them too, and everyone laughed. Some said, "See, they are really men like us. They, too, can speak like geese. We will show these dog children our ways. We will teach them to hunt like men."

From the coming of the geese until the darkness returned in autumn, people lost all track of time. The sun wheeled endlessly above our heads, and we hunted and ate and laughed and lay with our women. Only the rise and fall of the tide had any meaning for us during the short softness of summer.

LATE in our second day in the summer camp I saw Sarkak sitting on the gravel bank with the strangers, gesturing and talking to them as though they could understand him.

"Bring me one of the fish," he called to me.

Nowya's wife had gone up to the still-frozen lake and had jigged patiently for char, big sea trout, the best fish we have in our land. She had given Sarkak two huge ones. I laid a fish beside him, and he at once drew out the dead stranger's knife that was concealed in the top of his boot. "*Shavik,*" he said to the foreigners with a cutting motion toward the fish. The men nodded and reached for their knives, understanding that he wished them to cut the fish.

Kakuktak took out of his pocket a long thin stick and a flat brown-covered thing. Inside the cover were white smooth skins, with marks scribbled on them. Kakuktak looked at Sarkak and said, "*Sha-vik?*" while pointing at his knife.

Sarkak held it up and said, "*Shavik,*" and Kakuktak made some marks with the stick on one of the thin white skins.

Then Sarkak pointed at the fish and said, "*Ikhaluk,*" and Kakuktak nodded and scribbled again. It was the first time I had ever seen anyone marking on something other than bone or ivory.

With one gentle movement of the knife Sarkak then slit the big fish lengthwise, from tail to head, cut the two pieces in half and cleverly stripped the meat from the bones. Taking one quarter for himself, he grasped the pink slab of meat firmly between his teeth and with a reckless slash of the deadly sharp knife he cut off a slice just below his nose. The strangers stared in disbelief as he wolfed down the portion of raw meat and sliced again and again with the same breathtaking accuracy.

Portagee tried gnawing at his portion, but the tough silver skin held the flesh together and he got almost nothing. Pilee would not even look at the raw fish. Kakuktak tried imitating Sarkak, held the fish in his mouth and hacked away beneath his nose until he sliced a mouthful free. Sarkak was pleased. I could see that he believed Kakuktak might become one of us, for this yellow-haired stranger was very quick and willing to learn.

I looked at Kakuktak, as if I were seeing him for the first time. He was no longer ugly and frightening to me. I saw that he was lithe and graceful in all his movements, and when he smiled and his white teeth flashed, we all smiled back with pleasure. For

now, although we could not speak together, we felt like brothers in a family. After all, this should be so, for the earliest story I remember is about the young woman of our people who slept with a dog. Her father was ashamed and sent her to live on a remote island. There she had a litter of half dogs, half humans. When she tried to return to our people, her father killed her and she fell into the sea and became a goddess. Now here were three of the great-grandchildren of that litter, relatives returned to us. In my mind at that time it was just as simple as that. These strangers, having nothing and knowing nothing, seemed to us like overgrown children whom one must care for and protect against harm.

When the fish was gone, we lay together on the dry bank, watching the shifting clouds, and I saw that the dog children's eyes searched the waters of the fjord leading to the distant sea. Suddenly Pilee jumped up and pointed, shouting, "Dag-it! Dag-it!" for that was the name the strangers called Kakuktak. The others leaped up and stared, too.

Sarkak said to me, "They think it is the sails of one of their ships, but it is only a drifting piece of ice."

Portagee, Pilee and Kakuktak sat down slowly. Again we all silently looked now at each other and now down at the fjord, its whole length dead still, except when a seal would raise its black head above the water to breathe and then disappear.

Sarkak was the first to rise, stiffly, like an old man. He smiled at the strangers and at me. Then he turned slowly back to the big tent. We could hear Nuna humming to herself as she waited for him. She sang that tender wordless song women sing to comfort a baby in the hood. She had no child, but I knew she wanted one.

Portagee and Pilee also stood up and went to their own tent. But Kakuktak walked slowly to the water's edge and stared at his reflection, and I imagined that he was thinking of that far-off place that had been his home.

SARKAK's large summer tent was of an ancient style that has now almost disappeared. Hair had been left on the sealskins that formed the rear half of the tent so that it would be dark inside, a

31

good place to sleep during the bright nights of summer. The whole floor of the tent had been leveled with clean white gravel above the half-frozen ground. The summer rains would run beneath this gravel and leave the tent dry. The long entrance passage at the front was made of *mumik*, a thin seal membrane that allowed light to filter through. Here the women had a bright place to sew and gossip, and the children a place to play, safe from the dogs. The strangers often visited this porch, for they liked to be with people.

In our tent, one of those early nights, I heard Sarkak laughing and whispering in the bed with Nuna. They spoke of the brown man, Portagee, and the great physical differences that the women ascribed to him. Nuna said she could not believe them to be true. "You shall know," said Sarkak. "Tomorrow night I shall give him to you as a present. Later you can tell me what is true."

"I would be afraid," she said. But by the excited way she laughed, I could tell she would not be too afraid.

On the following evening Portagee found two children sleeping in his place in the bed. When he went to Sarkak's tent to speak of this, he found everyone lined up comfortably in the big bed, waiting for him. There was one snug place left, right beside Nuna. Sarkak smiled, gesturing, insisting that Portagee occupy the warm fur hollow beside his beautiful young wife.

Since Sarkak was master of the house, everyone knew that he had carefully arranged all of this. Sarkak sighed with pleasure when he saw Portagee crawl, fully clothed, into the bed. He rolled over, confident that his wife would have the exciting truth for him in the morning.

I saw Nuna smile at Portagee, her loose hair spread around her as she lay naked beside him. Portagee raised his head twice to stare across her at the broad snoring figure of Sarkak. He lay down again stiffly, perhaps with fear, for while I stayed awake he did not move or sleep. At dawn he hastily left the bed, still fully dressed.

"I think you frighten him," I heard Nuna say to Sarkak in the morning. "He touched me once, but drew his hand away as though I were made of fire."

"He must be afraid of you," Sarkak replied. "I still believe all the wild things I've heard about him."

She laughed. "I do not think he is afraid of me."

EARLY the following morning, when I hobbled outside, Kakuktak had left his small tent and was watching a big flock of snow geese set their wings and drift low over our heads. I could tell by the way they gabbled softly to each other that they had not seen us and were about to land. Just at that instant Kangiak, having also heard them, slipped out of our tent. Quickly, cautiously, he gathered a slim three-pronged bird spear, a throwing board and six throwing bolas newly strung by the women. He waved to Kakuktak to follow him. With envy I watched the two of them make their way up the river valley. My mind walked with them where my legs could not carry me.

There was much laughing and shouting when they came back, for strung around their necks and across their shoulders they each had more snow geese than I could count on my fingers and toes. Many women and children hurried out of their tents to see the catch. Portagee and Pilee came out, too.

"Oooh-ho!" cried Portagee as he lifted a big clump of birds from Kakuktak's shoulders. He rolled his eyes, laughing. "Heavy, heavy, heavy!" He pretended to stagger under the weight.

We all laughed and imitated him. "Oooh-oh! Hay-vee!"

Kangiak said to me, "Kakuktak must live life well, for the geese crowd in on him from the sky."

Everyone looked at Kakuktak as though there might indeed be magic in him, for we remembered that when he and the others had first appeared, more seals than we could eat had come to us. And now the hills echoed with the calling of countless geese.

That evening Ikuma cut into many pieces the first goose that Kakuktak had killed, for she was acting as his mother. She flung them up into the air, and everyone in the camp scrambled to have a piece of this sacred meat. For it was Kakuktak's first kill among us, and it meant that he would always share with us as we would share with him. Crowding around Sarkak's tent, everyone sat facing the

sea that had sent us such riches, and together we ate our fill.

Sarkak's eyes never stopped searching the foreigners' faces, and I knew he was trying to decide how to fit them into the life of the camp to suit himself. I saw Sowniapik and Poota also look at the *kalunait*. They told me later that they did not know whether to like or fear these men, since they seemed to give Sarkak too much power. I, too, looked at Kakuktak, Portagee and Pilee and wondered what they thought of my people, the real people.

When finally we had finished our feast of goose, an old man, the father of Atkak, rose and ran stiffly around us, shaking his bag of amulets at the spirits who lurk in the four corners of the world. Then, entering the circle we made for him, he sang a song, imitating the soaring flight of the great white birds. He sang slowly, often directly to Kakuktak, and everyone exclaimed in wonder at the gracefulness of his motions and the power of his song.

Whenever the three men sat in front of their tent, some of our people, usually the young, came and sat with them. Some older ones stayed away because they were angry at Sarkak's new power or because they thought the strangers lazy, and saw that only Kakuktak might learn to hunt for himself.

I could feel the camp breaking into two halves, as though there were a thickening wall of ice between our family and the strangers on one side and the rest of the hunters on the other. Such a thing had never happened before. If a person or family became angry with other people in a camp, it was the custom to move away rather than risk violence. But now, in spite of all the misunderstandings, everyone stayed. I think it was curiosity that held them. I wondered what would come of the growing distrust.

Most of the young people did not seem to notice this feeling. They laughed with the strangers and tried to teach them to speak in our way. Kakuktak kept making marks on his bundle of white skins and he also made images of things, like tall ships with wind sails, strange high houses with too many openings, and big-breasted women wearing ridiculous clothes. Always, when he drew pictures, people crowded around to watch, and one day he lent Shartok, Tungilik's son, his bundle of skins and the marking

stick. Kakuktak and Pilee and Portagee all seemed amazed at Shartok's clever drawings. He drew the three strangers so cleverly that they could easily recognize themselves. I was not surprised, for I knew that Shartok was a poor hunter, but good with his hands. He was a clever mimic, too, and always full of jokes. On this day he also made a drawing of Neevee, because he always wanted to lie with her. While everyone watched, he drew her naked. She laughed softly but ran away to her family's tent, because she was so shy. Portagee stood up quickly to watch where she ran. Outlined against the sky, he looked immense. He stood there kicking the gravel like a musk-ox, his legs stiff with yearning.

IT WAS during the fullness of the egg-gathering moon that the young women first started to work their wiles on the *kalunait*. One clear night I awoke and through my peek hole saw a pair of girls scratching cautiously on the sealskin flap of the strangers' tent. When the men did not wake, they hurried back to the tents of their families. But I am sure that more than one pair of curious eyes followed them on this first night visit.

The strangers soon found that, like ourselves, they could not always sleep during the long white nights of summer; so, hearing the endless calling of the geese and the laughter of our young people, they would get up and go walking. I, too, was often wakeful. Some nights I lay and thought of girls. I also dreamed about bears, which means that a man should try to lie with a woman as soon as the dream is ended. But I knew Sarkak would never ask any hunter to give his daughter to Avinga.

After one such dream I went out and, helped by Lao, the gray bitch who was my constant companion, made my way up to the top of the hill behind the camp. On the plain below I saw Yaw and Shartok with Kakuktak and Portagee, moving slowly, searching for eggs. As the sun's heat warmed the land and white mists rose everywhere like steam, I saw two girls come slowly through the mist, also searching the ground for eggs. I could tell by their careful way of walking that they already carried many in their hoods and in the front aprons of their parkas.

Suddenly I saw Shartok and Yaw, with Portagee and Kakuktak on their heels, racing toward the girls. Neevee saw them, too, and quickly knelt to empty her parka of eggs. I knew she didn't like Shartok. He was almost on top of her when she leaped up and threw two goose eggs at him. One burst against his chest and the other splattered on the side of his head. Laughing, she whirled and ran. I knew that he would never catch her. The other girl, Shartok's sister, did not try to run from my brother Yaw. She did not make a sound while he wrestled gently with her, and Portagee and Kakuktak stood watching with excitement.

On the following night all of the young people, the strangers with them, went up to the high plain behind the camp, and from their shouting, I could tell they were playing the kicking game. I could not make myself stay behind. Other people gradually came up to watch, too. Some woman had sewn up a sealskin ball that was bigger than a man's head, and I could imagine the fun they were having rushing back and forth, kicking at this ball.

Now Pilee and Portagee set up two stones, one at each end of the plain, divided the players into two groups, and showed them how to kick the ball violently and fight their way through their neighbors to reach their goal. Our young people were shocked, for this game was like men fighting in anger. They continued, in order to be polite, but they played our way, joking and only pretending to be violent, while the three strangers rushed wildly after the ball, smashing into each other and snorting like animals. Kakuktak's nose ran with blood. I turned my eyes away, for I did not want to watch their madness. At last they tired and played more gently. Perhaps, having run off their wild fighting energies, they began to understand our joyful way of playing.

Panee, the daughter of Atkak, the hunter who was famous for his wrestling skill, had been standing at the edge of the plain, whispering with Mia and Evaloo, Sowniapik's daughters. Panee was tall and quick, with narrow hips and full breasts. As I watched her, she darted out at Portagee and tripped him. He fell, then leaped up in surprise. She laughed and made no attempt to hide the fact that she had tripped him. I did not see how she

managed it again, but Portagee stumbled once more and she stood almost over him. He grabbed at her leg, but she leaped back and was off quick as a fox, Portagee racing after her. At the edge of the plain there was a great tumble of rocks that led up into the hills, and Panee scrambled over them with the swift sureness of an animal. Portagee was only halfway up the first terrace of rock when she stood on the second small plateau. Then she ran on, more slowly, into a soft mossy place surrounded by big boulders, and we saw him lunge in after her.

Some children started to follow them, but their mothers called them back, and the game continued. The women looked at each other and laughed a lot, for Panee was the first to catch a stranger.

WITH the waning of the egg-gathering moon, the tides carried away the last ice that clung to the shores. The sea was open. Sarkak sent Yaw and four other young men to bring the boats we had left in the winter camp. There was great excitement when they arrived with the women's boat—the umiak—and the eight kayaks. We were all longing for the taste of some dark red seal meat, and they had seen seals on the edge of the drifting ice.

The umiak belonged to Sarkak, and every kayak belonged to some particular person. Every young person knew someone well enough to borrow a kayak. This was our way, for we shared everything. Nuna's mother owned the one that had belonged to her dead husband. Being a women she could not use it, and because I often did favors for her she let me have it whenever I wanted.

So now Kangiak and Kakuktak helped me rig the hunting gear on the widow's kayak and held it steady as I slipped my crippled legs beneath the long slim deck. Kangiak then climbed into Sarkak's kayak, showing Kakuktak how to get into his without upsetting the delicate craft. One after the other they pushed away from the shore and followed me down the long stillness of the fjord. On the water my crippledness was gone. My arms seemed to sing with strength. That day we three shared in the killing of a great bearded seal. Although it was Kangiak's harpoon that had

caught it, it seemed to me that the beast had come to us at Kakuktak's bidding. As people said, he was a fortunate hunter.

I was tired, and I slept soundly that night until the giggling of girls woke me. I removed the small bird-skin plug from the peek hole by my head and saw that Panee was scratching the seal-skin flap of the strangers' tent. The other girl was Evaloo. She was young and red-cheeked and had a smooth close-kneed way of walking that always excited me. In a minute Portagee thrust his head out, and then Pilee. They smiled and beckoned to the girls.

Many thoughts raced through my mind before I fell asleep again. Panee had led Portagee up the hill and now she was back, bringing a friend for Pilee, perhaps also for Kakuktak. I could tell that both girls were wildly willing, and I had noticed from the day Pilee started to get well that the strangers were excited by our women. Such feelings are shared by men everywhere.

But it was all wrong. I felt that strange uneasiness again, as if something evil were creeping toward us. The girls were like wild children, and if this went on the strangers would gain power over them, learn to speak to them and advise them. I wished the girls were full-blown women, wise like Ikuma. She would know how to handle the men and still hold our camp together.

That they met secretly like this was Sarkak's fault. As he had given the strangers meat for their hunger, boots to wear and a bed to sleep in, so he should have lent them women, hunters' wives who would have known how to satisfy them and then return to their families without harm. This is the usual way in our camp. Now, because the hunters' daughters were meeting secretly with these giants who, Sarkak thought, belonged to him, it was dangerous. It could cause him to lose control over the foreigners, and if that happened everyone in the camp would suffer.

The girls' smothered laughter kept me awake all night. The foreigners themselves seemed half dead in the morning. Sarkak, for reasons of his own, was in a surly mood, and he watched as Pilee, having nothing better to do, picked up a dog whip and tried helplessly to flick the long lash out before him in imitation of a dog-team driver. Portagee lay by the tent, laughing at him.

"He cracks the whip like a woman," Sarkak said.

Pilee glanced at Sarkak and then, disgusted, flung the whip to the ground. At once he picked it up again and drove its handle down between the two big stones that weighted the entrance to the tent. Walking across the beach, he stretched the lash toward the sea and placed a stone on its tip to hold it straight.

"What is he doing now?" Sarkak asked me, but I had no answer. Pilee had started to throw loose rocks over the long straight line of the whiplash.

"Portagee!" he called, and the big brown man rose and ambled down to him. Pilee said something, and together, faster and faster, they threw stones away from the straightened whip until we could see a line of bare clay appearing along the edge of it.

Then Pilee walked up to the tent and got a harpoon line, which he fastened to the stone on the other side of the tent entrance. With great care he drew it also down toward the sea, so that between the harpoon line and the lash there was exactly enough space for two men to walk side by side. Now the strangers hurled the stones away from between the lines with surprising force.

"Look at them. Those two, they eat like four men and play like children," said Sarkak. "Son of mine," he called out to Kangiak, who was coming up with Kakuktak from the river, "look at those two using so much energy to destroy the land."

We were surprised to see Kakuktak hurry to join them. When the three of them had cleared the whole space between the lash and the line, they stretched the lines on to a farther point. Between the newly stretched lines I could see a large boulder buried deep in the hard clay. I believed they would have to go around it. But no. With a walrus tusk and a piece of driftwood, they dug and heaved and fought against it. Many of us gathered near them, but they did not seem to want our help. So we left them to their senseless wrestling.

Early next morning I awoke to the sound of stones clicking against stones. I hobbled outside. The *kalunait* were already up. Their path now stretched more than halfway to the sea.

Kangiak and Sowniapik joined me. "They got it out," said

Kangiak, "without any help from us." But we could see they were tiring and would now welcome help. So Sowniapik and my brother and I began clearing that crazy path, and soon many others, kayak-men and young people, joined us. Slowly, as the morning wore on, the *kalunait* stopped working and became our masters. Pilee shouted harshly at the young people, and when they slackened their work, Portagee strode toward them as though he might strike them. The work was not completed until evening, when gravel carried by the women in heavy sealskin bags had been spread along the whole path.

Pilee was the first to step into the finished path, and he caught Kakuktak by the arm. The brown man followed a few paces behind them, and they walked like gods down to the sea and back.

None of us, not even Sarkak, ever walked on that path. It is still there, although ice and tides have destroyed the lower half and our tents are long gone from that place. The geese do not come there to nest anymore, and the caribou do not pass in autumn. Some say the animals flee from that straight path in fear, for they know that it was built by men.

IV

FROM THE first day we brought the strangers to our village, every-thing started to change for us. We began to look at ourselves through their eyes. For the first time we started to see ourselves. Without a language to speak together, we had to observe each other carefully.

By the middle of summer the foreigners seemed to feel as safe as children among us. They were learning to live freely as we did, enjoying each day, not caring about tomorrow. They slept in our beds, laughed often and tried to make themselves understood. They sometimes seemed to compete among themselves for our attention.

One day I remember they pulled out three of their tent poles and disappeared up a rocky ravine. After a while they came to the top of the path, and Kakuktak shouted down to us and gestured for us to come. Sarkak, followed by most of the villagers, went up the path. There were the three strangers standing around a newly formed outline of stones in the shape of a boat.

When we were all silent, Pilee walked stiffly back and forth, as though his eyes were searching. Then suddenly he shouted, "*Tuga, tuga, tuga,*" the words we call out when a sea beast is sighted.

Quickly all three snatched up their poles and pretended to climb over the boat's imaginary gunwale and knelt down inside. Pilee sat at the stern, steering with his pole. Kakuktak sat in the middle, moving his pole back and forth with a long steady stroke; then he moved to another place, stroked briefly and moved again, until he had sat in four places, so we could see that it took four men to row the boat. Now Portagee, who was in the bow, picked up his pole and aimed it like a huge harpoon. Leaning forward, he gazed intently beneath the surface of the imaginary water, then swayed back, taking careful aim, and drove his harpoon forward and downward, deep into a great sea beast's back. At once all three held on to the sides of the boat and swayed back and forth as they let the whale drag them at great speed through the water. I could scarcely believe my eyes, for all of this was like our own sea hunting, but the strangers were using their boat as we use the sealskin float we attach to our harpoon line. They allowed the whale to drag them while he was still full of life.

In their clever pantomime we saw the whale surface three times; saw Portagee drive his blade in and out of the great beast, giving each thrust that skillful bloodletting twist we knew so well; saw Kakuktak catch the fin of the imaginary whale and

hold it while Portagee fastened lines to it; saw them tow the floating carcass, all three of them now rowing and singing.

Finally they jumped out of their stone boat and bowed before us, smiling. People blew out their breaths in surprise and pleasure, for we had all understood perfectly their pantomime.

But we had a question. We had found one man dead; here were three. Where were the other two? Sarkak walked up to Pilee and pointed at two empty places in the stone boat.

Pilee nodded his head. He walked away a few steps and started slipping as though on ice. Then he fell, grasping at an imaginary man, and they both appeared to slip into the water.

Thus it was that we discovered how the strangers had come to us and how their companions had died on the way.

For the two and a half moons of summer the entire world seemed full of the river's singing and the sky knew no darkness. Only in the mornings mist drifted in from the sea and crept like white smoke over the tundra, hiding the inland from view.

I have always heard that fog in summer is caused by young people carelessly lying out together on the open tundra. Young people should be more careful, since fog never fails to spoil the summer hunting. So careless were our young people and the strangers, too, that heavy fog came to us for five days, and then day after day of driving rain. With so many people crowded into the beds, it was hard to live in the tents. At first it was comfortable enough; we slept a lot and told stories. But too much sleep makes the head ache, and one's thoughts grow heavy. Someone coughs and spits and coughs again, always in the same way, and everyone grows nervous. And when we had all had more confinement than we could stand, the old widow, Nuna's mother, started singing that crazy song of hers again and again. I wanted more than anything to run out in the rain and get away from it.

Once we heard Pilee and Portagee shouting at each other in the little tent next to ours and Pilee rushed out cursing. Pilee and Portagee had almost nightly visits from Evaloo and Panee at this time. Kakuktak seemed to prefer our company. During most of

the long rain he lay on our bed next to Kangiak, who was now his best friend and adviser about our ways and language. It was exciting having the strangers among us, and yet I had misgivings, for I could see that the whole life of the camp was changing.

On the last two days of the rain Pilee could no longer stand the company of Portagee and Panee, and he had gone with Evaloo to Sowniapik's tent. To fill the time, he had ground the point of his sea knife until it was deadly sharp. Behind the tent he found a flat piece of driftwood almost as long as a man. As soon as the rain let up he began to play a game on the piece of wood with his knife. He would flip the knife in the air from one end of it and it would whirl three times and land, point first, quivering right on a mark he had made at the far end. He allowed Sowniapik and me to practice with his knife, too, and slowly we gained skill until we could sometimes hit the mark. The other kayakmen— even Sarkak—tried it a few times, but we were too far ahead, so they usually just stood by and watched.

One evening, after we had played for some time, Pilee held up his hands for attention. Carefully he cut a white button from the top of his pants, held up the precious button for all to see, then placed it in the center of the board. Looking around, he saw Sowniapik's new sealskin mitts. He pointed to them and got Sowniapik to place them beside the button. Then he showed us with his hands that if his knife struck closer to the mark than Sowniapik's he would win the mitts, but if Sowniapik's knife came closer, Sowniapik would have the button.

This was a very exciting new idea to us. Sowniapik was delighted to try it. We all gasped with wonder when he won the button and still retained his mitts. Bursting with pride, he jerked off his parka and got his wife to sew the button onto the very center of it. He looked around wildly for something he could bet against Pilee. Then he remembered his bound cluster of little ivory knives, the amulet he used to shake when he wanted to cut away bad weather. Pilee looked at them with disdain, as though they were a child's toy. To keep the game going, though, he accepted them and reluctantly cut away another button from

his trousers. Sowniapik won again, and yet again, until he had triumphantly had his wife sew all four of Pilee's buttons onto his parka.

Everybody was excited now, and looking at Pilee and Sowniapik. With a gesture I shall never forget, Pilee held the knife itself aloft, offering it instead of a button. People gasped, and Sowniapik's eyes narrowed. He wanted that knife more than anything he had ever hoped to possess. Slowly he began to take off his parka with the four buttons on it, but Pilee stopped him and took his hand and placed it on Evaloo's wrist.

It took us all some moments to realize that Pilee wanted Sowniapik to offer his daughter as a bet against the knife. Sowniapik glanced at his wife. He did not like what he saw in her eyes and started to release Evaloo's hand, but his hunting companions groaned with disappointment, so he jerked her hand upward. The bet was made.

Sowniapik crouched and spun the knife with all his skill. It landed right beside the mark. We all blew out our breath, believing he had won. But Pilee moved into place. Then, slowly and carefully, Pilee flipped the knife. It buried itself in the very center of the mark.

With his teeth clenched in a half smile, Pilee reclaimed his precious knife. Then he grasped Evaloo's wrist and hauled her roughly to him, staring at us in defiance. The thought came to me again that the foreigners were one thing and we were another and perhaps we could never understand each other.

Pilee looked at Sowniapik's wife. Her face was like a death mask, her eyes drawn into slits. Pilee quickly let go of the girl and lay back on the bed, hoping we would not see that he was trembling. Everyone started coughing, which is our way of easing a tense situation. I was glad I was not Sowniapik. He would somehow have to settle with his wife for the daughter he had lost.

I could scarcely believe what I saw next. Sowniapik was holding up the hand of his other daughter, Mia. No one was more surprised than Pilee, who sat up and looked hungrily at the second girl. He held his knife in the air again, but Sowniapik made him

grasp the wrist of Evaloo instead. So Sowniapik's first daughter was bet against his second daughter. I did not have the courage to look into his wife's face.

Pilee was deadly white. I saw him look around at the cold eyes of the kayakmen, and I believe our closeness suddenly terrified him. He knelt down and cut a new target in the board, then quickly he spun the knife into its very heart. He handed the blade to Sowniapik, who, like a man in a trance, spun it without hope or skill. It landed far from the mark.

Pilee did not reach for Mia. He did not move. Sowniapik, without looking, flung his daughter roughly at Pilee. Those of us who had been sitting on the edge of the bed moved away. We wanted to be in some other place.

Pilee must have known that every eye and every hand in the tent was against him, for he suddenly leaned forward and handed Sowniapik his knife. He handed it to him backwards, with the handle out and the blade pointed toward himself. This to us is a sign of surrender, a sign of giving.

We all started coughing again, and the terrible tension in the tent was broken. Now Sowniapik had the precious knife, and Pilee had the two daughters. We all knew that if Pilee hurt either of the girls, some relative would seek revenge upon him. If he could feed them and so truly call them his own, we would be surprised. Sowniapik had really won, for he now owned the shining knife. Later I heard that his wife went to bed with a needle in her hand for several moons, and he was afraid to go near her. But she did let Pilee sleep between her daughters, and even came to like him. He was always able to work a kind of magic on women.

So sleeping places for the foreigners were settled by the middle of summer: Kakuktak with us in Sarkak's tent, Portagee in the little tent and Pilee in Sowniapik's. We could see that the three strangers were breaking apart. Because of the bright metal buttons on his jacket and his position as boat steerer, we were aware that Pilee was somehow above the other two. Portagee with his smooth-muscled brownness and his booming laughter was no

brother to the two pale men, and I could see that he sometimes wished to break away. Kakuktak, even though he had yellow hair, was most like us. He melted into our lives and understood our language.

Sarkak had become very fond of Kakuktak. He liked to sit between him and his favorite, Kangiak, and talk to both of them, and he was bent on teaching them all his skills. "Sons of mine," he would call to them, for they were now always together. Kakuktak showed great ability with the three-pronged bird spear and with the bow and arrow that Okalikjuak, the archer, showed him how to make. Kakuktak was indeed material for a son. Tugak and Yaw could not have liked this, but they were slow to take offense; and we were at this time all relaxed in the abundance of food and summer weather. It was a pleasure to have Sarkak in such an expansive mood.

One evening when Kangiak and Kakuktak had gone hunting, Sarkak lay down between his wives and asked to see the boots he had ordered Ikuma to make for Kakuktak. He inspected them carefully. Young Nuna sighed as she looked at these masterpieces of Ikuma's. She said, "Now Kakuktak has beautiful new boots, and all the children in this camp act as though they were his children. Kakuktak does not need a wife."

Sarkak sat up, and I could see his excitement rising. His women were always clever at planting ideas in his mind at the right moment. He swiftly left the tent.

Nuna followed Ikuma to the tent flap and flung her arm affectionately over the older woman's shoulder. Looking after Sarkak, they both began to laugh. "He will ask Poota for his daughter Neevee," said Ikuma. "She is the girl Sarkak desires most for himself. He will have her now for Kakuktak."

As though her words propelled him, Sarkak made his way to Poota's tent. There he stopped and coughed to warn the family of his presence, while Nuna and Ikuma held their heads together and clasped their hands over each other's mouths to muffle their wild unruly laughing. Some say that men rule the women in this land, but I would not say that is so.

47

Of all the girls in our camp, I liked Neevee best. There was a gentleness and yet a feeling of strength hidden within her. She had a beautiful tanned face, with cheeks glowing softly red as the belly of a sea trout. Her hair was long and of that kind of black that appears blue in the sunlight. She was shy with men, but because I was crippled and different from the others, she would often talk to me. I used to watch her with longing.

Sarkak remained for a long time in Poota's tent; but when Ikuma asked about the marriage he only grunted.

That afternoon Kakuktak and Kangiak returned carrying big bunches of fat eider ducks, which they proudly flung down at the women's feet.

Ikuma and Nuna skinned the feathers from eight of the birds and crammed them into the pot of water boiling above the lamp. The two young men lay on the bed, savoring their hunger as the rich broth began to fill the tent with its delicious odor.

Sarkak reached into the pot and selected the two largest ducks. One he kept for himself and the other he offered to Kakuktak. Everyone else then took a bird, and with our fingers we stripped the steaming meat from the carcasses. When he had finished, Sarkak belched with pleasure and spoke softly. "Wife of mine, take those others," he said, pointing at the remaining ducks. "Give them to the family of Poota, saying that Kakuktak sends them."

Understanding Sarkak's intentions, Ikuma immediately did as he had asked. Soon after she returned, Sarkak said to me, "Avinga, go and say to my dear hunting companion Poota that Kakuktak, who is like a son to me, wishes to come to their tent to sleep. You also will stay in Poota's tent and tell me how it goes with them."

I found Poota and his wife and their smaller children and Neevee sitting in a straight row along the front of the low bed. There was also the widowed mother of Poota's wife, old Ningiuk, and a younger daughter of Ningiuk's who was not yet spoken for in marriage. To make room for me, Neevee's small sister ran out to find a place in a neighbor's bed. I could tell that they were all nervous.

Poota spoke the first word. He pointed toward the pot and said, "Some ducks have given themselves to Kakuktak."

"Yes. In a little while he may arrive," I answered.

It was some time before we heard footsteps on the gravel bank and then a coughing outside. Poota coughed in response. The flap was thrust aside, and Kakuktak bent low and entered the tent.

Poota's young son shoved against me as he made room for Kakuktak on the bed. He did not intend to leave and miss anything that might take place between this yellow-headed foreigner and his sister Neevee. When he saw Kakuktak sit cautiously between Neevee and her father, he blew out his breath in noisy delight. Neevee dug her elbow into his ribs to silence him.

The ducks were quickly skinned and shoved into the pot and the feeling of tension went out of the house. Poota's wife showed Kakuktak a complicated string game we call the flying owl, and Kakuktak took out his marking stick and white skins and began to draw animals like nothing we had ever seen. While he was drawing, Kakuktak told how these strange beasts bellowed, roared and jabbered, and as he imitated the sounds, everyone in the household shouted with laughter.

Kakuktak's eyes were shining and his face flushed with pleasure as he leaned back among them, feeling all the warmth of Poota's family. Neevee and her brother had pushed me into the circle as though I, too, belonged within this family, and my soul wished that it could have been so. Sarkak's tent could never be like this. In Sarkak's tent, we all lived for him.

Poota's wife put the stone pot full of ducks on the floor before us. When we had finished the meat, we passed the pot, each drinking his share of broth. Then we wiped our hands and mouths with the soft skin of a white hare and lay back on the bed. I could smell the sweet heather spread beneath it. Poota soon slept heavily. Neevee's brother tried desperately to stay awake, but his head soon nodded. I was too excited to sleep at all.

In the half darkness, Kakuktak sat up beside Neevee and drew off his parka, slowly exposing his shocking smooth white torso. He rolled the parka into a pillow and lay down again. Neevee

waited for some time, then sat up and in one smooth movement drew off her parka and shook her head; her hair spread over her naked shoulders. Then she slid quietly down beside Kakuktak under the skins that covered all of us.

I could hear them breathing and knew they were feeling the heat of each other's bodies. Neevee showed Kakuktak how to place his nose beside hers and sniff tenderly, a custom of our people. Then I saw Kakuktak place his whole mouth over Neevee's. I thought he was biting her and thought to grab his sea knife and stab him in the back, but Neevee's arms were pressing him tightly to her. They parted for breath, looked at each other and then placed their mouths together again in that unbelievable act. So shy were they that they had moved very little. They were like young children playing in the warmth of their family bed.

I must have grown weary with watching, for I fell asleep and dreamed of countless children with yellow hair and pale skins, but when I knelt among them, I could see that they had the dark quick eyes of our people. A white bear came in the dream and stood silently among us. When I awoke I was trembling, knowing that because of such a bear dream I should quickly lie with a woman. I pulled on my parka and made my way out of the tent to touch Lao, the gray bitch, hoping that this might be enough to fulfill the dream. Then I hobbled off to report to Sarkak.

Kakuktak, I thought, was like ourselves, although his goodness may have been learned from us. Now Neevee came to know him much better than anyone. She came to think of his smooth white skin and yellow hair as beautiful. She teased him about the hair on his jaws, and to please her, he honed his sea knife into deadly sharpness and shaved his face until it was as smooth as any of ours. The times when I slept next to them and heard them laughing and whispering were when I wished desperately that I could have been a whole man, with a woman of my own.

When summer was almost gone, I awoke one night and heard Tugak saying excitedly to Sarkak, "The fish have returned. If you come now, you can see them from the high bank."

Everyone left the bed, drawing on pants and parkas, and hurried to the river below the falls. Others were already there, watching in the twilight. I knelt on the bank, supporting myself on the bitch Lao, and watched school after school of bright sea trout flash their red-and-silver sides in the blackness of the racing river as they fought their way upstream. The fish goddess had called her children to her from the vastness of the sea and now carefully guided them up the river to leap the falls and make their way to the great depths of the lake that would be their winter home.

"Clear the openings to the stone trap, and watch it very carefully," said Sarkak. "Just as the tide turns we will roll the stones back into place and close the trap."

Dawn came and slowly the river rose with the huge tide until it flooded its banks, and the silver hordes were carried upward on their journey. As the incoming power of the salt sea met and mingled with the downward force of the river, I saw the water go slack. Our people long before us had built a false channel here, and into this weir slipped whole schools of shining fish.

On a signal from Sarkak, the four spearmen who had cleared the heavy stones from the opening quickly waded back into the rushing water and replaced them, closing off the narrow entrance so the fish could not escape.

Sarkak, taking a double-pronged fish spear, walked carefully out into the weir, slowly, his eyes adjusting to the sunlight that now flashed across the water. He held the spear lightly poised in his right hand. Then he struck downward with a thrust so swift I could not see it, and when he raised the spear again it held a huge thrashing sea trout.

Sarkak laughed with joy, for this was what every man lived for. Here he was with a whole camp of men, women, children and dogs to feed, and because we lived like true people, offending neither men nor spirits, the fish had come to give themselves to us. Carefully he handed the fish to the mother of Poota's wife, Ningiuk, who was the oldest woman in the camp. Crooning to the fish, she walked a few paces upstream, where swiftly she slit it open. Removing one eye and some secret parts of its entrails,

she cast these out onto the river and cried out, "Swim, soul, swim. Swim back to your dear father's house."

Then all the men were suddenly easing their bodies into the freezing water. Poota speared the second fish and Sowniapik the third. Then everyone seemed to have a shining sea trout on the end of his spear. The men flung them with wild abandon into the crowd of women and children, who carried the big, cold slippery fish to a mounting pile of shining silver bodies. The next day the women would clean them and hang the bright forms on long lines between the tents to dry.

But that evening was feasting time. We slit open and ate the beautiful cold pink flesh of fresh sea trout until we could eat no more. The three strangers were anxious to join us in the feast, though they had taken little part in the day's fishing. Only Kakuktak had any skill with the spear. Pilee and Portagee found a huge flat stone over a hollow place in the rocks, and there lighted some dry tundra moss and driftwood twigs. When the rock grew hot, they split open several of our fish and laid them on the stone. The delicate meat turned from pink to white to a burned black. Then they called Kakuktak to join them and the three of them, laughing like children, ate the hot crumbling flesh. We knew how to do this, of course, but we thought it a disgusting way to spoil meat, and the smell and the greasy smoke were offensive to us. We turned our heads away so we would not have to see them disgracing themselves by eating this ruined flesh.

Next day we watched for the tides again, but the fish in numbers did not come. Something must have offended them. Perhaps it was having their flesh burned black; perhaps some child had thrown a stone and angered them. And then the wind rose, and our fish lines fell in the night, and the dogs devoured the catch. The river went mad and flooded over our stone trap, so that the fish all passed over it and on up to the lake, where they would remain, locked away from us beneath the oncoming winter's ice.

It was a terrible thing to lose the fish. We knew whole camps that had starved to death because the summer fishing had failed them. It was just as well that our three visitors did not know this.

What people said about these *kalunait* was true; whenever we tried to like them, they would do something disgusting to remind us how outlandish they were. Perhaps they never could be one with us, not even Kakuktak.

V

NEEVEE's young brother saw them first and ran to his father Poota's tent. In a moment everyone was out, watching as two men and three heavily burdened dogs approached from the inland.

"My cousin Tunu and his son Nukinga arrive," Sarkak said. "Loaded with caribou meat. Look at the size of Nukinga's pack. No one else in this country could travel with a load like that."

"Even the dogs are bending bowlegged under their packs," said Poota. "And see the weight dear old Tunu is carrying. He must be glad to see this camp and know he is finished for today. I do not think he will bother much with women this night."

Sarkak could have sent a young man to help Tunu, but that would have been an insult, suggesting that he could not carry his load. It also would have made Sarkak appear too anxious to get his teeth into some of the fresh caribou meat.

Poota's wife turned and went into their tent and Poota darted in after her. I knew he was asking her if Tunu could sleep in their tent, sleep with her. She could easily have refused by saying nothing, and then he would not dare invite Tunu. But if she agreed she would answer, "It's only up to you." This she must have said, for Poota came out of the tent looking pleased.

Tunu walked up smiling, his eyes twinkling with delight.

"*Tikiposi*. You arrive," said Sarkak formally.

"*Tikipoguk*. I arrive," answered Tunu, and with a sigh he eased the big pack of meat off his back. Many hands were already helping Nukinga unload the dogs. Then Tunu looked up and saw the *kalunait* standing in front of our big tent. He touched his son's arm, and they stared in horror and disbelief. I realized all at once that we had almost forgotten the unreal appearance of our tall, gaunt visitors.

"Come, you will both sleep in my tent," invited Poota.

Tunu answered with a cry of pleasure, "*Eeee!* Yes!" For he and Poota had grown up together in another camp.

It was as Poota had said. Tunu and his son Nukinga slept and ate and slept again and did not bother the women. They had come to us after their hunt because our camp was closer than theirs, and they knew we would gladly load their caribou into a kayak and send it the three days' journey along the coast. They gave a generous portion of the meat to all our households.

On the following day Poota went away seal hunting and was gone all night. Tunu lay in his place. Kakuktak was very nervous seeing this, and Neevee and I laughed and tried to calm him. We told him again and again that it was all right—that, when agreed upon, it was our custom.

On the third day after the newcomers arrived, the young people gathered at the end of the beach for wrestling matches. Soon the men went and joined them. I saw Kakuktak looking at Nukinga's shoulders, which were as wide as those of two men, and I wondered what he was thinking. We wished Nukinga belonged to us, for he was good-natured, and there was no strength like his anywhere in our whole world.

Two young boys stepped forward and started cautiously circling each other. Then one grasped the other around the waist and gave a clever sideways lift, and the other boy lost his balance briefly. Although he regained his footing immediately, the match was over. The instant one lost his balance, the other man had won. There were four or five more such matches and then the men

turned and called to Nukinga, who just sat smiling. In spite of his strength, he was still young and not clever at the wrestling game.

Our Atkak, who had never been beaten during my whole lifetime, pulled off his parka and walked out, smiling at Nukinga, urging him affectionately to do likewise.

"I'm not enough for him," said Nukinga.

"*Ataii. Ataii.* Go on. Go on," called the watchers. Nukinga got up.

The two stood before each other, legs slightly spread, arms raised, smiling yet alert. Atkak slipped his arms around the youth's waist and heaved to force him off his feet. Nukinga seemed rooted to the sand. He locked his arms around Atkak and twisted only a handsbreadth and Atkak lost his balance. Instantly Nukinga released him. Atkak had lost! We gasped with disbelief.

Both wrestlers, smiling, started to leave the sand, but I heard a murmuring. There was Pilee, urging Portagee to pull off his parka. Why hadn't *we* thought of this, I wondered. How wonderful to see Nukinga and Portagee play the wrestling game!

"*Eeee, eeee.* Yes, yes," cried all the men. "*Ataii.* Go on!"

Glancing toward the tents, I saw all the women watching the wrestlers, as excited as we were. But Kakuktak stood up quickly, his face showing no pleasure. I saw that he was nervous, and I remembered that we did not always play games in the same way.

Young Nukinga waited, smiling. Suddenly Portagee leaped in, crouching, his fingers hooked like claws, and lunged. Nukinga seemed to be unprepared for the attack. But I saw his back arch mightily; Portagee went over and would have fallen if Nukinga had not saved him.

Nukinga smiled politely and said, "He is very strong, like a giant." Then he started to walk away. But Portagee sprang quickly after him and tapped him hard on the shoulder.

It is not our custom for adults to wrestle many times together, only young children do that; but the big brown man, not smiling, demanded to try again. Nukinga stepped back onto the sand. He seemed to wait unthinking for the attack, but when it came we could see how ready he was. His huge arms locked like a bear's paws around the sinuous waist of the stranger, and with a small

56

shift of his weight, he carried Portagee off balance. Again he held him to keep him from falling. Nukinga had won again.

But as he turned away this time, Portagee, to everyone's astonishment, shot his arm out and locked it tightly around Nukinga's throat, cutting off his wind, as one might do before a killing. Portagee then placed his long leg behind Nukinga's and with a sharp twist flung Nukinga to the ground, falling heavily on top of him. Nukinga fought back, for he must have known terrible fear. He must have thought Portagee had gone mad, for such a violent attack could not have come from a sane man. Portagee's eyes bulged, and he bared his teeth like an animal's.

Kakuktak and Kangiak and Tugak and Yaw ran out and together pulled Portagee off Nukinga. Nukinga stood looking first at Portagee, then at his father. "Someone should open him up with a knife," he said, "and see what kind of a soul a man has that makes him play a game like that."

But Sarkak said, "It is only that these strangers do not know how to play our way. Look how the big one is smiling at you. That means he likes you, because you are strong and he is strong. You must remember that these *kalunait* know very little about life. They are violent, savage people."

On the day following the wrestling, when Tunu and his son had left, Sarkak stood outside the tent staring at the flatness of the sea and upon the first pale edge of the autumn moon.

"Wives," he called, "are the boots finished?"

You could tell by the power in his voice, as he gave the cry that is heard in every camp, that Sarkak was in a mood to travel.

"*Eeee*," they answered. "The boots are finished."

"We shall go, then," he called, and walked slowly down toward the beach, allowing the idea of leaving to spread through the camp. Silver-gray clouds drifted across the horizon. Anyone could see that the sky would soon be full of whirling flakes.

Our people believe in moving. It is like searching for a new life. We always believe that each new place will be crowded with land animals or birds or sea beasts waiting to give themselves to

us. The very thought fills us with hope. So soon every tent was down, all possessions packed, and the boats had been carried into knee-deep water. And when they were loaded, and the children and pups thrown in after the load, the people laughed and groaned with pride. They did not believe that any other people in the world could possess such riches.

As we left, a light snow squall blew over the mountains. Sarkak had decided that instead of returning at once to our winter camp we should move down the coast to hunt for seals or walrus or any dead whale that might have washed ashore. Kayakmen spread out like water bugs, carefully searching every bay. When the wind whipped the water into waves, we could not see the seals. On those days we pulled into shore, upturned the boats and huddled under them. The hungry bowmen searched for small birds and animals. But they did not find enough to feed the children.

After ten days of this, the skin bags of fish we carried were empty. There was nothing left to eat. With the first hint of hunger, you could see how much the strangers feared we would all lose our lives. Each day they seemed more nervous. They spoke in whispers, their faces tight. I saw them searching secretly through all our bundles, unable to believe the food was gone. The wind blew and blew and we all felt our strength ebbing. Our heads ached, and our tempers grew short. The length of time between plenty and hunger is very brief. In good times one tends to forget this. We traveled on to a rocky peninsula called Tikirak, and near its tip we entered a small cove. From this place, Sarkak said, we would travel no more; we would live or die here. We pitched our tents, and for three more days we listened to the hungry children crying and watched the squalls play across the heaving sea. Then on the night of the fullness of the moon the huge tide flooded the cove almost to the entrance of our tents.

Before dawn, as the high water receded, the women hurried out to search the tidal flats. There they found tiny breathing holes, and digging with their powerful fingers and sharp pieces of bone, they gathered delicious long-necked clams. They had to work fast, taking advantage of this big tide which would occur only on this

one day. Their efforts gave the camp just one good feeding, but it brought back the hope of life to all of us.

For five more days gray fog and freezing rain swept in on us. Each morning, noon and evening, two kayakmen would climb to the highest place and search the sea for walrus. Barely visible was a small island where it is said that walrus come in the autumn moon to dig with their tusks for clams. But apart from looking, the kayakmen could do nothing, for this was not a seal-hunting place. When their harpoon points had been honed to deadly sharpness, they sat huddled together carving the likenesses of walrus in bone or stone. And every word they spoke was carefully chosen, for some walrus spirit might be listening. The strangers laughed at our carving, as though we were stupid children, and made motions as though we should go out and hunt from kayaks. But we knew there was nothing there to hunt.

On the fifth night of the waning moon Sarkak was restless. He said aloud that someone had broken a taboo, but I know that he blamed himself for not having left the summer camp as soon as the fish had failed us. Again and again he pushed himself angrily out into the night and stood listening in the fog. Once he remained a long time, then came to the tent flap and called softly, "Kangiak, Tugak, Yaw, Avinga. Walrus! Smell them. Smell the meat. They have come to the rock."

At first I smelled nothing. Then a faintly pungent odor drifted in from the sea. I breathed it in with ecstasy. For us it was the smell of life. All the hunters of the camp came out to join us. The *kalunait* came out, too, but they could smell nothing; nor did they remember why all around us was the sound of the clicking of little ivory knives, the amulets men shake to try and cut the weather.

I slept more soundly that night than I had since the first night that the moon had been reborn, which proves that it is not hunger so much as fear that drives away sleep.

WE WERE all stirring before dawn. The sea heaved with a long gray swell, as though some monstrous beast lay beneath the surface. Men and women carried the hunting gear out to the kayaks.

Poota and Sowniapik were the first to push their long slim crafts out into the powerful swell. Kangiak and four others followed, like a loose wedge of geese.

Each man had placed his harpoon in the ivory rest on the right side of the kayak deck and his killing spear on the left, and had neatly coiled the harpoon line in the shallow drum that lay in the center of the deck. On each back deck lay the air-filled sealskin float that was attached by a long line to the harpoon.

I followed the others in Nuna's mother's kayak. As I caught up with them, a light gust of wind opened a hole in the early morning fog, and for a brief moment I could see the rock, covered with a solid mass of walrus. I felt my heart pounding.

As we paddled forward, the air suddenly filled with a strange tenseness. The herd had become aware of us. The walrus stopped their endless swaying and peered warily into the patchy fog. Then we heard the first challenge. A deep-throated roar rumbled from the belly of a huge bull walrus weighing twenty times more than one of the men who hunted him. Clumsily shouldering the younger males and females aside, he heaved his bulk into the sea. All of us eased our harpoons from their ivory rests and waited.

Suddenly the bull rose out of the water and lunged toward Nowya's kayak. Nowya snatched up his harpoon and swung his right arm smoothly forward. The point drove deep into the thick skin that protected the bull walrus's neck, and the harpoon's heavy driftwood shaft collapsed, as it should, into three pieces loosely tied together. If it had remained stiff, it would have torn loose when the big beast thrashed in the sea.

The walrus dived, and Nowya knocked free the air-filled sealskin float that was attached to his harpoon line. It danced on the water, then disappeared beneath the surface as the great bull dove deep. At that moment Nowya turned and gestured to us, wild with the excitement of the hunt. He had been the first to set his harpoon into this great prize. But he should never have taken his thoughts from that enormous beast. As I watched, I saw his whole kayak thrust violently upward out of the water. It seemed to pause for a moment, then turn over, and I heard the

sealskin rip and saw Nowya's head snap back sickeningly as he disappeared. The walrus seemed to crash down on him and the sea turned pink in a tangle of wreckage. We saw only one boot raised above the water as Nowya slipped away from us forever.

The big bull sulked beneath the surface of the sea until his lungs were almost bursting. Then he flung himself boldly upward into our midst. Two harpoons struck him before he could draw in his second breath, and we shouted at him in our anger. His instincts caused him to duck again, without enough air. But there were now three floats attached to him, so we watched where he swam and paddled to where he would have to surface. Suddenly this killer of Nowya reappeared among us, red-eyed and roaring, white tusks deadly. Sowniapik snatched up his killing spear and drove it in and out of the bull's throat three times. Then he quickly drew back out of danger. The water turned almost black as the big bull's heart pumped dark rich blood into the sea. We turned away for we knew his meat was ours, safely held with three harpoons and floats.

With Kangiak beside me, I now followed a young bull who jealously herded a dozen females ahead of him, roaring and threatening them with his tusks. I pressed in upon him, and my heart sang and my hands trembled with joy. Every kayakman seemed to have a walrus harpooned now. In these few moments our camp had been allowed to push death away.

From far away on land I heard the faint, delighted screaming of the women, and then I saw the umiak. Standing up in the bow, with his harpoon aimed ahead, looking exactly as he had in the pantomime of the whaling boat, was the big Portagee. Rowing hard behind him stood Kakuktak and Pilee. In the stern of the boat sat Sarkak, his long hair blowing in the wind as he worked the stern oar with all the cleverness he possessed. They were moving fast. A bull rose before them, and Portagee sprung his whole body forward as he released the harpoon. I saw it drive deeply into the animal's back. A shout went up from Sarkak and the others.

Portagee should have flung out the big sealskin float, but instead he snubbed the line around the front thwart, as the three

of them had done in the pantomime. The big walrus plunged deep into the sea, and with horror I saw the line go tight. Portagee paid it out, a little at a time, but the old umiak shuddered, with its bow forced down almost into the water. I was amazed at this crazy man trying to hold a full-grown walrus tied to a thin-skinned boat. I could not believe he would ignore Sarkak's angry shouts. But he did. Kakuktak and Pilee were holding the sides of the boat and howling with laughter as the old umiak skidded across the reddened sea.

Portagee had no time to laugh. He worked like a wild man, his muscles straining as he fought to close the gap between the walrus and the boat. The slim boat shuddered as the line snapped downward, and the walrus fought to gain depth beneath the sea.

But slowly the beast's muscles and his huge lungs failed him. Mouth open, he rose almost beneath the bow and Portagee, neatly and swiftly, in a way I had never seen before, lanced him with the killing spear. It was over. The bull rolled belly up and floated just beneath the surface.

The three strangers roared, and Portagee slapped his own buttocks loudly. I was shocked to hear such laughing from a boat with a newly dead sea beast attached and surprised that our young boys were so quick to call out and laugh in shameless imitation of the foreigners. Sarkak sat silent in the stern, alone, an old man; for he, the great hunter and planner for us all, had only acted like a servant to these men.

Portagee, not Sarkak, gave the order to return to land. I heard them singing and shouting irreverently as they towed their great burden back. Each kayakman also pulled a great floating prize toward the women on the shore. When we reached shallow water we heard them wailing as they mourned the death of Nowya and comforted his wife and children. But on this day when we had all been given life again, we could not force our thoughts to rest for long with the dead.

By the time we had placed the umiak and the kayaks safely up on the rocks, the great walrus lay almost fully exposed on the rock-strewn beach. Sarkak walked down to the huge form and

called to the three foreigners to follow him. Borrowing Portagee's knife, he reached down and severed the huge right-front flipper.

"Wife of mine," he shouted. Ikuma came forward, and he handed her the choice flipper. It was so heavy, she had to lean sideways as she walked proudly back among the starving women. All of the kayakmen then cut flippers from their walrus and called to their wives. Sarkak then cut away the other flippers and gave one to each of the strangers.

Pilee was the first who thought he recognized the meaning of this giving away of meat, and he called out to Evaloo and Mia. Pushed from behind by others, they moved shyly forward. Everyone knew he should have given the meat to the girls' mother, for in our eyes these girls were only on loan to him from that family. But he knew nothing of this, and we no longer expected these people to do things in our way.

Portagee did not hesitate to call Panee, the daughter of Atkak, and even her father did not say a word, for Portagee now was himself such an incredible prize for that girl to win. When it was Kakuktak's turn, he called Neevee's name softly. Although she was very shy, she stepped forward. This new style of doing things, this ignoring of the parents and giving gifts directly to the girls, shocked the old and pleased the young. Certainly it would never have come about except for the foreigners.

The kayakmen now sliced neatly through the animals, dividing them into sections small enough to carry. They worked desperately to finish their task before the tide returned. At last, on the rocks above the high-tide line, a dozen severed heads with gleaming ivory tusks stared blindly out to sea. We trembled with cold and exhaustion and a hunger that could not be banished by a few strips of meat. But we knew that if we ate a lot at once, our stomachs would rebel. So, the butchering finished, we washed ourselves clean of blood, for it is not right to have the life of animals upon you. And then we crawled to our beds and slept.

Hours later, Sarkak awakened me shouting, "*Kakpunga.*" Portagee, knowing this meant, "I'm hungry," also bellowed it.

This time when Pilee arranged flat stones and lighted a fire and

burned the young meat black, no one even noticed, so intent was everyone with the great joy of eating.

When all our stomachs were filled, Portagee went to the up-turned umiak and struck the tight sealskin sharply. It resounded in the darkness like a huge drum. He smiled and went on hammering with both hands, singing out wild words, flinging his head forward and then snapping it up again, faster, faster, shaking his mass of tightly curled black hair. The sound he made excited us all, and some of the women tried to set up a chorus to answer it, but it was too fast for them. They all laughed so much that both the drumming and the singing ended. Portagee in his excitement whirled among the women, then flung himself beneath the great boat drum. A number of young girls scrambled to join him there, without secrecy. The older people blew out their breaths, scarcely believing the wild new ways coming to us through these foreigners, these big children who knew so little.

Suddenly Sarkak was gone, alone, to our tent. I knew he hated this new lack of control, for it was not his way. He had gained no command over the *kalunait* and could no longer prevent the things that were happening in his own camp.

The next day we filled the boats with as much walrus meat as we could carry and set out at dawn. We paddled for three days, scarcely bothering to hunt the seals, which had reappeared in great numbers. And finally we saw the sight we longed for, the two tall man-shaped images built of stone that marked the entrance to the bay of our winter camp. But as my kayak touched the shore, I wondered at how desolate, how unused, our campground seemed. This place where I had been born should have shown some marks of our laughing and dancing, but only the boat racks and high stone graves showed that we had ever lived here.

We made our autumn camp near the shelter of the north hill, where we always waited until the snows needed to build our igloos came again. The weather was cold though, even now, and the strangers shivered in their dark, thin clothing. Sarkak decided to have the women make parkas for them. Ikuma made Kakuk-tak's, for which Sarkak chose light and dark sealskin strips, a

64

distinctive design which would allow us to recognize the wearer at a distance. Pilee's parka was made by Sowniapik's wife, and Atkak's wife made Portagee's and a pair of pants for him as well. Both were much too large at first, for she had an exaggerated idea of the hugeness of the brown man. When he tried them on, we all laughed together, like people related to each other.

During the second moon of autumn the tundra moss turned softly red. The women went out with the children and gathered great bundles of sweet-smelling heather for our beds. The children made a game of finding the few red low-bush cranberries and frost-blackened crowberries that lay hidden in the tundra and filled their parka hoods with them. When they took them back to camp, they were amazed to see the strangers wolf down the berries as though they were the only food in the world. So the next day they filled three large sealskin buckets with berries, these not red but dark blue. Pilee, Kakuktak and Portagee ate a few handfuls of these and then decided to save the rest so they could have some every day while they lasted. Knowing that the dogs would not like them, they carelessly left the buckets outside their tent. That night I heard against the side of the tent a muffled sound that meant our first heavy snow. For the next four days and nights a blizzard whistled and screamed and whipped our frozen tents. On the fifth morning there was deathlike silence, and I looked out on a new white world. Everywhere great wind-packed drifts were carved into strange shapes.

I saw Portagee with Pilee, out searching through the snow around the little tent. Curious, I went to help them, and so did a few women and children. The strangers outlined the shape of the three skin buckets with their hands and pointed into their mouths, cramming in imaginary berries. We did not understand, for we believed they had eaten the berries during the storm and now perhaps were foolishly looking for more berries in the snowdrifts. And so, thinking they were joking, we imitated them, stamping our feet and swallowing imaginary berries, making a game of it. But they did not smile, and suddenly Pilee jerked off his mitt and pointed his finger at us and shouted, "You steal. You steal."

I did not know what the words meant then, but I could not forget the sound of them because of all the rage on the two men's faces as they turned and stamped back inside the tent.

That afternoon Sarkak and the hunters took their long thin probes across the wind-packed drifts to test the snow and select the best places to build our igloos. They cut straight down into the snow with their long knives, lifted big blocks and stood them upright one against the other in a ring. Slowly six houses rose in coiling spirals, each snow block cleverly cut to fit against the next. The builder of each house stayed inside it and never stepped outside. The waist-deep hole he first stood in became the floor of the new snowhouse. Finally the wedge-shaped key block was carefully fitted into place in the top of the dome, immediately giving the house enough strength to bear a man's weight.

Outside each snowhouse the women were working, chinking the cracks with fine snow, and a man was building a meat porch and a long twisting entrance tunnel to keep out the wind and cold. Finally, a fist-sized hole was cut in a short snow chimney for ventilation, and a large clear sheet of freshwater lake ice, the thickness of a man's wrist, was placed in the sloping wall above the entrance passage to let light into the house.

When the new igloos were finished, the women spread dried heather over the snow sleeping bench that stretched across the entire back half of each house. Over the heather they placed white bearskins and sealskins, and over these skins on which we would lie they placed caribou robes with the hair turned inward, to make a warm nest for naked sleepers.

At this time two new side igloos appeared in our village. One for Nowya's young widow was attached to the side of Okalikjuak the archer's house. Living beside her brother gave her his protection. Visitors would have to ask his permission to sleep with her and this he would give only with her consent. The other side igloo was attached to Sarkak's big snowhouse. It was made for the three foreigners, but they rarely used it for sleeping, so great was the hospitality of our young women and their parents.

At this time in the early winter Sarkak wished to have Kakuktak

live with him in his snowhouse. I do not know what arrangement
he must have made with Poota, but one night Neevee appeared in
Sarkak's igloo and a place was made for her in the bed. Kakuktak
smiled and came without complaining, but they must both have
missed the warmth of Poota's family as much as I did.

VI

ONE midday during the first moon of winter the shaman came.
Atkak had sent his oldest son to get him because his father was
very sick. The old man had fallen six days before and since then
had lain, scarcely moving, breathing badly. The older women
crowded around him assuring him that he was going to die. To
them death was interesting and only a little frightening. I believe
the strangers did fear the coming of death, for I noticed that
Portagee quickly moved out of Atkak's house. A fish was the only
thing we knew that might make the old man well again, so Atkak
had gone off to the big lake to catch one. He was carrying it by
the tail, a big frozen fish, when his wife came out of his igloo and
told him the old man was dead. He stood quietly for a moment,
then spun around and flung the precious fish at the dogs—a crazy
thing to do, for they were half starved after three days of traveling. They fought savagely over it and Atkak stood rigidly, doing
nothing.

While we all stood shivering in the stinging wind, watching
Atkak, we saw another team come up through the barrier ice,
guided by Atkak's son. The shaman, short and very heavy, lay

on the sled and clung to it like a favored wife, waiting for it to halt in front of the igloo.

"*Keenaoona?* Who is this?" said Kakuktak, who stood beside me.

"*Angokok,*" I said. But I knew he would not understand our name for this magic man, this healer, with the skin line tied above his ears and the fox teeth dangling down over his forehead.

During our lives Sarkak and the shaman had always been the two most important people in the land. They both knew this and because of it they competed with each other, one using his religious magic and the other his immense wealth of food.

The shaman had with him a dirty boy dressed in tattered clothing. A hunter had told us that this boy had fallen down in a fit during the first spring moon and that was why the shaman had chosen him as an assistant. Now many people gathered around the two of them, standing in a circle, their hoods hiding all their faces in shadows. At first no one spoke, and I watched to see what would happen, for the shaman did not know that the old man was dead. Finally Atkak told him, and started to lead him into the igloo. The shaman spread his arms and called out, "No, no," in his high unnatural voice. Then he called for a snow knife and clumsily cut a big block of snow, which he at once placed in the entrance to the porch, carefully sealing it. Then with a great show of ceremony he urinated in the form of a cross against the blocked door. He called to the dirty boy and he, too, urinated there.

The three strangers laughed at this, for they did not understand that the shaman was disguising the entranceway, cleverly hiding it from the ghost of the dead man.

The shaman turned away from the sealed entrance and looked around him, searching, I was sure, for Sarkak. He saw him standing outside our igloo and making no move to come and greet him. The shaman, as though he had seen nothing, ducked, without invitation, into the nearest house, Okalikjuak's. Here he and his boy would stay the length of their visit.

Everyone now crowded around Atkak and his family, and they were led into the warmth of Tungilik's snowhouse.

When we returned to our house, Sarkak had gone inside and the

three foreigners were in their small igloo. I looked in on them, and I cannot tell you how much I wished that I had the power to speak to them. They did not understand who the shaman was or why he was here. I worried that I had no way to warn them that there were old jealousies between Sarkak and the shaman.

The next day I pulled on my extra caribou-skin stockings, for I did not want cold feet to cause me to miss any of the events. Then I woke Kakuktak and Portagee—Pilee was with his girls in Sowniapik's bed. Since I could not tell them about the shaman, they would have to see his magic for themselves—how he would break the dead man's spells and guard us against his ghost.

When we reached Atkak's snowhouse the shaman was already moving around importantly. He in no way acknowledged that he saw the giant brown man and the white-haired Kakuktak who were with me, and called out sharply to the dirty boy, who was gawking in horror at them. He made the boy cut a small hole in the block that sealed the entrance and told him to cough loudly and call certain words into the passage to attract the spirit. While the boy did this the shaman cut a large new opening in the igloo wall. Our people drew back in fear, not wishing to be in line with the new entrance. But Kakuktak and Portagee crowded forward for a closer view of the dead man lying inside.

The shaman strode into the igloo, peering all around him, holding out his hands as if to feel for any unseen spirits. He stepped up onto the sleeping platform and looked into the dead man's face. Then he called Atkak and his relatives to carry the body outside. It was frozen stiff, and pale as a bleached bone. The real man we had known, the dancer and singer, had flown out of it.

They carried his body to the hilly place where the high stone graves were, and found a windswept place, almost free of snow. There they laid him on his side, facing the frozen bay, with his knife, his bow and a bone drinking cup beside him; and then, as is our custom, they covered his body with heavy skull-sized stones, forming a mound as high as a man's waist.

The shaman placed the last large stone on top of the grave, calling out as he did so, "Beware, for with the coming moons others

will die in this place. Be careful, for great harm may come to all of you." Then he shouted harshly to the dirty boy, who kept staring at the foreigners, ordering him back to the village.

The next morning it was as though nothing had happened in the village. Atkak and his wife were out early to build a new snow-house for themselves, and many neighbors came to help them. There was much joking, as this house was both wider and taller than the old one, built that way, everyone said, to accommodate the tall Portagee along with Atkak's daughter, Panee.

The shaman and the boy stayed on for half a moon to eat our food and in this way collect their payment. But we rarely saw them, except the day the white bear came.

Moving silently in off the dark sea ice in the early morning, the great bear ate two of our dogs without waking the others, which seemed almost a miracle to me. It was not the dogs but Ikuma who gave the alarm. She heard the bear rubbing its side against our entrance passage and woke Sarkak. Everyone was alert in an instant, and we heard the dogs begin their slow moaning, a sound they make only for a bear, and then just outside we heard the big dog Pasti, snarling, rush in at the bear. We heard the bear disembowel the dog, and we heard the snow squealing as the great beast shambled off toward the jagged sea ice. We rushed out and saw the running bear with twenty dogs around him. Just then he turned to fight. With the cunning of the white bear he had chosen a great slab of ice to be at his back for protection. Two dogs attacked him, and with one smooth motion he killed the first and hamstrung the second.

We stopped cautiously halfway to the ring of dogs. But Sarkak was anxious to end the bear's life before too many dogs were killed. He bound his iron knife to the end of a long ice chisel with a length of sealskin line. He borrowed Kakuktak's knife, too, and stuck it in his boot top, and waving the others back, started out alone, running lightly on his toes, and giving, as he ran, the wounded raven call, "*Cauk, cauk, cauk,*" which dog drivers use to excite their teams. Instantly all our dogs were yelping, darting, feinting at the bear.

70

The bear's black eyes watched the running figure. His blue tongue lolled between great yellow teeth, his breath steamed white in the freezing air. *"Harr, harr, harr,"* called Sarkak, and our lead dog, followed by my brave foolish Lao, rushed in at the bear. The instant the bear rose to kill the bitch, Sarkak stepped within arm's reach and drove the iron knife into his side once, twice. As he tried for a third strike, the bear came at him fast. It was the moment the dogs had waited for, and in an instant they swarmed in upon the huge animal, tearing mouthfuls of skin and hair from his back and sides. The bear whirled on them, and Sarkak struck again, his shoulders driving all his weight behind the spear. He must have cut the artery to the heart, for the bear fell. The dogs leaped on him again.

I have never heard a man utter a sound as terrible as that which Sarkak then forced up from the depth of his belly. It was a roar that had in it the sharp cracking of whips and the breaking of bones. It drove deadly fear into the dogs and broke their bloody passion. They drew back and made room for Sarkak. With swiftness and caution, he touched the staring eye of the bear to be sure that its soul had flown away.

Ikuma and Nuna skinned the bear quickly, while it steamed hot in the morning air. Its great white hide belonged to Sarkak alone, but the meat was divided among all the people in the camp.

The killing of a white bear within a camp was no little thing, and the shaman came out to see if there might be any magic attached to this so silent dog killer. As he bent to examine the entrails, he found himself standing beside Sarkak.

The conversation between them started slowly at first, but gradually it grew and fattened, and these two powerful men, who had known each other all their lives, became caught up in the pleasure of words, for each of them loved best to talk, to argue. For all their jealousy and mistrust, they were a perfect conversational match for each other, and they both knew it.

Sarkak began by mentioning the elaborate plaiting of a new dog whip, not because they were interested in the craftsmanship, but it gave them both the excuse to go to the entrance of Sarkak's

igloo. Then Sarkak easily led the shaman inside by asking a question, knowing that the shaman would have to follow to answer.

"It's dark, it's dark," the wives called out as they entered.

And the shaman twice replied, "It's light, it's light."

With this formality completed, Sarkak heaved himself onto the sleeping platform. Sure of this first small victory, he did not indicate, as he should have, where his guest should sit. This was the second move in their complicated game. The shaman had expected something like this. Sarkak would have to show some rudeness somewhere. Sarkak should have offered him the place of honor in the center of the bed, which would, of course, give him the privilege of sleeping there later. But he did not. So the shaman, without hesitation, heaved himself into the center place and then rolled slightly away from Sarkak, in a subtle gesture of disdain. They stared at each other with cold admiration, for each had given and taken an unseen blow. Each knew he would never find another such adversary.

Their conversation would take at least all of one day and a night. First they talked of the hunting and of the people living to the north and east. The shaman was an endless traveler, for he lived entirely by the food of other hunters. Even with his bright skill of magic he could wear out his welcome very quickly. It was widely known that he possessed great powers. He could break a spell of sickness or choke an unborn son with the child's own umbilical cord. It was said that he had sometimes caused the winds to guide the caribou toward the hunter, and that his soul walked on the moon. As the conversation went on, each man started to flatter the other while belittling his own power. In this way each boldly asserted his own importance. They knew that listeners would understand that they meant not one word of what they said.

Sarkak, secure in his wealth, called for food, and Ikuma dragged forth a rich red haunch of bear meat and placed it on a clean sealskin. The two men got up off the bed and squatted with their backs toward the others, as was polite. Without speaking, they ate the cold delicious meat, and the women nodded in wonder, for they knew they would never again see such a pair of eaters.

Portagee and Pilee came in, but the shaman did not look up. Then he raised his head, stared, spat a piece of gristle at their feet and went on eating as though they did not exist. They looked at Sarkak, and seeing nothing in his face, turned and left.

When Sarkak and the shaman had finished feasting, they slept like dead men until the gray dawn of midday came once more. Then the shaman quickly decided that he would have Okalikjuak and three other men, who were going caribou hunting, deliver him to his camp. He was anxious to leave Sarkak while they were on good terms. It had not been like that for ten winters, and he knew if he stayed for one more sleep it might be spoiled.

Sarkak was so pleased to see the shaman leaving that he gave him a slab of walrus meat that outweighed him.

MORE than half a moon passed before Okalikjuak and his three young companions returned. They had had to travel on foot because their sleds were piled so high with fresh caribou meat that they could not ride. They arrived walking proudly, and their success caused great excitement. Everyone said, "What shall we do to welcome the hunters?"

Tugak said to his father, "Should we dance?"

Sarkak saw the shining eyes of the girls and said, "Dance? Yes. Build a big house and dance until it falls down!"

The young people rushed noisily to the igloos of Okalikjuak, Sowniapik, Poota and Tungilik. The four snowhouses, forming a square, had been placed about ten paces apart from each other. Portagee and Pilee watched with wonder as a big circle was paced out, its arcs touching the four igloos, and as Tungilik, the most skillful snowhouse builder, stood at the center and took command. He hewed big blocks out of the snow, and the young men curved them neatly against the four snowhouses. When the walls spiraled upward beyond the height of a man's arms, they used the long sleds as ladders to put the roof blocks in place. Then, with a cry of delight, they cut an entrance into each of the four connecting houses so that the heat from their lamps would warm the space beneath the big snow dome.

The hunters were tired from their journey and the builders exhausted from their labors, so everyone slept into the long darkness of the winter afternoon. By early evening the young girls were up again, whistling in their excitement, rushing into each snowhouse calling everyone to the dance.

The *kalunait* were as excited as everyone else, and when they saw the new dance house glowing with light, they ran back to their small igloo and shaved their cheeks and jaws. Then they pulled on their high-necked sea sweaters and their black pea jackets, and over their trousers they drew on their high fur stockings and tight black sealskin boots. Pilee polished shiny buttons with spit and put on his neat little short-brimmed hat, and then they all swaggered out.

Inside the big house Kangiak and I were tightening the skin of the big flat drum. Sowniapik tested it with the short drumstick. It vibrated with a rich boom and people shouted with pleasure to hear it, for the drum meant eating and laughing and wild unseen women and good times of plenty.

I will always remember that dance, for it was the very best of times, when Sarkak was full of power and when my three brothers hunted both seals and women until they dropped over with the pleasures of fulfillment. It was a time when I could listen to the stars murmuring to me and sometimes feel the snow tremble beneath my feet as the hidden creatures shifted in their tunnels, and I seemed to be a part of the earth and the sky.

Sowniapik again struck the drum and began chanting. With that everyone in the village filed into the dance house. Every woman had on her best dance costume of summer caribou skins, and men wore elegant boots of bleached sealskin. Then Sowniapik made the sign that the men and women should separate, and Poota, Kangiak and I pulled the *kalunait* gently to the men's side of the dance house.

Ceremoniously and very slowly, Sowniapik danced each position of the hunting moons, moving bit by bit from east to west. I could see that some of the young people feared the real dancing would never start. But they were wrong. Suddenly Sowniapik

flung the drum at Shartok, our clown, who leaped into the air and began to imitate a mating raven. The words of his song were scandalous, and everyone laughed and joined in the chorus of the outrageous performance.

When he finished, some of the young men brought in meat, and we all squatted together, eating our fill, and afterward some people went off to the wide beds in the side houses to rest. But not for long. One by one, the men took the big drum and pounded on it and whirled it in the air. Everyone was caught up in the rhythm. You could feel the magic pumping your blood and shaking your bones. At the height of it all, when Poota was thundering on the drum, he fell like someone in a trance.

The drum was at once snatched up and forced into Okalikjuak's grasp. He was the greatest dancer who ever lived among us, and that evening he agreed, after much begging, to reenact the caribou hunt for us.

He started slowly beating a steady rhythm, the kind of beat that crawls inside you. His eyes closed as he shuffled his feet, imitating the men and dogs as they dragged through the deep snow of the mountain passes; then he became a year-old female caribou as she caught the first dread smell of dogs and men; in the next instant he was the hunter, crawling on his belly, with his bow and arrows in his mouth. Holding the big drum flat like a drawn bow, he seemed to launch the drumstick like an arrow through the air. Immediately he transformed himself into a bull caribou, rearing up in pain. With five trembling drumbeats, the rich lifeblood from the arrow wound drained out of him. We heard his heart falter, and stop forever, as he crumbled forward onto the snow.

When I could compose myself, I looked at the strangers. Portagee stood rooted to the floor in wonder, as did Kakuktak beside him, and I knew that they had been caught in the power of Okalikjuak's dancing. Pilee, for some reason, had not been touched. He was the first to walk out and help Okalikjuak to his bed. It was time to eat again, but people had been so moved that they crept silently to their igloos and slept until it was almost time to dance again.

IT WAS THE SHOCKING SOUND of a great dogfight that roused us. The unusual violence could mean only that strange dogs had arrived. Rushing out into the darkness, we found three big teams, with as many men and young women as the long sleds would hold, from the nearest camp, our favorite neighbors. Laughing with delight, we helped untangle the dogs and hurried these guests of ours into the warmth of our snowhouses. When their boots were drawn off and their feet warmed with dry fur stockings, they were fed blood soup and made welcome with the most honored places in each bed, for there was nothing the people in Sarkak's camp liked so well as guests to join them in a party.

The visitors had heard of our foreigners and when they saw them, they stared in wonder; we shuddered with pleasure to think that we alone possessed such unbelievable oddities. But with all the thoughts of feasting, their amazement did not last long. On this night Sarkak expanded himself beyond measure. He kept waving to me to bring in more and more meat from the entrance porch. I knew that if this went on we would have nothing left. Yet if Sarkak had not shown his guests our disdain for hunger, I would have been ashamed of him.

Then we heard the throbbing of the drum again and everyone followed Sarkak to the dance house. This second night was the one people looked forward to, because all formalities flew away, and yet we still possessed the strength and the passion that make a midwinter dance so famous.

On this night a tiny child started the dancing. In the center of the dance house he started jerking violently in imitation of Okalikjuak. Everyone roared with pleasure, and the boy's mother's eyes grew big with pride. Did this boy not possess his dead grandfather's sureness and his skill? So the spirit leaves the body for a while and then returns to live a new life among us.

Seeing before us this promise of continued life excited everyone; Sarkak called for meat and beckoned to the child. "Uncle of mine, come eat with me," he said, and with all the dignity of an old man the tiny boy accepted the piece of marrow that Sarkak offered.

Slowly the dancing began again with Atkak. Then a sly man from among the visitors sang a ribald song about the wildness of their women, and I must say it was very funny. Our women took up the chorus and started jigging up and down, and the men paired off and tried to dance each other down, until the house grew hot and the walls dripped and glistened.

Suddenly a new drum sounded inside one of the snowhouses and a wild figure wearing a tight sealskin mask and furs, and around his neck two dog fangs on a braided sinew, rushed in and took command of us. He held his hands up for silence. Then he made a pantomime of listening at three of the entrances. From the fourth, to the sound of a triple beat, a masked woman appeared, so small she must have been a young girl. She danced in a weird un-womanly way, for she represented the spirit of Tivajuk, who al-ways appears during the wife-changing game. I could see that Portagee, Pilee and Kakuktak had no idea what was about to happen, but they were fully caught up in the excitement.

The female dancer now herded the women against one wall, and the male, whirling as he beat his drum, led the men outside.

I, Avinga, was the only one who did not go. I could not run or dance, but I could see and listen, and perhaps this was almost as exciting. I lay on the bed in Sowniapik's igloo, where I could see all that happened in the dance house. I saw the women, trembling with excitement, unbraid their hair, and I saw the masked girl whirl, grab one of them and force her into the night. And I heard the men shout with pleasure. I waited. Pushing and joking eagerly, the women and girls lined up to go. Again and again I could hear shouts and laughing and squealing, and the slap of flesh and snatches of songs and always running feet.

Some of the couples burst into Sowniapik's house and onto the bed where I lay. One of these was Sarkak, laughing as gaily as any youth as he flung the girl up onto the bed and leaped after her. Then Kakuktak came in. He had a girl by the wrist and I saw that it was Nuna. Kakuktak just stood there, not knowing what to do, and I could imagine Nuna's embarrassment.

Sarkak called to him to come to bed with her, but Kakuktak did

not understand. Then Nuna gently tugged him by the sleeve, and I could see that slowly the meaning of the game came to him. He pulled Nuna close, and Sarkak laughed and called out encouragement. Kakuktak knew that I was lying in the shadows, but so filled with passion was he that he did not see me with his eyes.

I turned my gaze away and lay trembling, filled with the wild excitement of life. The dance house now was entirely empty except for the two masked dancers. Like the ghosts of foxes, with arms outstretched, these two circled each other slowly in a ritualistic dance.

It may be difficult to believe, but these neighbors stayed with us for more than half a moon; and during this long party so full of borrowing and lending of wives, husbands, daughters and sons, there was not one hint of trouble. A wonderful mood came over Sarkak, and he freely shared our abundance with the visitors. One by one our great walrus caches lay empty beneath the stars, until we were stripped clean of food. The *kalunait* grew nervous once more. They did not know that if you live a good life of sharing, somehow food will be provided.

The day we opened our last meat cache, two of the visitors hitched their dogs and journeyed out to the thin salt ice. The following day they came back with two small seals, saying they had cached many more. They said the ice was covered with seal holes and we need only go near the place to have the seals give themselves to our good hunters. Hearing of this great run of seals, the visitors, laughing and politely belching with gratitude, left our camp as suddenly as they had come.

Early the next morning, Sarkak prepared to move us, too. He sent Kangiak ahead on the first sled with Tungilik, the snowhouse builder, to choose a campsite on the sea ice and build a house for Sarkak. Kakuktak and I were to go and help them.

Our sled thumped steadily across the hard-packed drifts, and I felt that this frozen sea had no beginning and no ending. As we approached open water I could hear the ice scream and moan with the tremendous pressure of the rising tide. Twice Kangiak

and Tungilik probed the depth of the snow. In the second place we stayed, and the four of us built two snowhouses. We lit the big stone lamp, piled soft caribou skins on our big snow bed and fell into deep sleep. Sometime in the blackness of early morning the rest of the people arrived and started building their igloos. Sarkak, his wives, Nuna's mother and Neevee crawled under the fur robes beside us.

I awoke once and heard the ice crack beneath us. I seemed to feel the sleek round-eyed seals that swam under our bed, warm, too, in their thick layer of white fat. Men, I remembered, were not the only hunters in this place. I thought of the swift killer whales. They, too, perhaps had slipped beneath my bed and were hunting for me with their terrible teeth.

## VII

SARKAK was the first to rise. With a great hacking, spitting and grunting he struggled into the soft fur stockings and new boots his wives had given him and then stepped outside and started to draw his burning yellow cross in the snow. Wherever his urine ended, in that direction would he hunt. "There to the west," he said, knowing that his body juices had shown him the best place to find the seals.

I heard Neevee whispering as she helped Kakuktak pull on his inner parka. Perhaps she pinched him, for he laughed as, shuddering with cold, he hurriedly pulled his outer parka over his head. Outside in the half darkness the men were gathering, each with his

harpoon, coil of seal line and hunting bag. Three old women, each guided by a bitch on a sealskin line, walked out over the ice, letting the dogs sniff out the sea creatures' breathing holes beneath the snow. I went searching, too, with the gray bitch Lao, until she stopped and whined and started to dig. Then I gave her line to the old woman Ningiuk, so that she could take her back to the camp. It is best to be alone on the sealing grounds, for seals are very sensitive to sound.

Taking a stand directly above the mark that the bitch's hot muzzle had made in the snow, I opened my hunting bag and took out a square of thick white bearskin. I stood upon it, then lapped it up over my feet and tied it like a single warm boot. In the snow beside me I placed two small notched pieces of driftwood as a place to rest my harpoon. Then I moved my thin wooden snow probe around gently until I felt the seal's true breathing hole in the ice. I left the probe floating just inside the eye-shaped opening, and taking out a goose feather, dampened its quill and froze the feather to the upper end of the probe. This was to be my alarm.

I bent double, resting my elbows on my knees, making myself as compact as I could against the deadly cold. All day and night I waited, knowing that the seal had other breathing holes than the one I had chosen. A dozen times my mind commanded me to leave, but patience is the true art of the hunter and I watched until the first pale coming of dawn. Then the sense of someone listening awakened me, and I saw the feather tremble. I allowed the seal one breath. Then I drove my harpoon straight down through the snow into the water and felt its point strike deep into flesh and bone. I flung the harpoon shaft aside, knowing its sharp point was firmly set. The harpoon line whipped through my hands and I drew the end of it around my body, using myself as an anchor. The seal was almost as heavy as I was and fought desperately, but the point had done its work, and slowly I felt the line grow slack. Then, using the bone chisel on the butt end of the shaft, I chopped a hole in the ice and drew the dead beast up out of the water.

It was my first seal of the winter, and to show my gratefulness I cut away a small piece of flesh and placed it back into the water.

Our people say that this allows the seal's body to grow again. When I removed the harpoon head from the seal, I plugged a wound pin carefully in the hole to save the blood, for all food is precious in a time of hunger. Then I left my catch where it lay. Someone else would have to pull the heavy lifeless weight back to the camp.

I was looking for a new set of breathing holes when I saw Portagee walking toward me, by himself, moving carelessly across the ice. He carried a harpoon, but, foolishly, he was not using it to test the snow-covered ice. When he caught up with me, I pointed at my track in the snow and walked and pointed again until I was sure he placed each footstep in mine. He smiled and thought I was teaching him a game, which in a way I was—the game of staying alive. When I came to a round white patch of snow that I considered dangerous, I stopped and pointed, then took one more pace forward and stabbed lightly down with the harpoon. It disappeared up to the place where I held it, and black water flowed up around it. I tapped the snow lightly just beyond my feet, and a chunk as big as a man collapsed into the freezing water. Portagee stared in horror and disbelief. He now learned quickly how to test the treacherous ice himself.

We soon found a breathing hole, and I showed him how to place the wand into the hole with the feather attached, and how to strike down with the harpoon if the wand rose.

I had scarcely set myself at a nearby hole when I saw him strike down with great force. In a moment he was struggling violently with something on the end of his line. I hurried to show him how to use his body as an anchor and we played the line together, back and forth, until the seal tired. When we hauled this prize out of the water and saw it was a huge dog seal, Portagee gave a whoop of joy, and I saw other hunters straighten up from their seal holes and wave their arms, for they guessed Portagee had taken his first seal.

Portagee called softly to me, pointed at his seal and at his mouth, and took out his knife. But I did not want him to spoil his reputation by bringing in meat that had been eaten, so we tied a line to his catch and dragged it over to mine. The big brown man

easily pulled the two seals behind him. Then he took me under the arm and urged me to place one of my feet upon one of his. We laughed and walked like a three-legged giant, and Portagee sang a song to me and I sang one to him, and neither of us understood a word of the other's, but it did not matter.

In the semidarkness of midmorning the women were waiting to greet us, and there was wild cheering in the camp as the hunters came in with seals. This first day of good fortune was a wonderful sign. Of course, no hunter told the women who had actually harpooned a seal and who had not, for women have a foolish way of attaching importance to this. Generations ago it was decided that it is best not to tell the women too much about success or failure. So we all share in the meat without question. But when all the hunters were in, I did say that Portagee got the big dog seal, because it was his first kill, and much was made of it. It was the first to be cut open for our feast.

Next day we awoke to the sound of savage winds, as a great blizzard gathered its strength. Sarkak went outside, to assure himself, I knew, that there was no danger of the wind and tide breaking us away from the main ice and floating our camp away like a drifting island. The storm lasted four long days. On the fifth day the old women and the dogs went out again, and the hunters followed. So sure were we of their success that I did not even go with them. An endless time later they came back. Nothing, absolutely nothing, had come to the breathing holes.

For the next three days, when the hunters went out Portagee and Pilee did not go. They stayed, instead, in their igloo doing nothing. One afternoon, when Portagee was bored, he sent to Ikuma a sealskin boot for patching. Ikuma, when it was finished, asked Nuna to take it back. Nuna did not return at once to Sarkak's igloo. And many eyes marked the time she took, knowing that husbands become enraged when their wives see other men without permission while they are hunting. It was foolish of Nuna; and more foolish that neither she nor Ikuma had the courage to mention to Sarkak this incautious, if perhaps harmless, visit. They made the mistake of trying to keep it secret.

The next time they were bored, Portagee and Pilee borrowed our snow knives and built four immense snowmen, facing north, south, east and west, like winter spirits around our camp, perhaps driving the sea beasts away from us. That day, too, the hunters came home with nothing.

All of our meat was gone now. The dogs began roaming through the camp like starved wolves. Sarkak paced among the snow-houses like a bear, and that night, perhaps seeing some vision in the shadows, he called out to Kangiak and Yaw to go and get the shaman. Someone must have broken a taboo, and for this we might die. If we returned to the land without meat, we would never again feel the warmth of summer. Fearing now that anything we did might make the situation worse, we gave up hunting and waited for the shaman. When Kangiak's sled finally reappeared with the shaman and his dirty boy on it, we were all relieved.

The shaman marched straight into Sarkak's house before he was asked and went to sleep. When, at noon, he arose, as many as could find room gathered in the big igloo. The *kalunait* placed themselves boldly before this magical man and eyed him intently. Pilee had a half smile on his face, not at all friendly. Earlier, it had been as though the shaman had not recognized their existence. But now he spoke out. "Have you been visited by foreigners?" he asked, as if he did not know.

There was a pause. Then everyone answered, "Yes."

"Perhaps they have brought some evil that drives away the sea beasts," said the shaman. "No wonder the hunting is bad with those great snowmen in the camp."

He tied a band of skin around his head, grabbed up a snow knife, tossing another to his boy, and together they ran out. Everyone hurried after them to watch them hack and smash at each snow figure. When the last one had been kicked to bits, the shaman turned away in disgust and led us back to Sarkak's igloo. Every eye turned toward the *kalunait*. Some perhaps started thinking of them in a new way.

"We can only try to understand the signs," the shaman said. "I will tell you of the dog children again, for some of you may have

83

forgotten and some young people may not have heard the story." And he told about the young woman who mated with a dog and was banished to a far island. "Now look before you at these three," he finished, "the offspring of her dog children, returned to this land with their sharp iron knives."

I saw many people draw back in shock and horror. Our people had only vaguely thought of these three as dog children, though they had sometimes lightly called them so, but now the ghostly impact of the inhuman father came to them.

"*Ayii*," said the people, full of uneasiness. "We understand you."

The shaman held up his hands and said, "Someone is trying to speak to me. Listen. Listen." At that he went into a great fit of hacking and strangling. When he straightened up, his face was flushed and he growled like a dog and whined words we could not understand.

The shadows of so many people standing in the snowhouse made the light faint, but I clearly saw what happened next; and Sarkak and the three strangers saw it. The shaman swayed back as though he had been struck a powerful blow on the head, and he let out a horrible inhuman howl. As he opened his mouth, I could see great curved white dog teeth on either side of his jaws. He was snapping his teeth, and foam appeared at the sides of his mouth. It was flecked with blood. He was like a man gone mad.

The dirty boy leaped forward and grabbed him. They struggled violently; everyone drew back in fear and horror. Had we not seen the mysterious dog man appearing before us, half hidden in the fat body of the shaman? At last the violent struggling ceased, and the shaman lay pale and trembling, his face steaming with sweat.

"Open your mouth. Show us your teeth," many called to him.

The dirty boy took him roughly by the chin and pulled back his lips, but the great dog teeth had disappeared. A babble of frightened whispers raced around the snowhouse.

The shaman was given water, and slowly he revived. But suddenly he coughed again and then howled like a dog and curled his lips into a snarl, as though the dreadful dog spirit was tearing at his body. Then for an instant the expression was gone, and the

shaman gasped and begged for a harpoon. The moment one was handed to him, he placed its butt on the floor, and kneeling on the sleeping platform, he held the shaft with the point directed at his chest. Fascinated, horrified, our people drew back as he started swaying from side to side, singing in a high unreal voice.

> *"Ayii, ayii,*
> *Father of these dog children.*
> *Enter into me. Enter into me."*

Then he trembled and howled again and lunged forward, straight onto the upturned point of the harpoon. He screamed as it pierced his belly. He flung back his head and stared with terrible bulging, dying eyes. Blood gushed out of his mouth as he fell and twisted in death throes.

Women and children screamed, and even the men in the passageway rushed out in fear. Roaring, he followed them. He ran once around the snowhouse and then darted back in. We gasped. He was a whole man. He leered at us; then slowly he raised his parka and exposed his great round belly. It was smooth and unmarked, showing neither wound nor blood.

There was absolute silence. Then the shaman said in a wild strong voice, "The dog man is dead." And he stood in triumph, staring scornfully at the three descendants of the dog man.

I looked into the faces of Kakuktak, Pilee and Portagee as they examined the shaman with looks of horror, for they, too, had seen him fall upon the point of the killing harpoon. How could he now stand here before us unharmed? I could see that they were nervous and excited, for they had not known what to make of the shaman's performance. They were still with Sarkak, a part of his household, and yet they were becoming a part of all of us, and we also seemed to be a part of them. I wished now they had not seen the shaman perform his magic. I knew they did not understand him. Because he was dirty and sly, they thought he was deceitful. This was not so. His magic was very ancient and had come down to him from powerful shamans. Oh, yes, I have heard that some useless shamans dwelling west of us perform tricks such as carving

bearlike teeth out of bone and slipping these into their mouths to frighten people. We know there are many old ruses. But we had no words to tell these foreigners such things. They did not wish to believe what they had seen, yet they had seen it, as we had, and it would haunt them forever. And the end was not yet, for that night the shaman called the moon spirit into Sarkak's house, and then he chiseled a hole in the sea ice and invoked the female spirit who lives beneath the ice and hoards the seals, and he shouted at that unseen force, "Release the seals."

And the next day the big tide came to us, and with it an abundance of seals. The evil spell was broken. Our meat caches filled and our bellies grew fat and the women and children laughed again. We scarcely noticed when the shaman left, for we did not need him anymore.

A WHOLE moon passed, and the foreigners seemed to enjoy this time at the sealing camp more than any other, for they felt sure of themselves once more. They could again see around them our richness of meat, and they could feel the warm coming of spring as slowly the light returned to us.

It seemed to me there was no longer any place in the camp where one could sit and not be aware of them. They ambled endlessly among all our snowhouses, and the children ran after them like a pack of unruly young dogs. One day I heard Panee shouting coarsely to Portagee. She sounded like a foreign woman, so well had she learned these new bad manners from them. Yes, I thought, this had truly become their camp. They could not even feed themselves, and yet they almost ruled us. I was surprised that our people did not seem to resent this. Only Sarkak began to grow remote and cold toward the *kalunait*.

One night Kakuktak lay on his stomach on Sarkak's wide bed, with Neevee as always beside him, and began drawing pictures on the last of his precious bundle of white skins. We all knew that he had only three unmarked skins left. He looked at Neevee and smiled. Then he drew a kind of sharp angular house that he said was all made of wood. Outside of the house he put a path with

flowers growing along each side. Then he drew the inside of this
same house. In the center of the back wall there was a large stone
place with fire in it, burning wood. I wondered what place could
have so much wood. On each side of the fireplace he put a chair,
and in one he sat himself, straight and tall. In the other sat Neevee,
dressed in a long woman's parka that completely covered her legs.
Neevee laughed and said she could never run beside a sled in
that long parka.

In Neevee's right arm Kakuktak placed a baby in a long dress
like the one he had drawn on Neevee. Beside Neevee's left hand
was a box with a hood over it, and in this box you could see another
baby. Neevee seemed to understand every line. "*Oona uvunga?* Is
this me?" she said. "Are these our children? Is this our house?"

Kakuktak answered yes and then held his hand gently over her
eyes so that she would stop looking at the drawing. But she would
not, and so he closed his eyes and went to sleep beside her.

After a while I saw that Neevee was crying, but I could
not understand why the drawing should have made her sad.
Finally she stopped crying and said to me, "He says the sailing
ship will come again when the ice goes. If it does, I will go away
with him and live in that strange house. Oh, yes, I will go and live
with Kakuktak. When that time comes, I will not be afraid."

ONE MORNING when we awoke, we saw that the tide had opened
an immense crack in the frozen sea and a field of ice larger than
our whole camp had drifted away during the night. Sarkak ordered all the families to move at once off the ice and back to the
land. Pilee and Portagee could not understand why and rudely
refused to let their women go. This was the first time that I had
ever seen Sarkak's orders disobeyed. We harnessed the dogs and
broke in the snowhouses that evening. But it was only their girls'
crying and threatening to leave them that forced Portagee and
Pilee to fling themselves angrily on the sleds and come with us
back to our village.

The spring blizzards had covered some of our old houses with
snow, so most of us built new ones near the hill, though a few oc-

cupied the igloos beside the big dance house, to give it life again.

It is hard to describe the awful strain that came between our people and the three foreigners during the next moon. The differences that had seemed small at the fishing camp, and had grown stronger when we broke up the sealing camp, now became so terrible that the whole village was torn into many parts. Men would no longer hunt when the fog blew in, and I believe Sarkak could not forgive Kakuktak for going so often with Neevee to the warmth of Poota's house. People were beginning to lose their fear of Sarkak. He sensed that the *kalunait* were taking his power from him, crudely disobeying him in every way.

Mixed with Sarkak's greatness was a childishness, a fierce crazy jealousy, which he had kept well hidden. On the day that changed everything I could see it raging in him. In the morning, as we lay in the snowhouse, ugly foreign sounds seeped through the walls of the foreigners' igloo: Portagee's rough laughter and Pilee's cackling while their three girls screamed with laughter. "Dag-it! Dag-it," they shouted across the village. It was their name for Kakuktak, and I heard him answer as he strode to join them.

Sarkak sat up trembling, his eyes as cruel as an eagle's. "Where is Kangiak?" he roared. "I want to send him for the meat!"

Kangiak was sleeping with Nowya's widow, to see if she was material for a good wife. Yaw hurried to get him, but Kangiak did not appear quickly enough to suit his father. When he did, he stared in alarm at Sarkak's face, which was pale with rage. And at that very moment the foreigners crowded into the snowhouse, laughing and talking loudly to each other and ignoring us.

Sarkak snarled at them like a dog gone mad, and at Kangiak, too. "Ravens, all of you. Little hunters. Big eaters. Only good at sleeping late with women. These three whom I saved from dying on the ice, what good are they to me lying idly in every girl's bed, begging meat from hunters?" He spoke through teeth locked in anger. "Look at that wife stealer," he rasped at Portagee, "waiting until the husband goes hunting to lure the wife into his house, begging for his boots to be sewn. Have I no sons to defend me?" He spoke these last words slowly, aimed at Kangiak and Kakuktak.

"You, Kangiak, and you, little husband of the gray bitch"—Sarkak turned to me—"go now for the meat. Take those three useless orphans with you."

Kangiak left, and I rose to follow him, and Sarkak shouted to the *kalunait*, as though to dogs, "*Tuavee!* Hurry!"

Kakuktak whirled around, perfectly understanding the rude command. "*Aagii*," he said slowly, using our single word meaning no, rolling the word up from the bottom of his belly, using all our kind of guttural force. And I heard Neevee let out her breath, the way a woman warns of trouble.

Sarkak looked up into Kakuktak's eyes, and what he saw there must have unnerved him. Kakuktak's nostrils were pinched, and he was breathing hard; his face was drained of color. I saw Sarkak's eyes flicker to the right and left, and what he saw could only make things seem worse, for on Kakuktak's left stood the big brown harpooner, his whole body tense with anger, and on his right stood Pilee, red-faced and sly as a fox, his eyes not bothering with Sarkak as they searched the other people in the house, gauging where their weapons lay. Watching, I suddenly understood that these strangers, these people who had danced and played with us, were not, as they had first seemed to us, clumsy overgrown children. They were strong, dangerous fighting men.

Finally Kakuktak turned away, and the foreigners left the snowhouse. Sarkak stood motionless for some time, then heaved himself up onto the sleeping bench and sat there, staring. No one spoke. He seemed to slump slowly into himself, like an old, old man.

It was night when Kangiak and I returned with meat from the cache and heard the laughter of the *kalunait* coming from Atkak's igloo. Inside our snowhouse, Sarkak lay motionless. When Ikuma offered him soup, he did not speak. He was like a dead man.

THE OLD widow, Nuna's mother, had knelt on the edge of the bed through all the excitement without making a sound. But when things were quiet again, Nuna told me later, she bent and stared into Sarkak's eyes and whispered hoarsely, "Go while there is still time. Go while you have strength."

That night we could hear the savage winds whirling around the house, choking the entrance with drifting snow. Kangiak, Kakuktak and Neevee were all gone, leaving empty places in the bed. Yaw tossed restlessly, as did I; we could not sleep. The old widow had stopped her singing, but now she swayed back and forth without a sound, stopping now and then to stare at one of us. Her quick animal eyes frightened me.

Sarkak's eyes were half open, staring at nothing. Could you imagine that one single word—*aagii*—would destroy such a powerful man? If Kakuktak had only known our customs, Sarkak would have given a party and sung a song of ridicule against them all, and that would have driven them out of the camp in shame forever. But they were too ignorant. Because he could not sing them down, Sarkak was the loser: he would have to kill them or leave the camp. But killing was not our custom and had not been in living memory. And I knew Sarkak thought of Kakuktak as an unruly son.

Toward morning I finally slept. I was awakened suddenly by the screaming of Nuna. Her mother was gone. The old widow's tattered sleeping robes were drawn up neatly, and her clothes folded precisely on top of her bedroll. Seeing her place empty in the bed gave me a profound shock. Nuna darted into the entrance passage. I had only kicked my crippled legs to the icy floor when I heard her long wailing cry. When I reached her she pointed to the small footprints that already were filling up with snow that had drifted into the passage.

Outside, it was a terrifying world of wind-lashed snow. After I had taken only one step away from our house I could see nothing— no house, no dogs, no sleds. I felt Nuna brush past me, and I caught her and held her, for I knew that no one could live out there in that howling whiteness. I forced her back into the house, and Ikuma stroked her head and tried to comfort her.

You will not believe me, but Sarkak did not move or show in any way that he had heard all of this, though the house was full of women's screaming.

When the storm passed all the men in the village went looking

for the old widow. It was the gray bitch Lao who found her under a snowdrift, frozen white and peaceful, her knees drawn up as though she were sleeping. All of the women came and mourned, and the men bore her stiffened body to the high ground and covered her with stones, so that no animal could tear apart the grave and her ghost could not lift the heavy load.

Some say that we kill our old people. That is not true. According to ancient custom our old people have the strength and pride to kill themselves if they believe their lives should end.

When we went back to our snowhouse, we found Sarkak sitting up. He must after all have known all that happened. "This ground is poisonous," he said. "I shall go inland for caribou today."

I could scarcely believe my ears. It would be a long hard journey, for the spring sun would soon soften the snow in the valleys, and each step could drop a man thigh-deep through the crust. But he planned to leave instantly. Any action, however, seemed better than the long silence we had suffered, so we all got up quickly to help.

"Two sleds I want," Sarkak said to Kangiak. "Twelve dogs, both wives, and Tugak and Yaw. You," he said to Kangiak and me, "stay here and guard our kayaks and our meat caches, for there are bad people here, wife stealers, dog people. Beware of them."

Tugak and Yaw were icing the runners of the sleds and Kangiak and I were harnessing the dogs when Sarkak suddenly commanded me to tie Lao into the team. For a moment I was dumb with shock. I looked into his eyes and he glared back at me, daring me to say one word. I shall say no, like Kakuktak, I thought. But of course I could not do that to him. I made the bitch stand and started to pull the harness over her head.

"It doesn't matter," Sarkak called to me. "Choose a stronger dog for this team." In this way Sarkak showed me more kindness than he had since my mother's death. Quickly I released the bitch, and she sat down in her place by the entrance porch, licking her nose and smiling.

When the loading was completed, Sarkak, Ikuma, Nuna and Yaw stood waiting beside the two sleds. I saw the foreigners stand-

ing silently in front of Poota's igloo. Sarkak hurried, leaving no time for farewells. His face was set like a dead man's, and you could see that he wanted everyone to know that he was being driven out of his own camp by these three hard-eyed intruders.

VIII

Spring came, carried softly on the south wind. But there was little joy in the camp. With our women gone, the lamps sputtered out and our big snowhouse died in the cold. Kangiak went to stay with Nowya's young widow, and I was utterly alone. I killed a white fox and sent it to old Ningiuk, the mother of Poota's wife, and she came over with her young daughter and lighted the lamp and swept the hoarfrost off the sleeping skins and remade the bed so that the igloo became livable once more.

When this was done, Kakuktak moved back into the big igloo with Neevee, Kangiak came often to visit and Portagee kept his spare clothing there. It was a house without a proper wife, but it had heat, and it was a house once more. It may be hard to believe, but people started calling it my house, Avinga's house. Imagine me, suddenly possessing such a place. For the first time since I was young I started to think of Sarkak as my father.

I believed then, as I do now, that all our troubles were caused by the foreigners. They had come to us like helpless children, and we had fed and clothed them and shared our women with them. Yet they still believed themselves to be their own masters, three people apart from us—Portagee with his boisterous laughter, Pilee with his cunning and his charm for women, Kakuktak, who

was almost one of us. However, he quickly joined the other two when trouble came. So they had insulted Sarkak and driven him away in disgrace. Because Sarkak had saved them, our camp was without a leader. For the first time in our lives we feared the changing of the seasons. Sowniapik slowly took a kind of weak control, but he did not wish to lead. And the *kalunait* walked among us like alien gods, proud of their victory over the old man, not knowing that he had been their protector.

ONE sunny spring day Portagee and Okalikjuak noticed several objects that stood out in the melting snow. Digging lightly around them, they found the sealskin buckets full of berries that the children had given the foreigners in the autumn, not stolen, as they had imagined, but buried by the first autumn storm.

Portagee jerked one of them out of the snow and hurried to Sowniapik's house to show it to Pilee. Together they ate a few of the bitter berries and laughed with delight.

When Kakuktak returned from seal hunting with Kangiak that evening, Portagee and Pilee showed him the berries and they all laughed again. Then, without asking Kangiak or me, they borrowed a huge stone pot and one of our big stone lamps. They also borrowed two smaller stone pots from Sowniapik's wife. Then, in Sowniapik's igloo, they poured the rotten berries into the pots with some water and suspended them, tightly covered, over the flames of the lamps. Slowly a terrible odor of hot rotten berries filled the house.

In all the time they had been with us, I had never seen the foreigners so interested in anything as they were in this cooking. Kangiak and I went seal hunting for a few days, and when we came back they had taken the pots off the fire and I could tell that they were very excited. The sealskin covers of the pots were now puffed upward with some kind of pressure.

Late one night, Kakuktak urged Kangiak and me to come quickly to Sowniapik's house. We all stood around and watched Portagee as he carefully removed a wooden plug from the vent hole in one of the covers. It popped, and foam bubbled up out

of the hole. Pilee handed him a horn cup, and Kakuktak carefully tipped the pot. A trickle of dark red liquid partly filled the cup. Portagee sniffed at it, then he closed his eyes and took a small sip. He made a face, and his eyes watered. Then he said, "It's good, it's good." Kakuktak next took the cup and drank and gasped. Pilee snatched it from him, drained it and coughed until I thought he would fall down. The first word he said, too, when he had regained his wind was, "Goood!" I was glad they did not offer that hot red poison to Kangiak or me.

THE first soft light of dawn caught the side of the big dance house that still stood between the four igloos, though the inner entrances had long since been sealed up. I had watched Sowniapik set out, with six other hunters, for a day at the sealing grounds. Pilee, who should have gone with them, lay instead comfortably in Sowniapik's house between the two girls he thought he owned. At noon I found him there, planning his evening entertainment. Suddenly he jumped out of bed, and with the long ivory snow knife he quickly hacked an opening through the wall again.

We all peered nervously inside the half-forgotten dance house. Great festoons of frost crystals hung thickly down from the ceiling. The little broken drum of the masked dog man still lay on the wide snow floor. It seemed only a moment ago that we had shaken this place with our wild singing. But in that moment all the people I could call family had gone except Kangiak, and the camp was full of trouble, for we no longer had a leader. Some men hunted, some stayed in bed and slept, and we were not together in anything we tried to do.

Pilee picked up the drum and beat on it and sang and capered. I could see that Evaloo and Mia were embarrassed by his bad imitation of our dancing. He had not had the courage to dance among our kayakmen in the midwinter feasting.

Mia said to me, "We could have a dance tonight."

I found myself thinking that a good dance might help the people to unite again. Perhaps in the excitement some strong man might come forward and take Sarkak's place as leader.

Pilee hurried out to find Portagee and Kakuktak; he told them that the hunters—it is hard to believe, *our hunters,* at a time like this—had decided to have a dance. Mia and Evaloo ran to every igloo to say that the three foreigners had decided to have a dance. Because these girls were the daughters of Sowniapik the people believed that Sowniapik had agreed to this, for who would believe that two young girls would dare think up such a thing by themselves? As for the *kalunait,* they were nothing; they had no houses, no meat, no songs to give at a dance feast. So the dance house was reopened, and the women unwrapped their best fur costumes and ran through the camp, whispering and shuddering with delight at their possible fate.

The dancing had to wait until the seven men returned from the sealing grounds. Fortunately their sleds were loaded and they were in good humor, eager to believe that the tensions in the camp were at last broken. They dragged the young seals into the houses and split them open. Soon everyone was crowded into the igloos that joined the dance house, eating fresh meat.

I was feasting with Okalikjuak when Pilee started shouting: "Kangiak, Avinga. You come. Neevee! Panee!"

The people eating in the three other snowhouses became silent. Slowly we who had been called made our way into Sowniapik's igloo. It was hot and crowded. Portagee and Pilee were trying hard to talk our language, and I had never heard them do it so well. I saw that Kakuktak was bright red in the face and wondered if he could be sick with fever. He placed his hands on my shoulders and started singing, and his breath smelled of the rotten berries. I noticed that one of the three stone pots was already empty.

Pilee dipped a horn cup into the second pot, danced his way across the crowded space, careful not to spill a drop, and held the cup for Mia, who drank half of it. The other half he gave to Evaloo. Portagee filled a long bone ladle and gave it to Panee. Then he offered some to Sowniapik. Sowniapik took a mouthful, then spat it out violently. But his wife drank a full cup and in a little while she was singing, too. She had always been so shy that I could scarcely believe it.

Kangiak was given a cup. He drank and coughed and passed the cup to me, while Portagee shouted, "Driiink, Avinga." The red liquid burned its way into my stomach and then sent waves of heat through my whole body. I slowly drained the cup and passed it back to Pilee.

Evaloo called out dreamily, "It's hot." She dragged her parka over her head, and her hair hung unbraided over her naked shoulders. It was not the custom for a young girl to sit with her breasts exposed before guests. I thought her mother, Sowniapik's wife, would speak sharply to her, but she only went on singing in a gay crazy way.

I tried to understand what was happening to everyone, but I found I could not think clearly. My crippled legs felt suddenly strong and I tried to dance. Neevee was holding me, encouraging me. Sowniapik, who had drunk nothing, left the house.

I do not clearly remember anything about the rest of that night. But I do remember that for a while I felt like a tall giant with long straight legs and mighty arms.

LATE the next day, Kangiak found me lying in a strange bed with Tungilik's daughter sprawled out beside me. Lifting her limp arm off my chest, I felt for my clothes, and when I had them on, Kangiak covered her and helped me walk back to Sarkak's house. I drank cup after cup of ice water to put out the fire that raged within me. I hoped the whirling in my head might stop when I lay down. Pilee was lying on his side, as pale as death. Kakuktak was fast asleep, with her arms flung out across Neevee's empty place. As we lay there, Kangiak told me about the feast.

"The dancing," he said, "was wonderful at first, but then it changed into madness. The noise was awful. I fell down once crossing the dance floor, and two women fell on top of me. I crawled into Sowniapik's house. Sowniapik was there, and angry. His wife and one of his daughters were gone and the other one lay on the bed, crying that Pilee was lost in the snow."

"How did you find him?" I asked.

Kangiak said, "First I found Kakuktak and shook him back to

his senses. Together we staggered out and climbed the hill, surprised to find it was morning. From that high place we looked all around us, and finally we saw Pilee sprawled on the snow beyond the kayak racks."

"Was he frozen?" I quickly asked.

"Not too much," Kangiak added. "Only his fingers and one cheek were white. We picked him up and ran with him, bouncing and dragging him, trying to force the blood to move again in his body. Being still half out of our minds, Kakuktak and I laughed and fell down and struggled up and ran again until at last Pilee, too, started laughing and began to walk a little. As we came into the village, I saw a huge snow owl. I knew that was a bad sign, coming just after the dawning of a new day. Sowniapik was sitting grimly in his igloo when we went in, staring at the floor. On the bed was Portagee, sleeping comfortably between Pilee's Evaloo and Mia. Pilee gave a wild shout and whipped out his sea knife. Kakuktak jerked Pilee violently away from the bed. But Pilee had become a madman. He whirled around and slashed open the whole front of Kakuktak's parka. Kakuktak let go of him in horror.

"Portagee awoke, sensed danger and was on his knees in an instant. With a murderous lunge Pilee drove the knife toward his face. But the thrust was short, and Portagee's huge right hand closed over Pilee's throat. He lifted him up and shook him like a white bear killing a seal between his jaws. The knife fell out of Pilee's hands, and Portagee let Pilee fall gasping onto the floor. Portagee laughed aloud and lay down again between the frightened girls.

"Sowniapik had watched all this without moving," Kangiak continued. "He got up slowly and said to me, 'These people are dogs. Dogs of the dog children. And there are others, those who run with them.' Then, having said this insult, he walked out of his own house in disgust. Kakuktak and I helped Pilee back to this igloo. He was choking and very weak."

We slept for a long time after Kangiak finished talking. Hearing someone come into our passageway, I awoke. Suddenly all of Pilee's possessions from Sowniapik's house were flung onto the

center of the floor. We never saw who threw them. Kakuktak and I stared at the pile of clothes and started to laugh. What else could we do, with everything going from bad to worse?

ONE DAY had passed when Neevee came to me and said, "Sowniapik and the kayakmen who did not drink the berry juice have been sitting together in Tungilik's house for a very long time."

I did not like the sound of this. Such a secret meeting had never happened. Far from improving the feeling in the village, the dance had made things much worse, because of the berry juice. We stayed in the big snowhouse, separated from everyone, until we ran short of meat. Then Kangiak and Kakuktak and I went out to our seal cache. When we returned, Pilee and Portagee were waiting outside the entrance. "Neevee has taken her things," they told us, "and returned to her father's snowhouse."

Kakuktak went to Poota's igloo, but finding no one, came back with a puzzled look on his face. We ate our meat in silence, for we were now womanless, without a friend in the village.

One morning a dog team came out of the north with three men riding upon the sled. We stood out in front of our igloo and watched the sled sweep up through the barrier ice and stop. The shaman looked at the five of us and then turned his back. Without hesitating, he and his dirty boy walked toward the large group who stood near Sowniapik's igloo. The driver from the north continued on his journey south.

For five nights the shaman slept in the camp without ever once coming near us. Kangiak, who was strong in so many ways, could not stand this isolation. After the second night he went back to sleep with Nowya's widow, and the time he spent with her increased each day. One morning he told me that the young widow had told him that Neevee walked alone in the hills and cried much of the time. She slept little and ate almost nothing, but Poota had forbidden her to return to our house.

For three nights and days nothing at all happened to us, no one came near us. Kakuktak became as nervous as a sandpiper on the beach. His mind was far away, searching for every memory of

99

Neevee. On this third night he went over and sat by the stone lamp beside the woman's place where Neevee should have been. The yellow light lit his face and I realized that he had grown as thin as when he had first come to us, and that a yellow stubble of beard had begun to grow again. Carefully, he sharpened the end of what was left of his marking stick. Then he took the book of white skins from his pocket and began marking on the last one. His eyes narrowed as he lost himself in this dream he was drawing. When, a long time later, he finished, he held it up and examined his work. Then he did the only crazy thing I had ever seen him do. He violently tore his last piece of drawing skin from between the hard covers, crumpled it into a ball and held it into the dying flame of the lamp. I was surprised to see it blaze up so quickly, then turn black and collapse into ashes, not at all like caribou skin burning. He stared at me for a moment, then closed the book and tossed it gently across the sleeping forms of Pilee and Portagee. It landed beside my hand.

"*Tuyuktagit*. A small gift to you," he whispered.

I AWOKE early the next morning to the sound of the soft creaking of footsteps on the snow. The walking stopped. Because of what Neevee had told me, I feared danger and had slept with my boots and pants on, so it took me only an instant to pull my parka over my head and hobble up through the entrance passage. The whole camp was silent and all the snowhouses lay wrapped in morning mist. And then I saw the shaman. He stood still, very close to our house, staring at me coldly, like a fat bold raven. He seemed to be in a kind of trance. I shuddered and made my way back into our entrance passage.

I sat down on the side of the bed and listened until at last I heard once more the sound of footsteps on the snow. He was leaving. It was as though a great weight had been lifted from me. The shaman's presence had filled me with unreasonable terror. I fell into a deep sleep that lasted until midmorning.

The sound of girls laughing woke me. Pilee was calling out to them excitedly, Portagee was urging them to come in, and

Kakuktak was pulling on his sealskin pants and boots. I recognized Mia's warm voice.

"Come in," called Pilee, smoothing back his long brown hair.

Finally Mia came through the entrance, then Evaloo and Tungilik's daughter. They stood before the bed, red-faced and shy. Patting the soft caribou skins, Pilee said to Mia, "Come lie down here beside me."

All three foreigners were full of desire, for it had been a long time since any girls had lain in their beds. Portagee started to hum our favorite song, clapping his hands softly and weaving his big brown body in a way that always excited people.

The three girls laughed and shuffled their feet. After some time, Mia shyly reached into her hood and drew out a new pair of long mitts, and the other two also each drew out a pair, all of rich design, which could only mean that the people had decided to be friendly again. I wished Kangiak were here to see this.

Mia shyly offered the new right mitt to Pilee. "Perhaps they're too small?" she said.

Pilee shoved his hand inside eagerly and said, "It is enough. It is enough," and as soon as she held the left mitt up for him, he slid in his other hand.

At the same time, the two other girls fitted their mitts onto Portagee and Kakuktak. Pilee was the first to notice that there were no thumbs in them. "Hey," he shouted loudly.

"You didn't chew them," Kakuktak said. "The palms are stiff."

At that instant I noticed that all the mitts had leather drawstrings, like a boot, and before I knew what was happening, the girls had whipped the laces together, tangling them into loose knots. The three men started to laugh, each trying to jerk his two hands apart; but this only served to tighten the knots.

I saw Kakuktak look at Mia. Her eyes were wide. She screamed *"Tuavee!* Hurry!" And then in horror I saw Tungilik lunge through the entrance, the dead stranger's sea knife in his hand. Sarkak had owned that knife, I thought. How could this man have it now?

Pilee knelt on the bed in front of him, shouting, writhing, while Tungilik lunged straight at him, thrust the sea knife into his neck,

then, raising his parka, drove the blade up under his rib cage until it must have touched his heart. The girls, huddled against the wall, watched intently.

As Pilee fell, I saw Atkak, the strong man, leap into the snow-house and fling himself at Portagee. The big brown man rolled back on the bed, drew up his legs and with both feet struck Atkak in the chest, so that he fell against the wall and lay sprawled on the icy floor. Portagee roared and stamped over Atkak's body and threw himself against the side of the igloo until the wall gave way and roof blocks loosened and fell around him. So great was Portagee's momentum that he stumbled into the snow outside and fell, jerking wildly at his bindings.

Shartok, the comic, the fool, suddenly separated from the crowd of onlookers and ran crouching toward Portagee. He snatched up a long killing spear and reared back in that slow comical way that had often made people laugh. But this time he was not fooling. He aimed and launched the harpoon, driving it into the center of Portagee's back.

The big brown man stiffened in horror as he felt his death blow. Shuddering, he died without a sound.

I whirled around to see what had happened to Kakuktak. He stood upright among us, his eyes alert, his sea knife in his right hand, which magically he had freed from the mitt. As I watched, he rushed at the three girls. He could easily have cut them, and I believe he should have for their terrible treachery, but they fell down, screaming in terror, and he veered away from them. He leaped out of the broken snowhouse and ran, with the grace of a strong young caribou, changing his course again and again. I can still feel the terror that he must have known after seeing his two companions cut down and thinking that the whole village was against him, not knowing that one and only one executioner had been sent to kill him.

Kangiak now came running as fast as he could from the widow's igloo. When he saw what was happening, he drew his thin flintstone blade and shouted, cursing at the people who ran after Kakuktak. But Kakuktak must have believed that Kangiak

had cursed him, for he glanced back only once as he started running westward along the beach.

The others were after him like a pack of wolves, some anxious to see their executioner make the kill, but many of the women cried out, "Run, Kakuktak. Run," for they could not bear to think of his being killed. I caught the gray bitch by her ruff and hobbled painfully up to a high knoll, where I had a long view. I knelt there, clasping my arms around the bitch's neck in terror that she too would run away from me.

I could see Kakuktak loping gracefully across the big patch of spring snow with Kangiak behind him, the two of them slowly increasing the distance between them and the pack. Behind the crowd walked Neevee, slowly, stiffly, her long hair drifting loosely out on the breeze. When she saw the cliff that barred Kakuktak's path and knew his mistake, she let out a long piercing cry of hopelessness, a woman's wail that set my gray bitch into a crazy trembling. For Kakuktak had blindly chosen the wrong direction. He should have turned inland, for no man could climb the cliffs of the red stone canyon. Faintly, I heard Kangiak calling to him to turn across the land, but Kakuktak did not trust him or did not hear, for he ran straight into the rough tumble of stone. Desperately he searched for a foothold, and then seeing that all was lost, he turned slowly to meet the panting mob.

I saw Kangiak run close to Kakuktak, then turn and point his own knife toward the villagers. I heard Kangiak's voice boom over the snow exactly like the deep voice of Sarkak as it called, "*Aauuu!* Stop!" to halt a team of dogs. The sound rose from his belly with such power that many people took a step backward. As I hobbled on toward the canyon, I met the shaman's dirty boy running back toward the village. I wish now that I had grabbed him and choked the life out of him.

When I reached the crowd, they were listening to Kangiak.

"This man, what has he done that would cause us to kill him? What had Portagee done to deserve killing? I warn you that killing begets killing, and this man is like a brother to me. Which one of you has been appointed to murder my brother?"

Kangiak stared longest into the eyes of those he trusted least. Shartok, who had given Portagee the death thrust, and Tungilik, who had stabbed Pilee, walked away, for their work was done. And the crowd started to shuffle around and to talk.

"He's better than the other two," called Poota. "See, he still has good fortune. He still lives life."

"Let him stay among us," called Nowya's widow. "He has the will to live, so he lives."

I saw that Kakuktak could sense the change in the temper of the people. Children on the edge of the crowd started to play. One woman called her husband and her son to come home. Kakuktak put his knife away and stood tall and straight against the red cliff, his yellow hair shifting in the breeze.

I saw the dirty boy come back then and hand something into the crowd of kayakmen. I felt my breath catch in my throat. Too late, I saw Okalikjuak, the archer, kneel and draw the bow. I tried to shout, to warn Kakuktak. I thrust out my hands and lunged out in front of the murderous arrow. Okalikjuak released the slim bone shaft, and the broad hunting point sheared away my two fingers at the second joints. This may have deflected the arrow by a handsbreadth, for as I fell I saw it strike Kakuktak in the belly just above the right hip. Blood spurted from my fingers, and as I tried to rise, the second arrow whistled over my face and struck Kakuktak deep in the chest.

His blue eyes opened wide, and with his last breath he tried to call out. He looked wildly among us, searching, I knew, for Neevee. Not seeing her, he fell forward. Kangiak turned him over and held him gently as the life ran out of him. Kangiak sat in this way for some time, looking into Kakuktak's face.

Finally he stood up and said to everyone, "I shall not live among people who would do that. You, who used to sing and dance with him. Perhaps I shall not seek revenge on the one who shot that arrow, for he was appointed by many of you. But I tell you this," he said, waving his knife slowly back and forth, "if anyone touches this man's clothes, if they take his buttons or his belt, or his knife, I will kill him. Do not cover him with stones,

do not weight his body or his soul. I hope it will rise each night and stalk among you, for the wrong that you have done to him. This man, Kakuktak, has the power to avenge himself upon you."

With that, Kangiak slipped his knife up the sleeve of his parka and walked through the crowd of kayakmen. He stopped beside me, examined the mitt I held against my bleeding fingers. Then we two slowly started back to the village.

It was then that I saw Neevee stumbling toward us, wide-eyed with fright. She fell on her knees beside Kakuktak's body. She ran her hands along his arms until she lay outstretched on top of him, trying to warm him, not caring about the arrows or the blood. Then, kneeling beside him, sobbing, shivering like a sick animal, she hid her face from all of us.

Kangiak and I returned alone to our broken snowhouse and worked grimly together, removing the killing spear from Portagee's back. We pulled first his, then Pilee's body up the hill, where we covered them with heavy stones. So grieved was I that I felt no pain from my bloody hand. The others stayed inside their igloos as Kangiak and I flung our belongings onto the sled and hauled it halfway to the place where Kakuktak lay. There we stopped and built our new snowhouse. Its entrance faced the village, and we drove many spy holes through the walls to show those people that we watched them always with mistrust.

All that day and all that night I watched and waited, but Neevee did not come out of that place. Just before the false dawn came, I left the snowhouse, and gathering all my courage, made my way up the dark path. The whole place lay in shadows and I found myself almost upon him before I could make out his form, staring stiffly at the sky. Neevee was gone, but where? Then, at my feet I saw a sharp crude drawing in the snow. It was of a square house with a pointed roof and many openings. A man, a woman with a long dress, and two small children were walking toward it. And I saw where Neevee's small footprints led away from her drawing, down the embankment and out over the newly broken ice that drifted toward the open sea. Neevee was gone, gone forever, carrying her children within her.

IX

FOR THE first time in my life I felt utterly alone. Only Kangiak was left to me, and he moved stiffly like Sarkak, his face cold as stone. I knew he still carried a knife in his sleeve. But we knew that the killing was ended and how it was begun. We knew that after the drinking the villagers had met and decided that the foreigners were dangerous in the camp. For one thing, they had taken everything from us and given us nothing in return; and they had forced Sarkak, the strongest man we had ever seen, to leave us. The three executioners, all relatives of mine, had simply done what the community had ordered. Only Shartok, the fool, had not been appointed. When Portagee backed Atkak against the wall, he had murdered the brown man without permission, and for this the people would banish him. To them, unplanned passionate murder was the most terrible of all crimes.

The hot spring sun caused our snowhouse to collapse, and we pitched a small sealskin tent on higher ground. The only person who came to visit us was the old woman Ningiuk. She was always helpful and kindly and a comfort to us, since we had no woman in our house. Her young daughter, so shy she rarely spoke, came with her. They both liked to look at Kakuktak's book of drawings, and in return they helped us sew the kayaks and mended our clothes and gave us the village gossip.

One of the things the old woman told us was that the shaman had tried to trade that dirty boy for Sowniapik's two daughters, who were both with child. But Sowniapik had refused, for every-

one was anxious to see what kind of young they would bear. The shaman and his dirty boy had left early one morning and no one had stood near them to say good-by. People, Ningiuk said, were forgetting the taboos he had placed upon them. It was clear she did not like the shaman. She told us, too, that she had all along been against the killing of the three foreigners, although she had said nothing, for that is our way.

As the spring sun warmed, Kangiak relaxed. He watched the red canyon less, and told me we should repair the kayaks so we could travel up the fjord as soon as it was free of ice. There we would hunt, he said, until the first winter moon, when we would journey inland to search for our father. I was anxious to go.

But on one of the first days of summer I was rudely awakened by Kangiak. "A ship," he gasped, "a huge ship!" He half dragged me up the hill to look. There, indeed, lay an immense ship with three great masts and vast sails slack and yellow in the dazzling morning light. That first vision of the mightiness of the *kalunait* stands forever in my memory.

I watched in wonder as two figures in a small white boat detached themselves from the huge ship and rowed toward our beach. As they neared the land, we could see that they had the same dark clothing we had come to know on Kakuktak, Pilee and Portagee. I heard Kangiak draw in his breath. He started to move out into the sunlight from behind the rock that hid us from their view. I caught him by the arm. I could not stand another encounter. Kangiak looked straight at me, and I knew he understood my feelings, but I also knew he had to go down to them. I released his arm and instead held out my own to him. Gently he helped me down the boulder-strewn hill.

The men ran their boat up clear of the tide and jumped out to wait for us, talking together, exactly like Kakuktak and Pilee. We crossed the beach slowly, empty-handed, for our knives were concealed in our sleeves.

"Halloo," said the taller of the two men. They both smiled.

There was a long moment of silence. Then Kangiak said to them, "*Tikiposi*. You have arrived." But these new strangers of

course did not understand and we all laughed with nervousness.

These two seemed younger to me than either Kakuktak or Pilee. They gestured that they wanted fresh water, as any man would who traveled by sea, so we led them to where a mountain stream emptied into the sea. One knelt and drank. The other remained standing, watching us. Then they changed places. The knife cases on their belts were empty. Their sea knives must have been in their sleeves, as ours were. But when they had filled their water barrel, they seemed to gain trust in us. They sat on a rock and motioned us to sit beside them. Then slowly they spoke to us, but we understood none of their words. So the short man began drawing, with the handle of his water ladle, in the wet sand, and making descriptions with his hands.

There could be no question that he was trying to ask us about Portagee, with the ring in his left ear; about the three men we had never known; and then blond Kakuktak and Pilee, quick, and full of orders. So here they were, the very men who had lived in the ship with our *kalunait,* searching for their missing men. I thought, Yes, I could lead you to the graves of Pilee and Portagee. I could show you the scattered bones of the dear Kakuktak, his clothes, his boots and his iron knife rotting there with him. I could tell you he was "Dag-it," and show you his drawings. I did nothing, for I could not bear to have other *kalunait* here again.

While these thoughts moved through my head, I looked at Kangiak. He blinked his eyes at me, and I knew he agreed. So we helped them carry the heavy water barrel. We lifted their boat into the water, for the tide was running out fast, and the tall man climbed in at once. But the short man did not. Suddenly he touched Kangiak's shoulder and pointed at the ship. He made a motion of throwing a harpoon, and then with his hand clearly invited Kangiak to go with them.

For a moment Kangiak did not move. Then he turned to me, and I could see how much he wanted to see that ship and to hunt whales with them. He sucked in his breath, meaning yes, and I looked into his eyes and answered yes.

Kangiak stepped quickly into the little boat, gracefully, like a

kayakman, and squatted down between the two strangers, with his back to me. I was glad I could not see his face. The short man reached into his pocket and handed me a small box, and I took it and put it in my parka. He then leaped aboard, and with a single stroke of the oars he drove the boat away from the rocks. Then he paused, and Kangiak turned, and all three stared at me. "Goo-baay. Goo-baay," they called, and a great feeling of sadness came to me, for I could remember our *kalunait* saying this.

I shouted back, as best I could, "Goo-baay, goo-baay." And Kangiak called "Goo-baay" to me, already using their language.

I stood there until I saw the bottom of the little white boat flash in the sunlight as it was hauled aboard the ship.

I moved back up the long hill slowly, for now I had no person I wanted to see in this whole land. In a while I saw the gray bitch tracking me through the rocks. She came and rubbed against me, nudged me. I rose, and together we made our way down to our tent. But it was dark and cold inside, and so sad without Kangiak that I went out again and squatted on the tundra, trying to set my thoughts free of the place.

I saw old Ningiuk and her daughter coming toward me. Ningiuk asked if I had seen the ship, and I told her of the two men and of Kangiak's leaving. She thought it was all magic, and the strange men ghosts come to avenge their kinsmen. Only then did I remember the gift. I took out the shiny box and showed it to her. It was full of thin little wooden sticks with blue, waxy heads. Even old Ningiuk could see that these things were real. But I knew no more than she what they were for.

Sarkak would have known and he would gladly have told me how to use them, but Sarkak never returned. Visiting hunters told me that terrible winter storms had turned the whole inland plain into a place of death. Countless winters turned into spring, and other foreigners like yourself came to our land again before I learned how to strike those waxy little blue heads and found out that those two strangers had given me a box of fire makers in exchange for my brother. And he, like all the others, was lost to me forever.

There was one evening at the end of summer when I thought I would take the widow's kayak and go searching for Kakuktak and Neevee, Sarkak and my brothers, Ikuma and Nuna, Portagee and Pilee. But as I stood up to go and get the kayak, the sun's rays slanted across the hills in a way that made me catch my breath with joy, and I remembered a song of our people:

> *Ayii, ayii,*
> *There is one thing*
> *And only one thing,*
> *To rise*
> *And greet the new day,*
> *To turn your face*
> *From the dark of night,*
> *To gaze at the white dawn.*
> *Arise, Arise.*
> *Ayii, ayii.*

These words seem true to me, for I have an endless curiosity. So look at me, old and crippled, and yet still waiting for all the good things and bad things life will bring to me.

*Abstract from the log of the bark* Escoheag, *824 days outbound from New Bedford, Massachusetts:*

*Tuesday, July 20, 1897.* Big tide here and heavy ice. Dropped anchor offshore of island where whaleboat was lost. Sent the mate and Atkins ashore for fresh water and to look for Esquimeaux or any sign of the lost boat crew. They came back soon, bringing a little fresh water and a likely Esquimeau lad. No sign of the boat crew. God rest their souls. Wind shifted to SW. We are leaving on this tide. So ends this day.

# James Houston

James Houston, Canadian artist and author, was born in Toronto in 1921. He was a young student, twelve years old, at the Art Gallery of Toronto when one morning the greatest of his teachers, who had just returned from Africa, played African music through the halls and did an African dance, his face covered with a great carved mask. "It shook me to the core," Houston says, "and I was hooked forever on the art and lives of primitive people."

Houston continued his studies at the Ontario College of Art and in Paris. From 1940 to 1945 he was on Canadian Active Service with a Scottish machine-gun regiment. In 1948 he made his first journey into the Canadian Eastern Arctic. He found a vast, cold and hauntingly beautiful world inhabited by people who had, he discovered, a flourishing art of their own. Fired by the beauty of their carvings in stone, bone and ivory, he began working to bring this Eskimo art to the attention of the outside world. He went to Tokyo and studied printmaking with the great Un-ichi Hiratsuka, and then returned to the Arctic to teach the Eskimos this process which was new to them but closely related to their incised drawings in stone and bone. Eskimo prints and sculptures are now in museums and private collections all over the world.

Because of his intimate knowledge of the Eskimos and their language, Mr. Houston was appointed the first civil administrator on west Baffin Island, where the story *The White Dawn* tells took place. For nine years he lived there, traveling the sixty-five thousand square miles of his district with his own dog team.

James Houston now lives with his wife in New York City, where he is associate director of design for Steuben Glass, but he returns frequently to the Arctic, and on one recent trip he served as interpreter for Queen Elizabeth II when she and her family visited the Northwest Territories and Baffin Island.

PHOTO BY WATSON

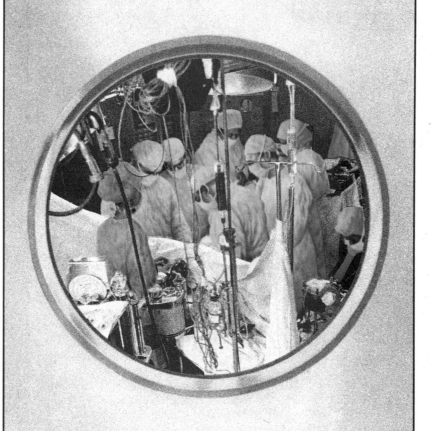

# RISK

A CONDENSATION OF THE BOOK BY

## RACHEL MacKENZIE

A remarkable
account of open-heart surgery
as the writer herself
experienced it

ILLUSTRATED BY
DON STIVERS AND HENRY RIES

Open-heart surgery is a wondrous medical advance, but what of the patient who undergoes it? The prospect of such an operation was frightening to Rachel MacKenzie, as it would be to anyone. But a steady commitment to life supplied her with the spiritual strength to undergo an ordeal which would take her to the very limits of her endurance.

*Risk* tells an unsparing, yet inspiring, medical story. It is an honest personal account of one woman's gallant struggle against human frailty—an experience suffused with peril and love.

# I

"I THINK it's time you saw a super-super heart man," Dr. Lewis said. "You remember, I told you I might want you to. We'll make the arrangements and be in touch."

The appointment with Dr. Jamison was for January 13th. "I have your September hospital record," he said when she called from the office where she worked, "and I've talked with Dr. Lewis and have his recent cardiograms and X ray. I guess that's everything I need."

"Except me," she said.

"Well, yes," Dr. Jamison said after a slight pause.

Now he perched himself on the desk in the hospital examining room and looked down on her. "Has Dr. Lewis talked to you about your situation?"

"Not as much as I'd like."

"Well, I'm going to. When I've spent this much time with a patient, I feel I should tell her what I think. It's congestive heart failure, as you already know. There's fluid. You have a murmur—two on a scale of six, not too bad. What I want to do is this: shift your medication around a bit"—he explained—"and if you aren't considerably better in six to eight weeks, then I feel we should do a much more intensive examination to consider the possibility of surgery. After all, you're a comparatively young woman."

It was such a shock she said nothing. She held her face very still.

"Heart X rays," he said.

"More than the X rays I've already had? I work, you know. Is it something I could come in and have done in a day?"

"No, no. You'd have to be *in* the hospital for them—I'd say a week to ten days. There are two: a heart catheterization and an arteriogram. We'd have to get you ready, and then you'd need three or four days to recover from the first before we did the second, and a few days to recover from that. They're quite different from anything you've had. They're done with dye and give us a look inside the heart, inside the coronary artery."

"Is there any risk?" she asked.

"There's always risk in a procedure that involves the heart. But if anything goes wrong you're with people who know exactly what to do and have the equipment to do it with. They're prepared." He smiled. He was a tall, handsome man, not personal but kindly, and everything he said was very clear.

"Why do I have to wait?" she asked.

"I want to try you on this change of medication," he said. "You might not have to have them done." He smiled again.

"Are you a surgeon?"

"No, I don't do surgery."

"I love being alive," she said inconsequentially.

"WHAT exactly are those X rays?" she asked Dr. Lewis when she saw him three days later. She'd known him longer, though not long, really—only a few months—but she found it easier to put her questions to him. Besides, it took time for her to find her questions. They always came late. Her mind turned things over, and there they were.

"A heart catheterization and an arteriogram, I would suppose. Didn't Dr. Jamison tell you?"

"Yes, and he explained them some, but I stopped listening. Taking it in, anyway. They run a catheter into your heart?"

"Yes," he said. "And take X rays. It's quite dramatic. Lots of

people around. You're in a big dark room, with an enormous light over you."

"Does Dr. Jamison do them?"

"No. It's a highly specialized department. Dr. Allen."

"Why do I have to wait?" she said. "Waiting is the hardest."

He was as cross as he got with her. "The tests would be meaningless in the shape you're in now. We want you in optimum shape."

"I mind waiting," she said.

Two days later Dr. Lewis called her at home. "I've been talking to Dr. Jamison," he said. "We've made a reservation for you for February twenty-second. We tried to set one up earlier, but the schedule was full the week we wanted, and then Dr. Jamison will be off for ten days, skiing. It's important that he be here. February twenty-second is the first date we could arrange. I'm sorry. That's a Sunday. The catheterization will be done on Wednesday."

"Wednesday!" she said.

"It takes some preparation," he said. "And we want you rested."

That evening she hung a large calendar on the wall at the foot of her bed and circled Sunday, February 22nd, and Wednesday, February 25th. It was the first that any of this seemed real.

The next time she was in Dr. Lewis's office she said diffidently, "Suppose they find surgery *is* possible, is there any chance that they'll move straight into it? I would need to do something about the office if there is—say something . . ."

He looked at her thoughtfully. "Yes," he said. "Or we might let you out for two weeks if there were personal things you had to attend to."

Another shock. "Where would the incision be?"

He reached across his desk and lightly traced a line down the middle of her chest, curving toward the left, low under her breast. "Here, I would think." His expression was fastidious.

She shivered, but not so that it could be seen. "Do you think it's going to be possible?"

"We have to wait for the results of the tests. But remember, if it

isn't, I can help you." He smiled. He had a lovely smile, warm and encompassing.

Help me adjust to a life in bed. Still, she smiled back.

THE weeks were slow. "Where do you suppose they run the catheter *from?*" she asked Ellie, who lived with her—an adopted sister. "The bend of the arm?"

"I haven't the faintest idea," Ellie said. "I think the wrist—no, maybe it's the shoulder. I think maybe I've heard that."

"But how could they possibly get into a *shoulder?*"

For some reason, she was shy about asking Dr. Lewis, even though it was the question they discussed most at home. Well, what else was there? To the people she worked with she said only that she had to go into the hospital for a week to ten days for some tests. They all knew she was in trouble, and how could you announce you were going to have something before you knew you were going to have it? But she made a new will, she transferred money to her checking account and executed a power of attorney so Ellie could draw on it. She got as much work in the office done ahead as she could, and papers at home put in order. And the waiting seemed to go on forever.

When they went to the hospital, she was having difficulty with her breathing. A woman from the admitting office came out to the waiting room with papers for her to sign, and a few minutes later brought the plastic identification band to fasten around her wrist. And then they were upstairs in a tiny dark box of a room, and the nurses took over.

Ellie was off buying a plant to cheer the place up when a nurse came in and sat down by the bed, holding a large red book open on her lap. "I've come to prepare you for your heart catheterization," she announced.

There didn't seem anything to say to that.

The nurse consulted her book. "This is a procedure by which catheters are introduced into the heart and X rays are taken."

"Catheters? More than one?"

The nurse looked down at her book. "Yes. Two."

"Can you tell me where they're inserted?"

The nurse consulted the book again. "I'm afraid it isn't a procedure I'm familiar with, myself. Your doctor can tell you. Yours is scheduled for Wednesday morning. Someone will come down from the department to go over it all with you. No breakfast. Nothing by mouth after midnight—the usual."

"Does that mean it's done under anesthesia?"

Another look at the book. "I really couldn't tell you. You'll have to ask your doctor."

"Is the catheterization done under anesthesia?" she asked Dr. Lewis when he came in for a visit in the early evening.

"No," he said. "Just a sedative. They have to have your cooperation for the X rays."

"I've been prepared out of a big red book," she said, "but it didn't seem to have all the answers." They laughed together.

"I have a horror of anesthesia," she said.

"I WANT to prepare you for your heart catheterization," Dr. Jamison said Monday morning after he'd examined her. He was wonderfully tanned from his ten days of skiing. "It's a little rugged. They run two catheters into the heart, one through a vein in here"—he touched the bend of her right arm—"and one through the femoral artery in your thigh. It's marvelous what the X rays show us; they're a marvelous diagnostic aid. The whole thing should take three, maybe three and a half hours. It may bother your back, having to lie in one position so long. They use a dye for the last pictures. Some people have a reaction to that, but there's no reason you should. We've stopped your anticoagulant and will be giving you some vitamin K. Do you have any questions?"

"No," she said. "I guess they're all answered."

He tweaked her toe and was off.

"HELLO. I'm Dr. Morris. I've come to prepare you for your heart catheterization," a very attractive young woman said on Tuesday afternoon. "I'll be in charge. The staff takes turns at it. Dr. Allen will do the X rays at the end. Has anyone told you what to expect?"

"Well, I think so," she said.

"I'll go over it again. We use two catheters. We cut into a vein at the bend of your right arm for one, and use the right femoral artery for the other. They usually go in quite painlessly—not always. We use a little Novocain. Once they're in place, we manipulate them around the chambers and get measurements—blood flow, volume, and so on—that are recorded on an electronic display. There's a constant cardiogram being taken. The X rays are done at the end. If you're interested, you can watch part of it on the fluoroscopic screen. Some people can't stand to, and we turn the screen away from them, but some people like to see what's going on—it helps pass the time. We're glad to explain things to you. We talk among ourselves. It's quite informal."

"I'd like to watch," she said.

"Fine."

"Dr. Jamison said three to three and a half hours?"

"At the most," Dr. Morris said. "I should think less. Now if you'll just let me examine you . . ."

"If anything goes wrong," Dr. Jamison said on Tuesday after Dr. Morris's visit, "remember, you're with people who know what to do and have equipment."

"You mean a heart attack?"

"It's a possibility. I don't expect it. But if you have trouble you couldn't be in better hands."

Dr. Lewis came that evening. "All set?"

"I should think so."

"Oh, one thing. Don't be reluctant to tell Dr. Allen when you've had enough. He'll ask. I've explained to him that you have a bad back. It's a long time to be in one position, and that X-ray table is *hard*. I have clinic tomorrow, so I'll be dropping in on you."

THERE were five doctors in the room, all young, and out in the corridor a number of nurses. Two of them came in and moved her to the cold, hard table, and Dr. Morris introduced her around. The light overhead was enormous, and so was a rectangle at the foot of the table. It looked like a great fluorescent light.

"What's that?" she asked.

"An electronic machine," Dr. Morris said. "It keeps records—cardiogram and so on. You won't be able to see them; the blank side is toward you." The room was lined with equipment. A large construction back of her head was for the X rays, they told her.

Two of the doctors covered her with sterile sheets. "Well, we might as well get to work," Dr. Morris said, and lifted her right arm. "I'm just going to cut into a vein. All you'll feel is the Novocain. We'll put a stitch in it at the end. We have a competition going to see who can come out with the smallest incision."

"Who's ahead?" she asked, terrified.

"It's a draw. Dr. Peterson here is pretty good. . . . *There* we are. By the way, be sure to let us know if at any time you have pain or feel odd in any way. I'm inserting the catheter."

"*That's* painful."

"Blast!" Dr. Morris said. "The vein's gone into spasm. I'm sorry, I'm going to have to hurt you."

She worked with the catheter for what seemed a very long time.

"The pain is quite bad."

"I know. Sometimes they slip through just like that. I'm going to have to get Dr. Allen," she said to the other young doctors gathered round.

"He won't thank you for interrupting him," one of them said.

"I can't help that—will you ask him to come in, please?"

"I'm Dr. Allen," he said to her. "I understand you're having some trouble." He took over the catheter. "I'm just going to have to force it through. Once we get past the axilla, we'll have smooth sailing. Oh, that axilla!"

The pain became excruciating.

"Hi." Dr. Lewis had come in. He spoke to Dr. Allen and went to the head of the table and put his hands through the shelves there and placed them one on each side of her head. "Is it pretty bad?"

She nodded. "How much longer?"

"Not too long," Dr. Allen said. "We're almost there."

"You're doing all right," Dr. Lewis said. "I'll be back."

"There!" Dr. Allen said finally, and sure enough the pain had

ended, though the word "excruciating" hung in her mind and wouldn't leave. "I'll see you later," he said to her, and to Dr. Morris, "Carry on. Let me know when you're ready."

"Now for the second," Dr. Morris said, "I'll just give you some Novocain. We have to push this one in—don't dare cut. It may hurt. Nothing like the other, though."

It hurt. There was a feeling of warmth running down her groin, and she thought they must be using warm water.

All the doctors were faced toward what looked like a television screen at her right. She turned her head to see, and there on the screen two long, thin, wormlike creatures moved in fluid in a vaguely chambered structure. Their movement was like a little dance.

"Is that my *heart?*" she asked.

"That's right," one of the men said.

"But I never felt the second catheter except when you pushed it in. It was so fast."

"Will someone get Pat to come monitor the cardiogram?" Dr. Morris said, and to her, "Do you feel anything?"

"I'm aware they're there."

"But no pain? It's important that you let us know immediately if you have any pain in your chest." She began to manipulate the catheter in the arm; Dr. Peterson was manipulating the catheter in the groin. They were using warm water again.

"Try turning it to the right," Dr. Peterson said, and on the fluoroscope she saw one of the catheters dance. "You have it," he said. "You're in."

In what? she wondered.

Out of her sight a voice began in a monitone, "Beep . . . Beep . . . Beep, beep, beep . . . Beep . . . Beepbeepbeepbeep."

Dr. Lewis's hands were on her head again. She hadn't seen him come in. "All right?" he said. "Is your back hurting?"

"It's beginning to. I feel as if I'd been here a long time. What are those beeps?"

"Oh, they're just keeping track of the beat."

"Do you see my heart?"

"I see it. Everything looks fine. I've been over watching the cardiogram. I'll drop by," he said.

"Beep . . . Beep . . . Beepbeepbeep," the voice droned on.

Dr. Allen was at her side. "We're going to take the X rays now," he said. "I'll just pull this machine over your chest. Don't worry, it won't crush you, though I do have to cut off your view. Lie perfectly still and hold your breath when I tell you."

It was a ponderous business, and it went on and on.

"I'm sorry, but I don't think I can stay in this position much longer," she said. "It's my back."

"Just five more minutes," Dr. Allen said. "Try moving that catheter—here, I'll do it." He came around to the side. "*Now* let's see what we get."

Plate after plate.

"I'm in too much pain to stand it any longer," she said half an hour later.

"Just five more minutes," Dr. Allen said from behind her head.

Dr. Lewis was there again. This time he stood at her side.

"My back's hurting," she told him.

"I'm not getting as clear pictures as I'd like," Dr. Allen said.

Dr. Lewis touched her lightly. "I have to go keep office hours. I'll be in to see you tonight. It shouldn't be much longer."

"Look, I really *can't* stand it," she said another half hour later. "If you'd just give me something to stop this pain in my back I'd be all right."

"We don't have anything of the sort up here," Dr. Allen said. "Just five more minutes now. We're ready to start the dye."

"You'll feel this the second we start," Dr. Peterson said. "Your mouth will dry up and you'll have a tingling sensation in your tongue and down your arms. Don't worry. It only makes a few people sick, but here's a basin, in case."

"Well, I guess that's the best I'm going to get," Dr. Allen said at last. "I'm sorry it took us so long." He shook her hand. "You were very patient." Three of the young doctors went out with him. Only Dr. Morris and Dr. Peterson were left.

"Maybe a pillow would help your back," Dr. Morris said. A

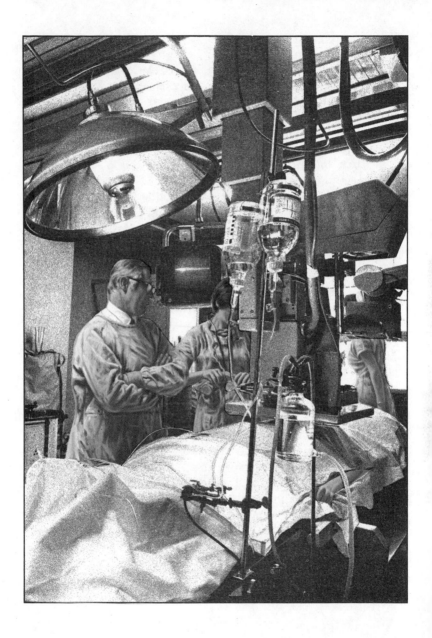

nurse brought one and wedged it under her left side. "We still have to take the catheters out and put a stitch in your arm."

She bent her legs to shift the pressure on her back.

"*Don't* move that leg!" Dr. Peterson said sharply.

"Could I have a drink?"

"I don't see why not," he said, and he went out and brought her a tall glass of cold water with a curved straw.

"There!" Dr. Morris said when the stitch was in. "Now we'll get rid of the second one." She moved down the table.

"It's been more than three and a half hours, hasn't it?" she asked Dr. Peterson.

"God, yes. Closer to five." Both doctors looked tired.

The warm water poured down her leg. "Bob, you'll have to help me," Dr. Morris said. "I can't put enough pressure on this artery."

It was only then that it occurred to her that the warm water was blood.

"Whatever you do, don't move that leg! Hold perfectly still!" Dr. Peterson said.

It took thirty minutes to get the bleeding stopped.

"Can't you put a stitch in it?" she asked at one point.

"And risk two more holes in this?"

"I guess that does it," Dr. Morris said. "We'll get you cleaned up and into a fresh gown."

She was two-thirds onto the stretcher when a violent wave of nausea swept over her. Dr. Peterson jumped out of the way.

"Oh!" she said. "How awful! I didn't have any warning."

"Don't think a thing about it," he said. "I'm in practice. I have a new baby. It's my own fault—I shouldn't have given you that water. We've never had anyone react to the dye *this* late."

There was a bright red stain spreading over the front of her clean gown.

She hadn't been back in her room long when Dr. Jamison appeared. "I've been looking at your X rays," he said. "You have an aneurysm of the left ventricle. That's a bulge—like a bulge you might have in an inner tube. It's still part of the heart wall, that is. The pictures aren't as clear as we'd like, but there's no doubt."

He seemed terribly pleased. "I've asked Dr. Rudd to drop round to see you tomorrow."

"Is he a surgeon?"

"He is," Dr. Jamison said.

DR. LEWIS was excited, too. "Yes, we've found the trouble."

"What does an aneurysm of the left ventricle mean?"

"Well, imagine a football, with one segment ballooned way out." He demonstrated with his hands. "The balloon is the aneurysm. It fills with extra blood, and the heart wears itself out trying to empty it. That's it, oversimplified."

"Did you know that Dr. Jamison is having a surgeon come see me tomorrow?"

"Dr. Rudd. There's a special thing about him. He's not only a very fine surgeon; he knows as much cardiology as any cardiologist. That's not generally true. Now we *really* have a team," he said with satisfaction. "Dr. Rudd, Dr. Jamison, and me."

"And me."

"Why, you're the most important member."

The intern who came round that night said, "I've been up to see your X rays. All of us on the floor had a bet on what they'd show. I lost. I didn't think it was an aneurysm. I thought it was muscle failure."

"Did anyone win?"

"Yes. Dr. Jamison."

DR. RUDD was in his surgeon's garb, a calm, avuncular-looking man, big enough to be imposing, with quick, amused eyes and a broad smile. He reminded her of someone. He shook her hand and sat on a chair beside the bed. "I've been studying your X rays." He was carrying a used envelope, on the back of which he'd made a little drawing. "The heart looks like this." He held out the envelope. "Here's the aneurysm. Upstairs they estimate that it's thirty-seven percent the size of the ventricle. I think it's larger—fifty, maybe. The pictures aren't very clear."

"Is that large?"

"Pretty large. We don't know exactly. I hope we can get a better idea from the arteriogram. We've put you down for that for Friday morning." He spoke in a relaxed, Midwestern accent.

"Friday!"

"Providing you feel up to it."

"Dr. Rudd, what would the surgery be?"

"Well, you cut out the aneurysm and stitch the sides of the ventricular wall together. I'd also plan to take a vein from your leg and attach it to the aorta and run it across to the coronary artery, to give you a better blood supply."

"It sounds like a long operation."

"Oh, I'd say around six hours. Maybe a little longer."

"Do you think you're going to be able to do it?"

"Perhaps. We won't be sure until we have the arteriogram. Do you think you'll feel up to it Friday?"

"Of course."

"I'll be seeing you," he said.

A NURSE she hadn't seen before came in next morning. "I'm Miss Josephson," she said. "Dr. Rudd's nurse. I work with all the open-heart cases. I've come to prepare you for your surgery."

"Physically or psychologically?"

Miss Josephson considered. "Psychologically, I guess."

"But nothing's decided," she said. "They haven't even done the arteriogram."

"Dr. Rudd asked me to see you."

"I must be going to have it," she told Ellie that evening. "I had a visit from the psychological-preparation nurse."

The arteriogram took only an hour and a half. And only one catheter at a time, run up from the left femoral artery. It was done by a different set of doctors. They used meticulous care and five variously sized catheters, whisking them in and out, to get pictures as sharp as they wanted. They had studied the catheterization X rays. There was no trouble with the dye, nor with the artery.

She was hardly downstairs again when Dr. Jamison appeared.

"They got wonderful pictures," he said. "The aneurysm is bigger than we thought. But the really surprising thing is that the blood supply's so good. It explains your color. You don't look like a heart patient. Practically no deposit on the arterial walls."

"*That's* good, isn't it?"

"It could hardly be better."

"We're set for surgery?"

"I don't see any reason why not."

They smiled at each other like a pair of conspirators.

Dr. Rudd came in the afternoon. In his hand was another used envelope, with another little drawing on the back. He sat down beside her. "There isn't any one man in the country who has made a specialty of this operation," he said, "but I'll be comfortable doing it if you would like to have me."

"I would," she said. "I've been hoping it would be possible."

"I have to tell you that we could open your chest and decide the risk was too great to proceed. It's large. The men who did the arteriogram figure the aneurysm is close to sixty percent the size of the ventricle. I still think fifty. It will depend on our judgment of the strength of what's left of the ventricle to carry on. Do you understand?"

"I understand."

"The blood supply's so good I shan't need to transplant the vein. That will cut the time down to four, four and a half hours. It takes an hour and a half just to open the chest."

"When can you do it?"

"We thought next Thursday, beginning around seven thirty. Tuesday and Thursday are my days. I could do it Wednesday, but you'd be fourth on the schedule. It will be best for you to be first. Dr. Jamison can be there. So can Dr. Lewis."

"That's almost a week. What do I do between now and then?"

"You stay where you are. I don't want to lose this bed rest."

"As open-heart surgery goes," Dr. Lewis said, "this is moderate to large. There will be about a dozen doctors in the operating room, perhaps more. A lot of preliminary work's going on already—using

the statistics from the X-ray studies to make graphs and charts that Dr. Rudd will need. Your back doctor has been over. He thinks your back should withstand things."

"Are you pleased?"

"Very." His eyes were bright. "It's what you want, isn't it?"

"You know it is."

After visiting hours that evening, an intern came into her room. He'd been drawing her blood every morning, but her only impression of him was earnestness. "I see you've decided to have the surgery," he said.

Something in his tone made her say, "Don't you approve?"

"No, I don't. I don't think you know what you're doing. If you were my—"

"Mother?" she supplied.

"Well, yes. I wouldn't *let* you. You haven't any idea of the risk and the awful complications of this particular operation, and I'm pretty sure no one has gone into them with you. I don't think you even know what this surgery *involves*. Of course I'm not the primary physician on the case."

"But Dr. Jamison approves."

"Dr. *Jamison?* Are you *sure?*"

"I thought I was."

"I'd suggest you talk it over with him tomorrow and *make* sure." At the door he said again, "Of course I'm not the primary physician, but I felt I had to give you my opinion."

"Yes. Thank you. I'll talk to Dr. Jamison in the morning." She kept her anger from showing, but she slept very little that night.

"Dr. Jamison," she said, "I've been thinking. Are there particular risks and complications in this surgery I ought to know about? Do you really approve of my having it?"

The expression of special pleasure that had been on Dr. Jamison's face gave way to one of reserve. "Nobody's rushing you into this," he said. "It's entirely your decision."

"That isn't what I mean. My decision was made before I ever came in here. But I *would* like to know what the risk is."

"It makes no sense to talk about risks in a thing like this," Dr. Jamison said. "Risks are statistics. Averaging. So far as you're concerned, they're one hundred percent or they're zero."

"DR. RUDD," she asked that afternoon, "what would you say is the risk of this operation?"

Dr. Rudd reflected. "Oh, I'd say around thirty-five percent or a little more—something like that," he said comfortably.

"I don't know why I asked," she said to Ellie. "I'd take it anything short of a hundred."

SHE told Dr. Lewis about the intern. He was indignant. "Why, that's one of the most bizarre things I've ever heard! Bizarre and inexcusable! Who was it?"

"I'm not going to tell you," she said. "I was furious, but I'm over it. He felt strongly and was acting on principle."

"I'm not against principle," Dr. Lewis said, "but he has to be told what to do with it. This is a teaching hospital. It would have been perfectly all right for him to bring his disapproval to me; we could have talked it over and I could have explained. To have come to you with it is inexcusable!"

DR. RUDD and Dr. Jamison came in together the following morning. "All the residents and interns on the floor are upset about your surgery," Dr. Rudd said.

"Why?"

"They don't think you look sick enough." He laughed. "We've just had to tell them we know more than they do."

Dr. Jamison laughed, too. "I told your intern that if you were *my* mother I'd want you to have it," he said. "In fact, I'd be pushing you hard."

One evening two doctors walking down the corridor stopped just beyond her door to discuss some changes in a patient's medication. One of them said in the saddest voice, "She's going to die, and she's such a nice woman."

"I could hear you saying something like that about me," she

said to Dr. Lewis later. "And I wanted to tell you, if anything goes wrong, *don't grieve.*"

"I won't," he said.

"You can't always have your own way."

SHE had been moved across the hall to a room with sun and a river view. All of her family came—Ellie, her sister Beth, and her dead brother's two daughters, whom she'd loved since they were babies and hadn't seen for a long time. She was touched. Sometimes the young surprise you, she thought. They were all so pretty. The room was full of flowers. They sat together, laughing and talking, and those days of waiting were like Christmas, when the family had been whole and together.

"There's always been enough love," she said to Dr. Lewis one night out of the blue. "I don't mean there haven't been disasters of love, and anguish, but there's always been someone to whom you mattered enough and who mattered to you."

Curious. She was a private person, really—covered—but these days she was quite naked.

DR. RUDD said, "I want to prepare you for the Intensive Care Unit. It can be a shock if you don't know what to expect. It's an open room with four beds and a good deal of equipment. Bright lights are kept on twenty-four hours. You can't tell day from night. There's constant activity. You'll wake up with a large tube in your throat—not very comfortable. It's connected to a machine that will be breathing for you. We'll get it out as soon as we can. There'll be a good many tubes. You'll be thirsty. We can't let you have anything to drink for a while. There'll be pain; we can't cover it entirely. You probably won't remember Thursday at all. After that, it depends."

"If I make it through surgery, am I safe?"

"No, the danger period lasts through the days in Intensive Care."

"I'm not afraid to die," she heard herself saying.

He made a dismissing gesture with his hand. "That's not the question," he said.

Later, Beth said, "Doesn't Dr. Rudd remind you of Father!"

"That's it!" Ellie and she looked at each other in amazement. But she didn't tell him. It would have been too much.

Dr. Jamison also prepared her for Intensive Care: "It's noisy. You won't get much sleep—just naps. Too much has to be done for you." And so did the psychological-preparation nurse, who came regularly to describe the world to which she would waken. "Everything of your own in this room will have to be taken away Wednesday," she said. "You can't have a thing with you except your toothbrush and a comb. There's no place to put it." A breathing machine was brought to her room on Monday; and Monday, Tuesday and Wednesday the psychological-preparation nurse instructed her in its use and conducted breathing practice.

WEDNESDAY, after lunch, the nurse in charge of the floor came into her room and announced formally, "As of four o'clock this afternoon, your name will be placed on the danger list."

"I'll see that you sleep tonight," Dr. Rudd told her. "They'll be getting you up early."

But she didn't. She was awake most of the night and glad to have a nurse come in at five thirty. "One of the doctors from surgery will be coming down soon to put in your intravenous and a stomach tube," she said. She was a motherly woman, and she took her in her arms and cradled her for a moment. "You're very brave," she said. "We'll all be praying for you."

They came for her at seven—no hypodermic, no sedative—and upstairs they wheeled the stretcher into a small room adjacent to the operating room. There were doctors and nurses coming and going, all in surgical garb. They paid no attention to her but bustled about, getting organized. Every now and then the door of the operating room opened and a blast of music poured out.

"Who's doing the anesthetic?" one of the nurses asked.

"Barnes," a doctor answered.

"Barnes!" someone said. All around the room eyebrows were raised and looks were exchanged.

"He's late. We're ready," the same doctor said.

Almost as he spoke, a frowning, black-browed doctor strode into the room and over to her. "I'm Dr. Barnes," he said. "I'm going to put you to sleep."

There wasn't time to say a prayer. There wasn't time to count one.

## II

SHE came whirling out of a long tunnel and knew at once she was in the Intensive Care Unit. A wide board was jammed across her throat. It kept her from asking what time it was, and it seemed important to know. There were people around her bed. Someone was calling her first name loud. She was thirsty.

"Prick. This is your antibiotic," a woman's voice said.

"Prick. I'm giving you morphine."

Every time she opened her eyes, a nurse was bent over the bed, doing something. Always the same nurse.

She felt splashed with ice water. "I'm going to turn on . . ." Slowly, cold spread through her back and up into her head. Her ears ached. Her teeth began to chatter.

"Prick." . . . "Prick."

There were other people in the room.

"I'm staying on an extra shift," her nurse said.

"But you can't," a doctor's voice said. "You'll be worn out."

"Please. Let's not argue. We're short."

There was something black dangling on her left wrist.

"Your sisters are here," the nurse said in the loud voice everyone said everything. "They're coming in for five minutes—OK?"

Ellie and Beth came toward her. They walked gingerly. Their eyes looked frightened. They took her hand. "You're beautiful," Beth said in her gentle voice. "Darling, you look beautiful." That was what their mother had said when she lay dying. In a hospital bed, a tiny, delicately boned woman, with her head tipped up like a bird's. "Beth, you're beautiful," and to Beth's husband, who was dear to her, "John, you're beautiful." "Mama, how about me?"

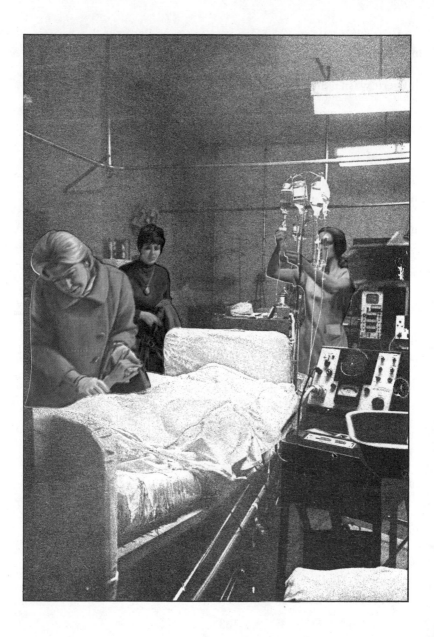

she'd asked, teasing. "Oh, *you!*" her mother had said with such tenderness it made her eyes fill to remember.

"Honey," Ellie said, "you're going to be better soon"—the very words and loving tone she'd used when they'd been made to leave the little dog they'd gone together to the animal center to have put to sleep a few months before. She would never get over not being allowed to stay with him.

So she wasn't going to make it. Fact. No feeling at all.

"Everything is fine," Beth said.

She raised her eyebrows in denial.

"It is," Ellie said. "It really is. You're going to be all right."

"All three of your doctors told us so."

They both looked stricken.

"Do you know you're hitched up to a machine that costs thirty-seven thousand five hundred dollars?" Ellie said. "It's on loan. They're trying it out on you."

She pointed to her wrist, the one with the black marks, wanting terribly to know the time.

"Do you want me to rub your arm?" Ellie asked. "I don't think I dare. You have intravenouses going."

She shook her head angrily. They looked helpless.

She made an effort and traced the shape of her wristwatch. Those black marks were the dangling ends of sutures. What were they doing on her *wrist?*

"Oh," Ellie said. "You want to know the time. It's eleven thirty."

Morning? Night? What day?

"I think that's enough," the nurse said.

"We'll be back tonight." They bent and kissed her.

What *day* was it?

The room was full of loud voices. "Joe! Joe! I'm going to . . ."

"Lucy, you've *got* to. Now try harder. You can do it—OK?"

"I want you to take some deep breaths, OK?" her nurse said.

She was too thirsty, and the board in her throat hurt.

"Have you got the gases on her?" A man's voice.

"I'm just getting them." Her nurse. Getting them where?

"Prick. I'm giving you morphine."

A LITTLE BLACK WOMAN in a bandanna turban came to the side of the bed and fell on her knees. "Oh, Jesus, Jesus!" She rocked back and forth. The nurse kicked her hard. "This is no place for praying," she said. "If you have to pray, find yourself some place where you aren't in the way. Get out!"

Had that little black woman really been there? Hallucination?

"I'm going to need more blood," her nurse said. "We're low. I ordered plenty."

"We had to use some for Joe," a doctor's voice said.

"But I ordered ten pints—more than enough. And we need more saline. I ordered plenty of that, too. Check with the clerk if you don't believe me."

"Joe's on it. Can't you use glucose?"

"I can't. Saline's what she's getting."

"Goddam it, and the weekend coming up!"

DR. RUDD was at her right side. She couldn't open her eyes, but she recognized his voice. Doctors were on both sides of the bed. "This is the Novocain. . . ." That was all she heard him say.

THE board in her throat was gone. She hadn't even felt them pull it out. But there was something dragging at her neck. It hurt in a different way; it was sore. She started to raise her hand toward it.

"You've had a tracheotomy," her nurse said, moving her hand away from her throat. "There's a plastic tube there. Now you'll be able to breathe better."

Both her hands were then strapped to boards.

They took out the plastic and with a thin tube suctioned out the trachea. "Cough!" they said. "Cough!"

DR. JAMISON said, "I know you're thirsty. You're dehydrated. But we don't dare give you anything to drink. It might make you sick at your stomach, and then all hell could break loose."

Her nurse brought her a lollypop of cotton batting soaked in glycerine and lemon. It was cool, briefly, in her mouth.

THE DOCTORS AROUND THE BED across from her were talking about Dr. Rudd. They were angry. "He's requiring so much care for"— she heard her name—"he's endangering the life of everyone else in this room," one of them said.

Dr. Rudd spoke up. "Please remember I'm the top man here," he said. "Any two-bit surgeon who can do a valvulotomy can have a patient in this unit. My operations are the big ones. So long as I have a patient here who needs care, she's going to get it." He was as calm as ever, but his voice was commanding.

What was he doing over there across the room?

"I'M turning on the thermal . . ." her nurse said. "We have to get your fever down."

The cold. The earache. The chill. She shook all over.

Dr. Rudd was at her side. "That's not a normal chill," he said. "Get the heater."

All of a sudden she was warm.

THERE were doctors at the foot of the bed. It was dark. ". . . three five-percent strokes during the operation," one of them was saying. "They didn't tell you *that*, did they! Or what the tracheotomy has probably done to your vocal cords."

Oh God, she thought, she wasn't going to speak again!

BETH and Jean, their younger niece, came. Only two could come at one time. Beth read her a letter from Ellie. " 'Remember Liz Taylor had a tracheotomy and it didn't mar *her* beauty.' "

Now she could move her lips. "Glasses," she said, and she pointed to her eyes.

"Do your eyes hurt?" Beth asked.

She shook her head.

"Do you have a headache?"

"Never mind," she said with her lips.

"I think maybe she wants her glasses," Jean said.

"Oh, I feel so stupid!" Beth said. She went off, and after a while she and a nurse came back with the glasses and a toothbrush and

comb. They put the glasses on her, and at once the blur around her cleared. There was a big clock on the wall to the right.

"Would you like to write Ellie a note?" Beth said.

She wrote dizzily at the bottom of Ellie's letter.

"We'll bring you something to write on tomorrow," Beth said, and they kissed her and went away.

THE foot of another bed faced the foot of hers. A man was in it—Joe? Bottles and tubes were strung along both sides, and she could see the machine that was monitoring his heart. The line of the cardiogram jumped up and down. In the bed at her side, a cameo face in a frame of waved black hair lay on the pillow, unmoving. Lucy?

"I'm taking away the oxygen for a while," her nurse said. "I want you to take deep breaths—OK? I know it hurts, but you have to." The nurse's name was spelled out in white stitching on her uniform: Carol.

"Have you got the gases?" an intern asked.

Nurses were arguing. A little blond nurse was saying, "But you could *show* me what to do. I'd be *glad* to work an extra shift. You can't manage as short as this."

"We'll manage," Carol said. "Betty's here and Dot's coming in."

"Please let me. I could take care of Joe for you. I'd ask about anything I wasn't familiar with."

"Will you kindly get the hell out of here?" one of the interns said. "Have you got the gases on her?"

"In a minute," Carol said.

"Prick." . . . "Prick."

"How are you going to feel"—it was her name the doctor was using—"to leave here knowing that three other people didn't make it because you got all the attention? How will you feel *then?*"

WHENEVER Dr. Rudd came into the room, everything grew calm. He was talking across the bed to Carol. He bent over and lifted two large tubes. They were full of pink fluid. "*These* aren't doing

any good," he said. "They might as well come out. This is going to hurt."

"Look at me! Look at me!" Carol said, and she turned her head. It felt as if half her side had given way.

Where had those tubes been? she wondered.

"DR. RUDD tells me the arterial line and both drains from the heart are out," Dr. Lewis said.

Arterial line?

LUCY was leaving. She had summoned her doctor from Westchester and demanded to be removed to another hospital where she would be properly looked after. There she sat in a wheelchair next to her bed, in a brown flannel suit and a beige satin blouse with French cuffs. "I'll sign you out," her doctor said, "but it is entirely on your own responsibility. I warn you, it's a matter of life and death."

Then Lucy was gone. Then she was back, still in her wheelchair, in her brown suit and fine beige blouse. But when she looked again there was the cameo face, unmoving, on the pillow.

"WE'RE going to get you into a more comfortable bed," Carol said. "You're still in the cardiac bed you came from the operating room in. Don't move—we'll do it."

A great gash above her groin at the left was pulled together with a long line of sutures. No one had prepared her for *that*.

Carol brought her a tray and started to feed her. Jello. Custard. She turned her head away.

"Dr. Rudd wants you to eat," Carol said.

She shook her head, indignant that the food was all sweet.

SHE heard her name from across the room. ". . . may make it or she may not, but Dave Rudd will get a brilliant article out of this, either way." So that was his first name: David.

*May* make it? She opened her eyes. She wrote on her pad, "Do you know I can hear?"

139

Carol gave her a speculative look. "Yes," she said.

The intern in charge was in the room. He came over to her bed. "You're some spring chicken, *you* are!" he said. He had not spoken to her before.

EXCEPT from the people taking care of her, she heard her name only one more time. Out of blackness, a Chinese voice called to her. "This is the year of the lion," the voice said. "And *you* are a lion and will fight your way through."

JOE's cardiogram was a straight line. A crowd of doctors surrounded him. They were wheeling his bed toward the door. But when she next woke up there he was as before. Another hallucination? Only they no longer called him Joe. They called him Sam, Tom, Jim, Hank—any old name—and Carol went to spend her time with him.

"Is that Joe?" she wrote.

The nurse said yes.

All the pricks now were antibiotics. There was no more morphine. Dr. Rudd said, "I've asked Dr. Williams to come in to see you. He's a lung specialist. He'll be in sometime this morning."

Dr. Williams brought another doctor with him. They were there for almost two hours. They sat her up carefully; they laid her down. "She should be having thirty-five-percent pure oxygen," Dr. Williams said to the intern. "There are air pockets. I want her waked up every hour and pounded on the back, then suctioned out. I'll go write the orders. We'll be in tomorrow. We'll need more X rays and cultures."

They took blood for the cultures three and four times a day from her veins or from her bruised right femoral artery. Both hands had swollen monstrously from the intravenous, and the needles were removed; her hands were wrapped in hot Vaseline packs.

"Are you coughing enough?" Dr. Jamison asked. "Here." He lifted her up. He put his hands on either side of her rib cage. "Take a deep breath. That's good. Now cough for me. I'll hold you. You're going to have to bring up whatever this is."

She felt as if she were split asunder, and was choking with the plastic tube in her throat.

"Again."

"I've asked Dr. Ellis from the Infectious Diseases Department to come see you," Dr. Rudd said. "To trace the cause of your fever."

Next morning Dr. Ellis came with two members of his staff. *They* sat her up carefully; they laid her down. Dr. Ellis had piercing blue eyes that looked at her with sympathy. "Do you hurt anywhere?" he asked.

Good God, she thought.

"We'll want cultures," Dr. Ellis said.

"When can I drink?" she wrote on her pad for Dr. Jamison.

"You should be drinking now," he said. "Just not too much at one time." He turned to the nurse. "Get her some ginger ale."

The nurse brought an icy bottle of Schweppes. She poured it into a tall paper cup and bent a straw and gave it to her. "Not too fast," she said, but she let her drink the whole thing. "Good?"

The fever was like a little tent. The chill, then warmth settled over her—a shelter—and she dozed. But the hypothermic blanket made her ears ache and brought on a chill of a different nature. She dreaded it, though the suctioning was worse. "Take a deep breath," they said. "Now cough!"

One night the intern who was on thirty-six-hour duty reeled into the room from wherever it was he'd been sleeping. "My God, what's the matter *now!*" he shouted.

Lucy had left and three people had come and gone from the bed across from where Lucy's bed had been when Dr. Rudd said, "Dr. Jamison thinks you'd do better in a room where the lights are out at night and you'd get more sleep and privacy. There's no place free I'd want to put you in today, but maybe tomorrow."

The next unit was across the hall, just beyond the nursing station. There were four beds here too, but more space between and a chair for each. There was less machinery. A familiar profile

141

lay on the pillow to her left. It was Lucy. But that afternoon Lucy was wheeled out in her bed and someone else was wheeled in.

She was off the monitor, though there was a tank of oxygen with a breathing attachment at one side of her bed, and a moisture-making machine with a mask that was kept on her face most of the time; there was medicine in it. The suctioning equipment was at the head of the bed. A bell was pinned within reach of her hand. Nurses were not in this room all the time. They came in, one for each patient, several times a day and at night. Voices were quieter. The other patients in the room could talk to one another. Visitors were permitted to stay longer. Tension was lower.

She sat on the edge of the bed and dangled her legs over the side, and the second day she was helped into a chair, where she stayed for a few minutes. That afternoon a small basket of flowers was brought in to her. Dozens of roses—cream and yellow and light pink and deep. The handle was twined with pale blue velvet, and baby's breath made a delicate veiling all the way round. The nurse put the basket on the windowsill beside her bed, a gentle thing to look at after these ungentle days.

Iᴛ was in this room that she began to write, "I can't get enough air." Pain burned from armpit to armpit through to her back. There was no relief from it, and one night she remembered a story about a simpleminded black woman who came home to find her mother dead; she couldn't move for the terror of it, and she dropped to her knees and repeated over and over, "Bless God, bless God" until she had enough space in her head to accept what she must.

"Bless God," she said, "bless God, bless God, bless God . . ."

Dr. Rudd seemed to know how she felt without her telling him. "Nothing short of Demerol or morphine will do you any good," he said, "and we can't risk what they might do to your breathing."

That night such a tearing pain came with a fit of coughing that the nurse called a doctor, and he called an X-ray technician, who came at once and X-rayed her chest. In the middle of the night.

"There's fluid in your lungs," Dr. Rudd said. "I want better X rays than we can get here," and she was wheeled down to the

X-ray Department. As she was waiting to be wheeled back, Dr. Rudd went by her. "I want a look at those X rays," he said.

"A section of lung has collapsed," he told her up in the room. "You're going to have to cough more. Don't be afraid. I have you put together so tightly you couldn't come apart if you tried."

"It feels like my idea of pleurisy *and* pneumonia," she wrote to Ellie, "but of course I've never had either."

When she coughed, Ellie held her.

They did the suctioning oftener. Dr. Rudd did it every time he came in, and he washed the plastic tube himself and replaced it. He was more skillful than the nurses; it was less strangling.

When night came and the lights were out, a nurse helped her sit up with her legs over the side of the bed and she put her head on the bedside table and recited "Bless God" endlessly—a litany to help endure what seemed unendurable. She dreamed that one of the doctors came and with his own hands gave her a hypodermic and a respite. She dreamed of a beaded glass of Schrafft's lemonade, with a sprig of mint showing cool over the rim. Fluids were restricted once more.

One night a nurse spent most of the night with her, working around the bed to make her comfortable. That night she slept. The morning after, the woman in the bed next to her asked to be moved from the room. "I can't get well beside anyone as sick as *she* is," she said. They wheeled her out as soon as lunch was over.

"WE'VE decided to take off some of that fluid," Dr. Rudd told her, and in the afternoon two interns came in with a trolleyful of equipment and bent her over her bedside table.

"Get a resident!" the first intern called in a loud, urgent voice when he saw the fluid flowing into the bottle. "Don't look!" But she looked anyway. It was red.

The resident was there with two other doctors in seconds. "It's all right," the resident said in an authoritative voice, and in a different voice to one of the interns with him, "Quick! Run this over to the centrifuge!" In his first voice he said to the intern with the needle, "I wouldn't take off more than two hundred cc."

When the job was finished, they all moved off, but the second intern—he had a round, jolly face—came back and wrote on her pad, "Bye Bye."

"This has nothing to do with your *heart*," Dr. Lewis said. "So far as your *heart* goes, we're right on schedule." He had brought her two new pads and two new pencils with fresh, sharp points.

Beth brought lengths of heavy yarn, and she or Ellie brushed her hair onto the top of her head and tied it with a small, bright bow. She couldn't lift her arms to brush her hair for herself.

Dr. Jamison said, "Things couldn't be better, especially now that you have your hair combed."

"I think they think I'm depressed," she wrote to Ellie. "They're all trying to cheer me up."

"Are you?" Ellie asked.

"No, I just can't get enough air."

An older surgeon on the staff—Dr. Hollister—came along with the interns on morning rounds and took the dressing off her incision. He poked and prodded. "You have an abscess under a stitch here," he said. "I'll leave it for Dr. Rudd."

Dr. Rudd appeared shortly. "This may be what we've been looking for," he said, almost with satisfaction. "The cause of your fever. I'm going to have to open it up. We'll get a culture on it and see." He opened it up at once—a long stretch in the middle of the incision. He came twice a day and irrigated and packed and dressed the opening. It looked like a piece of raw steak, and when she coughed, air whistled through it. "I want you to lie on your left side and cough for ten minutes every two hours," Dr. Rudd said. "I don't want to put a drain in unless I have to."

"I can't lie on my left side," she wrote.

"Can you lie across your bedside table? That would be all right."

"I don't think it's a serious infection," Dr. Jamison said. "You look too good."

"Your fever's up but the white count is not," Dr. Rudd said. "I'm not going to put in a drain."

"You're having some bad luck," Dr. Lewis said. "It will end."

But she was making progress. Every day she was helped into

a chair, and one morning she walked drunkenly across the hall to the washroom. She dipped her washcloth in water the nurse had drawn and lifted it up halfway to her face. The face in the mirror was a travesty of her own—thin, mostly eyes and cracked, encrusted lips. She looked at it briefly. Then she sat on the toilet seat and rang the bell to be helped back to her bed. That day she didn't get washed at all. The nurses urged her to walk, to cough, to eat more. "I can't swallow this food," she wrote. It was dreadfully cooked—a soft diet, gray, and without any seasoning.

TEN days after he had put it in, Dr. Rudd took the plastic tube out of her trachea. "I think things are healed enough now, and I know you'll be more comfortable."

She could speak at once, her voice not natural but her own.

"Listen!" she said to Beth that afternoon.

"Listen!" she said to Ellie. "I can *talk!*"

THERE were two more areas of fluid in her lungs. "We can't isolate anything of significance," the Infectious Diseases doctor said. "You've had too many antibiotics." The doctors debated drawing the fluid off. One day they thought they would; the next day they thought they would wait.

"One thing I *couldn't* stand—to go back to the operating room," she said to Dr. Lewis.

"There is no thought of *that*," he said sternly.

"I haven't any margin left."

Now that she had her voice, she told Dr. Rudd what she had heard in Intensive Care.

He sat down to talk. "It sounds to me like a bad trip," he said. "Anesthesia today is very sophisticated, and you had a fever of a hundred and four and a lot of morphine those days. No one in the world would have said that kind of thing to you—it's unthinkable. It was hallucination."

"Some of it," she said. "I even thought that at the time. But I'd bet you on a good part of what I heard. My mind was in order."

"Perhaps you don't know that I'm in charge of the Intensive

Care Unit. I'm in there a lot. The tension you felt was all from the patients—not the staff. I would know."

"But it's not there when you are. You bring quiet with you."

"It was hallucination," he said kindly. "And no wonder. I wasn't even near the room that time you heard me defending myself."

"Then someone must have spoken up for you."

He shook his head. "And I never do an article on just one case."

The next day he sat down beside her again. "I've been talking to Dr. Hollister about your experience. He says there were things said that you could have misunderstood. I haven't got hold of Carol yet, and I want to talk to some of the others."

Later Dr. Lewis said, "It had to have been a bad trip. Dr. Rudd told me about it and that was my first thought, too."

"Not all of it," she said stubbornly.

"It doesn't make sense. There's no such thing as a five-percent stroke."

She told Beth and Ellie. "I'll accept that Dr. Rudd wasn't in the room when I thought I heard him, and I know that little black woman was hallucination—I knew it at the time. And that Lucy couldn't possibly be out of bed and in a wheelchair—"

"But she was," Ellie said. "We had to climb over that wheelchair out in the hall when we came to see you Sunday."

"Did she have on a brown suit?"

"I didn't notice the color," Beth said, "but she did have on a suit and a beige satin blouse."

Two weeks after surgery she was moved to the room farthest from the nurses' station. Four beds, but the people in them were less sick. Oxygen went with her, and the moisture-making machine; the suctioning was over. She was walking rather shakily in the corridor, where there was a rail to hang on to. And still the examinations, the X rays; still the blood tests.

After four days Dr. Rudd said, "Wouldn't you be happier out of here and in a private room? I have one for you. Admissions said there wasn't a thing available, but I talked to the administrator,

and when I called Admissions again it seems there had been one all along. A mystery. The food up there is better—a different food service. We want to get you eating."

She was smiling so widely when Dr. Jamison arrived that he said, "Well, I see you've heard the news. This afternoon. I'm going to shift you to a freer diet. You can have some salt. In fact, except for a moderate sodium restriction, you can have anything you want." He went through his usual examination. "You still have that fluid and a collapsed wedge," he said. "And fever. We'd like to get rid of them."

The new room was large, with the most beautiful view of the river she had ever seen. And perfectly broiled lamb chops for dinner, with a linen napkin and a nicely appointed tray. She ate almost half the food.

"That's better," Dr. Lewis said.

"You'll have to cough more!" Dr. Rudd said. "Take a deep breath. *Cough!*" He patted her on the back as if she were a baby.

There was a large armchair to sit in by the window, and her own bathroom, though they didn't let her use it yet. Here she was not expected to wash herself but was given a bath in bed. She began to feel clean.

"I'm aware of those wires you've got me put together with," she said on an uncomfortable day to Dr. Rudd.

"No wires," he said. "You're much too thin. I used a very strong grade of Orlon."

He was still dressing the opened-up incision, and one morning he worked on it with forceps. The next afternoon the pain across her chest from armpit to armpit was beyond bearing, and tears began to roll down her face in a freshet. Just tears. It was the first time she had cried. She couldn't stop, even when Dr. Lewis came at dinnertime. "I seem to have lost my composure," she said, "and I can't get it back. I've hurt too long."

He left the room. "One of the nurses will bring you something in a minute," he said when he came back, and he stood by her bed and put the tea bag on her tray into the pot of hot water and

poured her out a cup of tea. "Drink this," he said. "Do you like anything in it?" He waited with her until she had taken the capsule the nurse brought in and was easier.

From then on she got Darvon on a regular schedule, and when her fever went over a hundred and one, two Tylenol. She welcomed the fever.

"I'm going to start pushing you," Dr. Jamison said. "I want you out in the hall walking. A nurse will take you."

That afternoon she walked half the length of the hall and back, and the next day she walked the full length. The third day she walked twice, and she walked Ellie to the elevator when she left at the end of visiting hours. "I've got to get out of here," she said.

In the night she felt the rhythm of her heart change. Dr. Lewis came early in the afternoon. It was Thursday, and he was going away for a long weekend. He listened to her chest. He went out and a few minutes later brought in a cardiograph machine. Moving unhurriedly, without speaking, he took a cardiogram. He studied the strips.

"It's different, isn't it?" she said. "I felt it happen."

"Did you tell anyone?"

"No, I didn't want any more fussing."

He went out again and came in with tubes and a hypodermic. He took the blood as silently as he had done the cardiogram, and he put the tubes and the strips in his pocket. "I'll turn these over to Dr. Jamison," he said. "See you Monday. Maybe Sunday evening."

Dr. Jamison came first thing Friday. He listened to her heart. He stood at the foot of the bed, looking down at her appraisingly. "I'm going to move you," he said. "There's a change, and while it may not be serious, it's potentially dangerous. I want you in Coronary Care. Our nurses know what they're doing; they can read cardiograms. I'll go make arrangements."

He was back shortly. "All set," he said. "They'll be right up for you."

"I can't just go in a wheelchair?"

"No. Wouldn't you like me to call your sister? It might be a

shock for her to come to this room and find you gone. If you'll give me her number, I'll do it after we have you settled in." He looked around the room. "You won't be able to take your flowers," he said. "I'm sorry."

Dr. Jamison stayed with her. A nurse came in to pack. "It's the best coronary-care unit in the world," he said. "I set it up myself. I'd better prepare you: we treat every patient who comes in as if he'd had a heart attack. I don't think you have, but I can't be sure until we run some tests, and I'm not taking any chances. We keep you on a monitor, of course, and under constant surveillance. It will be safer to have you there over the weekend."

"Just over the weekend?"

"That's all I anticipate."

A procession moved into the room: two aides trundling a narrow bed and an attractive, purposeful nurse pushing a monitor. Dr. Jamison introduced her. "And this is our battery-powered monitor," he said. "We use a different method for connecting the leads from anything you've had—needles in the arms and thighs. We get a better contact, and they don't slip out."

The nurse put the needles in deftly. Her manner was professionally reassuring. "There, that's not so bad, now, is it?" She spoke in a French-Swiss accent. "And I've brought you an intravenous gown. It makes things easier with the wires and tubing. Now we'll get you onto our cardiac bed. I warn you, it's hard!"

She started to move herself toward the bed.

"Don't move!" Dr. Jamison said. "I don't want you moving a muscle!" He came over and took one corner of the sheet she was lying on, the nurse took one, and on the opposite side each of the aides took one; she was transported to the narrow, hard bed without out a breath of effort.

Miss Townsend, the head nurse on the floor, came after her as she rolled down the corridor. "You'll be coming back to us, dear," she said. "Don't think you won't! We'll save your room for you."

They almost filled the elevator. She turned her head away from the curious eyes of the other passengers, embarrassed.

## III

CORONARY CARE was on a lower floor. She was wheeled into a little room right at the center of the station, where duplicates of all the monitors traced cardiograms and blinked their red lights on and off. The outer wall had two large windows, and except for the door, the wall facing the station was entirely windowed. The curtains around those windows and the bed were bittersweet. The little room was freshly painted; everything was immaculate.

"I'll be back in a few minutes," Dr. Jamison said, and he left her to the nurse and aides, who shifted her wires to a monitor on the wall behind her bed.

An intern came in and started an intravenous at the bend of her right arm. "I hate to put one here—you have to be careful not to bend your arm; the needle could break—and I hate to immobilize your right hand," he said. "But you haven't got another vein that's worth a damn. They've all collapsed."

"But why an IV?"

"Everyone has an IV for as long as he's in Coronary Care. We use it for medication. It can make as much as ten minutes' difference in an emergency."

"We want you on oxygen for your first twenty-four hours," the nurse said, and she clipped rubber tubing into her nostrils. "And since you have a fever we'll just turn on the air conditioning. Why don't you try to get a little rest? We'll be bothering you enough!"

On the wall behind her, red lights went on and off with a sharp ping-ping-ping, and the cardiogram traced its way noiselessly across the screen.

Dr. Jamison was in again. "I'm starting you on something that should take care of that arrhythmia," he said. "We'll be giving it to you in toxic dose, so speak up if you have any reaction. And don't worry! You're in good hands."

Dr. Rudd came in the afternoon. He looked down at her appraisingly. "We are mystified but not alarmed," he said.

"Was it the walking?"

"I hope not."

Ellie came after work. "Do you know I can only stay for five minutes? And you can only have immediate family? Five minutes out of an hour. Maybe we can ring in Sarah as a sister. She has time and would like to come. Jean can't make it every afternoon."

"Yes," she said. "I'd like that. Did Dr. Jamison call you?"

"Almost scared me to death, but I suppose it would have been worse if he hadn't."

"I can't have any flowers."

"Did you remember that this is Good Friday? Sunday's Easter."

"Your time's up," a nurse said at the door.

In Coronary Care they took blood more often and in larger quantities than they had anywhere else she had been. Some days four and five times; sometimes even in the night. Her veins got harder and harder to get blood from. "But why?" she protested. "I've been tested and tested."

"You're still running a fever, and there's still fluid in your lungs. We have to keep trying to find the cause. It might be something we could cure."

"I'm thirsty," she said often.

"I'm sorry, you're on restricted fluids. We can't let you have anything more to drink."

The food was like the food in Intensive Care. She couldn't eat, though aides offered to feed her and were careful to cut up her meat and butter her bread.

On Easter Sunday Ellie brought a large shopping bag. She took out the dear basket that had held the roses before, and a bunch of tiny, bright yellow chrysanthemums and wide white daisies. "They can throw them out tomorrow if they want to," she said. "You're going to have flowers for Easter!" She put the basket on top of the air-conditioner, and she took out a large bunch of little white grapes and washed them and put them on a table next to the bed in a bowl she had brought. "From South America, not

from California. You can eat them in the night. They might keep you from getting so thirsty. I'll rub your back before I go. Wouldn't you like your hair brushed?"

MONDAY morning Dr. Jamison said cheerfully, "Well, we haven't made it on our first try; I'm shifting to another drug," and he told her what it was.

"No change?"

"No change. Yet. Don't worry, we'll get it."

"How long do you figure it's going to take?"

"Oh, just a few more days. Give us to Wednesday. Remember, this is in toxic dose, too. Let us know about any reaction."

"THIS is Dr. Jamison's party," Dr. Rudd said, but he came every day and changed the dressing, and he explained with care that he was going away for ten days, and the date he would be back. "I get into town on Sunday," he said, "and I want to find you out of here."

"If the beat doesn't get corrected?"

"You can live with it. It's regularized now—a bigeminy beat, pretty steady. It just means a less efficient heart. I'd rather it got corrected."

THE second drug made her sick at her stomach, and Dr. Jamison stopped it and substituted a third. Then he combined two. That made her sick, and he tried a fifth. "Give us till Friday," he said. "That will just be a week. You're stubborn."

"Dr. Jamison doesn't like to be thwarted," one of the interns said.

Once more pain from her chest settled through into her back. When she woke up in the night she was unable to move and had to ring for help.

"What position do you want to be in?" the nurse would ask.

"I don't know. I hurt so much I can't imagine being comfortable," she would reply.

They were kind. They brought extra pillows. "Well, let's try

this," and sometimes it helped, but night after night, except for brief periods, she lay reciting "Bless God bless God bless God bless God" until she numbed her mind to feeling, or morning came.

The Infectious Diseases doctor began to bring her paperback mysteries, and though her eyes slid away from the print, she read them, one after another. She read them all day and into the night, but slowly.

"I DON'T mean to be ungrateful," she said to Dr. Jamison on Thursday, "but I'm not sure I can stand it here much longer. I think it's partly being tied down."

"No need to apologize. The normal tolerance for this unit is six days; a good many psychological studies have been made of it. We'll get you up into a chair for a bit. That ought to help."

Interns and nurses came in during the night. "Your blood pressure's dropped," a nurse said one night, and she brought in an intern and they took her blood pressure over and over. "I can't even get it," he said. "I'll ask the resident to come in. We'd better give you some oxygen."

With that, all her holds seemed precarious.

Friday morning Dr. Jamison said, "Do you think you could endure it till Monday? I want to try something entirely different: Dilantin. It's been used for years for epilepsy. About two years ago we found that it had an effect on heart rhythm. I'll be starting you on such a large dose I'll have to have you here. It wouldn't be safe. Monday is a fast promise."

"Whether it's corrected or not?"

"Whether it's corrected or not."

What could she say? But when a new intern came in to shift the intravenous and thrust his long, broad needle into her painful veins in ten different places without finding a place to let it rest, she cried. It was like the earlier time—all tears—and, like the earlier time, she couldn't stop. "I can't let you do it again," she said finally. "I don't care."

"Why?" she asked the nurse who came in as he left. "Why wouldn't he get someone else? Why would he keep trying?"

"Ego," the nurse said. "It's his damn ego. He wouldn't admit he couldn't do it. I can't *stand* it when they hurt the patients. Here, let me wash your face. I'll get you Dr. Kay. He's considered the best intern in the whole hospital."

The tears were still falling into her pillow when Dr. Kay came in. He didn't say a word, but he got the needle into a vein on the very first try and it scarcely hurt.

"You know that intern felt as bad as you did about what happened," Dr. Lewis said in the afternoon. "He was just telling me about it."

"Then why didn't he go get someone who knew what he was doing!" she said in an ugly voice.

Dr. Lewis looked shocked.

Around dinnertime Dr. Jamison stopped in. "Is there anything we could do to make things more bearable for you?" he asked. "Would it help if you could have more company and they could stay longer?"

"It might."

"I'll arrange it. The rule's adamant and the nurses won't like it, but if they say anything tell them to get in touch with me. I'll leave word with the clerk. Have your sister stay with you awhile when she comes this evening. And over the weekend."

"I'm so ashamed," she said. "But I feel like an animal in a trap."

"There's no reason to be ashamed," he said.

SATURDAY she walked twenty-five feet or so down the corridor outside her room. The procedure was elaborate. The battery-powered monitor was wheeled in, her wires were connected to it, two freshly filled hypodermics were placed on top—"Are those for an emergency?" she asked the nurse. "That's right."—the intravenous bottle was transferred to a pole on wheels. An aide supported her and pushed the intravenous pole; another aide pushed the monitor; the nurse walked backward, reading the cardiogram. "It's regular!" she called. "She's out of the bigeminy." The interns at the desk came to look and walk backward with the nurse. It was like a parade.

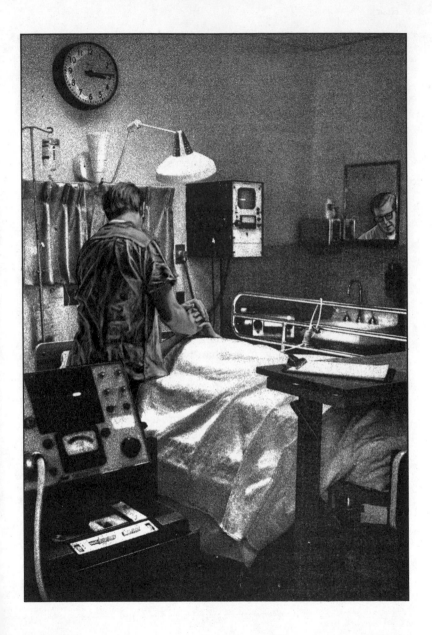

In bed again, wired to her own monitor, her heart returned to its irregular pattern.

"I guess we need to keep you on your feet," Dr. Jamison said.

SUNDAY two interns stuck their heads in her door. She braced herself.

"We've come to check up on you," one of them said.

"Dr. Bye Bye!" She held out her left hand.

They gave her the news of the Intensive Care Unit. "You were there for Joe's cardiac arrest, weren't you?" one of them asked.

"Was that why he was wheeled out of the room?"

"Yes, we had to take him to the OR."

"His mind was gone after that, wasn't it?"

"Yes."

"Did he make it?"

"No, poor devil, but it was just as well."

"I thought I imagined it."

"No."

"Remember when you took off the fluid and hollered for the resident? I knew that wasn't blood."

"If you did, you knew more than we did. You should have seen the resident's face—it was ashen. We thought I was in your liver."

"I'm going to get out of here tomorrow," she told them.

Dr. Jamison was late coming in Monday morning. "I have bad news for you," he said. "There isn't a room available, not in the section you want, where the food's good. I've just been to Admissions. They will have one tomorrow on your old floor. Miss Townsend said she'd hold it for you. I'm terribly sorry but there isn't a thing I can do."

She nodded, but she had no defenses left. She told everyone who came into her room that she was desperate.

THE nurse who brought her medication on Tuesday morning smiled and said, "Well, we're all set for eleven o'clock," and the nurse's aide who bathed her said, "I guess we'd better get *you* cleaned up early."

Eleven o'clock came, and twelve, and one, and two, and finally the head nurse came in and said, "They've given that room to another patient. Admissions wouldn't let Miss Townsend hold it. She tried. But there will be a room tomorrow on another floor."

"I don't know if they told you how upset everyone was," Dr. Lewis said. "Dr. Jamison went to Admissions. *I* went to Admissions. Interns called. Nurses called. Tomorrow *is* sure. I've checked myself with both Admissions and the head nurse on the floor. Tomorrow will come."

"I know," she said. "And I know I'm acting like a child. But I feel as if I shall *die* if I don't get out of here."

"Twelve days is a long time to be in this unit."

"The rhythm isn't any different, is it?"

"It has very brief normal periods, but no, not really. You can live with it, you know. It isn't something you can't live with."

SHE had been in her new room only an hour or so when the rhythm of her heart shifted back to normal. Dr. Jamison could hear it. The cardiogram he ordered showed the change.

"Was it the Dilantin?" she asked him.

"No. *You* did it." He sounded half disgusted. "I'm going to keep you on it, though, just as a precaution." He was leaving for the rest of the week, for meetings in the Middle West. "I've ordered some iron for you," he said. "We've taken so much blood your hemoglobin's dropped. You'll have to be on it for a few months. And you can go back to a regular diet. We want you to eat."

"ARE we on our own for the rest of the week?" she asked Dr. Lewis at dinnertime.

"It looks that way. And the intern who'll be looking after you isn't an activist. I've just been talking to him. Nothing but blood for prothrombin time and potassium. I want you to rest."

THREE benign days. The fever was lower; X rays showed less fluid in her lungs; the opened incision was definitely filling in. When she coughed, the air no longer whistled through it.

One evening the intern from the very first floor she'd been on, the one who had disapproved of her surgery, came up to see her. "I'm so glad you're all right," he said, and he sat on the edge of the bed and held her hand and he didn't say another thing.

Dr. Rudd walked into her room Sunday afternoon. She took his hand in both of hers, and after a few seconds he brought his left hand up and covered hers. "I've missed you," she said. "Dr. Rudd, why do you suppose I minded the Coronary Care Unit so much more than Intensive Care?"

"Because you were more alert." He smiled. "If you stay here much longer, you may be the first patient I've ever discharged to go back to work the next day."

"How much longer do you think it will be?" she asked Dr. Lewis.

"Oh, the day will come when all four of us agree that you're ready. A week or two, I'd think. You have to be a bit stronger."

"You've lost seven pounds," Dr. Rudd said. "Try to eat more."

"You've got some premature beats still," Dr. Jamison said. "But we aren't going to hold you up for those. They'll go away in time, we hope. And we won't hold you up for your fever; it's coming down. You'll probably have it for a few weeks after you get home. I'll want you to take your temperature regularly."

"Did you ever decide what caused it?"

"We never did."

"Or the arrhythmia?"

"That, either."

She was sitting up in a chair. With help, she was walking to the sun-room. She was restless. "Isn't it time?" she asked Dr. Lewis.

"Not quite. Soon."

One morning Dr. Rudd said, "Whenever the other two agree it's all right, it's all right with me. I want a last cardiogram taken at rest and immediately after walking, and a chest X ray, and that will do it so far as I'm concerned."

"I feel you've given me back my life," she said. It was some-

thing she'd been wanting to say to him. "How does it feel to give a person her life?"

Dr. Rudd made his dismissing gesture. "I don't think in those terms," he said. "I'm a surgeon. Surgeons are doers."

"I think you're ready," Dr. Jamison said. "It's going to take six months, you know—possibly a year—to reach your maximum level. Don't get discouraged. Remember, you're not sixteen. I'll want to see you in two weeks' time. You've been a wonderful patient—we couldn't have asked for more." He gave her an affectionate pat.

"How about Saturday morning?" Dr. Lewis said. "Would you like that? It would only be a few days longer in any case, and why be here over the weekend. I can come down to see you. I think you'll get better faster at home."

MONTHS later, back at work and beginning to be active again, she was in Dr. Lewis's office.

"You're well," he said. "Oh, it will be some months yet, but I don't have to worry about you anymore."

A question had turned up in her mind. "How many of those operations have they done?" she asked.

"Seventeen is the exact number, I believe."

Dr. Rudd had said the risk was thirty-five percent or a little more. She figured. Had they lost six? Seven?

"I ran into Dr. Rudd in the corridor today," Dr. Lewis said. "We stopped and congratulated ourselves."

"You mean I'm a credit to us?"

"To us and a good many others you don't know anything about." His expression was thoughtful—entirely serious.

They sat for a moment, unsmiling, looking at each other. Oh God, she thought, those nightmare days. Dear God, the miracle.

Risk *is Rachel MacKenzie's first book. She has taught at Radcliffe and at Wellesley and is now an editor at* The New Yorker.

## Preparing Patients for Surgery
### by William A. Nolen, M.D.

There are two goals to achieve in preparing a patient for surgery—I'm talking about psychological preparation, not physical preparation which varies with the nature of the operation.

First, I want my patients to be fully informed from the day they enter the hospital till the day they have fully recovered. I don't want them upset by some unexpected event. Second, I want them to be as free from fear as possible.

It's not difficult to achieve these goals; it's simply a matter of taking time to talk with patients. I routinely discuss such things as the necessary injections—no one likes needles; the shave and enema that may be given; the tubes that may be put in stomach, bladder or chest before or after surgery; how soon they'll be able to eat after the operation; how quickly they'll be up and about; when they'll be able to go home and back to work.

On two additional points I'm particularly emphatic because misconceptions about them are so prevalent. The patient will not say anything obscene or revealing when going under or waking up from anesthesia. I've performed about six thousand operations in the last fifteen years and I've yet to hear a half-awake patient say anything damaging or even interesting. Nor will a patient become an addict if "hypos" for pain are administered. Pain medication is usually good for patients because it enables them to move around and breathe deeply after an operation.

Sometimes, simply emphasizing the positive is enough to achieve my second goal, freedom from fear. But if patients ask, as they often do, "Is the operation dangerous?" I have one point which I always make: There is some danger connected with any operation; it would be silly to say there wasn't. But it's also dangerous to ride in a car. If the operation is elective—say, to straighten a nose or increase the size of a breast —then the danger is probably less than riding in a car. Otherwise the pa-

tient wouldn't want it and the surgeon wouldn't perform it.

If the operation is necessary and more serious—on a uterus or, as in Miss MacKenzie's case, a diseased heart—I point out that, though the risk of having the operation is real, the risk of not having it is greater. Knowing that he is choosing the lesser risk tends to reassure the patient. I see little point in going into percentages unless the patient demands them; the result in any particular case is a hundred percent for that patient.

I also tell my patients to ask me, at any time, any question they wish. I don't want them worrying or puzzling about things they don't understand or that I've failed to explain.

I should add that it's also important to prepare the family. I always arrange to meet with the wife, husband or children and explain, as completely as I can, what the operation is about and how to talk, or not to talk, in the presence of the patient. I remind them that though a patient seems asleep or under sedation, conversation may be heard and misinterpreted. I ask the family to join with me in doing what we can to get our patient through this period of stress.

Here's an example of the sort of important thing we surgeons sometimes fail to mention: Not long ago I operated on the wife of a friend. I'll call her Susan. She had gallstones. Even though she was a doctor's wife and probably knew what to expect, I went through my usual discussion prior to surgery. I thought I covered everything.

A few days after the operation she was sitting up in her room eating breakfast when I stopped to see her. "How's it going, Susan?" I asked.

"Fine," she said. "I'm quite comfortable and I'm very grateful. But," she added, "even though you did a good job, I'm a little bit mad at you."

"Why?" I asked.

"Because," she said, "when you told me about what was going to happen you never told me that the nurse would make me take my dentures out before the operation. Now all the nurses—and you—have seen me without my teeth, and I'm embarrassed half to death."

We surgeons just can't remember everything.

*Dr. Nolen, a Fellow of the American College of Surgeons, is the author of the bestselling book,* The Making of a Surgeon. *He is particularly concerned about what doctors can do to improve the morale of patients who must undergo major surgery.*

A CONDENSATION OF THE BOOK

# LIFEBOAT NUMBER TWO

BY
MARGARET CULKIN BANNING

As this round-the-world
luxury cruise proceeds,
passengers and crew
chart unexpected ways through
their own private seas

ILLUSTRATED BY
GUY DEEL

The first boat drill aboard the cruise ship *The Seven Seas* brought together at Lifeboat Number Two a curious assemblage of passengers. There was a widow whose newfound wealth could not appease her loneliness . . . an embittered ex-senator who thought his political career was finished . . . a disillusioned young girl who had lost her lover . . . a business tycoon and his glamorous traveling companion . . . a Catholic priest who was tortured by doubts . . . an aristocratic old lady who lived for her memories.

Mark Claypole, a writer, referred to his shipmates as "refugees," and as the luxurious round-the-world cruise proceeded it became clear that many of the passengers were indeed escaping from themselves.

An intriguing novel of human relationships by one of America's best-known, best-loved authors.

AT THREE o'clock, four hours after the ship had sailed, bells clanged through the corridors and lounges and bars. They were noisy, authoritative, summoning all the passengers to the stations by the lifeboats to which they had been assigned. The time of the drill had been posted on each deck of *The Seven Seas* but some had not seen it, some had forgotten it and there were always a few who would try to ignore it, as steward Jim Bates well knew. His immediate duty was to make sure that everyone in the cabins which he served attended the drill.

Alec Goodrich, who was in Cabin 4, was annoyed. He was in no mood to mingle with other passengers, but he was a lawyer as well as a defeated senator, and the habit of respecting regulations was strong in him. He threw down a magazine, which had been infuriating him with a smug postmortem on the November elections, took his life jacket and went out to find his station.

At the end of the hallway Mr. Howard Demarest came out of the Mandarin Suite, which was priced at twelve thousand dollars for single occupancy. But Mr. Demarest was not without companions. He pressed the buzzer on the door of a nearby cabin and a girl opened it. Jim Bates had seen her at Demarest's bon voyage party. Then she had been wearing white furs but now she had changed into slacks and a sweater and become a beautiful

tomboy. She was swinging her life jacket by its tapes and saying helplessly, "I don't know how to get into this horrible thing!"

Demarest, a big but still shapely man, took the girl's jacket and fitted her into it, handling her as if he owned her. The two handsome women who had connecting rooms 10 and 12 noticed that as they went past. The steward had been on the lookout for these ladies because he thought that Mrs. Barnes and Mrs. Hayward might feel that lifeboat drills were not necessary for them. They had impressed on him that they were experienced travelers. He had been asked to take some of their flowers to the refrigerator and to deliver a gift hamper of champagne to the wine steward.

All the passengers assigned to Lifeboat Number Two had to pass Jim Bates to reach the outer deck. As they streamed through he checked off the ones who were his responsibility. Only one had not appeared—the young woman in 9. Her parents had seen her off but since then Jim had had no glimpse of her. He hesitated, then tapped gently on her door.

"What is it?" she asked. "Come in."

She was sitting on the couch bed under her window, smoking a cigarette which had been one of many. She had not unpacked her bags and there were unopened letters and telegrams on the little desk. One opened letter lay on the couch beside her.

Jim Bates said respectfully, "Pardon me, miss, but there is a lifeboat drill. Your station is Number Two on the deck outside."

"I'll skip the drill," she said.

"I'm sorry, miss, but the captain is extremely strict about attendance of all passengers. May I get your life jacket for you?"

He took it from the wardrobe and held it open for her.

"Thank you. Are you my steward?"

"Yes, miss."

"Please tell me your name."

"Jim Bates. Just Jim."

"I'm Barbara Bancroft." She tied the strings of the jacket swiftly and correctly. Suddenly she smiled with disarming friendliness and said, "Thanks very much for keeping me in line, Jim."

The lifeboats had been swung out from the railings at intervals

around the enormous open deck. An officer stood by each one with a list in his hand, and over the loudspeaker a voice explained, "Ladies and gentlemen, please answer when your name is called. It is urgently requested that all passengers attend the drills. In the unlikely case of accident or emergency the bells will ring continuously. In that event put on your life jacket over a warm coat, wear a cap or hood, and report to the station where you are this afternoon. If you have any questions, the officer calling the roll at your station will be glad to answer them."

Over their bright orange jackets they eyed each other warily. The experienced travelers knew the hazard of making acquaintances impulsively and later finding it hard to disentangle themselves. The shy ones, like Mrs. Signe Goode, did not have the audacity to speak to strangers. And there were others who only wanted to be left alone. Alec Goodrich was already considering the possibility of leaving the ship at Lisbon, which would be the first stop.

"How many will the lifeboat hold?" someone was asking.

"One hundred and twenty people," the ship's officer said. He lifted his voice for attention. "Now—with your permission, ladies and gentlemen—I shall call the roll of those passengers listed for occupancy of Lifeboat Number Two."

It was a group introduction and Alida Barnes listened attentively, matching individuals to their names, sorting out the ones she might want to know. Julia Hayward did not seem to care.

To Alida, Mr. and Mrs. Julian Chilton were definitely interesting. They looked aristocratic, and a nurse in English uniform attended their little girl. The Eugene Beaufort couple were charming but very young—probably on their wedding trip. Mr. Howard Demarest must be very rich if he had the Mandarin Suite, but he had that blond starlet with him, and Alida Barnes did not want to get involved with messy affairs outside her own social bracket.

"Mrs. Hartley Barton," called the officer. An elderly woman supporting herself on two canes said, "Present," and Alida Barnes looked again. The lady had answered with a dignity and authority that spoke of firm social place and servants.

A tall man with dark red hair who watched the members of the group with an amused and cynical glance was identified as Mark Claypole. Barbara Bancroft's voice drew eyes her way, but all that anyone could see of her was bronze-gold hair falling uncurled down the back of her dark coat. Mrs. Signe Goode blushed when her name was called. The name of the Reverend Aloysius Duggan was called twice because the first time he actually did not hear it. He was deep in the continual dialogue he was carrying on with himself, the argument as to whether he should or should not leave the priesthood of the Catholic Church.

His bishop had said, "You must guard against impulse Father. You must reflect, pray—try to pray," he amended gravely. "It so happens that I can arrange time for reflection for you. I have been asked to supply a chaplain for a ship which is circling the globe. The passage is free, in consideration of the spiritual duties involved—daily Masses, confessions—and of course on such a cruise sickness or death may occur. Usually when such an opportunity has arisen I have sent a priest whose health would benefit from such a voyage."

"I am in good health, Bishop."

"You are in ill health spiritually, Father. On this journey you will have privacy and time to think. You can measure your problems in different atmospheres, against other backgrounds."

"Bishop, I don't deserve this trip. I know I'm a problem to the diocese and I honestly regret that more than I can—"

The bishop smiled. "I want you to do this, Father. I do not command you, but I request it urgently. Will you go?"

Father Duggan looked at his kind superior, and the thought of distance and change suddenly seemed infinitely desirable.

"Yes, Bishop. And may I say that I am very grateful."

"There is only one request I should like to make. The Church has not been so scrutinized and criticized for centuries. Among strangers you will be invited to argument, but the journey will be of no benefit to you if you indulge in futile discussion. I want you to search your soul in solitude; let your argument be inner, with

who might help you. Do not commit scandal by exposing doubts and criticisms of the faith in which you were ordained. You go as a Catholic priest. Will you respect this status?"

"Yes, Bishop," said Father Duggan, "I give you my word."

"HERE," said Alec Goodrich.

His name caused no great stir, though his defeat had been one of the notable upsets in the November elections. Several women looked at him, for there had been no mention of Mrs. Goodrich and he was a handsome man. Alida Barnes wondered if by luck he would be at their table in the dining room. The girl with Howard Demarest lifted her unbelievable eyelashes and would have smiled invitingly if Alec had shown any return of interest. He did not. Alec had been getting attention of that sort for years. It used to amuse him or give him a fillip of satisfaction; but not any more. That was what had defeated him in November.

Ex-Senator Goodrich had rarely felt so out of place. To go on a trip around the world had been an impulsive decision and he now felt it had been a preposterous one. His former colleague, Senator Marcus O'Brien, had first put the idea into his head.

"What are your plans?" Marcus had asked when it was all over. "What are you going to do?"

"I have no plans. I'm just beginning to find out what I can't do."

"It was a catastrophe for me too, Alec. I figured on our going on in harness together. But you have plenty of time."

"So has Whitlock. He has six years to entrench himself in the Senate and in the party."

"I don't think he'll wear well. And you're only thirty-seven now. In six years you'll still be younger than most of the men in the Senate. By that time all this will be forgotten."

"I doubt it. And they can always dig it up again."

"You're taking this too hard, Alec," the older man said gently.

"It's not the defeat. It's the way it was done. The way they used the death of that poor girl to discredit me. I couldn't fight back. The facts were there. She was working for me in the campaign and she did kill herself in my apartment. I couldn't defend myself by

attacking the character or mentality of a dead girl. So the newspapers had a field day and so did the opposition."

"You have to look beyond all that now, pick up the pieces and put them together again. Are you going back to New Alton?"

"There's nothing to go back to. My aunt died last year—a good thing she didn't live to be humiliated by this. My law business was a technical partnership, but Bill Warren has carried the work load for a long time. My being in the Senate lent some prestige to the firm and helped Bill. But now I'd probably be a liability."

"Then you'll be staying here?"

"There's nothing to keep me here," Alec said curtly. "My personal plans have changed."

"Too bad," muttered the senator.

Alec said compulsively, "It was a mutual decision. The whole picture changed when I was defeated under such circumstances." He stopped abruptly and then said, "I would like you to know that Cicely believed me when I told her that there was nothing between that girl and me. But here in Washington we'd be haunted by the whole miserable business."

"There are other places to live."

"Not for *the* Correll family. Her mother—well, you know her. And for Cicely, any other place would be exile."

"Alec," said the senator, "why don't you cut loose from everything? Maybe travel for a while. Get a new perspective."

"Take a Grand Tour, with my tail between my legs?"

"Not at all. With your head up. Go to places that are free from your habits and associations. Take a long sea voyage. On a ship you can separate yourself from pretty nearly everything for days. I've always wanted to do it but I never could find the time. Or the money. Right now you've got plenty of both."

Alec had laughed and said he'd think about it. What he really wanted to do was to find a place for himself, prove himself again. He put out feelers to law firms in New York and Philadelphia, but nothing materialized that would not have been demotion. He had never imagined how defeating a defeat could be. He frequented unfashionable restaurants and drank more than he intended. He

avoided his former colleagues, even Marcus O'Brien, and threw invitations in the wastebasket.

The senator's advice had been relegated to the back of Alec's mind, but not quite discarded. Every now and then someone's suspected pity pushed it forward. One day, after an encounter in the Statler barbershop with two men he had known well on the Hill, Alec stopped at the desk of the travel agent in the lobby.

"I'm considering taking a sea voyage. Can you tell me what is available right now?"

The agent looked over some charts and asked, "Would you be interested in a voyage around the world, sir? It just happens that this morning there was a cancellation on *The Seven Seas*. It's the flagship of the American Republic Line."

"How long is the trip?"

"Eighty-four days. Of course you touch a great many ports and can arrange shore trips to suit yourself."

AND here he was. Dismayed. The crowds of gay people, the bands playing, the flowers clogging the corridors—this wasn't what he had come for. He had never even seen the departure of an ocean liner. He had been abroad of course on several senatorial fact-finding trips, but always with political confreres, and always they had traveled by air to save time.

So, although he was well informed about the world, he was not well acquainted with it. Now, standing aloof from the group at Station Two, Alec felt he had made a ridiculous blunder. These people were looking for amusement, not adventure. To Alec life had never been trivial even when he enjoyed it. He was a serious man under his charm—Aunt Lucy had seen to that—and until recently he had thought he would be a useful one.

The bells rang again and with relief the passengers began to strip off their life jackets. Howard Demarest said imperiously, "Come on, Ruby. Let's see what's going on in the Mayfair Room."

Alida Barnes told Julia Hayward that they had better go up to the sun deck to be sure that their chairs had been put in the right place. Bettina and Gene Beaufort went to play shuffleboard.

171

Signe Goode did not know where to go. Her cabin had given her a terrible feeling of isolation, almost as bad as in the first weeks after Tom died. Later she had been kept busy with conferences with lawyers and bankers, the sale of the house where she had lived with Tom for twenty-one years and where she could not bear to be alone, and the subsequent move to her beautiful new apartment. The apartment was very expensive but she could afford it. It was hard to believe, but she could afford anything she wanted.

"Your husband was a wealthy man," said the bank officer.

"I don't think Tom thought he was rich," said Signe. "We always had to be frugal."

The banker smiled. "Of course it did come rather suddenly. Tom got in on the ground floor with a remarkably enterprising company, and then there was the merger and new oil discoveries."

Tom Goode had been a certified public accountant, and twelve thousand a year had been the top of the ladder for his position. Signe always did her own housework. She did not mind that. And there were no children. That was disappointing, but they grew used to it and would have been embarrassed to consult a doctor about that very private failure. So they had accumulated substantial savings, which Tom had finally decided to put into an expanding oil and gas development.

Signe knew that it had been a successful investment but she had no idea of its scope until Tom died. He had never wanted people to know he had money. "If they get an idea you've got a little extra," he'd say, "they're all after you with their hands out." And possibly he did not want Signe tempted to extravagance.

But the vice-president of the bank had said, "You're in a position to do almost anything you want to, Mrs. Goode. Someday I'd like to go into the matter of income-tax deductions with you."

"I don't know anything about them. Tom did all the tax returns."

"Well, for example, if your husband had given us the whole amount that we are trying to raise for the addition to St. Luke's Hospital, it would have diminished his estate very little, if at all. You would probably be quite as well off as you are today."

Signe was curious enough to buy a tax manual, and she found that what the banker had said was true. Now that rumors of her wealth were spreading, her mail was loaded with supplications. But she gave her usual ten dollars to the Red Cross, ten to the Cancer Crusade, twenty-five to the United Fund. Only at Christmastime she'd impulsively put a twenty-dollar bill into a Salvation Army kettle.

Christmas had been desolate for Signe this year, her first without Tom. She had always cooked a turkey or a goose, though it was only for the two of them after Tom's mother died. This year she'd had scrambled eggs for lunch, and in the afternoon she'd gone for a walk to see the lighted trees on lawns and in front windows. They gave her no cheer, so at five o'clock she was back in her apartment making a bourbon highball. She felt guilty at drinking alone but it dulled the cutting edge of her loneliness. Idly she began to read a column on the women's page. It was titled, "Is This Woman You?"

Astonishingly, on this dreary Christmas Day, it was.

The spendthrift woman who buys what she cannot afford is to be pitied, for the day of reckoning will come. But the woman who is the most pitiable is the one who has plenty of money and does not know what to do with it, the wealthy widow who could have everything and settles for little or nothing. If she ever had the spirit of adventure it has withered. She might be taking a voyage to the ends of the earth—but inertia or fear ties her to lonely monotony. Do you know such a widow? Is she by any chance you?

Signe put down the paper. Inertia—maybe that was what was the matter with her. She could go anywhere she wanted to. There was that travel place on First Street. She could go in there and just find out how much it would cost—to go to France maybe.

Almost before she realized what had happened, Signe was involved. "Would you be interested in a cruise? Let me make a little travel plan for you. No, there's no charge, Mrs. Goode. But if you'll give me your bank as a reference . . ."

And here she was on the ocean, more alone than she'd been

in the apartment. And she had bought all those clothes. Signe wandered through the public rooms, trying to look as if she were used to luxury. She wished she had a drink of bourbon. That might give her a little Dutch courage, as Tom used to call it.

CHAPTER TWO

THE five rooms that were equipped with bars on *The Seven Seas* differed in size, style and usually in patronage. The Mayfair Room had the best orchestra, but a good many people, especially those who were at the first sitting for lunch and dinner, preferred to have drinks in the Sky Room, with its blue furniture and enormous windows. The Embassy Café was quiet until a little before seven o'clock, and the Ritz drew its best crowd after late dinner.

Alec Goodrich asked the steward, "Jim, is there a quiet place to get a drink on board?"

"There's the Seashell, sir. That's very quiet. That's aft on the promenade deck."

"Thanks," said Alec. "I'll look in there."

Barbara Bancroft came out of her cabin a few minutes later.

"Where can I get a cocktail, Jim?"

"It's very pleasant in the Embassy Café, Miss Bancroft. And the orchestra in the Sky Room is very good."

"Is there a place where you can get a drink without music?"

She had not changed for dinner, knowing that it was not customary on the first night out, but she had brushed her hair into shining curves and it seemed to Jim that she belonged in the Embassy Café. He said, rather reluctantly, "There's the Seashell on the promenade. But it's not so popular."

"That's fine with me," said Barbara.

In the dimly lit Seashell there were a number of small tables, most of them unoccupied. At one, a man wearing a Roman collar was reading in the skimpy light from the lamp on his table, a long drink beside his book. At another table a middle-aged woman sat, looking out of place in a fur stole and satin evening dress.

174

Two men, obviously not companions, were sitting at the bar. Barbara took a stool at the far end.

She asked for a martini on the rocks but delayed drinking it. There was no pressure here. During the hours since her mother and father had gone ashore, and since she had read the letter from Boone, she had been conscious only of cessation, of emptiness.

She had tried to carry the departure off well for their sake. There was no point in destroying their hope that this junket would change her back again into the child she had been before that last year at college, before she met Boone, before she knew what tear gas and jail were like, before she knew what it meant to be rejected by a man. She took a sip of her drink and vaguely hoped that her mother and father would have a good time tonight, now that she was off their hands. Was it their fault that Boone did not want her? If they had not burdened her with what they considered privileges, might he have been able to accept her? These questions nagged at her.

"You'd ruin me, Barb," was what he had said.

"How can you say that! I only want what you want."

"You just think so. It would be impossible to go along with me."

"Because of the color of my skin?"

"I love the color of your skin. That's what would ruin me. I can't be on both sides of the fence. I belong with my people, the blacks."

"You didn't feel that way until lately."

"I know I didn't. I was fooling myself, going along with the white liberals and their pious, sentimental idea that desegregation would work out. I know better now."

"It's those people you go with now. They influence you."

"That's right, they influence me. They opened my eyes. Look, Barb, I could say that what I'm thinking of is your happiness, that I don't want to hurt you. It wouldn't be true. I'm thinking of myself, of my own redemption as a black man with no commitments that would make me conciliate or cheat."

When Barbara had found his letter in the pile of bon voyage notes, she had thought he might have changed his mind.

But Boone had written:

175

I saw Carrie the other night and she told me you were going around the world. She said you asked about me and if I was all right. I am. Put me out of your mind. I have given you a bad time.

I have gone through a personal evolution, changing from the person I was when we first met last year to the one I must now be. This person would not attract you. The man you liked thought that if there was enough interracial love and marriage, race problems would vanish. I know now that if there is any answer that is not it. And as we went along and your parents tried to face up to the possibility of our marriage, I felt a sycophant as well as a traitor. I began to dislike the future I was heading into. Of course I could stand up to the snubs of society. That sort of defiance can be exciting but it is really a kind of adolescent delight. We would have tired of it, and soon begun to chip away at each other. You didn't believe that but it is true.

I hope you get a lot out of this trip. I was a deckhand on one of those ships once, and most of the people went around the world without seeing it. I hope you won't. Carrie said you did not want to go but felt you had to get away from your family. And me, she implied. Personally I believe it is a good idea for you to get away. Stay away too—until you are sure of your own identity. It sounds corny but there's nothing to living except being yourself, doing your own thing.

He had struck her away as if she were an unwanted child clinging to him, and since then she had been without any attachment that meant anything. She had let her parents believe what they wanted to believe, that she had come to her senses. But she could not go back to playing around, to the vague search for a man to marry. Graduate work no longer interested her. Taking a job would be phony. She did not want to pretend she was being useful. For a year she had been living with a cause, with a crusade, and it had been ripped out of her hands.

She finished her drink and indicated to the barman that she would have another. He had just served a refill to the woman in the satin dress. As he put ice in another glass, the red-haired man sitting at the middle of the bar lifted his drink. In the silent little room his words came out loud and clear.

"Happy voyage to all the refugees on *The Seven Seas.*"

The others stared at him. Alec Goodrich frowned and Signe Goode looked frightened. The priest looked up from his book.

"That's a rather obnoxious statement," said Alec Goodrich.

"But it's interesting," Barbara said. "Are you a refugee, Mr.—?"

"Mark Claypole. Oh yes. I suppose most of the passengers on a journey like this are bound to be on the run from trouble or grief or disappointment. Don't you think so?"

"I know what you mean," the woman in satin said. Two drinks had made it possible for Signe to speak to strangers.

Mark Claypole glanced at her. "Won't you join us at the bar, madam?" he asked, and without waiting for an answer he went to her table and escorted Signe and her drink and fur stole to the bar. She hoisted herself to a barstool for the first time in her life.

"I'm very grateful to have you say that you understand me," said Claypole.

"Well—sometimes you want to get away from everything. My husband—Mr. Goode, I'm Signe Goode—died a year ago and when you live alone—well, after a while it gets on your nerves—"

"And you become a fugitive from loneliness," he prompted.

"I guess that's it. I read a piece that said travel was one thing that women like me should do. But it does seem very queer to be on the ocean on a ship and not know a soul."

"Something must be done about that. May I introduce myself—I'm Mark Claypole—and this young lady is—"

"I'm Barbara Bancroft."

"Senator Goodrich at the other end of the bar." And as Alec stiffened at being identified, Mark Claypole went on smoothly. "Father Duggan is also with us. Could you be persuaded to join our little group, Father? We are discussing refugeeism."

"I'm afraid I have nothing to contribute to the conversation."

Father Duggan spoke quietly and lowered his glance again to his book. But Claypole's words had struck home to the priest.

"I think what you say is terribly exaggerated," Barbara said. "Most people on this cruise are taking it to see the world."

"I'm sure that they'd tell you that. Maybe even believe it."

"Are you a psychiatrist?" inquired Alec.

"No. Only a writer. My job involves exploring motives."

"Or imagining them," muttered Alec.

He disliked people who wrote about others for a living. He had got along well with the press until the tragedy, but then the reporters had been merciless, slanted, draping the story in innuendo. They would not spoil it with the true facts that the girl had been a nuisance in the organization, that the senator had been embarrassed by her devotion but could not possibly have guessed that the announcement of his engagement to Cicely Correll would send her over the edge.

"Are you going to write about this cruise?" Signe asked.

"To that question there never is an answer," said Mark.

THE real question was, could he sell one if he did write it? A few years ago they clamored for anything he wrote. But now the editors were difficult to please and Milton Knott, his agent, said he didn't know why. The market had changed. He dwelt on that. "They want revelations, supertrue confessions. They don't give a damn whether you can write or not, Mark."

"Any word yet from Hollywood about *Summer of Fancy?*"

"They're buying nothing except the sexiest best sellers."

Claypole's first book had sold a hundred thousand copies. His last one had sold less than six thousand. "Where are you going to send *Bird of Passage* now that Phil Prentiss has turned it down?"

"It's pretty well made the rounds," said Milton uncomfortably, "but Prentiss did say he could use a story on travel. He feels that hundreds of thousands of people travel these days and they'd identify with the right sort of story."

So here he was, taking on a crazy, expensive gamble. He was in fact looking for a story, but without a contract for it. His reserves were all but gone and the alimony was bleeding him.

At the time of the divorce he hadn't objected too strenuously to Suzanne's demands. It was worth it to be rid of her. For if he was free he was sure that he could get back to the kind of work that had brought him notice and praise in his twenties. The years with

Suzanne had been one long drift in the wrong direction. It had turned out that all she was interested in was the glamour that went with a writer's success. When that had begun to diminish for Mark she had been resentful because he did not force his way back into the limelight. She believed it was a matter of keeping up contacts with influential people in the literary world, but Mark knew better. While they were breaking up he had a vision of re-creating his former industry, of spending long days and nights at the typewriter, of feeling the old verve and enjoyment in his work.

Now it was nearly twenty months and he had restored neither his diligence nor his success. If he had an idea it withered before he got it down on paper. He knew that today he should have pounded out his first impressions of the voyage. Of the tugboat pushing the great liner away from the dock, and the contrast between the men on the tug and the people watching from the decks of *The Seven Seas*. Of the lifeboat drill, assembling strangers who conceivably might die together—the exit of Howard Demarest with Mrs. Signe Goode would be an unlikely combination. But his typewriter was still covered.

Signe Goode took a cigarette from her bag and fumbled for a match. Claypole quickly snapped open his lighter. He noticed that her skin was quite beautiful. As she held the cigarette to the flame he saw her rings, a gold wedding band and another set with one small diamond. They told Mark Claypole that her husband could afford only a very little diamond at first. But he must have left her well fixed. Her stole was certainly Russian sable.

From the corridor came the sound of a bugle.

"The call for the second sitting," Claypole explained to Signe. "Tonight I suppose we have to find our regular seats."

"I'm at Table Twenty-four," said Signe.

"I forgot my card. I'll have to ask the steward where they have planted me," he said.

Barbara had already gone, leaving a half-filled glass behind. The priest closed his book and signed the chit for his single drink. Alec Goodrich was the last to leave, thinking with satisfaction that he would have a table by himself.

IN THE CAPTAIN'S SITTING ROOM, Commodore Rudolph James was talking to the social director, Mrs. Joan Scofield.

"When you have your daily program printed be sure to put in the usual item that during the cruise I shall invite all the passengers to have dinner with me at one time or another and that there is absolutely no order of preference."

"I'll make it the first announcement, Captain."

"I'm sure you'll arrange groups that are as congenial as possible. Mr. Howard Demarest is a director of the line so he probably should be at the first party."

"There is a young lady on board who seems to be a close friend of Mr. Demarest," Joan Scofield said, with so little emphasis that it was meaningful.

"Pretty?"

"Very."

"Then we surely can take care of her," said the Commodore, smiling. "Is there anyone else who should have special attention?"

"Mr. Alexander Goodrich was a United States senator. And the name of Mark Claypole is on the list. I'll find out if he's the writer. It looks like a nice crowd."

"Good," said the Commodore. "About the dinners—I was thinking that another year we might do it a bit more informally—"

He stopped. It was a slip of the mind as well as the tongue, because this was the last world cruise that Commodore James would command on *The Seven Seas*. He was being retired, and though he constantly reminded himself and everyone else that this was his final voyage, the fact hadn't quite come true to him.

He laughed. "Well, that won't be my worry. There's the bugle for the second sitting. You'd better get on down. Good night."

He was having dinner by himself tonight. There were details he wanted to think out, for he might have to omit a couple of African ports. The passengers always complained when that happened, but he had been told that trouble might be brewing, which could mean strikes on the docks, delay and possible shore dangers for the passengers.

He looked out the windows, savoring the sight. The ship was

alone on the ocean, casting beams of light on waves that were curled with white foam. The voyage was under way and after sixteen years of world cruises Commodore James knew all that it meant. *The Seven Seas* carried five hundred and seventy-six passengers, and the crew and staff numbered slightly more than six hundred. Twenty-four ports would be entered if the schedule was kept. Some of them were difficult to maneuver in and a few might be slightly hostile, with world conditions what they were.

His responsibility did not prey on Commodore James. He enjoyed its weight and intricacy. But he knew that only a man in his position could fully realize what was necessary to keep all these people safe and comfortable for a voyage as long as this one. Some were bound to get sick, a few perhaps seriously. The eighteen elevators had to be constantly checked, the plants that distilled seawater into fresh water had to be carefully tended, lifeboat drills regularly carried out. Thousands of details were delegated to the ship's officers and stewards and cooks and entertainers, but the ultimate power rested with the captain, as did the mood of the voyage. IIe had to be friendly enough and sufficiently aloof. He had to give the passengers an event to remember when they dined with him after the written invitations that Joan would send around. She was a great hostess. It would have been very easy to make his feeling for her more than admiration, but the Commodore did not permit himself that sort of indulgence.

He rang for a menu and ordered oysters and filet mignon. No dessert. He was careful to keep his tall figure trim. Commodore James did not look sixty-six. Nor feel it.

CHAPTER THREE

SINCE he had come this far and would probably have trouble getting his fare refunded, Alec Goodrich reasoned, he might as well have a look at Casablanca and Las Palmas, which was a matter of only three more days after leaving Lisbon. By that time he would have made up his mind whether he wanted to continue with the

cruise for the eight days it would take to get to South Africa. He could fly back from Cape Town if he felt like it.

The first week had gone fast. He liked all his stewards—Jim Bates, Dennis in the dining room, and Anatole, the wine steward, with the golden chain around his neck. The motion pictures were excellent and the young history professor who gave talks about the ports the ship would visit was thoroughly interesting. Alec usually drank at the Seashell but did not see there again any of his first-night companions. Sometimes he passed the priest on deck and exchanged a few remarks. He saw Claypole daily in the dining room, at a satisfactory distance, at a large table where Mrs. Goode also sat. The Bancroft girl was at what was obviously the star table, for Howard Demarest and his girl were there. Barbara was very beautiful in evening clothes.

Mrs. Barnes had asked Alec one night to fill in at bridge. It would have been rude to refuse and she and her friends played a superb game, so the competition was stimulating. But he managed to be inaccessible in the theater the next night. What he enjoyed most was walking on the high boat deck. The wind and the solitude seemed to take the sting out of the wound.

In Lisbon he had asked to be driven through the old city, where the streets were hardly more than ancient paved paths that wound up the hills. He sat with the driver, who translated the names of the streets—the Street of the Angels, the Street of the Sad Virgin, the Street of the Man Who Talks to Himself. I should get out here, thought Alec with amused irony.

It was surprising to feel, when he finally went back to the ship, a sense of being in place. To have Jim say that he hoped Mr. Goodrich had enjoyed himself and Anatole remark "Ah, tonight you must have a wine of Portugal, yes?" was oddly agreeable.

There was the same feeling when he returned from a ramble around Casablanca. He had known many historical and political facts about the city but he had not anticipated its astonishing whiteness and wealth. He found his way to the Anfa Hotel and went inside to look around, because he remembered that this was where Churchill and Roosevelt had met for their famous Casa-

blanca Conference. As he sat there drinking mint tea on a divan in the lounge, his mind dwelt on the two statesmen who had been at the height of their political power when they had met here.

Someone said, "Hello, Senator," and he looked up to see Mark Claypole's slightly satirical grin. Signe Goode was with him, carrying some kind of embroidered garment over her arm.

"This girl is a great shopper," said Claypole.

"I never have been, but the things are so beautiful and so different," Signe said. "It's all so wonderful!"

Alec beckoned the waiter. He said it was a very interesting city, and escaped as soon as he could after a few more flavorless remarks. To get back to the ship ahead of the other passengers and unlock his cabin door gave him again that pleasant feeling of having a place of his own.

"Wonderful city, Jim," he said in quite a different tone from the one that he had just used with Mark Claypole, "and now I'd like a double Scotch. I'm not much for mint tea."

When Alec left the hotel Signe said, "He doesn't seem very friendly. He even has a table all by himself in the dining room."

"Taking no risks. You can't really blame him."

"What do you mean?"

"He was caught up in a scandal that killed him off politically. One of the girls who worked in his campaign committed suicide and there was a lot of talk. My guess is that it probably wasn't his fault. Those girls who go political are very uptight."

"Oh," said Signe, "I think I did read something about it. But I don't know much about politics. Of course I always voted when Tom was alive. He was a Republican."

"I'm sure he would have been."

After ten days Mark knew a great deal about Signe Goode. He could see the little house, like all the others in the block, with the leather armchair "that Tom never would give up" before the television set. He also understood Tom better than his wife ever had. There must have been some quality of the miser in him and probably a basic distrust of society. As far as possible he had made his home a fortress against social and financial demands.

Signe had rarely talked freely to anyone, but perhaps because he had broken through her misery on that first night aboard she had talked to Mark almost without being questioned. Sometimes he would stretch himself out in the steamer chair next to hers and listen as the pattern of her life evolved. As he had been listening idly one morning a week ago.

"They are so good-looking." That was when Mrs. Hayward and Mrs. Barnes went by, in expensively casual sweaters and pants. "You know I was scared when I found I was at the table with those two." She gave a still timid smile at them as they passed.

"Scared? Why on earth?"

"Well, I've never known society women. We never went out much. Of course for a long time we couldn't. Tom's mother lived with us. It was rather hard on Tom—you know how old people think they're being neglected. We never left her alone the last year. I sometimes think of how different it would have been if we'd had more money then."

"Nice to have money anytime."

"Some times more than others. I wish Tom had taken a trip like this just once. He could have, but we didn't know what was going to happen. I never could get Tom to a doctor."

He didn't want to spend the money. And he distrusted doctors. It fitted into Mark's picture of Tom Goode.

"He was only forty-six. We'd just had our anniversary, our twentieth, and he always gave me as many roses as the years we'd been married. American Beauties. I was only eighteen when we married. But I never felt any difference in our ages."

There was no difference between her age and that of Mark Claypole. He wondered vaguely why he had assumed she was older.

"Anyway, I wish he had taken some of that money and spent it on himself. I certainly don't need so much."

"Is there ever too much money for a woman?" he asked.

That was when she told him about her interview with the banker and mentioned figures. "I was just astonished," she finished.

With no change of expression Mark too was astonished.

"Anyway, you've learned to spend it while you can."

"I just don't know, Mark. To buy things you don't need seems wrong. But I do worry about where the money would go if I died."

"Haven't you made a will?" he asked.

"Not yet. The vice-president of our bank said I should. He wanted to help me do it, but he is very interested in hospitals and charities and I rather thought—"

"That he hoped to feather the nests of his projects?"

"Well, Tom never liked what he called the do-gooders. And it's his money. I wanted to think it over. If anything should happen to me as things are now it would all go to his stepbrother. But—"

"But you don't like his stepbrother?" asked Mark.

She hesitated. "Tom and George were never close. Tom always took the responsibility and George—I've never told anyone this—"

"Don't tell me, if you're going to be unhappy that you did."

"It's kind of a relief. Tom gave George a great deal of money over the years. I didn't know how much until after Tom died, when I found a record of it. George never paid anything back."

"That happens."

"It wasn't the money I cared about. George didn't even come to the funeral. And he'd just had his last check from Tom."

Mark heard the resentment and the shame. She had been the only member of Tom Goode's family to follow him to his grave. For just a second Mark Claypole identified with her desolation. That plunge into loneliness—it used to happen to him. It hadn't, though, in a long time. The second passed. This was a very commonplace woman.

"Did George know about your husband's money?"

"Not until later. When he found out, he wanted to make a fuss but the lawyer and the bank wouldn't let him."

Mark lounged to his feet. He was not going to let Signe Goode begin to cling. "Better not think of it," he said.

HE INTENDED to spend the day at Casablanca on a beach, and when the ship docked he joined the crowd that was flocking to the gangplank. Then he saw Signe standing alone. She wasn't dressed right. She wore a checked suit that would be too hot for

the day. It should have been a cool plain sleeveless linen dress of the sort that Julia Hayward and Alida Barnes wore.

Signe smiled at him and said, "I hope you have a good day."

"You too," he said. "Are you off to Marrakesh or Rabat?"

"There weren't any tickets left. I'm just going to look around."

"You aren't tied up?" he asked against his good sense.

"No," said Signe and he could hear the hope.

"Why not go to the beach with me? Do you swim?"

"I just love to!"

"Then get your suit and come along. We'll have a swim and lunch at a beautiful hotel."

Signe said diffidently, "If you'll let me pay for the lunch."

"I'd be delighted."

He had been surprised at the litheness of her figure in her bathing suit. Also at her swimming. "You're pretty expert, Signe."

"I was a counselor one summer at a Girl Scout camp. And sometimes, when we could get away, Tom and I—"

"No, don't tell me where you went on Sunday afternoons. Don't make me jealous."

She knew he was making fun of her, but he could tease her as much as he liked. She wasn't going to be alone all day. They swam for an hour and afterward Mark fell asleep on the sand. Signe soaked in the bright beauty of the shore and watched the tiredness and defeat in Mark's face destroy his mask of cynicism. She noted how much gray there was in his thatch of red hair. And she saw that the raincoat tossed over his body to shield it from the sun was very shabby.

Later they wandered through the open stalls of the bazaars, and suddenly Signe caught the fever of buying.

"Wait until you get home," advised Mark. "You can get the same things at Macy's more cheaply."

But she bought the gold caftan. The persistent little native said it was very beautiful on the lady, and with his greedy eyes as a mirror the lady felt beautiful. It was expensive and she cashed a traveler's check, and asked for the change in American currency.

In the taxi on the way to the Anfa Hotel she took a bill out of her

purse, put it shyly in Mark's pocket and said, "It's my lunch, remember. But will you take care of it for me?"

At the hotel he took a look and found it was a hundred-dollar bill. Why not? he thought, and ordered an unforgettable lunch.

FATHER Duggan had gone ashore soon after the ship docked. He was restless. At times this journey to which he was committed seemed unbearably long. He had done the obligatory things, said Mass daily in the theater, where the stewards would place a temporary altar. A few people attended every day and a larger number had come to the Sunday service, when he had tried to give a sermon that would mean something. But it had seemed artificial to him and he had wondered whether, if the trappings and beauty of churches were taken away, religion would stand by itself.

He had no plans for the day but obviously most of the passengers were bristling with them. There were private cars, taxis and buses lined up, with their drivers accosting the tourists. Howard Demarest was paged and the priest watched him go to a limousine, his girl wearing the shortest possible blue dress.

Mr. and Mrs. Chilton, with the little girl who looked like Alice in Wonderland and the nurse in English uniform, also got into the car that was waiting for them. This was the only child on the ship and Father Duggan pitied her, surrounded by all that wealth and overprotection.

He saw the writer who had been so talkative that first night in the bar and he was with the woman he had picked up there. The beautiful Bancroft girl was getting on a bus, mingling with the others but as usual somehow not blending with them. She managed that very well, he observed.

Father Duggan had been ordained at twenty-six, and in fourteen years of hearing confessions, celebrating marriages, listening to human problems and visiting in houses of illness and death he had developed extraordinary insight. People did not have to tell him when they were carrying burdens. And he had begun to share the burdens. The sullen pregnant women whose homes were already crowded with underfed children, the black boys growing

up in hate, the hopelessly mismated husbands and wives denied divorce—all these things preyed upon him. And the advice he was obliged to offer often seemed hypocritical, for he knew that it could not resolve the tensions.

He tried to find satisfaction in the relaxation of some dogmas and precepts. Fasts were being abolished, services simplified, and there were folk masses where long-haired boys chorused ancient responses to the beat of pop music. But these changes seemed to Father Duggan to be almost bribes. He thought the Church was making small concessions and not attacking the major problems of modern living and deteriorating morality.

He knew he was only one of many troubled priests. Many younger men ignored their bishops' admonitions, argued against celibacy, joined and led demonstrations for peace or integration or better housing. But for Father Duggan such things had been an outlet to nothing.

The pronouncement of Pope Paul against birth control had shocked him to bitterness. "Catholics won't go along with it," he said to the bishop. "How can this be right when it will make women stay away from confession or tell lies? If there is a general breakdown in obedience on one point, there will soon be on another. If the Pope loses authority, the Church will dissolve. What I hear in the confessional—"

"You are on the firing line, I know, Father Aloysius. But you love the Church, don't you?"

"I have loved it all my life."

That was what made it so fearful. The thought that he might never again say a Mass overwhelmed him with pain. Yet to continue to use that privilege while doubting the judgment of the head of the Church would make him both traitor and sinner.

Someone spoke to him. "There is a seat left in the last bus, Father. You're going with us to Marrakesh, I hope?"

"Thank you—yes, I think I shall," Father Duggan said absently, and mounted the steps of the bus. He went down the aisle and saw that the only vacant seat was beside the Bancroft girl.

"May I sit here?" he asked. She glanced up and he saw her face

closely for the first time. Her smile was pleasant, but he knew that this was not a happy young woman.

"Of course," said Barbara.

JULIA Hayward looked through the stone arches of the hotel terrace at the sumptuous gardens. She had last been in Marrakesh five years ago, and her thoughts were drawn relentlessly into the past. Seen from the back by passing hotel guests, Julia looked like a girl, with a slim, beautiful figure and a crest of dark hair. There was no one in front of her to see the carefully tended face which was not young and the somber eyes which held no expectations. Julia did not travel for the same reason Alida did, which was that "everyone" in New York went away during the cold months. Julia traveled in the recurrent hope—always disappointed—that unknown places would give her life a new impetus.

Alida was in the lounge writing postcards to her son in Washington, to her daughter in Arizona, to the bachelor in New York who was her extra man at dinner parties, to friends in Palm Beach or California or the Virgin Islands, and to her cook and caretaker.

Julia never sent postcards. Although she had mailed her itinerary to Peter, there had been no letter from him so far at any of the ports of call. But Julia had disciplined herself to never being hurt by anything her son might do. Peter and Christine went their own way. Julia did not think they were happy. But what young married people were today? They didn't think in terms of happiness. They talked of communication and sexual variety and there seemed to be no rules. Ten years ago there had been a few rules left. Julia's husband had broken them all and thrown the pieces in her face. She hadn't been able to live with it.

Sometimes, now, with Peter and Christine and their child hovering in her mind, she wondered if she shouldn't have. At least if she couldn't put up with him she should have married again. She wished she could tell Christine that a husband was the best answer even if he was as difficult as she knew Peter must be. On the edge of being a manic-depressive, the psychoanalyst had said, adding that this had begun when Julia got her divorce.

She turned from the window and her thoughts. Alida was still writing. Julia had known Alida since they were young, before they were debutantes. Alida had been twice widowed, and a great deal of gay and expensive life had flowed under the bridge since they were beautiful girls. Alida had traveled with both husbands, and when the last one had died in a plane crash four years ago she had suggested that Julia take a cruise with her. The trip together was now an annual event. Julia was fond of Alida and grateful, for Alida often insisted on paying more than her share of the expenses. Julia never had quite enough money because at the time of the divorce she had refused alimony, stipulating instead that her husband set up an irrevocable trust for Peter.

She crossed the room to Alida. "I think I'll go over to the square and look at the snake charmers while you're doing this."

Alida shuddered.

"I won't be long," Julia said.

She took a taxi, and the doorman who called it said to watch her purse carefully. The driver also told her to watch her purse—there were many thieves. "Yes, I will," said Julia.

She saw the extraordinary snake charmers, gave them a few coins and then wandered to the end of the square, where an old gray-bearded Moroccan sat on a rag of carpet, telling a story to a circle of natives. She went as close as she dared, and stood there listening. She could not understand the language but the storyteller had the voice of a great actor who needed neither scenery nor costume to hold his audience. The faces around him grew serious and despairing as he told the tale. Suddenly Julia felt tears in her eyes. He seemed to be telling of her own lonely futile life.

The voice was sad. Then it condoned, forgave, ceased. As the story ended Julia felt a tug at her wrist and her purse was gone. She turned and saw a small brown figure running across the square.

"Did that boy grab your purse?" She turned at the question. It was the priest from the ship, and the Bancroft girl was with him. "I'll see if I can find a policeman," said Father Duggan.

"No," said Julia, "it doesn't matter that much. The courier has my passport, luckily, and I've a friend at the hotel who will pay for

my taxi. Let the little vandal have the purse. It's a small price of admission to that wonderful storytelling."

The priest gave her a smile of admiration.

"Wasn't it wonderful?" said Barbara. "Do you know Arabic?"

"Not a word. But I felt as if I knew what he was telling," Julia said.

"Sorrow is the same in all languages," said the priest.

JOAN Scofield had not left the ship at Casablanca. She needed a chance to work on her schedule and have her hair done. She had been a social hostess on passenger ships for five years. She was thirty-five years old and could look twenty-five unless the day had been too harassing. She had two assistants but most of the planning of activities was done by Joan herself. She was expected to know everyone and remember names when she received with the Commodore before his dinners. Her evening clothes had to be dramatic enough to give style to the innumerable shipboard parties. She had to be admired, gay and amusing but keep the men from making passes. It was a variegated job and Joan loved it.

She had been the wife of an army officer who was killed in Vietnam. The shock had brought on a miscarriage. Some months later her aunt took her on a Caribbean cruise to help her forget her double tragedy. On the ship, watching the efforts of the hostess, Joan had thought she could do a better job of bringing strangers together. Six months later she was sailing to South America, a hostess herself.

After the first week of a cruise Joan had the passengers sorted out in her mind, by their social usefulness on the ship as well as by name. She had been pleased on this trip to see that several men were traveling alone, for there was always a surplus of unattached women. But Howard Demarest had Ruby Canaday; and Alec Goodrich was not responsive to invitations. As to Mark Claypole, when she was sure he was indeed the writer, Joan remembered a book of his that she had read. One day in the first week she mentioned it to him with a smile that usually brought responsive warmth. "I loved that book. It was so beautifully written."

His look of resentment surprised her. "Thank you," he said. "That is very interesting, coming from the hostess of the ship."

His tone angered Joan. "Didn't you think that people in my profession could read and write?" she asked.

"Sorry," he said, "I didn't mean to intimate anything of the sort. But you seem so busy with all the games and general togetherness that I wondered how you could spare the time to read."

"It was quite a long time ago when I read your book."

"Yes, quite a long time ago when anyone read it." He switched the subject. "Is it amusing, your job of hostessing?"

"I don't laugh at it," said Joan.

"I'm sure you don't. But do you really enjoy presiding over all those antics—" He was interrupted then as someone stopped to speak to Joan. She was not sorry the conversation ended. She decided that Mark Claypole was probably spoiled by success and sophistication.

Sitting under the hair dryer while everyone was ashore at Casablanca, she looked over the program for the next day: trapshooting, flower-arrangement class, a lecture on Africa, rhythmic reducing, horse racing—plenty for Mark Claypole to satirize. Let him, thought Joan. Thousands of people look at cruises like this as the best times of their lives.

THE SHIP was due to sail at seven in the evening, and before six-thirty the captain was on the bridge checking final details with his officers. The passengers who had been on the Marrakesh and Rabat trips were coming up the gangplank. He recognized some of them—the two handsome women from New York, the priest, the Bancroft girl.

"Fifteen minutes," he said to Karl Van Sant, his chief officer. "The gangplank goes up on the dot."

"Calling Mr. Howard Demarest," came over the loudspeaker at almost the next moment. "Calling Miss Ruby Canaday. Calling Mr. Howard Demarest. Calling Miss Ruby Canaday."

"They can't be on board yet," said the chief officer. "I think they went off with some big shot."

"We sail at seven," said the captain. "If they aren't back in time they'll have to fly to Cape Town and rejoin the ship there."

"He'd make a hell of a row."

"We sail on schedule."

"Yes, sir."

There was no one on the gangplank now except a ship's officer. Twelve minutes after the captain's ultimatum a limousine glided up to the dock. Demarest got out, moving heavily. Ruby Canaday tumbled out after him, almost falling on the rough platform of the dock. Everyone who stood at the railings above saw Demarest grab her arm, slap her violently and pull her roughly after him up the gangplank.

Mrs. Hartley Barton, leaning on her two canes, was shocked. She had just been thinking of how many happy sailings she and her husband had known. She sighed. Others laughed.

Joan Scofield, at the side of the boat deck, glanced up at the captain on the bridge. He must have seen what had happened, but he had not moved.

CHAPTER FOUR

THE travel lecturer told his large and interested audience that Africa was four times as large as the United States and the second-largest land mass in the world. Great civilizations had waxed and waned there while Europe was still barbaric. He explained that Gao on the Niger had once been a center of the arts, and that the inhabitants of that city were reading and writing in Arabic for centuries before the era of exploration to the West.

"Africa contains more than fifty countries, many of which are larger in area than the few colonial powers that still occupy them."

Alec Goodrich suddenly found that most of what he already knew about underdeveloped countries was becoming alive. He had never realized the scope of the problems as he did now that he himself was on the coast of Africa. He had a feeling of being cut down to size and expanding at the same time.

"Mali," Dr. Hermann was saying with his faint German accent, "had been great for four centuries. It was tremendously wealthy and had a very effective political system. Then Songhai became great in the fifteenth and sixteenth centuries as Mali was fading."

As Alec left the theater he carried with him the question of why Mali had faded out. Going out on deck, he found himself holding the door for Father Duggan. "Did you enjoy the lecture?" he asked.

"Yes. It was very interesting."

"He knows his stuff certainly. I understand he is a history professor on sabbatical." Alec laughed. "I found myself listening to him as if I wanted credit for the course." The priest fell into step with him and Alec went on. "What I was wondering was why the political system of Mali lost out if it had been so effective. I suppose nobody knows when there's such a time gap."

Father Duggan asked, "Don't political organizations—perhaps all organizations—wear out?"

"If you don't mind my saying so, Father, your organization, the Roman Catholic Church, still seems to be going strong."

Father Duggan, who did not think it was going strong, had an impulse to discuss the trouble, the confusion he saw in the Church, with this obviously thoughtful man. But it was just this that he had promised the bishop not to do.

He said, "The Church has found it wise to make many innovations in its organization as times have changed."

"I've read about changes in ritual and the dropping of Latin," said Alec. "But I should think that the stand on birth control must make it difficult for many of your people. I mean that the cost of living and the crowding in the cities doesn't make it easy or even feasible to feed and house big families."

"It presents a serious problem," said Father Duggan.

I suppose he can't open up, thought Alec. But Alec himself had become hungry for conversation. "And divorce—so many kids get married without knowing what they're getting into."

"I am sure that they often don't know," said Father Duggan.

"But your church won't let them have another chance, will it? I mean there's no out, is there, if they want to stay Catholic?"

"The Church allows legal separation for sufficient cause. It rarely permits remarriage."

"Isn't that pretty hard on human nature?"

No one knew better than the priest how hard it was on human nature. All those troubled confessions, appeals for dispensations, and rebellions because human nature couldn't stand it.

"I'm speaking out of turn, I'm afraid," said Alec into the silence. "I apologize."

"There's no reason to. Personal problems—even tragedies—do exist. But sometimes we cannot see the wood for the trees."

Alec gave him a quick glance. What did he mean by that? And Father Duggan, not seeing the glance, was ashamed of the evasive answer his promise had demanded of him. Neither went on talking. At the next entrance to the lounge Alec said, "Well, I think I'll see what the stock-market report looks like today."

The priest continued around the deck, feeling more of a hypocrite than ever.

IT WAS an eight-day journey from Casablanca to Cape Town, and between the two ports routines became more deeply established. People found their own levels at the bridge tables. Buffet lunch was served on deck, and by the swimming pool groups of almost naked passengers browned and ate.

Cocktail parties multiplied. Jim Bates delivered invitations to his passengers and knew that Mrs. Barnes and Mrs. Hayward were invited to many of them. The Honorable Alexander Goodrich seemed to be asked to all of them, but he usually drank by himself. Mrs. Goode was asked to comparatively few.

Jim liked Mrs. Goode. He recognized her inexperience and was protective toward her, suggesting that when the sun was high it was well to keep out of it even if she liked to swim. He saw that she sunburned instead of browning. Jim admired Mrs. Hayward but kept a respectful distance from her. Mrs. Barnes made him a good deal of trouble. She was, however, generous at the end of the first week, when tipping was in order.

Barbara Bancroft was his favorite passenger, but Jim did not

197

think she was enjoying the cruise as much as she should. Invitations that he slipped under her door were sometimes lying there unopened when he made up her room hours later. She always looked right for any time of day or occasion, but she did not seem to enjoy attention or admiration. At the end of the week her tip was just the amount that in Jim's category it should be, and she offered it to him as one person to another who deserved it.

Howard Demarest was not methodical in his tipping but it averaged out all right. He would give him five or ten dollars when it was not expected and forget to tip when normally it should have been forthcoming. Jim had no illusions about the relationship between Demarest and Miss Canaday. He was often summoned to bring splits of champagne to the big suite before they went to dinner; and sometimes Demarest would act, as Jim described it, like the minister coming to call, and sometimes there would be the rough edges of a quickly silenced quarrel. The night they sailed from Casablanca there had been a noisy row. The girl rang for ice later and Jim saw a bruise on her cheek. But a few days after that Demarest gave his big party and she was there, looking very beautiful and acting as if nothing had happened.

SOMETIMES, as he shaved or knotted his tie, Howard Demarest would stare at his face in the mirror as if he were looking for something. Sometimes he would have a feeling of revulsion as he saw what the years had done. Then again it wasn't so bad. The bold courage was still there in the eyes; the features were thickened with flesh but still in good proportion.

He had begun his career with a number of natural assets. His ego never had been burdened with humility. He had an aptitude for mathematics. Also—and this he never underestimated—he had the body of an athlete and a very handsome face. The business scouts who came to recruit college students before graduation noticed him immediately. He chose industry, and in the next twenty years he learned almost all there was to know about industrial chemicals and coatings, electronic devices and computers. Naturally he became familiar with methods of financing and ad-

vertising as he went along. His picture was in *Fortune* twice before he was forty. He was a pioneer in building conglomerates and that was one of the reasons he was on *The Seven Seas*.

The American Republic Line, which had owned the big ship, had a long history of profit and self-sufficiency. But competition with air travel and the doubling and trebling of costs had finally made refinancing necessary. The line had been acquired by a corporation which also owned a railroad, a chemical division and an insurance company. It was at a meeting in November that doubt about the value of the shipping line had been expressed.

"Passenger ships are going to be obsolete," said Mr. Welch. "With the new superairliners they haven't a chance."

"I'm not convinced of that," said Mr. Davis. "There are still many people who prefer to travel by sea. *The Seven Seas* has had a world cruise for the last nine years. Always practically sold out."

"Does it make money with present costs?"

"It's more than broken even to date."

"Who takes these world cruises?" asked Welch.

"I don't really know," admitted Mr. Davis. "People take them for a rest, I suppose. Or to see the world. If they can afford it."

"We need a survey of costs, wastage, the labor situation too. Who do we get to do an expert appraisal of the whole picture?"

"Perhaps I could do it," said Howard Demarest. "My doctor has been breathing down my neck about getting away. I might sign on for the next *Seven Seas* trip and bring back a report on the makeup and so forth of one of these cruises. Of course the ship's officers would know I'm a director of the line but I'd go as if I were traveling like anybody else and see what the deal is."

"It would be very useful," said the chairman of the board, "but can you spare the time?"

"I've got my doctor's orders to spare it."

THE DOCTOR had surprised Howard Demarest more than he had frightened him. "I don't like the sound of your heart, Howard. Or the pain you describe. You have to let up."

"What do you mean, let up?"

"Get away from pressure for a while. I don't think this is serious yet. But it could be unless you change your pace."

"There must be medicines."

"Yes, I'm going to give you some nitroglycerin pills. They're very effective. If you get a pain put one under your tongue."

"And that will fix me up?"

"No. You should stop smoking and limit your drinking. Don't spend every night with a lady. Limit that too. But the main thing is to relax. Go off and fish. Or take a long ocean voyage."

It had seemed made to order. The day after the directors' meeting Howard Demarest had booked the Mandarin Suite.

Letters to persons of importance in New York and Washington had produced good introductions in each of the ship's ports of call. In Lisbon he had lunched with a leading banker and sent Ruby off to see the castles in Sintra. In Casablanca, Henri Latour had offered to be his host. He had now cabled the ship to add that any family or traveling companions would also be welcome. So he had taken Ruby along.

The Latours lived in the country, with elegance. Howard Demarest was aware that his host was a member of one of the great colonizing families, but he had not been prepared to hear the wife of Henri Latour addressed by servants as Madame La Comtesse. There were other guests, most of them bilingual but politely careful to speak excellent English to him. He soon sensed that life in the white mansion by the sea might be informal but was certainly not casual. He felt socially, even financially, out of his depth. And he wished he hadn't brought Ruby. Under the worldly, courteous eyes of these people she was embarrassing.

An aperitif was served before lunch, and Ruby, who had never tried French vermouth without gin or vodka, made a slightly wry face. One of the guests said quickly that mademoiselle would like a cocktail perhaps—he had learned the art in the States. She said she would love it, that she liked them six to one. The man made cocktails for Ruby and himself, and she had several, which made her flirtatious. It amused the men but Demarest could feel the appraisals of his hostess and the other very chic women.

At lunch two wines were served and he saw with controlled anger that Ruby was getting drunk. The afternoon was a long one. The Latours did not hurry anything. He was shown the grounds and the private beach and the stables. When it was past five o'clock Demarest said that they would have to leave because it was a long drive and the ship sailed at seven. Ruby said, "Don't worry, they wouldn't dare go without you!" She was then drinking a highball, supplied by the man who knew American habits.

Henri Latour had the car brought at once, and apologized for not being able to accompany them. In the car, Demarest sat without speaking until Ruby said, "They must be awfully rich."

"Better than rich," said Demarest. "They're distinguished."

"Well, I don't like French people very much."

"And what in God's name do you think they thought of you?"

"What do you mean? What did I do?"

"Shut up," he muttered so that the chauffeur wouldn't hear.

She turned her head away and Demarest stared out at the white city. He thought of Katherine. If she'd been with him—

Ruby had fallen asleep. When they reached the pier he shook her to wake her and she got out of the car after him. But the boards of the pier were rough and she stumbled. Then anger at her and at himself went out of control and he struck her.

HE HAD struck Katherine once and that had been the end of a marriage. It had lasted for nearly nine years, and though it had not been as happy a marriage as it looked to other people it had steadied him. He had been with an electronics company in Cincinnati when he met her.

She belonged to a wealthy and devout Roman Catholic family which had bred a bishop and a monsignor. Katherine was romantically in love and intended to convert Demarest to her faith after they were married. It was some time before she realized that neither her prayers nor her example would accomplish that. Her confessor said she should not reject her husband, but she did not welcome him and of course he knew it. One night his humiliation had risen to anger and he had struck her.

Katherine had left him. She had bought a small castle in Ireland and was bringing the children up there.

Demarest had not suffered greatly because of the break. A new business connection had been offered him in New York and he had been there ever since. Katherine would not divorce him, and although Demarest could have divorced her, he had not. In some ways having an undivorced wife was a protection. He was occasionally curious about the children, especially the boy, but the more he saw of adolescents in New York the more he thought they were better off in their Irish castle than in America. Someday he would look up the boy, arrange it through his lawyer.

He had very little social life except at his clubs, but there were always women available for a temporary relationship. Ruby had not been in his plan for this journey, but one night he had suddenly thought it would be fun to have her on the ship.

Things had been all right until Casablanca. To set them straight again he had given a cocktail party. Nearly everyone came, even the captain and Joan Scofield. But not Goodrich. Nor Barbara Bancroft.

Demarest had not been neglecting his job of inspecting the ship and analyzing costs and wastes. Some things were easy to put a finger on. For instance, the huge midnight smorgasbord feasts could be cut down. But he wasn't sure whether travel by sea was on the increase or not. He found that he liked being on the sea, and felt better than for some time. And in spite of the incident at Casablanca, it was worth having seen the city and the style those French people lived in.

### CHAPTER FIVE

BEFORE the ship reached Cape Town, Alec Goodrich had received a cable from Washington: LETTER MAILED TO REACH YOU CAPE TOWN IF NOT RECEIVED TRY TELEPHONE ME. O'BRIEN.

The letter was there. Jim Bates brought it in before eight o'clock. When Alec read it he was deeply touched.

I am writing by hand because very few people know of this project. A commission to reexamine the relations between the federal government and state universities is being set up. Problems of better financing, collaboration and discipline to be studied. Your name has been suggested as chairman because of your experience on the Committee on Education and Labor. No Senate confirmation necessary as this will be done under presidential authority. It should be a rewarding job—hard work, plenty of prestige and national notice. You'd have to return at once so cable me soonest. Miss you. Your shoes are badly filled.

Now and then one of these innumerable commissions caught the public imagination. This could be very useful. Alec knew it was needed. Better relations should exist between government at all levels and the universities which lived on state funds and federal grants. There was too much favoritism, too often political pressure. It would be a tough job but it should be done. And Alec gratefully realized that the old man had seen the chance for a comeback for his junior colleague and had wangled this. He went at once to the cable office on the top deck.

"We can't accept cables when the ship is in port, sir," a young man said. "You will have to send it onshore."

"Where do I go to do that?"

"The post office is best. Any policeman can direct you."

Alec went back to his cabin. Jim Bates was making up the bed. He said, "Have you been to Cape Town before, sir?"

"No, I never have, Jim."

"You'll enjoy it. It's different in a way, with all those mountains just about on top of it. Some people like it better than Durban. But you see more of the old South Africa near Durban."

Alec realized that he was not going to see any more of South Africa at all and a feeling of regret came over him. Tonight, or at the latest tomorrow, he would be on a plane.

The ship was in the usual medley after arrival in a port, but the crowds were on the lower decks and Alec stayed on the upper one, looking at the peak that he knew must be Table Mountain and at the surrounding summits which he could not identify. He

was astonished at how churned up he felt. He thought of Washington as he viewed the strange mountains, seeing the confrontations his acceptance of a new job would mean. He would have to face the newshounds. There would be jealousy, competition, the inevitable political struggle, no matter what his backing was. But if he put the job over in a big way, the people who had veered away from him would come back again. And if Cicely had not yet found another man . . . Suddenly he found himself resenting the whole idea of returning. He thought, This is the first time I've had the freedom to be my own man since I went into politics. Even before that. His early life had been shaped by Aunt Lucy's interest in politics, her own kind of patriotism, her pride in his victories. He had become interested in foreign relations, based campaign speeches upon them. But this journey had made the world real. He was moving about in it, not as a politician but as a traveler with no strings attached. He had not known how much he had enjoyed the brief freedom until he faced the loss of it.

The post office was big and bare except for a large writing table surrounded by red leather chairs. A sign on the table read FOR EUROPEANS ONLY. Alec had read about apartheid but to see it was something else. There was so much he should know.

"Where do I send a cable?" Alec asked a guard.

"The last window on the left, sir."

Standing at a window Alec wrote: RECEIVED LETTER DEEPLY APPRECIATE SUGGESTION BUT FEEL SHOULD PROCEED ON JOURNEY. YOU WERE RIGHT. IT WAS THE THING TO DO. EVER IN YOUR DEBT. ALEC.

THE SCHEDULE of the cruise allowed two days in Cape Town. Some passengers would stay there and go on with the ship to Durban. Others would take trains or planes to Johannesburg or Nairobi or Kruger National Park and rejoin the ship at Durban. Father Duggan's plan for the two days was to stay with the ship. Tomorrow he would take the bus ride that circled the mountains and the shores of both the Atlantic and Indian oceans. But on this first day he wanted to be alone and form his own impressions. He had read about a church that he very much wanted to see.

During the last few years he had organized desegregated Catholic groups in his own parish, and his sympathies with the blacks ran deep. Today he hoped to learn a little that might be useful when he went back to America, whether or not as a priest. So he walked through the city for hours, less interested in its surprisingly modern aspects than in the variety of color in the skins of the people and the obviously disciplined segregation. He rested in a small park while he studied his map. He found he was close to the church he was seeking. It was simply built, with wide wooden steps, from the outside an ordinary house of worship. But inside it was unlike any Catholic church he had ever seen.

The body of Christ on the crucifix above the high altar was black and the Virgin and all the saints had black faces. He knelt at the altar rail, deeply affected, and prayed for the people who wanted to claim Christ for their race. He prayed for understanding, compassion and an end to his own confusions.

The church had been empty, but as he rose he heard the door open. Barbara Bancroft was coming down the aisle.

She said in a still, hard voice, without smile or greeting, "They don't want even Jesus Christ unless he is black, do they!"

She turned then and fled toward the door. Father Duggan followed. She must not feel like that about this church. On the steps outside she stood with her hands over her eyes.

He said quietly, "It seems strange, of course, but you must not be shocked."

"Oh, I'm not shocked," she said. "I know exactly how they feel."

"What is it that disturbs you then?"

"It surprised me, that's all. I was tired of walking and I came inside to rest. Rest! There it was waiting for me, saying it again."

"Come out of the sun," he said. "There's a park down the street."

She came without resistance and he guided her to a bench shadowed by the huge leaves of an exotic tree. He sat and waited for her to recover herself. This was not the girl with whom he had spent a pleasant tourist's afternoon in Marrakesh. She had pressed her hands against her eyes and he was sure she was silently weeping. At last she lifted her shoulders in a gesture of control.

"It is wrong, isn't it?" she said, not looking at him. "The blacks cutting us off. Cutting themselves off from all whites."

"They are seeking to establish their racial dignity. They feel that they can only do it by themselves."

"I know," she answered bitterly. "Would you like to hear why I know?"

"I would like to know why you are unhappy, Barbara, but only if it would help you to tell me."

After a pause she said, "I had a black friend. More than a friend. I loved him. We were going to be married. Then he changed. He told me I would ruin his life. Because I was white! He said that to marry me would make him a traitor to his race."

"It must have been very hard. For both of you."

Barbara said, "We were in college together. He was older—a leader. Everyone thought he had terrific potential—even the people who objected to things we did. We were—you know—protesters. We struck because there was so much discrimination and injustice. The police were rough—they used a lot of tear gas and once I was in jail for a couple of nights. But I was never so happy in my life. I was working for something—and he and I were working together for the same thing. Then he changed, suddenly. He was in law school. But he left the university and started to go around with people who didn't believe that integration would work, who despised the very idea of it. Everything, everyone had to be black. When I saw that figure on the cross, rejecting me just as—"

"Christ was not rejecting you."

"It felt that way."

"Have you been alone in all this trouble and confusion? Without any help?"

"My parents and I don't talk the same language. Of course they were horrified when I said I was going to marry Boone. Then they tried to be broad-minded and civil to Boone and that was almost worse. I never told them he was the one who broke it off. Not because of pride. Because it was a thing I had to bear myself. But today in that church—have I shocked you, Father?"

"Of course not. I am only sorry for your anguish."

"Thank you. How strange to be telling you all this. I feel better than I have in a long time. Does confession always do that?"

"It should," said Aloysius, who did not feel like a confessor at the moment. He was very conscious of Barbara's beauty. He felt a personal desire to relieve her, to restore her happiness.

"Barbara," he said, "will you do something for me?"

"I'd certainly like to."

"Let's go back to the church. For just a few minutes. I don't want you to remember it as you saw it before."

She hesitated, then said, "All right, if you want me to."

MARK Claypole could not afford the excursion to Nairobi but he very much wanted to take it anyway. For Nairobi was the approach to Hemingway country and Mark had never seen Mount Kilimanjaro. He wanted to get the feel of the region that Hemingway had made so real. It occurred to him to ask Signe Goode to come along—she might help with expenses—but he rejected the idea. He did not want her interfering with his attempt to reincarnate the inspiration of a great writer. And he hoped to arrange to spend the second day alone in the Tanganyika territory near the mountain, bypassing the visits to game reserves and Johannesburg. When he saw Demarest and his girl at the airport early that morning he was glad he had planned it that way. The newlywed Beauforts were there also but they were so locked in their own company that they were never a nuisance.

Howard Demarest was in good spirits this morning and greeted Mark with welcome news, that he and Ruby were not staying in Nairobi but flying on to Johannesburg by private plane. Ruby was breathing in the admiration of the men in the waiting room. Her dress was the color of ripe watermelon, ending high above her smooth bare knees. Mark glanced at her as if she were the cover girl on a magazine that he would not buy. The story that went with the picture would be the same old one. He had no desire to write that story.

Mark looked at his watch and saw that it was past flight time. He asked the travel agent when they would take off.

"We're waiting for Mrs. Hartley Barton, Mr. Claypole."

As he spoke the waiting-room door opened and Mark saw the elderly woman pulling herself along on her two canes. She smiled— the smile of a lady who was gracious from long habit—and said in a voice that was surprisingly young, "I do hope I haven't kept everyone waiting. Just as I was leaving the ship there was a call from Nairobi that I couldn't ignore."

"She must be crazy," said Howard Demarest to Ruby, "a crippled old woman taking a shore trip like this."

But the travel agent was paying Mrs. Barton special attention. She chose a seat on the aisle, saying cheerfully that it would be easier to get out from there. The young Beauforts helped to make her comfortable, as if they were used to elderly ladies. They sat behind her. Demarest was across the way.

He leaned toward her as they took off. "This may be a hard trip."

Mrs. Barton had immediately recognized him as the man who had hit the girl at Casablanca. She answered pleasantly but not as if she intended to continue the conversation, "I've always enjoyed it. And it is not so difficult as it used to be."

The reply astonished him. "You've been here before?"

"Oh yes. I always enjoy Africa."

"You travel a lot?"

Her eyebrows lifted. "We've always traveled—at our pleasure. I would not know if it would be considered a lot."

Young Beaufort grinned and murmured to Bettina, "Just like Grandma. She put him in his place."

Demarest persisted. "I suppose it gets in some people's blood. I wonder how long these cruises will last. They're taking off a good many passenger ships. Planes get there quicker. And cost less."

"My dear sir, people will always want to travel by sea. As they will always want to ride horses." She turned away, dismissing him.

Demarest was irritated. The annoyance of not having someone realize his importance itched. Mrs. Barton reminded him of his wife's mother, who always thought she was better than anyone else. He was being met, in style, at Nairobi. He did not quite admit that he wanted that old woman to see how he traveled.

It was a long, tiresome flight and the relief could be felt when the plane finally touched down. Mrs. Barton reached for her canes, and the guard and Gene Beaufort carefully helped her to her feet. Demarest said to Ruby that it was a damned nuisance having a person in that condition on a plane.

Someone was being paged. "Mrs. Hartley Barton."

She stood waiting, her face serene.

A chauffeur hurried forward. A guard indicated Mrs. Barton, and Demarest heard, "The car is waiting, madam. Sir Maurice and Lady Mary send warmest greetings."

### CHAPTER SIX

THE bus in Durban which had been reserved for the ride to the Valley of a Thousand Hills was filled. Father Duggan had seen Barbara Bancroft mount the steps. He sat several seats back of her. She might regret her outburst of confidence in the park the other day. Also she had been very much—overmuch, he was afraid—in his thoughts since then. He had not had such a personal feeling about a woman since he had been ordained.

Signe Goode had reverted today to her original shipboard shyness. She did not want to sit by Julia Hayward, but by the time she boarded the bus there was the choice of taking the seat beside her or the one by the priest. That she could not face.

"May I sit here?" she said to Julia.

"Of course, Mrs. Goode."

They agreed it would be a hot day and then conversation lapsed. Julia was alone, for Alida had gone for two days to Kruger Park. She had urged Julia to come with her.

"It's a small, very nice group. That interesting couple from Canada are going, and the Julian Chiltons. Marcia Chilton didn't know what to do. They didn't want to take Hilary along for fear she might catch some infection. So they finally decided to leave her with the nurse to go on with the ship to Durban. The nurse is utterly reliable—but of course they had that awful experience."

Julia didn't inquire into the experience. Alida had established a connection with the Chiltons through friends in California.

"I'd really like just to wander around Cape Town," she had said. "And the day we're docked in Durban, before you get back, there's a long trip to native territory I'd like to take."

She could not afford the Kruger trip and did not want Alida paying for it. There had already been too much of that. Besides, Julia was glad to have a few days by herself. In Cape Town she found a bookstore and went to the theater. She also did some figuring about the increased cost of living in New York. She might have to move to a smaller apartment. If she could earn something—but how could she at her age and with no training?

The Durban run was pleasantly relaxed. It took only a night and a day, and Jim brought her meals to her cabin. And at Durban there was a letter. Not from Peter but from Christine.

Dearest Julia—

Pete says we ought to let you know what's with us. We're divorcing. Nothing has worked right for us for ages. He is terribly edgy, either indifferent or jealous, and frankly I've had it. I still love him but living with him is something else. He feels the same way—I haven't been much to come home to. So he's moved to the Field Club and I'm going to Mexico, which is handy and quick. It should be all over by the time you are home. We won't divide Tony. Pete agrees that I should have him, if he can see Tony now and then. Pete didn't want you to pick up the news from somebody else. I'll keep in touch and Tony and I will always welcome his grandmother any time you come our way.

All love,
Christine

There was nothing Julia could do about it. She wondered if Pete was still in analysis, if he was drinking more heavily. Would Tony be scarred by divorce as his father had been? The old questions swung through her mind as the bus lumbered through Durban.

The windows were wide and from where Signe Goode sat she could see rickshaw boys with their headdresses of feathers, horns

and beads, women in silk saris, bearded Mohammedans wearing red fezzes, half-naked boys holding monkeys.

The native guide used a small microphone. "Now we go to Valley of Thousand Hills," he informed them. "We take pictures when we see Zulus on road. Children dance."

Barbara Bancroft had been absorbed by the sight of this mosaic of color and race. It was unsettling. It proved something possible—something that she had made herself stop trying to prove.

Then she saw the first group of Zulu children. As the bus came closer they went into a frenzy of dance. All were nearly naked, and as they danced they shouted, "Money, nickel, dime, money."

"You want stop take pictures?" the guide asked.

Someone said, "You bet." The children jumped like animals, did special antics for the camera, and Barbara felt sick.

"Just like monkeys," a woman said, giggling.

A girl with a child on her back came under Barbara's window and stretched out her hand. She had one eye and broken teeth but her body was young, her breasts high and firm.

"And they call themselves people of heaven! Isn't that something?" There was a laugh from one of the front seats.

Father Duggan cut it short.

"Who knows? It could be true," he said with quiet authority.

Barbara turned to give him a look of gratitude. Signe Goode did not turn, but the priest suddenly seemed less formidable.

Where the group stopped for lunch there was a shop plastered with souvenirs and candy for sale. Barbara bought several bags of candy. If they saw more children she would have that to give them. Candy, not money, and she wouldn't throw it at them.

Like monkeys, that woman said. Boone had said bitterly once, "A lot of people think of us as apes. There used to be slave owners in the South who would dress up little black boys in red coats like the monkeys with organ grinders and teach them tricks. Plenty of people still feel like that about blacks."

On the way to the Zulu enclosure of the Valley of a Thousand Hills the guide talked incessantly. The Zulus bought their wives with cattle. For a good cow a man could buy a woman to work for

him for life. If he wanted to return her, he would want his cow
back. Laughter. The unmarried girls wore beads as love letters
and the colors of the beads showed if they were ready. Laughter.
The guide was condescending. But he too was black. Boone had
said, "We must be taught not to despise our own people."

The dancing was not beautiful. Unshapely men and women
capered around to the sound of a drum. Barbara wandered away
from it and found a tiny hamlet. It was a collection of round windowless huts with low entrances. A small thin child crawled out of
one as Barbara watched.

The tiny boy struggled to his feet and Barbara handed him a
piece of candy. The child sucked at it, a look of pleasure came
over his face, and he tumbled back inside his home. Barbara
started back along the path and suddenly there was a pack of
small boys and girls following her. She portioned the candy into
their little greedy claws and when she took out a third bag a boy
snatched it. The rest cried, "Dime, nickel."

She shook her head firmly and said, "No more." Then she smiled
at them as they repeated their chant for money. Father Duggan,
on the top of a hillock—for he had left the dances to look for Barbara—saw the smile and went down to be with her.

COMMODORE James had taken Joan Scofield to dinner in Durban
at his favorite restaurant. It was dark and cool, with walls decorated with filigree and rare birds in cages hanging from the rafters.

"This is the kind of place tourists never see," Joan said. "How
did you find it?"

"A Greek merchant told me about it. Do you like the wine?"

"It's perfect. You'll miss your favorite haunts, won't you?"

"Oh, Lord, yes."

"But you'll be free to travel where you please."

"Travel costs too much unless it's part of your job. No, I'll be
stuck. I'll sit on a bench and whittle."

"It's all wrong. It makes no sense. You're a wonderful captain.
Don't they know how stupid they are to lose you?"

"It's automatic. Not personal. If the line were independent, as it

used to be, things might be different. If seamen were at the top. But now men like Demarest run the show."

"I don't like him."

"He's sharp," said the Commodore. "Between ourselves, I don't think he's on the ship just to give his girl a boat ride."

"What do you mean?"

"He's a kind of scout, I think. For the holding company."

"If he's that, I like him even less. He does ask a lot of questions."

"Let him ask. We've nothing to hide. It's a good ship. The passengers get their money's worth. Maybe there's a bit too much plush but that has nothing to do with me."

Joan said, "I love the ship. But I don't know whether I want to stay with it without you."

"It's a good berth, Joan. And nobody does a better job than you. It's been a pleasure to have you around."

"Don't," she said. "You make me feel miserable. I've been so happy being your hostess."

"I wish you were more than that," he said. "I shouldn't say that but I'm not sorry I did."

"I'm glad you did," she whispered, and he reached to touch her hand. He poured more wine and they talked of Africa and the next run of the ship. It was late when they went back. *The Seven Seas* lay enormous beside the dock, gleaming white and with lights at almost every porthole.

"Isn't she beautiful?" said Joan.

"Hard to beat."

"It's funny," Joan said. "There's that mixture of strangers—most of them never saw each other until a few weeks ago—but when they come back tonight there'll be a sort of family feeling."

"A happy family?" asked the Commodore with a skeptical grin.

"I wouldn't say that. Most families aren't happy. But they thrive on their irritations."

MARK Claypole came back to the ship earlier than he had intended. His pilgrimage to Kilimanjaro had turned out to be a fool's expedition.

To be sure, he had seen that insolent snowcap rising out of a steaming hot country and had understood why Africans identified it with divinity. But he had not managed to be alone with the mountain, for tourists were everywhere. Nonetheless he watched Kilimanjaro for a long time, and then had dinner at a lodge at the entrance to the jungle. He spent the night within hearing of strange roarings and trumpetings. He felt stupidly safe.

In the morning he was lucky enough to hop a little six-seater plane to Durban. After a few hours of bumping and sweating he was back on the ship with mixed feelings of relief and lethargy. Nearly everyone, including the bartenders, was still on shore.

He wandered into the empty smoking room with a copy of *Time* and settled into one of the huge upholstered chairs. It was a moment before he saw that he was not alone. The ship's only child passenger was almost lost to sight in an adjoining chair.

Mark had noticed her many times, always with her parents or nurse. She pleased him. Like all people of intelligence he treasured *Alice in Wonderland,* and this child had the expectant, meditative expression of Alice in the Tenniel illustrations. Even her dress was right, the skirt full, the small sleeves puffed. She wore no apron, but a pocket on each side of her skirt served as well.

He said, "Well, hello. How are you today?"

She made no answer, looking steadfastly ahead.

"Won't you speak to me?" he said teasingly.

She said, "I am not allowed to speak to strangers."

"Oh," said Mark. "That's sensible, not talking to strangers. But people who are traveling on the same ship aren't strangers."

Hilary said, "I don't know. Nobody told me that."

"Where is your family today? And your omnipresent nurse?"

"My father and mother have gone on a trip to see the beasts. And Cora is sick. She was not supposed to let me out of her sight— so my mother will not worry and have a nervous breakdown."

She even talks like Alice, thought Mark. The same logic.

"That's a bad thing to have certainly," he said.

"Yes. She had one when they stole my brother."

Mark said quietly, "I hope you got him back."

214

"Well," said Hilary, "after a long while they did. But he was dead then. He was mutilated."

The fact, stated so calmly, and the incongruous word on the child's lips, gave Mark a twinge of horror.

"Cora is sick," Hilary explained. "She has to go to the bathroom all the time. She left me in there"—Hilary pointed to the library—"but the men came with vacuum cleaners so I came in here."

"It's comfortable here," said Mark, "isn't it?"

"I like it. I like being by myself."

"I often feel that way. Don't you go to school?"

"In New York I do. But Cora takes me and comes for me. I would like to go by myself but I am not allowed."

"Oh, well," said Mark, "when you get older they'll let you."

"Yes," agreed Hilary, "and when I get older I can run away."

"That shouldn't be necessary."

"Lots of girls do. I've read all about it in the newspapers."

"How old are you?" asked Mark.

"I'm ten. I think I would have to be about thirteen to run away."

"Did you get that advice from the newspapers too?"

She nodded gravely. "There are lots of girls under sixteen who run away. They take drugs. We don't have any drugs in my school."

"Look—" Mark began and was interrupted by a scream.

"But I left her here! In this chair! Hilary!"

Mark stood up. "The little girl is in here," he called.

The nurse rushed in from the library, her face green. She clutched the back of a sofa to steady herself, and fainted.

"Bring a shot of brandy," said Mark to a steward, bending over the woman.

"The bars are closed, sir."

"Then help me lift her to the sofa," said Mark.

"Is Cora dead?" asked Hilary.

"Of course not. She'll be all right in a few minutes."

The impassiveness with which the child asked the question was strange, and Mark quickly glanced at her. He did not like the expression on Hilary's face. She looked withdrawn, overly calm. She was not Alice in Wonderland now but a little girl who had

been touched by shock and fear in real life. Mark repeated that nothing serious was wrong with the nurse and, as he smiled at her, trust came slowly back into Hilary's eyes.

So THE elegant Chiltons were also refugees. Mark could not get them out of his mind even when he was finally sitting in the Seashell with a drink before him. And carrying with them their most valuable possession, as refugees always did.

When the nurse had revived, Mark had gone with her and Hilary to their suite to make sure that she did not collapse again. He had rung for their steward and, waiting for him, noted the evidences of luxury—the space and special decor, the dining alcove, the spread of books and magazines and newspapers. Hilary's reading matter, with its lore of what went on outside this rich privacy.

Her look of horror remained with him. He could not help imagining the waiting, the finality. Mutilated, Hilary had said, a word she must have accepted without comprehension. Hilary had been taught that she must not worry her mother. She had been threatened with that nervous breakdown, another calamity she would not understand. On the surface she was docile. But she was planning, in her cool, direct, child's way, to run away. She probably would. Alice in Wonderland would become one of those confused girls who fled their families to communal attics, drugs and the streets.

Mark's thoughts were stirring, wakened by a compassion he had not felt in a long time. He had gone to the edge of the jungle and found no story. And here was an obsessive one, stumbled upon in the smoking room of the ship.

"I thought I might find you in here," said Signe Goode, adjusting herself on the stool beside him.

"Hello. So you're back from your bus trip."

"Did you have a good time in Nairobi?"

"I did not. I haven't had a good time since I last saw you."

"You ought to have come," she said. "To see all those natives certainly makes you think how lucky we are. The way they live! It makes you wish you could do something. To help in some way."

"You help," he said rather absently. It was true. It was tonic to have her simplicity and honesty around. Mark wanted to stop thinking about that look on Hilary Chilton's face when she had asked if her nurse were dead.

THE DINING room was fairly well filled by the time of the second sitting. As Joan had predicted, the passengers were glad to be back. They had packed their souvenirs away and showered gratefully in their clean polished bathrooms.

Alec Goodrich was at his usual table. The always helpful Dennis had recommended rock oysters because the chef had taken some on at Cape Town, and Anatole was opening a bottle of dry white wine. Alec had not wasted the last two days after sending his cable to Senator O'Brien. He had wangled a flight to Pretoria and taken in some of the political atmosphere of the administrative capital of South Africa. He had been jarred and impressed. He had introduced himself at the American embassy, for he knew he could not dig even a little way into the politics of the Transvaal without help; and though he had not asked either for escort or special information, both had been forthcoming.

It was invigorating to feel organized again. The decision not to go back to Washington had made all the difference between taking things as they came and shaping them to his own wish. Alec had plenty to think about and, he knew, new experiences ahead, but it was comfortable to be back on the ship. He looked over the dining room to see who else was on hand.

The priest was there. Alec was curious about why such an intelligent young cleric had been assigned to unimportant work. Mrs. Goode and Claypole were both at their places. Demarest came in, not in the best of tempers judging by his scowl. Barbara Bancroft was not there. Alec was conscious of a potential between himself and Barbara, though he had no intention of developing it. But they were both unattached and probably spoke the same social language.

"Yes, very good, Anatole," he said, tasting the sample of wine.
Gene Beaufort and Bettina passed his table and gave him a

nod and smile. He felt a twinge of envy. It must be something to have a girl like that with you on a long journey, wedding trip or not, to talk to, sleep with, wake to.

And now Barbara came in. She was wearing a white dress tonight, very short and untrimmed, and as usual there was no jewelry clanking on her. Alec liked her clean brown throat. Why was a girl who looked like that traveling by herself? Howard Demarest rose with a fatuous smile to pull back her chair. Alec was irritated. Demarest had his little tart. Let him stick to her.

Aloysius Duggan was also watching Barbara. He too disliked the attentions of Howard Demarest. He was beset by his wish to give Barbara peace of mind. But he could not do for her what he had done for so many others, and not only because they did not share a faith. He no longer had a sure faith to offer her. And with her he could not keep the impersonality of a priest.

"Such an attractive girl, that Miss Bancroft," said Mrs. Hartley Barton, who was sitting next to him tonight. "The one who just came in. Have you met her, Father?"

"Yes. I've had some conversation with her."

"She is a graduate of Barnard, she said. That's Columbia University. But she seems to have escaped all the turmoil there."

She had been tear-gassed. She had told Aloysius that. Her throat still hurt sometimes. She had been put in jail. She loved a young black. She is unhappy because he walked out on her. The facts piled up in his mind as he said, "She shows no trace of turmoil."

"I'm sure she will get a great deal out of the cruise. Travel completes a good education. But frankly, I sometimes wonder why some of the people you see today do travel. They could drink and dance and carry on just as well at home."

"Mark Claypole, the writer in our midst, says they travel to escape. That most of our fellow passengers are fugitives."

"Fugitives?" she repeated questioningly.

"Escaping from problems. Difficult situations. Sorrows."

"Well, it's true of many widows of course. But they don't have the right approach to travel as a rule. So many of them are hoping for new attachments."

"What is the right approach?"

"My father used to say that a person should travel to measure himself against the world. Do you do much traveling, Father?"

"I've had very little opportunity."

"I am always glad when there is a chaplain on the ship, though I'm not a Catholic. We always visited the cathedrals, and even without understanding one was uplifted. By the atmosphere."

He did not reply. He knew and loved that atmosphere.

CHAPTER SEVEN

THERE was considerable indignation when the announcement was made that *The Seven Seas* would have to bypass Port Victoria, in the Seychelles, because of weather conditions, though the sun was shining over a sparkling sea. Shortly after breakfast several tenders which were to take passengers to the island had moored to the side of the ship and loaded up. When it took off, those who were watching saw that the brightness was an illusion. The tender was tossing about on the waves.

"Get those passengers back on the ship as soon as possible," ordered the Commodore, "and cancel any more shore trips."

So acute was the disappointment that Joan telephoned to the Commodore a half hour later and asked if it would be possible for people to take the trip if they were good sailors.

"We can't take a chance with a sea like this. If there were any broken bones we'd be blamed. Cheer them up, Joan. Run off a party or something tonight. Break out some free champagne. And I'll post a boat drill for this afternoon instead of tomorrow. That will give them something to do."

"Adding insult to injury. They think drills are unnecessary."

"I'll decide that. You keep them happy and I'll keep them safe."

He put down the telephone and resumed his conference with the chief engineer. "What do you think might be the trouble?"

Fred Timmins, the chief engineer, was a lanky man with a deceptive, leisurely manner. He was quick to react to anything that

concerned his job. "Possibly a damaged shaft bearing. It's been too long since this ship was in dry dock."

"I know that. And we both know that dry-docking costs a lot of money. And that the company doesn't make any while it's being done." The Commodore had asked the owners before this cruise to have the ship inspected in dry dock. They had replied with the question he put to the chief engineer now. "There's no immediate danger of trouble?"

"I shouldn't say so. Unless the propeller is bent."

The Commodore inwardly cursed the management. "I'll insist on dry dock when this cruise is over. Have any repairs we need done when we're in Bombay next week."

Two notices were posted on the bulletin boards within the next two hours. One read ALL PASSENGERS ARE REQUESTED TO ATTEND A LIFEBOAT DRILL AT 3 P.M. AT THEIR ASSIGNED STATIONS.

The other was gaily crayoned in red:

> MASKED DANCE IN MAIN LOUNGE AT 10 P.M.
> BE SOMEONE ELSE FOR A CHANGE!
> MASKS WILL BE DISTRIBUTED BY STEWARDS
> TO ALL CABINS BEFORE DINNER.
> CHAMPAGNE SERVED IN LOUNGE

By three in the afternoon the sun had disappeared and the gray sea was choppy. At Lifeboat Station Number Two the assigned passengers gathered, with Jim Bates noting names and faces as they passed him. It was now a familiar if not completely friendly group. Alida Barnes crossed the deck to speak to the Julian Chiltons when they appeared with Hilary and the nurse. Hilary looked around and then managed to maneuver her parents close to Mark Claypole. They spoke to him pleasantly, for of course they had been told the story of Cora's illness and his help.

Mark winked at Hilary. "Why is a raven like a writing desk?"

"I don't know. Why?"

"Actually nobody knows," said Mark to Hilary. "They never got the answer at the tea party."

"What tea party?"

"You haven't read *Alice in Wonderland?* Too bad. It's one of the best books in the world."

"Will you give it to me?"

"I'll think about that."

Barbara Bancroft and Alec Goodrich arrived at the same time. "It's turned out to be a mean sort of day," he said.

"Not a day for romping on tenders."

"I was on the one that tried it," said Alec. "It was rather fun."

"I suppose disappointment's the reason for the party tonight."

"Masks," Alec said with distaste. "Are you going to wear one?"

"I don't know. As they suggested, it is rather tempting to be someone else for a change. I doubt if a mask would do it for me. You don't usually join in the fun and games, I've noticed."

"Is it so noticeable?"

"Well, you manage to sit in solitary state in the dining room."

"I'd be glad to have you join me if your table companions—"

Barbara finished for him. "Bore me? Probably not more than I bore them. We haven't a lot in common."

She seemed to Alec more beautiful close up. There were highlights in the loose long hair, and the dark lashes were real.

"My table might be even more boring," he said, "but I'd be happy to have you try it. Shall I ask Dennis to set a place for you tonight?"

"Shall we wear masks?"

"Only our usual ones," he said.

She looked at him in surprise, then laughed. "Good guess. It really would be fun to talk instead of making conversation."

"Is it a date for tonight then?"

She hesitated, then said, "Thank you. I'd like it."

Aloysius Duggan had been watching with some surprise. The senator's aloofness had always seemed unnatural. Barbara had not mentioned knowing Alec. But the conversation between them now seemed very alive. Any man would enjoy Barbara's company. Not only because of her beauty but because she was so responsive. So straightforward. And Alec Goodrich was a free man. Celibacy had never irked Aloysius, but today, glancing at those two, he had a sense of being imprisoned.

THE MASKS WERE OF MANY KINDS and sizes. Some passengers had spent hours in changing themselves beyond recognition, but there were many who couldn't or wouldn't be disguised. Mrs. Barton, sitting at the side of the lounge, was very much herself in spite of a half mask. Mark Claypole wore a death's-head mask—until he became bored and went out to the nearest bar. He had danced once with Signe Goode, who was wearing the gold caftan she had bought in Casablanca and a gold wig she had found at the hairdresser's on the ship. It was astonishingly becoming.

The Commodore looked in after eleven o'clock. He did not come much farther than the door and was about to escape when Joan, in a white lace costume, came to his side and said, "Well, did I do all right?"

"You put it over. They're having a whale of a time."

"Most of them. Always a few misfits."

"You're looking very lovely."

"You've seen this before. I wore it to the party last year. And I'll wear it again next year."

"With some other captain to admire it."

"I'll remember that you did," she said quietly.

"Dance with me?"

She lifted her arm, then drew it back. "No, I think I'd better not. I think I'd better see how the champagne is holding out."

The Commodore turned to go, and ran into Howard Demarest.

"Quite a party, Commodore," said Demarest. "The champagne must run into money. Who decides on giving a blowout like this?" The criticism from a director was implicit.

"In this case I did," said the Commodore coldly. "To ease the passengers' disappointment."

He left and Demarest muttered, "I'll look into this."

"Don't get mad at the captain, Howie. He's such a doll," said Ruby, who was beside him, holding a glass of champagne.

"You're getting yourself drunk," he told her. "Do that once or twice more and I'll send you back home from the next port."

"I have my own ticket," she said sulkily, "all around the world."

He gave her an ugly look. It had been a bad evening. He had

had a chest pain while he was dressing for dinner. This was the third time it had happened on the voyage. The nitroglycerin took care of the pain but not of his fear. He had never told Ruby of his doctor's warning. Instinctively he felt it would diminish him, make him seem less powerful a man. And then he had been extremely annoyed at dinner to see Barbara Bancroft sitting with that broken-down politician Goodrich instead of at his own table where she belonged. He had gone over to them and tried to make something of it and come off poorly. The encounter had left him in no mood to be kind to Ruby.

IT WAS impossible to find a quiet place in any of the public rooms when Barbara and Alec looked for one after dinner. The big lounge was crowded with dancers and spectators. Bridge had been pushed into the smoking room. The library was locked. Even the Seashell offered no privacy.

"Six hundred and ninety-eight feet of ship and no place to go," said Alec. "Shall we go to the movie?"

"I don't think I could take that show again. It's a stupid one."

"We can't run up and down stairs all night looking for refuge." She laughed. "Maybe Mark Claypole had a point."

"Would you come up to my room and have a drink?"

"Yes," said Barbara promptly.

It was a large, comfortable cabin, with two armchairs and a cock-tail table at the far end of the room. Alec left the door slightly ajar and rang for service. It was Jim who came.

"There isn't room to breathe down there," Alec said. "So we came up here for a drink."

"Yes, sir. What can I get you, Miss Bancroft?"

"A gin and tonic, please."

When he had brought it, with an unrequested bowl of nuts, he mixed a Scotch and soda for Alec and left, quietly closing the door. Hearing that click, they exchanged a glance and laughed.

"I love Jim," said Barbara. "He keeps subtly encouraging me to have a fling. He wants me to enjoy the cruise."

"Are you enjoying it?"

"It's not bad. It's serving its purpose, and I'm learning a lot."

"We seem to be in the same boat as well as in the same ship."

"Didn't you want to come?"

"I had nothing better to do."

"When Demarest came over to ask why I was at your table tonight, your mask slipped. I like you without one. Why do you wear it?"

"I suppose to hide my scars."

"Are there scars? They aren't noticeable."

"Don't you read the papers? The political news?"

"I know you lost an election. But is that so disfiguring? Isn't it the chance you take when you go into politics?"

"Losing an election isn't disfiguring. But character assassination is apt to be. You don't look the way you used to look, to yourself or anyone else. So you cover up with a sour puss."

"I wasn't reading the papers much during the last campaign. How did they manage to smear you?"

"A girl who worked in my office killed herself in my apartment."

"Why did she do it?"

"It's a very unpleasant story, Barbara."

"Unpleasant stories don't frighten me. Did people think you were responsible for her suicide?"

"The majority of voters in my state apparently assumed so. And perhaps in a way I was."

"That needs to be explained. Don't leave it like that."

"All right, I'll tell you how it was. This girl had worked on my campaign more than six years ago when I was elected to the Senate. So when she got out of college a couple of years later she asked for a job and I found a place for her. Before long I knew that was a mistake. But I didn't want to hurt her feelings so I didn't fire her. I thought I was being generous."

"She was in love with you?"

"It was one of those common enough attachments that grow out of working in a campaign. Girls exaggerate their candidates. I was going to redeem the world and she would be the disciple. I tried to cool her off, but a man—especially a politician—gets hooked on

225

flattery. That's why I think now I may have been remotely responsible for what happened."

"You did tell her you didn't want her to work for you?"

"No—she saw in the newspaper that I was going to be married. She asked me if it was true. I said it certainly was and that I wanted her to come to the wedding. And thought no more about it. Later one of her friends said she had been taking pills at both ends of the day—sleeping pills at night and bennies in the morning. Naturally she couldn't think straight. And one afternoon she came over to my apartment. She'd often brought over papers from the office so the janitor let her in. She told him she would wait for me. And she did. She was full of pills and whiskey and dead."

Barbara was remembering the nights when she hadn't wanted to live. "Oh, poor girl," she breathed.

"I warned you that it was a horrid story."

"And you were defenseless, of course. I can see how easy it was to assassinate your character. And how cruel. Cruel for the girl you were going to marry too. You didn't marry her? Are you going to?"

"No. I'm not going to marry anyone. I'm grateful to you for listening. It's broken the suffocating silence to talk to you instead of to myself. Now will you tell me why you are alone?"

"I'd rather not. You've had enough experience with girls who deluded themselves. But it's been a good evening. Very real."

"It's not over. I'm going to ring Jim for refills." As he passed her chair he stopped and lifted her face and kissed her.

### CHAPTER EIGHT

SIGNE GOODE had been bewildered when she first looked over the land-travel booklet delivered with her ticket. To make a choice among all the glamorous shore tours was an exciting leap in the dark, for all the places were strange to her.

"I've been reading about the trips in India," she said to Mark Claypole, who found her in her steamer chair poring over the brochure. "Have you been in India before?"

"No. And I've always wanted to see it," he said as he settled himself on the end of her chair.

"Which trip are you going to take? I've signed up for Tour Twenty-three that goes by train. I want to see the Taj Mahal."

He took the booklet and scanned the tempting description of the journey to Jaipur, Agra and Old and New Delhi. "You will see quite a bit of India in five and a half days," he said.

"That's what Joan Scofield said. What are you going to do?"

"Stay in Bombay. Explore the city. Find a bookstore."

"You'll miss so much."

"So I'm aware. But I can't afford it. Not while I'm paying alimony to an ex-wife who likes to lunch at The Four Seasons." He gave his usual uncaring grin and stood up.

Signe said, "Mark. Please. Come along. I'd pay for us both."

"Oh no," he said, reaching for the booklet again. "It costs three hundred seventy-five even for an upper berth."

"Do you mind upper berths?"

"I mind your paying my way. It's out of the question."

"I don't want to offend you. But I have a lot more traveler's checks than I can possibly use. Let me at least lend you some."

"I don't know when you'd get it back. Or if you would."

"That doesn't matter really."

"Inhibitions linger. Let me think about your generosity."

"Please think about it and not as generosity. When the purser's office opens I'm going to cash fifteen hundred dollars, which is plenty for both of us. And nobody will ever know."

He said again that he would think about it, and promised to buy her a drink before lunch. As he passed the door of the travel office a half hour later he turned back and went in, and inquired about accommodations on Tour 23.

"Not much left," said the agent. "Let me see. Yes, there is one upper. In Nine. Father Duggan has the lower in that room. Shall I put you down for it?"

"I'll let you know."

"We can't hold any reservations beyond five this afternoon."

"Okay," said Mark, "put me down. I'll settle later."

THE SHIP'S CHAPLAIN was offered complimentary tickets on all sight-seeing bus rides, and Father Duggan had found those had been satisfying enough so far. But there were two big shore trips that he had decided to pay for himself. One was Tour 23.

He wanted to go to Delhi because he had a friend there whom he had not seen in years. Sebastian Clarke had been in the seminary with Aloysius and the two young men were as close friends as the rigors of that highly disciplined life permitted. They were both zealous and both dreamers. Sebastian dreamed of carrying the faith to distant places. After his ordination he had spent some years in the West Indies. A few years ago he had been sent to Southeast Asia. His letters showed his deep interest in the social as well as the spiritual problems he encountered.

A year ago Aloysius had had a postcard from Delhi: "Here among Buddhists and Hindus I have a small church and with the help of my Untouchable friends we have put a steeple on it to display the Holy Cross for which the parish is named. How I wish I could talk to you in these troubled times. Yours in Christ, Sebastian."

When he took off on the cruise and realized that he could go to Delhi, Aloysius wrote to Sebastian, simply in care of the Church of the Holy Cross, having no other address. Somehow he must be able to find this one person in the world to whom he could fully expose his mental agony.

THE TRAIN which was waiting for passengers from *The Seven Seas* in Bombay surprised them by its modern appearance. The Indians who watched them get aboard were obviously proud of it, Alec Goodrich noticed, and he gave them a wave of appreciation which delighted them. The members of Tour 23 had the first coach to themselves. They would be sleeping in it for the next four nights. The second coach was filled with those who were going only to Agra. Behind that one was the dining car, which looked luxurious with white napkins in glass tumblers and flowers on every table. A fourth coach, furnished with wooden benches, held a miscellany of people, brown, black and yellow.

Alec was sorry the accommodations were so segregated. He wanted to see Indians, not Demarest or Julian Chilton. Barbara was on the train. He did not know whether he was glad or sorry about that. Or whether she was. They had not met since that night in his cabin. There had been admiration and laughter and gratitude but no protestations of love. He knew that given opportunity desire would rise in him again. He was not sure about her.

The train rolled away from the station and began to make its way through the worst slums Alec had ever seen. There were miles of shacks, with roofs made of pieces of tin or scraps of canvas. Naked children and emaciated dogs roamed around. Women squatted beside small fires, cooking. There was a strange look of lethargy.

"Who are these people?" Alec asked the guard.

"Squatters. They come to Bombay from outside."

"What do they do for a living?"

"They steal. They are very good thieves."

"Why doesn't the government clean up districts like this?"

"If the people are sent away, they come back. They must live."

Mark Claypole, moving from another window to where Alec was standing, said, "This somehow disproves that bland statement that when you've seen one slum you've seen them all."

"I've never seen anything like this."

"Neither have I, though I did a piece on Chicago once that made my own hair curl."

"Washington has bad spots too, but at least we're working on it. Everyone's going to have some kind of income one of these days. But the guard implies the Indian government tolerates this."

"This, and caste, and sacred cows, and unbridled breeding."

"You know the country?"

"Only from reading. It should be an interesting trip if we can skip folk dances and elephant rides." And remembering to whom he was indebted, Mark went away to find Signe.

BARBARA also was looking with sickened pity at the packed, ragged slums. But the people seemed to have an ease, even in squalor, that she had not felt in Africa. She wondered if she was

imagining that. The ease might be in herself. It could have come—this she knew was possible—from those almost casual hours with Alec Goodrich. She did not regret them, but he needed no more from her than she had given and it was better to leave it alone now.

She watched India spreading out before her, little towns with windowless mud cottages. The roads were gray with dust and the piles of cotton beside many farmhouses seemed amazingly white in contrast. Barbara was liking India and it seemed a long time since she had liked any other place.

HOWARD DEMAREST said that the railroad was outrageously inefficient. That was after he found out about the dining-car routine. He was equipped with a flask of cocktails and was having his first drink at half past twelve when the train stopped and the guard summoned the passengers to lunch.

"We'll go in after a while," said Demarest.

"Sir, must go now please. Before train starts."

The guard explained that because there was no connection between coaches it was necessary to get off the train and walk to the dining car, then stay there until another station was reached.

"That's a hell of a note," said Demarest.

Ruby gulped her drink. "Let's go, Howie. I'm starving!"

During the lunch, which was elaborate, Demarest criticized the management of the train, the roadbed and the food. He told the priest, who sat at the same table, that he was a director of an American railroad. "We've set up buffet cars. Dining cars are obsolete. And here you don't dare eat the salad."

"I suppose," said Aloysius, "most people in India wouldn't feel that way about it. A large percent of them are undernourished."

He spoke sharply. During the ride this morning Aloysius had been seeing the country with Sebastian's eyes, imagining his early encounters with the poverty and habits of this vast country.

"The Hindus have a stranglehold on India, haven't they, Father?" Demarest asked.

"It's the prevailing religion. But there are also strong minority ones—Muslims, Buddhists—and Christians. Many sects."

"I suppose it depends on who is running the country."

"Mainly, I think, on tradition and faith."

"People break away from any religion after a while," said Demarest sententiously. "The Pope seems to be having quite a struggle holding his people together."

He always spoke loudly, as if it added to his authority. Across the aisle Signe Goode and Mark Claypole heard him.

Father Duggan did not answer and Demarest persisted. "I've read that a lot of priests and nuns are dropping out."

Father Duggan said, "Mr. Demarest, nearly six hundred million of the world's Christians are Roman Catholics. You have read about an infinitesimal percentage of them."

"Maybe so, but it could show the way the wind is blowing. Not that I take sides at all. But I've known some prominent Catholics— in the higher echelons—and I know that they have their problems like other men in big organizations."

"No doubt," said the priest. He was trapped. Until the train stopped again he must sit and listen to this insolence.

Demarest went on. "I look at it from a businessman's point of view. Now, any big, wealthy organization is bound sooner or later to be involved in a power struggle. The younger, modern executives resent the older ones, especially if power and say-so are concentrated at the top. From what I hear, a good many bishops and capable churchmen want a hand in making decisions. Not to have Rome call all the shots—isn't that a fact?"

"It is a distortion. And this is a very futile discussion."

"Well, if you feel that way—" Demarest renewed his attack on the lunch. After a minute or two he grinned, not affably. "But what was the Pope thinking about the day he spoke against birth control? Didn't he know most Catholic women do it anyway?"

Signe said indignantly to Mark, "Did you hear what he said? He shouldn't talk that way to a priest!"

Mark said quietly, "Of course somebody should push his face in. But don't worry about Father Duggan. He's quite able to take care of himself."

At the moment Aloysius could not. He was filled with revulsion

at the likeness between what Demarest said and what he himself thought. He questioned the power of the Pope over the bishops and the procedure for nominating the higher clergy. He had told the bishop that Catholic women would disobey on contraception. And many priests and nuns *were* breaking their vows.

But his concern came out of love for the soul of the Church, its Sacraments, out of a deep and mystic faith in God. With violent silent denial Aloysius rejected the notion of the Church as one big corporation. And he knew that even if he had not promised to avoid such arguments, it would be useless to try to explain to the worldly, probably corrupt man across from him that the Church had been kept alive through all the centuries not by acquisitions of wealth and power but by love. By the mystery of grace. And by loyalty? The question came to the priest cruelly as the train shuddered to a slow stop.

THE DECKS of *The Seven Seas* were deserted and her public rooms empty. Only a skeleton crew and staff remained.

Mrs. Hartley Barton was on board, for she had fallen in her cabin and her forehead and one eye were badly bruised. She could not remember the fall. "Was it a stroke?" she had asked the doctor calmly. "I have had a small one before."

"If it was, it was also small. There's no paralysis, and many people have occasional blackouts as they grow older."

"Perhaps I'll be able to go to Agra tomorrow?"

"That would be inadvisable. We must keep you quiet for a bit."

So Mrs. Barton lay in the narrow hospital bed, with the railings pulled up around it. She knew that precaution was because the doctor thought she might black out again. And sooner or later she would. But, as Hartley always said, it did not matter where you died. She smiled, recalling the first time she had seen the Taj Mahal with her young and handsome husband. They had waited for sunrise, which gave the white marble mausoleum a delicate flush. They had watched it with delight and she had said, "Imagine any man caring that much for a woman." Hartley had said, "I can imagine it, Sara." She would never forget his saying that.

Before they had docked in Bombay the chief engineer, Mr. Timmins, had been on the ship-to-shore telephone to summon a ship repairman whose expertise he trusted. The Indian machinist had been asked to bring a diver with him, for the engineer wanted to have the stabilizers below the waterline looked at. The two men had come on board in the morning. They had been working ever since, with the skill and concentration of surgeons examining before diagnosis. They were now inspecting the oil-fired boilers and the steam turbines which drove the ship's electric generators.

The chief engineer tapped the main shaft that worried him. "You think we might have trouble with this?"

"Cannot tell. Must be—" The Indian sought for a word.

The engineer gave it to him. "Yes, the shafts must be in perfect alignment. But the other propeller is okay, I'm sure."

The Commodore appeared in the engine room and shook hands with the Indian. "Find anything wrong?" he asked.

The chief engineer answered, "There's a funny sound—he heard it too. But we haven't the time to tear down the propeller." He spoke to the Indian. "How long would it take to fix it?"

"May need new part. Two—three weeks—"

The Commodore shook his head. "Can't be done. Not with six hundred or so passengers. Did you find anything else wrong?"

"Nothing that can't be taken care of while we're here. There's a small job to be done on the reduction gears, and he's going to do some work on the boiler that's hooked up to the shaft we're sure of. We can't have a flareback there."

"Have him get on with it," said the Commodore. "Did you get a diver to look at the stabilizers?"

"He's still down under—here he comes now."

The thin brown diver spoke no English. He stood in the doorway until the other Indian beckoned him in. They talked in some rapid dialect and the diver pointed to the right.

"Well?" asked the Commodore.

"He say"—he pointed—"that one not good. Is bad rust. He says maybe go all right. Not if typhoon."

"Then we'd better not run into a typhoon," said the Commodore.

"But stabilizers don't worry me too much. We used to get along all right without them. People nowadays expect no more motion on the sea than in a bathtub at home." He said to the Indian, "Thank you, sir. Good to have you on board. Do your best for us."

But his face was grim as he went back to his quarters. He smoked a cigarette, then called Joan Scofield on the telephone.

"I wanted to take you to dinner onshore, Joan," he said, "but we're having some repairs made and I think I'd better stick around. Will you eat with me up here?"

"I'd love to. I hope there's nothing seriously wrong."

"I don't think so," said the Commodore.

CHAPTER NINE

MARK Claypole would not admit to himself that he owed Signe companionship, but he did stay close to her as they visited the Palace of the Winds in Jaipur and looked from a balcony to the rugged hills that were crowned with forts.

"Everything is such a lovely pink," Signe marveled.

"It's pink paint on the buildings here. In Agra the buildings are actually made of pink sandstone."

Signe consulted the tour schedule. "It's about time to go to lunch. This afternoon we go to a place called Amber and ride on elephants up to another palace. That will be an experience!"

"I'm sure it will be."

He looked depressed. But he joined her at the communal lunch and then submitted to the hot automobile ride to Amber, where the elephants waited in a hangdog row. "Take the one on the left," he advised. "He seems to have a little life left in him."

"They put four people on each elephant. We can sit in front."

"Not I. I'll walk up the hill. See you when you get back."

On his way, alone, Mark tried to figure out his distaste for these expeditions. He knew that strangers needed guides in foreign countries. Was it snobbishness that made him dislike being in a group? Or frustration at being shown only the obvious things? He

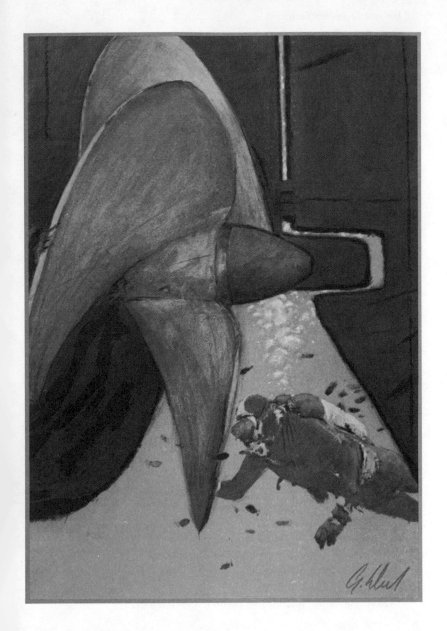

wandered through the palace, admiring the inlays which had glowed on the walls for centuries, then walked down the hill and saw that Signe was safely back, still sitting her elephant. She was a very pretty sight.

"You should have had that ride, Mark," she said as he helped her down. "Sometimes I think you don't like sight-seeing."

"It makes me feel a little like a Peeping Tom."

"Oh, Mark, you don't mean that."

"Probably not. But can I skip some of the rest of the routine without seeming an ingrate?"

"Why, of course! Do what you please."

He had taken a bicycle rickshaw to the old part of Jaipur, then paid it off and merged on foot with the native life. Sacred cows roamed the streets and camels and elephants were beasts of burden, not treats for tourists. Beggars were everywhere, though there seemed no one who would have anything to give them. He felt again the stir to write, not of the "sights" but of his own feeling of contact here with the core of India, and the curious pleasure of anonymity. He gave some coins to an old man and bought small bananas at an open food stall when he was hungry. It was dark when a rickshaw took him back to the train.

The plan for the next morning was for the party to be driven to the Taj Mahal in time to see it at sunrise. Mark managed to slip away from the group when the cars reached Agra, and again found a hotel which was *not* the day's headquarters for the tour. He spent some of Signe's money for a room and bath and then tried to record his experience of the night before. But the words would not come. He tore up the paper and went out to walk among the pink sandstone buildings. It was late afternoon when he came upon the Taj Mahal, and he realized at once how childish he would have been to miss it. He marveled at its perfection.

He was wandering toward the steps leading to the shrine of the tomb when he met the Chiltons, without the nurse for once. Hilary was happily surprised to see him. She wore a band to hold her straight hair back and she was very much Alice today.

"Have you gone through it?" Mark asked them.

236

"No," said Mr. Chilton. "Hilary doesn't want to."

"Why not, Hilary?"

She shook her head.

"Come, Hilary," urged her mother. "What's the matter?"

Hilary looked at Mark and told him. "There's someone dead in there. I don't like cemeteries."

Her mother covered her mouth as if to repress a cry.

"That's not what it is," said Mark. "This was built to keep some-one alive. Nobody can ever forget her. She was the empress Mum-taz Mahall. Come, let's see what it's like inside."

"All right," she said. "I'll go with you."

"Okay?" Mark asked Mr. Chilton.

"We'll be very grateful. We'll follow along," said Mr. Chilton.

Mark took Hilary's hand and she went with him willingly. "But I really don't like cemeteries," she said. "My brother—"

"We won't go into that," he answered firmly. "You look pretty."

"They say I will be beautiful when I am older."

"Perhaps," he said. "It's possible. But not if you run away."

"I will take myself with me," she said practically.

"You would get dirty. Your hair would snarl. You would smell."

"Why?"

"It would be inevitable. Now forget your future and let's go into the house that was built for the empress."

THE TRAIN jolted badly on the run to Delhi that night. They would have thirty-six hours there before the train took them back to the ship in Bombay. Alec Goodrich, pleased with the trip so far and all he had learned about India, knocked softly on Barbara's door. When he left her several hours later he met the priest in the corridor, but he was fairly sure that Father Duggan had not identi-fied the door from which he had emerged.

Aloysius had known whose door it was. They might have been only talking or playing gin rummy, he told himself. Possibly Bar-bara had been taking Goodrich into her confidence. He believed none of this but he needed the doubts and clung to them. He did not pretend that this was not stinging jealousy, personal desire of

a woman. And it was sin until he renounced his vow of celibacy. He should fly home from Bombay and tell the bishop that he no longer had the right to perform the duties of a priest of the Church. But he did not have enough money to do that. And if he did he would never see Barbara again. How foolish he had been to come to Delhi. Even if he could by some chance find Sebastian, he felt that he was now past help.

He was the last passenger to leave the train in the morning. Breakfast was to be provided at a hotel in the city, but he had no appetite for it and the thought of facing Goodrich and Barbara sickened him. As he was about to follow his companions he noticed a man in a cassock scanning the doors of the rear coaches.

"My God," said Aloysius, and it was not profanity but thankfulness for a miracle. "It's you, Sebastian! How did you know I'd be on this train?"

"It figured—and I didn't want to waste a minute. I've been counting the days since I had your letter. Now—you have no obligation to stay with these people, have you?"

"Not until tomorrow."

"Then we'll go home," said Sebastian. "It's only a short bus ride. If you wish you can say your Mass in my church and then we'll have breakfast."

But after they had laughed with the pleasure of reunion, Aloysius said, "I shall need absolution before I say Mass, Sebastian. And you may not give it to me."

Sebastian's smile vanished at the somber words. He said quietly, "I shall hope to. You do not look depraved. Perhaps a bit weary and tense. Shall we go immediately to the church?"

Sebastian's church was very small. It was made of wood, painted white, but the wall boards were rough timber. The little steeple, topped by a gilded cross, looked out of place among Indian huts and women washing clothes in a stream beside it.

Inside the chapel was clean and bare. There were no statues, and the pews were a few rows of wooden benches. But the altar was a table of white marble and there were polished brass candlesticks on either side of the tabernacle. Through the bars of the

window behind it the hot pink blossoms of flowering trees could be seen.

"I almost always have flowers for my altar, you see," said Sebastian. He genuflected and went on. "If your need for absolution is urgent, my dear friend, there is my box."

He entered the confessional and Aloysius knelt on the low, shaky bench behind the curtain. Their conversation went on for nearly half an hour before Sebastian said the words of forgiveness and dismissal of sin. Then, with his friend serving him at the altar, Aloysius offered his Mass and felt washed clean.

But the problems remained. Aloysius could not let them alone, and he found that Sebastian was as concerned about the Church as he himself was.

"It is not that I have lost faith in God or in the Sacraments," Aloysius said. "It is my faith in the infallibility of the institution."

"I know. There are times when it's hard to go along with doctrines that seem outworn. And harder for you than for me."

"We're both priests. Why should it be harder for me?"

"Because the Church accepts it that a missionary yield to the customs of the countries to which he is sent and make exceptions to some rules. I was eager to see as much of the world as possible— a thoroughly selfish motive—but also I had a hunch I might feel trapped in a diocese. Perhaps that trapped feeling is one reason why so many priests are dropping out."

"Partly, yes. But it's mainly that they are forced to support rulings which they do not believe are right. Against contraception. Against divorce. Against abortion, even if a girl is raped. Do you think such blanket prohibitions make sense today?"

"No."

"What do you do when you know the rules are broken?" asked Aloysius. "If you can't go along with the doctrines of Rome you should stand up and be counted."

"Counted as what? As a priest who is more concerned with sex relations than doing his own job?"

"What do you think his real job is?"

"Maintaining religion in the world," said Sebastian. "Without it

there's no hope for man. He will destroy himself. My job is to maintain Christianity. And the job of the Hindu priest is to maintain his religion. And the Mohammedan likewise. Read the Koran or the teachings of Buddha. They uphold almost the same virtues we do during life and believe that the soul does not die with the flesh. That's the great fear of man—it always has been. And the only hope. No, I don't think my priestly duty is first and foremost to fight a battle for the use of the pill."

"Don't you think it should be used in an overpopulated country?"

Sebastian said with a wry look, "Of course I think so. But the way I see it, we're getting off the track. Religious doctrine shouldn't be concerning itself with sex. Sex isn't spiritual. It's a function of nature. Our business, Aloysius, is not to argue about the act but to build up tenderness and devotion between men and women."

They talked in the cottage and then Sebastian took his guest to the open-air Moti Mahal, and they watched their lunch being cooked in clay urns heated with charcoal. They visited a Hindu temple, whose priest seemed to be a warm friend of Sebastian and gave Aloysius his blessing. For dinner they had a chicken brushed with spices and a delicious vegetable curry prepared by the old woman who took care of the meager housekeeping. There was wine.

Out of a companionable silence Aloysius asked, "Do you think priests should be allowed to marry?"

Sebastian said, "Well, a priest who finds celibacy too frustrating should marry. But I personally think he diminishes his usefulness to his vocation. A good priest cannot give too much of himself to one individual or to one family. He sets himself apart by his abnegation, and because he gives his life principally to God, people feel that he can link them with God. His celibacy makes him a secret person and his parishioners are therefore able and willing to come to him with their sins and secrets. Self-denial always came easily to you, Aloysius. I think," he added slowly, "that the desire you felt—may feel again—for this girl is more acute because it goes against your nature."

"Have you ever had such desires, Sebastian?"

"Oh, yes, God forgive me."

The old woman had spread blankets on a worn leather couch for Sebastian. He had insisted that Aloysius should have the narrow bed.

"Good night," said Aloysius. "It's been a grand day. There are no words to tell you how much it has meant to me."

"And to me. I shall hope and pray that you will not leave the Church. I know you are suffering but I am quite sure that you love the priesthood more than you could ever love life outside it. More than you could love any woman. Your bishop may release you but I do not believe you could ever release yourself. Good night. God bless you, Father."

AT THE hotel newsstand on her way to breakfast Barbara saw a copy of *The New York Times,* and a picture on the front page suddenly sent her into shock. It was one of three candid press photographs and the caption above them read BLACK TERRORISTS ARRESTED AFTER BOMBING ATROCITY. "The *Times,* please," she said numbly to the girl behind the counter.

She must hide somewhere to read this. She saw Alec Goodrich coming through the lobby, and as the door of an automatic elevator nearby opened she went quickly into it and pushed the button for the ninth floor. The hall into which she emerged was empty and there was a red exit sign at the end of it. On the fire escape outside she read about Boone.

The picture of him showed the splendid molding of his handsome head, but the face was angry, defiant, the face of the hard reckless character Boone Champion had become. He and his companions had manufactured bombs. They had planted them in several buildings, and a still undetermined number of people had been blown to pieces. The police had found the trail to the place where the bombs were made, and the city was outraged.

"No," said Barbara aloud, "not Boone." She stared at the picture and remembered how he used to look. She had met him first at a meeting where he had talked eloquently of justice and true democracy. He had seemed so noble—had been noble.

She imagined the reaction of her parents. They would be very glad she was in India. "She won't know anything about it," they would say. But on the fire escape of a New Delhi hotel Barbara knew all about it. She had seen him change. She knew that a crusader had become a criminal, but she also knew that Boone had once believed in making a better world, not in destroying this one. Through the haze of her horror she wondered if there was some way she could have kept him from this madness. If she had never met him would he have come to this? It was after they had decided to marry that he had begun to turn against her and to hate all whites.

It would be the death penalty, no question about that. The public was aroused and frightened. There would be nothing of Boone left, none of that brilliance and eloquence and hope.

She felt dizzy. She did not want to return to those strangers with whom she had been traveling carrying this hideous knowledge. Alec Goodrich—she had found it impossible to tell him anything about Boone, feeling that he would not understand. Father Duggan knew, though. Perhaps if she showed him this paper he would tell her if she was to blame. He would know. As soon as they were back on the boat she would ask him.

WHEN Howard Demarest announced at breakfast that he was about to present his letter of introduction to the American ambassador, Alec Goodrich had a sudden change in plan. It had been in his mind to go to the embassy because he had known the ambassador in Washington. But he did not want to be drawn into companionship with Demarest, so he decided to skip it and go instead to the House of Parliament.

Alec had also met the prime minister of India when she had visited Washington. It had been at a private dinner and he had been lucky enough to have a conversation with her, and though it was brief he had never forgotten it or her. He had been charmed by the great lady's beauty but even more impressed by the grace and simplicity with which she carried the weight of power. Since then he had taken a close personal interest in her career.

The intricacy of the political structure of India appalled Alec as he studied it. There were innumerable factions, separated by deep differences in religious belief, in habits and in language. The heavy problems of poverty and overpopulation hung over the whole country, but along with them rose the obvious efforts for reform and change and the ambition for beauty, wealth and sophisticated living. Alec was astonished at the contrast between the crowded picturesque squalor of Old Delhi and the almost exhibitionist modernity of New Delhi.

He bought some newspapers and read them as he lunched in an Indian restaurant—the New Delhi paper, printed in English, and *The New York Times*. He read the account of the bombings with anger and shame. Violence was out of hand in his own country. If he were in the Senate today he would demand action. But he was not in the Senate. That shamed and depressed him too.

The House of Parliament in Delhi was reminiscent of all buildings conceived for the dignity of lawmaking. There was no session going on and the guard allowed Alec to enter. He went down a wide hall, splendid with marble and mosaic. Several distinguished-looking Indians passed him, and a tall Englishman in a frock coat. Then Alec suddenly saw the prime minister. She came through a door held by an attendant and walked swiftly toward some other chamber. There was no way for Alec to avoid meeting her in the hall. But he felt sure she would not notice or recognize him and he gave himself the pleasure of observing the concentrated calm face. Her eyes lifted and, seeing him, a look of surprise and puzzlement came over her face. She smiled and stopped, close to him.

"Ah, Senator Goodrich," she said. "I am glad to see you."

He bowed over her hand very briefly. "I am very honored to have you remember me, Madam Prime Minister."

"I remember our conversation in Washington. I have often quoted what you said about the inevitability of a basic income for everyone in your country. From what I read you are making progress, Senator."

"Unfortunately I am not involved in the progress. I am no longer a senator. I was defeated for reelection last November."

"I am sorry to hear that. But it happens to very useful men. This I know well. And there is always another election to win. You will try again, of course."

He heard himself say, "Of course."

"How long will you be in India?"

"Only overnight."

"I would have liked to have a visit with you. But it is very busy for me today. I wish you success next time, Mr. Goodrich."

## CHAPTER TEN

THE lecturer told his audience the legend that God had given Ceylon to Adam and Eve to console them for the loss of Paradise. When they saw the whole island and went to Colombo and Kandy, he assured them, they would see how close to Paradise it was. There were not so many people as usual listening to him this morning. Many other events were competing with his talk. There was the final match of the golf tournament on the sports deck. In the lounge Joan Scofield was giving a lesson on the draping of saris. And a Late Risers' breakfast was now featured on the Lido deck. Signe Goode enjoyed every minute of those breakfasts, especially if Mark woke up before noon and joined her. He had not appeared yet. Although she would not dream of saying anything about it to him, she wished he would drink less. And write more. She had found one of his books in the ship's library and had read it, marveling. To know that much about people, what they thought as well as what they did, and put it all down was amazing.

In a corner of the lower promenade Father Duggan stopped by Mrs. Hartley Barton's chair to ask if she was feeling better. He didn't believe her when she said that indeed she was. The bruises were fading but her face was gaunt. "Another day that the Lord has made, Father," she said, smiling.

"Indeed it is. And how good to hear you say that."

Jim Bates in a very clean white coat came up to the priest and waited respectfully until he turned. He held out a note.

"Miss Bancroft asked me to give you this, Father."

"Thank you, Jim." He took the envelope and said to Mrs. Barton, "I must go along. Have a good day."

The note disturbed him. He had not seen Barbara since the last day on the train in India. She had not appeared for a meal since they had sailed from Bombay twenty-four hours ago. "Dear Father Duggan," she had written, "I have had some very bad news and would like to talk to you. Would you be able to see me in my cabin sometime today at your convenience? I would be very grateful. Sincerely, Barbara Bancroft."

Father Duggan went into the nearest public room and sat down to think. The television in the front of the lounge was turned on and a number of people were watching it. Vulnerable as he was to Barbara's beauty and charm, should he expose himself to temptation? It would probably be wiser to ignore the note and to tell her when he saw her again that he was sorry but he had been preoccupied all day with other obligations.

A staccato voice announced that this was the morning stock-market report. Julia Hayward sat staring at the screen, her handsome face not betraying the panic she felt. She had been aghast when she had seen in the paper in Delhi that one of the stocks she owned had omitted its quarterly dividend. And this unfeeling voice now stated that another of her holdings might do likewise. If she lost thirty-five hundred dollars a quarter how could she live? Not in New York on the twelve thousand a year that was all she'd be able to count on. As the weather report began she left the room.

It was a beautiful day, perfect for pleasure on shipboard, but Commodore James, Karl Van Sant and Fred Timmins were not relaxing. They were in conference. Timmins had reported that the fin on the right stabilizer did not seem to be performing properly, though the deviation from normal was small. "Of course on a sea like this the passengers wouldn't feel it," Timmins said.

"The weather's perfect in Colombo," said the Commodore, "and the long-range reports look as if it would stay that way until we reach Hong Kong."

"We'll have time in Hong Kong to fix the fin," said Timmins. "But by rights the ship should be put into dry dock there until we see if anything is wrong with the screw."

"And feed the passengers for two weeks at the Peninsula?" asked Van Sant. The chief officer was a man of fifty-odd, practical and unexcitable. He was less a seaman than a manager.

The Commodore said, "We haven't had any trouble yet. And you know we can't dry-dock in Hong Kong, Fred. The port is too crowded. But we certainly must get the stabilizers fixed. All these decks on the ship may increase everybody's fun, but they make her top-heavy, and if we run into a bad storm there might be some slight danger of capsizing."

"There sure might be," said Fred.

"Keep your cool, Fred," Van Sant advised him amiably. "We'll get back to New York with her all right."

"To San Francisco at any rate," said the Commodore. "If she does have to have extensive repairs there, we'll be on home ground. And more than half our passengers leave the ship at Honolulu and San Francisco anyway. Less said about this the better. I'd hate to have Demarest know that there might be a problem."

FATHER Duggan asked Jim Bates, "What is the number of Miss Bancroft's cabin, Jim?"

"Miss Bancroft is in Nine, Father."

The priest thanked him and knocked lightly on the door.

Barbara opened it immediately. She said, "Come in, Father. This is very good of you. Won't you sit down?"

She did not try to smile. Nor did he, after one glance at her face. He took the small armchair, noted the pile of half-smoked cigarettes in the tray on the table beside it, and waited.

"Father, did you see the New York paper in Delhi?"

"No, I didn't."

She lifted a newspaper from the desk and gave it to Aloysius. "There on the first page. About the bombings."

He read it and studied the pictures. Then he looked at Barbara. "That's the one," she said. "Boone. The man I told you about."

"It's a terrible thing, Barbara."

"Ever since I read it, I've been thinking. Thinking back. He wasn't like that, Father. He didn't want to kill. Like the rest of us he wanted to change things that were unjust and rotten—especially for black people. But he didn't want to kill anyone—"

"He must have changed greatly."

"He did. I told you he wasn't the same person. Father, could it have been my fault in some way? It haunts me. Could I have been to blame?"

"It's possible," said the priest.

Her eyes widened. Then she laughed.

"Why do you laugh?"

"Because I suddenly realized that I expected you to tell me I wasn't. I wanted to have you clear me and you don't!"

He said, "You mustn't allow yourself to become hysterical, Barbara. I said it was possible because you told me that this man came to feel that his love for you made him a traitor to his own people. Love is very close to hate, especially love that frustrates itself. His love for you turned to distrust—then he hated all white people—then it became hate for the world. Do you understand what I mean?"

"That if I had never had anything to do with him he might not have become a murderer?"

"I don't know that. You don't know it. And it's futile to speculate on what might have been. You have to face what has happened."

"Yes," she said more calmly, "that's what I have to do. I must go back and be a character witness at the trial."

"He wouldn't welcome you, Barbara. He'd resent you."

"You think so?"

"I'm sure of it. And think what the newspapers would make of your engagement to him. He would hate that. And you'd crucify your parents."

"But you say I may have been responsible."

"You couldn't atone for that by further exhibitionism."

"Exhibitionism!"

"It was probably more or less that from the beginning. You

wanted to be one of the far-out people, a rebel in public—rejecting convention—you still want to."

"No—it's not that. It was always more than that."

"Do you love this man now?"

She shuddered. "But I did," she whispered.

"You were determined to. You clung when he tried to get rid of you. As he did finally. You bolster your pride by thinking that you can never love anyone else. That's false. You probably never really loved him. He was your possession. In your own lingo, he was your 'thing.'"

He spoke firmly. Desire had left him. He saw this girl as she was, one of the confused young people in today's world.

"They will execute him," she said.

"Perhaps. But before that happens he may save his soul." He thought for a moment and then said, "When I go back to New York I shall arrange to see Boone. I'll try to help him."

"You will?"

"I promise that. I shall try to make him believe that there is a God who will forgive any sin that is truly repented."

She shook her head. "He doesn't believe in God."

"He may change."

"We all believed that the rules we were supposed to obey were wrong. Out of date. That if we protested openly enough they would be changed. We wanted to stand up and be counted. You know what I mean?"

He heard himself echoed. It was what he had said to Sebastian. "Yes," he said, "many of us wanted to do that."

"I still do want to. But how? Not by blowing people up."

"You'll find out how. So shall I. Barbara, you're very tired. If you could say a prayer, I think you could rest."

"Say it for me, Father."

"I shall. Tonight and again in the morning. Every morning."

THE STAY in Ceylon presented no problems for the excursion staff. Practically all the passengers would spend the first afternoon sight-seeing in Colombo and on the next day they would go

in a fleet of automobiles to Kandy, the town high in the green hills which always delighted tourists.

"The shopping district in Colombo is called The Fort," Joan Scofield told the women in the lounge, "and you'll see an absolutely priceless assortment of jewels—sapphires, rubies, emeralds. It's one of the biggest gem markets in the world. You will love Colombo but the big treat will be Kandy. I won't spoil it for you with my feeble description. You must see it for yourselves."

Signe Goode listened with a feeling that she would not enjoy Ceylon no matter how beautiful it was. And it was her own fault. She had only herself to blame. She should have known better than to talk to Mark about his writing. It was none of her business and he had a right to resent it.

It was on the train returning from Delhi that she had said, "Now we have four days at sea. You can get on with your writing."

"Is that a command?" he asked, and she knew she had said the wrong thing, sounded as if she thought she owned him.

"Of course not. I just meant you'd have time to."

"When Zola was lazy his mistress used to lock him in a room until he started writing. It's an idea."

He had left her blushing furiously at that word *mistress*, and she had not seen him since. He hadn't even appeared for meals.

She did not see him during the afternoon in Colombo. But the next morning as she was on her way to the tender which would take them ashore again she heard his voice. He was asking the purser if airmail went out from Colombo. Signe hesitated—perhaps she should go right over to him—but a tour director touched her arm and said, "The tender is about to leave, Mrs. Goode. We've reserved a place for you in the third car that will be waiting on the island." Barbara Bancroft had also been assigned to the third car and took the seat beside the driver. Julia Hayward was in back, and unhappily, feeling completely unwanted, Signe climbed in beside her.

The driver, a handsome young man, spoke cultivated English. "In Sinhalese my name is difficult. Please call me Joe."

He had an infectious smile and was so eager for them to be

interested in his country that the three unhappy women had to respond. Children dotted their route, naked and gay, waving at the travelers. They waved in return and Joe blasted his horn in salute, but he shook his head. "In Ceylon there are too many children. Many are always hungry. Many die."

"Could we stop in one of the villages?" Barbara said.

They stopped in one that was set beside a stream where children were bathing. The children rushed to the car, and girls and women came out of the huts to see the strangers. Everyone smiled.

Joe took his passengers into one of the huts, making courteous explanations to the people who lived there, and the visitors saw the lack of almost everything but shelter. A girl came close to Julia and reverently touched her gay chiffon scarf.

"You like it?" asked Julia, smiling, and she took off the scarf and put it around the girl's neck. Everyone was delighted, and Joe was proud of his generous Americans.

Back in the car Barbara asked what these people did for a living.

"The men work in the rice fields. Many women work in the tea fields because their touch is gentler on the tea leaves. Rice is their life. They eat rice in the morning and at night—there is never enough for all. Too many children," he repeated.

"No birth control?"

"We try to teach the women about that. It is very difficult."

"You're a teacher, Joe?"

"Oh yes. In Kandy I will show you my school. Also many of us work outside the school, teach in the villages, very practical things, how to plant other crops than rice, how to limit the family. But Ceylon needs more teachers—it is one of our greatest problems."

IT SEEMED to Barbara all day that she was lifting the brightly decorated cover off tourism and seeing what lay beneath it. While other passengers were entertained by dancers, Joe took her to see his school and the university campus. He introduced her to other teachers and she listened as they discussed their problems.

"When I first went to college," she told him, "I thought of becoming a teacher."

"But you decided not to?"

"I became interested in other things."

"It is unfortunate that the teaching profession lost you."

"I might go back to it. If I could teach in a place like this. Could I get a job here, Joe?"

"It is too bad but there is no money to spend for American teachers."

"Suppose I did not ask for money?"

He laughed at the joke. "That indeed would be the miracle."

Later at the guesthouse Father Duggan found her, watching the sunset. "It's beautiful," he said. "It would have been generous of God to send Adam and Eve here after they had sinned."

"After they had sinned," she repeated. "I would like to come back to Ceylon. It might be the answer."

She had Joe's name and address on a card in her handbag.


COMMODORE James was in a jewelry store in Colombo late that afternoon looking for the one gem that would suit her—and that he could afford. The manager hovered respectfully, pointing out the beauty of the jewels, but wisely not pressing too hard.

"That sapphire ring," said the Commodore finally.

"Very beautiful."

"The price?" the Commodore asked. When the merchant named it he raised his eyebrows and shook his head.

The price came down step by step. At last the ring was put in a small blue satin box and the Commodore went out with it in his pocket. He was annoyed at meeting Howard Demarest and Ruby Canaday just outside the door.

"Find something for the lady?" asked Demarest insolently.

The Commodore strode down the street, thanking God that Joan was not with him. He had been determined that there must be no slur on Joan's reputation or on his own as master of *The Seven Seas*. Of course there was no way in which even the prying Demarest could discover for whom the ring was intended.

His feeling for Joan Scofield was no longer casual. It had been growing for a long time and on the night they had dinner in his

quarters it had matured. They both knew now—and had decided that there must be no more dinners by themselves on board.

But the Commodore felt he must talk to Joan. So he had asked her to dine with him tonight at a hotel a few miles out of Colombo. He took a taxi and was waiting there when she arrived. She was wearing a white cotton dress and he told her she looked like a bride. Then he wished he had not said that.

"I do my best," said Joan. "I'm not a bride but I'm certainly looking at a man I'd like to marry."

"Don't make it too tough, Joan."

"You look a little tired. Is anything wrong?"

"We've had a few problems with the ship. We're undoubtedly safe enough, but things were not done that should have been done before we made this cruise. Penny wise, pound foolish—the owners may find that out when they get *The Seven Seas* into dry dock."

"If that man Demarest is a sample of the owners—"

"I don't know. There may be better men in the company."

"Rudolph, it's not fair. You should own the ship. You mustn't let yourself be wasted. What are you going to do?"

"I've given it a lot of thought. I might get a job with some ship-building company—maybe even the Navy could use me. And I'm going to ask my wife to give me a divorce."

Joan put down her glass, and her eyes asked the question.

"Yes, I think she will. I think she'll be glad to be rid of me. When I was younger and came home from voyages it was different. She rather liked to show me off."

"I'll bet she did."

"But the way it is now, I'd be in her way. She can live in the house—take someone to live with her, as she has before, or sell it—it's a nice piece of property. Joan, if I can't live with you I'm not going to live with anyone else."

There were tears in Joan's eyes but she did not speak.

Dinner was brought and when the wineglasses were filled he raised his toward her.

"But if you get a divorce—" began Joan.

"That doesn't obligate you in any way," he said quickly. "I'm

an old man and you're a young, beautiful woman. You should marry someone of your own age. And have children."

"I can't have children," Joan said. "And since my husband died I've never known anyone I wanted to live with except you."

"Aside from age we couldn't marry because I may not have any way to take care of you. I can't be sure I'll get a job."

"I can work. And you'll have a pension."

"I couldn't live like that, Joan, loafing while you worked. But I'll always remember our times together." He took the satin box out of his pocket. "I bought this for you today because maybe when you wear it you'll remember them too."

Joan slipped the jewel from the velvet nook and put it on her finger, then held it up for him to see.

"You said I looked like a bride. Maybe I will be one someday. But anyway I'm engaged to be married."

CHAPTER ELEVEN

THE DAYS were full to the brim on the run from Ceylon to Hong Kong. Although Bangkok was usually a port of call, it had been scratched from the schedule before the cruise started because of the political situation in Thailand. So for almost ten days *The Seven Seas* was on the ocean with unsurpassed good weather, and Joan Scofield and her assistants were busier than usual. There was tea dancing in the afternoon, the best movies were rerun, and all day long there were competitive games going on.

Nearly every night, before the clocks were set ahead an hour at midnight, a lavish buffet was set out on a long table at the head of the great staircase. The same people usually gathered around the feast for turkey or partridge, salads, cheeses, sweets, and of course highballs. Some occasionally walked on the boat deck for late exercise. Alec Goodrich always did.

Jim Bates came out periodically for a change of air.

"They're at it pretty late tonight, Jim," said Alec.

"It's quite different on our transatlantic passages, Mr. Goodrich,"

said Jim. "There's more people on serious business on the ship then. But of course you don't see the world the way you do on a cruise like this one."

"Yes, you see more of the world than I thought I would." Alec lit a cigarette and said, "I haven't seen Miss Bancroft around lately. I hope she's feeling all right."

"Miss Bancroft has been having her meals in her cabin. Sometimes passengers get tired of the big menus and just want a snack."

"I suppose so." Alec started to walk away and felt his foot slide toward the railing. He steadied himself and asked, "Jim, is the ship rolling a bit? She doesn't seem as steady as usual."

"I've noticed that myself, sir. It could be there's a little trouble with the stabilizers. They'll soon put it to rights. Mr. Timmins, the chief engineer, never allows anything to be out of order for any length of time."

Alec felt a slight tremor as he walked the deck, but paid no attention to it. His thoughts were on Barbara. Had he offended her? He went back to his cabin and telephoned her.

"Did I wake you up?"

"No, I was reading."

"How are you? I haven't seen you since breakfast in Delhi."

"I know."

"Barbara, is something wrong? Did I do anything to hurt you?"

"No, it's nothing to do with you."

"Will you come up and have a nightcap with me?"

"Alec—things have happened since I saw you—"

"I can tell that by your voice. Barbara, if you won't come up here, let me come to you."

"No, I'm sorry but I'd rather you didn't."

"You're in some sort of trouble. Let me come. I won't stay a minute longer than you want me to."

There was a pause. "All right, I'll come up for a drink. But, Alec, I'm not—there are things on my mind."

"That's all right. I just want to see you."

He had a drink waiting for her. She took it gratefully, and as she sat back in the armchair he asked, "What is it, Barbara?"

254

She shook her head. "It's hard to talk about."

"Did I let you down in some way? I'm afraid I did."

"No. I'll tell you so you'll know it's not that, know why— Alec, did you read about the bombings in New York?"

"I certainly did. Thank the Lord they caught those crazy black militants. They not only kill people and destroy property but they are ruining the chances of decent integration."

"I knew one of the men who planted the bombs. Six months ago I thought I was going to marry him."

"Good God! It's not possible—"

"It was possible until he ganged up with the *violent* blacks."

"And then you got rid of him?"

"He got rid of me."

"Incredible!"

"But true. Alec, you told me you felt you might have been responsible for that girl's suicide. Remotely, without knowing what you were doing. That's what's been haunting me—about this."

What she said gave Alec a bad jolt on several counts. He remembered very well how he had been tortured by the death of the girl in his apartment. Beneath his sense of outrage there had been the nagging, accusing doubt. Had he let her come to Washington because her hero worship flattered him? Had Barbara perhaps in a similar way led this man on to believe that things were possible that were not?

"You're building this up, blaming yourself unreasonably. I did the same thing. But you have to fight it. Did you come on this cruise to get away from the whole mess?"

"I had to get away. And it was doing me a lot of good, until I read that newspaper in Delhi."

"It's done me good too," Alec said. "I had a letter in Cape Town suggesting that I go back to Washington at once—and I nearly did. Then the thing here—the journey—pulled at me. I didn't want to leave. And not because I'm running away, as Claypole said most of us were doing."

"I don't want to go back at all."

"That would certainly prove his theory."

255

"Do you dislike Mark Claypole?"

"Oddly enough I don't. And he's certainly brightening the life of Mrs. Goode. You have to hand it to him for that."

Barbara laughed. "I rather like her. She's so unremarkable."

"Which makes her remarkable. Shall I freshen your drink?"

"No, I'm going to bed."

"And to sleep?"

"I think maybe I am."

"Make it a promise." He took her to the door of her cabin, pushed her hair back from her face and kissed her lightly.

THE SHIP's doctor was very busy on the day before *The Seven Seas* was due to arrive in Hong Kong. There were always hypochondriacs and people who wanted free medical attention. This morning there were some seasick passengers who said their stomachs could not stand even the very slight rolling. Or so they imagined, having read the notice yesterday that the stabilizers were turned off.

Dr. Sedgwick said, "I'll see Mrs. Beaufort first." He took out a folder with her name on it. Bettina Beaufort came in, looking excited and scared and very like a child bride. "Am I?" she said.

He smiled at her and said, "You're elected."

She gave a little gasp. "We didn't intend to—right away."

"Nature usually knows best. And sometimes putting it off means disappointment in the end."

"Well—we talked it over last night and Gene said that if I were pregnant he'd be glad. Now what do I have to do?"

"Nothing for the time being. Just go on as usual and if you have any worries give me a call. I'm right here."

"Thank you so much, Dr. Sedgwick. I'll always remember that I found out on *The Seven Seas.*"

"Good girl," the doctor said, and asked for Mrs. Barton next. She came in slowly, managing her canes, and as he said good morning he saw the difference, the failing.

"How are you feeling?"

"Oh, much better."

He made the examination, put down a few notes on her record and said, "I hope you're resting a good deal."

"I'm resting up for Hong Kong."

He frowned slightly. "You want to go ashore?"

"I can, can't I? I've had such good times there."

"Well, if you don't overdo. Where are you staying?"

"At the Peninsula. We always did."

"They'll take good care of you. Just don't go running around."

The telephone rang then, and it was Howard Demarest.

"I'd like to see you, Doctor," said Demarest. "Can you come up right away? I've had a kind of heart flutter."

Demarest was a table companion Dr. Sedgwick disliked. But he was a director of the line. And he was certainly not a well man. "I'll be back in a few minutes," the doctor told his nurse as he helped Mrs. Barton to the door.

Howard Demarest was in bed, wearing white silk pajamas. The doctor found nothing new in the condition of the heart, but the man was hung over and in a bad temper.

"Couldn't sleep, with the ship rolling," he grumbled. "They cut off the stabilizers. Damned inefficient. Things ought to work."

The doctor said, "They'll get them fixed in Hong Kong."

"And run up a bill for the company to pay."

"Stay in bed today," said the doctor. "I suppose you'll want to go ashore in Hong Kong."

"I have to. I'm meeting some very important people at the Peninsula Hotel for dinner."

"Well, take it as easy as you can." The doctor gave Demarest a tranquilizer and went back to his office.

Demarest soon fell into a heavy sleep and Ruby Canaday, coming in quietly, noted that. He didn't stir as she watched him thoughtfully, thinking not of him but of the Mikimoto pearls she wanted to buy in Hong Kong. She knew he had cashed traveler's checks yesterday. He had been very mean lately. He would not buy the bracelet she wanted in Ceylon. He would buy her some clothes in Hong Kong—he had promised to—but he would balk at the pearls. Noiselessly she moved over the thick carpet and

took his wallet out of his dinner coat. A few hundred dollars—she certainly had it coming to her. She replaced the wallet carefully and went from the bedroom to the sitting room, closing the door between them. She rang for the steward, and when he came she said that Mr. Demarest was not feeling well and must not be disturbed. Jim Bates said coldly that he would see to it. Ruby wrapped her yellow robe around her yellow bikini and went out to the swimming pool, rehearsing what she would say. "I looked in and Jim Bates was in your sitting room."

*The Seven Seas* LOOKED like the floating palace she was advertised to be as she sailed into Victoria harbor among the junks, freighters, sampans and warships. On board, the loudspeaker was calling Mr. Mark Claypole. "Please go to the radio office for a telephone call, Mr. Mark Claypole."

Signe Goode heard the summons and thought it meant that Mark had friends in Hong Kong. She wouldn't see anything of him but she hadn't expected to. He didn't want to be bored with her anymore. She knew it was wonderful to be about to see Hong Kong, but the ring of barren mountains and the crowded harbor did not seem welcoming.

Mark went to the radio office because it was certainly his name they were calling. But he couldn't figure it. His agent would have the manuscript he had mailed from Colombo by this time, but Milt Knott would never spend the money to call Hong Kong. Suzanne in Japan? She'd spend the money, all right—his money.

"New York calling, Mr. Claypole. You can take it in the booth."

The voice was distant but clear. "Hi, Mark!" It *was* Milt. "I wanted to catch you before you landed in Hong Kong. Your piece came. Phil Prentiss is nuts about it."

"'Pictures I Took Myself'?" asked Mark unbelievingly.

"The vignettes are great. Phil is going to feature it."

"Well—that's a pleasant surprise. What's he paying?"

"Twenty-five hundred. But the big news is that Giant is buying *Bird of Passage*. They want you to go to Hollywood and work on the film as soon as you get back."

"You're not kidding, Milt?"

"I'm not kidding when I telephone you on the other side of the world. I always had faith in that story. And 'Pictures I Took Myself' is a knockout, title and all. Been taking pep pills?"

"It's the sea air. Thanks a million. I'll try to believe it."

He put down the receiver, thinking of what he'd written—vignettes that were imaginary but stemmed from the truth of what he'd seen on this voyage. He'd put it over! He wanted to tell somebody. He wanted to tell Signe Goode. He found her alone on deck, looking at the nearing city.

"All set to go ashore?"

She started when she saw him, looking a little afraid. "Yes."

"We're going to celebrate in Hong Kong."

"Celebrate what?"

"What you did for me."

"I don't know what you're talking about."

"You told me I should get to work. And I did. For four days without leaving the cabin. I mailed the piece in Colombo. My agent just called to say he's already sold it."

"That's wonderful," said Signe. "I'm so glad!"

"And because you somehow shamed me into getting to work, I thought you'd like to know that it paid off."

"I thought you were mad at me," said Signe. "Sick of me."

"Never, dear. But after I mailed the thing I didn't want to talk about it. It's like that. When you're working on a piece it feels good, but when it's done you don't think it has a chance. I kept out of sight because I didn't want to sponge on you anymore and I was short of money. But now I know I can pay you back."

HOWARD Demarest said angrily to the purser, "You remember I cashed eight hundred dollars in traveler's checks yesterday."

"Let me look at the record. Yes. Eight hundred."

"And three hundred dollars was stolen from my cabin."

"That's a very serious accusation, Mr. Demarest. You probably just mislaid the money."

"It was not mislaid. It was stolen. And I know who did it. My

steward. Bates was in my cabin while I was under sedation. The money was in my wallet when I hung up my coat. It wasn't there when I started to pack for going ashore an hour ago. I want Bates searched and his quarters searched."

A voice behind him spoke. "You can't do that legally," said Alec Goodrich. He went on, speaking to the purser and ignoring Demarest. "I came down to speak to you about the same thing. Jim Bates came to me very much distressed at Mr. Demarest's accusation. I am confident that he did not take the money."

"What right have you to horn in on this?" snarled Demarest.

"To represent Jim as his lawyer if any action is taken."

"It will be taken."

"Think twice about that," said Alec coldly. "I don't know if you are familiar with the laws of libel but—since Jim is innocent—you might lose a great deal more than three hundred dollars."

"Gentlemen," said the purser, "nothing can be done about this at the moment. We are about to disembark and this office is always closed while we are in port."

Alec walked away as the purser closed the window. There was no doubt in his mind as to who had taken the money. Jim had told him that Miss Canaday had been in the room and said that Demarest must not be disturbed. But to accuse the girl was embarrassing and she was probably tricky enough to throw the money overboard if she knew she was suspected. He had assured Jim that he would take care of it if Demarest made trouble.

In Hong Kong the passengers from *The Seven Seas* went their separate ways. To tailors. To floating restaurants on the bay. To the top of Victoria Peak. Mrs. Barton did none of those things. She was weaker than she had thought she would be and she went at once to the Peninsula Hotel. From her room she called the housekeeper, who remembered her well. A small procession of special courtesies began. A floor waiter brought her a vase with a single orchid. Another came with a bowl of fruit, a third with tea and thin sweet cakes. Mrs. Barton was sipping the tea when the housekeeper came herself.

"It is good to have you with us again."

"It's been ten years since we were here," said Mrs. Barton. "The hotel is greatly changed."

"It is, but I think you'll find we've kept the old atmosphere."

"Yes," said Mrs. Barton, looking at the orchid, "you have."

Howard Demarest was impressed by the Peninsula. The place had class. He had calmed down after his anger. When he went back to the ship he would see that the Commodore took care of that thieving steward. Now he must telephone the people to whom he had introductions. Ruby could look out for herself. He told her tolerantly to pick out some clothes and put them on his bill.

Within an hour Ruby had found the shop she wanted. She looked at the beautiful cultured pearls on their black velvet cushions and desired them almost with love. Finally she bought a string of a hundred for exactly three hundred dollars and paid in cash. The salesman wrote a careful guarantee that they were genuine Mikimoto pearls, with the price and date of sale, and Ruby put it in her handbag.

Mark and Signe had lunch at Gaddi's, which, he told her, was one of the ten best restaurants in the world. He paid for it himself.

"What is your story about?" she asked over the coffee.

"It's just pictures of people—candid shots in words. A child who's known too much reality and had too little fancy. A worried priest. A rejected politician. And an elderly lady who lives in the past, not because she was left behind but because she likes it better than the present."

"It's about people on the ship?"

"Yes. You're in it. So is your Tom."

"Tom? But you never knew him!"

"I know him very well. I know just how he'd feel about a jaunt like this, how he'd hate the cost and manage to get his money's worth."

She stared at him in amazement. "He would," she said.

Mark laughed. "Let's find a bookstore. I want a copy of *Alice in Wonderland*. There must be one in Hong Kong."

Alec Goodrich had hired a car and driver. He called Barbara's room. "Wouldn't you like to drive to the border of Red China?"

"I'd like to see it. But I'm not very good company, Alec."

"Please come. It should be interesting and rather exciting."

They drove through the chaotic city, into the country, where the small gardens were cultivated in old traditional ways, and on into the hills. The low mountains of Red China beyond looked sullen and ominous. At the inspection point the driver borrowed field glasses for them, and they left the car and walked as far as was allowed. Through the glasses they could see the barbed wire and sentinel posts and the small settlement behind them.

"That's our ultimate problem," said Alec. "If we can't solve it politically, the jig is up."

She asked, "You're going to stay in politics, aren't you?"

"Well, I've been thinking. I could try for the House. The incumbent is going to retire next year. It would be tough. I'd have to make pretty much of a door-to-door campaign in my home district. Of course it's a comedown—somewhat humiliating maybe—but I'd have my foot in the door. Be in business again."

"You should," Barbara said. "Humiliation isn't the worst thing that can happen to a person. You can live with that. Or with rejection. But you can't live with bitterness or hate. They're like acid. They eat into you. They'll destroy you."

CHAPTER TWELVE

*The Seven Seas* WAS due to sail at two in the afternoon on Wednesday. Most of the passengers returned exhausted after two days of continuous sight-seeing and shopping.

Father Duggan and Mrs. Barton were among the few who came back refreshed. She had spent all her time in the hotel, sitting for hours in the great hall lounge where East had met West for many years. The flavor of travel on the grand scale was still there and Mrs. Barton had enjoyed it. Father Duggan had found a church where he was permitted to say his Mass each morning and had gone on a kind of retreat, contemplating his God.

Howard Demarest came on board in the morning, leaving Ruby

to wander among the shops a couple of hours longer. He showered and dressed in fresh clothes, and at one o'clock the bands began to play on the pier in honor of the ship's departure. He called Ruby's room but there was no answer, so he went and knocked on her door. She opened it, wrapped in a bath towel, and said she had been in the tub.

"Go ahead and finish your bath," he said, "but hurry up. There's quite a show on the dock."

He lit a cigar and moved her open handbag to give himself more room on the sofa bed. A small folder fell out of it and he glanced at it carelessly. On the white cover was printed in black letters:

THE ORIGINAL CULTURED PEARLS

MIKIMOTO

GUARANTEE

Idly he opened the folder and saw NUMBER OF PEARLS, and in ink, *100 (one hundred)*, LENGTH, *25 inches*, PRICE, *$300*. DATE SOLD —and the date was Monday, two days ago.

Ruby. It all fitted. That was the exact amount. And he had been fool enough to believe her story about the steward. In a gust of anger he started toward the bathroom door but a sharp pain gripped him. He felt for his box of pills and remembered that he had left them on his bedside table. He must get back to his suite. If he could make it. The pain had never been so bad.

A light went on in the steward's room; Jim Bates was wanted in the Mandarin Suite. His face became grim. He wasn't going to take any more stuff from Demarest. Let him ring his head off. He wouldn't answer. For five minutes he tried to make the decision stick but he couldn't. He went to the Mandarin Suite and knocked. There was no answer but he heard a groan inside. He opened the door and saw Howard Demarest lying on the floor.

"Pills," gasped Demarest, "box by bed."

Jim rushed to get them and knelt down by Demarest. He opened the box, and Demarest managed to put a pill under his tongue. "Don't go," he whispered.

"I'll just telephone for the doctor, sir," Jim said, and when he had done so he brought a glass of water and put pillows under the man's head. "I'd just lie there for a bit. You'll be all right, sir."

"Good boy. You didn't take the money. Found it. Sorry."

"That's all right, sir. I'm very glad you found it."

"I'll tell the purser. Goodrich too. If I get by."

Jim asked, "Would you like me to ring Miss Canaday, sir?"

"No." Demarest opened his eyes and looked straight at Jim. And Jim knew that he had found out where the money had gone.

Ruby was dressed, and slightly worried when she saw that Demarest was gone and the guarantee paper was on the floor. She tore it up and flushed it down the toilet. Probably Howard was on deck. She checked herself in the mirror and went on down.

Leaving Hong Kong was always an exciting sailing. The beautiful white ship had its largest audience here, a kaleidoscope of people waving from the dock, and the freighters and sampans saluting. Standing as always on the top officers' deck, the Commodore said a silent farewell to this harbor and that circle of mountains. Leaving each port on this cruise was a special wrench. Then he turned his mind to the problems that might arise between here and San Francisco. The wind was coming up.

Fred Timmins was dead tired. He left his assistant in charge and went to bed. He had been able to get divers to work on the stabilizers but he could not get the new parts he had hoped for, and they had done only a repair job. It would probably hold up for the rest of the voyage, though. Timmins fell asleep.

"This is a very funny book," said Hilary.

She ran to Mark with *Alice in Wonderland* in her hand. Under her blue headband her hair flew in the wind.

"It made you laugh?"

"No, not that kind of funny. I mean it is crazy."

"Why?"

"Because none of these things could happen. But of course it was just a dream."

"Not just that. What part did you like best?"

She thought a moment. "I think The Mad Hatter's tea party. With all the people and animals who didn't belong together and were always interrupting each other."

"Yes," said Mark. "It's like the makeup of the tables in the dining room on the ship."

She laughed. "My father said it was written to make fun of England and queens."

"People have had many opinions about why it was written."

"Why do you think it was?"

"To show the wonders of a young mind. Maybe to match the confusions of dreams against the confusions of reality."

"I like to hear you talk, Mark. But I never understand it all."

"Better that you don't, said the Dodo."

"If you're the Dodo, I'll be Alice."

Cora came up to them. She said, "You mustn't bother Mr. Claypole, Hilary."

"I do not bother him," said Hilary coldly.

"Not at all," said Mark.

"Your mother said you were to come inside when the chill came. And now the sun's gone. We'll go into the lounge and listen to the music until it's time for the lifeboat drill."

Hilary looked at Mark. "Off with her head," she said.

"Hey, you're not the Red Queen. You're Alice. Better go along. I'll see you at the drill."

He was pleased that she had caught the spirit of Lewis Carroll's fantasy. It proved, as he had guessed, that she had an imagination which could break through her stylized environment. When she ran away—as she surely would—it might be in the right direction. Mark began to feel the stirrings of a new story.

THEY had been at sea four days since leaving Hong Kong. The winds had been too high for games on the sports deck, and the semiconfinement created restlessness. When the notice of another lifeboat drill had been posted there was some complaining, but the bells at three o'clock were obeyed by almost everyone. With coats and sweaters under their life jackets, for the day was gusty and un-

pleasant, the group at Station Two assembled. They said that the sea was getting rough and, facetiously, that if it didn't let up they might really need those lifeboats.

Her steward had said to Mrs. Barton, "I'm sure you would be excused, madam."

"No indeed. I always attend lifeboat drills unless I am really ill. My husband always said it was inexcusable not to."

Jim Bates hastened to help her to the deck when she came out of the elevator, and she stood braced against a wall with Gene and Bettina Beaufort on either side of her. Demarest came out by himself today. When Ruby appeared he did not look her way.

Alida Barnes said to Julia Hayward, "You can see that something's happened to that affair."

Julia said, "Of course. And who could possibly care?"

Alec Goodrich stood by the rail with Barbara, watching the angering waves. Hilary was beside Mark, asking questions. Watching them, Signe Goode thought it was a pity he had no children. Father Duggan, conscious of the bleak mood of the passengers, knew he should be more of a pastor to these people. But he stood alone.

The familiar instructions were repeated and the bells rang for dismissal. As the passengers hurried from the deck there was a curious jerk, as if the ship had balked in its thrust against the waves. The Beauforts, who were taking Mrs. Barton to the elevator, instinctively reached to steady her.

"Seemed almost as if we hit something."

"Big roller, I guess."

"I almost tipped over!" exclaimed Hilary with excitement.

"Curiouser and curiouser, wasn't it, Alice?" said Mark casually.

FRED Timmins was playing gin rummy in the alley outside the engine room. He recognized the shudder which meant the ship had lost a propeller blade, and jumped to his feet. Within the first minute of his inspection he heard the voice of the Commodore through the communications system. "What is it, Fred?"

"Screw gone bad, sir. Shaft bearing. Turbine One."

"Build up more steam on Turbine Two and we'll count on her."

"It's all we can do now, sir."

"Everyone down there knows what's happened?"

"I expect so, sir."

"There is no need for panic of any kind. But no one is to give answers or explanations to passengers, or to any members of the crew outside the engine room. Those are orders."

"I'll see to it, sir."

"Have Boiler Two watched with extreme care. Build up steam but don't overdo it. When you have things fully under control come up here, Fred. We're a bit concerned about the weather ahead. I want you in on any emergency plans."

By FIVE o'clock every table and stool was taken in the Seashell and everyone was talking about the weather.

"The ship's moving smoothly again."

"I wouldn't call it smooth. My glass slides away the minute I put it down on the bar."

"They're putting up velvet ropes for people to hang on to when they walk."

"That's always done when it gets a bit rough. It's insurance against lawsuits. They don't want anyone to break a leg or a hip and sue the line. That right, Howard?"

"They'd have a hard time collecting," said Demarest. He did not usually patronize what he called "this little dump" but when he looked in at the Mayfair he had seen Ruby. He was teaching her a lesson. Let someone else buy her drinks from now on.

"Do you think we're in for trouble?"

"Not if the officers know their business," Demarest said, as if he had reservations about that.

"I'm sure they do," said Alec Goodrich, who was at the bar with Barbara. "It's a very competent staff in all ways."

The remark made the point. Demarest had grudgingly admitted to Alec that he had wrongly accused Jim Bates. The humiliation still stung. "The barometer keeps falling," he said shortly.

"Well, this ship is unsinkable," said a cheerful drinker.

"That was what they said about the *Titanic.*"

At the other end of the bar Signe Goode said to Mark Claypole, "Are you worried about the storm, Mark?"

"I don't worry. But there's uneasiness in this room. The refugees are huddling together."

A man with windblown hair came in. "It's really fierce outside," he announced. "The wind is getting much worse. I could hardly open and close the door from the deck."

As he spoke the ship rolled violently. Bottles toppled on the shelves and one on the bar spilled all over Demarest. He mopped the liquor from his pants and kicked away the barstool. "Hell," he exclaimed, "I'm going up to see if those fellows are on the job!"

The Commodore's private suite was at the bow end of the navigation bridge deck. The officers' quarters were fenced in and signs reading OFFICERS ONLY were on every entrance to them. Demarest ignored the signs and went through to the Commodore's sitting room. The Commodore was sitting in an armchair, looking grave but calm. Chief Officer Van Sant was on the telephone. One of the pilots was standing by as if waiting for orders. Van Sant turned from the telephone, stared at Demarest and spoke to the Commodore. "Mr. Timmins has cut off both stabilizers. The one that failed was the one repaired in Hong Kong."

"He told me he didn't think it would last in bad weather," said the Commodore. "Mr. Demarest. If you will excuse us, we are in conference."

"I'll join the conference, if you don't mind. I may as well tell you that I am expected by the holding company to report on conditions on this ship and on its handling by the officers and crew. I had intended to act only as an observer. But—"

"I have been quite aware of your observations, Mr. Demarest."

"What's wrong with the ship? It sounded as if she were breaking to pieces a few minutes ago."

"No, the ship is not breaking to pieces," said the Commodore icily. "But there is a wind of almost hurricane force, and one of the stabilizers has become useless. For your information, there are two fins, on either side of the hull below the waterline,

operated by an electric hydraulic system, and the fin motions are controlled by two gyroscopes. The fins are now inoperative."

"What's being done about it? Things were flying around in the bar."

"We shall have to adjust to some discomfort. Instructions have been given to rope off heavy furniture such as pianos. Ropes have been strung in the public rooms and on the staircases to assist passengers if they move about. We are going to advise all passengers to stay in their cabins after dining, and to stow away all breakables in their lockers. We are taking all possible precautions against personal injury. All stewards will be on duty continuously tonight."

"Have you contacted other ships in this area?"

"They will not be able to help us without endangering themselves if this storm gathers strength. Radar can work badly at times like this and we are having some electrical trouble."

"These things should have been seen to before the cruise began."

"You are quite correct," said the Commodore.

"You seem indifferent to the damage that might be done by your lack of foresight. I shall hold you personally responsible for damage to my company's investment of twenty million dollars."

The Commodore rose to his feet. He towered over Demarest.

"I hold you personally responsible, Mr. Demarest—you and the directors of your company—for the safety of my passengers—you and your penny-pinching group whose only interest is in your profits. I urged months ago that *The Seven Seas* be put into dry dock, thoroughly inspected and repaired. The answer I received from your company was a query as to whether the ship was in good enough condition for this cruise. I could not say that she would not stand the cruise. I simply did not know.

"The situation is that we have lost a propeller and are operating on one screw, which is possible but always has an element of danger. The electrical system is failing for some reason. I pointed out that it too needed a complete overhaul. The piling up of problems is due to the fact that your directors would not spend

the money to make *The Seven Seas* completely seaworthy under all circumstances. My personal fault was in not refusing to retain command of the ship unless she was dry-docked. I am going to do my best with the aid of my staff to come safely through this emergency and protect my passengers, you among them. Now get out of my quarters and stay out for the remainder of the voyage. Get out!"

Demarest looked from the Commodore to his chief officer and then at the pilot. He saw the same cold accusation in each face. He remembered the meeting at which the dry-docking question had come up. The general opinion had been that the captain of the ship was probably bellyaching—that maybe he got a kickback on repairs. He was an old fellow, about to be retired.

The Commodore did not look like an old fellow now. He was giving orders. The ship rolled violently again. Demarest grabbed at the edge of the sitting-room door and went out.

Commodore James turned to Van Sant. "I'm going to study the course a little more. It might be possible to weave around the storm. But I want every lifeboat rechecked."

"Getting the boats into the water and away from the ship would be tough in this sea," said the chief officer.

"They're good heavy boats, and we have skilled seamen to handle them. They've been thoroughly drilled. What we'd have to worry about is getting the passengers into them."

Fred Timmins came in.

"How's it going, Fred?"

"We're doing all right. Making only ten knots, but moving. We have better than a hundred and fifty miles of wiring on the ship, so locating the electrical trouble takes time. But we have the emergency diesel if we get a power failure."

"That will take care of the gyroscopic compass and the steering system. And the navigational lights and fire pumps."

"If the lights go out the passengers might panic," Van Sant said.

"We can't allow that," said the Commodore. "I'll ask Joan to circulate among the women with her assistants and keep them calm. She'd better come up and I'll have a word with her." He

had a second's lift at the thought of seeing her, then said to Van Sant, "I wish you'd make that announcement about people staying in their cabins after dinner. If they go to dinner. A lot of them are probably seasick. The doc will have his hands full."

FATHER Duggan also had his hands full. He knew now that he must do something. He had posted notices that he would have a service of benediction at five thirty, followed by an hour of confession. Mass would be offered at seven tomorrow morning. He added the final announcement as reassurance that he expected shipboard life to proceed in its usual way.

With the ship pitching and rolling he had expected a very small attendance. But not only were most of the few Catholics on board at the service; the theater was almost filled. The service was simple. He intoned the hymn in English, blessed the congregation with the Host and knelt on the swaying platform for the prayer.

"Blessed be God. Blessed be His holy Name."

They repeated the words after him. Finally he lifted his voice and sang the recessional, "*Holy God we praise thy Name.*"

The confessions he heard that evening were more sincere than any he had heard before on the ship, digging deeper into faults and failures. At the end of the hour he went back to his cabin, and Jim Bates came looking for him. "Father Duggan, a lot of people have been asking for you. I guess they're scared. I don't think you can see them all but I took the names."

"Oh, yes, I can see them all. It may take a little time."

"They took Mrs. Barton to the ship's hospital. She's one who would like to see you."

"I'll go there first."

The railings were up around Mrs. Barton's bed and she looked very frail. "Thank you for coming, Father. I wanted to speak to a man of God, though I'm not a Catholic."

"We are both Christians."

"And you believe in immortality?"

"Yes."

"It takes great faith. I am sure the doctor does not believe in

it. He and the nurses are kind, but I am sure they think too that there's nothing more."

"There is immortality, no matter what they think."

"I'm glad to hear you say that. I'm on the edge of it. Is the storm very bad?"

"The weather is very rough."

"I hope the ship comes through. It does not matter to me, but I've been lying here and thinking of these people who should go on. Young Mrs. Beaufort. She is going to have a child. I hope she is all right. Give her help if you see her."

"I shall if I can."

"And I think of Barbara Bancroft, who is traveling alone."

"She has great courage," said the priest.

"Some of these people I have liked so much. Some I disliked. But if the good Lord would take only me and spare the rest of the people on the ship—"

"I'm afraid the Lord doesn't make that kind of bargain," said Father Duggan. "I believe He will take care of all of us."

In spite of the Commodore's orders, word of the broken stabilizers soon went all over the place. The electrical problem was apparent. Lights flickered on and off for a few hours, then most of them went out. The elevators were not running. Joan Scofield and her assistants explained that the electricians were working and the lights might come back at any time; and that in the meantime the emergency generators were quite able to take care of the navigational needs. But as *The Seven Seas* shuddered and rolled, rumors spread through the ship. She was off course. The fire doors were inoperative. Alec Goodrich, holding fast to the window ledge in his cabin, saw towers of white spray fly a hundred feet into the air.

"In a way it's magnificent," he said to Barbara. They were watching the storm, not talking much, drinking a little.

Signe Goode and Mark Claypole were in a corner of the smoking room, sitting on a sofa that was bolted to the floor. He fell asleep and she was glad he did. She sat quietly, with him leaning

against her, telling herself that she wasn't sorry, no matter what might happen. All those places she had seen, all the things she had learned—she began to make lists of them in her mind as Mark snored slightly.

On the bridge the Commodore had been debating with himself, asking advice from Timmins and Van Sant, watching the course and the barometer.

"We can't take a chance," he said at three in the morning. "We're pretty badly battered and the passengers need a little time to get to their stations. It will be dawn within two hours and that will make it easier to get the lifeboats off, if we must. I'm going to talk to them." And he gave Mr. Van Sant the order to ring the bells.

Over the immediate shock and terror which permeated the ship the Commodore's voice came—calm, deliberate, and with complete authority.

"This is the captain speaking. I regret waking you and I do not wish to alarm you unduly. We are not in desperate straits but we are in a difficult and possibly dangerous nautical situation. It is a time for self-control and cooperation with your ship's officers. I am requesting all passengers to proceed to their lifeboat stations. The wind is brisk on the boat deck but with due caution there need be no accidents. Wear your warmest coats, hoods or caps and put on your life jackets. It is possible that we need not take to the boats, but it is wiser to be ready to do so. Thank you for your cooperation."

Jim Bates knocked at the doors of all the passengers for whom he was responsible. Alida Barnes was crying, but Julia Hayward was calm and he left her to take care of her friend. Father Duggan was first on deck. Alec Goodrich and Barbara Bancroft went up together and Jim was glad of that.

"Miss Canaday," he called through Ruby's door, "the orders are to go to your station."

"I won't do it."

He unlocked the door with his passkey and found her life jacket. "That sweater isn't warm enough, Miss Canaday."

"But it's the warmest thing I have except my white mink coat, and I won't wear my mink coat out on a night like this."

He almost laughed. Then he took the white mink from its hanger and wrapped it around her.

"I'm not going out there," she declared flatly.

Jim left her and knocked at Howard Demarest's door. The director of the line immediately appeared, looking very serious and wearing his life jacket.

"Please use your influence with Miss Canaday," said Jim. "She refuses to go on deck because she doesn't want to get her fur coat wet."

"The little fool," muttered Demarest. "All right, I'll get her out."

"And don't forget your pills, sir."

"My God, I would have," said Demarest.

The people gathering at Station Two, their figures distorted by the life jackets, looked grotesque in the weak light that glimmered from a few bulbs connected with the emergency system. It was a much larger group than usual, for members of the crew were here as well as some from the service staffs. Alec Goodrich saw Pat, the bartender from the Seashell, and Anatole, the wine steward, wearing a heavy sweater and no golden chain tonight. Joan Scofield carried a flashlight and helped people place themselves along the ropes as she watched for signs of hysteria.

Bettina and Gene Beaufort stood with clasped hands watching the officer checking the list of those assigned to Lifeboat Number Two.

The Chiltons appeared, the nurse following with a look of horror. Hilary said, "There's Mark. I want to be with Mark."

Julian Chilton moved cautiously on the wet deck with his wife and child to where Mark Claypole was standing beside Signe.

"Will you take her hand?" Mr. Chilton asked Claypole. "It will make her feel safer in this crowd."

"Of course." Mark tucked the child under his long arm and felt her shivering against him.

"Are we going to drown, Mark? Cora says so."

He looked down at Hilary and saw the same shocked look there

had been when she had asked if Cora was dead and when she had refused to go into the Taj Mahal.

"Of course we aren't going to drown," he said cheerfully, "unless you start crying. Remember how Alice nearly drowned in a pool of her tears?"

Someone heard that and tried to laugh.

The door to the deck opened and very carefully a nurse and Jim Bates propelled a wheelchair through it, in which Mrs. Barton sat with her usual composure. She was wrapped in an old-fashioned mink coat, its collar dangling mink tails. She wore a hat and had tied a black lace mantilla over it.

"Thank you, Jim," she said. "I'll be all right now."

Everybody stared at her. Her voice, her manner, the fact that she was on deck, gave reassurance. If she could do it—

Julia Hayward moved toward the chair with several others to be ready in case its brakes did not hold.

Mrs. Barton said, "Quite a bad storm, isn't it? I remember once when we were crossing the Tasman Sea we had to take to the boats. Lifeboats weren't equipped then as they are today."

Demarest said to Father Duggan, "You have to hand it to the old lady. She's certainly got guts."

"She has faith," said the priest, "so she is fearless."

Demarest spoke again. "My wife used to talk about faith. She wanted me to go along with her religion. She is a Catholic, and she's bringing up my boy and girl that way. In Ireland. But I never could catch on to it—what you call faith, I mean."

He was explaining a great deal to the priest, including the arrogance and the tawdry girl.

From where she stood Signe Goode said, "I wish Father Duggan would say a prayer. It would make us feel better."

There was a murmur of agreement as the priest moved from his place by Demarest closer to the railing. He did not hold on to it but somehow balanced himself and said in a clear voice:

"Dear God, we pray to You tonight, those who believe in You and those whom You care for even in their unbelief, that all on this ship may come safely through this storm. We ask that You

will give us courage if we must venture on the ocean in this life-boat. We ask that You will forgive our sins of commission and omission and give us true contrition for them. Let this angry sea and this tempest bring us closer to You and also reveal us more clearly to ourselves." He paused. "Now let us accept His will, without fear and with hope, and say together, Our Father . . ."

"That was a work of art," said Mark to Signe. "Glad you thought of it."

"The priest isn't scared at all," said Hilary.

Most of the group were silent now. Alida Barnes was crying softly and Julia put her arm around her friend with more affection than she had ever felt before.

Joan Scofield's lips moved. Under her breath she was praying, "Dear God, save his ship. Save his ship."

The minutes passed, built up to nearly an hour. There were sighs, occasional sobs, murmurs of encouragement. The spray still lashed as high as the boat deck but the ship seemed to shake and tremble less. Or was it their exhaustion?

"I think," Alec said, "that it's a bit better out there now."

"You think so? It hasn't been quite so terrible here on the deck since that wonderful prayer. You remember he said 'even in their unbelief'? He surrounded everybody with a kind of comfort, no matter what. I love Father Duggan," said Barbara.

Suddenly there was a flicker of bright light—out, on again, then staying steady. The lights stringing the decks illuminated everything. People looked bewildered and all at once began to exclaim and talk.

"Ladies and gentlemen," said the ship's officer in charge, "you must remain on deck until further orders."

They waited, obedient and tense. Then at last came the voice of authority.

"Good morning. This is the captain speaking. Electric facilities have been restored. We believe we have bypassed the eye of the storm. You may return to your cabins, exercising great caution in moving about until the weather is calmer. Thank you very much for your courage and cooperation."

CHAPTER THIRTEEN

THE LAUNCH that brought the customs officers aboard in San Francisco also brought mail and newspapers, and the people aboard *The Seven Seas* found that the ship's arrival was headline news. During the brief stop in Honolulu—only long enough to repair the stabilizers—the magnitude of the storm they had endured had become common knowledge among the passengers. Trawlers had gone down— "All night I wondered when we'd collide with one of those trawlers," said the chief officer. Two small cargo ships had disappeared and were being searched for by Navy planes. These facts had been kept from both passengers and crew until Hawaii, so that no further fears would be excited. Many passengers had been scheduled to leave the cruise at Honolulu. All the rest would disembark at San Francisco. Those who had intended to go through Panama were to be flown home. It had taken many cables between the Commodore and the line to complete the plans. Howard Demarest had sent a few of his own.

In San Francisco they found out that the eyes of the world had been upon the peril of *The Seven Seas*. Alec Goodrich picked up a couple of newspapers and gave one to Barbara while they stood in line waiting to have their passports checked. He glanced at the one he held and groaned. Barbara laughed. "You and the Commodore and Mark Claypole seem to be the big news."

"'Defeated senator on luxury liner.'" But Alec sounded more amused than angry.

The headlines read:

LINER SURVIVES WORST STORM IN 30 YEARS<br>
ARRIVED IN SAN FRANCISCO TODAY WITH MANY<br>
WELL-KNOWN AMERICANS ABOARD

There was a spread of pictures. A very handsome one of the Commodore, a youthful one of Mark Claypole and one of Alec which had been used in his last campaign.

278

"That picture of Howard Demarest must have been taken years ago," said Barbara. It was at the top of a separate column head-lined FINANCIER DIES AT SEA. There was a story about his career and his many holdings. Barbara was right. The picture had been used years before in a *Fortune* article.

"I never liked him," she said to Alec. "But it was a pretty desolate way to die. I heard it was hours before Jim found him."

"He died in his sleep. But he'd known his number was up."

"It must have been a shock for poor Jim."

"Demarest made up to Jim for any shock he gave him."

"How?"

"It's a curious story. I don't think there's any harm in telling you, though these things are usually kept confidential until an estate is probated. But you like Jim and I think it'll please you. It was the day after the big blow and we were limping along toward Honolulu when Demarest rang me up and asked if I'd come up to his suite. I liked him a lot less than you did and was going to brush him off, but when he said it concerned Jim I went, to make sure there was no more trouble. But there was none of that. He told me he had a heart condition and that it was touch and go. He was thinking of doing something for Jim and he didn't want to take a chance on waiting until he got back to New York. He said to me, 'That boy saved my life and I wouldn't have blamed him if he hadn't.' Anyway, he got me to draw up a codicil to his will and he's left Jim ten thousand dollars."

"What a lot! What a windfall for Jim!"

"Quite a bundle! That's what I thought. But he'd found out that Jim's great ambition was to take a course in hotel management. This money will see him through a three-year course and give him a profession."

"I'm astonished that such a man would do this."

"There was something to Demarest under all that bombast. He was always trying to prove he was the big shot and could get anything he wanted. And yet he knew there were things he couldn't have. Like the night he made an ass of himself when you were sitting at my table. My guess is that the storm shook him up.

279

There he was, no better than the rest of us, good only for a seat in a lifeboat. He couldn't demand his own life and he couldn't run the ship." Alec paused. "I'll tell you something else. He asked if I'd do one more thing for him. He had come on this cruise, he told me, partly for his health, but also as an observer for the company which owns the American Republic Line. Sort of a hatchet man to report on whether the ship was a good investment and where they could cut costs."

"He was always criticizing something. The food. The ship's officers."

Alec smiled suddenly. "Well, he'd made a report and had the ship's stenographer run off a few copies. He wanted me to take two of them so that if anything happened to him I could give one to the Commodore and mail the other to the chairman of the board. He kept saying all this was just a precaution. But he was obviously a bit panicked and he didn't look good. Once he stopped and took a pill. I think he may have had an attack that night. He told me he didn't want his report to get lost or to be delayed by a lot of formalities, 'just in case.' He insisted on my reading it so I'd know what he was getting at."

"I suppose it was sour, all criticism."

"No. That was what surprised me. He recommended that this ship be put into dry dock as soon as possible. And that Commodore James be retained past the usual date of retirement, at the discretion of the directors. This, he said, was because the Commodore had done such an exceptional job of seamanship which saved not only our lives but valuable company property. There would always be people who'd want to travel by ship, he told them, and cruises should be promoted with more advertising. They could be more profitable. Prices could be raised and costs cut." Alec chuckled. "Did you know *The Seven Seas* on this trip carried a thousand pounds of caviar and thirty-five tons of filet mignon, prime ribs of beef and steak?"

"Not really—"

"Yes, there was a lot of data. Demarest had nosed around and knew where the waste was. The company would know whose

responsibility it was. I think he had a point. Anyway it was quite a document. When I delivered it to the Commodore it certainly surprised him. 'My God, I kicked him out of here!' he said. I guess I wasn't the only one who had a run-in with Demarest."

"Strange he'd ask to have him kept on if they had a row."

"I don't really think so. He was paying the Commodore off for saving lives and preserving property in which he had a stake. But also that report let Demarest set himself up as an authority on seamanship—he was the one who knew what the master of a ship should do, he was the one who knew where the waste was. He was showing off as usual—but it was all to the good for once. And he couldn't help being the kind of person he was."

"Perhaps he was different when he was young. People change."

Alec knew that she was not thinking only of Demarest as she said that. He looked down at her thoughtful, beautiful face.

"Barbara, haven't you changed your mind this morning?"

"No."

"But you will keep it open? You won't slam the door on the possibility?"

"I won't slam it. But it has to be closed for now. We must be by ourselves to think things out. To try and work them out."

Last night in his cabin he had tried to persuade her. She had been tender, more responsive than ever before. They had talked.

"Why don't we go on together, Barbara? Get married? I think we could make something of it."

"Alec, I'm not right for you."

"I think you are. The other night on the boat deck, during the storm, I had a lot of thoughts. I was glad you weren't alone, that I was there with you—not that I could do anything."

"You *did* something. I wasn't facing the storm by myself."

"And I was proud that you weren't making a fuss but taking it as it came. I thought you were the kind of person I would like to die with—and then suddenly I said to myself, or live with."

"I like hearing that."

"Then will you take the chance and marry me? Right now I haven't a great deal to offer—"

281

"More than I would have to bring you. Two people who marry should not just want each other but want the same thing for the world. Share the whole job. I don't think you and I would."

"Why not? We both want a better world."

"I'm more impatient. You have more hope." She smiled, not happily. "I'm a girl without a country, in a way, and you're a patriot. Don't you see why, as it is, I'd be a bad wife for you?"

"You'll come back to your country."

"I may one day. But Alec, I wish you so well. And I'd be no help to a man in politics. I hate campaigns. To me they're false."

"I wouldn't ask you to campaign."

"Wives have to go along. Alec, I like you so much that I almost love you. But I couldn't marry you. For your sake more than mine."

"What do you plan to do?"

"For a while I'm going to stay with my parents. You know— try to please them, not frighten them. They've been pretty brave. They deserve a break."

"You're not going to try to see that man?"

"Boone? No. He wouldn't want to see me. He'd resent me. Father Duggan is sure of that and I think he is right. He'd know I was being loyal to his old self, the self he's shed with contempt. But Father Duggan will see him and perhaps he can get through. Help. If anyone can."

"I don't think you'll get much satisfaction out of being a dutiful daughter, Barbara. I don't like your plans."

"You haven't heard them all. I'll stay home only for a little while. Then I think I'll go back to Asia. Maybe to Kandy. They need teachers and I would pay my way. I had a curious feeling of being in a place that was right for me when I was in Kandy. When my unfinished business here is over—I have to know what will happen to Boone because I'll have to live with that—then I'd like to try Ceylon. It may not work."

"Will you keep in touch with me?"

She thought about that.

He said, "I won't bother you. Just a word now and then. So I'll

know where you are and how you are. And so I can tell you what's happening to me—you're closer to me than any woman has ever been, Barbara."

"I'd like that very much. It will be the way it was on the deck that night—neither of us will be alone to face the possibilities."

FATHER Duggan had said his early Mass and had his breakfast. He was packed and ready to go. To go back. He was writing to his friend Sebastian: "I didn't think at one point the ship would survive the storm. But it did. And I found out that any usefulness I may have in this life is as a priest. As a layman I could not have helped anyone in that time of danger and fear. So I survived my storm. There will be others, but I believe I have come through the worst one...."

It was a fat letter by the time he sealed it into its envelope. On the way to mail it he passed Julia Hayward and said, "Good morning."

"Good morning, Father," she answered, and there was a happiness in her voice that he had not heard before.

"Glad to be getting back?" he asked.

"Very glad."

"We've had quite an experience," he said, and went on.

She wished she could tell him about the letter that had come this morning. She wanted to tell someone, but not Alida just yet. Alida would say, "But you mustn't give up your lovely apartment!"

She was going to give it up. If she came back to New York she would live more simply. Now all she could think about was how glad she was that there *was* something she could do.

She had been reluctant to open Christine's letter. It would tell her that the divorce was final. It had told her that, but Christine had also written:

I hope you won't think I'm just a marrying fool. But in Mexico I met a man I used to know. He's in the Foreign Service. I always was a little in love with him— Anyway we are going to get married. Peter knows and I honestly think he's relieved. The thing is, Julia,

that Kent—his name is Kent Morrow—is due to go to South America in June for three months. He wants to be married at once and have me go with him and I don't know what to do about Tony. Peter suggested that possibly you might help us all out. If you could take charge of Tony for the months we'll be away it would solve everything. Would you be angelic enough to consider taking over . . .


In the lobby Signe too was reading the newspaper.

"You really are famous," she told Mark. "It tells all about you—your movie and when your article's coming out."

"I have a smart agent. Milt was right on the ball. He took advantage of our little squall to get some free publicity."

Hilary Chilton cut a path through the crowd of passengers, with Cora in tow.

"My father is waiting for me. We have to go upstairs and stand in line and then get off," she said. "I came to say good-by. I do not like good-bys."

"We won't fool ourselves with good-bys," said Mark. "When I finish my job in California I shall come back to New York and take you to dinner and the theater."

"To a musical?"

"If there's one worth our while."

"You really will?"

"Of course," said Mark.

Cora said, "You must come, Hilary."

"I am coming," said Hilary with dignity.

"You're so good with the child," said Signe. "She adores you."

He shrugged and she said nothing more. She was rather shy with Mark this morning. They had been in the Seashell last night and suddenly he had said, "How would you like to marry me, dear? I know I'd be a hell of a husband for a girl like you. But would you care to take me on?"

"Don't tease me tonight, Mark."

"I am not teasing you. I'm proposing the holy state of matrimony. Which can be more unholy than anything else in the world. Will you marry me, Signe Coode?"

"I don't like jokes about things like marrying."

"I am not being humorous. I have been considering this seriously. I need your steadying hand."

"Even if you meant it—why should you want it?"

"You want more reasons? Well, I like to be with you. You have a curious way of stimulating me. You're handsome and have a pretty figure. And then—there's all your money. Writers don't stay rich."

"I certainly wouldn't marry anyone who wanted my money."

"I gave you other motives. Don't you like the idea of marriage?"

She blushed under her sunburn. "I couldn't dream of marriage with anyone but Tom."

"I suppose he would be around all the time," said Mark gloomily. "Then you're turning down my offer?"

"Of course I am. And you didn't mean it seriously."

"Yes, I did. I anticipated possible rejection. But I don't like your going back to that apartment and being a lonely heart."

"Oh," said Signe, now on firmer ground, "the first thing I'm going to do when I get back is to get rid of it. I'm going to buy a house. Not a big house but one with an upstairs and downstairs and no elevator full of people I don't know. I want to find a place near a lake."

"Buy a lake," he suggested. "You've got the money."

"I'm going to spend money," said Signe. "I'm going to take more interest in things. Good causes. The night of the storm I kept thinking of all the things I could have done. Sins of omission, like the priest said."

"You're going to be a do-gooder? Take care, dear."

"I'll take care. And then I'm going to travel. Now that I know how to. I'll go somewhere every year."

"I feel better. Can I come to see you in the new house? And hear about the trips?"

"You'll be too famous. But it would be lovely if you did. And, Mark—I mean this. If you ever need any money—"

"I'll need you anyway, dear." He had leaned over and kissed her in full sight of the barman.

THE COMMODORE STOOD in his white uniform on the top deck. He felt, with a quiet exultation, the gentle shudder as the ship touched the moorings. They had made it. And Demarest had written that astonishing letter. *If they keep me on . . .* He saw Joan watching him from below, happily touching the sapphire in her ring. He had shown her the report of Demarest and she had wept. Ship or shore, he would not give Joan up.

The passports were stamped. All the luggage had been taken ashore, and the long line of passengers began to move down the gangplank. Reporters watched for familiar faces, and cameras snapped pictures. Alec Goodrich said, "Yes, it was a bad storm. Yes, certainly I expect to stay in government service."

Mark Claypole, when he was asked about the price for the motion picture, said, "You'll have to ask my agent."

Ruby Canaday had been singled out by a reporter and a photographer. She smiled enticingly.

"You were a friend of Mr. Demarest, weren't you?" asked the newsman. "That was too bad about him."

"Yes, it was sad about Mr. Demarest. I met him on board ship. I was traveling by myself."

Jim Bates heard. He turned and stared at Ruby Canaday with all the contempt he had tried to suppress during the voyage. His glance spoke, calling her a thief and a liar. Ruby's hand went to the string of pearls around her neck as the photographer snapped another picture.

# A Word from the Author

Travel has been a considerable part of my life and I have taken different kinds of journeys to many parts of the world. Often I was alone, traveling under difficult conditions in wartime, and I have flown over the oceans many times when I wanted to get swiftly from one place to another. But a sea voyage, especially a long cruise, has a quality of its own, and after taking a few of them I became interested in the reasons why people take such trips and how they are affected by them. That is why I wanted to write *Lifeboat Number Two*.

Some people go for escape from grief or failure, some from a desire not to be trapped in one place in the world. Others go to celebrate a marriage, or a solvent retirement, and many people take cruises to enjoy a luxury they do not have at home and for shipboard fun. When you put all these motives into a forced companionship—and sometimes a resented one—a cruise can be like a mirror held up to contemporary life with all its variety. Cruises have ridiculous features but they can be healing and can give some passengers new slants on life, renew courage and awaken a sense of the size and proportions of the world.

There are many books about ocean voyages but as a rule they are journals or diaries of travel. *Lifeboat Number Two* is a novel written not primarily to describe shipboard life but to tell the stories of a few people on board *The Seven Seas*, tying their past lives and their possible futures into the narrative. It also deals with some very contemporary social problems, such as the rejection of whites by blacks and the struggle some Catholic priests are going through in their decisions whether or not to stay in the priesthood.

MARGARET CULKIN BANNING

# BECAUSE I LOVED HIM

## THE LIFE & LOVES OF
### LILLIE LANGTRY

A CONDENSATION OF THE BOOK BY

## NOEL B. GERSON

ILLUSTRATED BY ARTHUR BARBOSA

She lived in an age of opulence, and
became its crowning splendor. Daughter
of an Anglican clergyman, Lillie Langtry
was an outstanding beauty who took
Edwardian London by storm. The Prince
of Wales was her suitor, the London
theaters her private domain. Headlines
blazed her name.

In America her triumphs were no less
spectacular. On one transatlantic crossing
she struck up a shipboard acquaintance
with Somerset Maugham. She told the
distinguished writer that the most celebrated
man in two hemispheres was Fred Gebhard.
Why, asked Maugham in surprise, was
Gebhard so famous? "Because I loved him,"
said Lillie.

Her ravishing beauty exalted or ruined,
but never left untouched, a multitude of
admirers. In this biographical novel
Noel Gerson records a life steeped in
success and tinged with scandal.

"Lillie Langtry," said John Everett Millais, the distinguished painter, "happens to be, quite simply, the most beautiful woman on earth."

"Lillie's beauty has no meaning," Oscar Wilde declared. "Her charm, her wit and her mind are far more formidable weapons."

"To look at Lillie," said the American artist James Abbott McNeill Whistler, "is to imagine one is dreaming. She is so extraordinary that not even I can do her justice in a painting."

When questioned regarding his supposed close friendship with Mrs. Langtry, His Royal Highness, Albert Edward, Prince of Wales, replied, "I neither affirm nor deny that I am acquainted with the lady."

"Lillie," said "Diamond Jim" Brady, "is the greatest there ever was."

"What I find astonishing about Mrs. Langtry," Mark Twain observed, "is that she has a genuine talent on the stage."

"It gives me a feeling of great pride," said William Ewart Gladstone, Prime Minister of Great Britain, "that Lillie Langtry acknowledges me as her friend."

"That woman is a real marvel," said Theodore Roosevelt, President of the United States. "And she's so pretty she takes away a man's breath."

*"Sure, we named our town after her," declared the Honorable Roy Bean of Texas, the self-styled hanging judge. "I dare any man alive to tell me a better name for a town than Langtry."*

*Artist Frank Miles, whose sketches of the fabulous Jersey Lily were partly responsible for her rapid rise to fame, was reluctant to talk about her. "Oscar Wilde usually speaks for Lillie," he said, "and her beauty speaks for itself."*

*Edward Langtry, the lady's first husband, for many years refused to speak her name either in public or in private.*

I

EMILIE Charlotte Le Breton lived her entire life as a contradiction of her era, and perhaps the greatest of incongruities was her background.

Her father, the Reverend William Corbet Le Breton, was dean of the Isle of Jersey and rector of St. Saviour's Church there. His wife, Emilie Martin Le Breton, was modest and self-effacing. Their sons grew up to be quiet men who took pride in their accomplishments and avoided the limelight. Their only daughter was an iconoclast who willfully smashed traditions, and became the most famous—some would say infamous—woman of her time.

The Isle of Jersey, the largest of the Channel Islands, has an area of less than fifty square miles. Although located only a few miles off the coast of France, near Saint-Malo, Jersey enjoys a subtropical climate, in part because the Gulf Stream sweeps past her, in part because her northern cliffs cut off Atlantic gales.

What nature initiated, the island's inventive natives developed. The use of seaweed as fertilizer has transformed the sand of Jersey into one of the richest soils on earth. Palm trees, tropical flowers and fruits flourish, tomatoes and potatoes grown there are prized by gourmets, and the famous Jersey cattle grow fat and sleek grazing on the extraordinary grass.

The people, about thirty thousand of them in Lillie Langtry's time, are even more remarkable than their tiny country. Long

isolated, Jersey was a part of the realm of the rulers of Normandy, and her "modern" history began in the eleventh century, when Robert the Devil established his summer home there. When his son, William, conquered England in 1066, at least two hundred Jerseymen were members of his personal regiment. An attitude resulted that persists down to the present. "We are England's conquerors," the Jerseyman says, and "technically, we *own* it." This spirit of independence is no laughing matter.

Jersey is self-governing, her parliament being an outgrowth of the old Norman feudal system. Her people are bilingual, and every Jerseyman speaks a Norman-French patois as well as English.

On this proud, individualistic island, Emilie Charlotte Le Breton was born on October 13, 1853, and welcomed into a family of five brothers. Another brother would be born within the next two years.

No one remembered how the girl came to be called Lillie. But one thing was certain: the name was spelled Lillie, and later the celebrated Mrs. Langtry reserved her greatest scorn for those who dared to spell it any other way.

Family recollections indicate that she was a tomboy from the time she learned to walk. Her older brothers protected her, but demanded that she hold her own in games and exercises. So she climbed cliffs and was an expert swimmer at four, and learned to ride a horse bareback before she was six.

Discipline was almost nonexistent in their home. Mrs. Le Breton, as the wife of the head of the Church of England on the island, as well as the mother of seven, was a busy woman. Dean Le Breton was so gentle and vague by nature that he rarely inflicted punishment on his children.

The family governess, one Madame Brisson, was largely responsible for Lillie's upbringing during her early years and taught her to read and write. But when the antics of the Le Breton boys became too much for Madame, she retired, and thereafter the girl was educated by tutors who worked under the dean's supervision. There were no schools for girls in Jersey at the time.

Lillie and her brothers were inseparable. Frank, William and

Trevor were very much her senior, but still admitted her to their races and other sports. She was closer to Maurice and Clement, and eventually her younger brother, Reginald, became her best friend. In the future, the glamorous Mrs. Langtry would feel at home with males but was usually shy and withdrawn with other women.

Lillie first achieved prominence of sorts when she sneaked out of the house one night with Maurice and Clement and helped them tar and feather a statue of Queen Victoria that stood in the center of Saint Helier, Jersey's capital. The deed was discovered the following day, and the culprits were identified by the tar on their hands, faces and clothes. The boys were spanked, but Lillie escaped lightly and was punished by being confined to her room for twenty-four hours.

Her later pranks, performed with Reggie, often made her a nuisance. The pair set up a raised trip wire that knocked off the top hats of visitors who came to attend the dean's annual tea. And neighbors complained because she and Reggie romped in the graveyard at midnight, pretending to be ghosts.

One practical joke caused her to be remembered in Saint Helier for years. At the beginning of the Christmas season, when people were paying calls on relatives and friends, Lillie and Reggie stole all the door knockers in the neighborhood. The finger of suspicion inevitably pointed toward the Le Breton children. For the first and only time in Lillie's life the dean intervened, and found the collection of door knockers in the cellar. He caused them to be returned, affixed to the appropriate doors, and apologies to be tendered. His children would not be permitted to participate in the holiday festivities that year. "But he relented on Christmas Eve," Lillie wrote in later years. "Papa couldn't help spoiling me, and I always knew it."

By the time the girl was fifteen she stood five feet eight inches tall, weighed one hundred and thirty pounds and was full-breasted. Her hair, described as Titian red, was worn in a bun at the nape of her neck. Her deep blue eyes were her most arresting feature, and Lillie discovered that when she stared at a boy he became flustered. She enjoyed the experience.

Reggie was disgusted by the change in her personality. When they went riding, as they had done every afternoon since they were small, Lillie now wore a big-brimmed hat and a long-sleeved dress to protect her from the sun. She smeared cream on the backs of her hands to shield them. And when he threatened not to go with her, Lillie told him, truthfully, that there would be no lack of escorts to take his place.

Her parents were introducing her into the limited social life of Jersey, and, always chaperoned, she attended dances, assemblies, beach picnics, and sometimes took walks with boys.

At fifteen Lillie enjoyed her first romance, although it was short-lived. Lieutenant Charles Spencer Longley of the British army, twenty-three years of age, was posted to Jersey, and as a son of the Archbishop of Canterbury he paid his respects to Dean and Mrs. Le Breton. There he met the girl with the Titian hair, blue eyes and mature figure, and promptly fell in love with her.

Lillie was too young and inexperienced to realize what was happening until he proposed marriage to her, and then she had to confess her age to him. The lieutenant was so shaken that he applied for a transfer.

This experience helped convince Mrs. Le Breton that her daughter needed the broadening experience of a trip to London. The following year Lillie and her mother went there, and the visit became an unexpected nightmare.

At first the girl was ecstatic; the world's largest city fascinated her. But she soon realized she couldn't cope with London. The people she met were polished, and she scarcely understood their aristocratic gossip, their talk of court and society, affairs and scandals. She had never seen an art gallery, never attended a concert or a professional theatrical performance.

The climax of the trip was a dinner party given in Lillie's honor by the daughters of Lord and Lady Suffield, part-time Jersey neighbors, at their London town house. "When I walked into the ballroom," Lillie wrote many years later, "I felt like a clumsy peasant. My one 'party gown,' which had been made for me in St. Helier, made me look like one of the serving maids. I had

never waltzed, and could follow the leads of none of my dancing partners. The food was strange, and never having seen so many forks and spoons at one's supper place, I had no idea which to use. I disgraced myself so often I could scarcely wait until the evening came to its abysmal end."

When Lillie returned to Jersey after that traumatic experience, she resumed riding with Reggie in the tomboy clothing of earlier years. She climbed rocks, she fished, she sailed. Above all, she avoided titled visitors from England. Young men who called at the rectory were turned away.

Lillie spent most of her evenings reading the plays of Shakespeare and Ben Jonson aloud to her father. "Between the ages of sixteen and twenty," she said in her autobiography, "I learned the magic of words, the beauty and excitement of poetic imagery. I learned there was something in life other than horses, the sea and the long Jersey tides."

All of her older brothers had gone off to various parts of the British Empire, and she understood their wish to leave Jersey. She saw no future for herself here, but she had no desire to live in India or to be stultified in the English provinces, which were no more interesting than Jersey. Her brief experience in London had taught her that it was to be the hub of her universe.

She intended to conquer it in her own way, once she was prepared for the renewal of the battle. She had had no training for a profession, and couldn't sew, cook or even clean a house. She had been reared to become the wife of a gentleman, and she would use marriage as her escape route. However, there was no one in Jersey who interested her, so her future husband would be a stranger. Until he appeared she continued to ride, climb, swim and fish. The exercise caused her figure to become even more supple, and she created a sensation when she wore one of her wasp-waisted dresses to Communion at her father's church.

Then, soon after Lillie's twentieth birthday, a large yacht from England, the *Red Gauntlet,* put into Saint Helier's harbor. In later years Lillie said, "One day there came into the harbor a most beautiful yacht. I met the owner and fell in love with the yacht. To

become the mistress of the yacht, I married the owner, Edward Langtry."

About five years Lillie's senior, Edward Langtry was a dashing young man with dark hair and black eyes, whose father was prominent in Belfast shipping. He was a widower, and was a friend of Lillie's eldest brother, William. It appeared that Langtry was very wealthy. His yacht was eighty feet long, and in his pay were a captain and a crew of five.

Hotel accommodations in Jersey were limited, so Dean Le Breton invited his son's friend to stay at the rectory. He accepted, and overnight Lillie mended her ways. As she accompanied their guest on walks, she wore her prettiest dresses and carried a parasol to shield her from the sun. She was so demure, in fact, that she even feigned seasickness when she went out for a sail on the *Red Gauntlet*. Her new attitude again disgusted Reggie.

An unexpected family celebration caused Edward Langtry to prolong his visit in Jersey. William Le Breton returned from India to be married, and all of his brothers came home for the great event. Langtry gave a ball for the bridal couple at the Jersey Yacht Club, and spent a small fortune. Lillie was enthralled.

Two days after William's wedding Edward Langtry approached Dean and Mrs. Le Breton. He said that his father had settled a handsome sum on him, and that he owned three yachts in addition to the *Red Gauntlet*. He had taken a degree at Oxford and had also studied law, although he had never taken the bar examinations. He was able to support a wife, he said, and asked for the privilege of proposing to Lillie.

The Le Bretons believed that their daughter was too young, and Mrs. Le Breton wanted the girl to enjoy the benefits of a season as a debutante in London. But Lillie told them that she was in love, and insisted on the right to be married. She did not reveal that she had already accepted a large diamond ring as a betrothal gift from Edward, and not until her parents gave their reluctant approval did the ring make its public appearance.

Dean Le Breton took charge of his daughter's financial affairs, and displayed unexpected sagacity. His future son-in-law, he dis-

covered through Clement, who had just been admitted to the bar, enjoyed an income of only three thousand pounds per year, which he realized as rent on properties he owned near Belfast. He also owned a fine house near Southampton. But his yachts had consumed virtually all of his capital, and the clergyman insisted that he sell all but one of them.

The dean also demanded that a settlement be made on his daughter, and Edward's father, Robert Langtry, was pleased to comply, for he was relieved that his son had chosen the daughter of an Anglican dean. So ten thousand pounds was put aside for Lillie, on the stipulation that she would receive the principal when her husband died. In the early 1870s that sum was equivalent to approximately seventy-five thousand dollars.

Although Edward wasn't as wealthy as Lillie had believed, she wouldn't consider postponing the marriage. He still afforded her the only means of escape in view.

The wedding was a small affair, held quietly on the morning of March 9, 1874. Dean Le Breton performed the ceremony in St. Saviour's Church, and Clement was the only one of his sons who attended. Reggie, who disapproved of Edward and was the only member of the family who recognized his sister's motives, had ridden off to the cliffs at dawn.

The wedding breakfast was held at the yacht club, and the bridal couple went off on the *Red Gauntlet*. After a month at sea, they went to Belfast for a visit with the Langtry family.

Robert Langtry approved of the shy but straightforward young beauty his son had married, and offered Edward a place of responsibility in his shipping business. Lillie was relieved when the young man refused. London was still her goal, and she had no desire to exchange Jersey for Ulster.

Mrs. Langtry, a quiet, passive woman, seemed to appreciate her new daughter-in-law, but they had little in common. Edward's young sister, Agnes, was awed by Lillie's beauty, and thereafter corresponded with her regularly. In all, Lillie's conquest of the Langtry family was complete.

Edward kept his word to Dean Le Breton and sold all of his

boats except the *Gertrude*, a yawl of eighty tons. He and Lillie spent most of their time on board the vessel during the next eight months, attending yachting regattas in Cowes and Le Havre and twice putting in to Jersey for brief visits with the Le Bretons. On both occasions Reggie left the house when he heard his sister had arrived, and did not reappear until she had gone.

If Lillie was truly in love with Edward she admitted it to no one, either then or later. But it was not until long after their marriage had foundered that she confessed he had failed to arouse her sexually. In all justice to Edward, it must be remembered that a wife in the Victorian era was not expected to enjoy marital intimacy; it was sufficient if she satisfied her husband.

In the late autumn of 1874 the honeymoon finally came to an end, and the couple went to Southampton, to a handsome mansion of seventeen rooms. Lillie was expected to supervise the activities of a trained domestic staff. She soon discovered that the housekeeping operation was smooth only if she left everything to the butler.

Now that boating no longer kept them busy, she and Edward enjoyed few interests in common. "We had so little to say to one another," Lillie later wrote, "that we began to eat breakfast separately. Edward usually went off to join friends in Southampton at noon, so we rarely spent much time with each other until we dined together in the evening."

Marriage, the young bride was learning, was not the escape she had believed, and London was still a distant mirage. Lillie had little patience with the Southampton ladies who called on each other every afternoon, played cards and filled their days with idle gossip. The provincial ladies never went out alone for brisk walks, and in their circle horseback riding was an unknown sport.

Lillie corresponded regularly with her mother and occasionally with her father. She also wrote a number of letters to Reggie, but was depressed to receive no replies. Bored, out of sorts and brooding, she lost her appetite and couldn't sleep. Then one morning she woke up with a raging fever.

When Edward discovered his wife was ill he jumped to the wrong conclusion, and announced to his friends that she was preg-

nant, a statement he was forced to retract when Lillie's illness was diagnosed as typhoid fever.

Her basic health was good and she soon passed the crisis, but her convalescence was as boring as it was long. As the days stretched into weeks Lillie had time to evolve a plan. Edward had rejected all her suggestions that they visit London, but he could not refuse the idea if it came from a physician.

Just how she achieved her ends with the doctor is unknown, but he told Edward that Mrs. Langtry's mental and physical health required a long sojourn in London, where the weather would be less severe and activities would keep her occupied.

Edward had no choice. He sold the Southampton house and its furnishings, and Lillie was ready to assault the city that had defeated her at the age of sixteen. They arrived there in March 1875. Not even she could have imagined what lay ahead for her.

II

LONDON, in the mid-1870s, was the center of the civilized world. The capital of Queen Victoria's still expanding empire was without a financial, industrial or artistic equal. It boasted more theaters and published more books than any other city on earth; its women were regarded as the most handsome and best dressed, its gentlemen the most powerful and influential.

Paris was still recovering from the disaster of the Franco-Prussian War. The Berlin of Chancellor Otto von Bismarck was still a country town. Vienna had music, medical research and a gay spirit, but its outlook was still provincial. The isolated Saint Petersburg exerted little influence on other cities. Across the Atlantic, New York, although pulsing with life, was brash, brawling and still crude.

So London shone alone, the mecca of all who sought power, fame and success. A step below the inaccessible Queen Victoria stood her eldest son, the plump, bearded Albert Edward, and his sweet, even-tempered wife, Alexandra of Denmark—the Prince

and Princess of Wales. Edward was the social arbiter, the patron of the arts, the titular head of the armed forces, the man who encouraged continued expansion of the empire. Alexandra worked tirelessly for charitable causes and showed a compassionate understanding of the poor that was unusual in her time.

Victorian London was not perfect, of course. The food, for instance, was execrable. "There is not one gourmet in all of Britain," wrote Victor Hugo, France's greatest living author and culinary expert *extraordinaire*. "Nowhere in the realm of Queen Victoria is it possible for one to sit down to a meal that includes a single palatable dish. But the Almighty has extended His infinite mercy to the English. He has created them without taste buds."

One of the strangest phenomena of the period was the cult of the P.B.s, or Professional Beauties. The name was a misnomer, for actually the P.B.s were amateurs; they were highborn ladies, most of them married, who dressed handsomely and indulged in exceptional grooming. Each inspired an enthusiastic following.

Behind the cult lay the new art of photography. The P.B.s were badgered by professional photographers, who distributed their photos by the thousands as advertisement for their talents. These pictures were seen in the windows of countless shops, on small billboards all over London and in the private homes of the poor.

The painters of London struck back by doing portraits of the P.B.s in oils and watercolors. They also made pen-and-ink sketches of the ladies which were reproduced in large numbers. A number of prominent artists made their reputations by these means.

These young ladies achieved considerable renown. They earned no money as models, they engaged in no work, but they did win status in socially conscious London. Certain unwritten rules were observed. Only ladies of impeccable aristocratic backgrounds were eligible. Under no circumstances were actresses, courtesans or professional artists' models allowed to become P.B.s.

Into socially competitive London, Lillie and Edward Langtry moved, renting an unpretentious flat in Eaton Place. For a month or more they were tourist sightseers, and each day they set out for a different destination, usually on foot.

Their idyll was interrupted when Lillie received a telegram informing her that her brother Reggie had been killed in a riding accident. She returned to Jersey immediately, and remained at home for several weeks. Before she left for London, her parents tried to cheer her by buying her a new dress. Always indifferent to clothes, Lillie was not interested in the black gown made for her by Madame Nicolle, Jersey's only dressmaker of standing. She and Edward led such a circumscribed life that she would have no opportunity to wear the dress.

After she returned to London, she and her husband resumed their sight-seeing. Life in London was so uneventful that Lillie must have wondered whether their move had been a mistake. Edward yearned for the life of a yachtsman, but he had sold the *Gertrude*, and could not afford to buy a new boat. And since he neither was engaged in business nor had any avocational interests, they met literally no one.

In later years Lillie hinted that her husband began to drink to excess during this period. At the time, however, she made no mention of his drinking in her correspondence with her parents.

When spring approached, the Langtrys had been living a stultifying existence in London for a year. Edward, grown desperate, was actually considering accepting his father's offer and entering the family's shipping business in Ulster.

Lillie was not yet ready to give up. She did not know what she wanted, but, as she subsequently wrote, "I was possessed by the conviction that my destiny lay in London. Not even the uneventful tenor of my life could rid me of the feeling."

With nothing better to occupy them, the Langtrys decided to attend the opening of the new Royal Aquarium in Westminster in April 1876. There, at last, fate intervened in the guise of Lord and Lady Ranelagh, one of the wealthy couples who sometimes visited Jersey. Lady Ranelagh invited the Langtrys to attend their Sunday afternoon tea. Lillie, who wouldn't have presumed to get in touch with the Ranelaghs, was delighted.

The grounds of the Ranelagh mansion extended downward toward the Thames on one side, and inland for acres on the other.

The guests, dressed in the latest fashions, laughed and chatted, and all seemed to know each other.

"Edward felt very uncomfortable," Lillie later wrote in masterly understatement, then added in strict candor, "As for me, I was badly frightened." But the daughter of the dean of Jersey looked like a remarkably poised young woman; she knew enough not to let anyone see she felt flustered. Wearing her unadorned black gown, with her hair fixed in a knot at the nape of her neck, she wandered through the grounds with her husband, then retired to a chair at one end of the gardens. She sat there for a long time, a simulated smile at the corners of her mouth, her hands folded demurely in her lap. She thought of herself as a detached observer, and had no idea that she was creating a sensation, that guests were questioning the host and hostess about the very beautiful young lady who displayed an air of aloof amusement.

Not until the following week did Lillie learn that she had been noticed. An invitation arrived from one Lady Sebright to a Sunday evening party. The hostess, Lillie knew from the newspapers, was a patroness of the arts. Lillie accepted the invitation, and only when she threatened to go alone did Edward agree to escort her.

Although clothes had never meant anything to her, Lillie realized it might be wrong to wear her one appropriate dress again. She was still in mourning for Reggie, however, so she made the best of the situation by lowering the neckline, and she changed her hair style slightly by twisting her long hair into a single braid and arranging it in a figure eight at the back of her neck.

The Sebright town house was a mansion on Lowndes Square. Lord and Lady Sebright greeted the Langtrys with vague cordiality, then left them to their own devices. Again Lillie sought refuge in a corner chair, and Edward, standing behind her, swore in a low tone that nothing would persuade him to be humiliated in this way again.

Then the greatest and most popular artists in London descended on Lillie in a body to admire her beauty and what was called "the artful simplicity" of her attire.

Leading the pack was John Everett Millais, the eminent por-

trait painter and member of the Royal Academy of Arts. A native of Jersey, he was delighted when he learned that Lillie was a fellow countryman, and before the startled girl quite realized what was happening, Millais persuaded her to sit for him.

Her second conquest was considered more significant, although the reputation of the artist has declined somewhat in time. Lord Frederick Leighton was a noted sculptor, and was soon to be

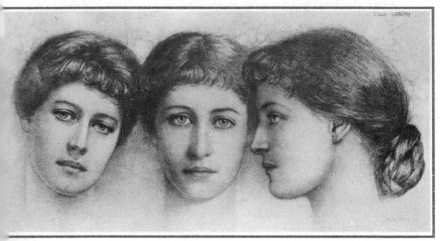

Frank Miles' drawings of Lillie

president of the Royal Academy. He made an appointment for Lillie to pose for a bust in marble.

A third artist who crowded around Lillie was James Abbott Mc-Neill Whistler, an American-born iconoclast. Homely, sardonic, and possessed of a razorlike wit, only Whistler took the trouble to present himself to Edward Langtry before bowing to Lillie. It was not accidental that Whistler subsequently was the only artist in London of whom Edward approved.

But it was Frank Miles, an artist still in his twenties, who stole a march on his colleagues. Miles earned his living by drawing pen-and-ink illustrations for newspapers and magazines. Taking a tailor's bill from a pocket, he drew two pencil sketches of Lillie

and presented her with one. The other, which was reproduced by the hundreds a few days later, was the first portrait of Lillie to appear in shops and to be made available to the general public for a penny. It was Lillie's initiation card, and made her a member in good standing of the exclusive circle of Professional Beauties.

THE following morning a steady succession of coaches drew up before the Langtry home as invitations from dukes and duchesses, earls and countesses were delivered. Mr. and Mrs. Edward Langtry were asked to attend dinner and tea parties, luncheons and formal balls, informal at-homes and formal receptions, weekends in the country. In one day they received invitations to keep them busy for at least six months. Perhaps the most significant was that sent by Lord Randolph Churchill and his wife, the American-born Jennie Jerome. The Churchills did not bother with people who didn't matter; there were members of the Prince of Wales' inner circle who had never been asked to their house. This invitation alone was a guarantee of Lillie's success.

She insisted on accepting every invitation. Edward protested. They were acquainted with none of their hosts and hostesses; the pace was too swift and they could not afford the wardrobes for such extensive party going.

But Lillie had her answers ready. Aware of the contribution made by her black dress, she would continue to wear it. She had waited all her life for the events of the past twenty-four hours, and although she had no idea what might lie ahead, she intended to find out.

Thereafter, his wife's new sense of independence caused Edward to retire permanently into the background. Although he escorted Lillie to scores of parties, flower shows, bazaars and entertainments of every conceivable sort, there were many ladies and gentlemen in London who, in later years, couldn't remember meeting him. He became the nonentity who was the husband of a celebrity.

The Langtrys frequently attended three or four parties in a single evening. Within weeks of her discovery, Lillie's presence was mandatory to ensure a party's success.

John Everett Millais canceled other appointments so he could finish her portrait quickly, and it was he who presented her to the great William Gladstone, who, out of office as prime minister for three years, was currently head of the Opposition. An exchange took place in the painter's studio that Gladstone delighted in telling. Learning that the lovely young woman with whom he was chatting had come from Jersey, he made conversation by asking, "When was it we conquered Jersey?"

Lillie's reply was swift, patriotic and truthful: "You didn't, sir. We conquered you, and England belongs to us!"

Few people dared to address Gladstone with such spirit, and he became Lillie's devoted friend. When scandal sent scores of aristocrats scurrying in the opposite direction, Prime Minister Gladstone, while in office from 1880 to 1885, and again from 1892 to 1894, went out of his way to be seen with her in public. He let it be known that he was her firm admirer. Lillie always claimed that her success was due to his help. Unlike many of his contemporaries, Gladstone saw the depth of character behind the lovely façade.

Millais, who first made that façade immortal, also gave Lillie the name by which she became known. For the sitting, he had her hold a crimson lily from their native Jersey. Everything concerning her had become news, so it was inevitable, even before the portrait was completed, that she should become known as the Jersey Lily.

Lillie was also posing steadily for Frank Miles, who turned out hundreds of pen-and-ink sketches, some of which were reproduced in magazines and newspapers, and many of which found their way onto penny cards. "My sketches of Lillie during her first London season," he wrote later, "earned far more than I've ever made on the largest commissions for my most expensive paintings."

Other painters also clamored for sittings. She could not refuse the request of George Frederic Watts, a member of the Royal Academy, who may have been the most distinguished portrait painter of the century. Still another painter who requested that she sit for him was Edward Burne-Jones. So many demands were

being made on Lillie's time that she tried to evade Burne-Jones' request, but he retaliated by serenading outside her bedroom windows at dawn, informing the entire neighborhood that Mrs. Langtry was a heartless vixen and an enemy of art. Lillie finally capitulated and the Burne-Jones portrait of her was painted.

Many went to great lengths to capture Lillie's interest. Perhaps none was so inventive as Lord Hartington, who interrupted a reception at his ancestral home to climb, in his formal attire, into a lily pond on the grounds. He pulled out scores of water lilies and piled them in the Langtrys' carriage.

Edward Langtry was not entertained, and on the drive home he threw the lilies out of the coach window. To his dismay a crowd formed and hundreds followed the coach, fighting for souvenirs of the Jersey Lily.

Overnight fame had its disadvantages, Lillie soon discovered. She could no longer go out walking or shopping without being followed by a large crowd. One day, to vary her appearance somewhat, she wound a band of velvet around her head and stuck a feather in it. By the following morning, every milliner in London was advertising the sale of the "Jersey Lily toque." And innumerable London hairdressers offered customers a "Jersey Lily knot."

What was astonishing about Lillie's sudden rise to fame was that everything she did was completely respectable, sanctioned by society. She did, in fact, nothing that could have offended even Queen Victoria.

Beauty alone was responsible for her renown. Her photographs found their way into the Paris press, and the readers of American newspapers soon became as familiar with her features as the British public. Within a year of her discovery at Lady Sebright's party, she had become the most dazzling Professional Beauty in London.

Among her new friends was William Morris, the noted Oxford professor, who was one of the most prominent authors and critics of the age. He always sought her out at London dinner parties, and was responsible, Lillie said, for the vast knowledge of contemporary literature she acquired.

Algernon Charles Swinburne, the moody, brilliant poet of re-

bellion, became attached to Lillie. "It was Swinburne," Lillie claimed, "who taught me the meaning of real beauty, the beauty of words and the images they form."

Dante Gabriel Rossetti, the poet and artist, painted her portrait, and she became friendly with him as well as with his Bohemian poet sister, Christina. Although the Rossettis were middle-aged they were young in spirit, and Lillie delighted in their literary arguments that often raged through the night.

Ellen Terry, regarded as the greatest actress of her day, became well acquainted with the Jersey Lily, and she predicted that Lillie's intelligence would someday surprise a great many people.

Two of Queen Victoria's children, Prince Leopold and Princess Louise, were friendly with many of the prominent authors and artists of the day, and Lillie met them at the flat of Frank Miles. She fascinated Leopold,

Famous painting of Lillie by George Frederic Watts

who broke royal precedent by calling on her at the Langtry flat in Eaton Place.

Once the prince expressed such admiration for a sketch of her done by Miles that the artist presented it to him, and Leopold had it framed. These facts gave rise to a story that may be apocryphal. Soon thereafter Leopold was confined to his bed by a cold, and his mother visited him.

Queen Victoria allegedly stopped short when she saw the sketch on the wall, and demanded to know the identity of the woman.

The prince told her.

Lillie's fame had penetrated the palace walls, and Victoria supposedly stared at the sketch for a long time. Then, according to the story, she climbed on a chair, and removed the picture.

One friendship which Lillie formed during the first year of her social triumph stood out above all others. Oscar Wilde was a flamboyant young Oxford graduate who was exerting tremendous efforts to attract attention as an author and personality. He wore suits of exaggerated cut and color to create talk.

Always conscious of publicity, he maneuvered so that Lillie's limelight reflected on him, too. What may have started as an attempt to advance himself soon developed into a lasting friendship. Wilde remained loyal to Lillie when her notoriety caused aristocratic London to drop her; and years later, when his homosexual activities sent him first to prison, then into disgraced exile, Lillie was one of the few who publicly defended him, and helped him with loans she knew he would never be able to repay.

Wilde conceived an idea for publicity purposes, and it caused precisely the furor he had anticipated. He wandered through London carrying a single large lily in his hand, and the thousands who saw him associated the gesture with the Jersey Lily. Cartoons showing him with the flower appeared in several newspapers, so he began to wear a lily regularly on his lapel. The flower continued to be an integral part of his appearance up to the time of his trial and imprisonment.

Lillie's life was not all adulation, however. On one occasion, she, who was almost totally ignorant of world affairs, made an error that created international laughter. In her favor, however, is the fact that she freely admitted the blunder.

A distinguished American, the bearded General Ulysses Simpson Grant, and his wife were guests of honor at a dinner party to which Lillie was invited. Grant was accorded the privilege of escorting the Jersey Lily to the table, and as they walked into the dining room she froze all who heard her by asking, "What have you done since your Civil War, General?"

A number of witnesses said there was a gleam of humor in Grant's eyes as he replied, "Well, I've served two terms as President of the United States, Mrs. Langtry."

Not until Lillie had completed her first tour of the United States did the American people allow her to forget her mistake, and the

newspapers in city after city invariably referred to it, relenting only when the editors and reporters had succumbed to her charms.

The successes of Lillie's social life were balanced by the steady deterioration of her marriage. Edward Langtry grew increasingly exhausted by the endless social whirl. Everywhere Lillie was the center of attention, and he remained in the background.

Within a year of Lillie's discovery, she and Edward slept in separate bedrooms. And Edward no longer acted as his wife's faithful watchdog. For propriety's sake he continued to accompany her to dinners, dances and other formal functions, sometimes falling asleep in a chair. Days, however, Edward vanished, and Lillie went alone for her portrait sittings, to teas and luncheons.

One of the fixed events of literary and artistic London was the weekly Sunday breakfast given by James Whistler. The painter cooked such typically American dishes as flapjacks and sourdough biscuits, and the food as well as the company guaranteed that his flat would be crowded. Lillie became a regular at these functions, and was soon recognized as the queen of the group. Everyone paid court to her, read poems dedicated to her or showed the progress he had made in his portrait of her.

Lillie relished her Sundays at Whistler's, but Edward Langtry refused to accompany her. The unceasing, undiluted praise heaped on his wife had become sickening, and he preferred to sleep late, then turn to the solace of his whisky bottle. It was an open secret now that Edward Langtry was drinking too much.

But Lillie remained loyal to her husband. She refused to listen to criticism of him, and said nothing that might be construed as antipathetic toward him. Any man who reasoned that the breakdown of her marriage made her more vulnerable to a new romance received no encouragement from the Jersey Lily herself.

At the end of Lillie's first season as a Professional Beauty, a change took place in her appearance. Until now she had worn her black dress to every social event. It had become her trademark, and her public had never seen her wear anything else.

Then, one night, Mary Cornwallis-West borrowed the dress to wear to a concert at Covent Garden. Lillie was indisposed, and

Mrs. Cornwallis-West, reputedly a close friend of the Prince of Wales, hoped the novelty of appearing in the dress of a rival Professional Beauty would restore her to the limelight.

The dress was worn and tired, and perhaps Mrs. Cornwallis-West failed to treat it respectfully. She returned a dress that had literally come apart at the seams.

Lillie faced a social crisis. She and Edward had been invited to

Lillie and her husband Edward Langtry

a grand ball, being given within forty-eight hours, by Lord and Lady Dudley in honor of King Leopold of the Belgians. It was rumored that the Prince of Wales would attend.

So she went to a Mrs. Stratton, one of London's leading dressmakers, and promptly learned a valuable lesson. Mrs. Stratton was so pleased she had been given the opportunity to dress the Jersey Lily that, knowing her business would boom, she charged only a pittance for a magnificent Grecian-draped gown of white velvet. Edward was so delighted by the price that he told Lillie to buy several more gowns.

The Jersey Lily was so ravishing in white that she created a sensation equal to that of her initial triumph.

That week marked a definite change in Edward Langtry's attitude. Money, which had been one of his principal concerns, no longer seemed to matter to him. First he gave Lillie a regular clothing allowance. Then he suggested they move to a larger flat, and seemed pleased when she found one on Norfolk Street, in one of the most fashionable districts in London. And he urged her to hire a second maid.

Lillie suspected, but could not prove, that several of her wealthy

admirers were paying Edward to arrange her schedule in ways that would enable them to be seen more frequently in her company, at the expense of their rivals. She confided in Frank Miles and Oscar Wilde, who exchanged notes on the subject, thereby recording the matter for posterity. But neither then nor at any later time was Lillie able to confirm her suspicions.

Certain straws in the wind made her believe she was right. She had unfailingly returned jewelry and other expensive gifts from her admirers, and Edward had been indignant when he learned of these attempts to buy her affections. But he displayed a far different attitude toward Moreton Frewen, a wealthy and dashing young aristocrat from Leicestershire, who presented Lillie with a spirited horse named Redskin.

Edward did not protest, and her own desire to own a horse finally overcame her. It had been a long time since she had ridden regularly, and she had missed the sport.

If Frewen had hoped he would have Lillie to himself on her morning rides, he was mistaken. So many men appeared to escort her that the group soon became known as Langtry's Lancers, and one of the most repeated jokes in town was that Lillie's bodyguard was larger than the queen's household regiment of Grenadier Guards.

Frewen complained bitterly, and then took Edward off on a three-day fishing trip.

The relationships were becoming complex, and Lillie's friends grew worried. She had been safe enough while her husband had acted as her watchdog, but his changed attitude weakened her position, and she might not be able to resist the advances of every suitor who pursued her. She was still young and impressionable, and many saw dangers ahead.

Lillie laughed at their fears. She was interested in all men, she told them, but wanted romance with none.

Their concern persisted, and Oscar Wilde wrote to Miles, "The nobility of human nature is confounded and mocked by our universal weaknesses, so I have cause to believe the Lily is ripe for adventure."

## III

ALBERT EDWARD, Prince of Wales, the second child and eldest son of Queen Victoria and Prince Consort Albert, celebrated his thirty-sixth birthday in 1877, the year Lillie Langtry turned twenty-four. He had been married for fourteen years to Princess Alexandra of Denmark, who was tremendously popular with people of every class in Great Britain.

The prince himself enjoyed considerable sympathy, and his future subjects agreed that his lot was not an easy one. His mother was stern and devoted to duty, and although she expected a great deal of him, she constantly displayed a reluctance to give him any authority. Her whims determined the patterns of his life.

In spite of this handicap, Prince Albert Edward worked hard to discharge his obligations. Thanks largely to his untiring efforts during his journey to India in the autumn of 1875, Queen Victoria was crowned Empress of India the following year. He was the first member of his family to show an understanding of the "Irish question" that had plagued Britain for centuries; he persuaded the government to adopt a more enlightened attitude toward the long-impoverished and oppressed people of Ireland. At home the Prince of Wales made the innumerable public appearances expected of royalty, taking the place of his mother at most events, since Queen Victoria had gone into semiretirement after the death of the prince consort.

The line of succession from Prince Albert Edward was assured. From 1864, when Prince Albert Victor, later the Duke of Clarence, was born, to 1869, when Princess Maud Charlotte Mary Victoria came into the world, Princess Alexandra gave birth to five children, two sons and three daughters. The second son of the Prince and Princess of Wales eventually became King George V, following the death of his elder brother.

The British people generously forgave the future Edward VII his weaknesses, which were those of the aristocracy of his day.

They placed bets on the champions in his large stable of racing horses. They read avidly about the magnificent royal yacht on which he cruised.

Full-bearded, more than six feet tall, and portly, Albert Edward had a discerning eye for feminine beauty. Certainly his attitude was no worse that that of other blue bloods. During the Victorian era, no one thought less of a gentleman if he strayed from home and hearth, provided his behavior was discreet. The wives of gentlemen who strayed were expected to smile, to remain good wives and mothers and to behave as though nothing had disturbed the even tenor of their marriages.

There were few ladies in England who smiled more steadily than Princess Alexandra. She had not only done her duty by giving her husband—and the empire—five children in as many years, but everyone knew, after all, that royal marriages were conveniences of state and not immortal romances.

The precise extent of Prince Albert Edward's dalliances is not known, for a heavy curtain of discretion surrounded him, and it was a tradition of the British press, abetted by some of the most stringent libel laws on earth, to maintain a total silence about the private lives of royalty.

Almost inevitably, the name of one or another Professional Beauty was linked with that of Prince Albert Edward, and at least some of them did not seem to mind. When the Prince of Wales paid special attention to a Professional Beauty, London's high society responded with extraordinary sensitivity. She was invited to every dinner, dance and weekend house party at which he, too, would be a guest. The meaning of the sobriquet "a friend of the Prince of Wales" was clear to everyone.

Oddly, ladies who had enjoyed this standing displayed no overt signs of jealousy when Albert Edward turned away from them. They had known from the outset that the relationship would be a fleeting one. What was more, the Prince of Wales never dropped a lady so hard that she felt bruised. He always remained attentive, courtly and pleasant, no matter how much time had passed since he had lost personal interest in her.

One of the favorite pastimes of social London, after Lillie Langtry burst onto the scene as a Professional Beauty, was engaging in speculation regarding what would happen when Prince Albert Edward met her. It was taken for granted that the prince, with his unerring eye for beauty, would be quick to develop an interest in her. But those who knew Lillie best, or thought they did, were convinced she would reject any advances he might make.

For more than a year she had spurned many men far more handsome and aggressive than the prince. Regardless of her arrangement with the nonentity to whom she was married, she was still faithful to him. And she was quick to cut any man who became too persistent in his advances.

There were many who agreed with the irreverent Wilde's prognosis. The prince was a mortal man, he said, and therefore would be smitten. Lillie would be flattered by his attentions, but he would never take a single step beyond the Langtry parlor. He would recognize her purity, and would be satisfied if he sat beside her at an occasional dinner party.

What puzzled many in London society was that Lillie and the Prince of Wales had never met. On the night of the ball for King Leopold, the prince had been forced to take to his bed with a mild upset and had sent his regrets. When the meeting did finally take place, it was totally unplanned. Lillie and her husband had gone to the home of Sir Allen Young for a small supper party. Suddenly, in the midst of the meal, the Prince of Wales appeared, loudly demanding a dish of the lobster curry for which Young was famous.

The Langtrys were presented to the prince. Lillie curtsied, the prince nodded, and then told a story to his host. Anyone expecting fireworks was disappointed.

According to the vague reports that seeped out later, the Prince of Wales offered the Jersey Lily a compliment before he departed, saying something to the effect that she was far more beautiful than her photographs and portraits. The party broke up, and a disappointed London considered the evening anticlimactic.

It was at this juncture that a burly English manufacturer in his sixties, C. J. Freake, entered the picture. A product of the working

class, the shrewd Freake had become a multimillionaire, and he and his wife were busy working their way up the social ladder. He owned a large home in one of London's most fashionable districts, and he was known to be a friend of the Prince of Wales.

Freake was one of a very few people whose company Edward Langtry enjoyed, and they often met for lunch. Freake was able to give the younger man advice on investments, and, according to subsequent speculation, it may have been through his help that Edward had been able to rent the larger flat, hire an additional maid and give his wife a substantial clothing allowance.

Lillie's friend Oscar Wilde

In the light of what happened in the months that followed, it has also been suggested that Edward Langtry received the beneficial financial advice in return for keeping his eyes, ears and mouth shut, and for accepting a situation that most husbands would not have been willing to tolerate. It was rumored that the glamorous Mrs. Langtry and the Prince of Wales were meeting fairly regularly for tea at the Freake home, and when Lillie and the prince met at various functions in the next few weeks, it was obvious that they were well acquainted.

It was apparent that a transformation had taken place in the clergyman's daughter from Jersey. Until now, in spite of the furor she had created, she had put off her suitors with a smile. The fact that she was meeting the prince privately at the home of a mutual friend indicated that there had been a change.

At least some of the reasons for this transformation in Lillie are clear. She was still very young, in her early twenties, and the adulation of the art and literary worlds as well as of the aristocracy undoubtedly went to her head. She was living something of a dream life. She had never been in love with Edward Langtry, but

had seen him as an instrument of her escape from Jersey. When he had sailed into the harbor of Saint Helier on his yacht he had seemed sophisticated and debonair. But now she was associating with men who were truly worldly, who were making history in the arts, in politics and in the development of industry. Edward, still lazy, did nothing and had no discernible ambition.

Lillie's wardrobe had been the least of her concerns, and her one black dress had sufficed for an entire London season. Overnight, however, she became the fashion leader of society. When she wore a pink dress to the Ascot races, pink dresses by the thousands suddenly proliferated. When she appeared carrying a muff, women of every class bought muffs. She displayed an infallible instinct for the dramatic, for ideas that had universal appeal and, above all, for what showed her off to good advantage.

The results were spectacular. Lillie, more than anyone else, was to become responsible for the simplification of women's attire during the final portion of the Victorian age and the Edwardian era that followed. She sensed the need for a change from the overly ornate and fussy, and she impatiently refused to follow the dictates of the time.

The first sign that Prince Albert Edward had developed a personal interest in her was a move devoid of subterfuge. When Lillie went out for her regular morning canter, the prince appeared on horseback and joined her, forcing the members of the Langtry Lancers to fall in behind them. The word traveled through the drawing rooms and salons of London, and was confirmed when the prince reappeared on the bridle path the next day, and the next.

Wise hostesses who sought to entertain the Prince of Wales made it their business to invite Mrs. Langtry to their dinner parties, receptions and dances. It soon became evident that if Lillie weren't asked the prince busied himself elsewhere. Furthermore, except on those occasions when his official duties occupied him, he and Lillie never went to separate affairs.

The proprieties were always observed. Lillie invariably arrived and departed with her husband, and the prince came to parties with a pair of his equerries. If he chose to escort Mrs. Langtry to

the table, if he elected to dance repeatedly with her, that was his prerogative. But the prince and the Jersey Lily never spent any time alone, never wandered off into a garden or conservatory.

The domestic arrangements in the household of the heir to the throne made it easy for the Prince of Wales to spend as much time as he pleased with the lady who fascinated him. Princess Alexandra accompanied her husband to all official functions, but they led separate private lives. Alexandra felt at home in the court circles Albert Edward found stuffy, and she spent most of her time there, while he escaped to the gayer life of London society whenever possible. They had followed this routine for many years, so it was taken for granted that an invitation to the Prince of Wales need not be extended to the princess, too. And if hostesses did invite her, they were not surprised when she refused.

Although Edward Langtry was often invited to go for fishing and sailing outings, the wise London gossips noted that he was always on hand to take his wife out socially. If he went off on an overnight trip, he left London only on a night when Lillie stayed at home and rested. She was careful to appear nowhere without him, and even envious critics were forced to admit that the Jersey Lily's husband seemed devoted to her.

Yet it was at this time, Lillie later indicated, that Edward's drinking became a real problem. On a number of occasions, she declared, he became too intoxicated to escort her to a social event, thereby forcing her to send last-minute regrets to her hostess. It was known that he was drinking too much, but there were many who sympathized with him. Lillie had become too popular too quickly, and her conquest of the Prince of Wales was the last straw. Although she was still faithful to her husband, she had developed a measure of notoriety, and seemed to go out of her way to make news. Once when she met Benjamin Disraeli at a government reception, she not only dared to joke with him, something that few wits of the day attempted, but actually twitted him about his archrival, Mr. Gladstone.

Lillie's sense of humor was suspiciously like that of her brothers when they had been schoolboys. One of her favorite stories con-

cerned Lord Malmesbury, a diplomat whom the Langtrys visited at his ancestral estate in Hampshire. He sat Lillie on his right at a dinner party, and insisted that she pass publicly on the main dish before anyone else ate it. She found it so hot that it burned her mouth, and tears came to her eyes.

"Well, Mrs. Langtry?" Lord Malmesbury demanded.

"It would be very good," Lillie replied calmly, "if it weren't cold."

Malmesbury was astonished, and, insisting that his chef had never erred, plunged his fork into the tureen, took a large portion and swallowed it. Gasping and sputtering, he drank both wine and water before recovering. He and his other guests thought Lillie's little trick very amusing.

A serious incident marred the peace of that visit in Hampshire. Lillie had just received a gift from the Prince of Wales, a brooch set with small diamonds, and she wrote to thank him. Edward Langtry, who had been drinking, read a portion of his wife's note on the desk blotter she had used, became wildly jealous and—for the first time—created a scene. Lord Malmesbury was annoyed with his staff, saying that his butler had standing instructions to burn all desk blotters daily.

Apparently Lillie reported her husband's behavior to the prince. Immediately thereafter Langtry received the royal gift of a pair of initialed gold cuff links, and arrangements were made for him to be presented to Queen Victoria at court. The queen seemed impressed with Mr. Langtry and engaged him in conversation for more than five minutes, which for her was unusual. Edward Langtry, it appeared, was mollified.

Arrangements also were made for Lillie to be presented at one of Victoria's "afternoon drawing rooms" at Buckingham Palace. No lady was considered to have made her permanent mark until she had curtsied to the queen, and Lillie had heard gossip to the effect that, because she had become so notorious, Victoria would not receive her.

Presumably Lillie reported the rumor to the Prince of Wales, and soon thereafter she received her invitation to the palace.

She had a new gown made for the event, of course, and her mother came from Jersey to help her prepare for the important occasion. One touch, characteristic of Lillie, was her own audacious idea. All ladies presented to the queen were required to wear feathers in their hair, and it was currently the custom to appear in tiny feathers, which, Lillie learned, irritated Queen Victoria.

So the Jersey Lily decided to wear three enormous white plumes, which bore a suspicious resemblance to the three large feathers on the Prince of Wales' coat of arms. If her mother or anyone else tried to dissuade her, their efforts were unavailing.

Presentations bored Queen Victoria, who usually made only a token appearance at them, leaving the Prince and Princess of Wales to do the honors in her stead. But Victoria must have been curious, so she stayed to see the Jersey Lily. Those who watched said that she studied Lillie closely, her eyes never wavering.

Princess Alexandra was present, too, sitting beside her husband. The prince, untroubled by the presence of his mother and his wife, made no secret of his pleasure as he looked at an exceptionally attractive young woman. The presentation was a success.

It is not known when Lillie became the mistress of the prince. They were discreet, but word seeped out to their social circle, and when they were invited to weekend house parties at various manor houses their suites were located, as a rule, in the same wing.

Whether Lillie was in love with the prince at any time in their relationship is a matter of conjecture, but she was surely flattered by his attention, and welcomed her new position in society as well as the gifts that he gave her. Albert Edward was one of the wealthiest men in the world, and he had a predilection for expensive jewelry. The rings, bracelets, pendants and earrings he gave Lillie, all in spectacularly good taste, became part of what grew into one of the world's largest private jewelry collections.

The prince was notoriously fickle and had never maintained an interest in any favorite for more than a year or two, so Lillie made the most of her time. She and her husband spent part of the summer at Cowes, where they were guests on Sir Allen Young's yacht, the *Helen*. It was berthed adjacent to the slip occupied by the

magnificent royal yacht, the *Osborne*, on which the Prince and Princess of Wales were enjoying a holiday with their children. The Langtrys were frequent guests on the *Osborne*, where they met the King and Queen of Denmark, various members of the Austrian royal family, assorted German princes and the exiled Empress Eugénie of France.

Edward Langtry was in his element on board ship. He struck up a friendship with the Danish king and queen, and every morning took them for a ride around the harbor in a rowboat. He participated in many of the races, and came alive for the first time in many months. Then the Prince of Wales loaned the Langtrys one of his yachts, the *Hildegarde*, manned by sailors of the Royal Navy. Lillie and her husband sailed off in style for a visit to Jersey. Lillie Langtry was not considered newsworthy in her childhood home; many years would pass before the good people of Jersey felt ashamed of the notoriety she had brought to the island.

So far, to be sure, Lillie's discretion had prevented the outbreak of any major scandal, but her attitude was changing. By 1879 everyone in England was whispering about her, while the rest of the world shouted.

IV

ALTHOUGH the future Edward VII had enjoyed numerous affairs with attractive ladies, he had been circumspect. However, he seemed eager to let the world know of his interest in Lillie.

The prince owned one of the world's largest stables of racing horses, and Lillie was devoted to the sport, so they appeared together frequently in the royal box at Ascot and at Epsom Downs. They also rode together daily on London's bridle paths, with his equerries following at a respectful distance.

Lillie's international reputation rapidly acquired a new dimension. She was no longer merely the reigning Professional Beauty of London, but was dubbed "the favorite of the Prince of Wales" by the world press. The reserved British newspapers managed to

keep their readers informed by subtle means. Whenever possible they published a list of guests at social functions, and the name of Mrs. Edward Langtry usually followed that of the prince.

The respectable ladies of London society were shocked by Lillie's blatant conduct; she even appeared at official royal functions. While she maintained her position as the prince's favorite, however, it was impossible for them to show their contempt. They continued to entertain her because they had no choice, but they were biding their time. Meanwhile, Lillie suffered no illusions regarding their attitude toward her.

A new scandal suddenly gave the Jersey Lily an even worse name. Late in 1879 Crown Prince Rudolf of Austria-Hungary, the heir to the throne of the Hapsburgs, paid a visit to London. Only twenty-one, the son of the Emperor Franz Josef was brilliant and handsome, but emotionally unstable. Prince Rudolf met Lillie Langtry at a ball given by Baron Ferdinand de Rothschild, and from the moment he saw her he went wild.

He danced with her repeatedly, refusing to relinquish her to anyone else. The Prince of Wales was present, and presumably Rudolf knew of his relationship with the Jersey Lily; but such delicacies were of no matter to the smitten Austrian. Albert Edward, always the gentleman, pretended to be unaware of the younger man's infatuation.

When supper was served, Rudolf, as the guest of honor, was expected to escort the Baroness de Rothschild to the table, while the Prince of Wales and Lillie fell into line directly behind them. But the Austrian took Lillie's arm and marched her off to the supper table. Albert Edward smiled quietly, offered his arm to the baroness and escorted her to her place. Perhaps his own strict upbringing made him tolerant of the youth's rudeness.

That was anything but the end of the matter. Each day thereafter Prince Rudolf paid a call at the Norfolk Street flat, and his advances were so bold, so insistent, that Lillie had to summon her husband from a fishing trip to be present when Rudolf appeared.

So much speculation appeared in print about Lillie and Prince Rudolf that Emperor Franz Josef abruptly called his son back to

Vienna. Lillie was spared further embarrassment, but there were many who believed, wrongly, that she had in Rudolf gained another royal lover.

Sarah Bernhardt paid a visit to London in the autumn of 1879, and Oscar Wilde, always eager to capitalize on publicity, acted as her constant escort. Through him the great French actress met his friend Lillie Langtry, and the two women immediately established

Lillie and Sarah Bernhardt

a rapport that lasted for the rest of their lives. Their paths frequently crossed through the years; they corresponded; and in interviews with the press each always spoke of the other with great warmth and respect. It could not have occurred to Lillie, when she first met "the Divine Sarah," that it wouldn't be long before she, too, would be earning a living on the stage.

In the spring of 1880 Edward Langtry went off on a month's yachting trip with Sir Humphrey Coyne, who was a member of what was called "the Prince of Wales' set." During this time Lillie and the prince made their boldest gesture.

Lillie announced that she was leaving London to visit her parents, and two days later she arrived in Jersey. But she remained there only a few days and then went on to Paris, where a suite had been reserved for her at the exclusive Hotel Bristol. A portly, bearded English gentleman happened to be staying at the same hotel, and the Paris newspapers said his suite was located on the same floor. The Prince of Wales, traveling incognito as a private citizen, used the name of one of his equerries and enjoyed a strictly private visit to the French capital.

He and Lillie were seen everywhere together, while tourists

gaped and well-bred Frenchmen pretended they were invisible. They danced together at Maxim's and, it was said in the press, kissed on the dance floor. They took carriage rides down the boulevards and in the Bois. They sat at sidewalk cafés and sipped liqueurs. And when they had nothing better to occupy them, they shopped; oh, how they shopped.

The prince bought Lillie an entire wardrobe at the House of Worth, the former dressmaker to the Empress Eugénie. The Paris press reported that Lillie was wearing two new diamond bracelets, a magnificent diamond and emerald ring, and a huge diamond and ruby brooch. Whether the prince actually gave her these gems on this trip isn't known, but she owned and wore them for the rest of her life.

Nervous British embassy officials hovered in the background whenever the couple emerged from the Bristol. Lillie and the prince led them on a merry chase. They bought perfume, visited the graves of Voltaire and Rousseau and went to Versailles to see the great palace of Louis XIV. They attended the theater on a number of occasions, and one night after her performance Sarah Bernhardt gave them a supper party at her apartment.

The following night they dined at the home of Victor Hugo. The great French author, now seventy-eight years of age, had a justly acquired reputation as a ladies' man that made the Prince of Wales rank as an amateur. Recently recovered from a heart attack, Hugo had given up his countless amatory adventures at the insistence of his "official" mistress of almost a half century, and was leading a quiet life.

But he had lost none of his wit. After toasting his incognito male guest, he offered a toast to Lillie, which immediately became famous. "Madame," he said, "I can celebrate your beauty in only one way, by wishing I were three years younger."

Lillie and her companion traveled north together as far as the French coast. Then she went on to Jersey for another brief visit, while he crossed the Channel to England. A few days later, when Lillie returned home, a domestic crisis awaited her.

Edward Langtry had visited his family in Ulster, and had

learned that his father heartily disapproved of the notoriety that Lillie was giving the family name. The elder Langtry had offered to assume all of his son's debts and give him a place in the business that would pay a handsome annual stipend, on condition that Edward divorce Lillie.

Edward Langtry had refused, and left Belfast without speaking to his father again. Regardless of what he either knew or suspected about his wife, he was adamant in his insistence that he would never divorce her or permit her to divorce him.

Lillie was riding the social crest. Dressmakers gave her unlimited credit, she could no longer walk in the streets for fear of being mobbed, and every change in her costume created a new fad. At the age of twenty-seven, having done little to deserve it, she was the heroine of millions.

The end came suddenly, unexpectedly, thanks to an indiscretion that Lillie herself committed. She went to a costume ball given by Lord Randolph Churchill and his wife, dressed as Pierrette. To the surprise of no one, the Prince of Wales came as Pierrot, even though Princess Alexandra, who accompanied him, wore a different sort of costume.

Ordinarily Lillie drank sparingly, and some eyewitnesses insisted that she only took a glass or two of champagne. Others, however, said she consumed wine at a far more rapid rate than was her custom. In any case, she and the prince were in high spirits and teasing each other when Lillie reached into a champagne cooler, picked up a piece of ice and dropped it down the back of the Prince of Wales' ruffled Pierrot collar.

There was a limit to the familiarity that anyone could take in public with the heir to the British throne, and Lillie far exceeded the bounds of propriety. Perhaps no one was more surprised than Albert Edward himself. He stared at Lillie for a long moment, then turned on his heel and stalked out of the room. Princess Alexandra hurriedly followed, and the other guests hastily departed for home. The party was ruined, and so was Lillie Langtry.

Not until the following day did the full import of what had happened dawn on Lillie. When she went for her usual canter in

the park, she rode alone. No invitations were delivered to the Norfolk Street flat, but before the day ended, cancellations of various social engagements began to arrive. Dinner parties were postponed, arrangements for weekends were unaccountably changed, and even the usual at-homes were temporarily terminated. Society had dropped her.

There were few aristocratic secrets unknown to London's fashionable tradespeople, and soon the bill collectors descended on Norfolk Street. Dressmakers and milliners, shoemakers and glovers demanded payment at once, and Lillie discovered she had been living far beyond her means.

Edward Langtry lacked the funds to pay all the bills, and was incapable of earning the money, so Lillie decided she would have to go to work herself.

Her only friends now were the artists, actors and authors who cared nothing about the disapproval of Lillie shown by the Prince of Wales and his friends. Because of their unswerving loyalty, from that time onward all of her lasting friendships were made exclusively in artistic circles. Only one woman of social standing, Mary Cornwallis-West, Lillie's predecessor as "the favorite of the Prince of Wales," demonstrated the desire and courage to remain friendly with her.

Bands of the faithful gathered at Norfolk Street to consider the future. Frank Miles, among others, thought Lillie would prosper if she opened one, then a chain, of Jersey Lily florist shops. James Whistler believed she could become an accomplished artist and offered to give Lillie drawing lessons. Mary Cornwallis-West and several others were convinced she could become an enormously successful dressmaker.

Oscar Wilde, at his persuasive best, told Lillie she would be mad if she contemplated any career other than the stage. She already possessed several exceptionally valuable assets. She was the most beautiful woman in Great Britain, perhaps in the entire Western world. She had been making headlines for years as a Professional Beauty, and therefore already had an eager audience.

While Lillie pondered, unable to make a decision, she was un-

expectedly restored to the Prince of Wales' favor. Whether he got in touch with her himself, or whether an intermediary notified her that she was forgiven is not known. It sufficed that the invitations began to pour in to Norfolk Street again, and the creditors agreed to wait for their money.

On the surface, at least, Lillie resumed the life she had been leading, but for her private purposes she had merely bought a little more time to make up her mind. Thinking about the advice she had received, she was inclined to go into the theater, even though she lacked any experience on the stage.

Henry Irving offered her a role in a new play that would open the 1880-81 theatrical season. The part was small but important, and she would be shown off to good advantage. Lillie declined, afraid she would disgrace Irving by being too amateurish.

Then nature intervened, and hastened at least one portion of Lillie's decision, forcing her to retire from society. She discovered she was pregnant.

V

PRINCESS ALEXANDRA paid a call on Lillie Langtry at the Norfolk Street flat, and showed the younger woman every consideration. At her direction the royal household physician, Francis Laking, called on Lillie, and thereafter attended her.

Lillie's immediate financial problems vanished. She received a check from the prince's friend Sir Allen Young for two thousand pounds, which was the equivalent of ten thousand dollars. For the sake of propriety it was called a loan, but Lillie actually considered it one and eventually repaid Sir Allen every penny. For the rest of her life she refused to be indebted to anyone.

Edward Langtry had gone off on a two-week hunting trip, and Lillie moved quickly. She wrote her husband a brief note informing him she was leaving him. Since they had not been intimate for more than a year, she made no mention of her pregnancy.

The funds supplied by Sir Allen easily took care of Lillie's credi-

tors, but her plans made it necessary for her to give up the London flat, so she arranged for the furniture, rugs, bric-a-brac and draperies at the Norfolk Street quarters to be sold at auction. Then she departed without fanfare for Jersey.

Mrs. Cornwallis-West passed the word that Lillie had "retired," and hinted that a marital break was responsible.

The news first appeared in a small London society paper, the *Figaro,* on October 2, 1880. Two days later *The New York Times* reprinted the London article in full under a headline, RETIREMENT OF MRS. LANGTRY FROM SOCIETY. Other newspapers around the world also carried every scrap of information available. Edward Langtry refused to comment.

In November *The New York Times* ran another story:

> Mr. and Mrs. Langtry have given up their London residence and for the present Mrs. Langtry remains in Jersey. Is beauty deposed, or has beauty abdicated? The result on London society will be the same. Public pets may be objectionable, but few could so well have survived the ordeal of public admiration and preserved so much of the natural good-hearted woman as Mrs. Langtry.

The Reverend Le Breton was in the process of leaving Jersey at the time of his daughter's arrival. Or, it has been suggested, the news she brought caused him to seek a transfer. He was given a London church, and took up residence in the Marylebone parish. Mrs. Le Breton remained in Jersey for a time with her daughter.

The next months of Lillie Langtry's life are a mystery. Whether she remained in Jersey and gave birth to her child there, or whether she moved elsewhere during her confinement, has never been revealed. It has been rumored that she went to a small estate owned by Mary Cornwallis-West in Wales. It has also been suggested that she went to Paris, or to Lille or to Rouen.

No records of the infant's birth or baptism appear in London, in Wales or in Jersey. There are none in Paris or the other French cities. Enterprising newspaper reporters have, over the decades, scoured every official registry of both state and church, but their efforts have revealed nothing.

It has been assumed that Lillie's child was born in Jersey, presumably in either March or April 1881. It was at about that time that Lillie rented a cottage near the Jersey cliffs, and was seen there with her mother and her maid, Dominique. The baby was a girl, named Jeanne Marie Langtry. London society and the world press knew nothing of her existence.

The people of Jersey who stumbled onto the secret kept their mouths shut. "My mother," said a lady who still resides on the island, "told me that, as a child, she played with Jeanne Langtry, but it was an unwritten law that her name was never to be mentioned to outsiders. I was grown before she told me the secret, and I don't like to talk about it myself. We may hold our opinions of Lillie Langtry, but when we're dealing with the rest of the world, we're loyal to our own."

One person, above all, had no idea of the baby's existence. Edward Langtry was in a deplorable condition. Dropped by aristocratic London the day his wife disappeared, he was a lost soul. The auctioning of the Norfolk Street furnishings had revealed his financial condition, he had no friends of his own, and his drinking caused even those who felt sorry for him to drop him.

Even when whispers of Lillie's secret began to make the rounds of London society, nothing reached his ears. He received a tiny allowance from his father, lived in a cheap London rooming house and spent his days drinking. He would be one of the last to hear about Jeanne.

Battered though Edward Langtry may have been, he refused to compromise his principles and would not grant Lillie the divorce she wanted. Nothing budged him, and the Reverend Le Breton wrote to his daughter from London, "I spent an uncomfortable hour with Edward today. He was in his cups, and blames you alone for the failure of your marriage. You would be wise to put aside all thoughts of divorce, which he will not contemplate."

Lillie would have to rebuild her life without thoughts of remarriage within the near future. Her limited funds were being spent too rapidly, and she faced the problem of earning a living, which she couldn't do in Jersey. So she hired a governess for the

baby; and her mother, who had joined the Reverend Le Breton in London, promised to spend as much time as she could in Jersey.

There was only one place Lillie could go, so she traveled with her maid, Dominique, to London, and engaged a small suite of rooms in Ely Place. The ladies and gentlemen of high society had no idea she had returned, and she had no intention of telling them. Instead, she called on Millais, Wilde and Miles, and confided to them that she had decided to become an actress.

Through these friends she received several offers, the most lucrative a tour through the United States. But she had no dramatic training, and would be paid only for the notoriety of her name. She refused, planning to become a qualified professional.

Through Oscar Wilde she met the woman who would influence the rest of her life. Henrietta Hodson Labouchère was a tiny, energetic woman who had achieved a minor reputation acting in secondary roles. She was married to Henry Labouchère, a member of Parliament, ardent follower of Gladstone and editor of a small liberal magazine called *Truth*.

Henrietta had enjoyed a fair success by giving dramatic lessons to several budding actresses who had managed to find roles on the London stage, but she wanted far more. Her great desire was to create her own theatrical company, and through Lillie Langtry she saw that it might become possible.

Lillie agreed to work with her, and went to live in the Labouchère home at Twickenham. They rehearsed a half-hour play, *A Fair Encounter*, in which they played the only two roles.

Their performance was held in the Twickenham town hall, and a number of Lillie's artistic friends came out from London to cheer her. They told her she exhibited the potential of an actress; and so did Henrietta, who insisted on preparing her for a bigger role before a more demanding audience.

Lillie returned to Ely Place, and found that social London had learned of her return. On several occasions the Prince of Wales called on her, but Lillie refused all society invitations. She was serious about creating a career based on talent and hard work, and would not be distracted.

Edward Langtry also discovered she was in the city, and after getting in touch with her through her solicitor, George Lewis, he came to see her. He not only rejected her demands for a divorce but tried to insist on a reconciliation, which Lillie refused. He still had no idea she had given birth to a daughter more than a half year earlier.

A number of theatrical managers offered Lillie roles in forthcoming attractions, but she was not yet ready to accept any of them. She wanted recognition as an actress, not as a former Professional Beauty, and needed more experience.

The indefatigable Henrietta Labouchère saw that she got it. Henrietta obtained a role for her as Kate Hardcastle in a charity performance of *She Stoops to Conquer*, which was to be held for the benefit of the Royal General Theatrical Fund at one of London's best theaters, the Haymarket. A number of England's finest actors and actresses had agreed to take parts, and the capabilities of the amateur would be tested to the limit.

The news that Lillie would appear in a leading role resulted in a rush for seats, all of which were sold long before the performance was given on December 15, 1881. At the age of twenty-eight Lillie Langtry was launching her career.

Realizing that the critics and reporters from London and foreign newspapers would be present, along with scores of her former aristocratic friends, Lillie labored incessantly to prepare herself for her role, spending ten hours a day working with Henrietta— after rehearsing in the theater for the previous ten.

The Prince and Princess of Wales occupied the royal box on the night of the performance, and the stalls were filled with the nobility and the domestic and foreign press. To the astonishment of everyone present, Lillie was more than adequate; she showed an instinct for the stage, and projected a strong and appealing personality across the gas footlights.

Princess Alexandra led the large group that hurried to Lillie's dressing room after the performance, and placed a rare, impulsive kiss on her cheek. The Prince of Wales, close behind his wife, was equally enthusiastic. Oscar Wilde announced that he would write

a play for the budding star, and Millais extracted a promise from her to pose for a new portrait in costume.

In all, Lillie achieved a triumph beyond her hopes. Only in high-society circles was she now not admired. By becoming an actress she had forfeited her place in aristocratic ranks, regardless of the gesture made by the Princess of Wales. The aristocratic ladies would have been shocked to discover that Lillie Langtry no longer cared.

The managers of the Haymarket offered her a small but important part in a melodrama, *Ours*, by Tom Robertson, which was opening the following month, and Lillie promptly accepted. She went into rehearsal thirty-six hours after appearing in *She Stoops to Conquer*, and the play opened January 19, 1882. Lillie took only one day of rest, Christmas, when she dined with her parents at the Marylebone rectory.

Clergymen of the Anglican church were not enthusiastic supporters of the theater in Queen Victoria's day, but the Reverend Le Breton evidently gave his daughter his full support. He attended her first charity performance at the Haymarket, and thereafter never missed one of her opening nights. "The loyalty of my parents," Lillie wrote years later, "sustained me in my darkest hours."

The darkness was beginning to lift. She was being paid the substantial salary of two hundred and fifty pounds per week, which enabled her to support herself and her child, start to repay Sir Allen Young, and replenish her wardrobe, which was her greatest publicity asset. Reviewers were critical of *Ours*, but treated her with kindness, and her future on the stage seemed assured.

Her personal life, however, was complicated. No longer protected by even the semblance of a marriage to Edward Langtry, she became fair game for every London man-about-town. The aristocratic ladies might shun her, but their husbands did not, and Lillie's dressing room was filled every night with flowers and other gifts. But she refused to accept private engagements with anyone.

Lillie needed no instructions in the handling of men. She accepted other advice, however. Prime Minister Gladstone came backstage to visit her, and for the rest of her life she followed, to

the letter, the suggestions he gave her. "Mrs. Langtry," she reported him as saying, "you have become a truly public person, so you will be attacked, maligned and slandered, in your professional life, and in your personal life as well. Never reply to your critics! Never explain, no matter what you've said or done! If you attempt to defend yourself, you'll keep alive a controversy. As the French say, speech is silver, but silence is golden."

When *Ours* began to falter at the box office, the management revived *She Stoops to Conquer*, and Lillie again played Kate. The two plays were alternated, and both did capacity business.

Henrietta Labouchère was still working with Lillie for several hours each day on diction and movement, and drilling her in the reading of roles. She never tired, and Lillie soon loathed the sight of Henrietta. But she continued to depend on her.

It was Henrietta who refused to allow the Haymarket to give the Jersey Lily star billing, claiming she wasn't yet ready for it, and it was Henrietta who put off the provincial managers who were offering large sums for a tour.

By the summer of 1882 Lillie was still selling out at the Haymarket, but a change in her personal situation made it necessary for her to earn more.

Edward Langtry had been coming to see her regularly, sometimes at the theater, sometimes at her flat, and begging her to take him back. His drinking had become a chronic problem, he looked seedy, and he was incapable of obtaining even menial employment. His father, hoping that stern treatment might cure him, cut off his allowance, and Edward was literally penniless.

He explained his situation to Lillie and demanded money. If she refused, he said, he would make trouble for her, perhaps even revealing more than was proper concerning Lillie's relations with the Prince of Wales.

Lillie capitulated to an extent, but insisted on her own terms. She agreed to pay Edward a monthly stipend on condition that he never come to see her again. Should he break the agreement, she would cut him off.

The provinces were beckoning, and Lillie needed the money, so

she and Henrietta formed their own company. Lillie would appear in four plays. She would do Kate again, as well as the lead in *Ours;* she would have the chance to show off her legs as Rosalind in *As You Like It,* and would do Tom Taylor's light comedy, *An Unequal Match.* In making these selections, Henrietta demonstrated her understanding of both the star and those who would pay to see her. The provincial audiences, anxious to gaze at the Professional Beauty about whom there had been so much talk, would have ample opportunity to revel in her appearance, but would not be required to think.

Lillie opened the tour in Manchester, playing in *She Stoops to Conquer,* and enjoyed an opening-night triumph at which the audience cheered so lustily she was forced to take twenty-three curtain calls, and the entire stage was filled with baskets of flowers.

Such an enormous crowd gathered at the stage door that police reserves had to be summoned. When Lillie left the theater she saw that the horses had been unhitched from her carriage, and it was being pulled by two dozen of her most enthusiastic admirers. At her hotel entrance, she had to mount the roof of the carriage and make a speech before the throng would release her.

Every performance in Edinburgh was sold out, and the success was repeated in every city of the Midlands and the North. Then the Prince of Wales, who had sent her flowers for each opening night, telegraphed a request that she return to London for two days. A state dinner was being given for a prominent African tribal king whose homeland was under British protection, and the monarch had expressed a desire to meet the fabulous Jersey Lily.

Lillie received the telegram during a Saturday-night performance, and apparently had no thought but to obey. Since no trains left Edinburgh for London on a Sunday morning, she had to hire a special train for the sum of one hundred pounds, an act which stunned the world. English and Scottish newspapers reported that she returned to London for the state dinner but they made no mention of the prince's request. The American and continental press was less restrained, and the name of Lillie Langtry once again was coupled with that of the Prince of Wales.

The day following the state dinner, Lillie returned to Edinburgh, having canceled only one performance. There wasn't a vacant seat in the theater for the rest of her stay. One member of the audience particularly liked what he saw. Henry E. Abbey, one of New York's more enterprising theater owners and producers, had been in private correspondence with Henrietta Labouchère, and had crossed the Atlantic for the purpose of making his own judgments. Now he made an offer: Lillie would pay the salaries of her company and he would give her fifty percent of the gross.

The offer was good, but Lillie held out for sixty-five percent, with Abbey guaranteeing all traveling expenses, including those from England to America. After several days of haggling, the producer capitulated. "Mrs. Langtry," he later wrote, "is as tough a businesswoman as she is a lovely lady. She may smell of a delicious perfume, but nothing creases her hide except dollar bills."

Shortly before the news was announced that Lillie intended to invade the United States, another storm broke. She became the first woman to endorse a commercial product. The Pears' Soap Company paid her one hundred and thirty-two pounds for signing a statement to the effect that she owed her flawless skin to her regular use of the product.

Ladies of quality were horrified, and it was said in high circles that Mrs. Langtry had sold herself with the abandon of a prostitute. As for Lillie, she calmly pocketed the money, and later wrote that she had requested the odd sum because she happened to weigh one hundred and thirty-two pounds at the time.

Henrietta prepared shrewdly for Lillie's invasion of America. She hired a small company, rented the Imperial Theatre in London for brief tryouts, and prepared a repertory of three plays, including the already familiar *As You Like It* and *An Unequal Match*. The third, *The Honeymoon*, was a frivolous new work for the star in which she would be required to do little except look lovely and speak simple lines. Henrietta was taking no chances.

The trial engagement opened at the Imperial, with the Prince and Princess of Wales in attendance. Their presence made it necessary for society to buy tickets, too, and the aristocrats who had

been damning Lillie had to swallow their pride. When the engagement ended in late September, the Prince of Wales gave a sumptuous farewell supper in Lillie's honor. The ever-discreet British press made no mention of the event, but Henry Abbey saw to it that the American newspapers learned the details of the party, and hundreds of columns appeared in print throughout the United States while Lillie was on the high seas.

The New York to which Lillie Langtry was traveling was a brawling, bustling, contradictory city; the census of 1880 had credited it with more than two million inhabitants. The center of town was Twenty-third Street, but the city was expanding northward on Manhattan Island, and land was already so valuable that new buildings were eight to ten stories high.

The contrasts between the classes in New York were marked. The poor lived in semistarvation, but the wealthy dined in restaurants where the menu was remarkably varied, and where the portions were amazingly large. Two of the most popular were Delmonico's, an ornate establishment where the rich and socially prominent dined, and Pfaff's, which had become an informal club for literary and theatrical people. Actors and actresses could dine there without being subjected to harassment by an admiring public, but would be sure to meet playwrights, producers and directors. Several book and newspaper publishers had regular tables, as did a number of authors. The management was loyal to its clientele, and the house quietly carried those who lacked funds. Walt Whitman had eaten there for years, even when his wallet was empty.

Visitors from abroad often were startled by the lusty vigor of New World living. After a lecture tour, Oscar Wilde had written, "America is a land of unmatched vitality and vulgarity, a people who care not at all about values other than their own, and who, when they make up their minds, love you or hate you with a frightening, passionate zeal."

Wilde was on hand in New York to greet Lillie. The day before her arrival he told the New York *World*, in an interview that was widely reprinted, "I would rather have discovered Mrs. Langtry

than to have discovered America. You have asked whether she is indeed a beauty, and I can reply to such nonsense only by saying that . . . she is the most beautiful woman in all the world, and will be a beauty still at eighty-five. It was for such as she that Troy was destroyed, and well it might have been!"

On the morning of October 23, 1882, Henry Abbey and his partner went out to the far end of the harbor in a rented boat to meet the Jersey Lily. Accompanying them were members of their staff, twenty to thirty newspaper reporters, Oscar Wilde, and a brass band playing "God Save the Queen."

Lillie awaited the company in the salon, and the first to enter was Wilde, who presented her with an enormous bouquet of white roses. She had dressed for the occasion in a simple, figure-hugging dress of dark blue, and had worn none of her jewelry. Her graciousness and charm overwhelmed the press, which had expected her to be haughty. She shook hands with each of the reporters, and she impressed them by remembering their names. She exercised extraordinary patience during the mass interview, and answered all the questions except one.

"What do you think of America, Mrs. Langtry?" was the first, inevitably, although she had yet to set foot on New World soil.

Lillie fielded it smartly. "I have spent nine days on board an American ship," she said, "so I already know your kindness and your hospitality. I am enchanted."

"What is your opinion of American women?"

"I have often been told they are the most beautiful in all the world, and I am sure the reports are accurate."

"Have you seen the Prince of Wales lately, Mrs. Langtry?"

Lillie's composure remained unchanged, but she suddenly became hard-of-hearing. The question was not repeated, and the reporters refrained from asking others like it. Thereafter, no matter where Lillie traveled, she suffered a hearing affliction whenever the Prince of Wales was mentioned.

A suite had been engaged for Lillie in an elegant hotel, the Albemarle. More reporters came to the hotel, and Lillie graciously answered questions for more than two hours. She went for a

drive with Henrietta that afternoon, and to her astonishment was recognized and followed by such a large crowd that traffic on Fifth Avenue became snarled, and the police had to rescue her from her admirers. Then she visited the Lord & Taylor dry-goods store on Broadway, and a near riot made it impossible for her to do any shopping. A squad of policemen escorted her back to the hotel.

Abbey had done his work well. Everywhere posters advertised the appearance of the Jersey Lily, and there were photographs of her in hundreds of shopwindows.

The song-writing industry tried to cash in on Lillie's popularity, and a number of composers turned out waltzes, marches and polkas in her honor. "Jersey-Lily Waltz" by Henry Le York became one of the most popular songs of the 1882–83 winter.

A dinner was given in Lillie's honor on her first night in New York by Pierre Lorillard, a financier she had met in London, and she found Delmonico's as sumptuous as any Old World restaurant. "The Americans," she wrote to her parents, "do not eat buffalo steaks and bear meat. The food here is superb, but I find the portions so large I shall gain weight unless I exercise great care."

One incident marred Lillie's welcome. At Delmonico's she saw several members of high society whom she had met in London, and spoke to them. But the ladies snubbed her, a reminder that she was now beyond the pale of New York's aristocrats, just as she was no longer received in London's best homes.

But there were limitless compensations, not the least of them the generosity of American business. A wine importer delivered a case of champagne, and all he asked in return was that she order a bottle at a restaurant. Two competing piano manufacturers insisted that she accept their products, and asked nothing in return. Dressmakers who had managed to learn her precise measurements inundated her with gifts of gowns. Milliners, shoemakers, glovers and corset makers did the same. The owner of a fleet of hansom cabs put a carriage at her disposal.

There was such a great demand for tickets to her opening in *An Unequal Match* that Abbey conceived of an unprecedented stunt. For all opening-night seats at the Park Theatre, except those

to be used by the drama critics, an auction was held. The usual price for orchestra seats was $2, for the balcony $1 and for the gallery fifty cents. Lillie made the front pages when a front box sold at auction for $325, and a group of ardent theatergoers bought a block at $17.50 per ticket. The cheapest orchestra seats sold at $10, those in the balcony brought $5, and $3.25 was paid for gallery seats. Not even lively New York had ever witnessed such a spectacle.

The wily, hard-bitten James Gordon Bennett, publisher of the New York *Herald,* assigned a reporter to cover literally every minute of every day in Lillie's life. Recognizing the publicity value of a limitless stream of stories, Lillie allowed the reporter, Bury I. Dasent, to accompany her on her rounds whenever possible. Dasent promptly fell in love with her, and his stories were ecstatic.

He was also an enterprising newspaperman, and one day he played a major role in the making of history—of a sort. As part of the publicity buildup for her theatrical appearance, Lillie was asked to sell tickets for a dinner at Sherry's restaurant that was being given for charity.

Lillie-inspired sheet music

At Dasent's suggestion, Lillie went down to Wall Street to sell tickets, with the reporter accompanying her. Streets were crowded and narrow in the financial district, and such a huge throng gathered that the police were called in to extricate Lillie.

At the Stock Exchange, Dasent guided her to the balcony. Word of her presence spread quickly, and transactions on the floor below were forgotten as members and their staffs hurried to vantage points. Precedent was smashed when business on the Exchange was suspended long enough for formal greetings to be extended

to her. The following day's *Herald* featured Dasent's story under the banner headline, MRS. LANGTRY PANICS WALL STREET.

Just hours before the opening of *An Unequal Match*, a fire destroyed the Park Theatre, and for a few hours it was feared that the catastrophe would force a postponement of the Jersey Lily's American debut. But the accident became something of a blessing in disguise when Abbey rented Wallack's Theatre, which was larger than the Park, and made more seats available.

The first-night audience included members of some of America's most prominent families, among them Vanderbilts, Goulds, Lorillards and Cuttings. Another spectator, who would play a role in Lillie's future, was the attorney Abe Hummel, who had successfully defended some of America's most notorious criminals.

Someone else in the audience did not go unnoticed by the press. Her name was Lillian Russell, and she was twenty-one, eight years Lillie's junior. She had made her own theatrical debut the previous year, and she was the American entry in the international beauty sweepstakes. Her admirers called her the loveliest woman on earth, and not until they saw Lillie did some of them desert her. At Lillie's performance, the exquisite Miss Russell was poker-faced, did not applaud and refused to express an opinion of her rival. She did not return to her seat after the last intermission.

Dasent's interview with Lillie on the subject could not have endeared her to her competition. "What is your opinion of Lillian Russell, Mrs. Langtry?" he asked.

"Who?"

"She is an actress, and is regarded as very beautiful."

"We haven't met," Lillie said, and that ended the matter.

Representatives of all the New York newspapers and many other parts of the United States were on hand. In all, Abbey put aside an unprecedented two hundred and fifty seats for the press.

The opening-night receipts were almost seven thousand dollars, a record in the American theater, and a long line at the box office assured the Jersey Lily of success, regardless of the critics' verdict. Two large horse-drawn wagons stood in the alley outside the stage door, loaded with floral tributes to the actress

who had just demonstrated her talent to an American audience.

No one, including Lillie, had any idea that the curtain would rise on a new era, and that she would spend the better part of the next five years in the United States. She would become an American citizen as well as a national institution. A town would be named after her, she would become independently wealthy, and a turbulent love affair would bring her fresh notoriety. She would suffer heartbreak, and in almost miraculous growth would achieve stature as one of the best actresses of her era.


## VI


WILLIAM WINTER of the New York *Tribune* was the dean of American drama critics. He had been the first to recognize Edwin Booth as a great actor, the first to hail the sensitivity of Helena Modjeska, the first to call Sarah Bernhardt incomparable. His reviews were respected in England, France and Germany as well as in all parts of the United States, and had he given Lillie Langtry a harsh review, her success would have been short-lived. Instead, he treated her with unexpected gentleness:

It is unfortunate that Mrs. Langtry has chosen to appear in her American inaugural in a play that shows its age, since her own youth and vitality are among her greater assets. On the other hand, she may have been wise not to attempt too much.

The crudities of her performance were obvious last night, although I may not be regarded as a gentleman for telling the truth. However, her freshness, charm and promise are equally great, and it is to be hoped that she will make progress in her elected profession. If she does, she will be hailed as an actress with the enthusiasm that now trumpets her appearance as a great beauty.

Other reviews were equally ambivalent. The *Times* complimented her beauty but damned her acting with faint praise.

In all, the reviews were better than any that Lillie had received in London, and she could not have been too badly disappointed.

But she was anxious to improve her image, and she evolved a plan to meet Winter, the most important critic, by "accident," and charm him. Henry Abbey arranged a dinner engagement for himself with the critic at Pfaff's. Lillie "happened" to be dining alone a few tables away. It was typical of the restaurant that no one paid any attention to anyone else. Virtually everybody who dined at Pfaff's was a celebrity, and it was the strict custom to mind one's own business.

William Winter made no objection, however, when Abbey discovered Lillie sitting alone and suggested that she join them. The lovely young woman who had melted the reserves of the stern Gladstone required little time to make Winter her friend. Her wit and intelligence surprised him, her beauty numbed him, and he was flattered beyond measure by her breathless attention.

Lillie and the austere Winter developed a genuine fondness for each other, and were close friends for the rest of their lives. Thereafter, Winter unfailingly gave Lillie glowing reviews.

Shortly after Lillie's opening in New York, she met the man who would mean more to her than anyone else she had ever known or would know. Many years later, in her sixties, she told Somerset Maugham that this man had been "the great love of my life."

Frederick Gebhard, Jr., was twenty-two when Lillie met him, which made him seven years her junior. He was tall, with black hair and dark eyes, and had the magnificent physique of an athlete who swam, played tennis, rode, boxed, fenced and sailed.

The son of a Baltimore dry-goods merchant who had died several years earlier, Fred had inherited a fortune conservatively estimated at five million dollars, and was believed to enjoy an annual income of approximately eighty thousand to one hundred thousand dollars. He had considerable social standing in New York and Baltimore, but had never played an active social role. Until he met Lillie he was rather retiring, and hostesses with eligible daughters had found it difficult to lure him to their homes.

Some of the more romantic reporters covering the Lillie Langtry story claimed that she and Fred fell in love at first sight, but they were exaggerating. Fred fell in love with Lillie, but she was indif-

ferent to him, and he was forced to pursue her. He invited her riding and ice skating. He took her driving, went with her on long walks, and they dined together.

The enterprising Dasent discovered that Fred purchased a necklace and bracelet of matching diamonds for Lillie at Tiffany's, and enlightened the *Herald*'s readers with the details. He sent her the gems in a huge bouquet of flowers, and she did not return the gift. Overnight Fred Gebhard was catapulted into international prominence, much to his annoyance.

He had been brought up to believe that a gentleman lived quietly, avoiding the limelight, but it was impossible to remain anonymous when one associated with Lillie. They were mobbed by the public, and whenever they went anywhere, one or more newspapers commented. Fred hated the press.

He didn't get along, either, with Henrietta Labouchère, who disapproved of him. Henrietta thought it harmful to Lillie's image for her, a married woman, to be seen so frequently with the young millionaire bachelor. She thought it wrong of Lillie to accept the expensive necklace and bracelet, and she wanted Lillie to spend more time rehearsing for *As You Like It*.

The reviews of *As You Like It* confirmed Henrietta's fears. They were the worst Lillie had ever received.

The critics granted that she looked the part of Rosalind, but called her portrayal stiff and unnatural. The *Times* declared, "The role requires the services of an actress, not that of a pretty elocutionist." Only William Winter was kind, and may have saved Lillie. He praised her beauty, grace and charm, but carefully refrained from commenting on the quality of her performance.

Henrietta felt that her own professional standing was being injured, and issued an unprecedented statement to the press. The following day's *Herald* led the way in proclaiming "The Langtry Scandal." Mrs. Labouchère, it read, "officially announced that she disapproved of Mrs. Langtry's proceedings in this country, had no further connection with her, personally, or with her theatrical engagements, and intends to return to England."

The press enjoyed the bonanza. The United States was, indeed,

a highly moral country, in which the principles of Victorian morality were observed. So Henrietta was presented as a champion of virtue, Lillie as a fallen angel and Gebhard as a conniving seducer.

Lillie took Gladstone's advice to heart and refused to comment.

But Fred Gebhard was less worldly, and made the mistake of writing an angry letter to the press. Fred said that Mrs. Labouchère's departure was caused by the harmless gift he had made to Mrs. Langtry. Things had come to a pretty state of affairs if a gentleman couldn't make a token gift to a lady admired by every man in America.

In the excitement the reviews of *As You Like It* were forgotten. The publicity made the public all the more anxious to see the Jersey Lily, and the advance sale at the box office for the next four weeks amounted to an unprecedented sixty-five thousand dollars. The controversy over Lillie's morals was better for business than the most splendid reviews would have been.

Lillie announced that she would manage the company's American tour herself. She was to demonstrate a great natural aptitude for the handling of business details. She was as hardheaded as the veteran showmen with whom she dealt, men who were not impressed by either glamour or beauty.

A flair for publicity also led her to make another bold decision. Fred Gebhard, she told Abbey, would accompany her on the tour, which was scheduled to begin in Boston, and would act as her bodyguard. The producer was shocked by the idea. In the 1880s such things simply weren't done. But Lillie was indifferent to criticism. As the boom in New York sales had just demonstrated, scandal was good for business. And, gossip to the contrary, Fred indicated to others that he had not yet had an affair with Lillie, who was still holding him at arm's length.

At this juncture one of the most colorful Americans of the age began to play an important role in Lillie's life. Diamond Jim Brady, ostentatious, vulgar and generous, was a part-time stockmarket gambler, part-time businessman and self-styled railroad magnate. He always wore a huge diamond stickpin and cuff links, and he gave his favorite gems to a remarkably large number of his

friends. He thought nothing of inviting forty or fifty people to dine at Delmonico's or Sherry's, and, a teetotaler, he compensated for his dislike of liquor by eating gargantuan meals.

He had met Lillie soon after her arrival in New York, and had already given her a large diamond ring and a diamond brooch, asking nothing in return except the privilege of being seen in her company at the restaurants he frequented.

It was Brady who told Lillie that someone of her stature could not go on tour in the railroad accommodations available to ordinary people. She needed a private railroad car, and he obtained the loan of one called *The City of Worcester*, which boasted a living room, three bedrooms and a private bath. Lillie enjoyed the luxury so much that she developed a taste for private railroad cars, with results that would be spectacular.

The actors who had accompanied her from England were badly upset by Henrietta Labouchère's defection, but it was Kate Hodson, Henrietta's sister, who saved the day. Announcing that she had no intention of abandoning the tour, Kate said in print that her sister was a lifelong troublemaker who couldn't get along with anyone. The rest of the company grew calmer, and accepted Lillie as the manager as well as the star of the tour.

A huge crowd gathered to see the Jersey Lily depart on board *The City of Worcester* in early January, 1883. At her side was Fred Gebhard.

Boston maintained its traditional reserve, and only a few people were on hand when the train arrived there. That night a dinner was given in Lillie's honor at the exclusive Papyrus Club, many of whose members were authors and artists, men with whom she always felt at home. The following night she opened her engagement at the Globe Theatre, and the audience responded so enthusiastically that she took ten curtain calls.

Yet the newspaper reviews the following day were brutal. The critics said she was an amateur, her acting was shallow and her performance lacked sincerity. She might be pretty enough, if one was attracted by her type of beauty, but her appearance on the stage was a sham and a disgrace.

Long lines that formed outside the Globe Theatre mocked the critics, however, and within forty-eight hours every seat for the two-week engagement had been sold. Lillie was an attraction, no matter what the critics thought of her.

Quick to sense Boston's conservatism, Lillie acted accordingly. Fred dined with her in her hotel suite before the evening performance, and sometimes took her to and from the theater, but made no public appearances with her. When she went shopping, sight-seeing, or merely took a walk on the Common, she was escorted by one or another member of the British consulate staff. The newspapers made virtually no mention of Fred, and he remained invisible.

Fred's presence would be even less embarrassing with a chaperon on hand. Lillie had been corresponding with her sister-in-law Agnes Langtry, who had long admired her, and she thought a great many problems would be solved if Agnes joined her. She sent an invitation by cablegram, offering to pay all expenses, and Agnes promised to come immediately.

The offer had been extended just in time to avoid additional trouble. A prominent member of the House of Representatives, Richelieu Robinson, made a virulent attack on Lillie in a speech delivered on the floor of the House. He accused her of demoralizing the American stage and corrupting American society, and suggested that she be deported. Lillie had now to behave with greater discretion.

The shy, retiring Agnes arrived and accompanied the troupe to Chicago. She had no idea why she had been summoned, but soon learned, because Lillie needed all the help she could get.

Chicago, the fastest-growing city in the United States, had already achieved the reputation it would maintain for a good part of another century. Tough, rude and incredibly energetic, it stood on ceremony with no one. Men fought for the sheer love of combat and shouted at attractive women in the streets.

Lillie had to endure a baptism of press crossfire when her train arrived. A reporter from the *Inter-Ocean* persisted in asking about her relations with the Prince of Wales, and not even her refusal

to reply deterred him. Others questioned her closely about Fred Gebhard. Then she repaired to the Grand Pacific Hotel, where Fred occupied a suite directly above hers. Reporters took up watch in the corridors, and Fred could not come to her sitting room without bumping into them. On several occasions only the intervention of the hotel management prevented a fistfight.

There were compensations, of course. The entire engagement was sold out, in spite of the usual attack by the critics.

More confrontations and accusations by the press and members of an outraged public took place on the next two stops of the tour—Saint Louis and Memphis. But Lillie broke box-office records everywhere, and her personal share of the earnings amounted to more than six thousand dollars per week. No entertainer in history had earned such a sum.

By the time Lillie reached Buffalo, she was openly having an affair with Fred Gebhard. One evening Agnes Langtry, who occupied the bedroom on the far side of the sitting room in Lillie's suite, saw lights burning, and went to investigate. She was astonished and horrified to find the lovers drinking champagne, with Lillie dressed in her peignoir and Fred wearing pajamas.

Agnes departed before breakfast the next morning, returned immediately to England, and disappeared into the anonymity from which she had emerged.

Oscar Wilde was reunited with Lillie in Buffalo, where he had a lecture engagement, and their joint visit to Niagara Falls provided the ebullient Wilde with an opportunity to publicize himself again. "Every American bride is brought here," he said, "and must content herself with the sight of vast amounts of uninspired water. The sight of this waterfall must be one of the earliest, if not the keenest disappointments of American married life." When Lillie posed in front of the Falls, his quip provided copy in hundreds of newspapers. "Mrs. Langtry," he said, "was photographed with Niagara Falls as an unpretentious background."

The tour ended late in March, and Lillie was now a woman of means, having earned a net of somewhere between one hundred thousand and one hundred and fifty thousand dollars. She was still

the strongest box-office draw in the United States, and Henry Abbey was reluctant to see her depart for England. She readily agreed to extend her tour, and went into rehearsals with a play never before presented anywhere but in England, W. S. Gilbert's *Pygmalion and Galatea*, the familiar myth about a lovely Greek statue that came to life.

Lillie opened in it at the Fifth Avenue Theatre in late April, 1883, alternating the play with *She Stoops to Conquer*. As Galatea, all she had to do was look beautiful. She spent six weeks in New York before playing short return engagements in Boston and Philadelphia. Then the time came for a major break in her life, a chance to get away from her increasingly complicated romance with Fred Gebhard, a chance to see her daughter and a chance to improve and polish her talents as an actress.

## VII

IN JUNE 1883 Lillie Langtry sailed for England. She had a great deal to occupy her thoughts on the voyage. Fred desperately wanted to marry her, and she herself was deeply in love for the first time in her life. George Lewis, her London solicitor, had written repeatedly that there was no chance that Edward Langtry would consent to a divorce, but Abe Hummel, the American criminal lawyer who had become her friend, suggested she become a citizen of the United States, and then file for divorce in an American court. She promised to give the matter thought.

Lillie stayed a few days in London, visiting her parents, and afterward went on to Jersey, where she saw her daughter for the first time in many months. She hired additional servants to help the governess, and rented a somewhat larger house. Jeanne could now walk, after a fashion, and was babbling baby talk.

On July 1 the Jersey Lily arrived in Paris, and astounded the theatrical world by enrolling in the conservatory of François Joseph Régnier, the leading dramatic teacher of his day. No one of Lillie's standing had ever reduced herself to the role of a stu-

dent, but she was determined to win recognition for more than her beauty. Régnier had agreed to work exclusively with Lillie for the entire summer.

Members of the Paris theatrical community hailed Lillie's arrival. Sarah Bernhardt gave a dinner for her, and the leading playwright of the day, Victorien Sardou, was the host at another. She was entertained in the Green Room of the Comédie Française,

Mrs. Langtry.

**8**

## MRS. LANGTRY'S RECEPTION

### THE JERSEY LILY'S FIRST EXPERIENCE IN AMERICA.

FACING A CRITICAL CROWD OF THEATRICAL PEOPLE AND REPORTERS—THE CRITICS DISARMED AT THE FIRST ENCOUNTER—BUCKINGHAM'S COMEDY TROUPE ALSO ARIZONA.

A woman seldom has a harder time through than Mrs. Langtry had in America yesterday morning. Arizona, that brought her across, bore down upon the coast late and felt her way slowly up where daylight found her anchored, daylight, that is, as could make a nasty cold fog that almost the Narrows from view. Ever ship was wet with the fog, slippery, and seem...

# A Flair for Publicity

PEARS' SOAP.

Testimonial from Mrs. LANGTRY.

*"I have much pleasure in stating that I have used PEARS' SOAP for some time, and prefer it to any other."*

*Lillie Langtry*

and invitations by the score were delivered to her at the conservatory, but she sent her regrets for virtually all of them. She had come to Paris to work. Her situation, as she well knew, was unique. Unlike the great actresses of the day, she had come late to the theater, and was just beginning to learn her trade. At the same time, she was the most popular star of the era, and her name guaranteed a tremendous sale. Lillie realized, however, that the novelty would wear off one day, that in time she would be judged on the basis of her talent rather than her beauty.

Régnier was a disciplinarian in his mid-seventies who had lost none of the energy that had made him renowned. Lillie was required to appear in his second-floor studio at eight a.m., ready for

work, and usually did not finish until late at night. Régnier drove her hard, but she drove herself even harder, and she quickly won the respect of the master.

One day Sarah Bernhardt dropped in to watch Lillie's lesson. Accompanying her was the star of the Comédie Française, Benoît Coquelin, whose fame was legendary.

The chance visit brought miraculous results. The best actor and

Lillie's image: on a postcard; in The New York Times; in an ad for Pears' soap; in the New York Sunday Telegraph; in an ad for Hall's Between the Acts cigarettes; in a Police Gazette cartoon.

actress of the French theater were so impressed by Lillie's determination and perseverance that they volunteered to play opposite her as part of her training. Régnier and a delighted Lillie immediately accepted, and for a period of two to three weeks the Jersey Lily worked on the conservatory stage each day with Bernhardt and Coquelin, a priceless experience.

"Coquelin is extraordinary," Lillie said in a letter to a friend, Dion Boucicault. "He says more in a pause than most actors can say in hundreds of words. He drops a hand, he raises an eyebrow, and one feels the controlled power of his gestures. As for Bernhardt, she is magnificent! I despair of becoming a real actress when I work on the stage with her, and I would gladly exchange my

353

beauty, such as it is, for a soupçon of her great talent. I know I will never be a Bernhardt or a Coquelin, but must emphasize as best I can my own assets. I can make you one pledge. . . . When I return to America I will not disgrace you or any of the others who have had faith. Even the assassins of the press will applaud me."

In spite of her heavy work schedule, Lillie found—or made—the time to buy a dazzling wardrobe from Jean Worth, son of the man who had founded the world's foremost dressmaking house. Each day, during the lunch hour, dressmakers and their assistants appeared at the conservatory carrying bolts of cloth. She insisted that everything made for her be original, and exclusive.

She continued to prove, too, that she was a hardheaded business-woman. Worth's clothes were expensive, and Lillie ordered more than fifty dresses. But she paid only a fraction of what the dress-maker would have charged anyone else. She remembered the deals she had made in London when she had been a mere Professional Beauty. Now she was a theatrical star, whose costumes would be seen by thousands, and she arranged to give Worth program credit in lieu of cash for the better part of her bill.

A number of London managers were clamoring for a Langtry season, and Lillie was tempted to return to England, where she would be near her daughter and her parents, but she decided it would be premature to assault the London stage again. She could earn as much in America in a week as she could in a month in London. So she sent a cablegram to Henry Abbey, agreeing to appear in a new comedy by Daniel Frohman, *The Highest Bidder*. The play was light and her own role was not taxing, but would show her off to good advantage.

She needed two handsome leading men, and through friends in London engaged Arthur Elwood and James Pygott-Smyth. The rest of her small company was also recruited in London, and Lillie would cross the Atlantic with them at the end of September. She gave a farewell dinner in Paris, presenting Régnier with a diamond stickpin in the shape of a horseshoe, the symbol that Diamond Jim Brady had made famous.

It was evident on board ship that there was a new Lillie Langtry

in charge. Instead of sleeping until noon, she assembled her company early every morning, and rehearsals of *The Highest Bidder* were well advanced by the time the ship reached New York.

There the usual crowd of reporters had assembled, and Fred Gebhard, who surprised the press by being restrained and almost friendly, was on hand, too. Arrangements had been made for Lillie to rent an apartment at 120 West Thirteenth Street that was owned by Harriet Hubbard Ayer; Lillie returned the favor by endorsing Mrs. Ayer's cosmetic line.

In late October the play opened in New York, and William Winter noted Lillie's improvement as an actress. The enthusiasm of the other critics was restrained, but at least they didn't treat her with the contempt they had displayed the previous year.

Thanks to the apartment, she could lead a truly private life in New York. Fred Gebhard could come and go without being seen by reporters, and if Lillie gave a supper party, the list of her guests didn't appear in print the following day. Her stay in New York was uneventful. Business remained good, and every performance sold out.

Lillie began her tour in Boston, and it continued until late June, 1884. Nowhere had there been an empty seat, and Lillie was richer by another one hundred thousand to one hundred and twenty-five thousand dollars. When she returned to New York, she went off to the Catskills with Fred to help him buy racehorses for his stable. During this sojourn she wrote to George Lewis in London, expressing her desire to own a stable, the first time she had mentioned the idea in writing. What made the matter memorable was her ability, within a few years of starting a career, to think seriously of participating in the inordinately expensive sport of kings.

Lillie decided that the time had come to attack London. She had two full seasons in the United States under her belt, and believed she would now be accepted as a serious actress by the British. Fred Gebhard made plans to accompany her, but was dissuaded by Abe Hummel and George Lewis, who felt certain that Edward Langtry would never consent to a divorce if Fred's name were linked with Lillie's in the British press.

So Lillie sailed alone for England in August 1884. One of the best leading men of the London stage, Charles T. Coghlan, agreed to become her costar in a season of repertory. She rented the new Prince of Wales Theatre on Coventry Street in Piccadilly, which was becoming the theatrical center. If the appearance of Mrs. Langtry at a theater named after the Prince of Wales was accidental, it was remarkably fortuitous. Gossip remembered about her and the prince, together with the name of the theater, did not diminish her drawing power.

The Prince and Princess of Wales attended the opening performance of each play in the repertory during the 1885 season. The prince returned to watch other performances of each play, and invariably went backstage to visit the star. It was widely assumed that Lillie and the prince had quietly resumed their affair. Albert Edward made his own rules when dealing with ladies. As for Lillie, Fred Gebhard was on the far side of the Atlantic. All that can be said for certain is that the name of the future Edward VII did appear frequently in Lillie's correspondence. "The Prince of Wales thinks my performance has improved since the opening," she told William Winter. "The Prince of Wales thinks Coghlan and I have achieved perfect timing," she wrote to Dion Boucicault.

Fred Gebhard, meanwhile, had sent her a magnificent diamond brooch for Christmas, and other gems crossed the Atlantic from time to time. Had she wanted to buy her own jewelry, she was rapidly acquiring the means. Her season was an unqualified success. Her repertory of three plays included *The School for Scandal*, and any actress playing the role of Lady Teazle needed a polished high-comedy style. The critics were astonished by Lillie's performance, and without exception praised her hitherto unsuspected gifts as a classical comedienne.

But the play in the repertory that really established Lillie's reputation as a professional actress was Sardou's *Peril*. Translated into English at her suggestion, it seemed written specifically for her talents. She created a sensation in the role of a beautiful, charming lady of culture and means. Eventually *Peril* became the heart of

Lillie's repertory, and over a period of years earned her an estimated five hundred thousand dollars. The playwright Sardou became her lifelong, devoted friend.

Lillie's success in London made it possible for her to take a bold step that the fear of gossip had previously prevented. She brought her child and the governess to London, and for the first time Jeanne lived with Lillie. In the presence of outsiders the little girl learned to address her mother as "Aunt."

Fred Gebhard frequently wrote that he wanted to visit London, but Lillie held him off. Edward Langtry, happily collecting the monthly allowance Lillie sent him, had resumed his previous life in Southampton, boating and fishing. But he was drinking even more heavily now, and might become ugly, creating unfavorable publicity, if he learned that Lillie had an ardent American suitor.

There was more than enough unfavorable publicity caused by two of Lillie's high-society friends on July 23, 1885. Her swains were Sir George Chetwynd, High Sheriff of Warwick, who was married to the daughter of the Marquess of Anglesey, and Lord Lonsdale, whose wife was one of the few society women with whom Lillie had kept up a friendship after abandoning her career as a Professional Beauty.

Sir George ardently desired an affair with Lillie, and she was equally anxious to deter him. Lord Lonsdale was the weapon she chose to fend him off, as she knew that he, too, in spite of her friendship with his wife, would become romantically inclined if she encouraged him. To play them off against each other, she arranged to meet them at the same place and time, and hoped that Sir George, in particular, would become discouraged when he realized he had a rival.

Lillie chose London's most fashionable promenade, Rotten Row, for her double rendezvous. One rode or walked there daily between noon and two o'clock to see and be seen, to gossip and remain in the social swim. Like a character in a farce of the period, Lillie told each of her admirers that she would meet him at one p.m. beneath the statue of Achilles. She arrived a quarter of an hour early, heavily veiled, and stood on the far side of some bushes.

357

Sir George and Lord Lonsdale, both on horseback, arrived more or less simultaneously. They chatted amicably for several minutes, until one or the other revealed that he was meeting Mrs. Langtry.

At that point the quarrel started, and a crowd began to gather. Sir George was the first to lose his temper. He shouted, and delivered a blow with his riding crop, knocking off Lord Lonsdale's hat. His lordship returned the blows, striking with such abandon that both horses began to buck. The crowd fell back, giving the combatants room. Lillie continued to watch from a distance.

Their horses became so unruly that both men were forced to dismount, and were wrestling when a squad of hastily summoned mounted policemen halted the fight. The combatants were sent to their respective homes in closed carriages. Even the most austere London newspapers reported the affair, and the ha'penny press went wild. Although the publicity barrage did not add luster to Lillie's name, it helped the box office, and she extended her London run for a month.

Apparently reasoning that the worst had already happened, and that no publicity could be more harmful, Lillie cabled Fred Gebhard. Telling him to ignore the fight, which had no real significance, she asked him to join her as soon as possible for a holiday before her eight-week tour in the provinces.

Fred had pride and a mind of his own, however. Refusing to be summoned at Lillie's convenience, he cabled that he was paying no attention to the press accounts, but that his business affairs made it impossible for him to leave the United States at that time.

Other results of the fight were even more unpleasant. Seeing Lillie's present vulnerability, a number of London tradespeople brought suit against her for money owed them in the days when she had been virtually bankrupt. During the trial, a deposition from Edward Langtry was read into the record. He was in no position to pay the alleged bills, he said, "because I have no funds other than the annuity allowed me by my wife on the condition that I do not molest her."

The court ruled in Lillie's favor, but the revelation of her private affairs during the trial had been embarrassing. As usual, though,

notoriety brought compensations. In York, Liverpool, Edinburgh, Lillie's public clamored for seats. Lillie extended her tour, and did not return to London until a few days before Christmas.

Fred Gebhard unexpectedly appeared. Mrs. Le Breton, who was visiting at the time, liked Fred enormously. Presumably the good lady knew nothing of the notoriety her daughter and Fred had attained. In fact, Mrs. Le Breton moved into Lillie's house as chaperon so Fred could stay there. Ordinarily, the wealthy and handsome Fred would have been welcomed by the British aristocracy. But the ladies who determined such matters, led by the American-born women who had married into the nobility, turned their thumbs down. Lillie Langtry was no longer acceptable in many of London's best homes, so her American lover was kept out, too. There is no evidence that Lillie and Fred felt hurt.

In the half decade of Lillie's theatrical career, she had taken no prolonged holidays. She and Fred decided now to take a grand continental tour, with him acting as her escort-bodyguard, a necessity on this tour, which began in February 1886. Police reserves had to be called out in Brussels to extricate Lillie from a throng of admirers. So many followed her in Amsterdam that she and Fred had to do their sight-seeing at night. Even in blasé Paris, where Lillie had become a familiar sight, crowds gathered to catch a glimpse of them.

In Vienna she discovered that Crown Prince Rudolf, who had embarrassed her with his attentions in London, had not forgotten her. She and Fred dined in the Austro-Hungarian capital with him, and the following afternoon the prince took Lillie on a personally conducted tour of his palace.

The hour Lillie spent there was one of the strangest she had ever known. Room after room was filled with enameled clocks, bric-a-brac and historical relics in glass cabinets. Lillie made the mistake of remarking that the place looked more like a museum than a home.

With his walking stick, Rudolf immediately began smashing cabinets, priceless crystal chandeliers and clocks. Two of his aides could not stop him, nor could Lillie's repeated pleas.

359

At last exhaustion forced Rudolf to halt, and he quietly led Lillie to a parlor for tea. Lillie wrote in her autobiography that he had gone on the rampage in order to please her, and that she had never before been so frightened. She could not have been surprised, a few years later, when she read of Rudolf's suicide.

In September 1886 she launched a new assault on the United States, accompanied by Charles Coghlan. Upon her arrival Fred Gebhard presented her with a gift, the deed to a house located at 362 West Twenty-third Street, in what was then New York's most exclusive residential district. The house had been built by Clement Clarke Moore, author of the classic *'Twas the Night Before Christmas*. It was a small, exquisite mansion, with a long driveway. Lillie had a high fence of grilled iron put in so her lawns, flowers and shrubs wouldn't be trampled by the daily crowds. Fred, ever generous, hired James Mitchell, New York's most high-priced contractor and decorator. For the first time in her life free to decorate as she pleased, Lillie had walls knocked down and rooms enlarged, ornate marble fireplaces and marble bathtubs installed.

Lillie played the same repertory that London had applauded, and the New York critics were even kinder to her than the English had been. The *Times* said she deserved and had earned her stardom. The *Post* announced that her acting was so superior the audience actually forgot her beauty.

But her beauty was not forgotten. Lillie, now thirty-three years of age, looked ten years younger, and the press knew she not only drank champagne regularly but that she and Fred Gebhard often gave parties that lasted the better part of the night. Lillie was a wonder, and the press sought her beauty secret. Sensing headlines, she revealed she was an exercise addict. She gave no details, and not until after her death was it revealed that she indulged in what came to be known nearly a century later as jogging. Every day, shortly after arising, she dressed in heavy woolens and had herself driven to some remote park or rural area, and no matter what the weather, she trotted for a minimum of two miles. In Lillie's day ladies were expected to be sedentary, but accustomed to sports,

in her childhood, she paid no attention to the notion. The Jersey Lily thus became one of the initiators of the youth cult.

Her New York run did not close until late March 1887. Lillie had been making plans for her most ambitious tour, which would take her to the shores of the Pacific, then back to the Atlantic. For personal convenience and maximum publicity she wanted a private railroad car.

Fred Gebhard offered to pay for it, and Lillie told the manufacturer what she wanted; she received an extraordinary railroad car. It was seventy-five feet long, and at either end was a platform of teakwood imported from the Orient. The rim beneath the roof was decorated with a bas-relief of brass lilies. The car was painted a color described as Jersey blue, and the curved roof was done in the heavy white enamel Lillie loved.

The principal bedroom was upholstered in a rich, green silk, and every piece of furniture was padded to prevent injury when the moving train bumped and jolted. Adjoining the stateroom was Lillie's bath with fittings of silver, her dressing room and a small sitting room, both of which boasted curtains of rose-colored silk. Beyond stood the parlor, a chamber filled with overstuffed chairs and a piano, and lined with bookcases. At the far end were two guest bedrooms, a maid's room, a kitchen, and a pantry complete with a large icebox.

Lillie named the car *Lalee*, which, she said, was the East Indian word for flirt.

The railroad car was the best publicity device she had ever developed. Tens of thousands of words were written about it over the years. Everywhere it advertised the presence of its owner, and in city after city large crowds gaped at it in railroad stations and yards.

More than the tour and her expensive new toy occupied Lillie's mind, however. Abe Hummel continued to prevail upon her to become an American citizen and obtain her divorce in the United States. She was proud of her heritage and reluctant to give up her English citizenship, but had grown desperate. George Lewis had gone to Edward Langtry and offered him a generous lump sum if

he would consent to a divorce, but the stubborn Langtry had again refused.

Lewis continued to advise against bringing suit in England. Lillie had left Langtry, which would tend to strengthen his position, and in any event, a divorce there could be obtained only on the grounds of adultery. She had no evidence against her husband, but he could make life thoroughly uncomfortable for her. And if he questioned the paternity of her daughter, of whose existence he and the world still knew nothing, the scandal could cause endless repercussions.

American citizenship appeared to be the only solution.

## VIII

LILLIE began her transcontinental tour in April 1887, and by the first of July she was in San Francisco. Everywhere the Langtry name guaranteed sold-out theaters, and the money poured in. The *Lalee* attracted so much attention that Fred Gebhard could not travel with Lillie. He reached San Francisco first, and conferred with the attorney Hummel had engaged to represent Lillie there, W. H. L. Barnes. At his recommendation Fred approved the purchase, in her name, of a ranch near the city. Armed with the deed, the lawyer filed an application for citizenship on her behalf using influence to avoid undesired publicity. But the ever-vigilant San Francisco press ferreted out the story, and on July 17, 1887, when her citizenship was granted, the news put her on the front pages. Americans applauded her move. But feeling ran high against her in Great Britain; her personal motives were unknown, and editorials suggested that English audiences would not forgive or forget her desertion of her native land.

The California property Lillie had purchased was a working ranch of more than four thousand acres. She hired a manager for it, Charles W. Aby, then bought several racehorses and housed them at the ranch. Apparently it was her intention to fulfill her long-standing dream of owning her own stable, but when distances pre-

cluded racing her animals in the East and stabling them in the West, she sold the horses.

Before departing on the eastward swing of her tour, Lillie appeared privately in the chambers of a California judge to obtain a divorce. She testified that Edward Langtry had been unable to support her, that he had left her for long periods to seek his own pleasures, and that, after declaring herself bankrupt, she had been forced to earn her living on the stage. Her divorce was granted.

Rumors of the divorce appeared in print during the following months, as did a persistent story that Lillie either had married or was on the verge of marrying Fred Gebhard. She denied the allegations. Why she didn't marry Fred now that she was free remains a mystery. She was in love with him, he had demonstrated his fidelity and loyalty and he wanted to marry her. Probably Jeanne Marie was the inhibiting factor. Edward Langtry was unaware of the fact that he had been divorced, and still didn't know of the child's existence. Were he to find out, he could stir up trouble, and Lillie didn't want vicious gossip to harm her child.

She had no desire to see her plans for the autumn disrupted. She was wealthy enough now to support her parents as well as her daughter, and her father had finally agreed to retire. The Reverend and Mrs. Le Breton intended to bring their granddaughter to the United States, and the whole family would live in Lillie's New York town house. Gossip could wreck that plan, and would mar Jeanne's entire future. However, while Lillie was still on tour she received word that her family's trip was postponed due to the serious illness of the Reverend Le Breton. His physicians were optimistic, and Mrs. Le Breton urged her daughter not to make the long journey home.

After reaching New York, Lillie went with Fred to Saratoga for a week to watch his horses run, and then returned to the city to make plans for the new season. Sarah Bernhardt had just arrived for a tour of her own, and Lillie entertained her frequently. They posed together for photographs, donning boxing gloves and pretending to fight.

Lillie now had acquired approximately five hundred thousand

dollars, the equivalent of four times that amount almost a century later, and Abe Hummel suggested that he invest it on her behalf. Lillie gave him a quarter of a million, keeping the rest aside.

Her play for the new season was *As in a Looking Glass,* and her part was that of a sadistic, domineering woman who used her beauty to tyrannize others. This was a departure from the sweet milksops she had previously portrayed. In order to bolster her company she hired one of the most dashing young stars of the day, Maurice Barrymore. They struck sparks together onstage; their love scenes were so realistic that it was rumored Fred Gebhard was jealous and threatened to challenge Barrymore to a duel. The story was absurd; in private life Barrymore was happily married to the talented and lovely actress Georgiana Drew, but the talk helped sell tickets.

When the company went on tour, Fred remained behind, "renting" Lillie's house. He joined her now and then for a few days, but he disliked the unending traveling of show business.

The theater was a gold mine for Lillie, and she struck silver elsewhere. Hummel had purchased real estate for her in Carson City, Nevada, and a rich vein of silver, allegedly worth five hundred dollars per ton, was discovered on the property. The newspapers speculated that she could sell the plot for at least a quarter of a million dollars; she did sell, but only she and Hummel knew the price. She was rapidly becoming one of the world's most independently wealthy women, and could retire whenever she wished.

When the company reached Chicago in February 1888, Lillie canceled several performances, announcing that she was ill. She was actually in good health, but had received word from London that her father had died. No one except Barrymore and a few other members of the company knew the truth. She successfully concealed her tragedy from the press and the public.

When she returned to Manhattan in mid-June, she barely had time to get her Twenty-third Street house in readiness for her seventy-year-old mother and seven-year-old daughter; they arrived without publicity. Soon Fred Gebhard was seen on the bridle paths with Jeanne Marie, whom he also took to the zoo, the circus and

other entertainments. Since Lillie was still stalling about marriage, he was perhaps seeking a new, persuasive weapon.

In July Lillie rented a house for the summer at Long Branch, New Jersey, for herself and family, and Fred Gebhard moved in with them. When Fred wasn't swimming with Jeanne, accompanying Lillie on her morning constitutional jog or escorting her to social functions, he was kept busy fending off the persistent questions of reporters about his marital status. Lillie herself kept interest in the subject alive by smiling enigmatically, while continuing to follow Gladstone's advice—maintaining silence regarding her personal affairs.

Another visitor that summer at the Long Branch house was Lillie's brother Clement. He had become one of London's leading barristers, and came to the United States at her request to review Lillie's legal and financial situation. George Lewis was on the verge of retirement, and Clement was taking charge of his sister's affairs in London. Their subsequent correspondence reveals that Clement believed Edward Langtry should be officially notified that Lillie had divorced him in an American court. But Lillie refused. She was earning so much that the monthly allowance she sent Edward meant nothing to her.

Before beginning her preparations for the coming theatrical season, Lillie hired a general manager, Frank C. Griffith, to look after her enterprises. He was efficient, sought no limelight for himself and remained with her for a long time.

*As in a Looking Glass* went on tour again in September, and remained on the road until mid-December. Mrs. Le Breton and Jeanne Marie saw something of America by traveling with Lillie in the *Lalee,* and the party included a tutor for the little girl. Fred Gebhard again stayed behind in New York; the newspapers hinted that their romance was growing cooler.

As soon as Lillie returned from the tour, she plunged into her most ambitious project. No actor or actress acquired real stature until he or she played Shakespeare, and she had made up her mind to do *Macbeth.* Coghlan would direct and play opposite her, and Lillie was listed as the producer. She spent an unprecedented eight

thousand dollars for costumes and scenery. Some newspapers criticized her before the opening, saying she intended to lull the critics and the public by drowning them in luxury.

Coghlan, who had played Shakespeare opposite Ellen Terry, closed the theater to outsiders during rehearsals. It was rumored that Lillie was encountering difficulty, that her role was too much for her, and the public held back for the first time. They would pay to see Lillie Langtry, looking and sounding like herself in a wardrobe by Worth, but they would not purchase tickets to see her playing Shakespeare unless the critics approved.

To the astonishment of the skeptical, the critics unanimously hailed Lillie's Lady Macbeth. William Winter set the tone: "She was admirable and rose to greatness; she was grand and exquisite." In the United States she was recognized as an actress of the first magnitude. Now she wanted to conquer England too. Besides, she was homesick for London, and she needed to replenish her wardrobe. Lillie engaged a large suite on a Cunard liner, the *Servia*, for herself, her mother, her daughter, the governess, two maids and sixty-three pieces of luggage.

When the boat docked at Southampton, Lillie astonished the press by greeting them with a lighted cigarette in her hand. At that time only men and prostitutes smoked. But Lillie had started to smoke onstage in one of her roles, and was a steady smoker in private. To her, later, would belong the dubious credit of being one of the first women, if not the first, to smoke in public, and to make smoking acceptable if not respectable.

One of Lillie's first callers in London was Oscar Wilde, who brought with him the manuscript of a play he had written for her. He called it *Lady Windermere's Fan*, and had assured her in a letter that he had tailored the role perfectly to suit her own personality. Lillie was shocked when he told her that her part was that of an upperclass woman who was the mother of a grown, illegitimate daughter. She refused indignantly to read the play. Her ostensible reason for rejecting it was that she was not old enough to play the mother of an adult daughter; her real reason, of course, was that it struck too close to home. Her relations with Wilde became

strained, and they were barely on speaking terms for more than two years. His feelings were somewhat assuaged when *Lady Windermere's Fan* became one of the greatest high-comedy successes of the era. Lillie, meanwhile, elected to present *As You Like It* at the St. James' Theatre. She chose the play because she had been an amateur when she first appeared in it, and now that she was a professional, she wanted London to see the difference in her performance.

A few hours before her opening, Lillie was bedded by a high fever. Her physician diagnosed the ailment as measles; the opening was postponed. While recuperating she caught influenza, and for ten days was seriously ill. The world press ran daily front-page stories on her condition. It was variously reported that Lillie was dying, that she had lost her hair, that she had retired from the stage and that she would be crippled for life. But after two weeks she began to improve and was able to reschedule the opening of *As You Like It* for mid-November, 1889.

News of her illness brought Fred Gebhard to London. He paid Lillie one visit which lasted thirty minutes, then turned around and caught the next ship for New York. What caused their break is not known, although there were persistent rumors that Fred encountered the Prince of Wales calling on Lillie, and that he made an ugly scene. They did not resume their affair. Years passed before they met again, casually, after Fred had married.

When *As You Like It* finally opened, critics were as lavish in their praise as they had been chary when Lillie first appeared in the role. *The Times* declared her a "bewitching Rosalind." The play sold out for its entire booking. Encouraged by her favorable reception, she purchased a house at 21 Pont Street.

Lillie's next decision was one of the shrewdest of her career; she would produce Shakespeare's *Antony and Cleopatra*, with Coghlan directing and playing opposite her. The greatest beauty of her age would be an irresistible magnet in the role of one of the celebrated beauties of all ages. She would also enhance the play with a lavish production in the style of her New York *Macbeth*.

As Lillie had anticipated, the bait of seeing her as Cleopatra

brought patrons to the box office in droves, and ten weeks of the run were sold out in advance. Lillie approached the opening with apprehension, for the role was complex, and would stretch her talents to the limit. Under Coghlan's imaginative direction she was attempting new approaches to the part, and was even refusing to wear the black wig traditionally Cleopatra's.

The play opened on April 28, 1890, with the Prince and Princess of Wales in their box. The sumptuous production overwhelmed the audience, and Lillie herself won the greatest applause of her career.

"Mrs. Langtry is dazzling!" *The Times* said. "She is the finest Cleopatra of our time," said the *Telegraph*. Lillie played Cleopatra to capacity audiences through the rest of 1890, her longest run. Eventually it became a staple of her repertory, and was estimated to have earned her more than one million dollars.

When it did finally close, an exhausted Lillie went off to Jersey, where she'd rented a house for her mother and daughter. She stayed there with them for two months, and in early March of 1891 took them to Paris. She showed them the sights, and they joined her at dinners given by Sarah Bernhardt, Sardou, Coquelin and others. During the three-week sojourn she spent many hours at the House of Worth, and when she returned to London in April she brought with her seventeen trunks filled with new gowns.

Damp weather may have been responsible, in part, for a brief but serious illness that forced her to postpone any thoughts of doing a new play. An attack of pleurisy sent her to bed for a week, and again the world press gave its readers an edition-by-edition account of her condition. When she recovered she decided to do no acting until the autumn, and instead turned to her favorite hobby, attending horse races.

As a direct consequence she became involved in the stormiest and most spectacular of her romances. Much later, in a remark to friends, she said, "It served me right for being lazy. How I wish I'd been spending my days in the theater, where I belonged!"

While attending the races, she met George Alexander Baird, Baron Auchmeddon. Possessor of one of the oldest and proudest of

Scottish names, he was the last of his line, and was one of the wealthiest men in Great Britain. His income, most of it from coal mines in Scotland, was estimated at more than a quarter of a million pounds per year.

Known as Squire Abington, a name he used as an amateur jockey, he was the darling of the ha'penny press. His father died when he was a small boy, and he had led a completely undisci-

Lillie's Impressive Possessions

plined life. A rebel who had never worked, he turned his back on high society, and consorted with jockeys, prizefighters and prostitutes. He was himself a pugnacious drinker, a brawler, an iconoclast, a gaudy dresser and, above all, a hedonist who never looked beyond the pleasures of the present.

Baird had seen Lillie as Cleopatra, and introduced himself to her by presenting her with betting slips on two of his horses. She tried to refuse, but he started to make a scene, and in her embarrassment she kept the slips. Both horses won, and she tried to return the one hundred pounds she had acquired. Baird accepted on condition that she accompany him to dinner, and he succeeded in spending the entire one hundred pounds that evening.

A psychiatrist might find it interesting that Lillie was older than several of the most important men in her life. As an adult she clung to her own youth. Beauty had made her famous, and one way to remain beautiful was to form attachments to younger men. Thirty-eight years of age when she met Baird, she looked like a girl in her mid-twenties, her beauty still unblemished.

She didn't care what anyone thought of her, and she made no

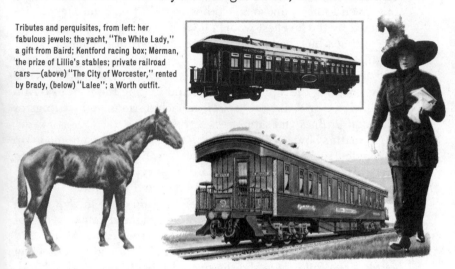

Tributes and perquisites, from left: her fabulous jewels; the yacht, "The White Lady," a gift from Baird; Kentford racing box; Merman, the prize of Lillie's stables; private railroad cars—(above) "The City of Worcester," rented by Brady, (below) "Lalee"; a Worth outfit.

secret of her relationship with Baird. Apparently they plunged into an affair almost immediately. Casting aside all conventions, she even allowed him to kiss and caress her in public.

What she, who had always shown taste in her choice of clothes, decor and men, saw in him is unknown. Whatever it was, she seemed mesmerized. For years the Squire had been seen in public with a succession of ripe young actresses with highly questionable reputations. A number of his affairs had ended abruptly after the unfortunate young woman had suffered blackened eyes and other assorted bruises. One actress had charged him with assault and battery after an evening on the town, and he had been forced to settle out of court.

Lillie's friends found Baird repulsive, her colleagues avoided him, and the good ladies of London so despised him that they snubbed Lillie openly. Her butler departed, and so did one of her maids. She knew better than to invite Baird to Jersey to meet her mother and daughter, and it is unlikely that he would have gone. In fact, nothing that had been important in her life mattered to him. He admitted that plays bored him; he had no taste for gracious living. Even Lillie's handsome clothes were lost on him. He was infatuated by the loveliest woman he had ever seen, but he rejected the setting which had become so much a part of her life.

Lillie and her new lover had two interests in common, fine horses and fine jewelry. During the racing season they could be seen daily, cheering the Squire's winners and visiting the paddock. And Lillie blazed with new bracelets, brooches, rings and earrings of diamonds, rubies and sapphires.

No matter how lavish his gifts, he did her career no good. He demanded so much of her time that it was impossible for her to prepare a play for the 1891–92 season. He even objected when she went to Jersey for visits with her mother and daughter.

A crisis occurred in the strange relationship early in 1892, when the Squire went off to Scotland for a hunting and drinking trip of uncertain duration. Lillie went to Jersey to see Jeanne Marie, and then traveled to Paris so she could add to her already overflowing wardrobe. While there she discovered that Robert Peel, a handsome and personable young man, grandson of the great statesman, and soon to inherit his father's baronetcy, was a guest at the same hotel. He was an old friend, and they dined together one evening. A few days later they lunched together, then came back to Lillie's suite for a chat.

While they were talking, George Baird burst into the sitting room. He had found Lillie absent when he had returned to London, and had followed her to Paris. He had been drinking, and lost all self-control when he saw her chatting with another man. First he accused Lillie of cheating, and when Peel tried to intervene, turned on him, knocked him down repeatedly, then threw him out of the suite. Robert Peel was no match for a drunken madman.

Lillie had no chance to call for help. The furious Baird assaulted her, blackening both her eyes and inflicting an ugly bruise on her cheekbone. When she screamed for help, he choked her until she lost consciousness. In unabated rage, the Squire made a shambles of her suite. Paintings and tapestries were ripped from the walls, furniture was overturned and smashed. Several new gowns had just been delivered, and he ripped them to shreds and then scattered the contents of her dresser drawers.

Lillie spent ten days in a hospital. The ha'penny press was quick to claim that she had been so disfigured she could never again appear on a stage. The actual facts were lurid enough, but the newspapers made them worse. Young Peel and Lillie both refused to press charges, and Baird, who had been held in jail without bail, was freed.

Lillie returned to her suite, which had been refurbished at the Squire's expense, and found a diamond bracelet from Cartier's waiting for her. She kept the jewelry, but refused to see the donor.

She remained in Paris for two weeks, convalescing, and each day new gifts arrived. One afternoon she received fifty gowns from Worth, the following day a ruby pendant. She was given three magnificent racehorses, all of them future champions. But her door remained closed to George Baird.

When she went to Cherbourg to take the Channel steamer to Dover, a steward was on hand to tell her that "her" yacht awaited her. She was conducted to a magnificent steamship of 750 tons, 220 feet long, that was riding at anchor in the harbor.

She went on board *The White Lady,* and there an abject George Baird awaited her. He handed her documents giving her ownership of the yacht, as well as a check for fifty thousand pounds for the vessel's maintenance and crew's salaries. Casually, with no strings attached, he was making her a gift worth one half million dollars.

Lillie knew the publicity benefits she had reaped from the *Lalee.* Ownership of *The White Lady* should prove even more beneficial, so she accepted conditionally. Baird could not drink in her presence, nor would she see him when he had been drinking. He could no longer interfere with her career or personal life, and she was free

to go anywhere or see anyone she pleased. He would visit her only by invitation, and if, in her opinion, he misbehaved or mistreated any of her friends, she would never see him again.

The penitent Squire accepted the conditions without question, and Lillie forgave him. They spent several days at sea before *The White Lady* put into port. Newspapers and magazines ran countless pictures of the ship, and disapproving publications indicated that Lillie deserved her association with a man of Baird's caliber. American newspapers called the vessel *The Black Eye*, and the name was picked up around the world. Society was aghast, and even some of Lillie's friends privately believed she had gone too far.

She finally returned to London, eager to work, and after renting the Criterion Theatre, went into rehearsals in a light comedy, *The Fringe of Society*. Her role, that of a bad woman with the proverbial heart of gold, was not taxing, and when she opened in early May, 1892, the critics said she had never looked lovelier than she did now at thirty-nine. The play sold out for eight weeks. Lillie had never appeared in a real failure, a record that few members of her profession could equal.

In June, with the still-penitent Squire accompanying her, Lillie went to the Kempton Park track to see the first race run by one of her own horses, Milford. The jockey wore her new colors, turquoise and fawn. Milford won, and Lillie, who had bet heavily on him, was one thousand pounds wealthier. The Squire happily admitted to the press that he had won ten thousand pounds.

Lillie's play closed in August. The yacht had been redecorated in accordance with her wishes, Baird picking up the tab. Mrs. Le Breton and Jeanne Marie joined Lillie and Baird on board. The press made much of the fact that *The White Lady* was not only larger than J. P. Morgan's famous *Corsair*, but dwarfed the yachts of Queen Victoria and the Prince of Wales.

A whole new series of rumors started. Lillie intended to make a trip around the world. She planned to sail to the United States for the theatrical season. She would give up her homes on land and spend all of her time at sea.

The Jersey Lily made no attempt to stem the ceaseless flow of

gossip by announcing her actual plans. She would say nothing that might pinch off her priceless publicity. When Griffith, her business manager, spent a week on the yacht, she told him that she intended to work hard and double her fortune. The world thought of her as a fortune-hunting glamour girl, and she would not destroy that image as long as it remained profitable.

## IX

THE theater season of 1893 was made more tolerable for Lillie because George Baird, still a boor, and still associating with disreputable people, went off to the United States to see the British heavyweight Charlie Mitchell fight "Gentleman Jim" Corbett.

Then, late in March, Lillie was informed that Baird had died in a New Orleans hotel room. He had caught pneumonia after a drinking spree, and had been too weak to combat the ailment.

Lillie's grief was restrained, and Griffith said years later that he thought she seemed somewhat relieved. She had grown tired of Baird's constant presence, and probably feared his uncontrolled jealous rages, despite his promises. She was forced, however, to rearrange some of her own interests. Her horses had been housed in the Squire's stables under the direction of his trainers, so she had to hire a trainer of her own. She also bought a three-story house called Regal Lodge in the tiny town of Kentford. The place had its own stable, and was known as a racing box.

The yacht was another big expense, with Baird no longer on hand to take care of the bills. Lillie put the ship up for charter. The shrewd maneuver paid handsome dividends, for there were many who wanted to say they had spent time on the Jersey Lily's yacht. Edward Michael, Griffith's assistant and the man who managed most of her personal financial affairs, aptly claimed that Lillie was congenitally incapable of losing money.

By the summer of 1893 Lillie believed that her daughter was old enough to tolerate any London whispers that might reach her, so the child and Mrs. Le Breton took up residence in the house on

Pont Street. Their presence made life easier for Lillie, since she was no longer forced to shuttle back and forth between London and the Isle of Jersey. But she kept the house there, using it as a holiday home, just as she did her Kentford racing box.

After devoting herself almost exclusively to Baird, Lillie was anxious to get back into the social swim. And she wanted to enjoy the experience of living permanently under the same roof with her daughter. So she took a year's sabbatical, and when London became boring she went to Kentford and bought more horses for her growing stable.

Many of the ladies of London had continued to snub her, but the gentlemen did not avoid her, and it was inevitable that her name be romantically linked with those of a number of prominent men. Two of her more frequent escorts were members of the diplomatic corps, the Portuguese ambassador, the Marquis Luis de Soveral, and the Austro-Hungarian chargé d'affaires, Prince Paul Esterhazy. Both were eligible bachelors. One or the other escorted Lillie to the more important and glittering social events of the season, and whenever the Prince of Wales was present he danced with her or chatted with her at length. Thus it was impossible for the good ladies to avoid her. Lillie was too proud to seek their friendships, but she deliberately made life more difficult for them, and spoke to them when in the company of the future Edward VII or a diplomat who could not be ignored. Had Lillie cared what society thought of her she might have been unhappy, but she had created a fantastically successful life of her own, and she was content.

Mark Twain, who met her on a number of occasions, was impressed, and wrote at length about her clarity of judgment. He said: "Contrary to what one would expect of a woman whose fame was based on her beauty, Mrs. Langtry is an exceptionally intelligent person. She must read constantly because she is able to discuss in detail any book, classical or modern, English or American or French, that is mentioned to her. I know she isn't shamming, because I questioned her in some detail, and she *knew* the books. She also reads the newspapers, and doesn't bother with the trivia. She can talk about world affairs or financial matters or whatever

with the good sense one would expect of a man who keeps up to date. She meets a stranger as an equal, and although she's so pretty her beauty is blinding, she doesn't rely on feminine charm. She's what she is, and she expects one to take her or leave her. She is good company with her friends, but it would be hell to be married to her. She's too damn bright."

She was also too wise to bear grudges, and by the autumn of 1893 she and Oscar Wilde resumed their friendship. Success had changed Wilde: he had grown fat, he lost his temper quickly and resented criticism. Lillie disapproved of the handsome young men who followed him everywhere and laughed at his witticisms. But his wit was sharper than ever.

He had just written *A Woman of No Importance*, but did not offer it to Lillie, undoubtedly wanting to avoid another rebuff. Lillie was seeking a new play, but did not blame him for not approaching her. She was one of the few in show business who refused to engage in long feuds, and she demonstrated to Wilde her affection and esteem by attending the opening-night performance. He returned the compliment in March 1894 by being present at Lillie's opening in *The Social Butterfly*, an inferior play which, nevertheless, offered her a long, emotional role.

The clamor in the United States for a return of the actress whose presence guaranteed box office was rising, so Lillie agreed to a new tour under the management of E. B. Norman. She would spend sixteen weeks on the road and then play for a month in New York. She hired James Pygott-Smyth as her leading man, and carried forty trunks of Worth clothes with her. Jeanne Marie accompanied her, but Mrs. Le Breton, who was ailing, remained in London.

New York was growing so rapidly that Lillie hardly recognized it in late summer, 1894. The theatrical district was inching uptown from Twenty-third Street to Thirty-fourth and even as far up as Forty-second Street. But some things were unchanged, and on her arrival the usual army of reporters met her to pay homage.

The house on Twenty-third Street that the now married Fred Gebhard had bought for her was unrented and run-down, and at Abe Hummel's suggestion she put it on the market. Hummel also

sold some property in Salt Lake City that brought her a net profit of more than forty thousand dollars. The sale of some lots in rapidly growing Chicago realized another eighteen thousand dollars. Hummel promptly reinvested the money for her. The theater was no longer her principal source of income.

She and Jeanne Marie traveled in the *Lalee,* which had been repainted and redecorated, and everywhere they went Lillie did capacity business and received excellent reviews. She decided to stay for the next season to appear in an American play, with an American cast. The time had come for a complete change of pace, and she didn't want to be typed as an English actress. She had no difficulty in finding the right vehicle. Clyde Fitch, who would become a most successful American dramatist, brought Lillie his new play, a comedy provocatively called *Gossip.*

The play opened at Palmer's Theatre in New York on March 11, 1895, and with the exception of the always loyal William Winter the critics attacked her. The play was good, they said, but Mrs. Langtry paid far more attention to her clothes, which were distracting, and to her ostentatious jewelry, than she did to her role.

The *Sun* became sarcastic: "Mrs. Langtry's brilliant company of diamonds, sapphires and the largest ruby in captivity is ably supported by Mrs. Langtry and several other living actors." Lillie did own the largest ruby in the world. It was set in a brooch she occasionally pinned to a gown just before going onstage. Thousands of women bought seats in the hope that they would attend a performance when she wore her fabulous ruby. The assault centered, however, on a diamond tiara; when she appeared in it every woman in the audience gasped, and the onstage action halted.

The playwright, Fitch, claimed that the jewels did detract from his play. Lillie told him the play's climax needed the diamonds to bolster it. Fitch insisted the drama would stand on its own. So Lillie agreed to an experiment. She would perform without the jewels, and if the playwright was satisfied with the reaction of the audience she would put away her diamond headpiece. Fitch stood at the back of the theater and watched the audience sit in a dull, semistupor when Lillie made her appearance in the big scene.

He hurried backstage to her dressing room. "Don't ever play that scene without your tiara!" he said.

*Gossip* sold out, and seats were unavailable at any price. Audiences came to see Lillie in the clothes and jewels that had drawn so much critical fire, and Fitch, hauling in his royalties, was happy.

The press estimated Lillie's collection of gems to be worth as high as two million dollars. Jewelry insurance was virtually unknown in the late nineteenth century, so only Lillie knew that many of her jewels were made of paste.

At least a few people learned the true value of the jewels later that same year. When she went off to Paris on her customary clothes-buying jaunt, she stored part of her collection in a prominent London bank. On the day of her return a messenger went to the bank and presented a note bearing her signature, asking that the jewels be given into his custody for delivery to her.

The next day Lillie herself went to pick up her jewelry. The officials presented her with the note, now seen to be a forgery. The gems had vanished. Lillie sued the bank for negligence. Its officials offered a settlement of forty-five thousand pounds, half the sum Lillie had demanded. But she accepted it gladly, indicating that she probably had not suffered a financial loss. Thereafter, until she rebuilt her jewelry collection, she wore only a thick rope of pearls. Perhaps as a consequence pearls became the fashion.

When Lillie's American engagement in *Gossip* ended late in the summer, she departed for England, leaving Abe Hummel an additional twenty thousand dollars to invest in real estate and securities. She thought of leaving Jeanne behind to attend an American boarding school, but rejected the idea, even though the move would have solved many problems. They had been separated enough in Jeanne's earlier childhood.

Their personal relationship could not have been a simple one. Jeanne was in her teens, an exceptionally pretty girl who more and more resembled her mother. In public she always called Lillie "Aunt," and everyone, including Lillie's close friends, believed the girl was the daughter of Maurice Le Breton, Lillie's brother who had died in India. A miracle had prevented gossip about her.

Since Edward Langtry still presumably didn't know of the child's existence, Lillie could not claim Jeanne as her daughter. Edward would have been certain to insist, publicly, that he could not have been her father. For the present, no changes could be made in an uncomfortable situation.

Lillie returned to her Pont Street house, hurried to Paris for a new wardrobe and, in the autumn of 1895, opened at the Comedy Theatre in *Gossip*. She played in it until May 1896, the longest single run she had ever enjoyed in London. Then *Gossip* went on tour for eight weeks and there wasn't an empty seat anywhere.

With her daughter, Jeanne Marie

When the play closed, Lillie went with her mother and daughter to the racing box in Kentford to put her stables in order. She owned six horses, four of them the winners of various minor races that made the operation solvent, but she was dissatisfied. Lillie Langtry had two constant demands: any project with which she was associated had to be the best, and had to earn substantial sums of money. Her first step was to discharge her trainer and hire one who had a long record of steady successes. She told him to sell any animal that failed to win consistently, and she imported two young horses from Australia, named Merman and Chesney. By the turn of the century Merman would become the biggest money winner of the decade on the English turf. She signed a contract with the leading American jockey, Tod Sloan, to ride exclusively under her banner.

Lillie wanted to buy a stud farm and raise her own champions. To finance it she decided to sell her yacht. It was her own idea to dispose of the furnishings and fixtures separately, as she believed she could make more that way. She was right. She picked

up twenty thousand pounds, and the yacht itself was then sold at auction for a whopping quarter of a million pounds. She immediately put fifty thousand pounds into her stables, and invested the rest. She was now worth approximately two million dollars, and was becoming wealthier every year.

Her plans to return to the stage in the autumn of 1896 were dealt a severe blow when a San Francisco newspaperman unearthed the hitherto hidden story of her divorce. The fact that Jeanne Marie was Lillie's child had been included in the divorce proceedings, as she was given custody of her daughter. Now almost immediately her worst fears were realized. An enterprising reporter for William Randolph Hearst's New York *Journal* went to Southampton and obtained an interview with Edward Langtry, who said, "However cruel it may be, I affirm that I never heard that my wife gave birth to a child of which I am reputed to be the father, until I learned of our divorce."

Although the London press maintained a thunderous silence on the subject, the public drew its own conclusions. And there was considerable speculation in print elsewhere regarding Jeanne Marie's paternity. British reticence, combined with British libel laws, made England the best place to ride out the storm. Since Kentford was remote, it was preferable to stay there rather than brave the whispers of London. So she stayed at the racing box and built up her stable until she owned thirty-six horses.

She and Jeanne went riding for several hours each day, and both were superb horsewomen. They appeared to be in high spirits. Lillie must have enjoyed one consolation: it was no longer necessary to hide Jeanne's identity as her daughter.

Edward Langtry was not yet out of print. One day in the spring of 1897 he was found wandering on the railroad tracks near Chester. His clothes were badly torn and filthy, and he spoke incoherently. He was emaciated, unshaven, and apparently he hadn't eaten recently. He smelled strongly of whisky. He was taken to the Chester jail, but even after he'd sobered up he made no sense.

The story was splashed in headlines, and Lillie paid three prom-

inent physicians to examine her former husband. They certified him as insane. In court he was committed to a county asylum. The news remained on the front pages for a full week, and several of Lillie's associates, among them Griffith and Michael, came to Kentford in order to hold reporters at bay.

Lillie courageously decided to show herself in public again when the racing season began, even though she would be subjecting herself to fresh barrages of criticism every time one of her horses won.

The prize horse of her stable, Merman, was entered in the Cesarewitch at Newmarket, the most important race in the entire English season. But he showed badly in his trials and in a number of lesser races, and Lillie was concerned about him. Then a friend told her that in Australia horses ran shoeless, so she experimented and had Merman's shoes removed. His speed improved, and he beat every other horse in the stable during his trials, never exerting himself.

Lillie kept the information to herself, and when the day of the Cesarewitch arrived, she bet the staggering sum of ten thousand pounds on her horse. The Prince of Wales also owned a horse running in the big race, and bowed to her from a distance. Members of society who were present believed he was snubbing her.

Merman won the Cesarewitch easily, beating the prince's horse and nine others. Lillie not only won the purse of thirty-nine thousand pounds, but the betting odds had been eight to one, and she collected an additional eighty thousand pounds.

The Prince of Wales conducted her to the paddock for the ceremonies that followed the race, and allowed the press to photograph him at her side. Then he escorted her to the Jockey Club, which no woman had ever entered before, and he toasted in champagne the first woman whose horse had ever won the Cesarewitch.

Then late that night she received the final blow from Edward Langtry. An hour before the Cesarewitch had been run, he had died, insane and penniless, in the county asylum. A torrent of press abuse was heaped on Lillie. The great coincidence of her victory at the track and Edward Langtry's death as a pauper was exploited by the newspapers. Had it not been against her principles

to comment on personal matters, she might have protested that she had supported him until the previous year, when news of their divorce was made public.

Clement Le Breton felt that the attacks could not be allowed to pass unchallenged. So, without consulting Lillie, he issued a detailed statement on Lillie's financial arrangements with Edward Langtry. She wrote her brother a furious letter, but he had managed, to some extent, to counter the unfair and thoroughly unsavory publicity she had received.

## X

A SHORT time after the death of Edward Langtry, Lillie announced what had been a fact for a year, her retirement from the stage. The brief statement, issued by Clement Le Breton, merely said, "Mrs. Langtry is fulfilling a desire to return to private life."

Lillie was forty-five in 1898. She had no need to work; her horses were winning her far more than she had ever earned as an actress. She wished to avoid subjecting herself to the publicity a public figure drew, and it was incumbent upon her to provide her growing daughter with a dignified home atmosphere.

In London she and Jeanne Marie began to be seen together for the first time, dining in fashionable restaurants and frequently attending the theater. Their resemblance was marked, and *Punch*, which published a sketch of them standing together, remarked that they looked like sisters. They both refused to grant the press any interviews.

It has been said that the Prince of Wales met Jeanne at a very small private dinner party given by Lillie. According to this story, the girl was presented to Prince Albert Edward, curtsied to him and then sat opposite him at the dinner table. Neither Lillie nor any of those who were present ever saw fit to discuss the dinner publicly.

However, Lillie, who had been in the public eye for so long, could not withdraw into comfortable anonymity. All of her move-

ments were duly reported by the world press. If she dined or went to the theater with a man, or even engaged in casual conversation at the races, it was reported that she was immersed in a new romance. Crowds gathered outside her door at all hours in the hope of catching a glimpse of her, and her house was as popular on sightseeing tours as Buckingham Palace.

According to the newspapers, Prince Paul Esterhazy was Lillie's favorite beau of the moment. A widower in his late fifties, enormously wealthy and socially impeccable, Prince Paul was a polished diplomat, a brilliant conversationalist and, like Lillie, was a horse fancier. He frequently bought racehorses in England for the Emperor Franz Josef, and was also a superb rider; he often joined Lillie on her daily canter. He made no secret of his affection for her, saying that no man could resist her charms or help falling in love with her. He let it be known that he had asked her to marry him and that she was considering his proposal.

Lillie wasn't in love with Prince Paul, but must have been tempted to accept. As a princess and member of Hungary's most prominent noble family, she would instantly regain the social standing that had eroded through the years. And some of the ladies who took delight in snubbing her would be forced to curtsy to her formally. Prince Paul's fortune was much larger than her own, so she had no fear that he was interested in her money.

But she put him off and continued to see others, one of whom completely escaped the attention of the press. It is probable that no one thought of Hugo de Bathe as a serious suitor, since he was only twenty-seven years old.

Hugo was tall, slender and elegant, one of the more eligible young bachelors in England. His father, a retired general who had played a prominent role in the Crimean War, was a baronet, and when he died Hugo would inherit his title. Like so many aristocrats, Hugo did no work, lived on a fairly small income and had no estate of any importance. He was charming, but he had no intellectual or other achievements, and what Lillie saw in him was something of a mystery. That mystery would deepen.

Meanwhile there were other things to occupy Lillie's time and

mind. Her horses continued to win, and her earnings grew larger. She bought a new cottage in Jersey overlooking the sea, and went there often with her mother and daughter. Hugo de Bathe, who resigned his commission as an officer in the royal infantry, went there for a quiet, unannounced visit, and the islanders who saw him with her raised their eyebrows. She was forty-six, nineteen years older than he; yet they seemed inseparable

Going to great pains to avoid publicity, Lillie married Hugo at her father's old church, St. Saviour's, in the summer of 1899. No word of the wedding leaked into print, and the Jersey Lily continued to be known privately, as well as publicly, as Mrs. Langtry.

By late summer Lillie was bored and considering a return to the stage. Marriage, like racing, could not oc-

Her London town-house bedroom, 1899

cupy all of the furious energies she had generated for so many years. Oscar Wilde was quoted as remarking on "a famous actress, who, after a tragic domestic life, has married a fool. She thought that because he was stupid, he would be kindly, when, of course, kindliness requires both intellect and imagination."

Wilde had been having his own troubles. Convicted on a morals charge after a spectacular trial in 1895, he had been condemned to a term of imprisonment at hard labor. He had been released in 1897, and had gone to France to live. Most of his old friends had cut him, although his literary reputation was enhanced in 1898 by the publication of what many consider his best work, *The Ballad of Reading Gaol.*

Lillie, who understood prejudice and was never one to avoid an issue, came publicly to Wilde's defense. His morals, she told the press, were his business, and she saw no reason for the furor that had been created. Her attitude was the better part of a century ahead of its time. Lillie saw Wilde in Paris in 1898 and, as his funds were pitifully low, gave him a substantial sum. Even when Wilde died in 1900, she refused to discuss the amount she had given him.

Lillie ended her supposed retirement in the autumn of 1899, renting the Haymarket Theatre to rehearse a new play called *The Degenerates* that Sidney Grundy had written for her. Lillie undoubtedly knew that many of the critics would consider it lewd and be outraged at her playing the part of a courtesan rejected by London society.

Hugo accompanied her to rehearsals every day. Before the play opened, news of their marriage leaked out and made headlines all over the world. Lillie refused to receive the press, so Hugo made a brief announcement, revealing so little that the representatives of the ha'penny press invented their own news, and Hugo was called a millionaire, which was far from the truth.

Hugo's family promptly made major contributions to the circuslike atmosphere. Sir Henry disinherited his son, and refused to receive Lillie under his roof. Hugo's three sisters made it clear that they did not expect to entertain Hugo and his wife. American newspapers added to the uproar, but for the most part wished Lillie the best of good fortune in their editorials.

The press printed juicy rumors that sparked the desire of audiences to see *The Degenerates*. It was said to be the "true, authentic" story of Lillie's own life, and the set, supposedly furnished with her own chairs, divans, lamps and tables, was purported to be an exact replica of the furniture in her own drawing room. Gossip-hungry theatergoers found it difficult to contain their desire to purchase seats.

Lillie celebrated the great success of the play by selling her house in Pont Street and buying a larger, even more elegant establishment at 2 Cadogan Place, a house previously owned by

Charles Dickens. The house became a showplace. Sitting rooms were done in Regency, Georgian and Louis XV styles. The trophy room included a stuffed bear, the gift of a group of Denver admirers. Lillie's bathroom was done in mosaic tiles, and the special wardrobe room had walls of double-damask silk. She could entertain sixty guests in the dining room, and in the adjoining ballroom was a platform for an orchestra. Her bedchamber was lined in satin, and the walls of Hugo's room were done in tweed.

Hugo dutifully accompanied his bride to the theater every night, then went on to dine with her daughter. Jeanne, now a striking beauty of eighteen, closely resembled her mother, and many who saw her in public with Hugo mistakenly assumed that the handsome young couple were romantically inclined.

Late in the autumn of 1899 war erupted in South Africa between Great Britain and the Boers, and the Crown asked for volunteers. Hugo offered his services, which resulted in a change in his family's attitude. Sir Henry and Lady de Bathe invited him to bring his wife to their house, and his sisters, along with their husbands, joined in the family celebration. Hugo would soon be going off to fight for queen and country, so his notorious wife became socially acceptable. Not surprisingly, Lillie's father-in-law found her charming. They became close friends, and remained so until the end of his days. She also managed to placate his sisters, and established firm, lasting friendships with them.

The twentieth century arrived, and Lillie went off to Paris for her new wardrobe. Hugo accompanied her, and then left from France for South Africa. His commission had not yet been restored, but apparently he expected the oversight to be rectified when he joined a volunteer regiment.

Meanwhile Lillie prepared for another tour in the United States. She was to travel alone. Jeanne would stay in London with Mary Cornwallis-West, who would introduce her, informally, to society. Jeanne's position was unlike her mother's, and no doors were closed to her. By now a great many people were conscious of her paternity. No aristocrat wanted to incur the wrath of the man who would soon succeed his now aged, ailing mother on England's

throne. Jeanne was a self-effacing young lady, and was welcome everywhere.

The welcome Lillie received when she reached New York in early April, 1900, was riotous. Fireboats steamed out to quarantine, spraying water high in the air. A police band played martial airs, and reporters who came out to the liner filled two boats. Lillie, wearing an ermine-trimmed suit, greeted the press in the salon,

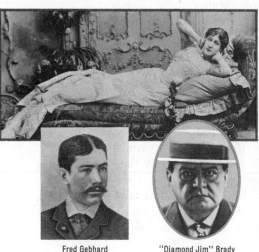

**Lillie...
Her Lovers
and
Admirers**

Fred Gebhard     "Diamond Jim" Brady     George Baird     Hugo de Bathe

ordered champagne for all and chatted with practiced ease. She said she was still an American citizen, and was delighted to return to her true home. And she was emerging from retirement because she could not bear to disappoint the many friends who had begged her to do another play.

The reception accorded *The Degenerates* was similar to that in London. Audiences were deliciously scandalized, and the star took more curtain calls than anyone cared to count. Critics hinted that the actress playing the leading role might be as degenerate as the play itself, and said it was a criminal shame that one who had delighted audiences as Cleopatra and Rosalind should consent to bathe in mud. Despite the critics, the Garden Theatre was sold

out for every performance, and after a successful run of eighteen weeks in New York, *The Degenerates* went on the road.

Following the opening in Philadelphia, one of that city's leading newspapers, the *North American*, attacked Lillie as she had never before been assaulted, claiming, among other things, that her heart was a cash register and that, "anybody who has a fortune to spend on her has been welcome to do it—raw boy, dissolute old

William Gladstone

Roy Bean          Prince Rudolf                    Edward VII

sport, rounder, prince, commoner, gentleman, blackguard, anybody." The attack was having far too serious consequences to be ignored. The police in Washington, D.C., and in Cleveland had already notified the theater owners that *The Degenerates* would not be allowed to play in those cities. Detroit, Cincinnati and Saint Louis were questionable. If the savage assault went unanswered, it might be necessary to close the play. So Abe Hummel and Lillie met in Philadelphia and decided to telephone the publisher of the New York *Herald*, James Gordon Bennett, long an admirer and friend of the Jersey Lily. The next day's *Herald* featured a long defense of Lillie by the British critic Clement Scott.

Many great artists, he said, had led scandalous lives, and he

named Charles Dickens, Thomas Carlyle, Edmund Kean and Sarah Bernhardt. Were the works of Dickens to be boycotted? Should pianists refuse to play the works of Chopin because he had lived with George Sand? It was necessary to make a distinction between the artist and his private life; besides, Scott declared, he could not share the opinion that Mrs. Langtry was herself degenerate. She was one of the loveliest ladies it had ever been his privilege to know.

Copies of Scott's article were sent ahead to every city on the itinerary, and most of them demonstrated their sophisticated hospitality by welcoming the Jersey Lily and *The Degenerates*. The play sold out in Boston, Buffalo, Louisville, Saint Louis, Memphis and Nashville before going on to Chicago for a run.

There, one night, moments before going onstage, Lillie received a cablegram informing her that Hugo de Bathe was seriously ill in a South African hospital. Later, when taking her curtain calls, Lillie's iron-willed composure suddenly broke, and she startled the audience by weeping. But her instinct saved her; she took the entire assemblage of sixteen hundred people into her confidence, and was awarded a standing ovation.

The following day she made a rare public statement, saying: "I confess that I have felt wounded at the attacks on the play and upon myself, but at nothing so much as the accusation that mine is a vulgar performance. Whatever people may say about me and my affairs, nobody who knows me could believe I would appear in a performance that was unrefined in spirit and tone. *The Degenerates* is harsh, perhaps, but is in no sense vulgar." It was the only time in a quarter of a century that Lillie had stooped to answer those who pilloried her.

While Lillie was creating a sensation in the United States, her daughter was enjoying a success of her own in London. Jeanne Marie was invited everywhere. Whenever the Prince of Wales saw her at a social function, he invariably singled her out for a chat, as did Princess Alexandra. Late in the spring of 1900 she was presented to Queen Victoria at a formal Buckingham Palace audience, which put the ultimate seal of approval on her respectability.

The name of Miss Jeanne Marie Langtry appeared regularly in the society columns of London newspapers. She was seen at dinners, at balls, at receptions and attending the races, where she loyally placed bets on her mother's horses. Then a rumor appeared in the ha'penny press that was echoed by American newspapers. It was said that Arthur Hill, nephew of the Marquess of Downshire and a wealthy playboy in his late twenties, was enamored of the girl and had presented her with a valuable gift of jewelry.

Lillie, still touring in the United States, learned via an exchange of cablegrams that the rumor was false. Jeanne had often been escorted by Hill, but had accepted no jewelry from him. Nevertheless Lillie decided to return to England to be closer to her daughter.

Hugo de Bathe also went home, coming from South Africa with a medical discharge. He had spent several months in a Cape Town hospital, suffering from a fever, and was being returned to civilian life. His military service had changed him, and a new experience confronted Lillie, a humiliation unlike anything she had ever before known.

## XI

THE romance of Lillie Langtry and Hugo de Bathe, if it can be called that, was short-lived. A bride and groom who had been married only a short time before being forced to undergo a military separation might be expected, under normal circumstances, to enjoy an ecstatic reunion. But Lillie and her husband had as little regard for precedent as, it appeared, they had for each other.

Within a week of Hugo's return to London, he was seen in public escorting other women. One, a generation younger than Lillie, was a chorus girl currently appearing in a musical comedy, who had achieved fleeting and questionable fame by sporting painted butterflies on her bare shoulders when she wore an evening gown.

Friends who reported to Lillie that they had seen Hugo with the girl also said he had been the girl's frequent escort prior to his marriage. But Lillie was not concerned. According to her friend

Mary Cornwallis-West, she approved of her husband's roaming; there were fewer strains on a marriage when a man strayed with his wife's consent.

These advanced theories were put to a sudden, embarrassing test one evening when Lillie was dining with a party of friends at one of London's most fashionable restaurants. Hugo and the chorus girl were seated opposite the party. Lillie's friends froze, and the girl looked very uncomfortable. Lillie, however, was equal to the occasion, and not only waved to her husband but smiled at the girl. Hugo, not in the least ill at ease, returned his wife's wave.

Whether Lillie suffered privately is not known. But it is a matter of record that Hugo did not accompany her when she went off to Paris for the Christmas holidays with Jeanne. Her husband remained at their London town house, and arranged evening forays with a variety of handsome young women.

Lillie's rift with Hugo ended abruptly after her return to London, and within a few days she departed again, this time taking him with her on a holiday journey to the Riviera. They spent much of their time at the Monte Carlo casino, where Lillie lost small sums almost daily. But she enjoyed the climate, and the excitement of the casino appealed to her so much that she wrote to friends that she hoped someday to retire to Monaco.

On her return to London she plunged into the biggest gambling venture of her life. She had long wanted a London theater of her own, where she could book other attractions when she herself wasn't playing. Now the proprietors of the Imperial Theatre came to her with an offer. They would give her the house on a long-term lease, with an option to buy during the next five years, for the trivial rent of only twenty-five pounds per week. But she would be required to install electricity and make a number of other repairs, which would cost approximately four thousand pounds.

Edward Michael, who was now Lillie's manager, protested the deal vigorously. The Imperial, which had twenty-five hundred seats, was one of the world's largest legitimate theaters. Audiences complained that it was barnlike, and producers and stars, who wanted a more intimate atmosphere, were reluctant to play there.

Michael believed that not even the Jersey Lily was a strong enough draw to fill the house regularly.

But Lillie not only accepted the challenge, she decided to have the entire theater redecorated. The royal box would be done in purple silk, the other boxes in yellow satin, and the auditorium seats in red plush. The lobby would be torn out and replaced with one she would help design. She was on hand every day to watch the most beautiful theater in London taking shape.

She paid dearly for the project. The venture marked the only time in Lillie's long career that she showed poor judgment and lost money. In all, the Imperial cost her more than a quarter of a million dollars, and its return in prestige was not worth it. But, as she wrote to Michael, she did not regret her efforts, as she had the satisfaction of knowing she had created a showcase worthy of the Jersey Lily. Somewhat to the surprise of others in show business, she did not rename the theater after herself. She wrote to Abe Hummel, "I have no yearning for a memorial of that nature, and if future generations wish to remember me, I trust they will look at my photographs."

While Lillie occupied herself at the theater, Jeanne was busy in the London social swim, and her name was linked with that of one or another young nobleman. She went to Paris again with her mother for the 1901 Christmas holidays and, soon after their return to London, Lillie announced Jeanne's betrothal to Sir Ian Malcolm, a prominent member of a wealthy Scottish family. Thirty-three years old, he was a member of Parliament, had seen service in the diplomatic corps and had been a secretary of Lord Salisbury, one of the leaders of the Tory party. He was considered one of the more important of the younger men in the Commons, and his political prestige, combined with his social standing and money, made him one of the marital catches of the decade.

The reaction of the Malcolm clan was emphatic. Jeanne was accepted, but her notorious mother was not. None of the usual premarital festivities were held, Jeanne loyally refusing to attend any function to which her mother was not invited.

On January 22, 1901, after Queen Victoria's death, the Prince of

Wales had succeeded to the throne as Edward VII, and there was considerable speculation regarding his attitude toward the forthcoming marriage. Queen Alexandra ended the gossip by pointedly seeking out Jeanne at a ball given by the Duchess of Devonshire, chatting with her, then leading her to King Edward VII to make her curtsy. If the universally respected Queen Alexandra openly approved of Jeanne and of the marriage, society was in no position to be critical.

The wedding took place at St. Margaret's of Westminster on June 30, 1902, and was attended by representatives of many of the great families of England and Scotland. The bride was given away by her mother. Following the ceremony, Lillie gave a formal bridal luncheon for two hundred at her house, complete with a string orchestra in the ballroom, and free-flowing champagne. On exhibition in one of the drawing rooms, guarded by private detectives, were some of the bride's gifts. Among them were a diamond horseshoe pin sent by the Rothschild banking family, a diamond necklace from the parents of the groom and an even larger diamond necklace from the groom. Along with gifts that Lillie gave her daughter, she settled the sum of five thousand pounds per year on her, making the new Lady Malcolm financially independent for life. No matter what the future might hold, Jeanne would never be forced to work for a living as her mother had. Conspicuous by its absence was any recognition of the occasion by King Edward VII, but the press later reported that he had given Jeanne "a splendid jewel," and had written a letter in his own hand to the girl "in whom he had been strongly interested since her birth."

The party ended soon after the bride and groom departed, and Lillie spent the rest of the afternoon at the races. One of her own horses was running, and she was observed placing larger bets than was her custom. It was also said that she was unsmiling and quiet. But her horse came in first, and she won six thousand pounds, which paid for the wedding and many of her gifts to the bride.

One of the curious features of the proceedings was the absence of Hugo de Bathe. Lillie, true to her tradition, offered no excuses to

anyone, but it was generally believed that Hugo had been requested by his wife to take himself elsewhere. He was younger than the groom, and his presence could have been an embarrassment to all of the principals. The American press reported that he was seen on the Riviera, but he eluded reporters. He reappeared a week later in London, and refused to discuss his journey. Hugo may not have been a model husband, but he was remarkably accommodating. Presumably that was all Lillie asked of him.

With the wedding out of the way, the Jersey Lily turned her thoughts to business. A young playwright with popular appeal, J. Hartley Manners, brought her a new comedy-drama, *The Cross-Ways*, which she saw as possible, but needing a great many changes. Manners incorporated her suggestions into the play and, with an eye on the box office, agreed to include Lillie's name as co-author. Rehearsals were to start in September, but were postponed when Lillie received word that her mother had died in Jersey. Lillie and Clement, the only surviving children, went to Jersey for private services, and Mrs. Le Breton was buried in St. Saviour's churchyard beside her husband.

Lillie went into rehearsal in *The Cross-Ways* early in October. Then just before she took the play to America, she received a mark of royal favor signifying to the world that her association with Edward VII had not come to an end, that he still held Lillie in high esteem. On the night of December 9 a command performance of *The Cross-Ways* was held at the Imperial, and only those approved by the royal household were permitted to purchase tickets. Lillie announced that the night's proceeds would be given to Queen Alexandra for distribution to charities.

The presence of King Edward and Queen Alexandra in the royal box was an extraordinary event, the first command performance since Edward had ascended the throne. To those who understood the subtleties of royal etiquette, the presence of Queen Alexandra meant that the sixty-one-year-old monarch and the forty-nine-year-old Lillie were good friends, but not engaging in an affair.

Although there had been no publicity, crowds began to gather at the Imperial shortly after noon, and by theater time the throng

was estimated at more than ten thousand. The curtain was late because the king and queen were delayed as they rode to the theater from Buckingham Palace. All of London seemed to have somehow learned of the command performance.

Immediately afterwards, Lillie and her supporting company sailed on the *Celtic*. The American press whetted its knives. Mrs. Langtry, said the New York *Sun*, soon would be fifty. If she tried

"Still as a barmaid
Lillie Langtry"

**Lillie ---**
**Her Famous Roles**

to rely on her beauty, much less the glamour of her relationship with King Edward, she'd be very foolish. She would be judged exclusively on her acting ability, if any. Mrs. Langtry, said the New York *World*, was no longer the radiant creature who had dazzled America; the public wanted to see a real actress, not a fading beauty who played at acting.

When the *Celtic* reached New York, the seventy-five reporters and photographers who came out to meet the ship were stunned. Lillie Langtry greeted the press on the open deck, attired in an ermine-trimmed coat of sable, and never had she been lovelier. Her figure was as slender, trim and supple as it had ever been, and her dress of soft, green wool showed off every famous line to

superb advantage. Her face had not aged in twenty years. She obligingly posed for photographers for a half hour.

The *Sun* ate a large helping of crow, admitting that Lillie looked only half her years. The *World's* portion of crow was even larger: "Mrs. Langtry's age is of no importance. She is still the most beautiful woman in the world."

The interview she gave the press was the most candid Lillie had

From left: as Lillie appears in "She Stoops to Conquer"; "The Young Tramp"; and "Macbeth," in which she wins status as a serious actress. A lady smokes in public in "As in a Looking Glass"; Lillie is a "bewitching Rosalind" in "As You Like It"; her role in "Antony and Cleopatra" earns her over a million dollars.

ever granted; she answered all questions with the deft poise of the true veteran. Why was she doing the play in the United States before playing it in London? "We didn't want to be subjected to English criticism. Americans are so clever that if they like a play it is sure to be well received in London. So we'll go there with all the laurel wreaths I'm sure our marvelous play is going to win here. You might say we're using good American common sense."

Was it true that she was intending to obtain a divorce while in the United States? "I am very well satisfied with my present domestic state, thank you."

Then why was it her husband had not accompanied her on her present trip? "My husband objects to extensive traveling. More-

over, American newspapers are so much freer than those in England, and he dislikes being interviewed."

Didn't he like America? "Since he's never been here, he's in no position to judge."

Didn't he want to become acquainted with it? "I daresay he'd have joined me if he had been curious. I assume he's content to stay in England."

Was it possible for a marriage to be successful when the partners were separated for long periods? "I can only speak for Mr. de Bathe and myself, and would not presume to advise others. Our marriage is a very happy one."

Did she know that a letter sent to her by King Edward and bearing his signature was on sale in a New York shop? "How extraordinary."

How did she account for this? "The servants, I daresay. I received twenty-five or thirty letters from the king when he was Prince of Wales, so I suppose one of them escaped."

Might she buy it back herself? "Certainly not! It was nothing more than a note from a friend. It couldn't have been anything more. But I suppose someone will want to buy it. There are souvenir collectors who will buy anything."

Would she explain her beauty secrets? "Gladly, although I wouldn't call them secrets. I've read all sorts of rubbish about a skin-peeling process I supposedly use, and about electrical massages I'm believed to take. My secret is work, plenty of sunshine, soap and water. I eat plain food, I drink very little, I inhale fresh air and I have a happy spirit."

Did she still engage in physical exercise? "Daily. I start my day with a cold bath after getting plenty of sleep, and I do exercises for an hour. When I'm in the country I go out for long walks, but I find it too difficult in the city, where people follow me. Any woman can do what I do!"

When *The Cross-Ways* opened, Lillie thought the reviews, which were only faintly scornful, were better treatment than the London critics would have accorded it. In addition to the reviews, special articles were written about her wardrobe, the furnishings

of her hotel suite, the identities of her visitors and the dishes on her breakfast tray. As always, partly due to this extraordinary publicity, long lines formed at the box office.

Lillie's behavior was impeccable during her New York run. Although she dined on occasion with Diamond Jim Brady at such popular establishments as the Gilsey House, she was seen less frequently in public places. Friends gave supper parties for her in their homes, and Lillie returned their hospitality in her hotel suite, since her former house on Twenty-third Street had been sold to the Pasteur Institute.

When she went on tour late in the spring of 1903, she continued to travel in the style that left Americans openmouthed. The *Lalee* had been destroyed by a railroad-yard fire, so she rented another private car.

When *The Cross-Ways* played for a week in Washington, D.C., the Jersey Lily received a dinner invitation from the White House, and President Theodore Roosevelt arranged the dinner hour to suit her performance. T.R. was as charmed by Lillie as she was fascinated by him. She sat on his right, and they chatted with great animation throughout the meal.

Afterwards, when asked her impression of the President, she replied, "I never discuss a host or a friend, and I consider the wonderful Mr. Roosevelt to be my good friend." Not until T.R. ended his second term as President did Lillie reveal to friends what had made the greatest impression on her at the White House dinner. Her host, she said, had astonished her by revealing that he thought of himself as a professional author who happened to be spending "a few years" in public service. Asked what they had discussed, she replied, "Why, Mr. Roosevelt's books, of course. I made it my business to read several of them before I went to the White House."

One of the highlights of Lillie's tour was her appearance in Providence, Rhode Island, although she had no advance notion of what was in store for her there. The previous year she had commissioned an English author, Percy Fendall, to write a play for her, and had paid him an outrageously high fee. Fendall had done a comedy,

399

*Mrs. Deering's Divorce*, which Lillie considered too frivolous. Her contract with Fendall made it mandatory for her to produce it within twelve months, or all rights would revert to the playwright. But she had delayed the presentation, intending first to discuss rewrites with him. Now she received a cablegram from her brother Clement informing her that Fendall was demanding she live up to the contract.

So the Jersey Lily and several members of her company made hasty preparations for a single performance of the play in Providence. She would fulfill the letter of her contract, and her reputation wouldn't be harmed by a production in a New England industrial city that was far removed from the mainstream of international theater.

She and her actors enjoyed themselves thoroughly, playing the comedy so broadly it became a farce. To her amazement the audience loved the play, and called her back for repeated curtain calls. The next day not only did the Providence press rave about the evening, but the Boston critics who had come to see her gave her the best reviews they ever had. Mrs. Langtry, they said, had found her true home in light comedy.

When Lillie returned to London in August 1903, unexpected complications caused her distress. The Imperial Theatre had been sold, and the building was to be razed before the end of the year. A study of Lillie's contracts with the previous proprietors proved her powerless to prevent the destruction of the place into which she had poured so much money. After a bitter fight she received a cash settlement, which was only a fraction of what she had spent; she suffered the worst financial reversal of her entire career.

What bothered her even more was the lack of availability of another theater. London was enjoying its best season in many years, and there were no theaters to book until the following spring. She had no intention of waiting, and decided to return to the United States later in the autumn to present *Mrs. Deering's Divorce*.

In order to ensure the success of the American engagement, Lillie conferred with Fendall, and at her suggestion the play-

wright added a brief new scene to the play. In it Lillie removed her dress, and would be exposed to the audience for a few moments in her underwear before donning a dressing gown. She well knew the effect she would create, the publicity she would receive, and she told Michael she was looking forward to the furor. As to the question of decency, or the lack of it, she intended to wear a full-length slip, and the audience would see less of her body than was revealed in an evening gown. Nevertheless the cunning maneuver was certain to guarantee sold-out houses in every city on the new tour.

Hugo detested publicity, but he did agree to spend a portion of the coming year in the United States with her during the particularly long tour. And so they moved into the greatest publicity storm the Jersey Lily had ever created. Her disrobing scene in *Mrs. Deering's Divorce* caused the heavens to open, and saturated the front pages of every newspaper in the United States.


## XII


Mrs. Langtry has made a career of shocking the American theatre-going public, and this time she goes too far beyond the bounds of good taste by unnecessarily removing her clothes on stage. She cannot be faulted for wanting to demonstrate that her figure would be the envy of a woman of thirty, but one expects a greater sense of propriety when an actress of Mrs. Langtry's stature steps on stage.

The review of *Mrs. Deering's Divorce* that appeared in *The New York Times* was austere in its disapproval, but other newspapers were less circumspect. Lillie was accused of being cheap, flamboyant and immoral, but she ignored the criticism and undoubtedly felt content when she visited the box office. Her entire run of sixteen weeks was sold out; women came to see her dazzling wardrobes, and their husbands came to see her undress.

Hugo de Bathe arrived in New York shortly after his wife's departure, early in 1904, timing his arrival to escape publicity.

The ruse was successful. He joined Lillie in Cleveland, and met her again in Chicago, in Saint Louis and in New Orleans. Then he returned to New York to buy himself a small racing sloop.

When Lillie reached San Francisco, she sold the ranch she had owned near the city for many years. She lost several thousand dollars on the investment, one of her few transactions which wound up in the red. But she put the money from the sale to good use by buying a number of lots in Los Angeles and Santa Barbara. Abe Hummel thought she was wasting her money, and that San Francisco was the only city of the future on the Pacific, but Lillie disagreed with him. The climate of southern California would attract many settlers, she believed, and she predicted that she would triple her money. She actually did better than that when she disposed of the lots after the First World War.

On her return across the continent, Lillie paid a long-promised visit to a town that now bore her name. It had been known for its first twenty years as Vinegaroon, and the man responsible for the name change was Judge Roy Bean, one of the most colorful of the Southwest's pioneers. Bean was a rancher as well as the proprietor of the town's saloon. A marksman with both rifle and pistol, he had maintained order in his district for many years, had been the combined mayor and chief of police and had gone on to become the judge of a circuit court.

When Lillie Langtry first came to the United States, Judge Bean had fallen in love with her photograph. The walls of his saloon were covered with her pictures and press clippings, and on her first tour of the country he had traveled to Chicago to see her act, and to obtain the autographed photo that was to occupy a place of honor behind his bar. Presumably with the consent of the electorate, he had changed the town's name. Lillie would be honored ceremoniously whenever she chose to go there.

Now, as the *Sunset Limited* was to pass through Langtry, Texas, officials of the Southern Pacific Railroad were sufficiently publicity-conscious to be delighted to honor Lillie's request for a halt.

Langtry, a typical turn-of-the-century cow town, was located in the cattle flatlands of Texas. There were no trees, and the grass-

lands and tumbleweed stretched to the horizon. Shacks were made of sandy, caked mud, or of wood that had been imported from two hundred miles or more. The station was a dilapidated shed, but a newly painted sign was nailed to a pole, announcing to the world that this was LANGTRY. The unofficial population was one hundred and fifty-seven persons, not counting the "young ladies" who made their headquarters in the two saloons on the rutted main street.

When the train came to a halt, Lillie thought a mistake had been made. She could see nothing but grazing lands, and not until she left her private car did she realize that the front portion of the train was at the station, leaving her car far behind in the open country. The entire town had gathered to greet her, and a delegation appeared to act as her escort.

Lillie was distressed to discover that Judge Roy Bean had died several months before. The welcoming delegation was headed by the new justice of the peace, a man named Dodd, and the new postmaster, whose name was Fielding. The owner of the general store, the blacksmith and other local dignitaries were presented to her, and were followed by the cowhands, one of whom outraged his colleagues by throwing his arms around the guest of honor and planting a grubby kiss on her mouth.

A serious fight was barely averted. The citizens of Langtry rushed to Lillie's defense, pistols drawn, forcing the amorous cowhand to reach for his own gun in self-defense. Fascinated passengers on board the *Sunset Limited*, who had been watching the ceremonies, hastily drew back from the windows.

The guest of honor herself saved the day by laughing, patting her enthusiastic admirer on the cheek and kissing the most belligerent of her defenders. Peace was restored.

The ceremonies continued. The married men brought their wives and children forward to be presented, and Lillie gravely shook hands with each. Then someone remembered the fancy ladies of Langtry, who were clustered together at one end of the little platform, and presented them. Lillie proved equal to the occasion, and again she shook hands, carefully asking each girl

*Because I Loved Him*

her name. The prostitutes were in awe of the woman whose reputation suggested that she was the world's most successful practitioner of their own profession, and they carefully studied her makeup and attire.

Then she was taken on a tour of the town. The largest and most impressive building was the late Judge Bean's saloon. It was called The Jersey Lilly, and the guest of honor commented on the spelling. A bar ran the entire length of the floor, and behind it were tacked twenty to thirty posters of the woman Roy Bean had idolized. Most of them were yellowed and torn advertisements for some of her earlier plays. A member of her entourage went back to the train for a set of new posters.

Justice Dodd, now the saloon proprietor, broke out whiskey for everyone, and Lillie was handed a shot. She forced herself to emulate her hosts, and downed the raw frontier liquor in a single gulp. Nearly everyone in the admiring throng noted that she didn't cough, gasp for breath or shudder, although she later wrote that she had been forced to exercise all of her considerable willpower to prevent herself from retching.

She was given an official gift, a pistol bearing an engraved plate, which read: *Presented by W. D. Dodd of Langtry, Texas, to Mrs. Lillie Langtry in honor of her visit to our town. This pistol was formerly the property of Judge Roy Bean. It aided in finding some of his famous decisions and keeping order west of the Pecos. It also kept order in the Jersey Lilly saloon. Kindly accept this as a small token of our regards.*

Lillie inspected the schoolhouse, and gave the schoolmaster one hundred dollars to buy textbooks. She was taken to the cemetery, and stood at the grave of Roy Bean, who, she was informed, was one of only fifteen persons buried there who had died a natural death.

Several housewives wanted her to sip coffee in their kitchens, so Lillie diplomatically proposed that everyone have coffee in the post office. That the respectable ladies and trollops sat down together under the same roof in Langtry was a matter of considerable controversy in the town for many months thereafter.

404

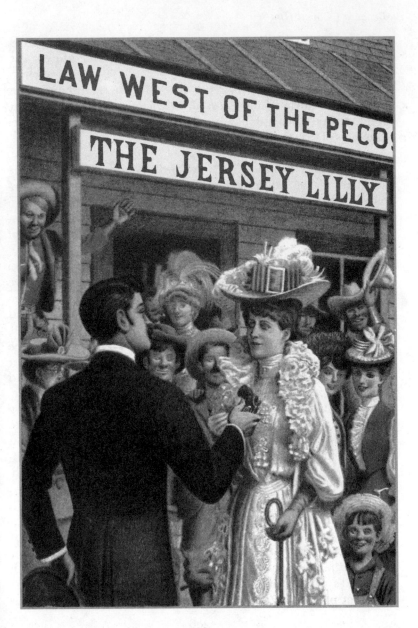

The engineer of the *Sunset Limited* blew a warning whistle. The entire population of Langtry accompanied Lillie to her car, and she made a brief address.

The cowhands fired their pistols and rifles in salute as the train pulled away. Lillie was so touched by the visit that she wept, retired to her stateroom and was not seen again by other members of her company that day.

WHEN Lillie returned to New York, where Hugo de Bathe awaited her, she had business matters on her mind. She had summoned her brother Clement from England, and they sat down with Abe Hummel to review her entire financial situation. Hummel had been urging her to consolidate her holdings, and Clement agreed that her extravagances were costing her a fortune.

Her brother returned to England and sold her London town house, complete with furnishings, for a staggering seventy-five thousand pounds. Some of her unmatched jewelry sold at auction for a sum in excess of one hundred and thirty-seven thousand pounds, and the story made new headlines.

The Jersey Lily, the newspapers of North America and Europe declared, had gone bankrupt, and was forced to liquidate her holdings. She was alone in the world, ignored by her friends and deserted by her daughter, paying the price for her dissolute life. Like so many tales told about Lillie through the years, the story was untrue. In fact, her financial situation had never been more solid, and she invested more than one hundred and fifty thousand dollars, her profits from the engagement of *Mrs. Deering's Divorce*, in additional New York and Chicago real estate. Quietly she had become a major property owner in both cities.

But the reporters, without knowing it, did tell the partial truth about one aspect of her situation. Lillie's relations with her daughter were deteriorating. Had there been an argument, Lillie might have found the break easier to bear. But what was happening was simple: the aristocratic Malcolm clan wanted nothing to do with England's most notorious theatrical star, and Jeanne was under constant pressure to keep her distance from her mother. The girl

had allowed her correspondence to fall off, and no longer answered her mother's letters. Lillie, always sensitive to slights and rebuffs, appears to have realized what was happening, and made no attempt to force her daughter to remain close to her.

The outside world knew nothing of these events, and Lillie maintained a tight-lipped silence. It is significant that even in her autobiography she made no mention whatever of Jeanne's existence. A reader who depended exclusively on that book for the facts of the Jersey Lily's life would never know she had given birth to a daughter.

But with a few close friends she was less reticent. Soon after her death, a quarter of a century after her estrangement from Jeanne, David Belasco declared that the break with her daughter caused her the greatest suffering she had ever known.

If Mrs. Langtry and Lady Malcolm had any contact for years after the daughter drifted away from her mother in 1904, there is no record of it. Mary Cornwallis-West and some of Lillie's other friends, writing circumspectly, indicated they never saw each other, and said that Lillie, after writing several letters that went unanswered, made no further attempts to revive the relationship. Jeanne, busily building her own life, vanished from her mother's existence, and either by accident or design, their paths did not cross again until the very end of Lillie's life.

Lillie learned she had become a grandmother when New York reporters telephoned to ask how achieving the milestone felt. At fifty-one she was the world's most glamorous grandmother—and a deeply hurt woman. She cabled her congratulations to Jeanne on the birth of a son, but is not known to have received a reply.

As always, the Jersey Lily sought solace in work, and accepted a new challenge. She received an offer to tour South Africa. The lure proved irresistible. De Bathe, remembering his own unpleasant experiences in South Africa during the Boer War, refused to accompany his wife there. Instead he returned to England, where his father was ill.

She had to go back to London, too, to prepare for the tour, and moved into the Savoy Hotel, which her presence made famous

overnight. She decided to present a number of her most successful plays in South Africa, among them *As You Like It*. London's theatrical set raised their eyebrows at a fifty-one-year-old woman's playing Rosalind, but Lillie had lost none of her business acumen. Her legs were still shapelier than those of most women half her age and, as new publicity photographs proved, she still looked spectacular in tights.

The guarantees she received from South African producers and theater owners enabled the entire company of seventeen actors and actresses to sail in style on the *Walmer Castle*. Scenery and properties filled thirty-six large crates. Edward Michael made the trip as Lillie's business manager, and her personal entourage included two maids, a chef, and a secretary for press relations.

There was no need for a publicity agent on the tour, however. The mere fact of Lillie's presence was news everywhere, and the tour was her greatest triumph. She intended to spend six months in South Africa, and instead stayed for a full year, returning to England in May 1906.

Rudyard Kipling, one of England's greatest authors, was making his fourth trip to South Africa, and it coincided with Lillie's tour. He met her, was charmed, and insisted on guiding her sightseeing trips. She was an enthusiastic and indefatigable tourist, as anxious to see everything in this land as he was to show her all the sights.

Lillie developed a great admiration for Kipling's work, which she'd never read before. He presented her with several volumes of his short stories, and she wrote to her brother that she had "discovered" an extraordinary talent. She hadn't quite discovered him herself; the next year Kipling was awarded the Nobel Prize for Literature.

When the company returned to England, Lillie was wealthier by more than one hundred thousand dollars, and this sum did not include the gifts of jewelry presented to her by a number of South Africa's wealthiest owners of diamond and gold mines. She had earned a holiday before setting out on her next venture, and went to spend the better part of the summer at her racing lodge.

The racing season was most successful, and the climax of the summer came when two of Lillie's horses won major races on the same day. The stable earned enough that summer to keep it in operation for the next two years.

Lillie took advantage of her stay in Folkestone to plan the most unusual venture of her career. Before leaving the United States, B. F. Keith, the vaudeville impresario, had offered her a tour on his circuit.

Until the turn of the century vaudeville had been universally regarded as a low form of entertainment, ranking only slightly above burlesque. The staple fare consisted of acrobats, trained-animal acts, third-rate comedians, inferior dancers and jugglers and an occasional singer. Keith, making an effort to change the medium's image, was offering enormous fees to the greatest stars of the day. Sarah Bernhardt had been the first to succumb to the lure of Keith's fat weekly wages, and had been followed by Lillian Russell. Between them they had given vaudeville a new dignity, a standing as a respectable theatrical medium. Now it was Lillie's turn.

Keith offered her the staggering sum of eight thousand dollars a week, for which she would play two performances a day, six days a week, of a twenty-minute sketch. She would carry her own sets and props with her, and would pay the salaries of her supporting cast out of the stipend she received.

Lillie shrewdly commissioned the writing of a skit called *Between the Nightfall and the Light*. Its theme was infidelity, and the writing was period melodrama at its best—or worst. At the final curtain the unfaithful wife was shot and killed by her jealous husband, but she did not die before a last, tear-jerking speech. To Lillie one of the most attractive features of the playlet was its small cast; she was required to hire only two supporting players, and a simple, inexpensive set was built for her. She estimated that she would be able to keep about seven of each eight thousand dollars she was paid.

Folkestone, like the other Channel resorts, boasted an amusement pier that jutted out into the water, and at the far end of it

was a small theater. The management was elated when Lillie decided to try out *Between the Nightfall and the Light* there.

The sketch ran only seventeen minutes, so she meticulously insisted that three minutes of playing time be added to make the full twenty minutes that her contract with Keith required. But that wasn't enough to satisfy her Folkestone audiences. Ticket buyers were under the misapprehension that they would be seeing a complete play, even though the billboards carefully spelled out the playing time, and during the week of the tryout there Lillie suffered a new experience. Audiences booed her vociferously at every performance.

Startled by the unexpected attacks, she thought of abandoning the vaudeville tour. But when she returned to London she attended the theater on several occasions, and the audiences, recognizing her, stood and cheered. The ha'penny newspapers had been filled with accounts of her Folkestone reception, and the London audiences wanted her to know they were loyal to her.

Heartened by their reaction, she sailed for New York on board the *Philadelphia,* the newest ship in transatlantic service. Two blooded wolfhounds were added to her entourage and she was always seen in public with them during the following months.

Her opening at the newly decorated Fifth Avenue Theatre on October 1, 1906, was the biggest event of the theatrical season. The mere fact that the Jersey Lily was playing in the medium enhanced the stature of vaudeville. The theater was jammed with the customary crowds of first-nighters—captains of industry, literary figures, society leaders, senators and congressmen—many of whom had never before seen vaudeville.

The newspaper drama critics all treated the event as a regular theatrical opening, too, and were on hand in full force. William Winter, still loyal, called the play and Lillie charming. The other reviewers were struck by her courage in attempting a new medium twenty-four years after her first appearance on the American stage. There was still another factor that accounted for the universal praise: Lillie was good in the role she played.

Richard Mansfield, one of the great actors of the day, discovered

the reason. He was so struck by her performance that he reserved a box every night for a week so he could study her techniques, and later he confided to various friends that Lillie was superb because, in spite of her limited training for high drama, the brevity of her playlet enabled her to sustain an intense emotional level from start to finish.

The happy Keith saw lines at the box office every day, and told associates he had never before had such a successful bill. He offered his star an open-end contract, enabling her to remain in vaudeville for as long as she pleased. Lillie, however, was content to play the single season for which she had been engaged.

Reporters and photographers insisted that Lillie looked like a woman still in her twenties, and she was besieged anew for her beauty secrets. A statement she made to the New York *Sun* was revealing. Asked if she was happy, she replied, "Of course I am happy, as happiness goes, for a woman who has so many memories and lives the lonely life of an actress. It is restricted, as all artistic life necessarily must be. I've often put in as many as forty weeks on the stage in a single year, so you might say I've had precious little opportunity to brood or feel sorry for myself. I've sometimes been accused of lacking sentimentality, a quality I haven't been able to afford, and I think that is all to the good. The sentimentalist ages far more quickly than the person who loves his work and enjoys new challenges."

Lillie's sojourn in vaudeville made her the reigning queen of the New York stage again, and she enjoyed more attention than she had received since her initial appearance in that city. She was equally successful when she went on tour. She sold out everywhere, and was amused when critics who had invariably disliked her treated her with new respect. She had been forced to turn to a new medium to win their praise, and she felt that she would do far better in the legitimate theater when she returned to it.

There were inconveniences she had to suffer because of her vaudeville tour. She could not travel in a private railroad car, but she made the best of the situation, always engaging two drawing rooms for herself, another for her maids and a compartment

for her butler. The butler walked the wolfhounds on the platform whenever the train came to a halt for a few minutes.

While she was on tour a long-expected change altered Lillie's life, but she seemed unexcited by it, thoroughly bewildering everyone who knew her.

## XIII

ON January 6, 1907, when Lillie was playing a vaudeville engagement in Cincinnati, she received a cablegram informing her that General Sir Henry P. de Bathe had died. Her husband inherited his father's baronetcy and became Sir Hugo. Lillie herself was now Lady de Bathe. The world's press, particularly in the United States and Canada, headlined the news on page one.

Lillie's social position was enhanced, but her title meant little to her. She didn't miss a performance, and she rejected the advice of Keith and his associates that she change her billing. She had made her fame as Mrs. Langtry, and refused to change her professional name. "Everything is precisely as it was," she told Richard Le Gallienne, the poet and critic. "I'm still supporting my dear husband."

Her comment was cruel, but accurate. Sir Hugo had inherited little of value with his father's title. He was now the proprietor of several small, debt-ridden estates in Devonshire and Sussex, and when Lillie wrote to him, suggesting that he sell the lands, he refused. But debts of any kind were anathema to her, so she sent him the sum of ten thousand pounds to pay off his creditors. Her title was expensive.

By the end of June 1907 Lillie was exhausted. She had been playing the vaudeville circuit for nine unrelieved months. She was also wealthier by a net that approached a quarter of a million dollars. She was in need of a rest, and sailed for England.

The racing season was under way by the time Lillie reached London, so she stayed in the city for no more than a few days before proceeding to her lodge. Sir Hugo, who had been wait-

ing for her in the city, accompanied her. They stayed at the lodge for four months, and Lillie's horses were such consistent winners that King Edward, who owned a larger stable, paid her a half-dozen visits at teatime to discuss the buying and selling of mounts that wore his colors.

London's theatrical managers were clamoring for the Jersey Lily, but Lady de Bathe was tired and decided to spend the late autumn and winter in Monaco with her husband.

Every day Lillie visited the Monte Carlo casino, becoming a familiar figure, and every day she lost heavily. It was estimated that, as the winter drew to a close, she had dropped approximately twenty thousand pounds. Then, at the end of February, on her last night on the Riviera, she plunged. The following day's headlines blazoned the news, JERSEY LILY BREAKS BANK AT MONTE CARLO. The newspapers exaggerated, but not by much. Lillie played roulette with abandon, and not only recouped her losses but showed a profit of more than twenty-five thousand pounds. And she stopped when she was ahead. The fascinated public agreed with an editorial in the New York *World* to the effect that she was as lucky as she was beautiful.

But her luck failed to hold when she returned to London. She was anxious to go back to work after her long holiday, and went into rehearsals in a new play Sidney Grundy had written for her, *A Fearful Joy*. It opened at the Haymarket early in April 1908, and the critics damned it with faint praise. Mrs. Langtry, they said, skipped through a familiar role, that of a high-society lady whose morals were dubious, and the play itself was weak. Most of the reviewers found little to commend other than her Worth wardrobe.

A new generation of sophisticated theatergoers had grown up in England, and the name of the Jersey Lily, as such, was no longer magical. Younger audiences had no desire to see the middle-aged Lillie on stage unless she appeared in a play worth their money and interest. Business dropped sharply, and after playing to half-filled houses for two weeks—an unaccustomed experience—Lillie closed the play abruptly and went back to her lodge for

the racing season. Her stable provided balm to her wounded ego.

When the season ended Lillie looked for new fields to conquer, and sat down to write a novel. In a surprisingly short time she completed an effort of approximately seventy-five thousand words, which she called *All At Sea* and had published under the name of Lillie de Bathe. It couldn't be called literature, but it was a light, amusing romance, tinged with just enough wickedness to titillate the early-twentieth-century reader.

Lillie commissioned the preparation of a one-act play, a condensation of *The Degenerates,* which she called *The Right Sort,* and she played it in British vaudeville during the 1909–10 season. She duplicated her American vaudeville success, and in the autumn of 1910 she returned to the United States with the playlet for another tour of the Keith circuit.

She had been in a subdued mood through the late spring and summer. King Edward VII had died in May 1910 and Lillie had gone into seclusion, seeing no one and refusing all interviews. She made no public appearances that summer, and after her return to America she turned a deaf ear to reporters' comments about her late friend and benefactor.

She was far less reticent, however, discussing her age. When a Boston reporter told her she looked like a young girl, she made her feelings very clear to him. "What rubbish!" she declared. "I am fifty-seven years of age, and I don't care who knows it. I don't look in the least young, as you and I well know. There isn't a woman in the world who doesn't look every day and every minute of her age. We can't be younger than we are, and we can't look younger than we are. The most any woman of my age can do is hope she's well preserved."

For the next three years Lillie followed the new pattern, playing a vaudeville sketch in England, then taking it to the United States. She spent her summers at her racing lodge, and each year made her usual trips to Paris for new clothes.

She was reputed to be the hardest-working actress of her day. The truth of the matter was that she had nothing but her work to keep her occupied. She and Sir Hugo were still married, and she

continued to support him, but they were drifting even farther apart and spent only a few token weeks together each year. Lillie had no contact with her daughter, who now had several children. And most of her old friends were either dead or occupied with their own interests. She was still remarkably attractive, and one of the most independently wealthy women on earth, but she was lonely.

Adamantly refusing self-pity, she continued to rely on work as a cure-all. In 1913 she again pioneered in a new medium, and following the recent example of Sarah Bernhardt, made a motion picture for Adolph Zukor's Famous Players Film Company. Produced and directed by her old friend Daniel Frohman, it was a comedy-drama called *His Neighbor's Wife*.

The motion picture was filmed in April 1913, and opened in New York in the autumn to reviewers' praise. It was, actually, no worse and no better than other films of its period. The acting was stiff, the lighting poor and the photography indistinct and jerky.

But Lillie was well satisfied with her efforts, and spent several incognito evenings watching herself on the screen. However, films were still a novelty, they paid only modest sums, and she had no desire to repeat the experiment.

Returning to England late in 1913, Lillie contemplated retirement, telling Edward Michael that, like Alexander the Great, she had no more worlds to conquer. But the outbreak of World War I in 1914 revitalized her. Sir Hugo went off to war with an army commission, as did Lillie's brother Clement. Lillie could not remain idle now, and opened at Drury Lane, London's largest theater, in a new play by Sidney Grundy, *Mrs. Thompson.* Her own salary and the play's profits, she told the public in daily newspaper advertisements, were being donated to the Red Cross. Neither the inconveniences of wartime living nor the German zeppelin raids on London could deter her, and she played in *Mrs. Thompson* for an entire season.

In the autumn of 1915 she brought the play to New York, still giving the profits and her entire salary to the Red Cross. Impervious to the German U-boat threat that made transatlantic

travel hazardous, she arrived in New York accompanied by a secretary and two maids, and carried forty trunks of new clothes.

She traveled back and forth across the Atlantic throughout World War I, sometimes doing plays, sometimes vaudeville sketches. One of her leading men was a young actor of rare promise, Alfred Lunt. She took part in innumerable war-relief drives, and gave scores of special benefit performances, acting as co-chairman with Will Rogers of a one-thousand-dollars-per-ticket affair at the Ritz-Carlton Hotel.

On one of her transatlantic crossings in 1916, a fellow passenger was Somerset Maugham, who had just achieved international renown as an author. Maugham recorded his impressions of the Jersey Lily in his autobiographical *A Writer's Notebook* published in 1949: "She still had a fine figure and a noble carriage, and if you were walking behind her you might have taken her for a young woman." At the time Lillie was sixty-three.

Lillie and Maugham struck up a shipboard acquaintance. When she mentioned the name of Fred Gebhard, the author had to confess he had never heard of the man. Lillie appeared to be astounded, and said Gebhard had been "the most celebrated man in two hemispheres."

Maugham asked her why he had been famous.

"Because I loved him," Lillie said.

In 1917 Lillie wrote a form of her autobiography for the Hearst newspapers, and was paid the enormous sum of one thousand dollars for each of ten installments. No other author except the Nobel Prize-winning Rudyard Kipling had ever commanded such a fee. But, aside from the use of her name, Lillie did not give value received. The work was stilted, formal and so discreet it was bloodless. At best it was a collection of loosely strung anecdotes about famous people she had known, most of them in high society. Whenever she mentioned Edward VII, which was infrequently, she carefully coupled his name with that of Queen Alexandra.

By the autumn of 1917 the U-boat menace had become so great that transatlantic passenger travel was difficult as well as hazard-

ous. In order to return to England from the United States, Lillie had to go to Spain, a voyage of more than three weeks. Then from Madrid she managed to get a train to Paris, and after almost six weeks of travel finally reached England.

She played another season in London while zeppelins regularly dropped bombs on the city; she did not miss a performance. By summer she was tired, so she went off to her racing lodge and devoted most of her time to raising vegetables, acquiring a suntan and thinking. She decided to make her own plans, and her husband would either fit himself into them or not, as he chose.

By the time World War I finally ended in November 1918, her plans were solidified. She had made her last appearance on a stage, and would not act again. Younger beauties and better actresses were appearing in the theaters of both America and England, and she had no desire to make herself look absurd.

Within a week of the war's end she sold her racing lodge and moved into the Savoy Hotel to await Sir Hugo's return. Perhaps he didn't care for her scheme, but she used her own method of persuasion. Lillie was buying a house for herself in Monaco, on the mild-climated Riviera, where she intended to live with a companion. She had already taken an option on a house in Nice, a half-hour's drive away, for her husband. She was as tired of scandalous headlines as she was of the grind of work, and preferred to avoid divorce. Sir Hugo was content to let Lillie support him while he led his own life, without obligation except to escort her on formal occasions. He agreed to the new arrangement.

Lillie's Monacan house was located on a steep mountainside overlooking the Riviera. She had it modernized and enlarged before moving in in the spring of 1919. Her companion was Mrs. Mathilde Peat, a widow with whom she had been associated in the theater. Lillie bought a limousine and an open touring car, and hired a domestic staff of five.

Her retirement, like her professional life, was hectic. She plunged into the social whirl of the Riviera's permanent residents, and a steady stream of famous persons made their way to her Villa Le Lys for lunch, tea, cocktails or dinner. Lillie became interested

in growing flowers, and competitive as usual, she eventually won a gold trophy as the best amateur horticulturist on the Riviera. One or two evenings a week she was driven to the Monte Carlo casino, and there played roulette and other games for about two hours. She gambled only modestly now.

Her many visitors soon learned that their hostess had no intention of lapsing into old age. She subscribed to a number of London and New York newspapers, and kept up with the news of the theater in both countries. "Anyone who limits his vision to his memories of yesterday," she told one visitor, "is already dead."

Twice each year she and Mrs. Peat sojourned in London for one to three weeks. Lillie visited old friends, dined at some of her favorite restaurants and often attended the theater. She was invariably recognized by audiences, and frequently was given an ovation.

On one of these trips the breach with her daughter was healed, and Lillie became acquainted with her three grandsons and granddaughter. "I was in awe of her when I first met her," the eldest later said, "but I soon learned to admire her, and then to love her." Subsequently the two eldest grandchildren paid a number of visits to the Villa Le Lys, and stayed for periods of a month or more. Photographs of all four children filled Lillie's bedroom, and the burden she had suffered for years in dignified silence was eased.

Always one to keep up with the times, Lillie bought modern wardrobes in Paris. The age of the flapper had arrived, so she shortened her skirts several inches, although she refused to bare her knees. She was one of the first to follow the example of the dancer Irene Castle, and bobbed her hair, abandoning the famous Langtry bun. When she discovered that her hair was turning gray, she had it dyed auburn, and wore it that way for the rest of her days. For a long time she had smoked cigarettes in private, but now that mores were changing she did not hesitate to smoke in restaurants or at the theater.

The escapades of Hugo de Bathe caused her occasional embarrassment. Now in his fifties, Hugo was one of the gallants of the

Riviera, and continued to chase girls with the fervor he had shown in his youth. He appeared regularly at the spas, casinos and yacht clubs with a chorus girl or debutante less than half his age on his arm. Occasionally one or another young woman expected him to marry her, and created a fuss when she learned he had no intention of obtaining a divorce from his famous, elderly wife. Some of his antics amused Lillie, and twice, when he was threatened with breach of promise lawsuits, she supported him by issuing statements that made it clear she intended to remain married to him, if only in name, for the rest of her life.

Lillie at seventy-five

In 1925 Lillie's autobiography, *The Days I Knew*, was published in New York. Those who expected scandalous revelations and inside stories of hijinks in high places were disappointed. The book consisted of a collection of harmless anecdotes, social and theatrical reminiscences and sheer trivia. In her discretion Lillie observed, to the last, the code of a lady.

Echoes of the past came alive in 1927. One Peter Wright wrote and published a book called *Portraits and Memories*, and in it he claimed that Lillie had been the mistress of Prime Minister Gladstone. Viscount Herbert Gladstone, the son of the statesman, himself now in his seventies, branded Wright as a liar and coward, and was promptly sued for libel. Lillie came to the younger Gladstone's defense, and sent him a cable saying, I STRONGLY REPUDIATE THE SLANDEROUS ACCUSATION OF PETER WRIGHT.

Lord Gladstone won his case, but Lillie, remembering the old days, feared being made a social pariah again. Times had changed, however, and her friends rallied to her. Yet there was a touch of bitterness in a newspaper interview she gave: "Sym-

419

pathy is charming, but it does not make up for the pain. I have always been willing to take the blame for the things I have done, but it is hard to have blame fastened on me for things I never did."

In the autumn of 1928, when Lillie was seventy-five, she suffered a serious illness. She was visiting London, and while a photographer was taking her picture she had to interrupt the session to go to bed. Her ailment was diagnosed as bronchitis complicated by pleurisy. Lillie summoned a lawyer and revised her will, which she had neglected to do in many years.

She recovered, but was still weak when she returned to the Riviera, and in the months that followed it became obvious that her mobility had lessened. It was a cold winter, so Lillie rarely left the house, usually entertaining her friends at tea.

Then in February 1929 she fell ill again, this time with influenza, and early in the morning of February 12, Lillie Le Breton Langtry de Bathe died.

The bulk of her estate was left to her four grandchildren, each of whom received a trust fund. There were generous bequests to Mrs. Peat and various friends, and she left each of her servants a year's wages. Jeanne received her mother's silver and china. There was no mention of Sir Hugo de Bathe in the will, but presumably Lillie had made provision earlier for his needs.

In accordance with a request in her will, Lillie was buried in the churchyard of St. Saviour's on the Isle of Jersey. Jeanne and her eldest son were present, but Hugo did not appear.

For the last time Lillie appeared on the front pages, and the New York *Herald-Tribune* published an editorial that said it all: "An era has come to an end."

## Noel B. Gerson

The steady sound of his own standard typewriter pounding away is music to Noel Gerson's ears. A reporter on a Chicago newspaper in the thirties, Gerson learned to live with deadlines. Now he sets his own: never less than ten pages a day—on a good day, twenty. His relentless three-fingered typing has piled up some one hundred books: fiction, biography, history, juveniles. "It's concentration," he explains. "If a fire broke out, I wouldn't know it."

To keep that typewriter moving, Gerson works on two books at once in his Clinton, Connecticut, home. When he gets stuck on one book, he turns to the other, such rotation keeping the writer's blocks melted away.

During the working week, Gerson's evenings are dedicated to the heavy research necessary for such biographical novels as *Because I Loved Him* and *TR*, his story of Theodore Roosevelt (Condensed Books, Winter 1970). A fast reader, Gerson can mentally bank for instant withdrawal up to seven hundred pages of research a night, his photographic memory recording the exact pages for facts and quotes. So he wastes no time on note-taking. Add to Gerson's impressive personal gifts a running file of twenty or thirty subjects which interest him, and you begin to get the broad factual base for his tremendous output.

His efficient use of working hours brings the fifty-six-year-old author leisurely weekends and long vacations at home and abroad with his family. He and his wife have three daughters, one son, a two-year-old granddaughter, three cats and a dog.

*Because I Loved Him* goes far back in Noel Gerson's life. When his father was the general manager for the Shubert theaters, he did business with Lillie Langtry. Gerson was too young to remember on which American tour or in which theater they met, but he remembers much family teasing about the famous beauty. "She was the only woman of whom my mother was ever jealous," he recalls. "And my mother was a pretty woman."

# The Sea of Grass

A CONDENSATION OF THE BOOK BY
## CONRAD RICHTER

The conflicts of a man who
passionately loves both his wife and his land.
A modern classic

ILLUSTRATED BY JIM SHARPE

In the last century the vast grasslands
of the American Southwest were the
lonely empires of the pioneer cattlemen.
Young Hal Brewton was the nephew of
one of these, and as he grew up,
Hal witnessed the long battle between
his proud, passionate uncle, Colonel
Jim Brewton, and the homesteaders
who coveted his range. Into this conflict
came Lutie, the Colonel's bride from
St. Louis, whose secret hatred for the
primordial plains would clash with
the Colonel's devotion to his kingdom
of grass.

This American classic, made into a
movie in 1947, has a particularly
powerful appeal today, when so much
of our country is threatened by the
shortsightedness of exploiters who
would break and tame the land.

I

## Lutie

THAT lusty pioneer blood is tamed now, broken and gelded like the wild horse and the frontier settlement. And I think that I shall never see it flowing through human veins again as it did in my uncle Jim Brewton riding a lathered horse across his shaggy range or standing in his massive earthen ranch house, bare of furniture as a garret, and holding together his empire of grass and cattle by the fire in his eyes.

His rude empire is dead and quartered today like a steer on the meat block, but I still lie in bed at night and see it tossing, leaping in the golden sunlight, stretching a hundred and twenty miles along the river and rolling as far into the sunset as stock could roam—a ranch larger than Massachusetts with Connecticut thrown in, his fabulous herds of Texas cattle sprinkled like grains of cinnamon across the horizons. His name was a legend even then, his brand familiar as the ABC's in every packinghouse, and his word the law, not dead sentences in a book, but a moving finger writing on a cottonwood tree where all who rode could read.

I can see his bedroom, just a bunk in the corner, with a fancy horsehair bridle and ropes on the wall. And I can see his huge parlor, without rugs or furniture, piled to the rafters with sacks of flour and burlapped hills of sugar and green coffee, and wooden buttes of boxed tobacco, dried fruits, and canned tomatoes—

provisions for his hundred hands and everyone else who passed that way, rancher or cowboy, Mexican, Indian, or outlaw.

But what moves across my eye unforgettably is his spring round-up when six or seven wagons working back from the Arizona line reached the headquarters range with a vast, almost mythical herd the like of which will never be seen in this country again. Farther than the eye could strain through the dust, the grass was colored with milling cattle, while bulls rode and fought, and cows and calves bawled, and sixty or seventy of us kept saddling fresh mounts and galloping here and there in a daylong excitement.

The free wild life we lived on that shaggy prairie was to me the life of the gods. And that there should be anyone who would not love it, who should even hate it passionately and secretly, and yet the memory of whose delicate presence in that violent land still stirs me with emotion, had not occurred to me. But I was only a boy whose face had never known a razor that early fall day I rode, with rebellious back, to Salt Fork to be shipped off to Missouri to school before my uncle would fetch to the ranch the scarcest article in the territory, a woman, the one we had never seen, who was coming all the way from St. Louis to marry him.

At the edge of town I scowled at an encampment of settlers' tents and wagons, the largest collection of nesters I remembered. They seemed to be waiting for something. Then I rode up to the hotel and heard someone say that the telegraph line was open after having been cut again by Indians in the Raton.

"You, Hal, can see the Colonel gets this," the station agent, red-faced, told me. And he handed me a sheet of gray paper, the writing in pencil and dated at St. Louis nearly a week before. It was the first telegram I had ever seen and for a moment I had the impression that the paper itself had come in some up-to-date manner over the telegraph wire and that the execrable writing was that of this woman who had signed it Lutie and who said with love that she was not stopping off in Denver as she had planned but would arrive in Salt Fork on a morning I knew was tomorrow.

I had not seen my uncle for more than two weeks, and with the telegram unpleasant as a perfumed handkerchief in my pocket, I

rode down to the shipping corrals, half expecting to see his herd of fall beef steers flooding the stock pens where, until shipped, they would fill the town with their bawling.

But no Cross B steers were there and neither was my uncle, and I went to the dim adobe courtroom where they were outrageously trying two of our hands for shooting at and running off a nester. I couldn't get any nearer than the door. But from there I could hear the oratorical voice of the young district attorney, lately from the East and close to the President, bitterly assailing the high-handed methods of my uncle and promising new justice for emigrants. Maybe this was what those settlers were waiting for.

When the trial adjourned until morning, I pushed myself through to Henry McCurtin, my uncle's lawyer, a ponderous man, who read the telegram over his great drooping dun mustaches.

"I haven't seen the Colonel since the trial opened," he rumbled. "I reckon, son, you better meet this woman tomorrow yourself."

For a long time I lay awake that night in the cavernous bridal chamber of the Exchange House, the corner room reserved for my uncle when he came to town, feeling my hate for this woman who was banishing me to Missouri, and thinking that I had never known the town quite so swarming with men, or the night so deafening with the clatter of pianos and scream of fiddles, and boisterous songs that paused only for the rap of the six-shooter.

But through it all I could hear, like the wild, unceasing heartbeat of this frontier town, the sound of boots pounding the wooden sidewalk from bar to bar. And I knew that not all these men, drawn from a hundred and two hundred remote miles, had come to ship beef. It was the trial, this new district attorney challenging the power of my uncle and other big cattlemen, that had drawn them. And sitting up in that enormous bed I could see through the long window the tents and wagons of the emigrants' camp.

When I awoke in the morning, I found to my regret that I had slept through another shooting. On the way to the depot I saw the dead man's oxen still hitched to his wagon, ten or twelve of them lying down patiently in the yoke, chewing their cud, while the stranger who had done it swung on the railroad's wooden water

tower, his boots already pulled off by some low wretch and the water dripping over him, his head to one side and one leg curiously longer than the other as if he were trying to reach the ground.

He was cut down by the sheriff under the indignant direction of the new district attorney and laid temporarily in the freight house. But as soon as the officers had disappeared, some of the dead teamster's friends dragged him out again just as I faintly heard a bell ringing. I stayed to watch them take a rope from a saddle and pull him up again. And when I turned, the train from St. Louis was in, coated with the dust of the Great Plains.

Up until now I expected that my uncle would surely appear. But he wasn't there, and I cast about harshly in my mind what I should say to this woman. In the territory my uncle attended strictly to business, riding the range as hard as any of his hands. But in Kansas City, where he went regularly to sell cattle, people said that he swung a wide loop, and once when a prominent man he disliked had solicited him too far for his business, even inviting him to a very elite party, my uncle had forever silenced him by coming in great style with a notorious and lavishly dressed sporting woman on his arm.

So now I looked for a woman bold and painted like Ready Money Kate from St. Louis, whom I had often seen sailing up and down the wooden sidewalks of Salt Fork in vivid silks with parasol to match and, when she crossed the dusty street, showing plenty of red and white striped stocking.

All I saw was one lady standing by the car steps and behind her a bearded brakeman holding a pair of valises. There was something unforgettable in the slender way she stood there, in a suit of unmistakable quality and a high flowered hat, a fragile feminine figure, alone and unmet, stared at by cowhands and loafers and shaggy teamsters, and back of them on the water tank the dead man swinging.

A loafer in a buckskin shirt with all the beading long since lost said something to her and pointed to me, and I saw her move toward me. She did not speak until she was so close I could smell the fragrance of violets about her, and although I was only a boy, I

felt that quickening emotion she was always to arouse in me until the last time I should see her.

"So this is Hal?" she said softly, and kissed me, and I stood there rigid with my face burning in front of everyone. But if she saw it she gave no sign. With the dead man slowly turning in front of her, she went on chatting in slightly incoherent but charming fashion, saying gay things that required none of my tongue-tied answers. And I realized that here was a finer-fibered creature than any my long black hair and callused hands had known.

When I stammered that her telegram had come only last evening and that I hadn't been able to deliver it to my uncle as yet, she took my arm with alive intimacy. "We'll find him together, Hal."

"He'll come to the hotel, if you'll wait there," I told her.

"The bags can go to the hotel, but not I, Hal," she answered. "I've been shut up in a train for days and days. I want to walk."

Very stiffly and thinking these St. Louis ladies a little mad, I guided her through the deep dust strewn with horns and the forelegs of sheep, between wagon hubs and saddle-pony heels, until we were up on the wooden sidewalk, where I took care to steer her away from the courthouse. But I couldn't avoid the wagon of the dead freighter, with boys climbing a wheel to stare at what we both could plainly see, a long figure lying on his back, his red beard sticking up defiantly from under the blue bandanna across his face. But Lutie Cameron's chatting never stopped. Only her soft live arm tightened in mine like a doeskin band.

I had the pride, common in the territory, that going about on foot was close to disgrace. And I was glad when the boardwalk came to an end. But there was no stopping Lutie Cameron. On and on we went, past a few scattered Mexican houses and up the sloping sandhills, where she exclaimed over the plants in blossom and pinned a yellow spray gaily across her coat.

But when we reached the top of the escarpment and, suddenly like coming on the ocean unaware, there in front of us stretched the vast, brown, empty plain, she stopped for a minute as if she had run into barbed wire. I tried to point out the general location of our ranch house, but she didn't seem to hear me, chatting al-

most breathlessly about a traveling acquaintance on the Pullman palace car, all the while striking out for the tents and covered wagons of the emigrants' camp, where life was busily going on.

She waved brightly to a score or more of children tumbling over the ground, and bowed charmingly to tired-looking women in sunbonnets who had been sewing and knitting on a circle of wagon seats and rockers set on the grass and who stood up now to receive her as some great lady who had deigned to visit their humble abode.

When they told her they had come all the way from her own Missouri and hoped to settle far out on this very plain, something came into her eyes that I hadn't seen before. She sparkled to wrinkled grandmothers, swung a gurgling baby high in the air, and ran and shouted with the children who clustered around her. And she climbed up into one of the wagons fitted up with a stovepipe, where, as I stood stiff and disapproving, I could hear her complimenting the delighted owners on what she found.

"If you see Colonel Brewton," she said gaily before she left, "tell him we've been looking for him everywhere."

I was conscious of a shadow instantly falling over us. Even the children seemed to freeze at the sound of my uncle's name.

"I reckon you'll find him at court today, ma'am," a gaunt Missourian answered.

Lutie Cameron said nothing until we were a quarter mile away. "Why didn't you tell me we might find him at court?"

"We couldn't get in anyhow," I answered sullenly.

And when we reached the square, I could see at the courthouse a crowd of men packed halfway across the boardwalk to the hitching rack. I would have gone on to the Exchange House, but she stopped and lifted her head in that gesture I already knew so well, a slight feminine figure against the rude backs of a score of men.

"May we pass, please?" She spoke clearly, and to my surprise that gentle lady's voice of hers turned rough men about and tumbled off their hats as if a bullet had whipped them. A narrow but unmistakable aisle opened in front of us, and presently I found myself inside, with Blackjack Kerns, a rustler and outlaw, rising to give the lady his seat, and others moving over to make room for me.

THE SALT FORK COUNTY court was stuffed and smelly as a stock corral at shipping time, a dingy adobe room with earthen floor and small Mexican windows darkened by men sitting on the deep ledges so that it seemed as if we had entered a kind of twilight.

"Is he here, Hal?" Lutie Cameron whispered.

But even before my eyes grew accustomed to the dimness I knew by the atmosphere that my uncle wasn't there.

"The jury's comin' in," a cowhand behind me muttered.

I saw now that the jury box was empty. Then I heard a stir at the doorway behind us and presently I thought I could feel a wave of restrained excitement passing from bench to bench until beyond the railing I saw our two accused cowhands twist in their seats and Henry McCurtin turn like a mountain suddenly come to life.

I felt my arm brushed by Lutie Cameron's gloved fingers.

"What is it, Hal?" she whispered.

Then I saw that she glimpsed something and I saw it, too, moving erect and towering down the crowded aisle along the wall, a familiar, proud, almost insolent figure in a gray broadcloth coat with tails and bulging on the side toward us with what I knew was a holster capped with ivory handles, his coal-black eyebrows and mustache white with alkali dust. In the abrupt quiet the fall of his boot heels was like the shots of a pistol. Since that day I have been in many a courtroom, but never any so quickly transformed by one man's vitality and power, so that today I can still see, as in the strongest sunshine, that fearless, moving figure of my uncle like some territorial czar.

Then I saw that those pitchfork eyes had found us. Deliberately he was crossing to our aisle, the men he chose to pass by scattering like sheep in front of him. And presently he stood beside us with bared head and a kind of mellowed dignity, pressing Lutie Cameron's hand, asking her welfare in quiet solicitude, his great lusty face gently warmed like the sunlight on a weathered cliff.

Saying he would join us later, he straightened, his black glance swept those close by who had been listening, and he moved majestically on, passing inside the privileged railing where Henry Mc-Curtin stood up in massive welcome and the two accused cowhands

432

grinned and the sheriff hastily brought him the bailiff's chair. The district clerk with a pen riding one ear stared respectfully and Judge White's glum face broke into a friendly smile.

Only one man showed him no deference, and I watched Brice Chamberlain, the new district attorney, standing there tall and impressive, his sack coat buttoned close to his white collar, his blond hair sweeping back, his brows frowning formidably.

"What's the case about, Hal?" Lutie Cameron whispered. "And who is the scowling gentleman?"

I didn't answer. The door beyond the railing had opened and men were drifting through, slouching Americans in unbuttoned vests and Mexicans in leather *chalecos*, one after the other pulling off his hat as he entered. Behind me a voice whispered loudly that for any man except Jim Brewton the jury would have stayed out with their verdict until they had had their dinner on the county. Then I heard leathery Eli Jones, the jury foreman, answering Judge White's question.

"We find," he drawled, "that Andy Boggs was shot at and run off the place he wanted to file on, by unknown parties."

I saw the strict face of the judge redden. "That's no verdict!" he reminded the foreman sharply. "The two defendants—"

"Oh, hell, they're not guilty," Eli waved.

I wanted to give the Apache war whoop while behind me a row of cowhands stamped their boots and jingled their spurs until Judge White pounded his pine bench. Then he demanded the formal written verdict of the grinning jury foreman and adjourned court.

"Is that the verdict you wanted, Hal?" Lutie Cameron asked eagerly, but I saw that her eyes were on the tall young district attorney, Brice Chamberlain, who had winced as if thrown by a horse. Another moment and she had swept me up the aisle, her arm in mine, and through the railing, where she stopped beside my uncle, slipping her free arm delicately through his, just as I saw Brice Chamberlain get himself in hand and stiffly congratulate Henry McCurtin.

Then the defeated young district attorney turned to my uncle. "May I ask a few questions that I had no opportunity for during

433

the trial, Colonel Brewton?" His manner was courteous, but there was a faintly challenging ring in his voice and a blue fire in his eyes that kindled the silent attention of those of us standing inside of the railing, and he went on without waiting for assent: "Is it true, Colonel Brewton, that your range runs a hundred miles or more north and south, and west nearly to the Arizona line?"

My uncle merely inclined his head.

"Is it true," Chamberlain went on, his voice rising, "that of this vast country, you actually own only a few scattered water holes? And that by far the greater part still belongs to the government?"

"Legally, yes," my uncle conceded.

"Is it true, then," Chamberlain concluded, his voice gathering force, "that this million or more of acres belonging to the government is the same land that Andrew Boggs, who only wanted a hundred and sixty for a homestead, was run off from?"

"No," my uncle said quietly but with great firmness and power. "He was not run off because he wanted to settle those hundred and sixty acres but because of what he wanted to do with the land."

I heard a strong murmur of approval from a press of cowhands and cattlemen against the railing. Brice Chamberlain did not glance around. But an appeal came into his face and voice, and even I for a moment thought him modest and almost likable.

"Let's forget about Andrew Boggs, Colonel Brewton. But waiting at the edge of this town of Salt Fork right now to see how this trial comes out are other settlers. Men with families, from babes at the breast to grandmothers. They have given up their homes in the East, driven their wagons more than a thousand miles across the plains, and left their dead from the Mississippi to the Rio Grande— all with the one purpose of finding homes for themselves in this great territory." His voice grew eloquent. "Now that you have won your case, Colonel Brewton, and can afford to show your sympathy and charity, I want to ask in the names of these families if you won't let them settle undisturbed on a few acres out of the million or more of government land on your range?"

Lutie Cameron glanced expectantly at my uncle. But he didn't see her. He had thrown up his head like an unruly lead steer.

"Chamberlain," he said, "I have sympathy for the pioneer settler who came out here and risked his life and family among the Indians. And I hope I have a little charity for the nester who waited until the country was safe and peaceable before he filed a homestead on someone else's range who fought for it. But—" and his voice began to ring in the small hushed courtroom, "when that nester picks country like my big vega that's more than seven thousand feet above the sea, when he wants to plow it up to support his family where there isn't enough rain for his crops to grow, where he only kills the grass that will grow, where he starves for water and feeds his family by killing my beef and becomes a man without respect to himself and a miserable menace to the territory, then I have neither sympathy nor charity!"

His eyes now were pitch-black, his great face written with power and almost dissolute ruthlessness. "I want to say," he finished, "that if I know the temper of these citizens, they'll keep running off every settler who tries to destroy their range!"

For nearly a minute more the two men faced each other, one older, rugged, fearless; the other young and white with emotion.

"They warned me," Chamberlain said in a low burning voice, "not to bring action against your men. They told me there was no justice here, that you dominated the country and would never share your land with your less fortunate fellowmen."

He turned on his heel and left, but all of us knew this was not the end. Lutie Cameron still hung on my uncle's arm, delicate, silent, rigid, her eyes on the stunned little group of listening would-be settlers from Missouri in the patched blue and striped jumpers of farmers. And when she and my uncle went out to the hotel for dinner, I saw her take the spray of bright yellow blossoms she had pinned so gaily across her coat and throw it away.

With my hat hot and uncomfortable in my hand, I waited as long as I dared that afternoon outside the ladies' parlor of the Exchange House. When I pushed in the door, I saw my uncle standing with dignity in front of the tall window. Beside him stood Lutie Cameron, her head thrown firmly up, her flowered hat at a high and gallant angle, making an unforgettable picture in that dark,

435

cavernous room with a single shaft of sunshine pouring over her, while Judge White in a long black coat with broad silken lapels kept sternly clearing his throat and compressing his lips as he read the unfamiliar marriage service.

Her cheeks were dusted as if with flour when she turned, but nothing else betrayed her as Dr. Reid, who I think must have denied himself liquor all afternoon for the occasion, bowed over her hand, like the Virginian he was, and wished her happiness. And Henry McCurtin, in fresh linen unsullied by a single tobacco stain, asked her jovially through his dun mustaches how she had managed to rope such a shy war-horse.

She and my uncle took me to the depot, and the last thing I saw of Lutie Brewton, she was standing with one arm outstretched waving her handkerchief gaily after me, a gesture I coldly declined to answer. But late that night when the train was puffing through the dark New Mexican hills, I kept thinking about her in that walled island of ranch house on my lost sea of grass.

I HAVE hated places in my life, but never any like that academy in Lexington where the woman who had waved me good-by so gaily had imprisoned me, with its brick walls and stone banisters and a winter of cold such as I had never known in the territory, with the sun not coming out for weeks at a time. When spring came and the eaves dripped a steady tattoo and strange birds cheeped in the wet trees around the school, the ice went out of the mile-wide Missouri with a roar. And I went, too, between two suns, as my uncle used to say of any man who disappeared. And late that afternoon I was in Kansas City, trying to keep my chin up and not to betray how bewildered I was in this cold young city with wagons and carriages clattering in every direction on the stone paving and no one paying me more attention than if I were a burro dozing in the dusty streets at Old Town in Salt Fork. The thought of those quiet, dusty streets sleeping in the yellow sun made me more homesick for the territory than I have ever been in my life except for a half hour later when I reached the stockyards and smelled cattle again and saw the familiar

colors of longhorns and listened to Nicholas Masters of the Masters Packing Company, the heavy flesh of his face quivering as he sputtered that if he helped me run home, my uncle would never sell him another trainload of steers.

But when I told him it had been the woman my uncle had married and whom I hated that had clapped me into this prison of a school, he stared at me thoughtfully as a companion in distress. And when I left, I had a pass and some money and had given a promise never to let this woman know who had befriended me.

All the way out to the ranch on a Salt Fork horse from Dagget's livery stable, with the range already greening up, with Canada geese rising from the ponds, with calves kicking and bucking in the spring sunshine and horses rubbing off winter hair, I felt the bitterness grow in me for the woman who would have kept me from all this. And I planned coldly how I would treat her and what curt speech she should hear from me.

Riding up Nester Draw so she should not see me coming, I cut across the rise and up to the rear of the ranch house, where a strange Chinese cook eyed me suspiciously as I entered by the kitchen door. Outside the house, I'd noticed a row of trees that had not been there when I'd left. Now I scowled to see that there were strange pine settees covered with Navajo blankets in the wide hall. And glancing into the storeroom, I saw with dull anger that the familiar mountains of flour and coffee and dried fruits had vanished, so that I hardly knew the room with a Brussels carpet on the floor and heavy dark red hangings at the windows and tufted horsehair chairs and sofa and a square piano polished as elegantly and offensively as the piano at school.

It all had an inexpressibly depressing effect on me, as if the old ranch house I had loved was gone. And I stood there lonely, bitter, and stiffening as a slender form appeared from the big front bedroom. Oh, she looked a bit paler, but her dark hair even here on these remote plains was done up in the latest St. Louis fashion; a spray of pink locoweed had been pinned freshly across her basque and she moved with undiminished sparkle and aliveness.

Then she recognized me. "Hal!" she almost screamed.

437

Her intense young arms hugged me as if she had seen no one for weeks. And with her delicate fragrance of violets about me like some sweet drug, I felt the hate go out of me as the ice had gone out of the Missouri only a week or two before.

Another moment and she was holding me at arm's length, delightedly looking me over, and laughingly exclaiming what a manly boy I was on the way to becoming, and chattering that she had not had a visitor since day before yesterday and what a wonderful winter she had spent here in this Western climate with blue sky and almost eternal sunshine, and that my uncle was looking more distinguished than ever, and had I seen the trees she had coaxed the hands to plant for summer shade; degrading work, my uncle had called it, that men who rode a horse would never do.

But with nearly every word I observed in her dark eyes the feverish brilliance of the first day I had seen her. And the following year when I came home a little older and taller, it still haunted her eyes although the parlor hummed with company. And I soon found out that scarcely a day was intended to pass without dinner guests or overnight guests or guests to stay the week. And most of them embroidered, or sang, or played whist, and were agreeable to almost anything except to ride out and visit the roundup, which Lutie Brewton kept finding charming excuses to miss. There were, I remember, the sporting English owners of the Bar 44 and the dancing officers from Fort Ewing, the lively Falconers and the important Netherwoods whose name Lutie Brewton loved to trill over her tongue, and Judge White and Brice Chamberlain on their respective rounds of the district court.

If I expected my uncle to resent their coming, I was mistaken. He rode his range no less hard, and it must have seemed to him as it did to me a kind of miracle to step from dark night into a lighted house, from a hard saddle to a cushioned chair, to come from the cold, shaggy plain into warm curtained rooms with Lutie Brewton bare-armed in a silken gown, with candles burning and silver sparkling and a mellow atmosphere of company around his table.

My uncle would bow with proud courtesy to everyone. But I

heard him talk very little, preferring to sit there with a faint glow warming his weathered face, his insolent eyes softening as he watched his wife. No matter who came or how large the dinner, Lutie Brewton was the tireless pure flame burning in the center of it, her face flatteringly raised to listen, her talk a highly seasoned language of its own, her headlong treble laughter leading into general bursts of merriment, and her ringed fingers skimming over the white keys of the piano, with the soft light from the tall marble, brass, and china lamp golden on her dark hair.

She never stopped, not even for a moment, and I had the curious feeling that she never slept, but, stimulated by congenial friends, could go on bubbling night and day.

Certainly she never stopped when she went to town with her fast team of bays to spend the night at the Netherwoods' or the Holdernesses', who were kin of Brice Chamberlain. Once or twice I drove her, and the moment we passed out through the dense wall of cottonwoods and tamarisks, she chatted incessantly, her face turned away from the wide sea of grass as if it were the plague, so that I began to understand that her cottonwoods and tamarisks had not been planted for summer shade at all.

"She'll settle down once she has babies," I heard Mrs. Netherwood say fondly to Judge White the day of the Holman wedding, when she wore diamond dust in her hair.

THE BABIES came soon afterwards. One after the other I found them in the big front bedroom of the ranch house when I came home from school; the first, a fat gurgling girl with dark eyes and scarcely any hair to start with; the second, an unsmiling boy with the blackest of hair and eyes; and the third, a boy whose eyes were an unexpected bright blue, with hair almost white.

Yet neither I nor anyone else could see a change in Lutie Brewton. With her first baby in the cradle, I felt that out of respect I should call her Aunt Lutie, but she turned on me quickly, her eyes black and flashing. "Don't you dare call me that, Hal. I shall never be old enough to be Auntie to anyone."

Black Hetty, who took care of the babies, showed the broad

white of her teeth. After the second child Lutie Brewton was still the same slender figure, alive, intense, her white skin without a wrinkle. And with the third baby scarcely in his cradle, she danced eight out of ten square dances and waltzes with Brice Chamberlain as her partner in the huge English hall of the Bar 44.

He was at my uncle's house now too often to suit me, driving out as a rule with his cousin, the young blond Mrs. Holderness, whether my uncle was home or not. The administration at Washington had long since changed and with it his and Judge White's appointments. Brice Chamberlain had opened a law office on the dusty Salt Fork plaza next door to Gidding's dance hall, where he specialized in the settling of titles to the huge land grants for profit and the filing of homestead entries as a passion.

My uncle paid him little attention, while he treated my uncle with unfailing politeness. But more than once when the latter wasn't looking, I caught Brice Chamberlain's blue eyes measuring him and seeming to say: "You're of the past generation now. Your time is soon over. We will run the world from now on, not you." And to Lutie he boasted: "Civilization is moving west fast. It will be here soon. And when it comes, the fertile plains around this ranch house will be dotted with farms and schoolhouses."

I paid him no more attention than my uncle. But once when I carried him an invitation to dinner, I saw his desk piled high with blueprint maps of township and correction lines and with stacks of letters from scores of land hungry Easterners he had circularized, a sight that gave me an angry, disturbed feeling.

I was in college at St. Louis when the Washington administration changed again. Almost as I was leaving for home I read with satisfaction in the Salt Fork paper, printed in both English and Spanish, that Brice Chamberlain was closing his office and going to Denver, where he had been promised the appointment of United States district attorney. Two weeks later when I found him still in Salt Fork, I scowled at his figure crossing the dusty plaza with that impressive stride, immaculately dressed as always with high-buttoned Eastern suit under an imposing silver-gray Western hat. I turned to see Henry McCurtin standing beside me, also watching

him from his inscrutable, deeply buried eyes. When we had shaken hands, I asked, "You glad as I am he's going?"

"I'm not so sure, Hal, not so sure. The town is full of rumors." Then, as if he had said too much, he turned away.

For the first time I became sensitive to things unsaid. I saw that the landlocked harbor of the square was taut and white with the crowded canvas of settlers' wagons from a dozen Eastern ports. And I remembered all the small emigrant trains I had glimpsed from my window across Kansas and through the Raton wherever the wagon trail lay in sight of the tracks.

And when I reached the ranch next day, I thought I had never seen Lutie Brewton more brilliantly alive. All afternoon her tongue poured out a stream of gay excitement, one minute warm and frank, the next coaxing and teasing, while my small cousins climbed on my shoulders and burrowed under my chair.

As a rule Lutie Brewton treated her children like some gracious lady who had consented to be their godmother. But tonight to my mild surprise she told Black Hetty she would put them to bed. And with me standing in the doorway silent at the picture they made, she poked tender fun at Jimmy's skinny freckled legs and arms, and called Sarah Beth's pantywaist a corset, which embarrassed her, and frowned with mock seriousness at the white skin of Brock, whom, she declared, God had intended to be a girl, all the while helping them into their long muslin nightgowns which covered their toes as they knelt on the brown sheepskin.

But when we were back again in the parlor, I saw her shudder, and I stared at her until she turned on me like a white tigress.

"Why must you look at me like that, Hal? Am I older? Am I sallow? What do you see? Have I pouches under my eyes?"

I lied to her that I had seen nothing, telling her the truth that she looked scarcely older than the day I had met her at the South Fork depot, and in a moment she had changed back to the sparkling person I knew. But during the night I heard someone moving about the great front bedroom, and when I awoke as the sun heaved up red above the plain, the one who hadn't slept was still walking.

Except for a few minutes at breakfast and noonday dinner, I

did not see her all day. I had planned to ride out to the roundup, but something in her eyes withheld me. All afternoon I could hear her moving about mysteriously in her room. About six o'clock I was lying on my back on the slippery horsehair sofa, staring up at the pine ceiling. I heard the swish of skirts in the hall. And when I turned my head, she was standing there, looking down at me.

"You are a man now, Hal," she told me. "You've been to St. Louis and Kansas City, and you know the way of the world. And I think you'll understand when I tell you I'm going away." The light in her eyes seemed almost blinding. "Run away is what people will call it, Hal. I'm running off. Leaving your uncle for always. I'm going tomorrow morning, and I shan't be back."

I sat up stupefied. I had heard of women deserting their husbands, but for Lutie Brewton to leave my uncle and her position in this luxurious ranch house was unthinkable. I remembered he was still out at the roundup, which on our range lasted from spring to summer, and she must have read my thoughts.

"Oh, not behind his back, Hal," she said. "I told him nearly a month ago. I told him I couldn't stand it another year. Not running the emigrants off again and perhaps killing them as they did that poor nester from Louisiana who shot at them last year. He was white trash, but he had a wife and six or seven children. Now, as far as I am concerned, it's all settled—all but the tearing out of a few roots and tendrils."

"But Jimmy and Brock and Sarah Beth?" I stammered.

The first white hardness came into her face.

"I went over it and over it with him, Hal! You know your uncle. He thought he could hold me by holding the children. My lawyer says I can't take them along. But I can fight for them after I'm away. Once we're settled. No jury, Hal, not even Mexicans, can keep three children from their mother."

Something between the lines of what she said troubled me.

"You're going *with* somebody?" I heard myself say coldly.

Unexpected warm color freshened her faintly wilted cheeks, and almost at once she was like a flower rooted again in rich wet earth with that unaccountable power we call life flowing through her.

"If I never knew it before, Hal, I'd know now you had the same blood as your uncle. You ask the same questions. But I shan't tell you any more than I shall him. Listen! He's coming now. Don't go, Hal!" she begged quickly as I stiffened and rose. Her slender fingers gripped my arm. "You'll break the ice between us. And don't look so frightened for me, you poor boy!" Something shining and irrevocable came into her face. "I'm not dying, Hal. I'm going where there's life, balls and theaters and shaded streets and up-to-date stores and parks to drive in!"

I could hear the hoofbeats. Turning, I saw through the deep windows my uncle riding toward the ranch house, sitting erect as always in his saddle. Presently he was in the room. But, contrary to what I feared, I had never seen him more quiet.

Lutie Brewton held up her face to be kissed as always and chatted brightly of some of the incidents I had told her of college, while my uncle shook my hand and inquired if I had seen Nicholas Masters in Kansas City as he had written me. There was a curious absence of time and hurry, as if utterly nothing was expected to happen. Only when I glanced closely to see if Lutie had really told me the truth did I feel the fine filaments of strain in the air.

"Supper's on, Miz Brewton," called Jeff Calder, the old chuck-wagon cook who had long since succeeded the Chinese.

I would have given a great deal that night to have avoided the dining room and the massive silver. My uncle ate gravely while Lutie Brewton single-handed kept conversation alive. But every moment I saw that she curbed her eyes from the windows.

The children, having had their supper, were out there, all astride the bare back of Old Cherry, with Black Hetty standing by. Jimmy sat in front; Sarah Beth, who was six or seven, behind him; and Brock to the rear, each holding to a share of the bridle reins. A strip of gunnysack had been tied over the gentle old barefoot mare's eyes, and she stood motionless until Jimmy yelled and pulled it off, when she came to life and bobbed up and down until each happily shrieking youngster was deposited on the grass.

I could not look at them myself tonight. I was thinking that I should ride to the camp at Cottonwood Springs, and stay there till

it was over. Then Lutie Brewton gave me one of her indecipherable glances. "If I don't see you anymore tonight, Hal, could you drive me to Salt Fork in the morning?"

My uncle had been sitting quietly, waiting for her signal to rise, the deferent courtesy he always had for her mellowing his face. Now his head was flung up in the gesture of a challenged wild stallion while his eyes flamed with sudden will and power.

"Hal will take your trunk in the buckboard," he told her proudly. "I'll drive you to the train myself."

"Thank you, Colonel Brewton," she said.

But I saw in an instant as she rose that an unusual pallor had swept her face.

For a long time I lay awake that night, listening at intervals to the faint bawling of a calf for its mother in some dim, starlit cañada. And when I fell asleep I dreamed that something vaguely beautiful had gone out of this massive ranch house like the kernel of life out of a prairie seed, and all that remained was the shell of adobe walls. And everywhere about the house in my dream, the sand was endlessly blowing, burying the print of the coyote and lizard, drifting close to the ground like barren snow.

At the first sound of morning I was up pulling on my clothes in the darkness and drinking coffee in the kitchen to escape the breakfast table, and lending a hand in the starlight to the hitching of the teams. And when I came back to the long dark hall, I glimpsed in a candle-lighted room, framed like a picture by the heavy doorway, Lutie Brewton, suited, hatted, and one hand gloved, sitting with three sleepy youngsters in their nightgowns. And I heard her promising in that clear, delightful, fun-loving voice she always used to children that she would see them all sooner than soon and would have a double present for each one that Black Hetty should say had been a little lady or gentleman.

Old Jeff helped me carry out her trunk to the sagging buckboard. And soon Lutie Brewton came, a slender, almost jaunty figure in the dim, blue-black light, answering the children's good-by before my uncle helped her up into the top buggy. Before the horses

444

started, she answered again. And from somewhere down beyond the spring I heard her voice a last time, high and clear above the thud of hoofs and rattle of spokes, like some incredibly sweet and lingering bell.

Old Jeff had waited by one of the buckboard wheels, never saying a word, but I could hear him draw hard and furiously on his pipe until the sounds of the buggy grew faint. Still saying nothing, he moved grimly into the house while I climbed into the rig and my horses without urging followed those that had gone before.

To the newcomer in our Southwestern land it seems that the days are very much alike, the same blue sky and unchanging sunshine and endless heat. But after he is here a year he learns to distinguish nuances in the weather he would never have noticed under a more violent sky; that one day may be clear enough, and yet sometime during the night, without benefit of rain or cloud, a mysterious desert influence sweeps the heavens. And the following morning there is air clearer by half than yesterday, as if freshly rinsed by storm and rain.

It was such a morning that I hauled Lutie Brewton's trunk through the crystal air to Salt Fork. An early purple light poured over the plain like wine, until it seemed that with every breath I could taste it. Most of the way across the vegas I could have reached out my hand and touched the fragrant rows of bee balm starting to bloom on either side of the trail. But all I could smell was the perfume of violets rising from Lutie Brewton's trunk.

The sun was a branding iron on the back of my neck when we came at last to the edge of the sandhills and I saw the cottonwoods standing already cool in shadow in the river valley below. My spent horses plowed the floury dust of the long street. And the red-faced station agent himself came bustling out to oversee the careful lifting out of Lutie Brewton's trunk.

Not until then did I look up and see with relief that everything about the station was normal and everyday, the groups of passengers through the open door of the waiting room, the loafers playing mumblety-peg with their knives on the plank platform, and out near the tracks a circle of friends surrounding Lutie Brewton,

445

laughing and chattering as always, wishing her a pleasant trip to
St. Louis and promising gay times when she returned.

Then I glimpsed lawyers Henry McCurtin and Archie Meade,
the one who was to take over Brice Chamberlain's practice, talking
together in low, grave tones, and was slowly conscious that all was
not what it seemed. I was aware now that the loafers kept peering
up stealthily from under their brows, and a group of passengers
whispered from the waiting-room doorway.

Now I was sure that all those happy friends were frantically
playing a part and that they really had no more belief that Lutie
Brewton was going to St. Louis than I had. And when I stumbled
by as if I noticed nothing, I saw that for all her gay animation,
Lutie's high lace collar was a pale branch whipsawing in the
pounding stream of blood at her throat and that the veins on one
of my uncle's hands stood out like whipcords of blue lightning.

I couldn't have left that spot now if I had wished. I could see
the grim bulge in my uncle's coat of gray broadcloth and an untamed violence flaring in his dark eyes. Several loafers had risen
to their feet, licking their lips. Following their eyes, I glimpsed up
the street the unmistakable tall figure of Brice Chamberlain in a
new brown suit coming out of the Exchange House and pausing
for a moment on the high stone steps, a Mexican behind him with
a pair of gripsacks. Then both approaching figures were blotted
out by a great gray clot of emigrant covered wagons.

II

The Colonel

THE SCENE at Salt Fork that long ago morning is still alive and moving in front of my eyes, and I can't wipe it away. I can see the small
red depot. I can hear the whistle of the eastbound train. And I can
feel the long-controlled but now overflowing passion of my uncle
standing there with his gunbelt buckled under his coat, while the
man Lutie Brewton had refused to name, but whom we all knew,
was coming toward us only a few hundred yards away. I noticed

that men were standing on the flat roof of the Baca hide and wool warehouse and that a teamster who had finished loading his wagon was making no effort to drive it away. And presently I became aware that young lawyer Archie Meade had left the side of the troubled Henry McCurtin as if he couldn't bear to see what might happen to his approaching friend.

The train was whistling now. Some of the silent crowd, I saw, tried not to look up the street, but it was plain that everyone was standing there in a kind of strained expectancy, waiting for Chamberlain's creamy Western hat and brown-checked Eastern suit to appear.

Only Lutie Brewton refused to be still, throwing herself into saying good-by to her friends with an animated gaiety that was almost incoherence. Some of the ladies were crying, although when Lutie Brewton turned to say good-by to me, I stood deaf and stony to hide everything I felt.

"Thank you for bringing my trunk," she said brightly, but when I was kissed, with the scent of violets swimming about me, she whispered in my long hair: "Say nice things about me to my babies till I send for them, Hal!"

And now without a sign as yet of Brice Chamberlain, the train was in, with black smoke drifting from the bulging smokestack, and with women passengers staring curiously at Lutie Brewton as their full skirts rustled to the train. My uncle himself carried her valises into the palace car, where I could see him standing by her seat as she gracefully chatted and laughed at her open window to her friends outside, her voice clear and charming as if nothing had happened or could happen and she might be only taking a flying trip to Santa Fe.

Even after the conductor, who had waited respectfully for my uncle to alight, gave the signal for the train to start, and when she and everybody else knew that the man who was to be United States district attorney in Colorado had not appeared from behind that tangle of emigrant canvas to join her, Lutie Brewton sat alone and gallant, leaning from the window to wave gaily and throw kisses to us all.

"Good-by! Good-by!" For a moment the air was filled with eager cries. Then she was gone. And suddenly the platform was silent and most curiously empty, and everyone stood there looking after the retreating train.

With his head up and his dark eyes a warning to all, my uncle walked toward the hotel, a lone, powerful figure to whom no one at the moment dared to speak.

As soon as he was gone, the crowd stirred and moved about like a pack of small dogs that had been cowed by the presence of a mastiff. Several men edged over to my uncle's lawyer.

"They say Brice Chamberlain's up with Archie Meade in his office now, Mr. McCurtin," one of them said. "What do you reckon Chamberlain'll do—take the train tomorrow?"

Henry McCurtin's eyes were pits of gray granite in the mountainous bulk of his cheeks. "Whatever Brice Chamberlain intends to do, he certainly would not inform us, gentlemen." He bowed, and moved stolidly up the street.

And so did I, as well as I was able. Contrary to my expectations, we stayed in town all next day and my uncle drew out a thousand dollars in cash. And when the time came for the next eastbound train, my uncle was on the plank platform again, with a tensely eager collection of human beings scattered for two hundred yards about the depot, trying to be casual and inconspicuous. One and all, friends or enemies, my uncle ignored them, pacing implacably up and down, that bulge still under his coat.

Henry McCurtin told me afterwards he believed my uncle had merely planned to take the train with Brice Chamberlain and stay with him until he made sure of his man. But Chamberlain did not appear that day or the next, yet common knowledge had it he was staying with his kin, the John Holdernesses, from whose house a stream of telegrams, it was said, was pouring to Washington. And for Lutie Brewton's sake I felt a kind of shame for him, holing up like a fox here in Salt Fork where everybody knew it. Even Archie Meade seemed embarrassed, crossing the square as if in a hurry to shut himself out of sight in Brice Chamberlain's old office near

the saloon. And my uncle wore a look of perpetual contempt.

The fourth day he disdained to go to the depot, and several evenings later as we sat at supper in the hotel eating room under the mounted heads of antelope, he said, I thought, a little wearily, "You can drive on back to the ranch in the morning, Hal."

All week I had slept on the red sofa in the cavernous bridal chamber, still my uncle's room when he came to town. I remember that when I went to bed that night it was not yet dark and so warm I threw the covers over the carved back of the sofa. I awoke after awhile and thought a bunch of cowhands must have arrived for a rowdy night at the dance halls. Then I was conscious of an unaccustomed light and, slipping over to the long window, I saw a procession from the emigrant camps winding around the plaza, all men, some on horseback, some on foot, in patched shirts and faded jumpers. A few carried long rifles, but most of them held up hoes and pitchforks and American flags and crude flares that threw waves of light over their unshaven faces, the faces of tenant farmers from Kansas, of Missouri backwoodsmen, of Louisiana steamboaters and artisans and tradesmen from half a dozen Mississippi and Ohio River states.

I watched them pass, then pulled on my clothes and ran down to the street, where I could see them massed in front of the Holderness house that stood with proud head and shoulders above all the squat adobe buildings of Salt Fork, the leaping flares lighting up its impressively mortared bricks.

As I stood in the shadows of the livery stable, a hoarse roar of enthusiasm rose from the emigrants, and I saw the familiar tall figure of Brice Chamberlain on the Holderness front porch, showing himself at last. A bit pale even at this distance in the flares, but still masterful in a long coat, his blond hair brushed vigorously back, he advanced to the ornate railing.

What he said at first I do not know, for he spoke in a low tone. Then his voice rang down the street. "This much I dare tell you," and I imagined I could see the blue fire in his eyes, "that the President is my friend. And he won't stand by in Washington while ruthless forces in this backward territory oppose and oppress you.

449

That I can promise you as surely as I can that the President of the United States today appointed me judge of your district court. And I have no fear but that he will see to it that the Senate confirms my appointment."

A thunder of approval with shouts of "Judge Chamberlain!" echoed in the dusty street. And I stood there incredulous, aware that something unexpected and tragic had happened, something that Lutie Brewton with all her quick mind had not foreseen. I could see that Brice Chamberlain, lawyer that he was, had moved to clear himself from my uncle's silent threat against the unnamed man going away with Lutie Brewton, and by the same stroke was vindicating himself in the eyes of certain Salt Fork people who would say now that the new judge had never intended to take the train to Denver at all.

All the way back to the hotel, I felt my anger rising against Chamberlain and wondered what Lutie Brewton would do now. And when I entered the room I was uncomfortable to find my uncle already there. He paid me no attention until he had worked off his boots and made himself ready for bed. Then, towering there in his long white nightshirt, he lifted a leather wallet from the inside pocket of his removed coat. "Put this under your pillow," he said. "You're going to Denver tomorrow. I want you to find Lutie and give it to her. She'll need it."

"Yes, sir," I stammered, aware now that he knew of Chamberlain's change of appointment and thinking I would give almost anything rather than find Lutie Brewton in her humiliation. And yet somewhere in my blood I felt an inexpressible eagerness that I was to see her again.

I wanted to tell him what Brice Chamberlain had promised the nesters, but I didn't dare. Even after I had blown out the light I could feel him there, motionless on his back, his eyes open, staring at the ceiling. But sometime during the night I heard him tossing and muttering. And once his voice came out thick and strong, although what he said was sinister and utterly incomprehensible.

"Drink your saddle galls, nesters!" it sounded like. "You've got to plow deeper than that to find him."

THE BRILLIANT SUNSHINE lay like a golden shawl over the rich mountain city the morning my train set me down for the first time in my life in young Denver. As I passed up Seventeenth Street, a babel of voices from the doors of clothing stores, auction houses, and pawnbroker shops coaxed and flattered me with "sir" and "young gentleman." There was something in the streets I walked that morning, in the costly dress of the ladies in passing carriages, in the very air that swept down from the mountains, something lavish, dashing and sparkling like Lutie Brewton herself, and I thought I began to understand a little of her fever for this prodigal place that was growing by leaps and bounds.

Even in the business establishment of my uncle's friend, George Twitchell, only a hardware house though the largest west of St. Louis, I felt I was walking on a silver floor. And when George Twitchell took me home to noonday dinner in his fabulous brick mansion, I knew that my uncle, who had said nothing of Lutie Brewton coming back, was aware that a thousand dollars would not let her stay in Denver forever.

That afternoon with the wallet in my pocket, with my hair freshly cut by a Denver barber, my boots shined, and an impressive card supplied and inscribed: "Mr. Harry Brewton" in George Twitchell's blue Spencerian flourishes, I stiffened my young back and pushed myself toward the new Brown Palace Hotel.

A lively bevy of ladies rustled out as I came in. In silks and satins, chatting like a group of brilliantly plumaged birds, they left the scent of violets floating behind them, and I was sure I should find Lutie Brewton here now.

An elegant clerk with a small, trimmed beard, a long tailed coat and immaculate stand-up collar took my card in his fingers.

"Mrs. Colonel Brewton?" he repeated. "Oh, yes, Mrs. Lutie Cameron Brewton." By the light in his face, I knew that he had surely seen her. Then I became aware that his face had clouded and he was speaking to me with genuine regret. "We all wished Mrs. Brewton might have stayed with us longer." I stood there stiffly, aware that something beautiful was slipping out of my grasp. "Mrs. Brewton was here until day before yesterday," the

451

clerk was saying. "I think she received a letter or telegram. I remember she was very gay, but I had the distinct impression she had been disturbed. She paid her bill and left the hotel and gave us no address. I am very sorry."

When I stepped out into the street, the golden air of the city had fled. All week I called at the other hotels and boardinghouses, and watched from the mule cars for a delicate face and slender figure. George Twitchell took me by night to the better restaurants, to the Tabor Grand Theater, and once to a quiet brick house where ladies and gentlemen gambled at a score of tables, none noticing the paintings on the wall that made me blush to my ears. And when the week was done, all I had for my pains was an endless gallery of ladies' faces that kept passing me in my sleep. But none of them had that rare something that was Lutie Brewton.

Monday morning I took my uncle's wallet from one of the tall iron safes in the hardware house.

"She's probably gone home," George Twitchell cheered me. "Where else could she go? You'll find her sitting on the ranch-house porch when you ride up."

He was a hearty man, tall and raw-boned, with an air that begat confidence. But when I reached Salt Fork and saw the old town with its dusty streets and plank sidewalks asleep in the yellow sun, I knew they had not been trod the last few days by the slender, alive foot of Lutie Brewton. And when I had passed through the wide-open doors of the Dagget livery stable, I noticed that Frank Dagget's eyes strayed at once behind me.

"Hullo, Hal," he greeted. "Hear the owl hoot up in Denver?" And when I nodded briefly, "Shorty Bowen took your buckboard. He said you could hire a buggy if you needed one."

"I don't need any," I said stiffly, knowing what he meant.

The liveryman looked indefinably disappointed.

"Shorty had to pack a couple cases of cartridges out to the ranch," he mentioned.

I felt my ears sharpen, but his face held no expression, neither then nor when he cinched up a horse for me.

As I rode out the straggling street Lutie Brewton had walked

with me that day now so long ago, I saw Brice Chamberlain driving toward me in a hired buggy and an impressive black frock coat like Judge White used to wear. He had always gone out of his way to cultivate my friendship, but today he greeted me with cool and scant ceremony, while I scowled at him in turn and wondered where he had been in a direction that led almost nowhere except to the remote ranches.

Then as my pony reached the top of the sandhills, I saw it, a new tent and covered-wagon city with horses and mules, oxen and cows grazing for miles on the mesa.

It was clear to me now where Brice Chamberlain had been. And if I hadn't guessed it then, I would have known it when I reached the ranch house that evening and found the bunkhouse almost an arsenal of six-shooters and Winchesters, while out on the ground around the supper fire sprawled more Cross B hands than I had ever seen together at one time, tin plates of steak and biscuits in their laps, and a look in their eyes I well knew.

I WAS glad for those dark war clouds as an excuse to put off reporting to my uncle about Lutie. But in the end I knew that all the time he stood there in the dim hall listening to what I had to say about the nesters' camp, and questioning me about their numbers, there was only one person who walked in his mind.

"You didn't see her?" he demanded at last.

I stammered what had happened in Denver. He made no comment. But when Black Hetty came in from the children's room to light a lamp, I saw that his great arrogant face was lined and his eyes held orange flames that I know now were hatred for the man who had failed Lutie Brewton. And the following day when one of our cowhands brought word that the nesters had left their camp and already, as if it were a fiesta, were swarming in wagons and on horseback over the eastern part of our fertile big prairie, the violence poured into his face like a living flood.

"Is Judge Chamberlain with the nesters?" he growled.

"I think it was him in a livery buggy," the cowhand stammered.

"Go out and tell the boys to saddle up," my uncle ordered.

453

I knew what that meant. And when the hand had gone, my uncle must have seen it in my face, for he fixed his fearful gaze on me.

"Remember, boy," he said, "there are times in your life you've got to be hard. No man respects you for being soft to him today and letting him ruin you and himself tomorrow. You're going to see things before sundown that aren't nice to look at and you better not come if a college education's made a woman out of you."

"I can be plenty hard to a nester," I told him.

Adamant in his gray broadcloth coat with its tightly fitting shoulders and tails spread by the saddle; his long, wrinkled boots, far different from the showy footgear of the modern West and unblacked since Lutie Brewton had gone away, he started for the corrals and the big buckskin I knew he would ride today.

Then as we passed through the green wall of cottonwoods and misty spraying tamarisks that Lutie Brewton had had planted, I saw the hands at the corrals and bunkhouse watching three horsemen riding over the rise, the sun sparkling like quicksilver on them and their saddle rigging. And when they rode closer, I could make out the blue uniforms and polished saber hilts and the slouch hats with gold insignia of officers from Fort Ewing.

My uncle waited there in a kind of insolent magnificence until the rider of the bald-faced horse in the lead turned into Major Wilberforce, a soldier of dignity and fierce red mustaches.

He drew off a gauntlet glove and reached down from the saddle to shake hands. "We're camping by the spring on your big vega, Colonel. We've got a troop of sixty-five men, and the Captain and I couldn't resist riding over to have dinner with you."

What he said was perfectly smooth and friendly, but I could see our cowhands stiffen and watch my uncle, who stood there now with utter dignity although his eyes were pitchforks. After what seemed to me an extremely long time, he inclined his head.

"Won't you gentlemen come in? Have your orderly feed your horses." With powerfully controlled steps and speech, he led the way back to the gallery of the ranch house.

I watched the major and the captain perspire in their efforts to bring back the friendship of old times as they sat there, drinking

whiskey on the tufted horsehair parlor chairs, with the children thumping and shouting at play somewhere in the big house, and dinner in the familiar dining room. No one mentioned Lutie Brewton's name, and yet it was plainly a mockery with her away and the nesters swarming at that moment over our big vega.

At the sound of their horses being led to the ranch house that evening, the officers rose with relief. My uncle stood up.

"May I inquire, Major, who ordered the troops to my prairie?"

The officer looked grave under his red mustaches.

"By order of the President, Colonel," he said in a low voice.

"The President," my uncle went on with pitiless irony, "wants you and your troops to stay for some time?"

"Until further orders, Colonel." The major cleared his throat and looked up. "I hope we shall still be friends."

My uncle did not reply. He stood there with lips tight and eyes pitch-black with contempt for the man who had pulled strings for others to fight his battles for him. I could feel the bitterness working in him and I knew that he would never send his men to fight against his country's troops, but would relentlessly put himself through the humiliation of sending them back to their respective camps in the morning.

"Good night, gentlemen," he said harshly to the officers when they left. "You can keep the nesters from being blown away, but God Himself can't the prairie!"

Long after they had gone, I watched him stand there in the bright June moonlight that was almost like day, staring toward the big vega. And that night as I lay in my sleepless bunk staring into the white haze that entered my deep window, I fancied that in the milky mist I could see the prairie as I had seen it all my life, and now would never see it again, with the grass in summer sweeping my stirruped thighs and prairie chicken scuttling ahead of my pony; with the ponds in fall black and noisy with waterfowl, and my uncle's seventy thousand head of cattle rolling in fat; with the tracks of endless game in the winter snow and thousands of tons of wild hay cured and stored on the stem; and when the sloughs of the home range greened up in the spring, with the scent

of warming wet earth and swag after swag catching the emerald fire, with horses shedding and snorting as they rolled, and everywhere the friendly indescribable solitude of that lost sea of grass.

It struck me as strange to see the sun come up as usual over the eastern plain next morning. And at breakfast I asked my uncle if I could ride west with the Red Lake hands to look for my missing B B mare. He raked me with his coal-black eyes, and I think he knew why I didn't want to stay, but he said nothing, and by the time we reached our Red Lake camp the summer rains were sweeping down on us. All night the water dripped from the camp-house roof with a steady clop; and suddenly I knew that I hadn't got away from it at all, and what I heard in my brain was the clop, clop, clop of the hoofs of oxen, of wagon wheels slopping in the sloughs, of the gutturals of men and shrill voices of women and crying babies and cackling barnyard fowl, of the baas of sheep and goats and all the despised chattels of the farmer nesters now scattering like a victorious army over the range.

When at last I rode reluctantly back to the ranch, I could see them squatting all over our big vega, digging holes for their dugouts, or plastering frames of cedar poles with mud; stringing barbed wire where our herds and the wild antelope had always grazed free; and yelling at their teams of mules and steers as they tore up the virgin sod with a breaking plow.

Hot and almost trembling with anger, I came through the wide hall of the ranch house at late dusk and halted, a little ashamed of myself, in the sitting-room doorway. My uncle sat with his great proud face over his tan leather account books as if there wasn't a nester within fifty miles, although I knew that from the nearby window he could have seen through the cottonwoods a half-dozen lights beginning to quiver across the dark prairie.

Sitting there that evening between the heavy walls of the old ranch house, with my uncle's steel pen scratching arrogantly or his two-weeks-old Kansas paper rattling in lusty gusts in his hands, with my young cousins stretched on the floor cutting out paper horses and cattle from old magazines, and all around us the familiar

curtains, furniture, and carpet by lamplight, the feeling kept creeping over me that Lutie Brewton was somehow still here.

A few days later Black Hetty whispered to me portentously: "Heah dem wagons a-rollin' by, Mistah Hal? Miz Brewton come back mighty soon now. It ain't lonesome round heah no mo'. No, sah. You wait and see if Hetty doan know."

It was true, I told myself half bitterly, that we weren't a peacefully remote ranch house anymore, forty or fifty miles from the nearest neighbor. From the bunkhouse doorway you could see fences and plowed furrows, and smoke rising from mud chimneys. Nearly every day nesters in spring wagons or in road wagons rattled by to town or to visit other nesters. And nester children began to ride up on the backs of old horses to borrow matches or sourdough for biscuits or baking soda for a cow with the colic.

They avoided the ranch house as they would a pestilence, going straight to the bunkhouse. I saw little Jimmy and Sarah Beth stand stiffly under the cottonwoods watching them. The tow-haired Brock ran right up and tried to get them to stay and play, but they were mute, staring, defiant yet scared, and as soon as they climbed back on their horses, they rode hurriedly away. I knew that Lutie Brewton would have coaxed them to stay and talk and smile with a glass of lemonade and a piece of democrat cake.

Once they were there as my uncle happened to come riding in, and they huddled together as if they had seen an ogre. But if my uncle saw them, there was no sign of it. In his eyes lately when he came riding up to the ranch house was a look as if he faintly expected someone. Tomorrow, always tomorrow, I told myself, we would glance up and there she would be in one of Frank Dagget's livery buggies as if she had just been to town. Dagget himself would be looking pleased and proud for the Colonel. My uncle's face would be grave, and he would inquire with unfailing courtesy of her health and not a word about where she had been or the skunk who had failed her.

But July passed and August passed, and the night before I went back east to college, my uncle called me into the big front bedroom. I hoped he would ask me to go to the convent in St. Louis to see

if they knew where Lutie Brewton was. But he did not mention her name. Once he glanced at her glove still lying untouched like a delicate part of her, sensitive, and crushed, on a shelf.

And when I lay down that night in my bunk I knew my uncle's inner convictions that wherever she was, the sensitive white hand of Lutie Brewton felt humiliated, dishonored, and crushed like its glove on the shelf, and that she would never come back and show herself to the ranch house and town that had idolized her—not even for her children.

For three long years, part of them in medical school, I didn't see the massive ranch house nor a grain of sand or blade of grass from the Cross B. I remember the weather as unseasonably dry those years at St. Louis, with the Mississippi gaunt as a trail-driven steer. But the Salt Fork weekly told in glowing italics of the heavy snows that fell west of Kansas and the unusual spring rains that soaked the ranges of the territory until they spouted like the rock of Moses with springs. And every issue there began to be more news of the nesters—settlers, homesteaders, and agriculturists, it called them—and less of the cattlemen, until a thousand miles away my thumbs would bite through the paper in anger.

More settlers were landing in Salt Fork by steam and wagon train. The settlers were crowding the Las Cruces land office. The settlers were plowing up the rich brown prairie loam. The settlers were harrowing and planting corn. From the sandhills above Salt Fork the townspeople could see the velvety green patches of the settlers' winter wheat and rye. Judge Chamberlain said as the rains continued that God was clearly on their side.

Not that anyone would have known the existence of a settler on the Cross B range from my uncle's letters. Brief as always, the handwriting was still spirited, erect, unquenchable as I had ever seen it, with the final letter of every word sweeping up like a whiplash, and every proper name underlined, not for emphasis, but from an overflow of will and power.

All those months he wrote me firmly that grass was good and beef high, that my B B mare had a pinto colt, that the hands and chil-

dren sent me their best and he remained my uncle, Jas. B.; but I knew from other sources that his favorite saddle horse, Pompey, had thrown and tangled himself in nester barbed wire until he had to be shot; that in sheltered cañadas his cowhands were digging up the telltale buried horns and Cross B hides of butchered beeves; and that a score of nesters were suing him in Judge Chamberlain's court for the destruction by his cattle of their gardens.

I expected the trial to be over before I came home. But in July when I stepped from the train, Salt Fork was like a nesters' holiday, with grain wagons choking the square, and the sidewalks crowded with men as distinct from cowmen as a draft horse from a saddle pony. In the stores the merchants were truckling to the nester women with the smiles and jokes I had thought they reserved for their cattlemen friends.

And Judge Chamberlain's new brick courthouse did not seem like the Salt Fork County court at all, with no buckled spurs swinging on the railing, with a floor of sawed pine, with pews for seats and all these stolid spectators standing up as in church while the tall figure of Brice Chamberlain swept up to the bar with his blond hair bright against the impressive black of his gown. Even the Henry McCurtin I knew had vanished. With sagging cheeks and sunken eyes, he defended my uncle's case like a man who had had his first stroke of paralysis and was calmly resigned to the second.

But it was when my uncle came in and the only notice these sluggish-faced men showed for that proud figure as he towered down the aisle were a few sullen looks that I felt the end had nearly come.

I tried not to listen to the court routine that followed, except when Judge Chamberlain, as if he were rebuking a Mexican cow thief, reviewed the nester evidence against my uncle to the nester jurors and charged them, as it sounded to me, that they must find my uncle liable and fix the damages. I was remembering a day twelve or fourteen years before when only the whisper that the owner of the Cross B was at the courthouse door had been enough to stir the crowd's emotion; when he had moved through the railing with as much right as Judge White himself, and the whole

courtroom had been charged with his presence. I realized that those golden wild horses of other days had slipped more deftly out of my uncle's rope than he knew, never to be caught again.

First to go had been Lutie Brewton, then the sea of grass. And now these people who had waited till the West was safe were barking and snapping around my uncle's legs like a pack of dogs. But after I had watched him seat himself again in the old, fearless way, without so much as a glance at the nesters beside him, I knew that although he had lost his case they didn't have him down.

From where I sat I could see only the back of his head like some dark, shaggy Jove. And yet I was sure that the red coals of his eyes had fastened themselves on Brice Chamberlain, who might not realize it but still had a debt to pay.

I remember that when I stepped out on the street I found that the two boys had come along to town with their father. When Brock saw me, he pulled off Jimmy's hat, waved it, ran up the plank sidewalk until he was about to be caught, and sailed the hat toward a nester wagon of wheat. For a moment the hat hung against the sky. Then it missed the wagon and fell into the deep mud.

Little did I think this night that the placid blue sky I saw was already returning to its old mysterious cycle, that this was the last deep mud and one of the last wagonloads of wheat that would be seen in Salt Fork for what the Navajos north of Red Lake called a land of snows.

WHEN the news reached me that the weather west of Kansas and Indian Territory had changed, it was as if the God few of us medical students believed in was in His heaven after all, and my eyes must have burned with a deep exultation in the dark halls of my school and hospital. The nester women were praying for rain. The nester men were hauling water from my uncle's ponds. The more responsible nesters were packing up to journey farther west and north, some to join the Mormons. And Judge Chamberlain had made a Fourth of July oration that it was the greatest drought in the history of the territory. But a letter signed "Cattleman" to the paper said it was no drought at all, just normal old-fashioned

461

New Mexican weather, and pointed to the native wild grasses wherever they had not been plowed under. With a desperate skill born of long experience in this dry land, they had caught the diminished rains and rushed into growth and seed while the nesters' corn and wheat scarcely sprouted in the ground.

On my way home the following spring, once the train had climbed the high plateaus, the skies were a dull blue and the plains toasted brown with sod. And when we came close to Salt Fork I had a glimpse of puffs of dust moving over the prairie that were nesters plowing and harrowing a dry land.

I hadn't seen my uncle since I left, and I felt he would be almost insolent with triumph to be vindicated at last. Then I stepped off the train at the familiar red depot and he was there with his buggy to meet me himself, and I wasn't sure of his feelings at all. With his great face plowed and harrowed, but his eyes still pitch-black as I had ever seen them, he drove me home over what had once been his fertile range and was now a waste of barbed wire and bare ground and squalid gates to open and close, with a few of the dug-outs empty and already falling in, and the song of an occasional mockingbird or meadowlark a mockery in the dead and dying young fruit trees. And I can still see him sitting in his buggy, silent and deaf, while a nester in an unwashed undershirt tried to sell him his barren fields.

It was long after dark when we reached home. The earthen ranch house stood deep in the shadows of its cottonwoods and tamarisks like a decaying fortress. Sarah Beth was east at convent school, the boys asleep in bed, and the spring winds had deposited miniature dunes of sand and nester field dust along the wall boards as if no walls were there. And that evening as we sat at the hulking supper table, bare of cloth and candles, with only the smoky light from a brass lamp trickling over us; and afterwards as I wandered through the hall with boys' ropes, spurs, bridles, and saddles scattered over the floor; and again next morning when I heard the two boys fighting and tumbling like young savages over the parlor floor and then riding off hard on their ponies, it seemed strange to think that there had ever been a gentle lady in the house.

"She's gone and nobody but my uncle remembers her anymore," I told myself. But when I rode out to the remote Cross B camps in the hills where nesters had not yet penetrated, and when I talked to some of her old friends in town, I found that they were still talking of the beautiful wife of Colonel Brewton.

Several thought they knew where she was. Young Mrs. Bob Kingman said she had seen Lutie Brewton's face, as young and beautiful as ever, in a nun's wimple on the streets of New Orleans. The gentlemanly wagon boss of the Bar 44, who had won a prize with her as his partner at whist, had seen someone he believed was Mrs. Brewton in a stunning black lace gown and diamonds gambling for high stakes in Tombstone. Myra Netherwood thought Lutie must be dead. But the story I clung to was told by Superintendent Bedford of the railroad, who had been at the famous Silver Ball given with full orchestra and waxed floor under a waterproof canopy at the bottom of a Colorado silver mine. During the evening a fall of rock in a nearby stope had frightened the dancers off the floor, all but a guest with another name, who was the image of Mrs. Brewton. For several minutes while the rocks continued to fall, she had kept on gaily dancing with her partner, encouraging the orchestra and laughing as if nothing had happened, until most of the guests were over their scare and back on the floor. Somehow I felt that had been the real Lutie Brewton, and the peculiar emotion I had always felt at the sight of her had welled up in me indescribably.

But later I found that there was something else they were saying about her, although they did not say it to me. All I noticed at first was that they took a great interest in young Brock when he came with me to town, laughing at his quick replies and provoking him to others. And all the while the ladies admired his feathery blond hair and treated him to slices of layer cake, and while the men bribed him to strut up and down the Kingman store porch like certain well-known characters of town, I could see them exchange veiled glances and knowing nods. And yet for a medical student I was very thick in the skull and thought nothing of it until in August when we had all driven to town to meet Sarah Beth, who was coming home alone by train from school in the morning.

The square swarmed as usual with nester wagons, as if having a poor crop year meant nothing to them. My uncle's old friend Dr. Reid, as one professional man to another, invited me into the White Elephant Saloon, and I found several nesters drinking next year's wheat, appropriating the front of the long walnut bar. A little group of cattlemen and cowhands kept themselves distinct at the other end, and while I shook hands with several of them, the doctor gravely waited for me. His face and manner were courteous and serene, but I knew his hand was twitching to wrap itself around a dark bottle, a long white hand marked with veins that as a small boy I was sure must flow with purple wine.

Through the open door I could see young Brock and Jimmy across the street, facing each other on the steps of the Holderness porch as if they had had one of their differences and the men around them were stirring them up to fight. They made a picture I can see now—Jimmy, slim and dark, a small, stiff image of his father, fists tightly clenched—and Brock leaning forward recklessly to hit him on the nose, his hair white gold in the sun.

Then it happened. A bushy, round-headed nubbin of a nester in a hickory shirt moved to the saloon doorway. "I'm a-bettin' on the Chamberlain young 'un," he called.

For a split fraction of a second as his meaning broke over me, I saw Lutie Brewton clear and beautiful. And when the nester turned and grinned toward a sandbox, it was almost as if he had spat in her face. I was aware of the grave silence of the cowmen and of a curious wild hate sweeping over me like prairie fire. I had thought myself a medical student soon to go out in the world and save human lives. Now I found that the thin veneer of Eastern schools had cracked and I was only a savage young Brewton from an untamed sea of grass, moving through the little gate to where customers' rifles and pistols stood or lay in their accustomed places. I was aware of the cowmen backing out of range and of the barkeeper ducking. And then I almost wanted to kill Dr. Reid, too, whose hand had with surprising force suddenly thrown up my barrel so that oil from a brass hanging lamp poured down on the bar.

At the sound of the shot, men from the square began to wedge their heads in the saloon doorway until they were brushed aside like flies and my uncle stood there, sniffing the smell of black powder like an old war-horse, his black eyes sweeping the room until they halted on me standing at the end of the bar with my unsuccessful six-shooter in my hand.

"What's going on, Hal?" he demanded.

I did not dare look at him now, only stood there rigid with my lips closed tight. He waited what seemed a half hour.

"What was said in here, Walt?" he asked a huge uncomfortable cattleman with open vest and silver watch chain.

The sweat poured from the cattleman's forehead, but he only shook his head. Something came into my uncle's face. For some little time more he stood there unruly and aroused, dominating the long dim room like old times. Then, following the direction of a half-dozen glances, he turned his head and I saw that Jimmy and Brock had squirmed into the jammed doorway.

Just whom my uncle looked at the long minute he kept his head turned toward them, I do not know, but I found it was Brock's eager young face and bright blue eyes I was staring at. In that short time I think there passed through my mind everything I had ever seen him do and heard him say, one minute mean and irrepressible, and the next charming and winning as Lutie Brewton herself so that you forgave him everything. I remembered how painstakingly impartial my uncle was with the boys, always buying two when he bought one, and dividing equally the lash of his quirt although I felt that Brock usually deserved the most of it. And I wondered if this unnameable thing could have been the source of the deep-seated enmity between the two brothers ever since they had been old enough to walk.

When my uncle finally turned back to the barroom, I saw that something unutterable and terrible had come into his face. "If any dog has something more to say, now is the time to say it!" he challenged them all, a wild violence fairly leaping from his eyes.

There was no sound in the long saloon but a chip someone dropped at a poker table, the jingle of a horse shaking his harness

at a hitching rack, and the slow drip of oil on the bar like a clock ticking off the last minutes of the one who would speak. Then with almost a grimace of pain, my uncle nodded at me, and with the boys ahead of me, and my uncle to the rear, we pushed out into the square.

### III

### Brock

IT WAS the boy Brock I couldn't get off my mind the next few winters as a student assistant of a high-tempered French surgeon who operated at St. Mary's and the Alexian Brothers' hospitals. And I can't smell chloroform today without some of those old questionings and doubts rising up in front of me like ghosts. All the baffling memories I had of the boy kept turning over in my mind. Young Brock leading the half-starved nester youngsters over to the ranch house for sourdough biscuits. And young Brock sharpening the rowels of his spur with a blacksmith's file. Young Brock's white hands galloping gracefully through "Black Jack Davey" and "The Gypsy Maid" on the keys of Lutie Brewton's square piano. And the same white hands keeping a tomato can rolling at fifty feet with the thirty-caliber, rimfire five-shooter my uncle let him carry because it was hard to get the odd-sized cartridges.

It was Brock loving to talk. And Brock loving to ride. And Brock trading forty-five cartridges from his father's stores for thirty-caliber rimfire. It was Brock shrewd as a judge and reckless as a Brewton and charming and magnificent as his vanished mother as he swindled his and Jimmy's tutor out of their lessons for the afternoon. And all the time his feathery blond hair kept blowing this way and that in my mind.

Peaceably as if he had been a bishop going to his reward, old Dr. Reid back in Salt Fork made ready to depart his life and his well-thumbed books of Robert Ingersoll in his room at the Exchange House, where the older guests would no longer hear his bedside glass and whiskey bottle striking the hours of the night.

And my uncle telegraphed for me to come home and take the practice.

I found the old doctor in a coma. I tried to make him comfortable, but there was little I could do for him. Even the bottle had been drained of its comfort, and he knew neither me nor my uncle, who, when I came in, had been sitting there for several hours quietly smoking, as the two old friends had often sat in health with only an occasional word between them.

"The thoughts of the *señor doctor* are not anymore on this world," the Mexican woman who had been taking care of him told me.

Once Brock burst eagerly into the room, startling me as some blond Lutie Brewton in boots and spurs, shaking my hand now like a grown man, showing the gold piece he had won at monte, and paying no attention to the bed and its burned-out ember of a man who had brought him into the world. But while the boy stood there laughing and talking, fetching into the sickroom an air like a fresh wind blowing from out of the past, I saw a vestige of life and consciousness struggle into the old physician's eyes. And after Brock had gone whistling down the hall, the old doctor tried slowly to sit up in bed.

"When did Mrs. Brewton come back?" he asked, staring at me, and I did not dare to look at my uncle, whose puffs on his cigar, I was aware, had suddenly ceased.

"I haven't seen her, Doctor," I said in a low voice.

The light went out of his eye like the flame of a candle blown upon and he sank back. But long after he was silent, the emotion I had always felt at a meeting with Lutie Brewton kept stirring me at the unexpected sound of her name.

We buried him a week or two later in one of those inexpressibly lonely and barren Southwestern graveyards, so different from the green graves he had known as a boy in his native Virginia. But the mourners did not see that. They were covertly watching the picture of blond Brock, taller than I, standing only a few feet away from Judge Chamberlain, now a bit portly and distinguished-looking in a long black coat, a shiny high hat in his hand, his yellow hair faintly touched at the temples with silver.

And from then on, everything I remember of my uncle and Brock is tinctured with iodoform and carbolic acid of the old doctor's office that became my own, with its green student lamp shining on the white shelves of drug jars and bottles, on the old leather operating couch strewn with surgical instruments, and on the skeleton that ever since I could remember had stood in a corner.

Before I was back in Salt Fork a year, I found that Brock was already becoming almost as well-known a figure in Salt Fork as Ingram Carter, the gambler, whose full-length portrait in oil hung in the White Elephant Saloon. It was blond, gentlemanly Brock Brewton, a favorite with all the dark-haired, dance-hall women in Madame Nana's *Sala de Baile,* and the same Brock Brewton never losing caste but sedately dealing whist and euchre from the best horsehair furniture in town. It was Brock Brewton playing "The Blue Danube" waltz on Myra Netherwood's grand piano, and Brock Brewton driving up and down the town streets with his Choctaw-blooded nester girl beside him.

I can still see him in a long-legged brown suit that reminded me of the one Brice Chamberlain had once worn, taking his mother's friend Myra Netherwood devoutly to mass. And I can see him in the same suit, his hat pushed back recklessly and his yellow hair curling, calling for two hundred dollars' worth of chips at the White Elephant or Dutch Charley's.

He didn't pay for his chips like ordinary people. He was a Brewton, and if he had called for a thousand dollars in gold, they would have tried to give it to him, the bartender marking it down as usual in his jawbone book. And when the Colonel came to town, he would have asked for his bill and there on the wet bar written out a check for it.

Brock's conflicting ways and my uncle's indulgence toward him were the biggest puzzle I ever tried to solve. Perhaps it was that I refused to see Lutie Brewton as others did, that to me she was still a young boy's beautiful lady. It was summer again when fate tried to make me see it their way.

I had been called to a prairie dugout where a nester woman had tried to kill herself. She was very low and I couldn't leave her with

her small baby fifty miles from a doctor. And several afternoons later when it was all over, I felt that I was no physician at all, only a tired and defeated ranch boy, and that I wanted nothing so much as to spend a night again under my uncle's roof.

I was glad I had come. It was dusk when I approached the old ranch house and found light gleaming from a dozen windows, as I had often seen it in the past. And when I stepped into the bare old hall, I had the strange feeling that a lady was there. The incredible notion came to me that Lutie Brewton had returned. Then Sarah Beth in a white dress with red sash sprang out of the dining room and cried welcome and said she had finished school forever and had come through Salt Fork the very morning I left.

They laid a place for me at the table. The white dinner candles and their shades which I had not seen since Lutie Brewton left, the great mass of pink bee balm in the center, and the familiar heavy silver on snowy damask affected me strongly. All through the meal I observed that my uncle sat very quietly on his chair, the faint desert glow warming his weather-beaten face as I had not seen it for many a year, his pitch-black eyes softening a little as they rested on Sarah Beth. But I had the impression that it was someone else with dark hair and slender bare arms he saw sitting here with other guests around a gayer and younger table.

We were in the parlor, Sarah Beth had opened the old piano and played some of her convent pieces, and my uncle said he wished Brock were home to hear them, when Jimmy was called outside. Sarah Beth's hands strayed into a waltz which her mother's white hands had often played. I saw my uncle hold his cigar motionless in his hand, and for a minute or two with that old melody in the room, it was almost as if the plague of nesters had never swarmed and that Black Hetty might appear with the three small children to give their mother good-night.

The feeling was so strong that I glanced up at the doorway, and found Jimmy standing there. He moved rigidly to his father.

"I just heard," he said in a low voice, "that Brock shot Dutch Charley in town."

Sarah Beth went on playing without hearing and my uncle sat

469

staring as if the boy had told him that several Cross B cows were bogged down in Red Lake and he was considering whether or not to send hands at this hour to pull them out.

"Brock shot who?" He lowered his head like a bull trying to protect himself from a deep wound already administered.

Guessing that something was wrong, Sarah Beth stopped playing. Somewhere on the trail we could hear a galloping horse. Then Jimmy's low answer came clear enough in the huge room.

"Dutch Charley. He claimed that black-haired woman that deals monte for him was in with Brock and favoring him. He said every time Brock came to the table the house lost money. They had an argument. Charley went for his gun, but Brock got him first."

Sarah Beth gave a little cry, but my uncle had hold of himself now. Only the faint gray showed through his deeply lined face.

"Is Charley dead?" he asked after a little.

"I don't know," Jimmy said. "They locked Brock up."

I knew that must have hit my uncle, but there was no change in his proud face as Jimmy gave him the story. Only at Judge Chamberlain's name did my uncle show any emotion.

"What did Chamberlain have to do with it?" he demanded.

By the whiteness of the boy's knuckles I knew that he guessed more than I had supposed. He tried to evade it, but his father's violent eyes were pinning him to the floor.

"Judge Chamberlain got Brock out," he said in a barely audible tone. "Because Brock was so young he wanted to make a private investigation of the circumstances. If Brock behaves himself, he said the case might not come up at the next term of court. But Brock's got to report to Judge Chamberlain as often as he says."

For a headlong, incredible moment it was as if I had seen the long arm of Brice Chamberlain reaching across all Salt Fork County in front of the nesters and the loafers, in front of the town ladies, the ranchers' wives and the dance-hall women, to pin a final ugly red brand on the gay, slender figure of Lutie Brewton.

I had seen my uncle angry many times, but never when his blood ran black in his veins as it did now. Even across the room I could feel the rising torrent of flame that, once aroused in him, burned

like a prairie fire that no man could put out or stand up in front of.

Then I saw that he was moving toward the door. I don't think he knew any longer that we were in the room, but we all knew where he was going. We watched him pick up his old gun belt where it hung from the post of a pine settee in the hall. And at the sight of it, Sarah Beth rose quickly from her stool.

"Don't go tonight, Papa!" she begged him. "Let Hal and Jimmy go in tomorrow."

He stood there bleak and unhearing, strapping the double buckles of the belt before he turned and swept the three of us with his violently smoldering eyes that told us he was still lord of his family, including Brock.

But he did not go. He stood there for a little in the wide hall as if listening. Presently we heard a familiar footstep on the gallery and Brock, his yellow hair curling like a child's, came swinging past him and into the room, fresh and gallant and unscathed.

He must have guessed from all our faces that we knew, and it only made him more charming and desperately gayer, throwing himself into lively banter at Sarah Beth as if she wasn't standing there with white cheeks in front of him, ready to burst into tears on his shoulder; chiding her for not waking him up where he slept in the hotel most of the day when she passed through town; teasing her about Tom Milledeaux's love letters; and penitently coaxing her to play a duet with him at the piano.

And I thought that perhaps no one anywhere but Lutie Brewton herself could have come in at a moment like this and so disarmed us and held off my uncle until I saw him take again his horsehair armchair, where he sat waiting for the festivities to be over, watching Brock with painful and unutterable affection.

At last Sarah Beth went to bed, and my uncle sat looking at the boy. "Is it true you shot Dutch Charley, Brock?"

The boy's face changed. "I had to or he'd have shot me."

"Is it true," the older man went on, "that the woman who deals monte for Dutch Charley was favoring you and you knew it?"

"All women like me. Like everybody liked—" Brock's lips closed, but he kept his veiled, almost derisive eyes on my uncle.

The slow color rose in the latter's leathery cheeks.

"I don't mind the shooting so much," he said with difficulty. "Boys will fight, and I wouldn't think much of you if you couldn't defend yourself. I told you I'd pay your gambling debts so long as you played fair and square. But I've always told you that cheating was the lowest form of animal life. Now you've cheated, and no matter what anybody else says, I want you to go through trial on your own feet until you clear yourself or take your punishment."

The boy was staring at him with a sudden curious, impersonal hatred. "No father," he said defiantly, "would send his boy to prison when the judge got him out of it. Besides, I have a job. That's why I'm out here tonight. I'm going to be a counterjumper for George Holderness and Company."

At the sound of the name of Brice Chamberlain's uncle and all it implied, my uncle sat up and the veins swelled in his throat and hands until even the boy backed across the room. But the bright blue eyes were burning in the boy's white face, and when he saw he wasn't going to be touched, he began to pace. "You can't keep me out on a ranch!" he was crying. "I'm eighteen. I wasn't cut out for ranching. I've got to be where there's excitement and people and lights and music and things going on. Sooner than stay in this Godforsaken place, I'd rather be stuffed in a coffin—"

I did not hear any more. There was something fatalistic in the scene and words, as if I was on the same horsehair sofa seeing Lutie Brewton pacing up and down this very Brussels carpet, her eyes burning, her lips speaking almost the identical words.

When I looked at my uncle, his face was drawn and he was breathing heavily as if he had seen a ghost. "All right, Brock," he brought out thickly. How much it cost him, I could only guess. "I stood in the way of somebody else years ago and I've always been sorry. I won't stand in yours."

Flashing a look of triumph at the dark silent face of his brother, Brock went quickly out of the room. Long after he had gone my uncle sat staring out of the dark window, and I could see him in the pane, and I never realized before how utterly furrowed his face was, like a worn-out field, the face of an old man at

last. Only his eyes were the same, burning black and unspeakably bitter. After a while he rose unsteadily, paying no attention to Jimmy and me standing helplessly by. Then brushing aside Jimmy's proffered help and planting his boots slowly but relentlessly in front of him, he went on, without speaking, to his lonely and barren bedroom.

THERE was a huge cottonwood that used to stand off the plaza in one of Salt Fork's crooked streets. Its bark was rougher than any tree I knew and its branches gnarled. It had seen Navajo and Apache raids and the long ox trains crawling on the Chihuahua Trail. But it still stood there green and cool. And when of a morning I crossed the plaza to my office, I found myself glancing to see if the old tree had weathered last night's storm. Back in my mind it was not the tree I looked to see, but an old man who had also known the Navajo and Apache raids and the ox trains on the Chihuahua Trail.

One evening just before the fall term of court, Dutch Charley died of his gunshot wounds. And sometime that night Brock left the dim lights of Salt Fork and an empty money box of Holderness and Company behind him. I had not seen my uncle since the evening after the shooting. It had not been pleasant to think of him coming to town where everyone would see for himself how deeply he had been stricken. And now it was my conviction that he would not be in Salt Fork, if at all, for a long time to come.

But only a day or two later I met him walking across the plaza, slower, grayer, not much more than a shadow of his old powerful self, yet still painfully erect and implacable in his gray broadcloth tails. And the men looked sober when they saw him coming, and said with respect: "Gettin' dry, Colonel," and "Yessirree, Colonel," and looked after him thoughtfully when he had passed.

And when the news came that Brock had been seen in El Paso and called himself Brock Chamberlain now, everybody said it was all over and you could take one look at Jim Brewton and know he himself admitted it. Certainly I seldom heard him mention Brock again. But it wasn't over. At Sarah Beth's wedding I thought

I saw those burned-out eyes staring dully at the guests as if there were someone missing in that ranch-house parlor, although exactly who was missing I could never be quite sure.

I believe now that every piece of news about Brock my uncle read in the Albuquerque and Denver papers was a secret Apache lance in his heart. His forehead was incommunicable as an old rawhide and branded like one with the mark of the band of his hat. And of what went on behind it he never spoke. All I know is that as months passed and the stories kept coming in about Brock raking eight thousand dollars from a Cripple Creek gambling table and Brock holding up a Mexican sheepherder with three pesos on his person; of Brock shooting up White Oaks and riding south into old Mexico ahead of the sheriff; of Brock riding west with Cochran's Wild Bunch and Brock riding east alone to bring a jeweled necklace to his Choctaw-blooded nester girl in our next county, Brock wasn't real to me anymore. He was just a glittering idea, a name printed in papers from Omaha to Oregon, talked about over wet bars and dry trails.

And when they came and asked me to drive forty miles to dress the wounds of a fugitive the White Oaks sheriff had shot, I sent word to Jimmy to keep it from my uncle. It was all still unreal to me. This Brock Chamberlain, wanted for a dozen things over Arizona Territory, now making fools of a county posse nearer home, holding off twenty or thirty men from an abandoned shack until the sheriff had sent for Judge Chamberlain to come and talk him into giving up, could not be the Brock whose feathery white hair had blown with my breath in his cradle.

Then suddenly I knew I was mistaken. The morning train had come and gone, and I was refilling the small bottles of my medicine valise and picking up my surgical instruments when a step sounded in the outer office; and when I looked up, Lutie Brewton was standing there. Oh, her veil hung heavy and I could not distinguish a feature beneath it, and she wore clothes I had never seen before, but there was something special in the straining high angle of the plumes of her hat. In the voice I hadn't heard for fifteen years, she said, "Hal!" And she hugged me, in that silent inte-

gral part of speech of several generations ago which told things the lips neither would nor could. The familiar scent of violets closed around me, and I was still a boy. Lutie Brewton had never gone away, and my uncle rode the range in his lusty prime.

She pinned back her veil, and I saw that with all her struggled erectness, her face, dead white against the lifted black plumes, had begun to show the first branding marks of her hated arch-enemy, age. As if she knew I had seen, she threw herself into holding me at arm's length, inspecting me with that critical yet flattering air, telling me almost feverishly how proud she was of me as a doctor, that any woman just to see me must throw herself in my care, and that as a physician's ears must be filled with the woes of his patients, she knew I should never ask her the weary question where she had been all these years.

And I found myself gazing at that brilliant, animated face and asking under my breath if it were true that a few minutes ago I had seen any signs of age. But all the time she plied me with questions about Jimmy and Sarah Beth and Sarah Beth's husband, whom she had never seen, I knew it was Brock that had brought her. And it was strange how I could feel him now for the first time in years, one of those three sleepy youngsters around her in their nightgowns in that early, candlelit room so long ago.

Out of the window I could see across the street men watching from the gallery of Gaylord's saddlery, and I knew that someone had recognized Lutie Brewton. Then there were quick steps in my outer office, and Myra Netherwood, tall and gray-haired, an excited look on her dignified face, was there. "Doctor, they tell me—" she began. "Lutie!" And they were in each other's arms.

Out in the plaza I heard the rattle of my phaeton's wheels.

"You comin', doc?" called the messenger from the next county.

I moved to finish packing my doctor bag.

"I've got to make a little call—on a sick man," I told Lutie with my back turned. "I know you'll want to be with Mrs. Netherwood. I'll come over as soon as I get in."

I tried to put it as if it were only a nearby nester patient, but I knew when I turned that her sensitive mind had guessed where

I was going. And all the long trail down into the South Prairie country, while the rancher who had ridden all night to get the doctor dozed beside me, I could see in the endless heat waves two unforgettable looks in Lutie Brewton's brilliant dark eyes. One of them was when she had seen on the wall the photograph of my uncle, an old man, a great frame without flesh, sitting in his buggy, holding the reins of his pair of sorrels. The other look she had given me when I left. It concerned nothing of this world, only a small boy in a long nightgown and tousled hair white in the candlelight of a world that had vanished like last year's snows.

It was Sunday morning when my horses' shoes splashed silently back again in the dust of Salt Fork streets. The shutters were up on mercantile houses, the doors of business places closed, and that strange Sabbath stillness hung over everything as if these whitewashed galleries and brown adobe walls had not heard only yesterday the untamed roar of dance hall and six-shooter. And when I turned in my team at Dagget's, it was Sunday even among the peacefully munching horses in their stalls.

All the while I drew my straight razor above the wooden washstand in my room and while I made my way across the plaza with the Spanish bells from the adobe church clanging in my ears, I dreaded meeting Lutie Brewton. I knocked on the paneled Netherwood door, and Lutie Brewton opened it herself, slender and rigidly erect as I had ever remembered her. Only the plumed hat looked as if it were bearing down too hard on that fragile head and throat, and the eyes burned in the white face.

"Don't tell me anything—yet, Hal!" she said. "Just take me to mass. I don't want to be stared at alone."

My uncle and I seldom went to church. And I would have given a great deal to escape it this morning. I had never been out with Lutie Brewton before when the nearness of other people had not been the stimulus for the most animated conversation to her companion. But today the only emotion at their approach was the tightening of her arm in mine as it had that first day so long ago when together we had passed the murdered teamster lying on his

back in the straw of his wagon with a bandanna over his face.

Once we were sitting in the dim church it was as if she no longer knew I was there. The click of her beads was strangely like the click of six-shooters, and the sibilants of her lips like those of the wind drawing through rusty barbed wire. The whitewashed walls of the church kept passing away like mist, and instead of the altar, there in front of me was the South Prairie I had driven through the last several days, naked in the pitiless Southwestern sunlight, with discouraged nester families watching my phaeton from the doors of occupied dugouts and the doors of the empty houses half-fallen from their hinges. I saw plows rusting and gaunt horses standing motionless where there had once been grass. And sand drifted along the crazy pattern of abandoned fence posts.

And at the end of the journey wounded men stupefied with whiskey lay half-undressed under a leafless, sapless apple tree. A fresh mound of earth dried and cracked in the sun like a giant adobe brick. And I knew that around a rough circle of sandhills, hidden men with rifles watched the cañada where a deserted nester's shack stared sullenly from its empty windows.

Chamberlain had not yet arrived, and we had no idea then that he never expected to come, that even at this hour he was boarding a train for Santa Fe on some unnamed judicial business. And after the sun went down and a horse's hoofs sounded on the trail, we thought it was the judge or news of the judge at least, even when the sound told us there was no buggy. Then as it drew closer through the twilight, there was something familiar about the rider hunched on the saddle of a weary, raw-boned roan.

"It's the old Colonel," someone muttered after a little.

The men stared at each other and back at the apparition. And now I could make out clearly enough the unmistakable figure of my uncle on his favorite, silver-horned saddle, a weary old man in a gray broadcloth coat too large for his shrunken girth and shoulders, unarmed, his coattails spreading behind the cantle, his trousers tucked into boots brown with dust. Who had told him about Brock I had no idea, but he had ridden a direct line across the country from the Cross B, over malpais and timbered ridges

where no buggy trail ran. His roan was caked with mud far above the knees where he had plainly forded the treacherous Puerco, and the blanket protruding from the saddle was dark with sweat.

He halted beside us presently, his great head with its long gray mustaches forward on the soiled linen of his chest. His burned-out eyes seemed to peer at us from far back in his head where life had taken a final stand. And if there was a sign of recognition for any of us, I didn't see it, and for all the attention he showed me, I might have been a stranger instead of Brewton flesh and blood.

"Where's Brock?" was all he asked.

The men stirred uncomfortably. One of them indicated the cañada. For several moments the old eyes peered at the squalid deserted nester's shack, a symbol of all that he hated and that had brought him tragedy and pain. Then the gray wrinkled knees nudged his mount; his old fingers, no more than bone, veins, and skin, twitched the reins, and the tired roan started.

A dozen sheriffs could not have held him, and none of us tried it, or said anything as we watched him, rigidly erect in the saddle, ride down alone into the cañada where a low deadly voice we could barely hear hailed him from the nester's shack, warning him he would never give himself up alive for trial, that the old man wasn't his father anyway, and that if he came any closer, he would drop both horse and rider in the trail.

No answer came from my uncle, and the only change in that lone, riding figure was that he seemed to tower in his stirrups.

He had been in the shack only a few minutes when he was outside ordering me in his old-time thunder to come. When I got there, an unshaven man sat propped up against the wall with rifle and pistol on the floor beside him, mocking and grimacing at me, his yellow hair curling like a child's. And all the time my hand wanted to shake as I tried in the dim light from the doorway to stop the bleeding from a wound in his lung, and while my uncle stood there with tortured stolidity, Brock lay on the dirty floor, paying no attention to my command to be quiet, jibing and mimicking me, calling me a horse doctor, begging tobacco and smoking cigarettes, bantering about Jimmy and Tom Milledeaux and coaxing me to say

nice things about him to Sarah Beth, so that no one, not even the sheriff, standing silent and listening some feet beyond the door, could help being won over to him now.

And in the firelight that evening, when he couldn't talk anymore and there was no sound but the yapping of the coyotes, I thought I saw his sardonic blue eyes pointing to something behind me. The shack had been systematically riddled with lead by the posse until it was almost a sieve. Only one conspicuous place on the four walls remained untouched by bullets, and I found now that he was derisively drawing my attention to what hung pasted by unknown hands to the center of this spot, a faded, Christmas newspaper print of Christ in the manger, with the well-known words: "Peace on Earth, Good Will toward Men."

The ringing of a bell somewhere and the rising and dipping of the congregation brought the whitewashed walls of the church back again with Lutie Brewton beside me. And when I looked about I was aware now that most of the people around us must have already heard of what had happened on the South Prairie. Their stares at Lutie Brewton carried a questioning as if they were not so sure but that yesterday they had wronged her.

When she went out she lifted her veil and smiled gently to the little Mexican girls admiring her as they kept dipping their knees at aisle and door, and spoke, as she had in the old days, to a sightless, black-shawled Mexican, now an old woman known as La Ciega. The latter, I am sure, had never understood one of Lutie Brewton's sparkling English sentences, although a look had always come into her blind, wrinkled face as if she had talked to someone who had seen the Blessed Virgin.

But today at the sound of that charming, unmistakable voice she had not heard for fifteen years, La Ciega let go of her *rebozo* and reached out to the speaker, and her hands were tight lumps of brown copper against Lutie Brewton's white slender ones.

"*Ay de mí, señora!*" she began, and poured out a stream of Spanish from one woman to another.

Lutie stood there delicately responsive and sympathetic, glancing questioningly at me. But when, without translating any of it, I

tried to urge her quietly on, she turned attentively to a Mexican youth. "What does the blind woman say?"

"She say," the boy said, arching his back with pride to be speaking to Mrs. Brewton in front of everybody, "she say she have a boy too who is kill by a bullet. She said thank to God her boy and your boy don't suffer anymore."

"Yes," Lutie Brewton said, drawing in her breath. "Yes, thank her for me."

She was erect again and very white as she took my arm and went on, steadily clearing the multicolored stream of churchgoers.

"Now I am ready to go to the ranch, Hal," she said. "Will you have someone from Dagget's livery drive me?"

"I wouldn't go until the funeral," I begged her in a low voice.

The plumes of her hat were suddenly and rigidly higher.

"May I go right away this morning, Hal, please!" she asked, and I found that her clearly modulated voice impelled me toward the livery stable as effectively as twenty years ago.

A hundred times since she had gone away I had pictured Lutie coming back to the Cross B. In my thoughts I was always there, feeling that extraordinary, quickening emotion just the sight of her had always called up in me. But today the old ranch house was the last place on earth I wanted to go with Lutie Brewton.

Frank Dagget gave me a queer look when I asked him for a pair of fresh horses for my phaeton to drive to the Cross B. And I knew he had guessed who was going with me, for he lifted his best black harness from the long pins, laid it on the back of his fastest team, and said that the boxing of one of the wheels of my old dusty phaeton was loose and he would give me today the fine green-seated buggy he had only last week unloaded from the railroad. And before he let me go, he combed again the manes and tails of his team and flecked the fine particles of dust from shiny black spokes, leather dash and whipstock.

"Is she well?" he asked, not looking at me.

"I think so," I said.

"It takes spunk to go to the old Colonel now," he said as I climbed into the buggy. "But then she always had it."

There are days in our Southwestern country that people call brassy but should be called steel. The sun beats down with a merciless white fire until the cloudless sky is scarcely blue but rather like the blade of a knife that for days has been ground to the stone.

It was such a morning I drove out of the wide front doors of the livery, and I felt for Lutie Brewton and how she would flinch. But I had no need to. Although Myra Netherwood in a silk wrapper gave me an anguished glance, Lutie Brewton came out of her room delicate and fragile but up and never to be turned back now, showing me the valises to carry to the buggy as if she had been away from the ranch no more than to come to town and would find everything on her return as she had left it a few days before. She gave little sign that the townspeople watched her as we drove away, and once we had reached the prairie, she kept her face turned from all the nester sores and scars, talking in a low incessant voice as if she could not halt if she wished. But although I listened for any touch here or there that would reveal the pattern of her hidden years, I knew no more afterwards than before which of the stories was the true one.

Only at dusk when, after pushing the team, we saw the ranch buildings and trees swimming ahead of us like an oasis in a purple desert, was she silent. And she didn't speak again until we had driven through her own wall of cottonwoods and tamarisks and had stopped by the dark familiar walls of the ranch house.

I learned that my uncle had not yet returned from the South Prairie, from where he was expected an hour or two ahead of the wagon. But under the candles that Lutie Brewton went about lighting, the whole house was grimly eloquent with his presence: his implacable, sweated gun belt hanging from its accustomed corner of the pine settee in the hall; his wrinkled, unyielding boots standing along the wall in the big front bedroom where Lutie directed me to set down her valises; the inflexible shape of his pipes lying about; and the fierce spartan barrenness of everything.

I wished to God that Jimmy might come in from somewhere in the cedar country, where, they told me, they had sent a rider with the news. As the evening went on, there was no sign of him. But

after an hour the older hands who had known Mrs. Brewton moved in a body from the bunkhouse to greet her, lining up on the front gallery and pushing the foreman first, all grave and embarrassed, ceremoniously shaven and in clean shirts, holding their hats in their hands, feeling tremendously sorry for her about Brock and all that had happened before and all that might happen when the old Colonel came home, but the farthermost notion from their minds that of expressing a word of it.

Soberly each one spoke as he shook hands.

"Nice day, Miz Brewton."

"You have a nice trip from town, Miz Brewton?"

"Find the road pretty fair, Miz Brewton?"

And after that they just stood around respectfully until such a time should elapse that it would be fitting for them to go. What few remarks they managed to make they chose with extreme care, avoiding anything that might assume that Brock had ever lived or died or that she had gone away. And all the while Lutie Brewton, her face very pale against her dark hair, tried to make them less uncomfortable, cross-stitching and embroidering their simplest subjects, picking up in her white fingers the most ordinary sentiment spoken with sawdust and awkwardness, and breathing upon it till it grew golden and exciting and important so that the others looked with surprise at the original speaker for having uttered it.

And when the time they waited for had elapsed, it was as hard for them to go as it had been to come. Then even without ears I would have known by the way they stiffened that a step had sounded on the front gallery. And when I looked up, my uncle was towering in the doorway, an untamed shape in the shadows, charged with turbulent will and power.

When I glanced back, the cowhands were solemnly taking their leave, mumbling: "Good night, Miz Brewton," going as they came, in single shuffling file, until at last Lutie Brewton stood there alone, a frail figure rooted against the approaching storm.

My uncle came forward slowly, still a kind of king in his tailed gray broadcloth, and when he was under the lights I could see that the forked veins stood out in his neck as he bowed over her

hand, asking about her health. But his furrowed face was a mask and his voice granite, and I knew that while all the others in Salt Fork County might tactfully shy from the subject where she had been all these years and what she had been doing, my uncle now would not for a moment avoid it.

And I think Lutie Brewton knew it, too, and resolved in her mind that she would not be compelled to explain as if she were a child, and it only made her eyes more brilliant and tilted back her fragile head piled with its black hair at a defiant angle, while she threw herself not into her old gaiety but a grave and desperate incoherence, asking about his welfare, and where was Jimmy, and telling him that Myra had shown her Jimmy's and Sarah Beth's photographs, and mustn't he be terribly tired from his long ride, and couldn't she get something for him to eat and drink? And when my uncle's eyes grew darker with dammed-back questions, she spoke the faster, and her face became very thin and intense.

Until at last I couldn't bear it any longer and, while my uncle's eyes flared at me, I leaped to my feet and begged her to make us some coffee or rouse the cook to build a fire. Certainly I expected her to seize the chance to leave the room, but she only stood there with an indecipherable look in her feverish eyes, till I was the one who escaped, bolting to the bunkhouse, where I found the hands up far beyond their bedtime, smoking, talking in low tones, waiting for the wagon.

When an hour or two later I went stiffly back across the front gallery, some chemical change had taken place in those ancient walls. The air of the massive old ranch house hung with the elusive scent of violets high on the peaceful fumes of cigar smoke. In the wide hall the brightly colored Navajo blankets had been laid again over the pine settees. A great white cloth hung low from the heavy dining table set with four places for tomorrow's breakfast. And the parlor I could see was swept and dusted in readiness for the coming visitor who had not been home for many a day.

Then my uncle, who had been sitting quietly on a horsehair armchair, raised his head, his half-smoked cigar held motionless in his hand. Through the door to the front bedroom I saw Lutie

Brewton stand perfectly still while she clutched folded clean sheets in her bare white arms. After a moment, far away on the lonely trail under the Southwestern stars I could hear the tolling rumble of the approaching wagon.

There is little more to tell except that the last time I was back the stone my uncle raised was still standing near the broken walls of the old ranch house.

"Brock Brewton, son of James B. and Lutie C. Brewton," it is carved in unequivocal letters that all who ride may read.

I remember well the first time I saw it. In Salt Fork, people were still divided about Brock and where Mrs. Brewton had been. I knew that Lutie Brewton herself would never reveal the truth to any of them, perhaps never to me. On this particular day she and Sarah Beth, who was home for a month, had driven to the Bar 44. My uncle was sitting alone on the ranch-house gallery from where he could see the stone. And from what he said to me while his eyes rested on it, his motives were as clear to me at last as a Cross B brand.

"Have you noticed how young she still looks, Hal?" he asked, filling his chair again with that iron dignity and pride I remembered as a boy. "It was a hard thing for a lady to go through. But she's one in a thousand, Hal. No one else will ever be like her." And his deeply lined face warmed like the late afternoon sun mellowing the rugged western slope of an old mountain.

# Conrad Richter

Conrad Richter, whose novels about American pioneer days earned him a host of readers and literary honors, was born in 1890 in a small town in the heart of Pennsylvania. His great-grandfather, a major in the War of 1812, had helped settle Pine Grove, and his father kept the general store there until he, like his father before him, became a preacher. His mother, grandmother and several aunts were all born storytellers who made the past of his native countryside as lively to him as the present.

At fifteen Richter finished high school and went to work, lumbering, bank clerking, and reporting for Johnstown and Pittsburgh papers. In his early twenties, a story he sold to the *Forum* was chosen "best of the year," but the magazine paid him only twenty-five dollars. "I had just been married," he wrote later, "had sober obligations, and told myself stubbornly that if this was what one got for the 'best' story of the year, I had better stick to business. . . ." The business he chose was running a children's periodical—writing, editing and publishing it himself.

In 1928 he moved to New Mexico and there he settled down to serious writing. He was fascinated by the people he met who had lived through the early days of the Southwest. *Early Americana and Other Stories* (1936), based on what these men and women told him, launched his reputation. *The Sea of Grass* (1937), equally authentic in background, was his first novel and one of his most successful. In 1940 he began a trilogy about the settlers of Ohio with *The Trees. The Fields* followed in 1946. And the third, *The Town,* won the Pulitzer Prize in 1951. *The Lady* appeared in Reader's Digest Condensed Books, Summer 1957. *The Waters of Kronos* won him the National Book Award in 1960.

He was back in Pine Grove, its most eminent son, when he had a fatal heart attack in 1968. Perhaps the essence of Conrad Richter's work was best summed up by one critic: "It has the American heartbeat in it."

# The Possession of Joel Delaney

A CONDENSATION OF THE BOOK BY

## Ramona Stewart

The dead cannot
possess the living . . .
or can they?

ILLUSTRATED BY

## Marvin Friedman

Norah Benson's house was on a
tranquil block in New York's East Sixties.
Just over a mile away, yet separated as
by a continent, was teeming Spanish
Harlem—El Barrio—where primitive
rites were still practiced, dark shrines
still worshipped. For Norah, the
chilling link between these two worlds
became her brother, Joel, and his
baffling behavior, which began with an
unkept date for dinner. Why did she
glimpse in him a person unrecognizable?
What could account for the fearsome
and mystifying events that followed?
At a beach cottage, where with her two
children she had sought safety, Norah
found an answer.
A story of demonic forces, charged with
suspense, superbly crafted, and soon to
be a major film.

CHAPTER ONE

AT THE START I had no premonition of disaster; but then I haven't the slightest gift for prophecy. Even when I was a girl my expectations never came to pass. At college, the test questions weren't what I'd crammed for; the telephone call wasn't from the man I thought I'd impressed. And instead of going on for an M.A. in anthropology, I married a microbiologist and joined that band of migrant workers who travel from one university to another.

My children came, unplanned for, as we moved from N.Y.U. to the University of California at Berkeley and then to M.I.T. Between Carrie's toilet training and Peter's teething, I wrote a novel that sold twenty-five hundred copies and disappeared. But once the habit had set in, I wrote others. They do well enough, but at parties, people are still apt to ask me what name I write under.

Then Ted was transferred to Rockefeller University and we were back in New York and soon after, unexpectedly, divorced. Ted had announced he wanted to marry Marta, a young blond Swedish geneticist with the lab next to his. I fought it for six months, then capitulated. There were talks with lawyers over trust funds for Carrie and Peter—Ted's family made oil-drilling equipment, so we had an income above the university appointments. I flew back from Mexico to find myself a divorcée with two children to raise in a converted carriage house in the East Sixties.

So I can make no claim for woman's intuition. It's when I'm skating along on smooth ice that a crack splits open at my feet.

Certainly, the night the trouble began with my brother Joel, I had no prickling sense of the extraordinary. Not even when he was late for dinner, as he usually was now. So I had asked him for earlier than I'd really planned, leaving the steak ready to broil until he arrived. I'd invited him often since we returned East and found him two years out of Columbia with a string of jobs already behind him—a magazine, an encyclopedia, a trade-book house. Next came a broken love affair and a trip to Morocco that exhausted his savings. He'd sent me a cable and I'd arranged for his passage home. Since then he had been a free-lance editor.

That night, waiting for Joel, I was exasperated. The children had met their father after school at his laboratory, where a new strain of bacillus had just arrived from the Texas Department of Health. Normally, the children would have been restive wandering about the lab, but this particular strain was plague and stirred medieval fancies, so that even Carrie's thirteen-year-old cynicism about Ted's indifference to his family wavered. Peter, of course, was wild with interest. Already, at twelve, he had decided to be a microbiologist like his father.

The children had arrived home chattering professionally about antibodies just as I had finished a bad day at the typewriter and was writing out a weekly paycheck for Veronica, our Puerto Rican maid.

"Wash up now, will you, Carrie, Peter? Your Uncle Joel is coming for dinner."

"But we're going to the movies!" Carrie cried in distress.

"Afraid not. Tonight is Joel. See you Monday," I said to Veronica, trying to strike an easy note. I added, "Take the Baron for a run, will you, Peter?"

"I can't," Peter said cheerfully. "It's snowing."

We have probably the only Hungarian sheep dog in the world that is afraid of snow. I believe in Hungary they wade shoulder-deep in it. "Well then, just drag him to the curb."

As Veronica went out the door, the Baron shrank back and

whined. The sight of his great craven form meant the sidewalk was already whitened over. I felt awful. Mean and self-pitying. Trapped with two disappointed children and a neurotic sheep dog.

By seven, there was still no sign of Joel. I made the salad, garlicked the French bread, took the baked potatoes out and watched them shrivel. At least I hadn't broiled the steak. We sat about the living room, snow falling past the windows, a fire blazing in the fireplace. But inside our hearts were rotten. Carrie sighed in martyrdom and glanced at the mantel clock. I jumped up and went to the window, hoping to see Joel hurrying down the street. But all I saw were refaced brownstones, converted stables and carriage houses, and clouds of snow driving past the streetlamps.

"Do you see him?" Carrie asked.

I shook my head and she gave another sigh, twisting a lock of her long blond hair around one finger. It was really too bad of Joel. He'd not been this thoughtless until recently. As a boy, he'd been a lot like Peter. The same dark good looks and quickness to understand. Our family hadn't been the cheery thing of children's books. After a series of breakdowns, our mother killed herself in a sanitarium. Our dad was good-natured and charming, but he was a stock promoter and our financial future was uncertain. We had the Westchester trimmings—a lawn and trees, summer camps; our teeth were straightened. But the big comfortable house was rented, and sometimes I had to hold off the landlord while we waited for a check to come. Dad died broke finally at seventy, showing a prospect around uranium mines in Canada.

Because I was ten years older, I ended really being Joel's mother. I saw that our laundry went out, cooked our meals, washed the dishes. He was a grand kid, bright, with a lovely sense of humor. And then when he was ten I left him flat. Ted and I had met and married and soon flew off to the University of California. The house was too large for a boy alone and a man who was away so much. Joel was sent to boarding school. I felt guilty about it for years. Perhaps I might have taken Joel with us, though I doubt that would have worked with Ted. The next year was hard for Joel. He got pneumonia and I flew East when we thought he'd

die. But he pulled through, thin and weak but tougher. It seemed to me he had a new wary look about his eyes.

He came to us on vacations, and later when we moved to Cambridge he took weekends with us from Columbia. He did wonderfully at college. The rapid series of jobs afterward might have been just a young man trying to find the right spot. The broken love affair didn't alarm me. Better find it out early than later. But his flight to Morocco made me uneasy, and the feckless way he let himself run out of money. When he came back from Tangier and didn't look for another regular job, I really grew worried. I'd wake him if I called in the afternoon. One day, I pulled a book from his bookshelf and dislodged a ball of tinfoil that came apart and exposed a chunk of nougat. But when I broke off a piece, Joel said, "I wouldn't. It's kif."

"Kif?"

"Hashish."

I examined the stuff. "So that's what it looks like. Whatever are you doing with it?"

He shrugged. "I brought it back from Morocco."

"And are you into the mind-expanders?" I asked, making my voice casual. But he turned the conversation, and I had been left with my troubled feelings.

It all came back to me as I stood by the window—the running away, the recklessness, the pad on Second Street—and I didn't like it. On impulse, I set down my drink and crossed to the phone.

From just the sound of dialing, Carrie made out the number I was calling. She said, "You don't think he's still home!"

"He might have taken a nap and overslept."

"That's just fine," Carrie said with irony. "I think I'll get a piece of bread."

"Perhaps you'd better," I answered. The ringing continued in my ear and I hesitated to hang up because I knew no other way to reach him, had no idea who his friends were or if he still had any. There had been a few pretty girls but they had married. And there was Sherry, the big romance. But that was over long ago. While running over the past, I nearly missed the phone being answered.

Though not quite answered. No words, just the phone being taken off its cradle, and the sound of cool jazz, soft and far away.

"Joel!" I cried into the phone. "It's Norah!"

There was a peculiar hiccup as if he were having difficulty using his vocal cords. A thick strange voice repeated, "Norah."

I called his name again, but I had no idea if it was Joel. The voice did not remotely have his timbre. And after that, I heard only the jazz, cold and wailing.

Peter was by my side then. Across the room, Carrie was starting to be frightened. "What's wrong?" she asked.

As I laid down the phone, my mind raced for solutions. I could call the police, but then the ball of tinfoil floated before me. Hashish was a narcotic. If they found it, Joel might go up on charges.

"Joel's phone is off the hook," I said. "Will you be all right if I run down?"

"I'll go, too," Peter said. Carrie put a hand on his shoulder. They looked tense and resolute, standing together, but of course it was out of the question. I had no idea what I'd find. They protested when I told them. So I moved quickly to get my coat and snow boots from the closet.

"If he's sick, you'll need a doctor," Peter reminded me.

"I'll see first. I can call your father for help."

Before they could argue with me I pulled open the door. There were no cabs in sight but on Park Avenue I found one. Shifting fears rose around me as we drove downtown. Joel had been beaten by robbers. Or something weirdly worse. His strange voice had unnerved me.

"Sure this is the place?" the driver asked.

We'd pulled up before Joel's tenement. Two bearded youths in leather jackets were sheltered in the door under a NO LOITERING sign in English and Spanish. Garbage cans lined the wall.

"This is it," I told him, groping for the cab fare.

I went in the front door, across the broken tiling and up the cracked marble staircase, past scrawled obscenities. Joel lived up five flights, and my breath was failing as I pounded on his door.

"Please!" I cried. "Joel, open the door! It's Norah!" I tried the doorknob and, to my surprise, it gave.

I could see the entire room: divan, canvas sling chair, a lighted copper lamp, Joel's ginger cat, Walter, in a fright, crouched flat to the bookcase. Joel was sprawled against the wall, the disconnected phone in his lap.

"Joel!" I cried. I walked in cautiously and knelt beside him. There was no blood, no sign of attack. If there had been a struggle, it had been an inner one. Joel's fine-boned face was contorted. I switched off the radio, leaned close and smelled his breath. He'd not been drinking. There was no glass, no signs of pills or telltale tinfoil. I searched his arms; to my relief, there were no marks.

I reached for the phone and dialed Ted. As quickly as I could, I told him what had happened. "What's wrong with him?" I asked. It was stupid, of course, even though he was a doctor.

"How can I tell? There are a dozen things he could have taken," Ted said.

"You don't know that he's taken anything. He might be ill." But as I glanced at Joel again, I trailed off. His face was working in a way I'd never seen before, hitherto unused muscles coming into play. His brow lowered and his lips curled; he looked oddly sly. He tried to speak.

I couldn't understand him so I bent closer to hear the thick new voice labor, "Are you Norah?"

THROUGH the shock-blur, I took in disconnected parts of the next hour. Sirens, dark blue uniforms in the hall. Pieces of memory come back like crazily spliced film. A fatherly sergeant saying, "What's your relationship?" as he wrote in a black notebook. Two white-clad attendants arriving and thrusting Joel into a jacket with arms bound to his chest. An ambulance ride. Then the doors were pushed open at Bellevue, and my mind was back in focus.

They put Joel in a wheelchair and took him into the brightly lit Emergency ward. I tried to follow but a nurse stopped me. "You wait here. We'll be needing information."

A crowd was clustered at the admitting desk: police, doctors, a

knot of sad-faced, worried Puerto Rican women looking as if they'd waited there too often. Interns and attendants wandered by carrying clipboards, a squad car drove up, the swinging doors let in gushes of night air.

Then Ted came striding in, and relief went through me. A highly organized man may not make a comfortable husband, but in an emergency he is like the marines arriving.

As usual, he didn't waste time on niceties.

"Where is he?" he asked.

"Around there," I said vaguely. "They wouldn't let me in."

"Wait here," he said and plunged into a knot of white coats. He moved with the doctors around the corner. Research men like Ted are apt to be heady stuff for young residents. As I waited more ambulances pulled up, taxis and squad cars disgorged drunks and blood-stained accident victims. Half the city seemed to be in trouble that Friday night.

At last, Ted reappeared. "Okay," he said. "We can go. He's checked in and on his way to Psycho."

The word ripped into my stomach. I was on the verge of crying, an unwise state around Ted. Nothing drove him up the wall like a crying woman.

Outside, the smooth snow had softened the lines of the great Bellevue complex. In the chilled air, the word "Psycho" ceased clanging inside me and I felt I could trust my voice again.

"What's wrong with him?" I asked.

"Looks like he's taken a bad trip. It's probably one of the hallucinogens. He has no psychotic history."

"Of course not," I said and he glanced down at me thoughtfully, reminding me of Joel's behavior the past few years—the love affair, his flight to Tangier and, on his return, the run-down tenement, the strange life apparently without friends. There was the memory of our mother, too. I spoke quickly to drive away her ghost.

"Can't they bring him out of it?"

"They're working on him with Thorazine. It's not my field." He flagged a cab for me and it slid to a stop. "I'll call the ward psychiatrist tomorrow."

I let myself be put in the cab, but as he slammed the door, I cried, "Ted!" and rolled down the window. "Will you phone me when you've talked to him?"

He gave a quick nod. I knew he feared tears. "Driver, take the lady to East Sixty-fourth Street."

As we lunged forward in the snow, I viewed through the rear window the great brick-and-stone complex where my brother Joel was a prisoner.

NEXT morning, Saturday, I woke to sun glittering on the iced trees of the back garden. For a second it was beautiful, and then the night came flooding back. To impose order on my nervous system, I sat up and poured coffee from the automatic pot on the nightstand. I turned on the news, but my mind kept slipping back to Joel. I saw him sprawled on the floor, his face distorted, then in Bellevue Emergency. Finally I rose and went to face the children.

They were in the foyer, dressed for ice-skating. The winterless California years had left them snow-happy, and Central Park would be lovely after the storm, bushes dazzling, hills frosted white.

"What was wrong with Uncle Joel?" Carrie asked.

I'd decided to tell the truth. It might serve as an object lesson. "He had a bad reaction to something he took."

Carrie gazed at me through a strand of long blond hair. "You mean a drug?"

"Something like that."

Her eyes widened in what I hoped wasn't admiration.

"How is he?" Peter asked.

"I'm not sure yet. I called your father and we put him in the hospital." I deleted the police.

"A man on this street took LSD and disemboweled himself," Carrie told me.

"Carrie!" I began to understand why parents packed up and left the city. In the timeworn manner of mothers, I fell to issuing directives about their trip to the ice rink. "Get your lunch at the zoo. If it's cold, eat indoors."

497

"If Uncle Joel's in the hospital, who's taking care of Walter?" Carrie asked as they trooped out.

I remembered the ginger cat crouched by the bookcase. Someone had to feed Walter.

After breakfast, I went back downtown.

In Joel's neighborhood, I left the cab to shop for cat food. I stocked up on milk, canned tuna and cat litter, hoping Joel's superintendent would agree to cat tending. At his tenement, I pushed past the unlocked front door and noted the super's name and apartment number on his letter box. The corridor was dark and dirty. A wine bottle lay smashed on the tile floor. I stepped over the shards to reach the super's doorbell. I rang and heard a television set go dead, but nothing else happened.

"It's about Apartment Five-D," I tried calling.

No answer. I rang again. Silence.

Then I saw the door to the basement standing open a few inches. I was far from eager to explore it, but I put down my shopping bags, strode over and threw open the door. Then I froze. A man was ascending the basement stairs.

He was broadly built, dark-complexioned, his air menacing. "What do you want?" he growled in an aggrieved way.

From his proprietary air I knew that he must be Mr. Perez, Joel's superintendent.

"I need the key to Apartment Five-D," I said. "Mr. Delaney's in the hospital. I'm his sister and I've brought some food for his cat."

He swayed a bit and steadied himself on the railing. "Cat?" he said, as if he were unfamiliar with the word.

"I thought you might agree to feed it. I'd pay."

"Get back," he said.

"I beg your pardon?" The man was drunk, of course. I stepped back and he lurched up the remaining steps. Besides being drunk, it occurred to me he might be crazy.

I said, "I'd pay two dollars a day to have you feed his cat. And I'd supply the cat food."

"No!" he shouted. "I don't go in there."

I had touched something strange, but the solution was beyond

me. I wondered if I dared ask Perez to keep an eye on my shopping bags while I found a locksmith. I was going to have to get in and take Joel's cat home. Then he unexpectedly capitulated.

"You wait," he snapped. He pounded on his door and shouted angrily in Spanish till the door opened and he went in. Through the partly open door, I heard a furious muttering. I recalled from my days as an anthropology major that it wasn't really Spanish that they spoke in Puerto Rico. I could see a living room, artificial flowers, a statue of a black saint, probably Saint Martin of Porres. On the wall was a picture of Christ's nail-scarred hand. And underneath, a glass of what looked like water. I smelled incense and heard the tinkling of a bell and something began to tease my memory. It was espiritismo, the religion involving air and water spirits. The water caught and held the evil ones. The bells were to draw the benign. Fascinated, I moved closer and caught a glimpse of a small darkskinned woman.

The extra step was my undoing. Mr. Perez came rushing to drive me away. "Here. Go now," he cried. He thrust a key at me and slammed the door.

As I climbed the chipped staircase, I began to wonder if his mood was really anger. I paused on the landing, recalling the way he'd balked at feeding Joel's cat. I sensed that he was a man in the grip of fright.

Walter was mad with hunger when I got to him. He'd been a stray Joel had found in the rain. He probably feared he'd been dumped again. I made a difficult trip to the kitchen with him weaving in and out between my legs, found a can opener and put down some food. As he hurled himself upon it, I searched about in the hall closet and Joel's workroom for a makeshift cat carrier. Then I noticed there was a small storage space above the hall closet.

I carried a chair from the kitchen and, standing on it, I managed to sight a navy nylon flight bag. I reached for it, pulled and the bag tumbled to the floor. I stepped down from the chair and saw I'd dislodged another object.

It was a switchblade knife.

I gingerly pushed the spring and the honed edge appeared, ten

inches long, razor-sharp, murderous. I couldn't imagine what Joel was doing with it. He was the least aggressive person I knew, the typical philosophy major, sedentary to the point of languor, defender only of stray cats. Solitary meals over a book, afternoons spent in museums, dinner-hour patron of art movies. A boy like that didn't fit with switchblades.

Then it occurred to me that a boy like that didn't fit with straitjackets either, or hallucinogens or tinfoil balls of hashish. It seemed odd, too, his hiding the knife so carefully.

A knocking interrupted my troubled reverie, a playful tattoo, insistent and demanding.

"Just a moment," I called. I dropped the knife in my pocket and pulled open the door.

"Hi, Norah." It was Sherry Talbot, the ill-starred love. She looked the same, with her long straight blond hair, turned-up nose and the ready smile of the politician's daughter. She was wearing a leopard parka, its hood thrown back from the shining hair.

"Hello, Sherry," I managed, recalling that, last time around, she'd reduced Joel to abandoning his job and fleeing the country. She wandered past me into the apartment. She was as beautiful as the leopard she was wearing, and as dangerous as it had been.

Sherry stood with her hands in her pockets and her feet spread apart in their low-heeled shoes. She seemed as brightly bland as any member of a 4-H club.

The hayride-and husking-bee effect was hers by birthright. Her father was a Wisconsin farm boy who had risen to be senator. For the past six years he had been a member of the powerful Foreign Relations Committee, and his rugged face topped by a snowy crest was familiar on millions of television screens. Sherry had spent her teen years troubling him with radical ideas and then, at twenty, she about-faced and joined the international set.

She dabbled in working for a living, and briefly held jobs in Washington and New York—one at the publishing house where Joel was working. He took her to museums and art galleries. They spent idyllic hours on the Staten Island Ferry, went for walks in Central Park, and then one day she just vanished. After a distracted

and sleepless week, Joel got a transatlantic phone call saying she'd joined an Italian racing driver for skiing in Gstaad. Next time, it was a Sorbonne activist. Sherry had been in analysis for years.

Looking at her now, I wondered at her clear scrubbed look and shining eyes. The long bright hair clasped with a barrette could have belonged to a child.

"Where's Joel?" she asked. "We have a date today."

"Joel's in Bellevue." I told her what had happened and she sank down on the divan. "They aren't sure yet which one of the hallucinogens," I said. "Have you any idea?"

But she shook the shining head.

I tried again. "Have you seen him often lately?"

"I've been away a lot," she hedged. "I went on the Laos trip with Dad last month. Before that, I was in Kenya. I got this coat there, on safari."

"I see," I said. I saw, too, that we weren't getting anyplace.

"I didn't make the kill myself. There was this Frenchman, a terrific shot."

I sighed and walked into the kitchen. Walter had finished his tuna. I picked him up, put him in Joel's nylon bag, and Sherry helped me carry shopping bags and cat downstairs. She had a little Porsche wedged between hills of snow at the curb.

With Walter on my lap in the flight bag, we took off with a screech of tires. While we raced up the street, I told myself not to backseat drive. "It's a fine car," I said with self-restraint.

Sherry said, "It's not mine, you know. This man I met loaned it to me last night."

APPARENTLY nothing had prepared Walter for the sight of a black Hungarian sheep dog. When I unzipped his bag, he sprang out, saw the Baron, then shrank from view behind a wing chair. But the Baron is a cat charmer. As he sat up with his eyes glistening through his bangs, I felt it was safe to leave them together and call Ted. His lab assistant said he'd made an unexpected flight to Washington, so I sat and fumed. But reason returned. I'd been out all morning and he'd probably tried to reach me then.

501

With him gone, it was up to me. I sat staring at the Baron, figuring. At last, Erika Lorenz came to mind. I called, told her about Joel and arranged to see her.

She was lying on her stomach, naked, when Charles, the houseman, ushered me into the terrace greenhouse. Surrounded by pre-Columbian stone figures in a jungle of foliage, she looked like part of an ancient Maya exhibit. What she didn't look like was a psychiatrist—though she had a stunning practice of actors, painters and writers.

"Hello, sweetie," she said, winding a scarlet towel around her slight, tanned body. "Charles, can we have another pot of coffee?"

As he glided away with the tray, I asked, "Are those really his eyelashes?"

"Yes and no. They're his but he curls them," she said.

Erika's dark hair fell loose to her shoulders. Time and money had made her beautiful in the stylized way of a tropical bird.

Ted had met her at N.Y.U. when she appeared in a bacteriology class he was teaching. She was clearly well-off but it was also clearly new money that ran to mink jackets, spiky heels and diamond bracelets. Ted thought she might be a racketeer's girl friend with hankerings toward culture.

Six years later, in Berkeley, he came home and said, "I ran into Erika Lorenz."

"Who?" I asked.

"The gangster's moll from N.Y.U. She's interning at Veterans Hospital." It was a startling announcement. The Veterans Hospitals' appointments were great plums. He added, "She's asked us for dinner next Saturday."

She had turned out to have an apartment on Russian Hill, teakwood modern with picture windows overlooking the lights of San Francisco. Ted had been wrong about the gangsters but not by much. Her father was Crazy Harry, a used-car dealer who advertised his mad generosity on billboards, in newspapers and even smokily across the sky.

As I stirred the ice in my drink that night in California, I wondered at the force that drove a rich girl to struggle through years

of med school. An intern's life was rigorous. An evening like this with friends must be rare. While I considered, the doorbell had rung and Erika looked suddenly uncertain. "I meant to tell you— he's here on a trip. He hasn't seen the apartment yet. I felt if there were friends—" She broke off and went to the door.

Erika's momentary nervousness was gone and she was again the graceful hostess as she introduced us to Dr. Hans Reichman. He was a most celebrated psychiatrist, a kind of Svengali to the rich and famous. The mystery about what drove Erika was solved.

But that was six years ago and a continent away. Now, in the rooftop greenhouse, I asked, "How's Dr. Reichman?"

"Ah, you know, my poor old Hans . . ." She reached for a cigarette, lit it and blew out smoke. "He's gotten old and lazy. He doesn't practice, only consults, and writes his book on demons."

"What kind of demons?" I asked.

"Oh, everything—were-tigers, Chinese fox spirits. At the moment, it's Caribbean obeah. Last year, as you see, it was Yucatecan." She waved her hand at the stone sculpture. "Now tell me about this trouble of Joel's."

By the time I'd finished, Charles had come in and out with the fresh tray and Erika was on the phone to Bellevue. At last she hung up and said, "He's come out of it."

My knees went weak with relief. "When can I see him?"

"Anytime. They've moved him to a ward called PQ1. I've arranged a pass for you."

I don't recall the rest of the visit, I was in such haste to get to Joel. As Charles held my coat for me, I slid my arms in the sleeves and reached in a pocket for my scarf. Then I realized I'd not told Erika everything. My fingers slid by the switchblade knife.

OUTSIDE PQ1 was a sign forbidding visitors to give patients matches, glass containers or razor blades. Inside, faded men in shabby bathrobes circled me like goldfish inspecting a foreign object that had been thrown into their pond. Someone had written an obscenity on the wall; somebody else had tried to rub it out. Across the way, a man began to sing; others shouted for him to shut

up. At last, Joel came down the corridor. He was unshaven and he looked thinner, but he was clearly the old Joel again.

"Hi, Nor," he said, and only his gaze not quite meeting mine let me know he was embarrassed. As we kissed, the other patients began to drop away as if their crumb had been snapped up.

"I brought cigarettes," I said.

"Thanks," he muttered. Then making an attempt at jauntiness, "Won't you take a seat in the conservatory?" He nodded toward a steel-netted window and we walked over and huddled on a wooden bench. After that, there was a long tough silence. The hand that held his cigarette was trembling as I lit it for him. A forthright question might crack him.

"I took Walter home with me," I said instead.

"Thanks." He studied his spiraling cigarette smoke.

"I used that old flight bag of yours."

"That's fine."

"I found it in that place above your closet."

He nodded vaguely. There was no sign he'd recalled the switchblade. I discarded the roundabout approach and asked him directly, "What was it you took?"

The handsome haggard face was strained. But, at last, he brought himself to look at me. "Look, Nor," he said. "I didn't take anything."

I stared at my oldest, greatest love, and it seemed as if I were seeing him down a long, depressing tunnel of knowledge, through the years of childhood when the ways of dodging are transparent. He never spun lies like other children. As long as possible, he evaded. It was only when he was caught that he lied, stupidly, flouting the evidence.

I wanted to shake the truth from him. Instead I lashed out. "Why do you always deny the obvious?" He shrugged. It was the old gesture that made me want to hit him. Except we are not a striking family, our weapons are words.

"If you didn't take anything, why are you here?" I waved toward the window mesh, the seedy drunks, the barbiturate addicts. "You didn't know me when I found you on the floor, and you fought

504

the ambulance attendants. They make official reports on every-thing. If you start denying what you took, you'll be here for years."

He drew in his breath in fear or rage, but before he could re-taliate, Sherry Talbot appeared, swinging an enormous basket of polished apples, grapes and pears nestled in green cellophane. She smiled at us sunnily.

"How did you get in?" Joel asked her.

"A boy I know on the administrative staff."

"But how did you know where I was?"

"Norah told me," she said.

He gave me a piercing look of betrayal and I knew how he must feel to be caught unshaven in the frayed hospital bathrobe with paper slippers on his feet. As Joel and I sat locked in misery, Sherry perched on the bench beside us and told us about a guest column she'd been asked to write.

As she went on chattering, Joel gave a long, unconscious sigh. I remembered our mother's sighing like that the last time she'd been at home. She'd lain all day in the warm May air, sighing, her auburn head turned toward the television set. That night, Dad drove her back to the sanitarium, and the next day she was dead. She'd found scissors in an attendant's sewing basket.

I glanced at Joel while Sherry chirruped. His eyes seemed scared, his face too pale. I couldn't leave him here.

When the attendant came to end our visit, I blurted, "I'll arrange for a private psychiatrist."

"What for?" Joel sounded threatened. Then he said, "I've been thinking. You're probably right. I'll say I took LSD last night."

"Oh Joel, that's good," I said. Yet I recognized the subtle pride-ful games of childhood. He was telling that to them but not ad-mitting it to me.

"So I won't need a psychiatrist," he said with a clever air.

"But my dear, I'm afraid you will. It's the hospital's way of making sure you won't take it again." Then in a rush to stem his arguments, "Look, Joel, it's just Erika Lorenz."

He brightened. He'd met Erika during college vacations with us

505

on the Coast and liked her. Perhaps her surface air of frivolity took the threat from psychiatric care. "Well, if it's only Erika," he said.

I was eager to be gone before he made more difficulties. As I kissed his cheek, he patted my shoulder and I felt myself forgiven. Yet, as Sherry and I walked away, I felt distressed that our agreement on Erika was an unspoken pact to cheat the hospital.

CHAPTER TWO

JOEL WAS formally released. I picked him up on Wednesday afternoon and with fresh clothes, his wristwatch, keys and money, he radiated youthful confidence.

But somewhere between PQ1 and the street, a shadow flickered over him. As we went through the waiting-room doors into the cold bright air, it seemed to me that he had altered. There was a kind of dying of eagerness. When we flagged a cab, he hesitated over giving his address. "Don't you want to go home?" I asked.

A muscle jumped beside his mouth and I suddenly saw that he was frightened.

"How about staying with me?" I asked.

"Would you have room? For a few days?" The brightness was back.

I told the driver to go to East Sixty-fourth Street and we drove uptown in silence, while my mind grappled with rearranging my workroom to make Joel comfortable. The children were in school and our arrival was subdued. Veronica gave him a shy welcome and bustled off to make coffee. As we sank into chairs in the living room, the Baron checked us out and wandered off. Walter must have been sleeping.

"Want a fire while we have coffee?"

"Fine," he said abstractedly. As he made no move to build it, I crumpled newspaper, laid out kindling and put two logs on the grate. As I lit the fire, I said, "Erika doesn't see patients at home, you know. Her office is at the hospital."

I must have thought that was an allusive feminine way of send-

ing him rushing to the phone to set up appointments. But he only nodded vaguely, and I handed him his coffee. It occurred to me that his reticence might be financial. He couldn't be doing too well free-lancing. "Don't worry about money with Erika," I said. "I'll take care of it and you can pay me back."

But at that, he got to his feet. "Did you put me in the workroom?" He looked suddenly gray and fatigued.

"Are you all right?" I asked. I had a sense that something had changed in him.

He didn't turn around, just continued toward the stairs. "I'm tired. I'll lie down for a while."

I watched him go with a feeling of dismay. He was clearly shutting me out. It came to me that in managing his release from Bellevue, I might have tampered with a condition beyond my ability to control.

The children trooped in soon after. When they heard Joel was staying with us, they came alive with interest because he'd been in Bellevue. "I'll bet he had horrible experiences," Carrie said. "Madmen attacking him." She pantomimed a dangerous madman and Peter followed with his own version.

I finally broke up the performance. "He's lying down now, so do try to be quiet."

The afternoon wound on interminably. I corrected proofs for my new book. Veronica peeled the vegetables for dinner, then bundled up to go home to Spanish Harlem. Since the children were going to a hockey game, I started to fix dinner early.

I went to wake Joel at six thirty. I was about to knock on his door when I heard him talking on the phone and I paused. What was odd was that he was talking in Spanish. And the timbre of his voice was rough, almost brutal. The conversation ended. I knocked and when Joel answered, I found him lying on my studio couch.

"Hello," I said, snapping on the overhead light. "I didn't know that you spoke Spanish."

He shielded his eyes and viewed me sleepily.

"Weren't you just talking on the phone?" I asked.

He stared at me as if I'd lost my mind. "Go away," he said and turned over on his face.

I discarded the telephone mystery. "But it's dinnertime!"

"I'm not hungry. I'll eat later." An arm went across his head to shut me out.

"Joel!" I cried, but he didn't respond.

The suspicion leaped to mind that he'd been calling his LSD supplier. But even that was no solution. If Joel spoke Spanish, he'd learned it in a recent crash course, and it was odd he hadn't mentioned it. But I backed away from a confrontation until the children had left for the hockey game.

As soon as they went, I made a plate of sandwiches, then advanced upon my workroom to make it clear we'd have no more nonsense. I knocked and when he did not answer, I opened the door. Joel was not there. I set the sandwiches on the desk and looked in the bathroom. It was empty. Yet he couldn't have gone out. He would have had to pass me on his way to the front door.

The workroom was oddly cold. The window was wide open on one of the coldest nights in February. I crossed to close it, wondering if he had left that way. It was very strange, a grown man climbing down the side of the house instead of using the front door, but it was possible, I supposed. The workroom was on the second-floor front and there were strong wisteria vines that ran down to the sidewalk. But Joel was scarcely the athletic type; swarming down vines was not his style at all.

Yet Joel was gone. For an instant, looking out the window, I thought I saw him near a streetlight. It was a man almost running. Still, one knows the body movements of one's brother, husband, children; it was a stranger's gait. I was trembling with apprehension, but I made myself close and lock the window. If Joel hoped to return unnoticed, he was going to be out of luck.

I built another fire in the living room, found the playing cards, and with shaking fingers laid out a game of patience. But I found myself putting red queens on red kings and throwing clubs on the spades pile, while I polished an imaginary dialogue with Joel.

The children returned home about ten and went to bed. Only the

Baron seemed to sense something odd. He usually slept with Peter or Carrie, but tonight he settled at my feet. The mantel clock was chiming two when he raised his head and started growling. He never growls and the sound gave me an eerie sensation. I told him to be quiet, but he jumped to his feet, barking. I supposed it could be Joel climbing back up the vines. He'd find the window locked, perhaps grow confused and fall to the street. As I ran to unlock the window, the front doorbell rang.

Shaking with fear and rage, I got the Baron quiet and unslipped the door chain. I found Joel standing nonchalantly with his hands in his overcoat pockets.

"Hi, Nor," he said. "Forgot to ask you for a key."

Infuriated, I said, "Joel!" and then I stopped. His face was pale and his mouth was working as if he were fighting tears.

"Where were you?" I asked him quietly.

He shrugged; perhaps he didn't trust his voice to answer.

"You could have been killed climbing out the window," I said.

He ran a hand across his forehead, then thrust it quickly back in his pocket. But not before I saw blood trickling from three parallel lines on the back of it.

"Who clawed you, Joel?" I asked.

That seemed to break him. He shook his head. "I don't know," he said. "I can't remember."

I frowned, thinking it was a new feint.

"I was here. It was afternoon. Then I was there. By the front door. It was night."

I watched him with the conviction growing that he was telling the truth. "You don't remember climbing down the wisteria?" I asked.

He gave me a sick look. "My God, Nor, I'm scared to death of heights." I recalled how I'd had to help him down a beach cliff one vacation in California. The drop hadn't been as far as from the window.

"Joel, what did you take? LSD? That kif from Tangier?"

He shook his head. "Nothing. I didn't the other time either."

I believed him.

509

He pulled his clawed hand from his coat pocket and we both stared down at the blood on it.

"I'll call Erika tomorrow," he said.

JOEL settled into regular Tuesday-Thursday appointments and soon we all began to feel as if Erika, single-handedly, were lifting some great weight from our house. He showed no sign of moving back to his own apartment. In fact, he brought over more clothes, his transistor radio and his portable typewriter. He had taken on new editing assignments.

One day, strolling into my old workroom to consult *Webster's Unabridged*, I saw he'd moved my desk. I looked up my word and was returning, slightly out of sorts, to my own typewriter, now in my bedroom, when he said, "Nor, those blanks I pulled—they weren't unusual."

"Really?" I said cautiously. Since Erika was my friend, discussing his case was delicate.

"They're some kind of trick reaction to the hallucinogens."

"I thought you said you didn't—" I started.

"I didn't say I'd never tried LSD. The last time was a full day before I didn't show up for dinner. It turns out there can be trips later without LSD. Spontaneously."

"I see," I said with what I hoped was friendly interest uncharged with family reactions.

"Usually you remember the experience, but there are all sorts of reactions. In my case, I just pulled blanks."

"Of course," I said, disconcerted by his cheeriness at having drug-induced amnesia. Then as he continued to look pleased with himself, I decided to tell him about the switchblade knife. I went to my bedroom and returned with it.

"What's this?" he asked as I tossed it onto the couch beside him. It was evident he didn't remember it. He picked it up and regarded it curiously, touched the spring and started as the long blade leaped out.

"I found it in your storage closet. When I was looking for a bag for Walter."

"Where? The one above the hall closet?" I nodded. "I never cleaned it out," he said, "just threw the bags up there. The tenant before me must have put it there."

That could be the explanation, since Joel was a slipshod housekeeper. Still, I worried. "You didn't pull other blanks?" I asked.

"And went out and bought this? But why would I put it there?"

"Hiding it," I suggested.

"Who from? The police? In case of a raid?" But the idea of Joel being raided was so silly we both laughed. When the phone rang and it was Sherry, I slipped out with a sense of relief.

Relief was the word for the rest of February and most of March. The children were wrapped up in school, hockey, movies, their friends. And I submerged into writing my next book. It was a pleasant time, tapping away at my card table, vaguely conscious of Veronica's vacuum cleaner, looking up to find the children were tramping in from school.

If there was a worm in the rose, it was Sherry. With uncharacteristic constancy she rang up daily or stopped by for Joel, and they whizzed off in the little Porsche she was still borrowing. They left and returned at all hours, and the bits Joel dropped concerning Sherry's parties—rich swingers, addicts and the discotheque scene —didn't strike the wholesome note I'd have chosen for a man in therapy.

When I ran into Erika at the Parke-Bernet auction galleries, her attitude was reassuring.

"Joel's doing marvelously, sweetie. Just leave him to me and don't worry."

With a sense of receiving good news, I fell in beside her as she strolled across the red carpet past green-uniformed attendants, all bowing. "You must be a tremendous customer," I said.

"It isn't me. It's my poor Hans. He's spent a fortune here. He loses his head at auctions. But at least I make him view the stuff on exhibition first. He's meeting me at three."

We circled through Oriental art, past jade wine cups and silk scrolls, and finally came out at Caribbean primitives to find Dr. Reichman waiting. He was studying a picture as Erika steered me

to him and announced, "You remember Norah Benson, of course."

Moslems call it *baraka*, the combination of energy, warmth and spiritual charm that makes a holy man or healer. It also makes for a rich psychiatrist. As Dr. Reichman clasped my hand, his pleasure in seeing me and obvious concern for my well-being had the general effect of several martinis. He hadn't changed in the six years since San Francisco. He took my arm and turned me about to face a painting.

"What do you make of that?" he asked.

It was a primitive. A white fairy-story hearse drawn along a tropic street. Two-dimensional, of course, with lively reds and blues in the background. "Look closely at the hearse," he directed. "In this old European hearse you notice cowrie shells!"

I saw a horizontal line of shells painted carefully around the coach. It seemed a strange thing to cause excitement.

"Voodoo," Erika told me dryly.

"You can't explain it so simply," Dr. Reichman protested. "These shells turn up in magic practice from Oceania to Harlem. You recall the little fetishes stuck with cowries that came from One Hundred and Tenth Street?"

"Haitian refugees," Erika said.

"No, my dearest, it's not only Haiti. What of shango in Trinidad, santería in Cuba, obeah in the islands?"

Drawing me into their argument, he steered me to another painting, a picture of a row of cabins hemmed in by sinister palm trees. A greenish light played over the scene. At the lower right was a ball of bluish flame. "That's Guayama, Puerto Rico, the town of witches," he said. "The fireball is a *bruja*—a witch. She flies at night to seek her victims."

"There's something crawly about it," I admitted.

He turned to Erika. "This isn't voodoo either, my dear. It's Puerto Rican. And you'd find it in El Barrio in Spanish Harlem, transplanted to New York by a thirty-year migration."

I remembered the bells and magnetic water in Joel's building.

"I know about the spiritist churches," I said. "Espiritismo."

"And do you know that in all the *botánicas* you see around the

city they sell powders to call up the spirits, rue to guard against the evil eye, mimosa baths to ward off death spells?"

I'd seen *botánicas* in the East Village and had taken for granted they were just herb shops. Veronica came to mind, so brisk and modern, and yet she lived in El Barrio. The thought gave me an uneasy feeling, as though she were hiding a secret life.

"There's a supernatural city all around us," Dr. Reichman said. "It abounds in séances, summoning the dead, *brujería*—witchcraft. And all the counterspell protections."

"Such interests will ruin you professionally," Erika said.

THAT conversation came back to me a week later as Veronica and I were helping Joel move from his old apartment. He had suddenly decided to give it up and find another in the West Village. In the meantime, he informed me, he'd store his furniture at Sixty-fourth Street. I found the news disquieting, for there is a permanence in the arrival of furniture.

Still, he was my only brother and he had been through a tricky period, so Veronica and I pitched in to pack him up. While I was scouring the kitchen sink Dr. Reichman's remarks returned to me, perhaps because the cleaning powder was named Magic Power. I glanced at Veronica scrubbing the stove and longed to ask what she knew of spells, but I couldn't devise a reasonable opening.

Beneath her New York gloss I knew there must be a residue of early knowledge. She was born on the island; I even knew she'd spent her infancy in the slum called La Esmeralda. As I worked at the sink, I recalled the shacks of corrugated zinc and tar paper beyond the San Juan walls. I'd seen them when I'd flown down one Easter vacation from college, and wandering through the old cemetery, I'd been caught by the sudden Caribbean sunset. Surrounded by pale marble angels, I watched the ocean turn dark and as the sky lowered, the tar-paper cabins clinging to the cliffs turned abruptly strange. In an instant, I was afraid and fled back toward the safety of the city. I didn't stop running till I reached the old cathedral on Calle San Sebastián. I was left with a memory of an encounter with the altogether alien.

Yet Veronica had toddled those crooked lanes among the broken bottles and squawking chickens. It was because I knew as much as I did of her childhood that I was hesitant about speaking of *brujería,* afraid of seeming to deny her modern identity. I gave it up. We locked the door and, carrying odds and ends of cleaning equipment, descended the cracked stairs to drop the keys at the super's apartment. But when we rang, there was no answer. Recalling my last visit, I checked the basement door, but it was locked.

"I suppose we could mail them," I said to Veronica. And then a small darkskinned woman entered the front door carrying a grocery bag. I'd only seen her once, huddled among her saints' statuettes and trappings of espiritismo, but I recognized the haggard woman. I stepped to greet her, extending Joel's key ring. But she glanced at me with a frightened expression and then dug frantically through her bag for her own key.

Veronica was having a strange withdrawn reaction to the encounter with her fellow islander, but I directed her to ask where the super was. Unwillingly, in stilted fashion, she said, "*Dónde está su esposo?*"

"*Muerte.*" I recognized the word but felt I must be mistaking it.

"What did she say?" I asked Veronica.

"She says her husband is dead," Veronica said and she plucked my coat sleeve as if to force me to come away.

"But he can't be," I protested, remembering the wine-reeking Mr. Perez. "I spoke to him not long ago."

I turned and met the woman's gaze. Small, brown, sad eyes. For an instant, we were free of the blinders our separate worlds had fixed on us and we examined each other with curiosity.

"He go off the roof. Three weeks ago," she said in English.

"Go?" I asked stupidly.

"Roof," she said. She made a queer shoving gesture.

Alarmed and confused, I asked, "How did it happen?"

But she jammed her key in the lock, scuttled in and slammed the door. I had an afterimage of Christ's scarred hand, the scent of incense, the faint jingling of bells dying away.

A FOG OF MISERY AND queer distaste hung around my memory of the scene. Not the least of the queerness was Veronica's withdrawal from a poor old Spanish woman. But she neither apologized nor explained.

By the night of Joel's birthday, I was once more thankful to have a jewel like Veronica. She spent the morning cleaning the house and the afternoon baking his birthday cake. When Joel returned after a day of scouting work from publishers, the children sprang out shouting. It was very Louisa May Alcott—young, favored uncle, paper horns and party favors—until Sherry drove up with a quantity of champagne and there was a frantic hunt for the champagne glasses.

The ceremony then proceeded in the undeviating way of family customs. Enthroned in a wing chair and wearing a gold paper crown, Joel set to unwrapping birthday presents.

I found myself wondering what really lay beyond Sherry's shining hair and the sweet, easy ways of campaign platforms. I supposed only her psychoanalyst might know. I had to admit there was evidence of improvement. She'd recently gone to work again, this time at a newsmagazine. She was furnishing an apartment in the East Eighties, which might be another sign of settling down.

"Champagne, Nor?" Joel was saying. I came out of my meditations to find the birthday king a bit too grandly playing waiter. But at that moment, Veronica announced that dinner was ready.

The shrimp-cocktail course was lively, but the roast beef began to take the edge off Joel's ebullience. Then Carrie made her discovery, "Sherry, did you know you're only wearing one earring?"

Sherry clapped her hands to her ears. "Damn. And they're my new ones." But she slipped the remaining earring in her pocket and continued cheerfully with dinner. Her carelessness struck Carrie as unnatural.

"Let me look in the chair you were in." She ran to the living room, but she returned shaking her head.

"It'll turn up," Sherry said with good humor.

"I'll find it for you!" We turned to Joel. His eyes were sparkling. I shot a look at his champagne glass but I couldn't tell if he'd

refilled it. As we watched, he drew his water glass to him in a gesture filled with portent. He gazed into it deeply and then, as Veronica hung back uncertainly with the salad course, he lifted his head with an air of satisfaction. "Come," he said.

"Joel, wait until we've finished dinner," I protested.

But he paid no attention. Pushing back his chair, he signaled us to follow, and with the children crowding after, he led the way out of the dining area, through the living room and out the front door into the freezing night.

"Joel, quit. We'll all catch cold," I said, but he was going across the sidewalk, half walking and half dancing, as if he were leading a conga line.

The little Porsche was drawn up at the curb. As he reached it, he turned around and spread his hands like a stage magician about to draw out a rabbit. Then he pulled open the door, leaned into the driver's seat and held up the earring. The children applauded, Joel handed it to Sherry and we all ran inside the house.

Back at the table, we took our seats, with the children demanding explanations. "Could you really see it in the water glass?" Carrie asked.

"I'll bet he palmed it and pretended he found it in the car," Peter said. Joel shook his head, very excited.

When Veronica circled, clearing off the plates, he told her to fill up the champagne glasses. I signaled her to pass him by.

"I'll have more," he said defiantly. Veronica glanced at me, caught between counterorders. Suddenly angry, he rattled off a barrage of Spanish, and not the tourist kind, either. It rolled out curt and brutal, like family rows overheard in Puerto Rican neighborhoods. I sat stunned. It was impossible for him to be speaking so, and yet he was doing it.

"Joel!" I cried. But it didn't stop him. He grabbed the bottle and filled his glass.

Veronica stood regarding him with astonishment, then turned and ran to the kitchen. I hurried after and found her putting birthday candles in the cake.

"You see, he's never been much of a drinker," I apologized. She

516

nodded, but was barely listening. "What did he say to you?" Veronica wouldn't tell me.

She struck a match and soon we were all standing around a blazing birthday cake. Joel's mood had veered again. He rose and, making a show of hesitation over choosing a wish, settled on one. His meaningful glances toward Sherry left us in little doubt of its nature. Finally, he blew out the candles. My anger gave way to embarrassment for him. It was so overt, not at all Joel's style.

To my dismay, I saw he was not done yet. He took off the gold paper crown and, with what must have struck him as dashing gallantry, set it on Sherry's head. I sensed disaster in her manner even before his hand caught in her upswept hair. He clumsily dislodged some essential pinning and a shining cascade came tumbling to her shoulders.

As she put up her hands to repair the damage, he took hold of the gleaming hair. For a terrible moment, he stood staring down at it as if hypnotized.

Sherry kept her grace. Moving slowly, she removed the paper crown, then rewound her hair and pinned it up.

"I'm so sorry," she said in a soft voice. "I have a dreadful headache. I hope you will excuse me." She rose, and soon we heard the Porsche driving away.

The children and I sat stunned at the spoiled birthday table, the burnt candles still upright in the cake. "What was that all about?" Carrie asked, but Peter shushed her. Suddenly, Joel stalked upstairs.

I was torn between exasperation for the wreck Joel had made of the evening and pity for his idiocy. At last, I went up to his room and tapped on his door. He was standing at the window when I entered, one hand clenching a wrist behind his back.

"Joel," I said, "I'm truly sorry." An abrupt movement of his head dismissed me. I had the sense he didn't want to turn and let me see his face. "Do you want a sleeping tablet?" I had some left over from the troubled period before the divorce.

But he shook his head again. I was clearly agitating matters. I backed out, closing the door behind me, and went down to placate

Veronica. But she had left without doing the dishes, a sinister sign as to her ever returning.

I washed the dishes, Peter and Carrie drying. As I sloshed in the sudsy water, I began to feel guilty about my children. They had had a rough enough time without my involving them in Joel's problems. I sent them off to bed and, as I did the pots and pans, I made my decision that Joel could not go on living with us. I would call Erika and see when he could move into his own apartment.

"Hi, Nor," Joel said, standing in the kitchen entrance. "Could we have a peace drink together?"

I had to smile. It was one of the rules of his childhood that the sun not go down on our wrath. A cup of cocoa before bed had been the unspoken apology.

He sent me out of the kitchen and got the cups and saucers himself. Then we sat by the living-room fireplace and drank the last of the coffee. It was the dregs of the pot and terribly bitter but we pretended it was fine. The bitterness suited our reconciliation. I loved him still but he was going to leave my house.

Afterward, as he said good night, I had a rushing sense of how forlorn his life was becoming. But perhaps Sherry wasn't past recall. I touched his sleeve and said, "Don't telephone too soon."

I'll never forget his look then. There was darkness in it but also a kind of prankishness I'd never seen before. I was suddenly unsure about him.

"Joel," I tried. "Don't do anything—at all—tonight."

He simply turned and went to his room.

I woke groggily the next morning. My mouth tasted metallic; when I tried to read the time, the hands of the little clock were blurred. I forced myself to pour coffee from the automatic pot. As I sat sipping it, my gaze fell on the sleeping-pill bottle on the nightstand and I wondered if I could have taken some without knowing it. The level seemed lower, but I wasn't sure.

And then something made me get up and put on my robe. Moving softly, I went down the hall to look in on Joel. He was sleeping soundly on the workroom couch. My heart lightening, I returned

to my room, poured my second cup of coffee and flicked on the bedside transistor.

"The weather forecast for metropolitan New York. It is clear in Manhattan. The present temperature is twenty-eight degrees. Humidity is eighty-three percent."

I reached for pad and pencil and began the day's shopping list. Steak, oranges, dog food, liver for Joel's cat.

Then I was reaching over to turn up the volume.

"The daughter of Senator Kenneth Talbot of the Foreign Relations Committee was murdered early this morning in her East Side apartment. The victim, Sherry Talbot, twenty-two years old, slashed and decapitated, was discovered by her father who had flown into New York last night from Washington. The medical examiner tentatively set the time of death at about midnight, pending closer examination. . . ."

Time began to seem endless. The announcer's voice washed over me.

". . . entering the apartment, he and the building superintendent found her head hanging by its long hair from an ivy planter. The police said there was no sign of a forced entry. . . ."

The next I knew, the Baron was barking. When I reached the front door, I found the police.

CHAPTER THREE

THEY WERE two plainclothesmen from the Fourth Division, one darkly taciturn, one keen-featured. The dark one, named Brady, showed his badge. I led them numbly into the living room. This can't be happening, was what I most remember feeling.

"I heard it on the radio," I said. "I can't believe it."

Brady regarded me bleakly. "You had a party here last night."

I wondered how they knew. Perhaps Sherry had kept an engagement pad. I said, "It was a birthday party for my brother."

"And where is he?" Brady asked.

"Upstairs. He's still asleep."

Brady nodded. "Miss Talbot was a guest?" he said.

"Yes."

"Was she engaged to your brother?"

I managed to say, "Nothing so formal. They were just good friends."

"We want to drive you to the station house," Brady said. "The inspector has a couple of questions."

It was at that moment that the shock began wearing off. I had a sudden vision of Sherry bleeding on her bed. And then the part about decapitation. I felt I might be sick. "I'll have to get dressed," I said to halt the picture.

"You can dress while we're talking to your brother." Of course, they'd come to get Joel. I remembered the way he looked sleeping on the couch. But the workroom had been in early morning shadow. If there had been blood, I'd not have noticed. I told myself that I mustn't think of that.

"I'll let him know you're here," I said to Brady.

But they were rising. "We'll break the news ourselves."

They trailed me upstairs and when I pointed out the workroom, they knocked, entered and shut the door. I stood in the hallway.

"Are those guys cops?"

I turned to face Peter and Carrie in wrinkled nightclothes. "Please," I begged. "Keep your voices down." I was going to have to let them know, I saw. They would hear it soon on the radio. I tried to think of a way to phrase it.

"Sherry had an accident."

They were waiting.

"She's been killed." I refused to speak about the ivy planter.

"*Killed*," Carrie said. "Did Uncle Joel do it?"

"My God, Carrie, no," I cried out.

"How should I know? Last night there was so much trouble—"

"Watch it, stupid," Peter said, jerking his head toward the workroom. The expression faded from Carrie's face.

"I'm not asking you to lie about anything," I protested.

Two young masks regarded me, flat-eyed.

"Don't worry about our talking," Peter said.

521

AT THE STATION HOUSE, Joel went into the inspector's office before me. From my chair in the squad room, I could see the door behind which his destiny was unraveling, but I couldn't catch the tone of the voices.

The ride over in the unmarked car had told me nothing. Joel was ashy but, I gathered, not bloodstained. Far from hauling him away in handcuffs, they were treating him with remote deference, but I supposed that could be a bad sign.

A revulsion against my own suspicions went through me. It wasn't possible that my gentle brother could have done such a thing to anyone. I knew him as I knew myself, or Carrie, or Peter. Not one of us could kill a chicken.

As conviction coursed through me, I shifted on the chair and tried to decide what to tell the inspector. Perhaps I'd leave out certain details: Joel's champagne change of personality, the gold-crown incident, even Sherry's angry departure. Perhaps the Bellevue stay need not come out. It wasn't a question that would normally come to mind: Has he been in a psychiatric ward recently?

A buzzer sounded. Brady got up and went into the inspector's office. When the door opened again, Joel appeared, still gray, beside him.

"You next, please, Mrs. Benson," Brady said.

As I stood up, trying to look confident, my memory betrayed me. Joel's switchblade knife came back. I faltered, recalling his clawed hand the night he'd climbed down the wisteria vines.

Assistant Chief Inspector Russell was sandy, bony and friendly. All too friendly, under the circumstances. But I made myself smile back as he seated me beside his desk.

I looked to see if smoking was in order, but the bare desk didn't have an ashtray. There were no pictures and not even a window, only the grid of an air conditioner.

"I'm sorry to bother you at this hour," Russell said. "I hope your children won't be late for school." He must have heard about the children from Brady.

"They'll be all right," I told him. "They walk to school from the house."

"My wife has to drive our two everywhere," he confided. "We live out on the Island."

It wasn't my idea of a police interview. I was almost starting to like him. I put myself on alert. And just in time, for locking his freckled fingers, he asked if I knew why I'd been brought in.

"Sherry," I said, and stopped abruptly.

"What do you know about it?" he asked.

"Just the radio report," I said. "She's been killed. They said that her head—" I broke off again, and frantically dug into my purse. He didn't protest when I scrabbled out a cigarette. He even produced an ashtray from his desk drawer. "I'm sorry," I said. There was silence while I drew in smoke.

"Do you know who might have done it? Her father says that nothing was stolen. Chances were she knew her killer."

"I didn't know any of her friends," I answered faintly. "That is, of course, except my brother."

"I understand she liked men."

I reflected on the bait he was offering. With Sherry's proclivities, the suspects could be infinite. Watching me hesitate, he sighed. "This was an especially ugly murder. It won't help Miss Talbot to pretend she was selective about her acquaintances."

I nodded, weakening.

"Would she admit a stranger after midnight?"

"I don't know," I said with reluctance.

"I see. Had she mentioned anyone lately who . . . interested her?"

I told him about the Porsche's owner. He made an entry in a notebook. "Suppose you tell me about last night," he prompted.

It was the moment I had been dreading. "I'm afraid I haven't much to help you. We gave birthday presents to my brother. Sherry brought champagne and we drank some. Then we had dinner and she left."

He led me carefully back over the evening. Gifts, gold paper crown. Even the lost earring came out, though I managed to put a gay face on it. I said Sherry had left early, but used her own excuse of a headache. I left out only Joel's fracas with Veronica and, of course, the crowning of Sherry.

523

When I was finished, he asked for Veronica's address. My heart sank but I had no choice. He entered it in the notebook, and then regarded me thoughtfully.

"Who put your brother in Bellevue last February?"

My heart began a tattoo. "I did."

"I'm sorry, but we have to know. He's in therapy for these blanks of his?"

"Yes." A dark suspicion had begun to come over me.

"We have to ask this, Mrs. Benson. Did you realize your brother has no memory of his birthday party?"

"No." The word came out small and breathy.

"Think carefully before you answer my next question," he said. I had the sense he already had the facts and was testing me. "What time did your brother go out last night?"

"He didn't!" The words came rushing out. Then came the memory of my dopiness that morning, but I hurried on. "We have a sheep dog who barks his head off. Your own men found that out this morning." Even as I spoke, I realized that the Baron knew Joel so well he'd not bark at his going out so long as Joel did nothing odd like climbing down vines. Yet *I* would have awakened. Unless I had been sedated.

But to my surprise, Inspector Russell accepted it. "I guess that does it," he told me. "Of course, we might have to ask you more later."

I went back to the squad room. Joel stood up shakily and we left. On the way out, I touched his arm and felt him shivering.

When we pushed through the station-house door, a bank of television lights was switched on. Below us on the stairs, a crowd of newspapermen was waiting. Besides being Senator Talbot's daughter, Sherry had been a conspicuous jet-set swinger.

"What did he ask you, Joel?" a man yelled.

I took Joel's arm and when I felt him steady, we descended. Newsmen gathered about us holding up microphones.

"What do you have to say, Joel?" someone shouted.

The apparently immovable wall of flesh melted as we pressed on, though it kept regrouping around us. As we reached the curb I

heard someone shout, "Any leads on The Chopper?" A vague echo, then the crimes came back. Last year several girls had been decapitated. One had been found in Central Park, her long hair tied to a tree branch. The papers had named the unknown killer The Chopper.

They thought that Sherry was his latest victim. Oh God, I pleaded, don't let Joel be The Chopper. Don't let it be a series of butcherings.

A taxi drove up and still I stood stupidly. Last spring was coming back to me. We were opening the summer house on Fire Island then. We'd been buying it when Ted met Marta. Spring and pain, the smell of grass and wet May earth, interwoven with headlines on the murders.

But Joel was missing from that kaleidoscope.

"Tangier," I murmured. I started to breathe again. Because when The Chopper was stalking, Joel was in Morocco.

WE WERE barricaded in the living room against the horde of rubberneckers and reporters who were lounging about our sidewalk. Carrie read aloud to us from the newspaper a noted psychiatrist's profile of The Chopper: "He is a lonely young man, deeply repressed, probably as the result of an ambivalent love-hatred relationship with his mother. The victims have all been young pretty girls with long hair. In none of the cases has there been a sexual assault; no weapon has been found, and robbery does not appear to have been a motive. His bitterness against women has shown itself in sexual rejection. He has acted out his contempt by slashing his victim's throat and then, in a gesture of defiance against authority, has decapitated her and hung the head, like a trophy, where it will immediately be seen. The long hair is probably a primary factor in his selection of a victim. . . ."

Carrie lowered the paper to her lap and said, "If we cut off our hair we're safe. Let's get the scissors."

"Don't be silly," I said automatically, while worrying about Joel. He was sitting in the wing chair rereading Proust's *Guermantes Way*. At least, he was staring at it. As soon as we'd returned from

the station house, he'd picked it from the bookshelf and hidden behind it a good part of the day. I'd fixed him lunch, since Veronica didn't show up. I had been right in my foreboding about her. When I telephoned, her aunt said a family illness had taken her to San Juan. So I began calling domestic agencies and, by three o'clock, I had the promise of a Mrs. Clara Grievy.

Carrie went to the window to inspect the crowd outside. "There's a news car stopping opposite," she said.

"Will you get back behind the curtain?" I began, and trailed off as the phone rang.

Peter answered, then laid his palm across the mouthpiece. He said, "It's Dad. I never heard him any madder!"

Ted was mad, all right; he'd seen the newspapers. "This jet-set slaying. Is Joel involved in it?" As always, he cut to the heart of the matter.

"It depends on what you mean by involved," I hedged. "She was here to dinner."

" 'Mrs. Benson is the ex-wife of scientist Theodore Benson, professor of microbiology at Rockefeller University.' " He was reading, I gathered, from a paper.

"I'm sorry. Still, they can hardly hold you responsible. It does say 'ex'," I pointed out.

"What in hell is going on with you?"

"Just a moment, Ted," I said. "I'd better take it upstairs."

A minute later I was on my bedroom extension. "Sorry, Ted. They were all sitting around."

"Let's see if I've got it straight," he said. "This Sherry is the same one who drove us all crazy last year?" He meant Joel's flight and subsequent breakdown.

"She's the same one," I said. "They'd been seeing each other again."

"I hear that Joel's moved in on you." The children must have told him on their weekly visits.

"Just until he finds another apartment," I said.

"And I hear he's going to Erika. How come?"

"To get out of Bellevue it helped to be in private therapy."

"Has he been having posthallucinogenic reactions?"

"There's a bit of that. But Erika is being helpful."

"What form are the reactions taking?" he asked with heavy patience. "Flipping out? Unexpected trips?"

"Not exactly." I paused. "He's had a few spells of amnesia."

"Amnesia?" He sounded surprised. "That's not typical." There was silence while he thought about it. I felt myself tightening. Ted was dangerously intelligent. "Did he have a spell last night?" he asked.

I was like a mother grizzly seeing her cub attacked. "Damn it, Ted," I heard myself exploding. "He only took LSD, like a million other young Americans. As long as you're reading the crime news, you'll notice that there were earlier similar crimes. The police are looking for—the newspapers call him The Chopper."

"Exactly," Ted told me grimly. "I won't have Carrie and Peter endangered in this fashion."

"What fashion?" I was shouting. "When the other crimes were committed, he was in Morocco."

"Norah," he said wearily. "Are you sure *when* he really got there?"

We fell silent, hating each other.

"Get him out of your house," he said.

THE NEXT few weeks were a nightmare. It was impossible to do as Ted had ordered. You don't evict your brother in the heat of a homicide investigation. And Joel had gone limp. He went for his sessions with Erika, but did little else. Half the time when I looked in his room, I found he had fallen asleep. I'd take his reading glasses off so they wouldn't break, and I'd stand gazing down at his defenseless face, trying to lay the suspicion Ted had unloosed.

I knew he'd been in Morocco and received the money I sent him there. But I developed a need for more evidence. I ransacked the house for old postcards, but in the end all I turned up was his final letter written from a hotel in the Tangier Casbah, saying he was sick and broke.

I was standing by the window staring at a spray of budding for-

sythia in the garden, when it came to me that I wasn't sure about the dates of the three Chopper murders either. The first one was surely in May. But perhaps not, maybe it was late April.

I went to check in the public library, and in *The New York Times Index* under "Murders and Attempted Murders, New York City," found the dates. I copied the information on an old envelope, then went to the microfilm room to read the stories.

The murder of María Sánchez, a nineteen-year-old girl found slain in Central Park, ran only two inches on page 30 of the April 21 issue. Theresa Ruggiero, eighteen, decapitated in a school playground, was given more space. She had six inches on page 26 on June 15.

The livelier press, the *News* and the New York *Post*, would have splashed the stories more fully and they dubbed the killer The Chopper. But even the *Times* gave the third murder, that of Victoria Díaz, a front-page story on September 30.

### Third Girl Beheaded In New Park Slaying

A young woman was slashed to death last night near the boat lake in Central Park.

The victim, Victoria Díaz, 19 years old, of West 110th Street, had her throat cut. Her severed head was discovered hanging by its hair from the branch of a tree by Daniel Hoey, who was walking his poodle early in the morning. The torso was found in a clump of bushes twenty yards away.

This is the third decapitation of a young girl in five months. The first victim, María Sánchez, was discovered in The Ramble of Central Park. The second victim, Theresa Ruggiero, was found in a school playground near the park.

The chief medical examiner said that the Díaz girl was slashed once across the throat. There had been little struggle. She had apparently not been raped. The time of death was tentatively set at about midnight. The girl's purse, still containing her week's wages, was discovered near the body. An autopsy will be performed today at Bellevue Hospital.

Police are seeking a possible witness, Tonio Perez, 17, of 405 East Second Street.

I sat staring at Joel's East Village address, trying to comprehend its meaning. At last, I consulted my notes and rolled the microfilm ahead to October 17.

The story was headed SEEK MISSING WITNESS, and it reported that the police were still trying to locate a boy who had been questioned near the boat lake by a park patrolman who was at the time unaware that Victoria Díaz had been murdered. By the time the police had gone to the Second Street address, Tonio Perez had vanished.

I left the film with the librarian, and as I strolled across Bryant Park, the name Perez slotted into place. It was the name of Joel's superintendent. I recalled the harried woman with the Espiritismo water, bells and incense. Tonio Perez was probably her son.

I pictured the detectives coming to her door, asking questions. Mrs. Perez must have known the same fears I had myself, shielding Tonio as I had shielded Joel. For where the cautious *Times* said "witness," it was obvious they meant "suspect." The police must believe Tonio was The Chopper. That explained why Joel had received such gentle treatment.

My mind leaped to the way Mr. Perez had been frightened the day I'd arrived to feed Walter. Perhaps Tonio had been hiding somewhere about. Joel might have known him. There was the strange phenomenon of Joel's fluent Spanish. And Sherry's dependable interest in thrills. I could easily see them befriending him. And finding they had a fearsome pet on their hands.

At that, my imagination began to run wildly. Had Tonio frightened Joel into obeying him and using amnesia as a cover? But the night I'd found him, Joel had been helpless, not running sinister errands. My mind spun dizzily about the mystery. I recalled standing with Veronica outside the Perez door while the small darkskinned woman searched for her key, and I was startled again by Veronica's expression, her withdrawal.

At that, my mind finally stopped circling. Spanish Harlem was a Puerto Rican village; as an insider, Veronica would know its secrets. She'd know what threat Tonio Perez was to Joel.

I hailed a cab and gave Veronica's address. As we approached

her corner in El Barrio at One Hundred and Fourth Street, I watched a scene that could have been in Old San Juan. Even the fruits and vegetables were different here. As we stopped in front of a *bodega*, I recognized the small finger bananas I hadn't seen since my trip to Puerto Rico. Beside them was a box of speckled mangoes, boxes of plantains, cassava roots and peppers.

The sidewalks were crowded with leather-jacketed youths, women wheeling baby carriages, and unshaven drifters. Children were playing in peril from two boys racing bicycles.

At Veronica's red brick tenement, an old lady with whiskery chin and twisted stockings was slumped in the doorway. "Sorry. *Perdóneme*," I said as I stepped over her and the half-empty wine bottle beside her.

The inner hall was like Joel's on East Second Street. Broken tiles, the smell of cooking fish, scribbled walls. On the second floor, I found Veronica's door and knocked; it opened and I was looking down at a small girl in flounced panties, gold earrings and huge pink plastic curlers.

"*Quisiera ver Verónica*," I began in murderous Spanish. She turned and fled.

As I stood there indecisively, a puppy rushed out of the apartment into the hall. I ran after him, scooped him up and took him back in, shutting the door behind me so he couldn't escape. With an apprehensive sense of trespassing, I surveyed Veronica's trove of treasures. A large doll dressed in tulle stood on a television set. Tinted photographs cluttered the mantel of a false fireplace. Crocheted doilies decorated tables and chairs.

At length, they came filing in to regard me reproachfully: the child in panties who'd let me in, a curly-headed boy, and an older girl.

I said, "I brought the puppy back in from the hall. I'm looking for Veronica Zayas. Is this where she lives?" There was a pause while the hope that they spoke adequate English left me. "Veronica Zayas?" I repeated.

At last the oldest child whispered, "Yes."

"Will she be home soon?" I asked. "May I wait?"

This only brought a smile. I seated myself tentatively. The little girl turned on the television and we watched a detergent commercial together. After a hospital drama, we watched another serial, and I grew increasingly uneasy, doubting that the oldest child had really understood my English. Veronica might be in Puerto Rico as her aunt had told me. Or working somewhere until dark.

At the end of an hour, I rummaged through my bag for a pen and a scrap of paper. Without much hope, I wrote: "Veronica, please call me. Norah Benson."

They watched me to the door with detached interest.

I strolled up the street to the sound of *disco* music. I passed boys with guitars and skirted a group of children who had chalked out a game of hopscotch. As I turned the corner to Lexington Avenue, I met Veronica hurrying home.

She was carrying the familiar bag containing her work shoes and housedress. I felt a pang of envy for the lucky unknown who had profited from my misfortune. Then I was busy trying to keep her from running away from me.

"Please, Veronica," I said. "I've been waiting to see you."

She stopped and gave me a small tight smile. But there was no missing the recoil in her eyes. "I can't come back," she said with defensive roughness.

"We've all missed you, but I know you can't. I understand that."

She looked relieved, but with that settled, she was at a loss to know why I was in El Barrio. I couldn't think of a way to ease into asking for help, so I blurted out, "There's a young man named Tonio Perez ..."

At that, the look of recoil was there again and she edged away. Catching her arm, I told her how I'd come on his name in the newspaper.

"Is he Joel's super's son?" I asked, and as Veronica was stubbornly mute, "Joel must have met him when he was hiding out."

"Let it go, Mrs. Benson," she said. Her eyes were black and hard as volcanic glass.

"Veronica, I know Joel was terrible to you. But there's no one else who can help me. He's in trouble and he's my brother."

For an instant, the black gaze wavered.

"You have two children," she said, recovering. "Take them and run." It was like a pronouncement from a stone idol. I caught my breath. "I got to go now," she said.

"You can't!" I suddenly saw that she thought Joel had done the butchery. And I found myself babbling out the dates of the murders that coincided with his trip to Morocco.

"The cops know who killed those girls," she said.

"It was Tonio," I insisted.

"Oh yes. Everyone knows that." It was as if I'd been battering on a door that had all the time been unlocked. I felt light-headed. After her stony warning about my children, her easy admission was bewildering.

"If it was Tonio, it couldn't be Joel. Why do you say to run and leave my brother?"

This time the dark gaze was troubled.

"Do you know where Tonio is hiding now?" I asked softly. "If the police could find him. . . ." Her face had tightened. I was afraid she'd turn and run. I bit my lip for mentioning the police.

"If Carrie and Peter are in danger, you have to tell me." She sighed at that, from deep inside.

"Come," she said, and without another word, she headed down Lexington Avenue. I hurried beside her past cafés, photographers' windows and *farmacias*. Soon we turned a corner into a grimy street. Tenements, garbage cans, a whitewashed church. Beside it, a shabby gray building housed a *funeraria*. A spray of artificial calla lilies was thrust in a vase at the clouded window.

The warmth seemed to drain from the late April sun and I had a desire to turn and run. The panic that had come over me that afternoon long ago at La Esmeralda was back. Only now I was fighting for my children and my brother. El Barrio's shadow lay over my snug life.

Veronica stopped and touched my arm.

We were outside the Botánica Tropical. Through the dusty window I made out religious statuettes and a row of candles.

"You got to be quiet now."

She pulled open the door, and to the tinkling of bells I was led into the shop. It was cool and dark, smelling of herbs. I had an impression of peculiar plants and boxes of dried and twisted roots. Then a man appeared at a black dividing curtain. It was hard to judge his age. I guessed he was some Caribbean mixture of black, Indian, and perhaps Spanish. He was dressed in island fashion with sport shirt outside his trousers. On a leather thong about his neck, he wore a small bundle of animal teeth.

I did not like him and he did not like me—a strong obvious instinct on both sides. "Madam, we are closed," he said.

Veronica addressed him so rapidly, I couldn't even pick out familiar Spanish words. While she spoke, he shot me a look. His glance held a strange compound of respect and malice, as if he were watching some unpleasant animal fall into an impaling pit.

But when Veronica urged me forward, he did not stop her. Suddenly realizing I was being pushed toward the black curtain, I tried to pull back for explanations. "Go, Mrs. Benson. You ask my help, I give it to you," Veronica whispered.

Bewildered, I let her thrust me through the draperies. I found myself in a large dim room filled with cartons of gnarled dry roots, *botánica* stock, statuettes, an iron Franklin stove. It was so dim that at first I didn't see the little woman huddled in a corner.

It was Mrs. Perez, tiny, haggard, more worn even than I remembered. Her small brown eyes met my eyes sadly. She came toward me and put out her hands like some timid beseeching animal. Her fingers were cold. But even more chilling was my realization that she was treating me as her fellow in misfortune.

### CHAPTER FOUR

In nightmares, even yet, those next few hours in the *botánica* return. Shadows and queer herb smells mingle with uneasy rustlings till I have to rise and walk about my room before I can persuade myself that time is truly past.

The rustling sounds, incidentally, were lizards. Don Pedro, the

533

proprietor, kept them in a cage near the Franklin stove. He flipped off their covering cloth for me to see, then reached in and captured one. He turned it over and, grinning, ran a finger down its belly in a slicing gesture.

I found from Dr. Reichman subsequently that a disemboweled lizard was part of a *hechizo,* the spell for bringing on illness or death. Don Pedro was a *brujo*—he worked with evil, and dealt in lizards, black cock's blood, and dirt from new graves which he used to summon dead men's spirits.

As I turned away from the lizards' cage, I saw a picture of Saint Michael hanging upside down. I didn't make the connection then with *brujería* but it was odd and somehow unpleasant. It was unsettling, too, that Veronica had left me. I was alone with Don Pedro and Mrs. Perez. Don Pedro translated for us and I was keenly aware that he was strangely patient with her ramblings. Even I, for all my urgency to find Tonio and help Joel, understood she must find her own way to give that help.

Her way began with a defense of her past. She had been raised in a fishing town on the east coast of Puerto Rico, where her father owned a little store. They were poor but she had shoes and went to school. When she was sixteen, she went to San Juan to stay with a cousin for a fiesta. And on the beach, by the leaping flames of the bonfires, she first met Tonio's father.

"He was black, not like me, a real Negro. He was bad, too, *con muchas malicias.*" She thought he had cast a love spell on her. They were married, I gathered, not in a church but in free union. He was a sailor and while he was in port, he drank, but he was in port increasingly seldom. Tonio was born while he was away and after that support money dwindled. She had no food and couldn't pay the rent. Then she met an older man who seemed fond of the baby. He was a waiter in a San Juan café. He was clean and sober and they lived together in La Esmeralda in reasonable content. When Tonio was nearly two, her sailor husband unexpectedly turned up, drunk and amorous. When he learned of his rival, he burst into her shack to kill her for her perfidy.

She was put in the hospital with a broken pelvis that prevented

her having further children. This was the last she saw of her husband. She lay in the hospital for months with no visitor except a neighbor named Teresa. Her aging lover had left Tonio with Teresa and decamped for New Jersey.

When at last she left the hospital, there was no one but Teresa to turn to. And Teresa led a gay life. She worked the bars up the hill from the plaza. She brought men home to her shack, where they were separated from Tonio by just a curtain. In time, Mrs. Perez became a bar waitress too.

Tonio was six when she met her next husband. His name was Ramón; he didn't drink or gamble, but unfortunately, Tonio hated him. After trying to mediate between them, she boarded Tonio with an old aunt of Ramón's who lived outside Guayama.

"It was in the country, you know. I thought it would be good for him."

I supposed she did, but I'd seen those tar-paper shacks settling into the mangrove swamps, the stinking mud alive with crabs, lizards darting up the shack walls. Chickens and hogs ran about the palm groves, and between cane crops the people lived on wild breadfruit, plantains and yucca root. I pictured the angry six-year-old, abandoned in a strange old woman's shack. Dread and rage must have alternated.

"She was a bad woman," Mrs. Perez said. "She made illegal rum." But that wasn't the worst of it. Tonio began to have what I gathered was a form of epilepsy and the old aunt's remedy was beating him. Or she tied him to the bed and stuck him with pins.

"When I found out, I begged to have him back," Mrs. Perez said. "But Ramón wouldn't let me."

It was six more years before the ordeal ended. Ramón stabbed a sailor and was himself shot and killed by the police.

Her next savior was Mr. Perez. He said he'd make a home for her in the States and even take Tonio, but when she went for him at the old aunt's shack, Tonio wasn't there. The old woman wouldn't say where he could be found until a five-dollar bill loosened her tongue. It turned out Tonio had gone bad. At this point, a grin spread across Don Pedro's face.

535

"He'd been hanging around a *bruja,* a witch."

"I know the word," I said. I recalled the painting of Guayama in the Parke-Bernet gallery. Dr. Reichman had called it the town of witches.

That afternoon, Mrs. Perez tried to fetch Tonio. She ruined the pair of new pink pumps Mr. Perez had bought her, picking through the mud till she came to a cabin isolated in a palmetto grove.

The *bruja* was formidable. A huge dark woman wearing a black turban, she poked her head out her smoky kitchen window and watched Mrs. Perez's attempt to lure her son away. But Mr. Perez's offer of New York with its ready money, television sets and real snow falling wasn't enough to make a wary Tonio leave his *bruja.* For with her he had the delicious sensation of throwing fear into his former persecutors. He was probably also picking up the tricks of *brujería,* with its spells and herb lore. So Mrs. Perez would have to leave without him, paid back for having deserted him.

But the day before the Perezes' flight to New York, Tonio had gone home to La Esmeralda, blood-crusted and swollen-faced. Stones had been thrown at him when he went to the settlement to shop for the *bruja.* A young girl had died the night before and the death had been laid at his door.

"*Mal de ojo,*" Don Pedro explained. "They said he had the evil eye."

Tonio had gone along to New York. For the first month, Mrs. Perez regretted leaving San Juan. It was March; she thought she'd freeze to death, and she missed the intimate bustle of La Esmeralda. She couldn't seem to learn English and, unlike most newcomers to El Barrio, she had no relatives to fill the vacuum. She sat huddled by the radiator dreading the daily trip to the store.

Mr. Perez had lived in New York before and spoke a fair amount of English, so he got a job right away in a shoe factory. Tonio, too, took to the new life. Though he was of school age, they didn't press him to go and he was free to wander the city. He was fascinated by the photograph booths around Times Square. Mrs. Perez fished in her purse and handed me some old picture strips. Even at thirteen he was different-looking. His eyes were slanting

and their gaze was too fevered to be quite sane. He was darker than his mother and I got a sense of wild unstable gaiety as he struck dramatic attitudes. In all the pictures, he was wearing a black garment with a stand-up collar.

"That cape. He always wore it. It made him look like he had wings," Mrs. Perez said. It suited the *brujería* history. He himself may have believed that he had the *mal de ojo.*

For a while it looked as if he was outgrowing the past. The epilepsy faded away. He picked up English, and went to work delivering for a butcher shop. Eventually, though, the job went. Mrs. Perez didn't know exactly why, except to say the butcher grew frightened of him. Perhaps it was nothing more than a queer way of looking at the knives or hints about his life with the *bruja.*

After that, he just hung around by himself, wearing the black cape, reading comic books. Mrs. Perez used to find him sitting on the tenement stoop, looking hotly at the passing girls. By this time, he was seventeen. "But he was innocent as a holy angel," she said.

One morning when Mrs. Perez started for the store, she found police cars parked along their street. The neighbors were crowding around the entrance to the next tenement, the home of María Sánchez, whose head had just been found in Central Park. Mrs. Perez remembered her clearly, a pretty girl with long hair. Only yesterday Tonio had been sitting on their stoop staring after her.

Later while she was making his bed she found his bloody shirt stuffed under the mattress. When she unrolled the shirt, a switchblade knife fell on the floor. When she confronted him, he said he'd had a nosebleed, and he'd found the knife.

Two months later, he was missing overnight. That was when they found Theresa Ruggiero in the playground on One Hundred and Fourth Street. There was no blood on his clothes this time, but Mr. Perez found his wife in hysterics and forced her suspicions out of her. He stormed about and beat Tonio, who remained silent and aloof. It never occurred to them to go to the police.

Then Perez took a job as super in the East Second Street apartment house. They put the past behind and started life again in the East Village.

But they were shaken. Perez drank more heavily than ever. Mrs. Perez took up espiritismo. Tonio said the religious pictures made him jumpy and they moved him into an empty apartment. Just temporarily till a paying tenant was found. Remembering the switchblade knife in Joel's closet, I asked, "Was it Five-D?" and she nodded.

That September, Victoria Díaz was found near the boat lake. This time Tonio had been questioned by the Central Park patrolman who didn't know there had been a murder. Later, the boy with slanting eyes and black cape wasn't hard to trace, and that evening, two detectives turned up on East Second Street.

"They didn't find him," she said.

"Where was he?" I asked.

There was a nervous hesitation. Mrs. Perez looked from Don Pedro to me. To help my brother, she'd have to sacrifice her son.

"Please," I begged.

She looked at Don Pedro and he turned to me.

"By that time, madam, he was dead," he said.

I sat in the dim room, trying to absorb Don Pedro's news. Just when I was getting a sense of Tonio, they were telling me he was gone forever. The shock made me dull-witted. But I caught glimpses of what it meant for Joel. If Tonio had died by the end of September, he could not have known Joel, who hadn't moved in until November. And Joel was on his own in Sherry's death. I had a terrible vision of an ivy planter gently swinging beneath its burden. Instinctively, I rebelled.

"Dead?" I said. "How could he be? A boy of seventeen doesn't just die. Why didn't the newspapers report it?"

"They don't know," Don Pedro said. He consulted with Mrs. Perez and then turned to me.

"Now, madam," he went on, "listen close to me. The night of the death of Victoria Díaz, Mr. Perez was drinking. He was in a bad temper, and coming home late, he found Tonio going in. It was one o'clock, no good for a boy like Tonio. His fear blazed up and he followed Tonio to his place. They shout and fight. Tonio pulls a

knife. But Mr. Perez is strong, and drunk, you know. He hit him with a piece of plumbing pipe. He hit him hard."

Belief started to sink in. And yet I grasped at unexplained parts. "Why didn't the police find the body?"

"Mr. Perez put it in a trunk and dumped it in the East River. He got it over there in a pushcart."

I had a harrowing picture of that dark mission. A Puerto Rican pushing a cart wouldn't attract interest in that neighborhood. I supposed he'd gone straight to East River Park and dumped his burden in the black waters; the trunk must have been weighted, too, to stay down. It was the historic New York solution. There must be hundreds of antique trunks settling in that mud.

Suddenly, Mrs. Perez spoke up. As Don Pedro translated, her pinched face was beseeching.

"She says she don't know this till much later. She thought Tonio ran away."

So that was how she got through the police questioning, by thinking Tonio had escaped. But then she must have waited, expecting to hear from him. October had gone by; November had brought Joel. Mr. Perez had cleaned the apartment. He must have tossed the switchblade knife up in the closet. "Mrs. Perez don't know what's happened till the phone call."

I was lost again. "What phone call?"

Don Pedro leaned forward with his face masklike. "The call from Tonio."

I looked from him to Mrs. Perez. "Wasn't Tonio really dead?"

"He is *dead*, madam," Don Pedro told me with simple emphasis. "On the last day of September. And all the rest, the way I said. After that, time goes by, months, you understand?"

I gave an uncertain nod.

"Last winter, Mr. Perez answers the phone and it is Tonio." He raised a hand to hold back judgment. "It is not someone pretending. It is Tonio. He speaks of the fight, of the trunk. Things nobody else knows."

I waited till Don Pedro continued.

"He says he's come back to punish Mr. Perez." He hesitated.

"A big shock, you see, for Mr. Perez. He is home that day and drinking. In terror, he finally tells Mrs. Perez that he killed Tonio." He paused again. "And that night he is dead himself."

I recalled that he had fallen from the tenement roof. Still, a drunk falling off a roof is not much of a case for the dead returning.

"There is more," Don Pedro said. "That night late, he gets a call that the roof door is banging. He got a hangover, he don't want to go, but the caller insists. He goes upstairs. Mrs. Perez waits. There's a yell and a bad sound outside. She runs and finds him on the sidewalk dead."

There was a silence while I tried to absorb it. Perhaps someone had hurled Mr. Perez to his death.

"The cops come when she screams. A crowd is around. She is on the sidewalk beside Mr. Perez. And then she sees your brother."

"It's not possible," I whispered. By then, Joel had left Second Street. He was either in Bellevue or at my house.

"Your brother," he repeated surely. "He leaves the building and walks up the street. He turns and waves to her. Then she sees it is really Tonio. He's walking with Tonio's—" He hesitated over the right word. "Movement?"

At that moment, a memory came back to me. The night Joel had climbed down the vines I'd seen out the window a familiar figure with a stranger's gait.

I tried to tell myself that the dead don't come back and take people over. But sitting in the dim strange room, I seemed to hear the voice in my workroom speaking Spanish. Other memories came crowding around me, the climb down a vine by a boy afraid of heights, the amnesia, his scratched hand.

"No," I said firmly. "I don't believe it was my brother."

I jumped up and stood clutching my handbag. "I'm sorry," I said. "Thank you for your trouble but I have to go now. My children will be coming home from school."

"Take care for your children, madam," Don Pedro said. I refused to show I understood.

The store bell tinkled as people entered and I said, "I'll slip out. I won't disturb your customers."

540

"They are not customers," Don Pedro said.

As I turned, I saw them coming through the black curtain. They were a mixture of Indian and Spanish, touched with African. One was a handsome boy, wearing an expensive-looking sweater. They all stopped uneasily when they saw me. Don Pedro spoke to them in Spanish, then turned to me. "You must stay now, madam."

I hesitated. I had heard him say the name Joel Delaney, and the eyes about me had sharpened with interest.

Mrs. Perez drew me down to her and whispered in the limited English she could use when pushed to it, "Stay. They try to catch Tonio."

I was startled.

"We try to lift him off your brother. To find out how to give him rest," Don Pedro said.

It has all become part of my nightmares, the smell of incense, the hypnotic flickering of candles, Don Pedro laying out a black cloth. On it he set a small figure.

"Who is that?" I asked.

The handsome boy was standing next to me. "San Marcos," he whispered. "The saint of the *brujos.* This Don Pedro is very good."

At the makeshift altar, Don Pedro raised his voice, chanting. He turned, squaring the compass, calling spirits from the world's four quarters. He took out a bottle of rum, poured some into calabashes and handed them out. I touched the gourd to my lips and the gesture seemed to satisfy him.

They formed a circle and began singing, a short refrain endlessly repeated in response to Don Pedro's chant. I felt that I did not belong; my revulsion grew as the singing picked up strength.

The boy beside me glided, dancing, to the circle's center, and my alienation increased. His cable-knit sweater and flannel slacks were crazily irrelevant in the squalid dim room with its lizards' cage and religious statuettes.

Suddenly, he gave a shout, dived forward and then, as he struck the floor, went rigid. But instead of running to help him, the singers only changed their chanting to a slower tempo. When I

541

tried to move, a woman touched me warningly, and I saw that Don Pedro was tying a large silk handkerchief about the boy's slender waist.

Slowly, the boy raised his head. His face looked different, as if the muscle play had changed.

Don Pedro addressed him and then the boy went white with fury. He took a breath and rattled off an answer I couldn't understand, but from the look of shock around the room, I gathered it was threatening. There was a hesitation in the chanting.

The boy rose and jerked the black cloth beneath the figure of San Marcos. The image, candles, calabashes, rum bottle, all went flying. The next second we were scrambling to prevent a fire.

As soon as the candles were safe, the singing began again while Don Pedro approached the boy's figure crumpled on the floor. He spoke softly till the boy moaned and painfully sat up. He seemed dazed. Don Pedro raised a hand for the chanting to end. Somebody turned on the electric lights and we saw the saint's figure in pieces, the rum bottle broken and the lizards' cage overturned, the little reptiles scurrying for cover.

Overcome with revulsion, I turned to leave. Then Don Pedro stepped to my side, saying, "He don't want to come out. You bring your brother and we try again. With your brother I have more power. Maybe we even kill a cock."

I had a mad sense he was about to quote prices. Blood sacrifice, of course, would be extra. My knees went weak and before I could be sick, I ran.

ON THE ride back downtown, I felt so queasy I had to roll down the cab window. Crazy bits of the afternoon kept coming back, the scent of incense, the candles' flicker, the distorted face of the boy as he snarled at Don Pedro from the floor. I marshaled my reason to grapple with them.

Don Pedro's disciples may have thought Tonio had taken over Joel's body but that didn't make it so. Don Pedro made his living building up such belief and selling his services as intercessor. It was even possible that saying Tonio was dead was part of a trick

to call off the police search. But they could scarcely think I'd tell the police Tonio was dead when that would make Joel their chief suspect. Besides, I didn't feel Mrs. Perez capable of sustained deceit. The last part of the taxi ride, I sat sodden, staring out the taxi window.

We had already passed the children before I registered their presence. They were standing with the Baron on our corner. Turning to look out the back window, I saw that they were trying to flag me, so I stopped the driver.

The Baron jumped on me as if I'd been away for years. As I returned his greeting, I tried to seem the same as always.

"Let's walk a ways on Lexington Avenue," Peter said as I turned toward the house.

"What's wrong?" I asked. We'd turned the corner but when I tried to stop, Carrie propelled me along.

"Uncle Joel is drunk," she told me.

"Or turned on," Peter added. "Unless he's gone crazy."

"Tell me what happened," I demanded.

"I don't know for sure. He was in your workroom. And suddenly we heard a lot of crashing like he was smashing furniture, roaring and shouting."

"What was he shouting?"

"We couldn't tell. It was in Spanish."

"I hope you didn't go near him."

"Peter did," Carrie said.

"Just to see if I could help," Peter admitted. "But then he came rushing out on the landing."

I felt like crying. "What happened then?"

"He shouted down at us," Carrie told me.

"In English?"

"Yes. But he didn't make much sense. About how we weren't going to send him back to a dark place. Bellevue isn't dark, is it?" she asked me.

I couldn't answer. I shook my head. I was struggling with a new horror: the timing could have been just a coincidence, or else Don Pedro's ceremony had had a real, material effect!

I drew Carrie and Peter into the shelter of a drugstore and went to a phone booth. I tried Erika's apartment and, when there was no answer, I called her office at the hospital but only got her secretary. She wanted my number so Erika could phone me back. That brought it home to me—I didn't have a number.

I replaced the receiver and sat staring out at my two children and a big black sheep dog, feeling like some heavy-laden matriarchal gypsy. I realized that with the Baron along, I couldn't even take them to a restaurant, or a movie. And I didn't want to call on Ted and have to explain.

Suddenly, I remembered Hans Reichman. I called him. He was uncertain about Erika. "I think today she goes to Rockland State Hospital. She is writing a book on drug-induced schizophrenia. A young musician there she finds interesting."

In a fright that he would hang up, I gave an account of the children's story laced with disjointed bits about Don Pedro and his trying to lift a dead spirit off my brother.

At last, he said, "There *is* a *brujo* named Don Pedro who runs a *botánica* in Spanish Harlem. I think you'd better come have a talk about it."

"I've got my children and the sheep dog with me."

He sighed. "Bring them all. But come at once. I have a plane to catch."

HANS REICHMAN was one of the old-line psychiatrists who still colonized the Upper West Side, scorning the glass-and-chrome of Park Avenue. To my modern American children, the aged housekeeper, walls of books and monstrous furniture were uncanny.

While the housekeeper set out a tray of black bread, cream cheese and red caviar, Dr. Reichman chatted about the trip he was to make that night. "I fly to Lima. Then on to the Peruvian coast towns. I study cases there of *mosuelo*."

"What is that?" Peter asked politely.

"*Mosuelo* is magical fright. The belief is that the soul leaves the body when the victim is startled, a syndrome in Latin countries."

I was relieved when the children went to buy a can of dog food

and Dr. Reichman led me into his consulting office. He settled behind the desk, and I told him about Joel, beginning with his stay in Bellevue, his climb down the vines, even my suspicions about waking drugged the morning that Sherry was murdered. At my account of Tonio's death, he groped for a pen. With Don Pedro's séance, he was writing swiftly across a pad. I finished with the children's report of Joel's refusal to return to the dark place.

"*Ja,*" he said and considered his notes. When he raised his face, I saw that his eyes were bright with interest. "This birthday party. Do you notice in him a change of features?"

I tried to recall how Joel had looked that night. Flushed, but I'd thought it the champagne. And then I remembered the night I found him in his apartment, his face working strangely, the change of voice.

"Not then," I said. "But the night we took him to Bellevue."

"Long sighs? Odd hiccuping?"

"Yes, I remember that."

He went back to examining his pad. "Loss of consciousness. Amnesia, classic. Only the medieval religious cases do not seem to have had amnesia. A curious variant."

"Is it—what Don Pedro thought?" I couldn't bring myself to say "possession."

"Let us say a weakening of the personality to the compulsive process." I looked up hopefully, but then he added, "What has historically been called possession. Alternately, called demonical somnambulism."

The phrase went ricocheting about my mind, with demons shrieking, gravestones overthrown, the weird panoply of a bygone age. I felt that either I wasn't hearing him correctly or his researches with folk magic had driven him over the edge. I remembered Erika's warnings about his professional reputation.

Still, he looked so sympathetic, sound and sane that I found myself asking him quietly, "But does it really exist?"

"Oh yes, cases exist," he said matter-of-factly.

He rose and went around the desk to the bookcases. "It has a long history." He touched a large calfbound book. "It begins, as

far as we know, in Babylon. The cuneiform writings on clay tablets give conjurations for possessing spirits. During the Babylonian captivity, these beliefs passed into Judaism and from there into Christianity." He tapped another set of books.

"There was a parallel development along the Nile. The priests of Egypt were famous exorcists. At the end of the Hellenic period, even the Greeks went in for it. We have descriptions of possessed persons in Lucian and Philostratus."

"But that was long ago."

He smiled. "Let us come to now." He crossed to the bookcase on the opposite wall. "This shelf is on Africa. Missionaries and ethnologists report possession by spirits and ghosts." He moved along a few steps. "Next is Asia. In Japan, possession is mainly by animals. But in China we come to our sort, possession by the recently dead. In *Demon Possession,* John Nevius, a missionary for forty years, says it's a daily occurrence."

He looked at me. "But they are foreign? Then let us take William James's *Principles of Psychology.* He tells of a fourteen-year-old girl living in Watseka, Illinois. She was possessed by a neighbor's daughter who had died in an insane asylum."

He moved on. "The whole next shelf is modern American spiritualist literature. And here we come precisely to our subject, the possessing dead from the Caribbean. The expert is Dr. Myal Singh of Trinidad. And we are most fortunate. He visits now the United States, teaching tropical botany. After I spoke to you, I telephoned him. He is expecting us. The children can wait here."

THE ST. GERMAIN was one of those decaying hotels on upper Broadway, cut up now into domiciles. Dr. Reichman in his tailored suit and Bronzini tie was out of place but he seemed cheerfully unaware of it. At the fourth floor, the smell of curry led us to Dr. Singh's quarters.

He met us at the door, a thin brown man in a pale blue turban, somewhere in his sixties. His education was evidently British.

The first few minutes of our visit were taken up with the preparation of mint tea and the passing around of sesame-seed cookies.

Then Dr. Singh seated himself opposite me and said, "I hear you have had perplexing experiences."

Beginning to feel like a child who recites for company, I ran once again through my story.

When I ended, Dr. Reichman said, "I find the *botánica* session most provocative. The image of San Marcos, the rum drinking and chanting."

"Yes, it is the Bella-bella," Dr. Singh said. "The circle of power, the *ballade* with responses, the young dancer possessed. It is a way of finding grievances of the departed."

"But *ballade* is French. Does that mean it's voodoo?" I asked. It was a mistake.

Dr. Singh undertook to clear up my ignorance. "What has occurred to your brother has nothing to do with voodoo, more properly vodun," he said, "which is a magical system performed by a priest and priestess in the presence of the sacred fetish. It is largely centered in Haiti and is distinct from obeah or espiritismo."

"I see," I said.

"Obeah is a system of magic based on spells, charms and communication with departed spirits. It has spread to all of the Caribbean islands and strongly tinges Puerto Rican espiritismo. A scarf around the possessed dancer, rum drinking, chanting, are all marks of obeah."

With a desperate sense that he was only warming to his subject, I plunged in. "Should I let Don Pedro try exorcism?"

Dr. Singh's face blazed with indignation. "Don Pedro is an impostor. The practice of true obeah needs no dog's teeth, gourds or lizards, only study with a qualified teacher."

Dr. Reichman seemed embarrassed. "My dear Mrs. Benson, it is not so simple. The history of exorcism is largely one of failure. Not only does it often increase the state of possession, but the exorcising priests risk falling victim to the state themselves. In a famous episode at Loudun, four exorcists were possessed. Even spectators are liable to it. In every culture this is considered dangerous."

Impatience about Joel made me tackle him directly. "Dr. Reichman, do you believe Joel is possessed by Tonio?"

Dr. Reichman chose his words with care. "We have, I believe, a compulsion which forms the kernel of psychasthenic crystallization," he finally answered. "Naturally, the view of possession that is current in the victim's society determines the interpretation of such a compulsion." I felt relief that he seemed to be coming out for psychiatric disorder.

But Dr. Singh, shifting restlessly, said, "Tell me how this interesting theory explains phenomena associated with possession—the voice and accent of the possessing spirit being different from the host, and his often speaking in a language he doesn't know, as in this case?"

"There is no great mystery about the Spanish," Dr. Reichman answered. "The boy has spent time in Tangier. In New York, he lived in a Puerto Rican district. The unconscious has remarkable potential for learning." There was the jagged silence of disagreeing experts. Dr. Reichman smoothed over troubled waters with affability, but Dr. Singh's words were sinking in. We said our good-bys with civilized blandness, while fear tightened again about my heart.

WALKING away from Dr. Singh's house, Dr. Reichman set himself to fill me with confidence. "A compulsion that has developed into a second personality is not so rare as you might think, my dear. There have been such cases and the patients recovered."

"Do you think he could have killed Sherry?"

In the twilight, I could not see his face but he pressed my arm in a gesture of compassion. "*Ja*, this is what we must discover. He is a disturbed boy. There can be no prison, no last mile, you understand. The worst would be protective custody."

"Matteawan?" It was the state hospital for the criminally insane.

"It is possible. We must face it squarely. If he did this act, he is ill, but he is also dangerous. You must not see him until after he is hospitalized."

"How will it . . . happen?"

"That is a matter for Dr. Lorenz. You should see her immediately. I wish I could stay on a consulting basis. Quite apart from

my concern for you, it is of profound interest. However, I must fly to Lima tonight."

"I understand," I said as he led me past a twilight group of dog walkers to a telephone booth. He called Erika, then I phoned Peter and Carrie to say I'd be a while longer.

Erika herself, in blue jeans and bare feet, opened the door, carrying a coffeepot. I followed her across white fur rugs to the kitchen.

"Is it Charles's night off?" I asked, while the coffee perked.

"Don't speak his name. I'm absolutely furious. He flew to Amsterdam when I told him most particularly he couldn't. If I knew how to reach him, I'd fire him." The notion of a flying houseman made me heady.

At last, carrying fresh coffee, she led me up the steps to her study. She slid a Steuben ashtray across her desk toward me and sat cross-legged on a wool-covered divan.

"Hans tells me Joel is possessed by Tonio Perez, The Chopper," she said ironically.

I didn't deny it. "It seems that Tonio's dead," I told her.

"You're sure?"

"They couldn't have made all that up."

She lit a cigarette and blew out smoke, considering. "He somehow picked up data on the death subliminally. Perhaps from the way the super acted."

"Joel?" I asked. "He didn't know Tonio existed. Much less that he was dead."

She gazed at me, not accepting it. "Don't sell the unconscious short, sweetie. He picked up something that fitted his need to split off from the past. He'd tried the breakdown, the flight from the country, then hashish and LSD. None of it worked, so we have a second personality."

"Why?" I asked.

"Why not is more likely. Depressive mother, suicide, an absent father, changing fortunes. To say nothing of your abandoning him."

"Erika!"

"There's an embarrassment of riches in his history. The chances for rage and guilt are enormous."

"What will you do with him now?" I asked her.

She adjusted the tortoiseshell pins that held up her dark hair. "Pentothal to locate causes. Then hypnosis and suggestions that his guilt is, after all, forgivable. It depends on what we dig up."

"How do you plan . . . to get hold of him?"

"He has an appointment with me tomorrow. And by the way, you must not return home. Not after this afternoon's episode." When I nodded, she asked, "Where will you stay?"

"I suppose I could find a hotel." I hesitated. "What do you think, though, about Fire Island? Next week is spring vacation anyway. We might open the beach cottage early."

She considered. "Good idea. Better to have the children out of town. In case there's some nuisance with the newspapers."

I'd forgotten about the papers. And it was likely that they would get hold of it. SHERRY'S BOYFRIEND TO SANITARIUM.

"I'll connect the phone first thing so you can reach me," I said. "It's only two and a half hours to town if you need me." I moved to get up and then I hesitated. "Will it be dangerous for you?"

She shook her head. "There's a good transference. He likes me."

"He liked Sherry, too," I heard myself say.

"Anyway, he'll be coming to see me at the hospital," Erika said. "There are guards in the hall."

I still hesitated and she smiled at me.

"You know, he's only possessed because he thinks he is. There are no demons with supernormal powers."

"You haven't met Dr. Singh," I said.

"That old fraud. Really, Hans should be ashamed of himself."

CHAPTER FIVE

I'D PICKED UP the children and the Baron at Dr. Reichman's and we were sitting on the 9:49 train to Bay Shore, when I realized we'd better not complete our trip that night.

Fire Island is a spit of sand a few hundred yards wide and thirty miles long, connected by ferries with Long Island. Our house

is on the beach in Ocean Bay Park and in the summer season we catch the ferry direct to it from Bay Shore. But out of season we should have to go to Ocean Beach and walk a mile of sandy paths to reach our house. I decided to stay in Bay Shore and go over in the morning.

"We have no nightclothes," Carrie pointed out. We kept a supply in the house.

I was silent. On the train, only the Baron's mood remained undampened. He sat up, pleased with all the unexpected moves. Carrie leaned on him broodingly.

"Poor Walter," she said. "It was wrong of us to leave him."

"He's Joel's cat. He'll take care of him," I said. But who was Joel now, I wondered.

"Do you think he will if he's gone crazy?"

"Carrie!" I said.

We all fell silent, staring out at the passing night while we reflected on private horrors. At Bay Shore a local taxi driver found us a motel that would take the Baron. In fact, I think we had the dog suite. The furniture was battered and the rug redolent of canine accidents. It was a miserable night. I turned and twisted, reliving the séance in the *botánica*. Then, toward dawn, I slipped into vaguely oppressed dreams.

We woke to wet white beach fog. It rolled past the windows and dripped from the trees like rain. Clammily depressed, we dragged on our wrinkled city clothes and walked up to the snack bar at the ferry landing. After eating, we stared through the fog waiting for the boat to appear. When it finally nosed into the bay, we huddled below deck, chilled and numb, and only stirred when we tied up at the wharf in Ocean Beach.

Arrival at the beach in fog is muted. My children, who usually land like the marines, were unnervingly decorous. I sent them to the grocery store while I stopped at the telephone and electric companies.

Then I dropped by Mr. Olsen's house. He was our handyman and plumber. Mrs. Olsen said he was at the marina painting a boat and she'd send him over when she saw him. I got our spare

set of house keys from her, then hurried after Carrie and Peter. As I walked into the grocery store, I judged by their purchase of huge tins of popcorn and marshmallows and packages of frankfurters that they had planned their day around the fireplace.

At last we set out, with promises of an early delivery. Few houses were open. Through the screened porches, we could see dust sheets covering furniture; here and there bicycles and wagons from last season were rusting. As we left Ocean Beach behind us, the path grew narrower, the reeds and grasses taller. A sudden flight of seabirds set the Baron barking.

At Ocean Bay Park, we turned from the bay side and made our way past the empty beach cottages toward the ocean. We couldn't see it in the fog but we could hear it restlessly moving. Then we turned and confronted our house—ungainly and brown-shingled, built forty years before when Fire Island was an artists' colony. So far, we seemed to be the only summer people in residence but some would arrive during spring vacation.

The kitchen was dark as night. To help the cottage survive the winter storms, I'd had shutters placed on the inside and held by braces. The electric company hadn't gotten into action, so there was a hunt for matches and kerosene lamps. At last, we paraded into the living room casting lamp shadows before us.

It was depressingly cold, but our fireplaces are the kind you see in photographs of Teddy Roosevelt's lodges, trimmed in rough stones and large enough to roast a side of beef. While I lit the one in the living room, Peter made fires in the upstairs bedrooms.

After that, we dug out sweaters and corduroys and changed from city clothes. The children had found their surf-casting rods and were examining them by firelight. "They say the blues run great in fog," Peter said.

"It's too cold to go fishing," I protested. But soon slickers appeared and they stamped off to provide us with a fish dinner, the Baron running after them. I told myself we'd soon be back to normal family life.

But Joel's troubles still hung over us. As I went upstairs to make the beds, I found myself growing edgy as the hour approached

for his appointment with Erika. I didn't doubt he would keep it, though I was far from sure of his reaction when he learned she planned to put him in a sanitarium. Don Pedro's Bella-bella dance kept returning, with the saint's image thrown over and the candles blown out. If that had been a taste of Tonio . . . And then I stopped, confused to find myself believing in Tonio.

It was only in Joel's unconscious mind that he still existed. Tonio was only a second self, built of Joel's compulsive processes. Suddenly that seemed to require a greater faith than belief in possession. But I still couldn't see how Joel had known of Tonio, much less known that he was dead.

The lights came on while I was making Peter's bed. The electric company had thrown our switch in Ocean Beach. Hopefully, I went to the hall and tried the telephone, but we weren't connected yet. Still, with lights, we were progressing.

I was digging out a checkers set from a downstairs closet when the boy came with the groceries. I recognized him from last year. "How are the blues running?" I asked.

"Too early for blues."

"Carrie and Peter are on the beach trying for them," I said, delaying him to fight off my sense of increasing isolation.

His look said he would not be surprised by any lunacy of city children. As soon as I tipped him, he marched out dourly. I heard my back door slam and the beach pickup zoom away.

I found a transistor radio and turned it on, but the batteries were dead. When I saw by my wristwatch it was past noon, I tried the phone again but it was still off. Since the children would be returning hungry, I went to the kitchen and started to fix lunch, which was difficult; the winter's kerosene was in the plumbing and I had to work without water. I opened cans of clam chowder and began to make sardine sandwiches.

It was while I was opening the mayonnaise that I heard logs falling. Most Fire Island summer houses have wood stored under simple rain shelters. Now it sounded as if someone were into mine. It occurred to me that Mr. Olsen might have come up without my hearing and brought us another load of wood.

I looked out the door but, while two logs had been dislodged, I saw nothing but dunes and drifting white fog.

"Mr. Olsen!" I called. The only answer was the ocean below, breaking on wet sand.

I supposed it must have been an animal, but the fog and isolation had got their opening. When I was reaching into the refrigerator, I had the crawling sensation that someone was staring at me through the shutters. I whirled about but all I saw was slats. The prospect of night seemed suddenly unbearable and I was viewing this new development in myself, dismayed, when I heard the approach of a pickup. It was really Mr. Olsen, come to help with our storm shutters and make our water run again.

He entered, tall and lanky, carrying his toolbox, and I was struck anew by his resemblance to a beardless Abraham Lincoln.

"You're early this year," he greeted me. "If you'd given me a ring, I'd a had your place ready."

"We only made up our minds to come last night."

"Well, let's get some light in here." He opened the toolbox, took out some tools and began prying off the shutter braces.

When the kitchen shutters were off, he moved about the rest of the house. As I was putting the chowder on to simmer, he reappeared. "I'll have your water on in a jiffy. Where's the baking soda? I'll flush out the pipes."

But a search turned up no baking soda, just a stained and empty box. "Only take a few minutes back to town. Can't use the water till I flush out the kerosene."

As he pulled himself into the cab of the truck, I asked, "Could you stop by the telephone company? They haven't turned ours on yet and I'm uneasy without it."

He regarded me kindly. "No need to worry on an island. It's safer here than New York City. All them robberies and muggings, fellas running around cutting folks' heads off."

I was shocked by his striking on it. I wondered, had he seen our name in the papers when Sherry died?

"He got another last night," he told me. "Some kind of lady doctor. You can bet nothing like that happens on Fire Island."

I was still staring at him when he switched on the motor. By the time I cried out, he was driving away. Though the trip itself would take only a few minutes, he might stop at his house for lunch, too. I decided I couldn't wait without knowing if it was Erika he meant.

I would have to go to Ocean Beach and call her office. But I would have to tell the children I was going. At that, my anxieties took a new direction. The children were late. I ran along the sandy path to find them.

Fire Island has a great wall of sandy dunes protecting the houses that lie behind and above. To reach the beach, you have to descend the dunes and, for this purpose, each townlet has a flight of stairs. Normally, when you stand at the top, you see miles of white beach, rollers breaking, and wide blue ocean as far as the horizon. But today, through the fog, I saw only the next few wooden steps below me, a spray of grass, a clamshell dropped by a gull.

I tried calling their names, but there was no reply. With the fog coiling slowly about me, I clung to the rail and, reaching the beach at last, crossed to the wet sand. A skirt of water swirled to my feet, wetting my espadrilles, and I jumped back.

I decided I might be trying the wrong direction. I turned and went the opposite way, calling. The Baron, at least, ought to hear me. For years, my patience had been tried by his barking. The one time I wanted to hear it, he was silent.

Blinded by the fog, I banged against a piece of driftwood and the pain set off panic. My face wet with tears and fog, I screamed the children's names.

Suddenly, a black cannonball was upon me. One moment, there was nothing and the next, a rescuing sheep dog. He jumped and barked, tore into the fog and disappeared, then came dashing back.

Carrie and Peter were trudging back up the beach, dangling a small fish between them. "What are you doing here?" Peter asked. "I have to go to Ocean Beach to call the city," I said. They accepted it without curiosity "You'll find clam chowder on the stove," I said. Now that I'd found the children, my anxieties were flying wildly around Erika. I wondered about the hospital guards,

then recalled Mr. Olsen had said that it had happened last night. At the top of the stairs, I announced I'd be back soon.

"Maybe by now the phone's on," Carrie said. They nudged me toward the house. As we gritted up the walk, I realized I couldn't leave them until I knew what was going on.

"Let's all go to Ocean Beach," I said, as Peter threw open the pantry door. "We'll have a big lunch, clams and lobster."

But Peter had stopped at the kitchen threshold suddenly. I moved to see over his head.

It was Joel. Or Joel-Tonio. He was standing by the kitchen sink watching us.

"Come in," he said and we filed in.

In his hand, he held an open switchblade knife.

## CHAPTER SIX

THE LONG blade caught the light with an evil glitter as he held it almost playfully. The playfulness increased the horror.

He smiled and nodded that we should sit down. I gave a look toward Carrie and Peter, and they moved into place about the kitchen table. It crossed my mind that we might make a run for it, but in the close quarters of the pantry surely someone would be caught and fall to the knife. He seemed to sense my thoughts. "Now, Nor," he mocked, "don't be silly."

Somewhere before, I'd heard him strike this self-congratulatory note. Then I recalled his birthday party. I'd thought him high on champagne when he'd led us to Sherry's car and flourished the earring he claimed he'd found on the car seat. That was the night Sherry had had her throat cut. The recognition sent a chill through me. To force it back, I asked, "What do you want here?"

"Why, sister, you know I go where you go."

In all our life, I don't think Joel had ever called me "sister." It made me feel a stranger stood before me.

"When was it you came back to the house and picked me up?" he asked. "About nine thirty?"

I stared at him, trying to understand. It was as if another face were coming through, a face I'd seen in the Times Square photo strips, a boy with slanting eyes and fevered gaze.

"Hey, listen!" he said. The tone brought me up sharply. "We came out together last night."

I began, at last, to understand. He was going to claim he came from New York with us. My sick sense grew that Joel himself was vanishing.

Then we heard Mr. Olsen's pickup returning. Our captor lifted his head to listen.

"It's our handyman," I told him. "He's coming back to flush the drains."

As soon as I spoke, he was beside Carrie's chair; he'd caught her long blond hair and looped it about his wrist. My breath stopped as he touched the blade to her throat.

"Now," he said, "we'll play a game."

In terrible stillness, we waited.

"See that checkers set?" he asked. The checkers set I'd dug out of the storage chest lay on the kitchen table. "Open it."

Peter reached out and unfolded the checkerboard.

"Pronto, now. Put on the pieces."

Peter set the blacks on one side, the reds opposite.

"You're going to play a game of checkers," Joel said. Or Joel-Tonio. There was nothing left now of my brother, no air or manner reminiscent of him.

He gave Carrie's head a little shake. It was like a cruel child shaking a rabbit. "You'll play good. Understand?"

Carrie whispered, "Yes."

"I'll be right beside you, watching." His voice was soft, almost caressing. "I'll have my friend here in my pocket. It only takes a second to spring him."

Slowly, he released her. Then in a gesture I found troubling, he reached out and smoothed her hair. There had been that same gentleness with Sherry when he'd disarranged the birthday crown.

The Baron began barking ferociously, protecting us from Mr. Olsen. "Let him in," Joel said. "And don't try anything."

"I won't," I said. I made my way to the back pantry and opened the door for Mr. Olsen.

"Something sure smells good," he said, brandishing a huge box of baking soda. I realized the chowder was still simmering.

"We haven't had lunch yet," I heard myself saying. It's odd how at the worst moment of my life, with Carrie's life in the balance, I still managed to walk about and chatter. "Get down, Baron. You know Mr. Olsen."

"Good boy," Mr. Olsen said with reserve.

"He's just greeting you," I said. "He's friendly, really."

Mr. Olsen gave him a cautious pat, then he straightened and looked around. "Hello, Peter. Have good fishing?"

Peter nodded. I saw the little fish in a puddle of wet beside his chair. He'd not had a chance to put it in the sink.

"Hello, Carrie," Mr. Olsen said. His gaze touched Joel and then I realized that he'd never seen him before.

"This is my brother, Joel Delaney," I said.

"Glad to meet you." Mr. Olsen nodded.

Joel gave him a dazzling smile. "You always get fog like this?" he asked with a disarming air of wanting information. "We had a bad time finding the house last night." He was establishing that he'd arrived with us but his move was uninformed.

Mr. Olsen looked at me, puzzled. "You mean you been here since last night without water?" Then he stopped. I remembered I'd told Mrs. Olsen that morning that we'd just got off the ferry.

A cloud darkened Joel's face. I had a sense of crisis.

"We stayed overnight in Bay Shore," I said quickly. "But Joel's right. The fog was terrible. We had a hard time finding the motel."

"Is that a fact?" Mr. Olsen asked. It was the fog that caught his interest. "We didn't have none here till morning."

I dreaded any more about the fog.

"I see you got the baking soda," I said, trying to redirect his attention.

"Yes," Mr. Olsen said. He seemed to be reflecting and I felt myself tense. But all he said was, "I'll just fix up the drains. Don't let me stop you from your lunch."

559

He turned to the sink. As he knelt to reach the drainpipe elbow, I looked at Joel. He seemed dissatisfied.

"How about it, sis? Lunch? Hey, Carrie, it's your move."

Like an automatic player in an arcade, Carrie raised her hand and moved a piece. As he gazed down at the checkerboard, I remembered him standing above Sherry. I saw the corn-silk hair, so close in shade to Carrie's and, choking back a rising terror, I made myself start for the chowder bowls and set them around the checkerboard. Joel pulled an empty chair over and sat beside Carrie.

Mr. Olsen finished with the sink. Ordinarily, I'd have written him a check, but I didn't want Joel to suspect me of trying to add some message. While I hesitated, the telephone rang.

I looked at it. I didn't know if Joel would let me answer, and yet with Mr. Olsen watching, my hesitation seemed peculiar.

But Mr. Olsen said, "Go ahead, Mrs. Benson, I'm leaving. Pay me later when you're not so busy." He glanced at Peter. "The sink's clear now. You can set that fish in it." With the sad Abraham Lincoln eyes, he looked wise and all-seeing, but he had seen nothing. "Hope you'll like Fire Island," he told Joel. Then he went out through the pantry.

I realized the phone was still ringing. "Answer it," Joel ordered. As I rose, he turned his chair to watch me. I picked it up.

"Are you all right, Norah?" Ted's voice shouted.

I wondered if they could hear him at the kitchen table. I looked over and saw they could. The switchblade knife had reappeared.

I forced myself to sound natural. "I'm fine," I said. "We came out to open the cottage."

There was a pause. "Who is we?" Ted asked.

"Carrie and Peter," I said, and looked at Joel. He gave a nod to tell me to include him. Then he pointed out something on the floor to Peter. Puzzled, I saw Peter bend and hand him the fish. "And Joel," I said into the telephone. "We all came out together last night."

"What time last night?"

I wondered if I might let him know something unusual was hap-

pening. There was a chance it might work. "We took the nine forty-nine," I answered. "We were too late for the ferry. So we spent the night in Bay Shore." He'd know we could have caught a ferry later, if we'd been willing to walk to the house in the dark.

"All of you?"

"All of us." My voice fell away as I stared at the fish. As I watched, the switchblade laid it open, boned and gutted it. Joel had gone fishing when he was eight, and he'd caught the hook in his thumb. As far as I knew, he'd never fished again. Yet now he was boning Peter's porgy with the ease of an expert. My mind gave a leap. I saw a Puerto Rican boy in a butcher shop. I almost saw the fish laid out on a bed of cracked ice.

"Are you there, Norah?" Ted was demanding.

"I'm here," I answered faintly.

"Have you heard about Erika?" he asked.

I hesitated. "I'm not sure," I answered. "Mr. Olsen mentioned something but without names, you know."

"Well, it's Erika. The same as those girls in the park and Sherry Talbot."

A picture of a swaying ivy planter blurred into Erika's apartment. I shuddered away from knowing where they'd found her.

"It happened last night," Ted was saying. "She didn't come to the hospital this morning for her ten o'clock session."

That session was Joel's. I steadied myself against the wall.

"Her secretary went over and found her," Ted said. "But you *all* went to Fire Island last night?"

"On the nine forty-nine."

"Well, now I know where you are, have a good time," he said pleasantly. And with that, he hung up the phone.

I stood holding the instrument as hope drained out of me. "Hang up," Joel's voice was saying.

Still, it wasn't Joel's voice. The timbre was very like, but the tone was different. It was too lively, too self-congratulatory. And yet somewhere beneath the new lethal personalty was my brother. A psychiatrist would take months getting through to him in a sanitarium. Now, in desperation, I had to try it myself.

"Joel," I said firmly. "It won't work."

"Sure it will," he told me.

"The track leads to you again with Erika," I said, trying to sound reasonable rather than accusing.

It was hard to know how much the children understood, but if they had not known Erika was dead, they did now. They were quiet as fawns in danger.

Joel nodded at the cleaned fish lying on the table. "Put that in the refrigerator," he told Peter.

Peter slid from his chair and picked up the fish. As he came away from the refrigerator, Joel said, "Sit down," and Peter took his place again.

"The cops will go on looking for The Chopper. And that couldn't be me," Joel said easily. "I was in Tangier when it started."

"The Chopper was Tonio Perez," I said.

He smiled. "Then let them find him."

I set myself. "I know Tonio's dead, Joel." I was dangerously reaching the level of his obsession, his belief that he was possessed. If I could persuade him that the Tangier alibi was wearing thin, he might give up peaceably. Providing he knew he would escape punishment. "Half of El Barrio knows Tonio is dead," I pressed. "And they aren't the only ones. Dr. Reichman knows now." He needn't be told that Reichman had flown to Peru.

He regarded me with great composure. "Try to make a jury believe that! Erika and Sherry went just like the others. There were little touches that weren't in the newspapers."

The jury talk was pointless. He wouldn't stand trial with his psychiatric record. Though now with Erika's death, he would have to be in public custody. Bellevue prison ward and then to Matteawan.

He broke the silence sharply.

"I won't go there. Forget Matteawan."

I heard him unbelievingly. Our thoughts had arrived at the same place at the same time. Or it was some kind of mind reading.

He was looking at me intently. The resemblance to the hectic boy in the photo strips was marked. Joel's features seemed to melt beneath the force of a wilder, more vigorous temperament.

"You're really scared, aren't you?" he asked. "More scared than you were at Don Pedro's."

I sought frantically for explanations. Perhaps Erika had had a chance to talk about Don Pedro before her killer . . .

"You looked so stupid in that ring of idiots." He gave a sharp laugh. "And that old *brujo*—how he flew around picking up the candles. It's too bad I didn't burn his store down."

That was the moment psychiatric interpretations vanished. I looked on the face of my tormentor and knew I was confronting not my brother, but a possessing spirit.

My opponent was a dead boy, killed last fall.

### CHAPTER SEVEN

PEOPLE can accept anything. Not just endure, but actually make terms with any situation. The first hour of our captivity was the most shocking. Seeing the switchblade without screaming, having Mr. Olsen go off and leave us, knowing Ted was hanging up without suspicion. After that, by degrees, we began to adjust. We ate our chowder. Tonio offered me a cigarette and I took and lighted it. I even decided it was a hopeful sign he'd made Peter refrigerate the porgy. As if he expected us to cook it later.

The children were behaving almost naturally. Carrie even managed to ask if he'd fed Walter.

"Walter? Oh, the cat. I guess I did," he said.

"You mean you don't remember?" she asked.

"Don't get fresh," he warned.

"He has a catport, Carrie," Peter said quickly. "He'll be all right till we get back."

She sat watching our captor intently. He was obviously throwing off the Joel-mask. "Have you taken over Uncle Joel's body?" she asked him at last.

"Carrie!" I said. But he moved his hand at me to be silent.

"I thought you might be from outer space," she offered.

"I'm not from outer space," he said. I saw with surprise that he

was intrigued. After all, Tonio had been only five years older than Carrie. They'd seen the same movies, watched the same television programs of UFOs and monstrous alien invaders.

"Does that mean you died?" she asked.

"More than just died," he said. "You mean you can't get the answer? A smart rich kid like you?" The mockery was taking on a bitter ring that made me uneasy. It was then we heard the motor approaching the house.

"Mr. Olsen must have forgotten something," I said.

"Yeah?" he said. He took out the knife. "Go look out the window."

Moving cautiously, I rose and followed instructions. Hope laced with fear shot through me. It was the police station wagon. The Baron began barking crazily.

"Cops?" he asked coolly, and I nodded. The local police chief got out and, after him, our old friends from the Fourth Division, Brady and Assistant Chief Inspector Russell. They passed my window on their way to the front door.

I wondered if Ted had telephoned them. Or they might have been with him already when I spoke to him. Even if they'd accepted Joel's alibi, they might have decided to ask a few questions. I supposed they'd flown to Ocean Beach by helicopter.

I began pleading with Tonio to admit them.

"We'll do exactly what you want," I said. "We'll say that the four of us came out together."

"Like hell you will," he said sardonically.

He was right; once they'd captured him, I would have told the truth. I recalled how he'd known what I was thinking when I'd decided he'd be sent to Matteawan. When the knocker struck, I feared for Carrie.

"Tonio, look—the safest way is to give yourself up."

"Is it me you're thinking of?" he asked. "Or are you worrying about Joel's body?"

He spoke as if he had borrowed an overcoat. I thought of my brother, the growing up, the little quirks that were Joel's own. He was a person, not an object you could borrow. A raging grief dimmed my thoughts.

565

He frowned as the rapping grew louder. "Shut that dog up," he said, "or I'll slit its throat."

I said, "Quiet, Baron!" He must have sensed we were at a crisis; for once in his life, he obeyed.

"Tell them to go away," Tonio said. And when I hesitated, he shouted, "Tell them!" He rose and grabbed Carrie's hair. "I'll come with you." Our little party made its way into the living room. As I paused undecidedly, he touched the switchblade spring and the wicked blade came sliding out.

I cried, "Inspector Russell! I can't let you in. He has a knife. He says if you come in, he'll kill Carrie."

There was silence. Then Russell's voice replied with the coolness I remembered, "Who is *he*, Mrs. Benson?"

I realized the impossibility of explaining. "It's my brother, Joel," I called. I'd never felt so hopeless.

"Tell them to go away now," Tonio said.

NATURALLY, they didn't go away.

They surrounded the cottage and called for reinforcements. Within an hour, photographers and reporters began arriving in panel trucks and pickups. Now and then we heard a helicopter trying to make a landing. To save his life, I locked the Baron in an upstairs bedroom. We heard him pattering back and forth above our heads.

Far from upsetting Tonio, the growing force outside heightened his spirits. It was as if he were giving a party and the size of the crowd measured his popularity.

I had a nerve-racking sense of his swift ambivalence. When he laughed, I felt giddy with relief. When his eyes clouded, I scarcely breathed. The children appeared to feel the same. Our desire to live created new dimensions. There were moments when I felt a mad fondness for him, when he seemed to care for us, when we inhabited some strange night-island that the world outside could never understand.

Then television spotlights glared whitely through the windows and Tonio ordered, "Make them turn them off!"

The room's mood altered as if a knife had slashed a canvas. I went to the window and demanded darkness. The television men were stubborn, but Inspector Russell called out and the glare dimmed. I realized the horror had nearly been precipitated. But I knew, too, we were only delaying it.

"They won't go away, you know," I told him softly. "You'll have to give up."

"Shut up," he said. "I'm not going to Matteawan."

"You don't have to," I said. "You can clear out."

He looked startled.

"Let Joel go," I begged him gently.

"But what would become of me?"

"Can't you go back where you came from?"

He stared at me in shocked silence. I saw he was remembering.

"I was in a dark box," he finally said. "There was no air and my head hurt."

I didn't understand.

"I called but nobody answered. I kept being bounced about."

The cold suspicion came that he was describing Mr. Perez's journey to the river, trundling a trunk in a pushcart. Perhaps he'd thought Tonio was dead till that moment, hearing the cries and the pounding of a boy trying to escape.

"I was falling, far, far. Water flooding in." Perez dumped his burden. Let the river keep it forever.

"I couldn't breathe. My chest was bursting."

A bad death, a death by drowning. Even now he glanced down as if he would find his hands bleeding from trying to break from the trunk. But they were Joel's hands.

"What happened when you were . . . dead?" I asked.

"Mist and water. Nothing more. Mist and water. My *bruja* said there would be spirits, friends who loved me." He stopped. Even now I could feel his hurt and disbelief at finding himself stranded in some borderland between the dead and the living.

"Then I found my way back," he said. "I don't know how. Maybe it was being mad at Perez. That was bad, you know; the way he threw me in the river."

"Somehow I got back to Second Street. I saw Perez. I saw my mother. I tried to let them know, but I couldn't work up much strength. My mother was scared and she got protecting incense. It didn't keep me out. But I got tired of their not seeing me. I wanted to kill Perez and I didn't have a body to act through. I started going back to my old apartment. They'd got a new tenant."

"Joel," I said.

"I looked him over awhile. It was funny watching an Anglo. He read a lot. He fooled with LSD once or twice. That's how I finally did it. He was lying there, his mind wide open, and I slipped in, looked through his eyes, made him move his hand. It was like stealing a car. The LSD wore off, but by then I was running him. When you called that night, I'd been in control since the day before."

Even at the time I'd thought Joel wouldn't have taken LSD so close to our dinner date. He'd lain there almost twenty-four hours while Tonio experimented with his will-less body. The knowledge sickened me.

The next part was unpleasant too. We had taken Tonio out of the hospital to freedom, and he had stolen down the vines to revenge himself on Mr. Perez. After that, he'd been content to watch Joel's sessions with Erika and go with him to Sherry's parties, see the swingers, the beautiful turned-on people.

Of course, in the end, it hadn't been enough to watch. He'd been himself at the birthday party. And when Sherry had walked out, an old rage began burning.

"I gave you the pills in your coffee," he told me. "Then I walked to Sherry's apartment. Her doorman went off at midnight. I pushed the buzzer and somebody let me in. And Sherry hadn't even locked her door. I just walked in and grabbed her.

"There's a trick to how you hold them," he told me. "I grab the hair and pull them back. The blood goes outward. Five minutes, and it's all over." He took a technician's pride in the skill involved. "I killed pigs and chickens when I lived with my *bruja*. After Sherry, I buried the knife in the park and marked the place so I could go back for it."

I tried to absorb it. I saw Joel sleepwalking through the city, unaware it was his hand, slashing, cutting.

"She was no good," Tonio said. "Men, that's all she thought about. Those parties where she went—" He cast a look at Carrie. "I did nothing with her, you know. Even there, that night, I never did. Not with one of them." I had the sense of some elaborate code that embraced murder and abhorred unchastity.

"Those other girls, the ones in the park—all the time, they just think about men," he said. I understood then his obsession with the beautiful mother who'd gone from man to man. It was hard for me to take that view of Mrs. Perez. She was for me just frightened and aging. But for him she had been the only woman and he was still punishing her betrayal.

I didn't notice he'd grown silent until Peter leaned forward and, following his gaze, I saw that Tonio's eyes were half shut. His head began to droop and bob slightly.

Peter said, "He's asleep or something. Hurry, get the knife!"

Nerving myself, I reached to take it. But his arm jerked. It was as if a gust of wind had struck him. The long blade slid out.

Our chance was gone. Wherever he'd been, Tonio was back.

HE confronted me, his breath coming hard. For the first time, he looked harassed.

"Why don't he mind his own business!" he said.

I wondered if Don Pedro were conducting another séance. He might have managed to recall Tonio as he had when the image of San Marcos had been smashed.

"I don't even know him. A thin old man in a blue turban."

"Dr. Singh!" I said. My recognition drew Tonio's anger.

"You're a tricky lady. You bought you a *brujo*." Rage made the switchblade tremble.

I denied it wildly. "I bought no one. If you mean Dr. Singh, he's not a *brujo*. He's a botany teacher."

That surprised him. The switchblade steadied, but I recalled my own sense that Dr. Singh practiced *brujería*.

I tried to erase that memory before Tonio picked it up. But an-

other gust seemed to catch him so his very self appeared to flicker. For an instant, there was vacancy, and desperate ventures moved within me, but his will painfully reasserted itself.

"He's good," he said. "Damn good. But I'm better."

Still, the struggle had cost him something. There was apprehension in the way he looked about.

"It's time to get out of here," he said.

I wavered. If he went, we would be free of him. But he'd be taking Joel with him. "The house is surrounded now. You'll never make it. They have guns. They'll shoot."

"No, they won't," he said. "I'll take Carrie."

I pleaded, then stormed at him. But he was dazzled by his vision of himself. The floodlights and television cameras would center on him. The superboy in the cape would defeat them all.

"We'll need coats. And money. Get them!"

We fell to making preparations for the journey. I dug out a slicker and gave over the money in my purse.

"Please," I tried again, "don't be foolish. Wait and think it out some more."

"And have your *brujo* get me?" He grinned. "Not on your life." So Dr. Singh had only increased our troubles. As the night passed, Tonio knew he must eventually fall asleep, and then his defenses would be lowered. He'd chance acting before that happened.

He ordered Carrie into her coat and, shrugging into my slicker, buttoned it with his free hand. Then he pushed Carrie into place before him.

"Go tell them nobody comes close or Carrie gets it," he commanded me. "Tell them to clear a path. We're leaving by the kitchen." It was nearer the marina than the front door.

As I hesitated, he grabbed Carrie's hair and jerked back her head. He drew the sharp blade along her throat and she gave a soft, hurt gasp. I stared with shock at the line of welling blood.

"Tell them," he said. His eyes were hard. "Remember what happened to the others."

In horror, I moved to the door.

As I swung it open, the floodlights went on. Men shouted and I

could hear the surf behind the roar of a hovering helicopter. "Please," I cried. The lights went off. I found Inspector Russell beside me. "He wants to leave. He's taking Carrie as a hostage." The helicopter landed and its engine cut off. In the quiet I filled him in on Tonio's instructions. He tried only once to make an argument. "Don't make him angry," I said. "He's already cut her."

He had children himself. He nodded, simply asking, "Where is he headed?"

"I don't know," I said. "He'll have to get a boat. The marina's just a short way over, on the bay side."

"Tell him he has an all clear," he said.

I went back inside to Tonio.

"Ready?" he asked.

"He's giving his men orders," I said.

He regarded me acutely. Under that dark gaze, I was glad I'd not tried any double-dealing. "How do you tell what I'm thinking?" I asked.

"I'm partly on this plane, you know, and partly out of it. My vibrations are faster than yours. It helps in picking up the pictures."

He pushed Carrie through the kitchen, unlocked the back door and threw it open. Then he urged her through it, standing close behind her. The police guard had been drawn back. I could see nothing through the door but cable equipment, beach pickups, panel trucks, the swirling fog. Carefully, he prodded her forward.

Then suddenly, he stopped and held on to her. They swayed as he leaned upon her.

It came to me that Dr. Singh was renewing his assault, drawing the spirit of Tonio to a Broadway hotel room. Which meant that Joel might be returning. He'd wake to find himself standing with Carrie. He'd have no warning of his armed audience.

"Joel!" I cried. "Stay where you are!"

So, in a way, I am responsible for what happened. Hearing my cry, he freed one of Carrie's shoulders to swing around and Carrie dove clear of him, hit the sand and rolled free.

In the instant, men were yelling, the floodlights went on and Joel was lit as if he were on a stage. I don't think he even realized

571

he held a knife. But as he turned, he moved blindly toward Carrie. She screamed and a rifle cracked. And then two more.

I'll always remember that endless moment, Joel swaying in the blue-white glare, Carrie screaming, the *chug chug chug* of the floodlight generator.

At last, he fell and lay curled in the sand, moving slightly. I ran toward him. The local doctor was already kneeling beside him. I could see blood spreading in a shocking pool and I knew that he was dying.

I knelt beside him and spoke his name but he didn't answer.

Strangely, then, I had a serial sense of his life. I recalled the summer he'd raised rabbits in the backyard, the way I used to take him to the movies and buy popcorn in the lobby. Even the last troubled years in New York returned, a lonely young man searching for a way he'd lost, trying books and arts and the hallucinogens. While another lost boy was also seeking a way back to a world that had crowded him out.

Toward the end, there was a tremor. A violent will seemed to rush into him and he tried to lift himself. It seemed to me that Tonio had come to add his strength to Joel's.

I said, "No!" and he sank back. The lips twisted. There was a bravado about that grin that wasn't like Joel. In any case, it was the final moment. They both were gone. The wounded body couldn't support their struggle any longer.

Then Ted was there. He caught my arm and raised me roughly. "This is no place for you, Norah."

Dazed, I looked back toward Joel and saw they were throwing a blanket over him.

"Your daughter's all right, Mrs. Benson," Inspector Russell said. "Scared but okay."

I heard Carrie sobbing. She sounded weak and frightened and strangely far away.

CARRIE's throat wound turned out to be minor, just enough to draw blood. Ted treated and bandaged it and became, for him, a sentimental father. When Carrie wanted the Baron brought

downstairs he suffered it, though ordinarily barking irritated him.

Actually, the Baron was nearly barked out. After the first bliss of reunion, he lay across Carrie's feet exhausted, oblivious to the noises outside, reporters shouting, detectives milling about, taking pictures and measuring distances.

When the children finally unwound and staggered up to bed, I sat staring into the fire while Ted called his wife, Marta.

"I'll spend the night here," he told her. "I'll be back when they release the body. They took it to the hospital in Bay Shore for an autopsy."

Joel was just a body now; there would be funeral arrangements. I felt tears coming but I forced them back.

"The kids are fine," Ted was saying. "They've gone to bed. No trouble there." It sounded as if he were still expecting trouble. Then when he hung up and turned around, I saw that he'd meant me. He sank his hands in his trousers pockets. "I'd never have guessed," he said, "that Joel would turn aggressive."

"But it wasn't Joel himself," I began and stopped.

He'd heard about Tonio's possession. The children had been full of it. So he was telling me he didn't accept it and was deliberately warning me that I was not to give that version.

Just then, Dr. Reichman phoned. Called by the police, he'd flown back from Lima to help talk Joel into giving up. But by the time he'd landed, Joel was already dead.

"I'm sorry," I said. "So sorry about Erika." There was silence. Perhaps he was thinking back to San Francisco, to that room overlooking the harbor.

"*Ja,*" he said finally, and gave a deep sigh. Then he asked about Joel's death, but when I tried to speak of Dr. Singh's part in it, he interrupted. "My dear, you work with the creative faculties. You must make allowance for your imagination."

I said, "But Joel described Dr. Singh, whom he'd never seen."

He went on as if he hadn't heard. "These secondary personalities are alarming. One sees how primitive societies come to believe."

"But Joel was in Morocco when the first deaths took place!"

"He heard of them later. We know he must have from what hap-

pened." I began to see at last what Ted had been trying to tell me. If I persisted, I'd join the ranks of crazy ladies who summoned ectoplasm and received messages on their planchettes.

By the time Inspector Russell came in to question me, I had made up my mind. I wasn't ready to be written off as crazy.

I WAS content for months that I made that decision. With the mystery solved, the killer caught and brought to justice, we dropped back to being private persons. I had times of grieving for Joel but I forced myself back to writing the book that had been interrupted.

We sold the Fire Island house before the start of the next season. After that April night, every time I went out there, I saw the place where Joel had died. Time never wore away the floodlights, the reporters waiting, the hovering helicopters, the police.

Our last link now with the island is the *Fire Island News*. I read it to keep up with the beach parties, the struggle over bay-front pollution, the raids by the local police force searching for drugs.

That's how I know about the strange young man. He was found lying on the beach one morning, unable to give an account of himself. He spoke as if his voice box were partially paralyzed. At first, they thought he was speaking Spanish. But he denied knowing any Spanish. He was taken to the hospital in Bay Shore, but before he was formally released, he vanished.

I decided to write this book, to put down the way the whole thing happened to us—in case it's happening to somebody else.

I hope I'm wrong.

But I think Tonio is back.

# Ramona Stewart

"Roll 'em. Action." It sounded like a movie set and in fact it was—*The Possession of Joel Delaney*, filming on location in New York. As star Shirley MacLaine faced the camera, the author of the gripping novel watched. "I think I prefer the nice loneliness of a writer's workroom," Ramona Stewart said. "Not that I haven't had my share of adventure."

During her growing years Ramona Stewart's family traveled from California to Texas, Louisiana and Nevada, and she remembers life in a tent on an oil-drilling site in Utah. After attending the University of Southern California, she held an adventuresome first job as Girl Friday to a wild and woolly movie-serial unit. Then, at twenty-two, Miss Stewart was the author of a successful novel, *Desert Town*. "I got scared I'd never turn out another book. And for several years I didn't."

Ramona Stewart came to New York and took a furnished room over a raucous vegetable market at the edge of Greenwich Village. She worked at temporary office jobs and one day plucked up the courage to try another book. "Also, I'd found a friend—a cat from the vegetable market wandered in one evening and hasn't left yet. I call her Lolita, but actually she's very ladylike."

Still a resident of Greenwich Village, Miss Stewart has written a total of eight novels. She credits New York's mixture of types and locales with the germinating idea for her first thriller, *The Possession of Joel Delaney*. "A friend of mine was in love with a girl in Spanish Harlem who was under the influence of a spiritualist cult there," she told us. "The cult was able to frighten the girl into breaking off the romance. And so I began reading about their practices. I discovered that nearly everyone in Spanish Harlem knows someone he believes has been possessed."

By now Shirley MacLaine was concluding a scene from *The Possession of Joel Delaney* in front of the camera. As the actors paused for a breather, Ramona Stewart smiled. "Well, this is one movie's ending I won't have to wait breathlessly for," she allowed. "I do know how it comes out."